TRIAL BY FIRE

VOLUME TWO OF
THE TALES OF THE
TERRAN REPUBLIC

CHARLES E. GANNON

BAEN

TRIAL BY FIRE

This is a work of fiction. All the characters and events portrayed in this book are fictional, and any resemblance to real people or incidents is purely coincidental.

A Baen Books Original

Baen Publishing Enterprises
P.O. Box 1403
Riverdale, NY 10471
www.baen.com

ISBN: 978-1-4767-8077-1

Cover art by Bob Eggleton

First Baen paperback printing, September 2015

Library of Congress Control Number: 2014020207

Distributed by Simon & Schuster
1230 Avenue of the Americas
New York, NY 10020

Pages by Joy Freeman (www.pagesbyjoy.com)
Printed in the United States of America

I dedicate this book to the
love of my life, my peerless wife
Andrea Beder Trisciuzzi.
Without her, this book and all which
shall follow would never exist.

Fellow-citizens, we cannot escape history....
The fiery trial through which we pass,
will light us down, in honor or dishonor,
to the latest generation.

—Abraham Lincoln,
December 1, 1862, message to Congress

CONTENTS

Interstellar shift links operative as of July 2118
(max shift range: 8.35 ly)

(Biogenic worlds are labeled in **BOLD FACE**)

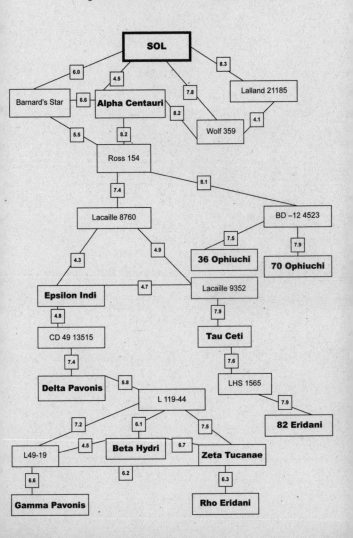

TRIAL BY FIRE

BOOK ONE

CONFLICT

All warfare is based on deception. Hence,
when we are able to attack, we must seem
unable; when using our forces, we must appear
inactive; when we are near, we must make the
enemy believe we are far away; when far away,
we must make him believe we are near.

—Sun Tzu

CONFLICT
Part One

November 2119

Chapter One

The maglev began decelerating. As it did, the light seeping in through the overhead plexiglass panel increased sharply: they were now beyond the safety of the base's tightly patrolled subterranean perimeter. Caine Riordan, newly minted commander in the United States Space Force, glanced at the young ensign beside him. "Are you ready?"

Ensign Marilyn Brahen looked out the even narrower plexiglass panel beside the door, checked the area into which they were about to deploy. There was blurred, frenetic movement out there. "Were we expecting a lot of—company?" she asked.

"No, Ensign, but it was a possibility." Caine rose. "So we improvise and overcome." She stood beside him as the doors opened—

—and they were hit by torrent of loud, unruly shouts from a crowd beyond the maglev platform. The group swiftly became a tight-packed wall of charging

3

humanity, their outcries building before them like a cacophonic bow-wave.

Ensign Brahen eyed the approaching mob, news people already elbowing their way into the front rank, and swallowed. "Sir, you think those crazies will stay outside the car?"

"Not a chance." *And given the automated two-minute station stop, they'll have us pinned in here before we can leave.*

"I gotta confess, sir," she continued, "this wasn't what I was expecting when they told me I was going on a field assignment with you."

"Well," mused Caine as the reporters closed the last ten meters, "we *are* off-base. And technically, the civilian sector is 'the field.'" Caine smiled at her, at the charade which was to be his one and only "command," and stepped out the door.

The moment his foot touched the maglev platform, an improbably shrill male shriek—"Blasphemer!"— erupted from the center of the approaching crowd, followed by a glass bottle spinning lazily at Caine.

Behind him, he heard Ensign Brahen inhale sharply, no doubt preparatory to a warning shout—

But recent dojo-acquired reflexes now served Caine better than a warning. Without thinking, he deflected the bottle, which went angling off to smash loudly against the side of the passenger car behind him.

As Caine sensed Ensign Brahen moving up to cover his flank, he scanned the rear of the crowd for the presumably fleeing attacker. Instead, he discovered the assailant was standing his ground, right fist raised, left arm and index finger rigidly extended in accusation—

—which disappeared behind the surge of newspersons

who surrounded Caine as a wall of eager faces and outstretched comcorders. Somewhere, behind that palisade of journalists, the attacker shrieked again. "Blasphemer!" But his voice was receding, and then was finally drowned out by the mass of jostling reporters and protestors who threatened to shove Caine and Ensign Brahen back against the maglev car. Their inquiries were shrill, aggressive, and rapid.

"Mr. Riordan, is it true you're the one who found the remains of an alien civilization on Delta Pavonis Three?"

"Caine! Caine, over here! Why wait two years to announce your discoveries?"

"Who decided that you'd announce your findings behind closed doors: the World Confederation, or you, Caine?"

A young man with a bad case of acne and a worse haircut—evidently the boldest jackal in the pack—stuck a palmcom right under Riordan's nose. "Caine, have there been any other attacks like the one we just witnessed, by people who believe that your reports about exosapients are just lies intended to undermine the Bible?" Ironically, that was the moment when one of the protestors waved a placard showing a supposed alien: a long-armed gibbon with an ostrich neck, polygonal head, tendrils instead of fingers. Actually, it was a distressingly good likeness of the beings Caine had encountered on Dee Pee Three, prompting him to wonder, *so who the hell is leaking that information?*

The young reporter evidently did not like having to wait two seconds for an answer. "So Caine, exactly *when* did you decide to start undermining the Bible?"

Caine smiled. "I've never taken part in theological debates, and I have no plans to start doing so."

A very short and immaculately groomed woman extended her palmcom like a rapier; Caine resisted the impulse to parry. "Mr. Riordan, the World Confederation Consuls have declined to confirm rumors that you personally reported the existence of the exosapients of Delta Pavonis Three at this April's Parthenon Dialogues. However, CoDevCo Vice President R. J. Astor-Smath claims to have evidence that you were the key presenter on the last day of that meeting."

Caine labored to keep the smile on his face. *It would be just like Astor-Smath, or some other megacorporate factotum, to put the press back on my scent. But how the hell did they find me out here at Barnard's Star?* Caine prefaced his reply with a shrug. "I'm sorry. I'm not familiar with Mr. Astor-Smath's comments, so—"

Another reporter pushed forward. "He made these remarks two months ago." The reporter's palmcom crackled as it projected Astor-Smath's voice: composed, suave, faintly contemptuous. "I wish I could share more with you about the Parthenon Dialogues, but the late Admiral Nolan Corcoran prevented any megacorporation—including my own, the Colonial Development Combine—from attending. However, we do have reliable sources who place Mr. Riordan at the second day of the Parthenon Dialogues."

Behind him, Caine heard a warning tone announce the imminent departure of the maglev passenger car. It would be ten minutes before the next would arrive, ten more minutes surrounded by harrying jackals. *No thanks.* "I'm sorry," he said, "but you'll have to excuse me." *So much for my "first command."* He started to turn back to the maglev car.

"One last question, Caine. Who's your new girlfriend?"

Ensign Brahen started as if stuck by a pin. Caine turned back around, foregoing the escape via maglev. Instead, he searched for the source of the question, asking, "Besides being grossly unprofessional and misinformed, just why is that a relevant inquiry?"

"Well," explained Mr. Bad-Skin Worse-Hair as he reemerged from the mass of faces and limbs, "we were expecting to see you with Captain Opal Patrone, your personal guard. And, some say, your personal geisha."

Enough is enough. Caine planted his feet, kept his voice level, his diction clipped. "I feel compelled to point out that, in addition to raising a thoroughly inappropriate topic, you didn't even manage to frame it as a question." Caine looked out over the faces ringing him. "If there are any competent journalists here, I'm ready for their inquiries."

The group quieted; the mood had changed. Their quarry had turned and bared teeth. Now, the hunt would be in earnest. The next jackal that jumped in tried to attack a different flank. "Mr. Riordan, is it true that you were present when Admiral Corcoran died after the Parthenon Dialogues?"

Caine pushed away the mixed emotions that Nolan's name summoned. The ex-admiral-turned-clandestine-mastermind had arguably ruined Riordan's life, but had also striven to make amends and forge an almost paternal bond. Caine heard himself reply, "No comment," just as the maglev car rose, sighed away from the platform, and headed off with a down-dopplering hum.

"Mr. Riordan, do you have any insights into how Admiral Corcoran's alleged 'heart attack' occurred?"

"Why do you call it an 'alleged' heart attack?"

"Well, it's a rather strange coincidence, don't you

think? First, you were reportedly present for Admiral Corcoran's heart attack in Greece, and then for the similarly fatal heart attack suffered by his Annapolis classmate and crony, Senator Arvid Tarasenko, less than forty-eight hours later in DC. Comment?"

"Firstly, I don't recall any prior assertions that I was near Senator Tarasenko at the time of his death—"

"Well, an anonymous source puts you in his office just before—"

An anonymous source like Astor-Smath, I'll bet. "Madam, until you have verifiable information from verifiable sources, I'm not disposed to comment on my whereabouts at that time. In the more general matter of the heart attacks of Misters Corcoran and Tarasenko, I cannot see any reasonable explanation *except* coincidence." Which was superficially true; Caine had no other explanation for the heart attacks that had, within the span of two days, removed the two leaders of the shadowy organization which had sent him to Delta Pavonis Three: the Institute of Reconnaissance, Intelligence, and Security, or IRIS. On the other hand, Caine remained convinced that the two deaths had been orchestrated. Somehow. "Timing aside, there's not much surprising in either of these sad events. Admiral Corcoran never fully recovered from the coronary damage he suffered during the mission to intercept the Doomsday Rock twenty-six years ago. And Senator Tarasenko was not a thin man. His doctors' warnings to watch his weight and cholesterol are a matter of public record."

Tasting no blood, the jackals tried nipping at a different topic. "Mr. Riordan, our research shows that you spent most of the last fourteen years in cold sleep. And that your 'friend' Captain Opal Patrone was cryogenically suspended over fifty years ago. What prompted each of you to abandon the times in which you lived?"

As if choice had anything to do with it. "In the matter of the recently promoted *Major* Patrone, she's the one you should ask about her reasons." *Hard to do, since Opal's on Earth by now.* "But I can assure you that she did not 'abandon' her time period. She was severely wounded serving her country. In that era, her choice was between cryogenic suspension and death."

"And *your* reason for sleeping into the future?"

"Is none of your business." *And is a* non sequitur, *since it wasn't my choice.* Caine had simply stumbled across IRIS's secret activities, which had earned him an extended nap in a cold-cell. "Next question."

"A follow-up on your long absence from society, sir. Some analysts have speculated that, as a person from another time, you were just the kind of untraceable operative needed for a covert survey and research mission to Dee Pee Three. What would you say in response to that speculation?"

Caine smiled, hoped it didn't look as brittle as it felt. *I'd say it's too damned perceptive.* Aloud: "I'd say they have excellent imaginations, and could probably have wonderful careers writing political thrillers."

Bad-Skin Worse-Hair jumped back into the melee. "Stop evading the questions, Riordan. And stop playing the innocent. You knew that the Parthenon Dialogues were going to be biggest news-splash of the century. So did you also advise the World Confederation on how to shroud the Dialogues in enough secrecy to pump up the media hype? Which in turn pumped up your consultancy fees?"

Caine stepped toward the young reporter, who hastily stepped back, apparently noticing for the first time that Caine's rangy six-foot frame was two inches taller than his own and decidedly more fit. Riordan kept his voice low, calm. "It's bad enough that you're plying a trade for which you haven't the aptitude or integrity, but you could at least check your conclusions against the facts. Without commenting one way or the other about my alleged involvement with the Parthenon Dialogues, it must be clear to anyone—even you—that the world leaders who attended were grappling with global issues of the utmost importance, and that the secrecy surrounding them was a policy decision, not a PR stunt. In short, whoever brought information to the Parthenon Dialogues may have delivered a sensational story, but not for sensational purposes."

But if that admonishment curbed the jackals momentarily, Caine could already see signs that they would soon regroup and resume their hunt for an inconsistency into which they could sink their collective investigatory teeth. And there were still at least five minutes before the next passenger car arrived. Five minutes in which even these bumbling pseudo-sleuths might begin to realize that the real story was not to be found in the storm and fury of Parthenon itself, but rather, in the surreptitious actions that had been its silent and unnoticed prelude. They might begin asking how the mission to Delta Pavonis had come to be, and—in the necessary nebulousness of Caine's responses—discern the concealed workings, and therefore existence, of some unseen agency. An agency that was unknown even to the world's most extensive intelligence organizations—because its select membership dwelt amongst their very ranks. An agency, in short, like IRIS—

From behind Caine, the maglev rails hummed into life, braking and hushing the approach of a passenger car. Surprised by the early arrival of the train, Caine turned—and saw that this passenger car was a half-sized private model, furnished with tinted one-way windows. The pack of reporters fell silent as the doors hissed open—

—to reveal a shapely blonde woman, sitting at the precise center of the brushed chrome and black vinyl interior. She smiled. It was a familiar smile.

Caine grimaced.

Ensign Brahen looked from the woman to Caine. "Isn't that Heather Kirkwood? Isn't she a reporter? A *real* reporter? On Earth?"

Caine resisted the urge to close his eyes. "She is that. And worse."

"Worse?"

"She's my ex."

"Your—?"

Heather cocked her head, showed a set of perfect teeth that were definitely more appealing—and far more ominous—than those possessed by the half-ring of jackals surrounding them. She crooked an index finger at Caine. "You coming? Or are you enjoying your impromptu press conference too much to leave?"

If possible, Ensign Brahen's incredulous eyes opened even wider. "Do we go with her?"

Caine sighed. "Do we have a choice?" He led the way into the car.

Chapter Two

It was typical of Admiral Martina Perduro that she started talking as soon as Trevor Corcoran opened the door. "Well, Captain, ready to ship out?"

The admiral's tone was jocular, so Trevor replied in kind. "Not at all, ma'am." He attempted to conceal his slight limp with a bouncing stride. "Heck, I was just getting used to the luxury billets here at The Pearl."

Perduro's answering grin was crooked. "Glad you've liked the accommodations."

"I've always been partial to the narrow bunks and dull steel fixtures, but it's the weather and the scenery I like best. Poisonous atmosphere, lethally low atmospheric pressure, hard rads due to the lack of a magnetosphere, and not a living cell except for the ones we brought with us into this gray-walled rat warren."

Perduro leaned back. "Okay, but smile when you say all that, Captain."

"I *was* smiling, ma'am—wasn't I?" Trevor glanced at a chair.

"Sit, sit already." Perduro waved at it. Then, not looking at him: "How's the leg?"

"I beg your pardon, ma'am?"

"Captain Corcoran, do you really think I don't get training updates on command grade personnel? Or that I don't read them?"

Trevor felt a little less jocular, now. "My leg is fine, ma'am. Never better."

"Hmph. Not what the base CMO said a few days ago. Fractured left tibia, if I recall."

"Hairline stress fracture," emended Trevor. "A small one."

"Yes, but enough to warrant them going in and poking around, evidently."

Trevor shrugged. "Which is, I suspect, the source of my discomfort, ma'am. I don't know why the CMO felt the need to get busy with a knife. I talked to the medtech who took the scans. Hardly anything to see."

"Hm. Is it the leg that's dented—or that SEAL ego, Captain?"

"Technically, I'm no longer in the Teams, ma'am." It annoyed Trevor that a chief petty officer had tagged him that hard during hand-to-hand drill.

Perduro was smiling at him with one raised eyebrow. "I'll be sad to see you go, Trev. Your visit brought a bit of color to the navy-gray of Barney Deucy."

Trevor stared at the files on her desk, at the screens that surrounded her. Caine Riordan's name or image was on at least half of them. "Well, Admiral, to be frank, it wasn't really *me* who brought the color, was it?"

Perduro's smile was small but genuine. "Don't sell yourself short, Trev. Besides, being with you is a bit like old times for me. Your father—God rest him—was the BELTCINC when I was a shave-tail HQ staffer during the Belt Wars."

Trevor nodded, did the math, was surprised that Perduro was that old, considered her very well preserved indeed. "But still, ma'am, I'm not the novelty around here." Trevor pointed at Caine's face on one of the screens. "He is. Understandably."

"You both met five species of exosapients at the Accord's Convocation last month. That makes both of you celebrities in my eyes."

"You're very kind, ma'am. But I just went along to carry the figurative shotgun. Caine was the liaison, the communicator. And the guy who found the first exos on Dee Pee Three."

"Yes, and who I've now had to make a naval officer to boot. As per Richard Downing's orders." She frowned. "About Downing: what intelligence agency is he with? And how the hell did he get the clearance and command-equivalency rating that he waved in front of my nose when he dropped you two off here a month ago?"

"Admiral Perduro," Trevor sat up very straight and cleared his throat. "I regret to say I have no information pertinent to the assignment or disposition of Mr. Richard Downing, nor would I be officially disposed to share it if I did. Ma'am."

Perduro's other eyebrow rose to join the first. "Ah. The Holy Creed of Plausible Deniability."

"Sorry, ma'am."

"I'm sure you are." She fiddled with a palmcomp stylus for a moment. "Downing is your godfather, isn't he?"

"That is correct, ma'am." *And he's the new chief*

of IRIS. And a direct advisor to President Liu. And the sonofabitch who turned my father's body over to the same aliens who sneaked some kind of organism into his chest. Yes, that's my friend-buggering, skull-duggering Uncle Richard.

Perduro nodded, might have detected the overly crisp tone in Trevor's reply since she changed topics. "And what's your take on our thirty-day wonder, Mr. Riordan? Will he cut it as an officer?"

"Ma'am, I'm sure you must have all of Caine's scores." *I can see them right there, in front of you.* "His lowest performance index is still a three-sigma shift above the center of the bell curve. Can't ask for better than that."

"Trevor, don't be obtuse. You know what I'm asking. He looks fine on paper. I need a human perspective from someone who knows him but can be objective."

Trevor frowned as if he was mulling over his response while his brain raced in a different direction. *You think I can be objective about Caine Riordan? Gee, that might be a little hard, seeing as how he's the guy who fell in love with my sister Elena fourteen years ago, the guy my dad then mind-wiped, who is the father of my fatherless nephew, and who is now romantically involved—well, entangled—with one hell of a wonderful coldsleeper from the past, Opal Patrone. Who my late father all but stuck in Caine's bed. Yeah, sure, I can be impartial about Caine Riordan, aka "Odysseus." Not a problem.*

"Captain Corcoran, are you uncomfortable giving your assessment of Riordan?" Perduro's tone had grown slightly more formal. "Is there some failing not indicated on his OCS results?"

"Oh, no, ma'am, just trying to find the right words."

"The right words for what? Either he's going to be a good officer or he isn't."

"With all due respect, ma'am, I don't think it's that simple in his case."

Perduro steepled her fingers, breathed out a slow sigh. "I'm probably going to regret asking this, but I am duty-bound to do so: please explain why the assessment of Riordan is not 'simple.'"

"Ma'am, to start with, he was an impressed civilian. A draftee in an all-volunteer force. So he's not wearing the blue because it's the fulfillment of lifelong dream."

"So he resents it?"

"No. In fact, he was preparing to volunteer. But only because he thinks it's necessary." Trevor wondered, despite Perduro having been briefed on the disastrous outcome of the Convocation, just how much he should reveal. "Riordan thinks that we could be at war pretty soon, and he wants to 'do his part,' as he put it."

Perduro's eyes grew harder behind the now-rigid pinnacle of her fingers. "So Riordan and Downing are on the same page about the disputes at the Convocation, that they could be precursors to war?"

"Ma'am, I think that's how all of us who were at the Convocation felt. The superficial purpose for that all-species meet-and-greet was to talk, but some of the members came to pick a fight. And I'm pretty sure they're going to get what they came for."

Perduro folded her hands. "A sobering assessment, Captain. But back to Riordan: will he freeze in a fight?"

"No, ma'am. He's already handled some pretty tough situations since being pulled out of cryosleep. You've probably seen the reports of the assassination attempts he foiled on board the *Tyne*, then at Alexandria, then at Sounion, and then on Mars."

"Hmmm. Yes. Although it looks like he had considerable help at Sounion. His fellow sleeper, Major Opal Patrone, seemed to be quite the one-woman reaping machine, there."

Trevor made sure that neither his voice or his eyes changed. "Major Patrone was assigned as Caine's close security, although he didn't know it at the time. She's a top-notch soldier. She has also been teaching him karate. Shotokan tradition." But Martina Perduro had no need to know that poor, future-stranded Opal Patrone had also been assigned to become Caine's paramour. *Which will make for an interesting reunion, if Elena and Opal are both in the room when Caine reveals that he has remembered the one-hundred-hour romance he and Sis had on Luna. And that Connor is his child. I'm not quite sure how Opal will take that—*

"So who's trying to kill Riordan, do you think?"

"I beg your pardon, ma'am?" *But with any luck, Caine will pick up where he left off with Elena fourteen years ago, and my sister will want to do the same. Which even makes sense on the chronological level, since his time in cold sleep has allowed her to catch up to his greater age. And then, once Opal has gotten over Caine, and started to move on, maybe then I'll—*

"Captain Corcoran, are you paying attention?" Perduro's voice startled him. Trevor almost blinked as his awareness returned to the gray-walled office.

"Sorry, Admiral. I was thinking about your question."

"Of course you were. But how about it, Captain? Who do you think is trying to kill Riordan? The megacorporations, maybe? He certainly ruined their attempt to dig up alien artifacts on Delta Pavonis Three."

Trevor drummed his fingers slowly on the arm of his chair. "Admiral, the various assassination attempts on Riordan might not all originate from the same source. And not all of the sources might be—familiar—to us."

"You don't have to tiptoe around the topic, Trevor. Downing highlighted the possibility that exosapients have suborned our own people to carry out covert actions on Earth. I suppose it's also implicit that some of the efforts could have involved both mega-corporate and exosapient assets. But there's been no clear motive for such collusion, and absolutely no hard evidence of it."

"That is correct, Admiral, although—" And then, motion on one of Perduro's monitors caught Trevor's attention. He pointed. "Admiral, is that Caine, next to that maglev?"

Perduro waved a desultory hand behind her. "Yes. Part of the charade of his being an officer. A four-minute command. To conduct a security check in the civilian sector, with our youngest shavetail, Ensign Brahen, as his 'unit.'"

"Well, Admiral, that little bit of theater might be veering towards hard-edged reality." He pointed more forcefully.

Perduro turned—and her eyes widened. Riordan was ringed by a posse of reporters, backed by a mob waving placards and trying to decide just how ugly it wanted to become.

"Damn it! I should have been watching—"

"No one else is on real-time oversight?"

"For a joyride to the civilian sector?" snapped the admiral, but she turned red as she said it. Coming from the same service ethos, Trevor could read her mind: *"My watch, my fault."* At that moment, a small maglev car—a private rental—pulled up, and after a moment's time, Riordan and Ensign Brahen entered it.

"Was their escape in that little car part of the plan?" asked Trevor.

"No. Not part of *my* plan, at any rate." Perduro punched a virtual stud on her desktop-screen. "Duty Officer, get me the Shore Patrol."

Chapter Three

Off-base sector, Barnard's Star 2 C

The doors of the private maglev car closed abruptly, terminating the outraged cries of the reporters. Once Caine and Ensign Brahen had found seats as far from their rescuer as politeness allowed, Heather Kirkwood tapped her outsized palmcomp. A gentle hum arose, as did the car, floating up an inch or so before they felt the smooth acceleration that would carry them toward the end of the civilian sector's rail spur.

Brahen eyed Heather again, and then Caine. "She's your ex-wife?"

"No, no. Ex-girlfriend." Caine managed to suppress a shudder at the notion that he might ever have married Heather Kirkwood.

Who had turned toward Caine. "So, it seems there was a nice reception waiting for you, now that you've decided to stop playing soldier. Surprised?"

Caine leaned back. "Not really. It was just a matter of time before the local stringers and hack journalists found me." Which was only a partial truth. That they knew Caine was on Barney Deucy was only mildly surprising. Knowing when and where he would emerge from the naval base was somewhat disturbing. What was alarmingly suspicious, however, was the sheer number of reporters on the platform: way too many. Barney Deucy was an infamously dull news post. The entire system typically had one-fifth the number of correspondents that had accosted the two of them.

"Okay. But that doesn't explain why *she*"—Ensign Brahen gestured at Heather without looking at her— "came all the way from her high-profile job on Earth. Just following a deductive hunch?"

"Oh, it wasn't guesswork for Heather. She knew she'd find me here."

"How?"

Heather twirled a golden lock with a desultory middle finger. "Yes, how did I know to find you here, darling?"

"You picked up my trail on Mars just a day or two after I left. Easily done, since I was seen by quite a few people at Nolan Corcoran's memorial. And I'll bet you learned that I'd been attacked in my room by a pair of Russian servicemen—despite attempts by both the Commonwealth and Russlavic Federation officials to hush it up."

"So far, so good."

"But all your leads came to a dead end: you found I'd been shipped off planet. No word where, no reason why. So you checked to see if any other persons of interest had been on Mars at the same time as me, and then left the same time as I did."

Heather smiled. "And what a crowd of luminaries I turned up. Two World Confederation consuls, two

Nobel-prize-nominated scientists, India's top computer whiz, the late Admiral Corcoran's kids—commando son Trevor and brainy daughter Elena—and, last but not least, Richard Downing, affiliate of America's two recently deceased heroes, Corcoran and Senator Tarasenko. Who were old Annapolis chums. Who both employed Downing at different times to do—what, exactly?" Heather's smile was wide and bright. Her eyes were every bit as predatory as the ambulance-chasers they'd just eluded.

Caine ignored the all-too-accurate intimation that Downing was up to his neck in clandestine activities. "Now here's the tricky part," he resumed, picking up the explanation to the wide-eyed Brahen. "Having traced all these people to Mars, Heather knows she's on the trail of something interesting. She finds indications that all of us have shifted out-system, but the transit logs indicate that there were no shift carriers outbound from Earth at the right time. But at some point, she makes—or is helped to make—the incredible intuitive leap which tells her I have left the system by other means."

"I didn't need any help coming to that conclusion, thank you very much," Heather retorted, chin elevating slightly. "Ever since you announced the existence of exosapients at the Parthenon Dialogs, some of us in the press have speculated that maybe not all of the exosapients are primitive. That maybe the focus on the aborigines of Dee Pee Three is just a stalking horse to take our attention away from contact with much more advanced exos."

Her concluding sentence did not end on as firm a note as it had begun. *She doesn't have any facts, just hunches. She hasn't been told about our group's travel to the Convocation.* Caine continued narrating Heather's journalistic adventures to Brahen. "Of course, Heather's right. A special shift carrier was, in fact, waiting to take us out-system," A half-lie, since the shift carrier had been "special" because it belonged to an alien species. "But where had we gone, and why? Alpha Centauri is the most developed system, and would be a logical first stop for all the missing VIPs, no matter their ultimate destination. But instead, Heather somehow deduced that we would wind up at the most closely controlled piece of real estate in human space: The Pearl, here on Barney Deucy." Seeing the slightly theatrical nature of Heather's smug answering smile, Caine knew she was trying to act knowing, confident, but had not reasoned it out this way at all. "Or," he added, "a helpful informant aimed her inexplicably but confidently at the base here. She never learned *how* the informant knew, but that didn't stop Ms. Kirkwood from booking herself on the first outbound shift-carrier." Heather's smile faltered as Caine asked her, "Is that about right?"

Heather recovered quickly, though. She shook her head; long gold tresses swept from side to side. Her extraordinary—and, Caine knew, artificially—lavender eyes engaged him for a full second before she spoke. "I heard rumors that the coldsleep had damaged your memories, Caine. But evidently it didn't affect your intellect, or your ability to be aggravating, to push my buttons. Occasionally." She leaned back; on the surface, it was simply a shift to a more relaxed posture. Somehow, Heather made it the inviting recline of a courtesan. "So—have you missed me?"

"Haven't had the time to miss much of anything, Heather."

"My, my, you never used to wake up this testy. But I suppose sleeping through fourteen years could make one a little more arch than usual."

"Or maybe I just woke up with a decreased tolerance for reporters."

Heather remained quiet for a second. "Such a semicivilized insult. But I suppose we've both grown old and boring. Which reminds me, are you in touch with any of your friends from the Independent Interplanetary News Network?"

Caine managed not to roll his eyes. "Oh, yeah, all my IINN 'colleagues' who loved me so much."

He felt Brahen's eyes move sideways to study him. "Actually, sir, wardroom scuttlebutt says you were a pretty successful—"

Heather tossed a bang aside. "Oh, he was very successful, Ensign. A bit too successful, actually. You see, he didn't go to the news networks: they went to him. On bended knee."

Caine made himself laugh. "You still don't mind a bit of exaggeration if it makes for a more evocative story, do you, Heather?"

"And I never will. You see, Ensign Brahen"—her sudden inward lean and facetiously intimate tone were Heather's most antagonistic provocations yet—"when I was at IINN, the senior editors were big fans of Caine's first book and his way with words. And then they discovered he was good on camera, even though he was shy about being in front of one."

"That wasn't shyness. That was aversion."

"See? He *is* good with words. So there he was, on an open-ended contract, free to come and go as he pleased, allowed to snatch up the choicest research projects involving the Pentagon or the cloak-and-dagger types a few miles away in Langley.

"But of course, not all of us girls and boys who had worked and sweated and lied and slept our way up the ladder were happy when Caine became the darling of the aging news chiefs who rediscovered, in their near-senility, that journalism was still about informing the public. As if it ever had been. But Caine Riordan was the perfect salve for their pangs of career-end guilt: a bona fide public intellectual who was self-effacing, honest, energetic, eloquent, even charming. And the rest of us could only look on in envy."

"Or hatred," added Brahen, fixing Heather with her own assessing gaze. "Sounds like you still haven't figured out exactly how you feel about your old boy-friend, Ms. Kirkwood."

Heather leaned back with a clap of her hands. "Bravo! Rising to the bait at last, are you, Ensign?"

Judging from Marilyn Brahen's lowering brows, Caine suspected he'd better steer the conversation back to the original topic. "Heather, you already know I'm not in touch with anyone in the media. That's the first place you'd try to pick up my trail."

"One of the first. I tried tracking down your family, but no contact there, either."

"Never had much to be in contact with. Less now." *As in "zero."*

"What about your college friends? You had a pretty close circle of them from your undergrad years, if I remember correctly."

"You do—and you'll leave them out of this. As I have. I keep a low profile so that people who knew me *can't* contact me. It might not be—healthy—for them."

Heather leaned back with a frown. "So the rumors are true."

"What rumors?"

"That what you know is worth killing for."

"The Pearl," Barnard's Star 2 C

Martina Perduro turned away from her commplex with a sigh. "Damn it. I didn't even know we had half that many reporters in the civilian sector. And of course we just happened to send Riordan right out into the midst of them."

Trevor watched the monitors, tracking the progress of the blip that denoted the private maglev car which had whisked Caine away from the journalists and protesters. "Don't worry, Admiral. Riordan can handle the press."

"Handle them? He was one of them, wasn't he?"

"No, ma'am, not really." Trevor tapped the monitor as the interactive maglev-system diagram flickered uncertainly, then reasserted. "He just took some freelance reporting gigs to make ends meet in lean times."

"What did he do for a living?"

"Different things. Worked for *Jane's Defense Weekly* as an analyst for a while, then wrote books. Consulted, too. Defense and intelligence: all the major three-letter agencies. A few others, besides."

Perduro made a huffing noise. "I know those consultancies and their fees. How 'lean' could the times have been?"

"Pretty lean, because Caine has a serious flaw when it comes to working for the government."

"Which is?"

"Well, he has this real bad habit of telling the truth."

"Ah."

"Yeah. So he had an irregular career because he was always willing to wonder out loud about the so-called experts'—and his own—methods of analysis, and about the conclusions derived from them."

"So he got in trouble for doing his job properly?"

"Yep, particularly when his observations ran afoul of Ancient Agency Traditions. One time, he pointed out that age stratification in the intelligence organizations was crippling their counterintelligence analysis. Specifically, the generation gap had senior experts unaware that contemporary ciphers were incorporating pop-culture memes and semiology—which the under-thirty junior analysts could have recognized and decoded in their sleep. Caine wound up getting two supreme recognitions for that discovery."

"Which were?"

"Well, first he got a huge consultancy bonus."

"And the second?"

"They let him go. Never hired him back. Buried the files and findings."

"So he was the proverbial prophet, unwelcome in his own land."

"Well, there's that—but frankly, he's also not your typical beltway type."

"How so?"

"Admiral, have you ever worked with a polymath? A *real* polymath?"

Perduro smiled. "I served under Nolan Corcoran—remember?"

"Touché. But Dad—well, he liked managing people. Not Caine."

"Strange. He doesn't seem antisocial."

"He's not, Admiral, but, well, you know how artists don't work best in groups?"

"Sure."

"Yeah, well, that's kind of how Caine works, too. He's a team player, but he often does his best work independently. Probably because he doesn't think like most of the team."

Perduro picked up a hardcopy report printed on the light blue letterhead of the Med-Psych section. "'Subject Riordan evinces unusual balance between right and left lobe thought; demonstrates real-time syncretic problem-solving. Does not alternate between data intake and revision of situational contexts, but engages in both processes simultaneously.'"

Trevor raised an eyebrow. "Ma'am, if you had all that psych-eval data on Caine already, why ask me for my extremely inexpert assessment?"

"For the reason I indicated before, Captain: to get a human perspective that isn't all numbers and graphs and psychobabble. Thankfully, what you just shared confirms most of what the so-called experts have observed."

Trevor shrugged, turned to check the real-time rail system diagram for the progress of the private maglev car that was carrying Caine—and jerked forward to scrutinize the screen. "Admiral—" he started.

"I see it, Captain. Where the hell did that other car come from? Where's its transponder code? And what in blazes is it doing on the same track?"

And then the screen went dead. A moment later the security monitor feed blacked out also—followed by every light in the room.

Perduro punched the button to call the Duty Officer just as he came through the door and the red emergency lighting began to glow. "Admiral, we've got a widespread blackout on all—"

The power came back up, the lights flickering sharply before their luminance stabilized.

Perduro rounded on the hapless D.O. "Mr. Canetti, what the hell is happening on my base?"

"Ma'am, I don't know."

"Admiral," murmured Trevor. As Perduro turned toward him, he pointed to the security monitors and the maglev tracking screen. They, alone of all the electronic devices, were still dark.

"Son of a bitch," Perduro breathed.

"Came in to tell you about those systems in particular," Ensign Canetti blurted into the silence after her profanity. "Those systems went down first. And they went down hard."

"Okay, so get the techs on it. What went wrong, and where?"

"That's just it, Admiral. We don't know. The whole maglev tracking system—and the station and platform monitors—just seem to have, well, disconnected."

Trevor looked up sharply at the young ensign. *The system had just "disconnected?" Where had he heard* that *before?* Trevor jumped out of his chair, made for the doorway in the long, gliding leaps made possible by Barney Deucy's low-gee environment.

"Trevor, where the hell are you going?"

"Admiral, we don't have a lot of time. That kind of 'disconnection' is exactly what happened when the airlock on Convocation Station failed and almost sent Caine and one of the friendlier exosapients into hard vacuum. Similar electronic failures enabled a number of the other assassination attempts made against Caine, like the one at Alexandria."

"So where are you going?"

"To the last station stop on the maglev line." He looked at the D.O. "Do you have the main comms back yet?"

"Only the hard-wired system, sir."

"As soon as you can, get a message to the Shore Patrol to meet me at the last station on the civilian branch of the maglev line."

Perduro stood, frowning. "Why there?"

"Admiral Perduro, correct me if I'm wrong, but the track into the civilian section only extends a dozen meters or so beyond the final station. And they use that extension as a kind of shunting track: they leave cars there, or send them back the other way."

Perduro's frown deepened. "That's true."

"Then it's also like a dead-end canyon. Once there, the only way out is to come back along the stretch of track that the rogue car has already entered."

Perduro swallowed. "Putting Riordan between a speeding rock—"

"—and the very hard place at the end of the tunnel, Admiral. So with your leave—"

"Get the hell out of here, Captain. I'll have the SPs meet you at the last station if I have to find them and drag them there myself."

Off-base sector, Barnard's Star 2 C

Heather reclined again. "So, Caine, about these secrets of yours—"

Riordan looked out the windows, saw three amber lights pass in quick sequence. "Stop the car. Now."

"I don't take orders from you, Caine, and I—"

"Stop the car now or you won't hear another word from me."

Heather frowned, modulated a control on her palm-comp's screen. The car began to slow. "And I won't hear another word if I let you out, either."

"I'm not getting out. Ensign Brahen is. Those yellow lights we just passed mean we're within a few hundred meters of a maintenance siding. She's getting out there."

"Not exactly the safest place to leave an innocent child, Caine."

"Any place is safer than here with you," Riordan snapped back, waving down the ensign's inarticulate sputtering.

"Sir!" Brahen finally shouted, "I'm not going to leave you with this—"

"Ensign, there's only one thing you're going to do, and that is to follow my orders."

"But, sir—"

"Don't argue with him, little princess," cooed Heather, who smiled broadly when Ensign Brahen's fists balled up. "The grown-ups are going to talk about secrets, now. Secrets that would complicate your poor little life if they entered your poor little ears at this early stage of your poor little career."

Some combination of the taunting tone and probable truths coming out of Heather's mouth caused Marilyn Brahen to turn very red. "Ma'am, when I get back to the Pearl, I am going to make it my personal quest to find anything—*anything*—irregular or illegal in your actions while on Barnard's Star Two C. And if I find something, heaven help me, I'll—"

Heather brought the car to an abrupt stop. The ensign almost fell face down on the floor of the car. "Oops! So sorry! You were saying? Oh, but wait—you have to leave!" She pushed another control on her palmcomp; the maglev's door hissed open. A grimy, half-meter-wide access shelf, lit by a single blue-white LED lamp, was revealed. "Out you go, sweetie!" Brahen did so, fists still clenched, eyes hard. Heather pushed the control. The door shut and the car began moving again. She tossed her bangs, surveyed Caine for a long moment. "Well, well, alone at last. Time to spill your secrets."

Caine shook his head. "I promised to keep talking, Heather. Nothing more."

"Oh! A challenge! But not a very hard one. Because if you don't give me the leads I want, I will locate your old friends, ask them what they know."

"Which is less than nothing."

"Oh, I'm aware of that. But I also know that you'd probably do just about anything to protect them. And according to what you've said, a well-publicized research visit from me could be almost as unhealthy for them as if you had contacted them yourself."

Caine made himself remain calm. "I always knew you were a hard-nosed investigator, Heather. But when did you add extortion to your bag of tricks?"

"One has to be ready to use any leverage available. Particularly when it comes to you, Caine. You don't leave many loose ends." She paused, became sly, but no less serious. "And I'm sure that's why you were recruited to begin with."

"'Recruited'?"

"Don't play innocent with me, Caine. It's more than just an aversion to publicity that still had you sitting on the full story of what happened at Dee Pee Three and dishing out 'no comments' like they were party favors. After which you and a bunch of world-class movers and shakers disappeared into thin interstellar air for about a month. And now here you are on Barney Deucy, but not a hint of your high-profile pals. So I've got to wonder, what were you all doing, light-years away from where you belong?"

Caine didn't change his expression, couldn't afford to. *She may not have been told about the Convocation, but she's on the scent. Careful, now.*

Heather leaned forward. "I know you're not alone in this, Caine, that you're not an independent actor. You're covering for someone. But I'll disappear—right now, forever—if you just tell me who they are."

Damn, she was a manipulative monster, but she was good. Caine raised one eyebrow, "'They'?" he echoed. "There is no 'they.' I'm just a researcher doing my job."

"And I'm the Tsarina of all the Russias. Look, even if you can't tell me what's really going on, don't insult me with that 'I'm just a researcher' bullshit." Heather seemed genuinely frustrated, now. Her Northern New Jersey accent and diction were starting to bleed through. "Honey, they yanked you out of an icebox that you never agreed to enter, sent you on a top-secret research assignment almost twenty light-years from Earth, and then put you up as the main attraction at the Parthenon Dialogues—all achieved despite numerous attempts to kill you. And you want me to believe that you're still just a 'researcher,' no permanent strings attached? Horseshit."

Caine smiled. "You were ever the charmer, Heather."

"And you, Caine, still don't know who your real friends are."

His smile widened. "You mean, 'friends' like you?"

"You could at least show me a little gratitude. I *did* rescue you from those underemployed hacks back at the maglev station."

"Rescue me? From those ambulance chasers who you fed an 'anonymous tip' so that they'd accost me as soon as I emerged from The Pearl? So that I'd feel some subconscious gratitude, and be more pliable, when you serendipitously 'came to my rescue'? Nice try. Better luck next time."

"Knowing you, probably not." Heather leaned forward. "But I'm not depending on luck. I have facts. For instance, fact: you had twenty-four/seven access to both Nolan Corcoran and Arvid Tarasenko."

"So, having a close professional association with those two men automatically makes me—what? Their devoted servitor?"

"I'm not sure what it makes you, Caine. But you're more than just a researcher when your employers start hiding your work behind some pretty dark curtains of secrecy."

"Well, that's hardly surprising, Heather. After what I discovered on Delta Pavonis, they had to give me pretty high security clearances. At least until Parthenon was over."

Heather smiled. "No, that's what you'd *like* me to believe. But you're telling the tale a little bit backward, aren't you, Caine?" She leaned forward. "They had to give you those clearances and bring you into their shadowy world *before* sending you to Dee Pee Three.

You needed access to classified files, rank equivalents, and actual authority to get the job done there. All of which indicates that you were some kind of operative for them. And you're still working for whoever is in charge now." Heather frowned, thinking. "I'd bet a week's salary that Tarasenko's primary successor is Richard Downing. Some say he was the one who summoned that group of VIPs to Mars, where he just happened to be attending Nolan Corcoran's memorial service. Coincidence?"

"Why don't you ask Downing?"

"I would have, except, by the time I arrived, he'd been on a preaccelerating Earth-bound shift-carrier for two weeks, the one that finally shifted out a few days ago. But here's what I *don't* understand, Caine. Why should you be so loyal to them—to Downing, Corcoran, Tarasenko, whoever—given what they've done to you? And taken from you?"

A faint vibration started ascending through Caine's feet, buttocks, abdomen as a gentle down-spinning hum arose and the arrival tone chimed. *Saved by the bell.* He smiled at Heather. "Our stop? So soon?"

Heather was frowning down at her palmcomp's control screen. "Faster than I intended, actually."

Caine's smile did not change. "Thanks for the ride, Heather." He rose, noticed a sudden bloom of red light beyond the window at the rear of the car. The track warning light had flashed for a moment, then died suddenly. The green light—signaling a clear track—did not replace it.

"If you leave now, Caine, you leave me no choice but to contact your friends."

"Heather," said Caine, watching for the green—or

red—light to reappear, "the track signals are malfunctioning and we're at the dead-end of this spur. You
need to get out of this car. Now."

"I think you've got the situation reversed, Caine. I
don't have to leave, *you* have to *stay*. Assuming you
want your friends to remain safe."

Neither track status light had reilluminated, and
Caine felt a faint, growing tremor rising up through
the center of the floor, where the car had settled on
the rail.

One quick look at Heather's stubbornly rigid jaw
told him she wouldn't listen to reason in time. He
turned toward the door, spotted the emergency exit
panel. He smashed it with his elbow and hit the red
panic-release button.

As the door was rammed back into its recess by
the sudden discharge of a compressed-air cell, Heather
reared up. "What the hell are you doing, Caine?"

"We have to go, Heather," he shouted, grabbing
toward her. *"Right now!"*

Heather's reflexes were extremely swift but perfectly
wrong. As Caine closed with her, she swung back,
bringing up her legs and kicking, hard.

With his focus entirely upon getting her out of the
car, Caine didn't realize what Heather was doing until
her spiked heels jabbed sharply into his abdomen like
a double-barreled nail-gun. With a grunt, he found
himself stumbling backward, falling as his heel caught
on the rim of the exit. He landed half in the car, half
out the open door—

—and discovered a palmcom shoved into his face,
red recording light on, a bizarre tableau around him.
He had fallen out at the feet of yet another crowd

of shouting protestors. Each brandished a placard emblazoned with a crucifix being menaced by "little-green-man" aliens, who had also sprouted satanic red horns and black tails.

The girlish reporter who was leaning over him stuck her palmcom down so energetically that it bumped his lips. As she began her oblivious mantra—"Mr. Riordan, Mr. Riordan. Janel Bisacquino, Reuters Interstellar"— Caine scrambled to get his legs back under him, to get back into the car, to get Heather out—

But the reporter grabbed his shoulder as he rose, causing him to stumble farther away from the maglev car as she chattered into his ear, "Is it true that you were abducted by aliens on Delta Pavonis Three?"

"Heretic!" one of the protesters yowled over her shoulder from the lee of a long kiosk that paralleled the platform.

Caine shook off the reporter's hand, spun toward the open doorway of the car—beyond which Heather stood, her features softening into uncertainty—

With an up-dopplering screech, another maglev car shot out of the transport tube and rammed into Heather's half-size rental—just as Caine grabbed the reporter and dove for the ground.

The metallic shriek of the impact seemed to propel debris savagely outward, heat-hissing shards of metal and plastic corkscrewing over the two of them even as they fell. Screams arose from the protesters. One had gone down, hands clutched to a face shredded by a wave of shattered glass from the kiosk. Others, panicked, fled wildly. One journalist who had evidently been hidden behind the placards was fleeing with the mob. Another was already getting footage of the crash, as well as the blood gushing from the face of the wounded protester. Ms. Bisacquino looked at the smoking ruin of the two cars—a pair of crushed tin cans forever fused and frozen in some savage mating frenzy—her mouth open, mute, and motionless.

"Come on," said Caine, as the flash-heated synthetics in the cars began to smolder. "We've got to get off this platform."

Chapter Four

Off-base sector, Barnard's Star 2 C

The last station's collision klaxon began hooting as Trevor reached the outer gate area. The emergency access portal dilated and spat out a torrent of terrified humanity. Fighting against the outflow of bodies, the stink of panicked sweat and the choking fumes of smoldering plastic, he pushed his way toward the station's long, narrow platform—

—and entered a tableau of chaos. Dodging broken glass and smoking metal, the remaining crowd converged upon the main exit, with a few of the rearmost changing direction toward the portal Trevor had just used. No sign of the Shore Patrol—the wireless comm channels had not reactivated yet—and only a handful of people were still on the platform itself, most of those wounded or just rising from where they had taken cover—

Caine swayed up into Trevor's field of view at the far end of the station, just a few meters away from the mauled remains of the two maglev cars. As he reached down to help a young woman back to her feet, Trevor saw movement a few meters farther down the platform.

From the shadows near a bank of ticket dispensers lining station's far wall, a tall, lean, knot-muscled man emerged with a knife in his right hand, drawn back for an overhand slash. Trevor took a long leap down to the platform level, yelling "Caine, behind you!"

But Caine was already changing his direction of movement. In the same instant that he released the arm of the young woman he had helped up, his turn accelerated into a fast pivot, spinning him fully around. His right arm cocked back even as his left arm rose swiftly—

—and caught his attacker's descending forearm. Caine's imperfect but serviceable rising block pushed the down-slashing knife-hand up and out of the way. Without any break in motion, Riordan closed the distance with a quick step and his already-cocked right hand came forward like a pile driver. The heel of his palm rammed into his assailant's face, just beneath the nose. Blood spurted, the knife wobbled, the man staggered back a step—

Caine's momentum carried him through a sideways stance and into a fast left-foot-forward shuffle. As he did so, he drew his right knee up high and, in a blur, shot that leg out straight as his torso leaned back.

Caine's step-through side kick caught the reeling attacker in the sternum. The man crashed backward into the ticket machines and then down to the ground, groaning faintly. By the time Trevor reached Riordan two seconds later, the platform was empty except for the two of them and the corpse of one protester whose chest had been transfixed by two lengths of blackened metal.

Trevor put out an arm to steady the suddenly swaying

Caine, looked down at his would-be murderer. "I guess Opal was a pretty good karate teacher."

Caine rose, glanced at Trevor. "Oh. You knew about her giving me lessons back on Mars, then?"

"Damn it, Caine." Corcoran sighed. "Everyone knew." He gestured toward the prone attacker. "What the hell is going on here?"

"Based on prior experience," muttered Caine, straightening up, "I'd say that was an assassination attempt. Two of them, actually."

"Yeah, but how—?"

"Trevor, 'how' doesn't much apply to the attacks we've been dealing with since Alexandria. Nor do the words 'impossible' or 'unimaginable.' Because whoever is behind them has trump cards that we didn't even know were in the deck."

Trevor heard movement behind them. The first members of the Shore Patrol trotted through the emergency portal, weapons out. Trevor waved them over, pointed down at the feebly moving attacker, then leaned closer to Caine. "Guess you've got eyes in the back of your head, seeing him coming at you."

"The reporter I helped up saved me, I think. She saw him over my shoulder, and I saw her eyes move. But also, I had this feeling—" Caine stopped.

Trevor waited while the Shore Patrol hauled the attacker to his feet and dragged him toward the exit. "What do you mean, 'I had a feeling'?" he muttered.

Riordan shook his head. "I don't know how to say it. Just before he got to me, it felt as though the whole universe was no longer fluid; like I was a small cog in the middle of a very fast, but very stiff and very big machine."

"And that—feeling—warned you that some guy was about to carve you up from behind?"

"No, just that something nearby was—was, well, *wrong* somehow. So I defended the place I was most vulnerable: behind me, where I couldn't see."

Trevor grabbed Caine's arm and started moving him toward the exit. "Man, I know twenty-year veterans who don't have reflexes like that. Didn't think you had them, either."

"That's because I *don't* have them. I wasn't following a fighting instinct, Trevor. It was more like a—a premonition."

"Well, whatever it is, it sure as hell saved your bacon. And we sure as hell have to get back to the Pearl."

Caine nodded. "Absolutely. Because there's one additional thing that needs to be reported, and quickly."

"What's that?"

"The guy who attacked me was on the first platform, too. He threw a bottle at me, then ran like hell."

"What? But how could he know you were going to stop here or—?"

"I don't know, Trevor. And I don't know how he managed to sprint through four kilometers of tight tunnels to get here before my maglev. Or how he went from religious zealot to..." Caine's voice trailed off.

Trevor watched the S.P.s shackling the attacker to a restraint bar. "How he went from being a zealot to—what?"

Caine swallowed. "A madman. No, that's not right: a killing machine. He was a wild-eyed screamer when I saw him at the first station. But here—" Caine turned to look over his shoulder. Trevor followed his gaze. The hollow eyes of Caine's would-be assassin had been following them steadily, calmly, empty of reason but full of a lethal, insatiable hunger.

Off-base sector, Barnard's Star 2 C

The CoDevCo special services liaison who oversaw corporate operations on Barnard's Star Two C stared at the last, frozen image that had been pirated from the maglev security system: Riordan and Corcoran hurrying away from the crash site. The liaison's jaw worked unevenly; his face grew steadily more red.

His mounting fury was defused by a slow, steady voice from behind, which ordered as much as intoned, "Calm yourself."

The liaison turned toward the man whom he served, at the behest of his superior CoDevCo Vice President R. J. Astor-Smath. Although having worked under this tall, sunglass-wearing man for almost three months, he still knew almost nothing about him, other than that he had a profound penchant for olives. "I do not know how you can be so calm. Two failed attempts in the course of a single minute? This is preposterous."

"Riordan is not as easy to kill as he might seem to an unprofessional observer. He may lack training, but he reasons quickly and has almost infallible instincts in a crisis."

"So you consider today's outcome less than disastrous?"

The tall, sun-glassed man leaned back in his seat with a sigh. "I find it interesting how many of you, when watching a plan go awry, are so blinded by your frustration that you are unable to learn from what you have witnessed."

The liaison mastered his annoyance at the man's customary, languid arrogance, in part because it was his job to do so, and in part because the man was usually—and infuriatingly—accurate in his observations. "And what was to be learned from what we witnessed today?"

"Why, that it was good fortune that today's attempts were failures. Your superior's ill-advised machinations to encumber Riordan by focusing the interest of the press upon him has produced troublesome results—precisely as I warned. Riordan is now an item of journalistic attention and scrutiny. Kill him, and inquiry will follow. And that inquiry would result in closer investigation of a variety of phenomena which you—and I—wish to remain merely puzzling anomalies in the minds of our adversaries."

"Such as Tarasenko's and Corcoran's heart attacks?"

"Those too, yes, but the failed attempt to assassinate Riordan in Alexandria is of greater concern to me. There, we left them with too many unsolvable puzzles. If your news services, or intelligence communities, are repeatedly agitated by such mysteries and 'baffling coincidences,' they will eventually begin to consider explanations that they now dismiss as not merely improbable, but impossible. This would be a grave development for us. We wish our opponents to remain complacent, content to follow the forensic pathways to which they are accustomed, which their science deems 'rational.'"

"If Riordan were to die because of a very conventional knife in his chest, that would not raise any such suspicions."

The tall man shook his head, took a green olive from a small bowl located at arm's length. "All of you think too linearly. To you, the universe is comprised of infinite rows of dominoes, each ready to be tapped and set in motion. Yet you assume that each row is almost entirely independent from the others." He chewed into the olive as if he had never tasted one before, and sighed. "But a few of you do see the truth of it: that the dominoes are arranged in sweeping curves that intersect, spread, double back, terminate each other, or engender new vectors, new events. So, if you eliminate Riordan in a place where the press is present or has ready access, there is an excellent chance that you may set other, deleterious events in motion."

The tall man evidently noticed the uncertainty creasing his liaison's brow. He deigned to explicate. "A society's entrenched attitudes and predilections are balanced upon a broad cultural fulcrum: they are robust and stable, but if pushed and stressed far enough, they tip and change—often becoming the opposite of what they just were. If you kill Riordan in an inexplicable accident—the kind you persistently pressure me to create through my Reifications of quantum entanglement and uncertainty—our adversaries are likely to detect that pattern. Their present tolerance for unconnected coincidences could convert into a fierce resolve to get answers, no matter the cost, and no matter how strange those answers might be.

"And they just might succeed. Not all of our opponents see the universe in the simplistic one-cause, one-effect paradigm that most of you are trapped within." The man nodded at the frozen image of Caine, fleeing the platform, looking over his shoulder. "He is one who sees more expansively, more completely. Nolan Corcoran, his companion's father, was another."

The liaison folded his arms. "Let us presume all you have said is true. It is also true that you yourself have asserted that Riordan may now be able detect the onset of your Reifications—which must be why he detected today's attacker. He felt you 'push' our man. Add all this to your observations that Riordan is particularly hard to predict, and that now, he is likely to depart for Earth before we do. Taken together, these things put us on the brink of failure. Riordan might soon slip beyond our collective grasp."

The tall man stopped chewing an olive and smiled— an expression which reminded his assistant of a tiger baring its teeth. "Riordan might slip beyond your grasp. But not mine."

"The Pearl," Barnard's Star 2 C

The first thing Caine saw when the door to the secure debrief room opened was Admiral Martina Perduro sitting at the other end, her body as still as a graven idol's, her face as pale and immobile as a slab of sun-weathered oak. Caine snapped his best salute a second after Trevor did.

Perduro waved them to chairs. As soon as they crossed the threshold, she touched her dataslate. The doors sealed and the breathy whirr of a white-noise generator rose up from the peripheries of the room. Then she indicated the screens around her. "I've got all the technical reports on today's nonsense with the maglev cars. None of which can explain the failures in the system. But I'm guessing you two have heard similarly 'impossible' reports on prior occasions. You particularly, Commander Riordan."

"Ma'am?"

"The assessments are very reminiscent of those Mr. Downing shared with me regarding the after-action reports from the assassination attempts you dodged at Alexandria and the Convocation Station: circuits uncoupling, polarities reversing, breakers tripping, computer controls being overridden without any evidence of hacking." She tossed down her dataslate and passed a hand across her brow. "It doesn't make a damn bit of sense."

Caine shrugged. "It never does, ma'am. And we never even have leads as to who's behind these incidents."

Perduro arched forward. "Well, at least we've got a lead this time."

"You mean, the attacker?"

The admiral scoffed, surprised. "No, Heather Kirkwood—who, if rumors hold any truth, may have had both personal and professional motives to set you up, Caine."

Caine made sure that his differing opinion did not come out as a contradiction. "Admiral, I know it might seem that way, but I think Heather may have been a patsy as well."

"Why? Because whoever she was working for was willing to kill her, too? Commander Riordan, after a mission, covert operators frequently prevent security leaks by eliminating any free-lancer they hired to carry it out. 'Burning assets,' it's called."

"Yes, ma'am, I am familiar with that concept."

"And according to your report, Kirkwood was attempting to extort highly classified information."

"Absolutely."

"So how does that not add up to the following scenario: she tries to extort information from you, she fails, and her handlers kills both of you to cover up their identity and interest in those particular secrets?"

Caine nodded. "I agree it looks that way, Admiral, but I've got information that problematizes the hypothesis."

"Which is?"

"Personal knowledge of Heather Kirkwood. Would she take a tip from a shady source in order to get what she wants? She wouldn't bat a lash, doing that. Would she actually, or at least threaten to, endanger old friends of mine if she thought it might get me to cooperate? Sadly, yes. And would she selectively reveal the time and place I was going to emerge from the Pearl to ensure that the local press and activist groups would be there to generate a more provocative scenario and story? Unquestionably. But here's where the hypothesis breaks down: Heather wasn't a killer."

Perduro shrugged. "So you say. I'm not convinced. And from what Ensign Brahen told me, you might have been at the top of Kirkwood's death list, if she had one."

Caine shook his head. "Heather Kirkwood was ambitious, vain, selfish, and couldn't stop trying to outdo everyone at everything—particularly the people she was closest to. But she hadn't the stomach for murder and frankly, had every reason not to be involved, directly or indirectly, in any attempt to kill me."

Trevor glanced at him, frowning. "Why?"

"Because she did not stand to gain anything by my death. Quite the opposite. If she was in any way connected to an event in which I was killed, she'd come under investigation simply because of our prior contact. And here's a cardinal rule in the journalism business: you can report news only so long as you don't *become* news. So if she was ever implicated, even tangentially, in the murder of a politically significant former lover, that could have ended her career. Even if she was ultimately exonerated."

"So again, we've got no leads," sighed Trevor, "just another closed room mystery. Just like Alexandria."

Perduro's gestures became sharp, testy. "Yes, and it's rife with the same kind of logical gaps. How did they know that either of you had gone to the still-secret Convocation? And, beyond that, how did they know that you had returned to human space? How did the assassin's handlers know which maglev car Caine was in? How did they have Kirkwood's private car ready to follow it into the first station? And how did they manage—on that short notice—to override our supposedly unhackable maglev traffic-control software to get another car to follow, and then ram Caine's car?"

Trevor frowned. "Well, this time, at least you've got one survivor you can interrogate: the religious fanatic."

"Except it turns out he's not a religious fanatic," Perduro snapped.

Caine stared. "What—ma'am?"

"The man who attacked you had no known affiliations with the local extremist sects. None of them know him. In fact, the 'fanatic' has no identity that we can determine."

Now it was Trevor's turn. "What?"

"He is a nonperson, as far as the ID system is concerned. And here at the Pearl, we maintain a very up-to-date registry."

Trevor was frowning now. "Have you interrogated him, Admiral?"

"We wanted to."

Caine heard the frustrated tone. "Admiral, what do you mean 'we *wanted* to'?"

"I mean he was found dead in his cell fifteen minutes before you walked in here."

"And let me guess. The probable cause of death was a heart attack?"

"No, Commander. This time, it was a stroke. Massive. He was dead within a minute. There was no response to either immediate CPR or more heroic methods."

Trevor leaned back. "Ma'am, as you say, these are just the kinds of mysteries that seem to accumulate around the attempts on Commander Riordan's life."

Riordan shook his head. "Except that there's an even larger mystery that hasn't been mentioned yet."

Perduro turned toward Caine. "And what mystery is that?"

Caine looked at Perduro uncertainly. Even though she was asking about a piece of data she'd overlooked, she still might resent having it "explained" to her. Riordan considered how best to ease into the topic—

However, Trevor's patience was exhausted after two seconds. "Well, what are you waiting for, Caine? A drum roll?"

"I don't need a drum, but it would sure be handy to have a crystal ball like the one the opposition is using. Because there's no other way to explain how they got all the press here in time to meet me coming out of the Pearl."

Perduro made a face. "The presence of the press can

be explained by a simple intel leak. No one needed a crystal ball to predict your movements."

Caine spread his hands. "Admiral, Trevor, I know enough about the journalism field to be familiar with its basic workings. And here are some facts about field reporters. They are not lurking everywhere, just waiting to pop up with a palmcom set to record. They are assigned to, or string as freelancers in, high-activity news zones. Which Barney Deucy is not. However, they can also be found in locales where an editor has sent them, on the hunch that a newsworthy situation is brewing there."

"Like a special task force," supplied Trevor.

"Exactly. Now here's the hitch. I did some checking while we were waiting to outbrief you, Admiral, and it seems the journalists who mobbed me at the first monorail station only arrived here eight days ago. Now, doing the reverse math of how long it took them to travel to Barney Deucy after they shifted in, that means they left Earth about four days before that. Of course, before they could shift out from Earth, they had to preaccelerate for at least thirty-three days—"

Perduro's face became even more pale than it had been when they entered: her eyes opened wide as the calendar implications drove in upon her. "Jesus, Mary, and Joseph, that means most of the surplus reporters here today got their marching orders to come to Barney Deucy at least forty-five days ago. At a minimum."

"But—" started Trevor. And then he stopped, his own eyes widening.

Caine nodded. "We hadn't even shifted out to get to the Convocation yet. In fact, their travel had to start just a few days after Nolan's memorial, about fifty days ago, to be here for today's freelancer feeding frenzy. And fifty days ago, we had no idea how the Convocation would turn out, or that we'd only be there for a few days, or that Downing, Trevor, and I would detour here, instead of returning directly to Earth, as the rest of the delegates did."

"So someone knew what we were planning before it was planned?" Trevor's voice climbed to a surprisingly high pitch on the last word.

Caine shrugged. "That's why I'm half-convinced they have a crystal ball, Trevor."

"Either that," muttered Perduro, "or whoever is behind all these closed room mysteries can send information faster than the speed of light."

Caine nodded. "Or can shift between the stars much faster and much farther than we can, and slip that information to human collaborators."

"What a reassuring set of alternatives," grumbled Trevor.

"Isn't it, though?" Perduro's voice was almost as rough and deep as the ex-SEAL's. "I'll code this into a report and send it out to the *Prometheus* ahead of you. She—and your cutter—are due to get to her Earth-optimized shift point in about three weeks, but you never know what might happen between now and then." She stood. "And I think I'd better run a general defense drill."

"A drill, ma'am?" asked Caine.

"Yes, Commander. I believe Mr. Downing told you he put us on Defcon Three. We've kept it from the civilian sector, as per orders, but I wish we didn't have to. People don't react well to news of an unexpected threat if you spring it on them at the last second."

Trevor's grin was wry. "Must be darn hard to prepare people to deal with exosapient invaders you don't have permission to talk about yet, Admiral."

"Trevor, get out of here before you make my brain hurt any worse than it already does. Now, have both of you filled out your resignations from active duty?"

Caine and Trevor produced the carefully folded papers, handed them to Perduro.

Who scanned them with a scowl. "Damn idiotic charade, this. I hope Downing knows what he's doing. I promote you yesterday, and pack you off into the Reserves today? Insane."

Caine shrugged. "As I understand it, his primary reason is so that, coming back as civilians, we can slip in under the press's radar. At least they won't have any immediate knowledge that I'm part of the Navy, now."

Perduro shook her head, put out her hand. "Commander, Captain. I hereby accept and duly record your departures from active service. It's been a pleasure having you here, gentlemen." Releasing Trevor's hand, she suddenly looked her full age. "After today's events, and what it implies about our undisclosed adversary's ability to run rings around us on the calendar, I'm seriously considering moving this facility to Defcon Two on my own initiative. And I think you gentlemen should move up your departure time to catch the *Prometheus*, just in case she has to fuse a little extra deuterium to get out of town ahead of schedule."

Caine nodded at the ominous implications of that precaution. "And when do you recommend we depart, Admiral?"

"Five minutes ago, Commander. Get the hell out of my sight, grab your gear, and Godspeed to you both."

Chapter Five

Outbound from Barnard's Star 2 C

Fifty minutes later, while settling into the accommoda-tions on the modular cutter that was set to sternchase and catch the *Prometheus* before her shift, Caine fin-ished folding the dress uniform he had worn precisely one time: yesterday, when he had been commissioned in the Space Force. He stared at the silver oak leaf on the jacket's shoulder. *God damn, how the hell did I get through four weeks of combined basic and OCS? And zero-gee ops and logistics? And combat simulators and live-fire range time whenever I wasn't up to my eyeballs in refresher calculus and space physics?* Between the trip-hammer pace and never more than five hours of sleep a night, it had become an absurdist comedy by week three. And then, with a salute and a step back, it was all over. Mustered out into the Reserves. As if it had never happened at all.

From the other side of the cramped cabin, Trevor's voice was wry. "Thinking great thoughts?"

"Hell, just thinking. I forgot what that feels like."

Trevor emitted a short laugh. "Yeah, they kept you busy. Kept shifting gears between brain-work and body-work, too. Although that can help."

"Why?"

Trevor didn't look up, kept entering security codes into their shared commplex. He was determined to finish changing the habmod's registry from military to civilian/diplomatic before the cutter got underway. "When I went into the Teams, the hardest thing about hell-week was that it was almost all physical. They just kept hammering at you, at the same strengths or weaknesses. Half the battle for me was finding a way to cope with the monotony." Trevor turned away from the commplex. Now when the module arrived at Earth, it would not indicate its passengers were military personnel. "Fortunately, I had a very colorful instructor."

"Colorful?"

"Stosh Witkowski. Never cusses, but he has a rare talent for inventing the most elegant insults that I have ever heard. And of course, I got a particularly rich share of his attention."

"Why?"

"Why?" Trevor looked at Caine as if he was yet another new species of exosapient. "I was an officer, an Annapolis legacy, and the child of a celebrity father." The last word threatened to catch in his throat; Trevor rose and exited their stateroom briskly, waved for Caine to follow. "Let's get something to eat before they make us strap in."

Caine followed Trevor into the small galley that was opposite the module's combination entry hatch/docking ring. The small observation port—still unsealed—offered a memorable view: framed by the top-and-bottom grid-work of the cutter's module-laden trusses, the system's second gas giant loomed as a great black arc, backlit by the dim red glow of the occulted Barnard's Star. A blood-washed white dot winked near the shoulder of the dark planetary curve.

Trevor nodded at the speck. "Say goodbye to The Pearl. They'll be shutting the viewport any minute now."

"Why?"

"Meteorology detected a flare, just as we came on board. Nothing too rough, but in addition to the rads kicked off by the gas giant, you'll want more than a layer of sunscreen between you and the Great Out There."

"Has The Pearl changed much since the last time you were here?"

"Does a 'Force base *ever* change?"

Caine snagged a cube of water, unfolded the integral straw. "You tell me. It seemed—well, almost deserted."

Trevor nodded, perching on the countertop across from Caine in the excessively cozy space. "Yeah, and I had expected the opposite. Given all the traffic that's been through here, and all the carriers and combat craft that the rosters say are in-system, I was sure the place would be overflowing, not a ghost town."

Caine looked at him directly. "Galley scuttlebutt says that it's because almost all the combat hulls are already deployed and double-crewed. Waiting."

Trevor sipped his water, waved a dismissive hand: "Yeah, yeah, the Defcon Three that no one mentions and everyone knows about. Great cover-up, too: lots of threadbare bullshit about 'routine maneuvers.' Meanwhile, it's common knowledge that assets are being dispersed to undisclosed groupment points or are shifting out-system to the 'training reserve' at Ross 154. Some secret."

"And all that precautionary activity wouldn't clear the bleachers?"

"Not like this, no. It wasn't just the lack of shipside ratings cycling through the base. It was the constant reduction of dirtside techs. Do you know that there were fifteen hundred cryocelled maintenance and construction personnel sent back on the last carrier that went out?"

"Are replacements on the way?"

Trevor shook his head. "I went down to the slips, asked around. Nada."

"So what do you think the brass is up to, and why aren't they telling us?"

"They're not telling us because we're not in the need-to-know loop." Trevor grinned ruefully. "And since no one here is aware that we're IRIS operatives, no one is aware that we have the clearance to hear the secrets they're not going to tell us, anyway. On the up side, we also never had to use those goofy, Odyssey-based code names my father hung on us."

"Admiral Perduro knows about our clearance levels."

"Yeah, but I'm not so sure she's fully in the loop herself. Look how she reacted to your commissioning orders: an official posting to Naval Intelligence but with a track for unrestricted line promotions. I don't think she saw that coming, judging from the way she frowned when she read it out to you."

Caine nodded. "I think you're right. Downing cut the orders; she just cut the ribbon."

"Thereby authorizing you to wreak havoc amongst genuine military personnel."

"Smile when you say that, Captain."

"I was."

"Didn't look like it."

"I was smiling inside."

"Uh huh."

Trevor did smile now. "Look, nothing against you, Caine, but Uncle Richard seems to be making this stuff up as he goes along. My promotion, your commission and 'training,' our immediate conversion to reserve status: this is so nonregulation, that I'm past being surprised. For all I know, he might try to appoint someone as Grand Fez-Wearing Poo-Bah of the God-Emperor's Armada. What he's been doing with ranks and titles and clearances—hell, it's just not done."

"Well, maybe not, but Downing had sign-offs from the president and the Joint Chiefs."

"Yeah, but just because it comes from so high up the chain of command that no one dares question it doesn't mean that it's in trim with the regs. And I'm telling you, based on eighteen years of first-hand experience, that it is all non-reg. Sooner or later, someone's going to insist upon an explanation."

Caine nodded, watched as the incandescent crimson edge of the planet's terminator rotated into view. "Yeah, there are a whole *lot* of explanations that would be pretty welcome right now."

Trevor glanced at Caine. "You mean, explanations for all the attacks on you?"

"Yeah, and on your dad and Tarasenko. And Elena's abduction on Mars. Every time I try to make sense of the incidents, the unanswered questions come hammering down like I'm hatless in a hailstorm."

Trevor smiled ruefully. "Judging from your tone of voice, you're getting pelted by those questions right now."

"Not all of them, but there's one incident that has started to trouble me more than the others," Caine admitted.

"Which one?"

"Remember those two Russians who broke into my room on Mars and tried to kill me? That attack just doesn't make any sense at all."

Trevor's voice was mildly incredulous. "You mean, it makes *less* sense than the others?"

Caine nodded. "Yeah. Actually, almost all the others were conducted by faceless assassins, people who—like the guy today—don't officially exist. But the Russian I killed on Mars not only had an identity, he was part of their consulate's security force. And Russians, Trevor? *Russians?* That makes almost as little sense as my living through the attack."

"You mean because the second guy left you alive when you were out cold?"

"Damned right. What the hell was that about? He had at least three minutes to kill me while I was senseless on the floor, before the police showed up. But all he does is cut my left arm?" Caine stared at the now almost-invisible four-inch scar, and shook his head. "It doesn't make any sense."

"Yeah, well, at least you'll be able to get some updates on the investigation, now that we're heading back to Earth—"

Their habitation module's main access portal rammed shut with a metallic slap. Blood-red emergency flashers strobed in syncopation with the alarm klaxon.

"—Or maybe not," Trevor finished. "We've gotta move. That's an automated call to general quarters."

Caine rose to follow Trevor—and crashed into the right side of doorjamb face-first. The cutter had ceased acceleration, and without the thrust to hold Caine in place, the world had tilted out from under him in mid step. Drifting backward, Riordan struggled to remember his zero-gee training, flailed his arms, caught the left side of the jamb, steadied himself. From beyond the hatchway coaming, Trevor's voice was sharp. "Goddamnit, Caine: move! We've got to get out of this can."

"Wha—?"

"Just shut up and follow me to the module access tube."

"And then?"

"Just follow me for now."

Small drops of his own blood swimming up past his eyes, Caine grabbed a handhold, propelled himself through the combination hatchway and docking ring—and stopped just before crashing into Trevor's extremely broad back. "What gives?"

Trevor was squinting up the cutter's spinal access corridor, to which all its modules were attached like ribs to a sternum. He shook his head and started pulling himself hand over hand in the opposite direction. "Follow me. Fast as you can go."

Caine trailed Trevor inexpertly, but noticed that it became rapidly easier to use the handholds. Sort of like crossing monkey-bars underwater. But the arm-over-arm half-swim, half-climb rhythm was broken when Trevor turned ninety degrees "down," plunging through a hole in what Caine was still thinking of as the "deck." Caine followed awkwardly, looked around as he came through the docking-ring coaming and then the hatchway: the Auxiliary Command module. "Why are we here?" Caine asked.

Trevor was already activating various systems, bringing up monitors, screens, relays. "From here we can tap into bridge comms, sensor data and—"

"—and run the ship if something happens to the bridge crew."

Trevor glanced at Caine, who was watching his actions closely. "I guess you were paying attention in some of those classes."

"Well, yeah." Caine dogged the hatch, which doubled as an outer-airlock door when the module was in free space. "But I wasn't thinking about access to auxiliary's redundant controls."

Trevor spun open the inner airlock hatchway. "No? So what *were* you thinking about?"

"Er . . . I was thinking that it's the only module really capable of autonomous operations."

Trevor stopped in the hatchway. His look of surprise quickly became one of grim affirmation. "You're right. Auxiliary command is the best lifeboat on this barge. Certainly the only one with any sustained maneuver capabilities." Trevor moved to the command console, powered it up, moved his hand toward the fusion plant's initiation switch.

Caine caught Trevor's hand before he could light it up. "Not a good idea."

Trevor looked at Caine's hand restraining his own, then up into his face. "Have a good reason."

"Survival."

"What do you mean?"

"Trevor, if we're at general quarters because some of

our interstellar neighbors have decided to come calling with their equivalent of shotguns and machetes, then I think we might not want to be sending out radiant emissions—of any kind—from this module."

Trevor's frown subsided slowly. "Christ, you're probably right. But let's not guess, let's find out." Trevor tapped his collarcom. "Bridge."

A delay, then a babble of background voices—too many of which were rapid and high-pitched—before they got a direct response: "Clear this channel and stay off—"

"Son, this is Mr. Corcoran. Status?"

A pause. "Oh—Captain. Sorry, sir. I—"

"No need to be sorry. I'm just asking for a courtesy sitrep."

"Yes, sir. We don't have all the info, sir. We're pretty far down the intel food chain from CINCBAR-COMCENT. But it looks like something shifted into system. Not running a transponder signal."

"You mean, not running an Earth transponder signal?"

"No, sir. I mean whatever it is, is dark. Completely dark, except for neutrino emissions."

"You mean, its shift signature?"

"No sir, I mean its pumping out neutrinos and—well, subparticulate garbage."

"In a beam?"

Caine got Trevor's attention, shook his head.

"Stand by." He turned toward Caine. "What?"

"Trevor, that doesn't sound like a weapon signature. Sounds more like a field effect of some sort."

"Yeah, like a shift signature."

"But since it's done shifting, and the signature is

never more than a brief pulse, it's got to be something else."

"Like what?"

"Some kind of engine or power plant. What else would create neutrinos?"

"I don't know; let's find out." Trevor called up the feed from the bridge sensors. Nothing except a red blinking cursor which marked the mystery ship's real-time location within the star field.

"What's its range?" Caine asked.

"Tell you in a second." Trevor reconfigured the screens slightly. "Lying out at one hundred kiloklicks, doing nothing."

"Yeah, sure. Ten to one it's running passive sensors and making a list of the active systems we've lit up to assess it: what kind of emissions, where from, phased or single arrays."

Trevor nodded. "Essentially, they're building a target list. And testing our response, maybe hoping to draw some fire."

"Which would also be invaluable intel."

"But it's too goddamned small to be a shift-carrier."

"Trevor, who says the Arat Kur—if that's who's come calling—have to work on our scale of shift carriers? You saw how small the Dornaani hull was that carried us to the Convocation. What if the Arat Kur can make something that's only two or three times larger?"

"And so they send it ahead to gather intel. But how do they go home to report? Say 'pretty please' and then go tank up at one of the outer gas giants?"

"No. They're not going back home."

"What do you mean?"

"Trevor, this is not a 'scout and withdraw' mission. This is a probing force that's also playing Judas goat. It has to be, because in the next few minutes, they must either use, or lose, their tactical surprise."

"Which means that a follow-up force—"

"Can't be far behind, particularly if they want to make good use out of the target list they're compiling. And since their first ship might get a powerfully unfriendly reception—"

"—they had to assume that it might not survive too long if left on its own. And that means—" Trevor tapped his collarcom again. "Bridge."

A different voice. "Sir, this is Lieutenant Hazawa. I don't mean to be rude, but—"

"Lieutenant, shoot this message up the chain using my name and reserve rank, marked for Admiral Perduro. Message begins: urgent that we presume enemy fleet inbound—"

And then it was bedlam on the other end of the channel: contact klaxons; shouted orders; a loud, steady recitation of a long string of bearing and range marks. Sensor ops cut in. "Skipper, we're getting direct feed from The Pearl's arrays and remote platforms. Major gravitic distortions above the ecliptic, registering at regular intervals, accompanied by bursts of cosmic and gamma rays. High confidence these are multiple shift signatures. Estimating fourteen and still counting—"

Caine felt a fast flush of panic. *Fourteen? Good God—*

"Mass scanners and high-end EM emission sensors confirm presence of large spacecraft, apparently in two groups. Range to first group is approximately two hundred kiloklicks. Range to second group is

approximately four hundred kiloklicks. Awaiting definitive range estimates from active arrays."

Trevor frowned. "Two waves."

"Or the fleet's direct engagement elements are out
in front, screening its supporting auxiliaries and landing forces. How are we responding?"

Trevor spent a moment more listening to the comm
chatter. "Sounds like we're moving seventy to eighty
percent of our heaviest and fastest hulls to a direct
intercept. Probably most of our drones and control
sloops as well."

"The others? In reserve?"

"I don't think so. The chatter makes me think that
they're a trailing escort for the shift carriers."

"Which are where?"

"Well, four were in far orbit after refit and upgrades.
My guess is that they're moving at best possible speed
toward the shift points and have activated the automated tankers for rendezvous during preacceleration."

"Do you think they can make it?"

"They've got a better chance than the two older
carriers that were in the slips. They'll be lucky to cast
off before the hammer comes down."

"If they can cast off at all; I heard some scuttlebutt that the work crews hadn't even received the
new drives, yet."

Trevor nodded sourly. "It figures, if it's true. The
repair and retrofitting work has been so extensive
that it's been getting backlogged—and you never want
to have that many ships tied up in one place at the
same time."

"So, given The Pearl's current traffic jam, a worst-
case scenario today means—"

"It means we lose six military shift carriers and most of their fighting-ship complements: the majority of the Commonwealth and Federation fleets, combined."

Caine looked at the nav screen, followed the pencil-thin orbit plots of the various human vessels against the black circular backdrop of the gas giant, saw them all spiraling out from the now golf-ball-sized orb that was The Pearl. The name had been a bad omen, after all—except this promised to be even worse than Pearl Harbor. There, the most important ships, the fleet carriers, had been out of port when the Japanese Zeros and Kates came out of the sky and put the rest of the Pacific Fleet at the bottom of the stretch of water known as Battleship Row.

And at least there had been something to do, in those days. You saw your enemy. You could pick up a rifle or a submachine gun and fire your own small counterattack—and expression of rage and retribution—into the sky, trying to gouge the red, rising-sun eyes that stared down from the bottom of each aircraft's wings. But here, in space, the enemy appeared at a distance of almost one full light-second. And you waited and listened and did nothing. You sat in relative comfort, with access to reams of data that might mean one's own—or one's species'—death and were absolutely unable to do anything about it except watch, reassess, and watch some more. And whereas Caine had been frustrated by that "sit on your hands" aspect of how events proceeded in space, Opal Patrone had been nearly driven to distraction by it.

Caine smiled. Opal was just about the most direct person he knew, often bordering on the impetuous.

A trait she proved not only in the staff room but the bedroom. And yet, despite her forthright manner, her innermost feelings remained a mystery to him. Perhaps because they were still a mystery to her as well; Opal was all about action rather than reflection.

Caine felt his brow wrinkle, his smile sadden. His feelings for Elena notwithstanding, by the end of the Convocation he had already begun to realize that he and Opal were simply not the same kind of people, did not speak the same kind of language. Perhaps, by the time he saw her again on Earth, she would have realized it herself. But even if she hadn't, and even if Elena had not reemerged into Caine's memory and life, it was far better to let things end now. The alternative was to have his and Opal's fledgling relationship slowly erode into mutual misperception and the desperate approach-avoidance sine wave of two people whose genuine attachment and intimacy nonetheless refused to coalesce into a sustainable love.

Oddly, that was the moment that Trevor tapped the sine-wave dominated screens showing the long-range sensor results. "The energy signatures are starting to settle into discrete point sources. We'll have final results soon." Caine stared at the screens over Trevor's shoulder, wished he had had more time to become familiar with the various crew stations and control systems of a modern spacecraft. But he was just a pretend-officer, given a rank so that he could give orders to people who had more training and skill than he did. It was no longer just a farce; it was a black comedy.

Trevor leaned back. "So, twenty-eight shift signatures confirmed. But they're not all headed our way.

Only the probe ship and maybe half a dozen more are coming straight for us. At three gees."

"Three gees? That means the leading ship will make intercept in—"

"—in just under thirty-one minutes. Although I don't think that detachment is heading for us at all. Like the rest of the local traffic, we're just a nuisance to be brushed aside in their race to get to The Pearl. The rest of the invaders' fleet is moving to engage our already-deployed forces. There's gonna be one hell of a big fight about ten light-seconds farther out."

Caine did some rapid math concerning the detachment that was heading for them. "If their lead ship has drones, and they're no better than ours, that means that their first weapons platforms will be zipping past us in just under nineteen minutes. That means they'll probably be able take us under fire in no more than twelve to thirteen minutes. Less, if their drones and weapons are better."

"Which is probably the case." Trevor activated his collarcom again. "Lieutenant Hazawa?"

It took Hazawa about ten seconds to respond. "Yes, Captain Corcoran?"

"Have you been given orders?"

"Just came through now, sir."

"And?"

"And we are to commence stern-chasing the shift-carrier *Prometheus* immediately, sir. Silent running."

Trevor checked his nav plots. "Lieutenant, have you looked at what that means?"

"I have, sir."

"It's going to have us paralleling the OpFor's

approach trajectory to the Pearl—and unless we move to four gee immediately, they're going to overtake us. As it is, if they've got drones, their remote units *will* overtake us."

"Big Lady's direct orders, sir: to get you two gentlemen out of this system. So we need to make rendezvous with the *Prometheus*, and that trajectory is the only way to do it. But we'll push the engines and burn to four gee."

"What sort of countermeasures are loaded?"

The extended pause was not promising. "A Level Two ECM package and two point-defense fire pods."

"Ship-to-ship ordnance?"

"None, sir. Sorry. We came to this party equipped to be a racecar, not a gunboat."

"Then put the pedal to the metal and get us the hell out of here, Lieutenant."

"Yes, sir. We'll be informing the other passengers in a moment, and give them four minutes to get into and flood their acceleration compensation tanks. Then we'll—"

"Son, every minute you give your passengers to get comfy makes it that much more likely that you will not outrun the OpFor and that, in consequence, we will all die. Recommend you hit the accelerator in one minute and tell the biofreight they've got that long to strap in, wherever they can."

A pause. It was a nonregulation procedure suggested to a twenty-five-year-old who'd never been in a shooting war. Then, "Aye, aye, sir. Strap in."

The shipwide blared Hazawa's warning overhead. Caine strapped in slowly, deliberately.

"You okay?" Trevor was looking over at him.

"Yeah—yeah, I guess I am." Caine was suddenly more aware of the perverse calm he felt than any fear of personal harm. It was either a helpful precombat reflex or a pathological level of traumatic dissociation. Or maybe those were the same thing. He couldn't believe that he was smiling, but the stretching pain in his injured lower lip confirmed it.

Trevor was staring at him. "You *sure* you're okay?"

"Well, I'm not about to start drooling or run around shrieking, if that's what you mean."

"Yeah, that's what I mean. Okay, then. Any second n—"

Trevor didn't complete the word "now" because four gees of force suddenly crushed them in their couches as irresistibly as a trash compactor. *Jesus Christ. How the hell do the regular crews take it?*

The force abruptly shifted to the side, like a hammer had hit the starboard side of the cutter. The lights flashed off and came back on in an environment that was once again weightless. A shuddering rumble tremored through the deck, then another two in quick succession. "What the—?"

"I think that was combustive venting of some tankage baffles."

"And the first big slam?"

"Well, either we had one hell of a malfunction or their capital ships have a hell of a lot more range than we do. And if their main weapons can disable us at their current range"—he checked—"which is about one hundred thirty kiloklicks, then whatever they just hit us with would tear apart our biggest cruisers at normal engagement ranges. Which means that if our fleet waits to get into optimal range—"

"—they'll never get off a shot," finished Caine. "They've got to concentrate long-range fire on a few select hulls and try to keep distance."

"Hard if they're already on course for direct engagement."

"Yeah, but that's for the admiral to decide. Either way, the whole fleet needs this information."

Trevor nodded. "Bridge."

Caine could hear the chaos clearly over Trevor's collarcom. "Captain—Mr. Corcoran—please. Not now. We've lost the preignition toroid and power to the starboard plasma thrusters. If we don't—"

"Son, has anyone else been hit yet?"

"Erm—no; we're the lucky first."

"Then you have to break silence and send this tactical update out on general broadcast. Give our current range to the enemy's capital ships and attach the damage report."

"Sir, I don't under—"

"Just do it, Lieutenant. The admiral and line captains will know what to make of it."

Hazawa signed off. Trevor brought up a screen which duplicated the bridge's engineering board. He shook his head. "Not good. The portside pulse fusion engine is completely gone. We still might get away if they fix the preignition torus for the plasma thrusters."

"That's a big 'if.'"

"You bet," agreed Trevor. "Half of everything else is fried. Countermeasures are gone. So's one of the PDF defense pods. At this point, they could finish us off with a few thrown rocks and sharp insults."

"Structural integrity?"

"Hard to say. No problem amidships or up at the

bow, but to aft, most of the hull sensors in engineering are out."

"Usually not a good sign."

"No, not at all."

"Sensors and commo?"

"Not much damage there. They're all up front, near the bridge module."

"One last question: how many friendlies are in scanning range, and how close are they?"

Trevor shifted to the close range plot. "Nothing big: an autonomous drone carrier deploying its complement, two tenders, a tanker, another cutter. And a missile frigate, coming up from The Pearl, probably trying to buy time for evacuation and for getting the carriers out of the slips."

"Any pattern to the vectors of those ships?"

"They're all over the place, although the frigate and the drone carrier are heading to engage."

"Which means they'll be coming right through our current position."

"More or less. The others are maneuvering away, but every one of those ships is still going to be in the neighborhood when the party starts."

Caine checked his chronometer. "Okay. If our first guesses about the enemy's speed are correct, we've now got between five and six minutes before their drones can start pranging us. And let's assume they've got better range, too."

"Okay, so that means we've got three or four minutes. What's your point?"

"Right now, what do you think this ship should be doing?"

Trevor looked sideways. "Well, not standing toe to

toe with drones, let alone battlewagons. We've got one remaining PDF system for knocking down missiles that come within five hundred klicks. It might put a few dents in a small craft, *if* one strays within a few kiloklicks of us. But that's the extent of our offensive potential."

"Do you think that's how Hazawa is going to see it?"

Trevor looked down, considering. "Probably not. He's young, true-blue, eager to prove he's not scared—so he'll have a tendency to try to fight his ship. And kill himself."

"And us."

Trevor nodded. "So I'll have to talk him out of that, and also out of maneuvering. Because if Hazawa gets mobility back, his immediate reflex will be to run or hide. And they're both suicide. Even if we get the preignition torus running, we still can't pull ahead of their main hulls, even if we jettisoned all the modules. And their drones—at eight gee minimum—will be all over us long before then."

Caine shrugged "So, with no place to hide, no way to fight, and not enough speed to run, we've got only one choice left."

"You mean we should play dead? How's that going to help?"

"Well...it might not. But it has this advantage over the other three alternatives: it *might* work. Remember, at Convocation the Ktor categorized us and the Hkh'Rkh as warlike, but indicated that the Arat Kur were merely more advanced. So, given the superior tech we've observed, let's assume we're being invaded by the Arat Kur. Being busy and not innately savage, they might survey the wreckage, see no activity, no emissions, and then push straight on to their primary objectives at The Pearl."

"And maybe we can still make the rendezvous and shift-out, if the *Prometheus* can slow down a little," Caine added.

Trevor shook his head. "With an invasion under way, the *Prometheus* can't slow down. Not enough, anyway. This attack, and our need to wait until the coast is clear again, are going to put us too far behind to catch her."

"Okay, but if any of our military shift carriers make it to the outer system, we could plot an intercept course for them. They're probably going to wait as long as they can for their combat complements to make it back to their berthing cradles, and that might give us enough time." Caine shrugged, waited a moment. "So, what do you think?"

Chapter Six

Outbound from Barnard's Star 2 C

Trevor resisted the impulse to roll his eyes. *What do I think? I think you're a civilian who's been turned into a toy soldier. I think that sometimes you're too damned smart for your own good—but thank God we've got you on our side. I think it pisses me off that the woman I'm always thinking about is in love with you, not me.* "I think your idea is just crazy enough that it might work."

Caine nodded slowly. "Can you talk Hazawa into it?"

Hazawa: another contestant in today's Amateur Hour Follies. "Probably, but it'll be faster if I just take command—"

Trevor had not expected Caine to interrupt, but he did. "Which means you'd have to self-activate out of reserve and take the conn."

"So?"

"So, you might want to retain your current civilian status and stay here in Auxiliary Command. Just in case this craziness doesn't work out."

"You mean, in case we're captured? Well, yeah," he admitted, "you've got a point. So"—he checked his watch—"we've got about a minute before things get lively. Get on your collarcom with Hazawa. Explain your idea quickly and convey my recommendation that he follows it."

"*I* should call?"

"Yes, you. If something happens to me, he's got to know to listen to you, too. He's too green to realize that you don't know half of what you're talking about."

"Thanks for the pep talk, Trevor."

"Don't mention it. Get going. I've got some *real* work to do."

As Caine started explaining his idea—and rank—to Hazawa, Trevor reconsidered the cutter's own passive scan plot, and the composite data being relayed from the CINCBARCOMCEN radio shack on Barney Deucy. Half of the Pearl's deep space battle group was now retroboosting to maintain distance. The other half—all lighter ships—had adjusted course and piled on the plasma, evidently trying to three-dimensionally cross the T ahead of the enemy's main body, albeit at a rather steep angle. Perduro had adopted a reasonable two-tier strategy. She would hold one of her groups back to duel with the enemy heavies as long as possible, perhaps showing their heels if the shift carriers got far enough away that the Arat Kur couldn't catch them anymore. The other part of Perduro's force was probably going to seed mines and sleeper drones—maybe even a few of the nuke-pumped, X-ray-laser ship-killers—in the path of the enemy. Which would present the invaders with Hobson's choice. Slow down to optimize scans and minimize damage from the autonomous and remote-controlled munitions deployed by the closer, lighter battle group; or rush through that kill zone in an attempt to close quickly with the heavier, but more distant, main fleet elements. Either way, there was a chance that significant parts of Perduro's flotilla would survive to fight again another day.

Or maybe not. As Trevor started reading the transponder tail numbers on the fleet plot, he wondered if there was a computer malfunction. Half of the missile frigates, including the one drawing near their crippled cutter, were of the Spear class, the last of the fission-drive buckets. Now officially reserve vessels, they had been shipped to The Pearl for training purposes. What the hell were they doing on the line? In fact, only Perduro's flagship—the President-class battle cruiser *Jefferson*—was a truly modern ship. *Goddamnit, where are all the—?*

The cutter shuddered.

Caine, just finishing with Hazawa, looked over. "Were we hit, or—?"

Trevor checked the plot. The blue triangle that denoted the tanker *Baton Rouge* faded away. "No, Caine; that was the farewell song of a nearby ship. From the look of it, hit by another shot from their lead ship. Did Hazawa go for the plan?"

"Yep, he's got the distress signals on now. And it looks like he'll have the preignition toroid repaired in a few minutes. He's taken the plant offline, so we're on battery backup and looking pretty dead. Just for good measure, he vented a little coolant from the starboard ignition chamber."

"So it looks like we've got a radiation leak, too. Nice touch. Hazawa's idea?"

Caine was silent, staring at the sensor plots.

Trevor smiled. Of course it wasn't Hazawa's idea.

Caine leaned closer to the plots. "Where are their drones?"

"I've been wondering the same thing. They should have opened up by now."

"Hell, if they're traveling under their own power, we should have seen some thermal signatures on our own passive sensors, right?"

Trevor frowned. "Well, if they were our drones, yes. But the invaders could have some stealth capabilities that—" Caine looked like he wanted to say something, but suppressed it. Trevor sighed. "Okay, spill it."

"Trevor, do you know of any way to conceal high-temperature exhaust in space?"

"No."

"I don't either. I can't even think of how you'd do that. But instead, what they *could* have done was—" And then Caine was on his feet. "The ships near us. Send them a warning. They're going to get hit point blank—in minutes, maybe seconds."

"What? How the—?"

"If the invaders' technology is both better and more compact, they've got more uncommitted hull volume to play with."

"So?"

"So, they could build in big mass drivers to launch their drones. So if they shifted in and the drones were launched immediately, we wouldn't see them because they're just inert metal traveling towards us at God-knows-how-many gees. But when they get close enough—"

Trevor completed the sentence as he put his hand

on the open comms. "They go active at point-blank range, firing and evading while they're in among us. And then they continue right on through us to serve as the advance strike force against the Pearl. Where they'll cause just enough havoc to further delay any evacuation." Trevor's finger was poised above the "send" relays, ready to broadcast in the clear—but he took his hand back. Slowly. And felt like a murderer as he did it.

"Trevor, what are you—?"

"You said it yourself, Caine. We've got to follow orders. We've got to get out of here and report. If those drones are close by, and if we go active—if we even juice up the tight-beam laser relays—we're likely to be vaporized before we can send."

And then it didn't matter. Without having to listen to Hazawa's nervous sitreps, it became quite evident that their theory was horribly correct. The nearby ships started taking crippling damage from drones that popped up on their sensors at only two and three thousand kilometers range, making targeted strikes on engineering sections, missile bays, sensor arrays. Secondary explosions of munitions and fuel were reported on every hull.

Trevor had only heard one thing like it before: when he had been coordinating the ROV oversight for a combined Spetznaz-SEAL operation that ran into an ambush in Uzbekistan. The casualties came so thick and fast that there was no time to think, to reconfigure the mission, to plan an extraction. It was like listening to an announcer doing play-by-play for a demolition derby. He had only been able to hope that, at the end of that litany of destruction and death, someone—anyone—would be left alive. That hope had been forlorn.

So it was here, too. The missile frigate was the first hit—naturally—and her skipper evidently knew he didn't have much time left; he salvoed his bays in the direction of the enemy's lead ship. He unloaded sixty percent of his ordnance before Trevor's passive sensors registered a split-second, white-hot thermal bloom where the frigate had been a moment before. Then the invaders' drones picked off the much slower human drones and their control sloop. Finally, the remaining enemy craft tumbled so they could keep firing at the human auxiliaries which were now aft of them as they kept arrowing toward The Pearl.

Hazawa's somber voice broke the extended silence. "We have the toroid back online, sirs."

Trevor rubbed his brow. "Which, ironically, makes us the most intact and capable ship in this entire sector."

Caine frowned. "How long do you think we should wait?"

"Before trying to make a getaway? Depends on what I see here in the next fifteen minutes." Trevor tapped the proximity passive sensor sweep.

"What do we want to see?"

"Wrong question. The right question is, what do we *not* want to see? Answer: we absolutely do not want to see a second wave of drones that are moving more slowly, because those could retroboost and come back for us. We don't want their main hulls to retroboost either, or even slow down, because that means they're willing to make sure that they've finished business out here, even if that delays them in their push to The Pearl. And no small craft. They'd be the worst, because whereas a big hull usually can't loiter because it's been tasked with key strategic objectives, smaller craft are more likely to be sent on more generalized patrol or picket missions. And that's my biggest worry: that they leave behind a sloop or a frigate to sift through the junk that used to be our ships, trying to gather technical intelligence."

"How's the rest of our side doing?"

"I can't tell. When Hazawa shut down power, our tight-beam gimballing servos went offline. But that's not a big loss. I think the niceties of lascom are about to become a thing of the past."

"Because they're going to be hitting The Pearl soon?"

"Yes, which will whack the snot out of precision communications. Not that The Pearl wants to talk with us anymore, anyway. They'll have cleared their tracking and comm arrays to maintain redundant C4I with our effective fleet elements. And we no longer qualify as such. We're on our own, for now."

Caine was oddly silent. Trevor looked up, discovered that he was staring intently at the passive scan plot. "Trevor, what do you think that might be?"

Trevor followed Caine's extended index finger to the thermal bloom that marked the drive of the approaching alien main hull—except now it was trailed by two small pinpricks, one of which was dropping behind very rapidly.

"That?" Trevor rubbed his eyes but could still see the decelerating pinprick. "That's trouble."

❖   ❖   ❖

And, thirty minutes later, it still was. Caine was looking at the shining mote that was now plainly visible at the center of their view screen. "Still coming toward us?"

"Yep. It's ignored the wreckage of the frigate."

Something's wrong here. Trevor tapped his collarcom. "Lieutenant, are you sure our power plant is cold?"

Hazawa sounded more collected than he had when, twenty minutes earlier, the main attacking vessel had virtually grazed their hull at two hundred kilometers range. "Fusion is offline, sir."

"And we're not the only transponder in the water?"

"No, sir. Four others in our area alone." Hazawa's voice rose slightly. "Sir, this small enemy craft—it's getting awful close, two hundred klicks and still retro-boosting. Now maneuvering to match vectors with us." Hazawa's voice tightened. "Sir, if they close to within fifty klicks, my orders clearly stipulate that I must take them under fire. And if they attempt to board, I must—"

"We'll cross that bridge when we come to it."

"Yes, sir."

Trevor turned to Caine, who hadn't taken his eyes off the craft's now visible outline. "How long?" he asked.

"They'll be alongside us in three or four minutes, tops. But *how* did they come straight to us?"

Caine looked out at the debris-field, most of it just winking bits of distant, rolling scrap metal, a few close enough that their tattered outlines were visible. He shook his head. "It doesn't make any sense. We *are* in slightly better shape than the remains of the closest fleet auxiliary, the *San Marin*, but she's a bigger hull, and so should be more interesting to them. I think they'd be eager to get a look at the contents of a tender with half of her lading intact."

Hazawa's voice was slightly tremulous over the ship-wide. "All personnel, all sections: watch personnel to the weapons lockers to distribute sidearms. Stand by to repel boarders. Enemy craft at one hundred kilometers."

Repel boarders? In space? It was too ludicrous to imagine, but it was about to happen. The enemy craft, a rounded body bloated by a large number of fuel tanks and furnished with a sharp, inquisitive prow, kept approaching. The proximity alarm triggered automatically, set up a shipwide ululation which underscored Hazawa's order: "PDF battery: acquire target."

Trevor rose. "Okay, so no one has any idea how they found us. Any thoughts about—?"

Caine turned quickly. "Trevor, our distress signal: will it be the same as the type emitted by, let's say, the frigate?"

"Yeah, except it'll be a lot longer. The frigate is a single hull: one registry code. But this ship carries modules, each of which has its own registry."

"So all the registries of all the carried modules are transmitted along with that of the carrier?"

"Yeah, they're appended to the end of the basic transponder signal. That way, if there's a wreck, rescue teams can figure out if any of the modules are missing, or—"

"And how does the cutter's transponder know the registry of all the modules?"

"Well, as long as they're attached, it polls their individual registry chips, and—"

Caine shook his head and interrupted. "Trevor, you changed our habmod's registry, right before the attack, didn't you?"

"Yeah. Since we're just civvie diplomats again, I had to change the module's designation from military to—" Trevor stopped. "Oh, Christ."

Caine nodded. "You changed it to a diplomatic code."

Hazawa's voice announced, "Enemy craft closing

through fifty kilometers. Stand by to—" Static surged over his last order.

Trevor felt a flash of hot moisture rise on his brow. He slapped his collarcom, noticed that the cutter's PDF pod had powered up. "So the attackers think—"

"—that we're flying a diplomatic pennon: a white flag. One of their commo officers must know how to read our data streams and noticed it embedded in either the transponder code, the distress signal, or both."

Trevor nodded. "Lieutenant Hazawa, please respond." Nothing. *Where the hell*—?

And just as Hazawa responded—sounding more confident, relieved, and excited—the bridge back-chatter confirmed what Trevor saw happening on his subsystem activity monitor. Behind Hazawa's energetic, "Yes, Captain?" was a whoop that almost drowned out the background report that Trevor dreaded hearing. "Direct hit on the enemy ship, sir. The bogey is venting atmosphere and angling away erratically. Reacquiring—"

"No, Lieutenant!" Trevor shouted into his static-ridden collarcom. "Stand down, stand—!"

Hazawa's "Say again?" vied with another excited report. "Multiple hits in her stern, sir. She's corkscrewing badly. I think we hit her engines—"

"Cease fire, cease—!" Trevor was shouting, when Caine's hand came down hard on his shoulder. Trevor yanked away. "What?"

Caine's voice was eerily calm. "We've got to detach."

"What the hell are you—?"

"We've got only seconds now. What's the procedure?"

Detach? What the hell was Caine talking about—?

And then Trevor saw two new bogeys light up, one only one hundred twenty klicks away.

Caine nodded toward the two red triangles. "The enemy left drones laying doggo out here. And we've just made ourselves a target."

The EM emission sensor shrilled throughout the cutter.

"They've acquired and locked. Trevor—"

Not even the time to say goodbye to Hazawa. What a shitty business this is—Trevor pulled open a red cover to his lower left, grabbed the recessed handle, turned it sharply to the left so that he could pull it straight up. And did so.

The blast of the emergency jettisoning charges—only twelve feet behind them—was deafening as the hab mod blew itself away from the cutter's keel. Caine lost the grip on his seat, spiraled off at an angle, slammed into a bulkhead, and floated free: stunned, unconscious, or dead.

The external viewing screen showed a slowly somersaulting image of the crippled cutter, now bookended by two explosions in rapid succession, one at the bow and one in the stern. Modules and pieces of her went cartwheeling in all directions. Trevor saw another flash back in the engine decks: a small secondary, back near the containment rings. Meaning that any second now—

Trevor scooped his feet under him so that they were on the seat, twisted and kicked off toward Caine. He cinched him around the waist as he passed, bumped to an awkward but fast stop, reverse kicked. He regained the acceleration couch, pulled Caine on top of him, pulled a strap across them both—

—just as the cutter's engine decks erupted outwards into a sudden, angry, blue-white star.

The screen blanked the same instant that the shock wave hit.

Chapter Seven

Washington D.C., Earth

Richard Downing entered the office he had shared with Nolan Corcoran for more than a decade, and stared wistfully at the couch in the waiting room. Sleep would be very welcome and would come all too easily. He had been planetside less than six hours and had already briefed the POTUS, the Joint Chiefs, and the intelligence agencies. And only now could his real work begin.

Once in the conference room, he activated the commplex, told it to place a call, dropped into a chair, and rubbed his face so he would appear alert and fresh. Well, alert. Mostly.

The commplex checked Downing's identity and then indicated that the requested individual was on the line. "Mr. Rulaine," he said, stifling a yawn, "I trust you've found your early retirement from the Special Forces relaxing?"

"Yes, sir. A little too relaxing."

"Well, we'll remedy that soon enough. Now, about

your team: their medical discharges went through without a problem?"

"Yes sir, although the clerk did eyeball the five of us pretty strangely."

Downing imagined the scene: the five men—a Green Beret (Rulaine himself), three SEALs (Jacob Winfield, Stanislaus Witkowski, and Carlos Cruz) and a bear of a Secret Service agent (Matthew Barr)—clustered around a desk to "medical out" of their respective services. "Medical cause, sir?" the clerk would have asked. "Unspecified," Bannor Rulaine would have answered in the flat baritone that was his all-business voice. And that first question would have been the last that the clerk asked the five of them.

"And you are satisfied with the authenticity of the fictional security firm that is now retaining your services?"

Bannor nodded. "Yes sir. Incorporation papers, contact data, client lists, transactions, all perfectly legit, even if scrutinized by a Congressional subcommittee. And by the way, I would like to convey the group's collective thanks for the very generous employment terms."

Which you will earn many times over, you poor sods. "You are all very welcome. I'm short on time, Captain, so let's review the OpOrds. My system will require a real-time biometric security check, so please activate your video pickup."

"Will do, sir." The screen on Downing's commplex faded up from black, revealing Bannor Rulaine's thinning sandy hair and calm hazel eyes. Downing nodded a greeting, watched the OpOrd file upload begin, and reviewed Rulaine's hardcopy record, located out of the commplex's visual field.

According to his atypical dossier, Bannor Rulaine

had gone to Dartmouth—gone, but never graduated. He found information imparted by drill instructors vastly preferable to that offered by professors. Instead of flunking out of the Fort Benning School for Wayward Boys, he had exceeded its expectations. His first posting had been to OCS, with more than a few of his trainers grumbling that the brass always ruined the best soldiers they produced by adorning their shoulders with shiny metal bars instead of honest fabric stripes.

Rulaine was already scanning the ops file. "So all five of us are to drop out of sight as soon as we've picked up the equipment here in Baltimore."

"Yes, all of which is 'defective' Army issue. It is fully functional, of course."

"Of course. What are you giving us, sir?"

"The lot. Everything you could want, except EVA gear; that's as scarce as hen's teeth right now. The cache—enough to support two fire teams for a month of extensive operations—has been sealed in a secure commercial container, waiting for you on the docks."

Bannor nodded, then frowned. "Sir, I know I shouldn't ask, but I have to anyway. Why all the cloak-and-dagger maneuvering?"

"A fair question. Here's the frank answer: if there is a war scare, every official asset—material or human—could get commandeered. So I am precautionarily setting aside some cells of independent operatives—prepositioned and presupplied—that cannot be usurped by higher authorities later on."

"I read you five by five, sir. Logically, you'll want us to drop out of sight until you need us, so I presume you've set aside a specific location?"

"Yes. Caribbean. Lesser Antilles. Nevis, just south of

St. Kitts. Friends of mine have a house there, and I think your men will enjoy a little time in a tropical paradise."

"Well, sure. Sir."

"They are to stay current on their dive ops and zero-gee equivalency qualifications. They are also to get to know the local rental agencies for VTOLs. And they will need to become friendly with the crew of the open-water vehicle ferry attached to the Season's Classic resort property—and must prepare an ops plan for the possible seizure of that vessel."

"Why, sir?"

"Because it may also become necessary for you to commandeer some VTOLs. In that event, you'll need the ferry's deck space to carry them if you have to move to your area of operations by sea."

"So if the balloon goes up, we close to target by surface craft, and then VTOL off the deck?"

"Best if you beach the ferry first, but yes, that's the plan."

"And what's our target?"

"That's the great unknown. That's why we're keeping your men in ready reserve on an island."

Rulaine's grin was lopsided. "That's the typical life of a soldier, Mr. Downing: hurry up and wait."

"'Fraid so. The Nevis address is at the end of Appendix B. It is a summer home, and the owners—friends of mine who have Langley connections—have agreed to let your group 'look after it' in their absence. No close contact with the locals, though."

"Right. We're there because we're a bunch of dive junkies. And if someone asks us if we know the owner, or his friend Richard Downing, we just answer 'who?' And we send you a picture of whoever did the asking."

"Good lad. Enjoy your stay in the Caribbean. Good speaking to you."

"And you, sir. We'll be awaiting your signal."

"Or Captain Corcoran's. He will be your direct CO, so you may get your final activation orders from him."

"Roger that, sir, and good luck."

"You, too, Captain." The link dissolved.

Before the light had fully faded from the screen, there was a knock on the door. Downing sighed. Chatting with Rulaine had been easy, even relaxing. But the rest of the day's agenda was devoted to an official briefing with other members of the delegation that had accompanied Downing to the Accord's Convocation, and who, for different reasons, now brought headache-generating issues with them. Young genius physicist Lemuel Wasserman was significantly more abrasive than sandpaper. Biologist Ben Hwang and cyber whiz Sanjay Thandla were usually even-tempered, but Lemuel was completely capable of setting either one of them off. Major Opal Patrone had been compelled to leave behind her security charge—and paramour—Caine Riordan and clearly loathed Downing as the architect of that separation. Elena Corcoran—Nolan's daughter and Richard's godchild—still believed herself the only person in the room who knew that, fourteen years ago, Caine had fallen in love with her and fathered her son Connor—all in the one hundred hours that Nolan had erased from Riordan's memory. Erased, that is, until those memories had been restored a month ago on Barney Deucy. But Elena didn't know that, and didn't know that Downing and her brother Trevor had learned that ticklish secret, too.

All of which was sure to be complicated by the

intellectual posturings and airs of the most insufferable French diplomat Richard had ever met: an old-school, Sorbonne-style wanker named—

"It is Etienne Gaspard, Monsieur Downing," a voice beyond the door announced, "along with, er, others."

"Please come in, Mr. Gaspard. And do bring the 'others' in with you."

Gaspard was the first through the door. Lemuel Wasserman was right behind him, his eyes already boring ferociously into the Frenchman's back. To Downing's knowledge, the two had never met each other, but it was entirely possible that Gaspard's suave, aloof superiority could have run afoul of Wasserman's blunt and vitriolic arrogance in the few moments they had been waiting together.

Opal Patrone, Ben Hwang, and Sanjay Thandla filed in, and lastly, at a slightly greater distance, Elena. And now that Downing knew what to look for, he realized that Elena had always put a little extra space between herself and Opal, but had been friendly and gracious, even while doing so. Her ethics allowed her no other course. Since Opal was thoroughly unaware of Elena's prior connection to Caine, animus was both patently unfair and utterly illogical. And so far as Elena knew, Caine still had no recollection of their own whirlwind lunar romance. But, eventually, Caine would return, and then the matter would have to be addressed and settled, one way or the other. Richard devoutly hoped he would be in another city—preferably another state—when it was.

"It seems you have been quite busy since the Parthenon Dialogs, Mr. Downing."

Gaspard's almost truculent comment startled Downing out of the contemplative haze into which he had fallen. "You are referring to our visit to the Convocation last month, I take it?"

"I am referring to everything, Mr. Downing. There are your trips to Mars, to the Convocation, then Barnard's Star. You have had your hands very full from the moment Admiral Corcoran died. Or so it seems to me."

Downing nodded diffidently, schooled his features to calm agreement as he watched Gaspard's face for any sign that the diplomat was probing after the possibility that Nolan's death had put some burden—some unseen and unnamed mantel of responsibility—upon Richard's neck. Specifically, had Gaspard heard whispers of a secret organization named IRIS, and was he snooping around to get confirmation that Downing was now its director?

But Downing saw no hint of incisive purpose in Gaspard's face, and so, felt safe enough to indulge in a genuine smile. "Yes, Mr. Gaspard. It has been a busy time. For everyone in this room. Yourself not least of all, as I understand it."

Gaspard's eyes rolled in exasperation. "*Oui, vraiment.* But my seventy- and eighty-hour weeks have not come with the exciting novelties that arise from unprecedented contact with exosapients. Mine has been the same dull routine of politics; only the names have changed."

"The names of the politicians?" asked Opal.

"Unfortunately, no. The same collection of cutthroats, crooks, and incompetents are still steering our planet's various ships of state. But the names of everything else—agencies, treaty organizations, even the blocs themselves—are in flux. I spend half my time just trying to discern which new names go with which old institutions. It is utter madness."

And you spend the other half of your time exercising your considerable gift for hyperbole, Downing added silently. Aloud: "Nevertheless, you and the rest of the Confederation Consuls are to be congratulated. From what I hear, the transition to global coordination—at least on military and industrial matters—seems to be progressing nicely."

Gaspard snorted. "Simple lies for simpletons. The 'transition' is a maelstrom of endless, petty bickering. Do not believe the optimistic analysts or headlines, Mr. Downing."

"Well, it's a good thing you know the global state of play better than the rest of the world's experts," drawled Wasserman.

Gaspard looked down his lengthy nose at Wasserman. "You may discover, Doctor, that my cynicism, which you presently elect to insult, shall later prove to be an asset for which you are grateful. To be more specific: I do not 'know better.' I am merely unwilling to be swayed by what I *wish* to be true. And since the issue at hand is nothing less than the fate of our planet, I contend it is ludicrous to assess the actual state of our readiness with the same rosy optimism that children adopt when anticipating the arrival of Father Christmas."

Downing raised a hand. "For now, let's ignore the political merits of morale-building PR versus pitiless rationalism. We are here for one reason only: to brief you, Mr. Gaspard."

"Just so. I require your detailed impressions of what occurred at the Convocation, with particular attention to what you learned about the other species of the Accord, and why you believe the meeting ended so disastrously." Gaspard's eyes narrowed as he indulged in a thin, unpleasant smile. "I would hear from Dr. Wasserman first."

Downing intervened, seeing that Gaspard was spoiling for a fight. "I think a round-robin debrief will not only be faster, but develop a better pool of knowledge for you, Mr. Gaspard, particularly if you'd start by telling us what information you already have."

Gaspard sniffed, turned away from Wasserman. "Only the basics. That there were five other species present—the Arat Kur, the Ktor, the Hkh'Rkh, the Slaasriithi, and the Dornaani. That the first three of those were not friendly, and that the Arat Kur were decidedly hostile. That the Dornaani are charged with being Custodians, a kind of overseer/peacekeeper duty, as I understand it. And the three unfriendly races— but again, particularly the Arat Kur—were laboring to exploit every possible procedural irregularity to ensure that Earth was denied membership in the Accord. However, their ultimate purpose for doing so remained obscure."

Elena shifted in her seat. "Mr. Gaspard, having been present for those exchanges, I have to report that their reasons seemed anything but obscure. The Arat Kur, aided by the backroom machinations of the Ktor and the intemperate behavior of the Hkh'Rkh, were pushing us all toward war. And there's an excellent chance that they will succeed. If they haven't already."

Gaspard tilted his head. "I seem to recall reading that the pretext upon which the Arat Kur based the majority of their procedural disruptions was the matter of our settlement of the 70 Ophiuchi system, no?"

"That is correct," Downing said. "The Arat Kur claimed this was a violation of the Fifteenth Accord, which requires that all members of the Accord remain within their approved pathways of expansion. However, since we had commenced settlement of that system before we were first contacted eighteen weeks ago, the failure was not ours."

"Which the Arat Kur accepted, no?"

"Yes, they accepted it. But they also wanted the Accord to order us out of the system."

"But the Accord had no authority to do so," objected Gaspard. "It may not dictate territorial policy to a species that has not been confirmed as a member of the Accord."

Elena spoke over steepled fingers. "Of course, all these juridical details may become moot."

Gaspard lifted his patrician chin. "How?"

"The Arat Kur may decide to forcibly evict us, regardless of the Accords. Which they suggested were not worthy of continued compliance, when the Custodians revealed the location of their homeworld to be Sigma Draconis. Of course, that may have been precisely the *casus belli* that the Arat Kur wanted. Throughout the proceedings, they were indirectly daring the Custodians to cross that line."

"And there's another clue that they were spoiling for a fight," added Ben Hwang. "Whereas every other species allowed some cultural exchange, the Arat Kur refused to share any information about themselves. They gave us no clues as to their physiology, their biosphere, their interstellar distribution, or their civilization."

At the word "civilization," Richard saw Elena frown. "El," he prompted, "what is it? What have you deduced about the Arat Kur?"

Elena shrugged. "I don't have facts, only a hypothesis." Silence and six pair of eyes invited her to amplify. "I believe the Arat Kur are primarily a subterranean species."

Gaspard leaned forward. "Why do you think this, Ms. Corcoran?"

"Because of their idioms. The Dornaani translation technology is extremely sophisticated. Most pertinently, it uses semantic equivalences where it must, but transliterates axioms and colloquialisms that would make sense to the listener. Consider these two expressions from the remarks of the Arat Kur leader Hu'urs Khraam, who stepped in for their senior ambassador Zirsoo Kh'n when the political breach between the Arat Kur and the Custodians became imminent. Listen: 'Your words dig tunnels in sand,' and 'your ultimatum leaves us no middle course: you force us to either scuttle back or shatter bedrock.' In addition, consider the title of their polity—the Wholenest—and their apparent tendencies toward conservatism, bureaucratic proceduralism, and caution."

Gaspard leaned his chin upon his palm. "And why would these be traits of a subterranean species?"

"Not just any subterranean species, but one which has achieved sapience. Consider the challenges they'd face in terms of population control, waste management, construction, water and food distribution. They can't just fold up their tents and seek a better life over the next ridgeline. Indeed, they may not even have a word that combines the concept of being a 'nomad' with 'sapience.' All the particulars of a subterranean race's existence would be dependent upon careful, logical, premeditated action."

Ben Hwang was nodding slowly. "And they would tend to perceive anything less than that as irresponsible, impulsive, childish."

"Or, possibly, insane."

Lemuel grinned wickedly. "Won't *they* have fun with the Hkh'Rkh if they become allies."

Hwang frowned. "Just because the two species are dissimilar doesn't mean they wouldn't be an effective team. Each has what the other lacks; although Hkh'Rkh don't evince the discipline and planning of the Arat Kur, they certainly seem to make up for it in daring and decisiveness."

Gaspard leaned back. "If correct, your theories suggest key features of the Arat Kurs' basic psychology. That is crucial strategic data."

"Sure." Opal stared into space as if she were thinking through the military and operational practicalities. "They'd probably be comfortable for long stays in space. No claustrophobia. Probably have comparatively poor eyesight: invariant light conditions and no need to scan a horizon. However, other senses might be enhanced. Also, I'll bet they tend to build downward on the z-axis, not upward like us tree-dwellers. And I'd lay odds that their evolution did not include an aquatic phase, at least not as recently as ours. In fact, they might be highly hydrophobic. Underground, water becomes a real threat. Hit it while digging and you'll kill hundreds, thousands. That also means they're less likely to be seafaring at an early point in their social evolution, therefore slower to spread to other landmasses. Hell, I wouldn't be surprised if they can't swim, or maybe can't even float—"

Gaspard beamed. "Excellent. This is precisely what I came to hear: useful extrapolative information about a potential foe. It may all be hypothetical, but it is infinitely more than we had when I walked into this room."

"While we are on the topic of the Arat Kur," murmured Thandla, "I have another piece of information I think you will appreciate."

The group looked at him, surprised—Gaspard most of all. "Dr. Thandla, have your research efforts been shifted to the Arat Kur? I was told that you were working on decoding the 'child's primer' that the Slaasriithi gave us as a means of becoming acquainted with their race."

Sanjay's answering grin was very broad. "Oh no, you are quite right. I am working on the Slaasriithi primer."

"So what does that have to do with the Arat Kur?"

"Everything. You see, the Slaasriithi also used the primer to pass us encoded information about the Arat Kur."

Downing sat upright. "How much information, Dr. Thandla?"

Thandla looked sideways at Downing. "It is nothing like a dossier, Mr. Downing. It is far simpler than that, almost a puzzle, if you like. Indeed, I only thought to look for it after Ms. Corcoran noticed the Slaasriithi ambassador's marked emphasis upon the importance of the primer's supplementary information."

Downing nodded. "And that is where you found the puzzle?"

"Correct. It is subtle. And quite tricky. Which I think was entirely intentional."

Gaspard peered over folded hands. "What do you mean?"

"I believe the data was hidden not only to protect the Slaasriithi from being accused of sharing information pertaining to another species. I think their message was also a test. If we did not take the time or were not clever enough to pass that test—well, that served their purposes, too."

Elena smiled faintly. "So being able to find and decode the hidden message also meant that we were worthy of it."

Thandla nodded. "Yes, and this is what I found: a single graphic comprised of multiple overlays." An insanely irregular 3-D polygon appeared on the room's main display. It looked vaguely like a cubistic python digesting a pig.

Hwang frowned. "What is that? Arat Kur genetics?"

Thandla smiled. "No, it's—"

"Hot damn!" Lemuel Wasserman's tone was triumphant. "That's a 3-D map of interstellar space. Specifically, of the limits of Arat Kur space, judging from the buildup Sanjay's given us. Which means that all the angles in that geodesic solid must be centered on stars, and the connecting lines between each pair of angles must be proportional to the distances between the corresponding stars in Arat Kur space."

Downing frowned. "But if you don't know the distances—"

Lemuel shook his head and rode right over the top of Downing's puzzlement *and* Thandla's attempt to clarify. "You don't need to know the distances. As long as the proportions are precise, that shape is like a fingerprint. And we know that, somewhere in there, is Sigma Draconis."

Thandla smiled. "Just so. And here's the next layer of the puzzle." Now, at each of the polygon's articulating points and intersections, a bright star winked into being. Similar bright stars faded in from the darkness within the interior of the shape. Then, the lines joining all those star-points that were relatively close to each other illuminated slightly. Thandla pointed to an orange-yellow point near the jaw of the python. "That's Sigma Draconis. The stellar color, the angles of incidence and the ratio of the distances to each of the adjoining stars are a precise match."

Downing folded his hands to keep an eager quiver from becoming evident. "And you know what else those bright lines tell us."

Wasserman grunted as he started racing through calculations on his palmcomp. "Their maximum shift range. Which will be a value somewhere between the longest illuminated line and the shortest nonilluminated line. Which will be a pretty small numerical range."

"That conjecture assumes they can't conduct deep space refueling from prepositioned caches," Hwang pointed out.

"True," Lemuel agreed, still hunched over his palmcomp, "but that's a reasonable assumption."

"Why?"

"Well, first off, the Slaasriithi would anticipate that question, right? So they'd build a clue into the graphic that some of these lines were not 'one-shift transits.' Maybe put some kind of special marker at the midpoint, where the two shifts would be joined end to end. Secondly, we know that both Slaasriithi and Arat Kur technology are an order of magnitude behind the Dornaani and Ktor. So I think we can project that the Arat Kur shift drive, like ours, depends on stellar gravity wells to function as navigational bookends for each shift. You need to start at one star and end at the other."

Gaspard had folded his hands. "Mr. Wasserman, it is strategically crucial that we do not underestimate the Arat Kur. But your extrapolation—that they are unable to shift to deep space because we cannot— seems based upon a dangerous presupposition regarding the essential parity of their technology and our own."

Wasserman's smile was wolfish. "Wrong—because even the Ktor, who are the second oldest members of the Accord and have had FTL capability for millennia, apparently, can't pull off deep-space shifts, either."

Downing blinked. "How can you be sure, Lemuel?"

Wasserman shrugged. "Simple logic. The Dornaani have assured us that they can prevent the Ktor from entering our space. But if the Ktor *did* have the capacity for deep space navigation, then they could get around the Dornaani by going from one prepositioned deep space fuel cache to another, and show up unannounced in our back yard. And if they did that, then we'd know the Dornaani are liars and wouldn't support their interests anymore. So, if the *Ktoran* technology can't handle deep space shift navigation, then we can be sure as hell that the less advanced races—like the Arat Kur—can't pull it off, either."

Downing was determined not to let his admiration for Wasserman's swift deduction show in his face. "So what can you tell us about their shift range?"

"I've run all the stellar pairs that are joined by shift-lines. No distance is greater than nine point five light-years."

"And what is the shortest distance between any two stars that are *not* joined by a shift-line?"

"Nine point seven. So their maximum shift range is someplace between nine point five and nine point seven light-years. And that confirms our suspicions that they're operating at something like our level of technical ability. At least within the same order of magnitude."

"Equally important," Downing mused, "it allows us to predict their preferred strategic option."

"What do you mean by that?" Gaspard asked.

"I am referring to the places they are most likely to attack first."

"And given that shift range, what do you project as their most likely path of attack?"

"They'd start with Barnard's Star."

"And then?"

Downing shrugged. "Why, Earth. Of course."

Chapter Eight

Washington D.C., Earth

Gaspard stared at Downing with wide eyes. "What do you mean? Why are you so sure they would attack our homeworld—and in violation of the Twenty-first Accord, no less?"

"It is a rather straight-forward deduction, Mr. Gaspard. Firstly, any place where one of their stars is within nine point seven light-years of one of our stars is a possible jumpoff point for a general invasion."

Wasserman frowned at his palmtop. "I've already run those numbers. Unless the Arat Kur were going to take a circuitous route through their most far-flung system"—he pointed to the tip of the 3-D geodesic python's tongue—"then they've got to jump into Barnard's Star from across the nine-point-two-nine-light-year gap at 61 Cygni. That's the only place where they can cross the gulf of deep space in one hop, and it brings them right into our home systems."

Downing nodded. "And Barnard's Star is also the

key system when it comes to isolating us from our best colonies."

"Okay, I get the danger to Earth," Opal said with a frown, "but how could they cut us off from all the best green worlds by taking just one system?"

Wasserman's stylus stilled. "Because all of our traffic and contact with the worlds beyond Alpha Centauri and Barnard's Star runs through Ross 154. From Barnard's Star, it's one shift to Ross 154. Once they're there, they've got the run of our house."

Gaspard's faintly contemptuous demeanor had become far more serious. "Very well. So we have some idea of how our most likely adversary would proceed against us. Perhaps it is time to consider other threats." He turned to Hwang. "Doctor, what have you learned from the Ktor environmental tanks you scanned at the Convocation?"

Hwang frowned. "Not much. Any further conjectures regarding Ktoran biology are going to require much closer analysis of the data. Or maybe better data."

"Why?"

"Because all we've got to go on is respiratory wastes, and those results are inconclusive."

"What do you mean, 'inconclusive'?"

Hwang looked vaguely embarrassed. "I can't tell which are the gases they inhale and which are the ones they exhale. Assuming they breathe at all."

Gaspard shook his head. "More simply, please."

"Let me use a human example. If I were to collect the gases you exhale, how would they differ from what you had inhaled?"

"There would be a higher concentration of carbon dioxide."

"Exactly. That's the primary waste gas. And there'd be a lower concentration of oxygen, the metabolically necessary gas. And, if I knew nothing about human physiology other than those respiratory gases and the temperature at which we exist, I could be reasonably sure that humans are carbon-based, and therefore, use water as a transport medium and solvent."

"But with the Ktor—?"

"With the Ktor I can't tell from the results which gas they need and which is their waste gas. And there's no guarantee that their respiration is based upon gases at all. They could be metabolizing what they need from liquids."

"Which means that we know nothing about them, either?" Gaspard asked, his fingers spread wide in frustration.

Downing shrugged. "That's not quite true. Dr. Hwang's study of the PSI limits of their tanks indicate that the gases they breathe are at a maximum pressure of two point four atmospheres. Also, there are some brief mentions of the Ktor in the Dornaani self-reference materials."

Gaspard cocked his head. "But there is a prohibition against sharing information about another race."

"Perhaps this is a special case, since the Ktor are inextricably bound up in the founding of the Accord. They were the first race that the Dornaani encountered, and had a major impact upon the Accords themselves and thus, Dornaani history."

Gaspard ran a finger under his jawline. "Did the Ktor coauthor the Accords, then?"

"No. The Accords' principles were inherited from an earlier epoch that Alnduul has mentioned fleetingly. But the Ktor were the source of most of its privacy requirements. They refused to share any biological information on themselves. They refused to indicate their world of origin, claiming that it was very distant and had long ago become unable to support life. But the most troubling aspect was that the Dornaani were unable to verify the number of systems that the Ktor had settled."

"Why?"

"Because the Ktor already had FTL capability and refused to let the Dornaani within their borders. So the Dornaani either had to accept their word, or wait for some other race with which to found the Accord. Evidently, the vote to found the Accord with the Ktor was very narrow indeed."

Wasserman smirked. "You've gotta wonder if the descendants of the ones who lost the vote have been saying 'told you so' ever since."

Elena was shaking her head slowly. Downing let his voice drop to a slightly softer pitch. "What is it, Elena?"

"According to Ben, the sensor data indicates that the Ktor must inhabit an environment where the temperatures are so low that any of our worlds—even Mars—would be utterly uninhabitable for them. Which means that Ktor-suitable worlds would only exist in the farther orbits, which are usually dominated by gas giants and iceballs, like Pluto. True?"

"Yeah," agreed Wasserman, who was watching Elena with considerable attention now.

"And how many worlds in those orbits have we discovered which would have seas or atmospheres of the right composition?"

Lemuel frowned. "Three or four—maybe."

Elena nodded. "So these are among the most rare of all planetary types."

"Yeah, I guess you could put it that way."

"Well then," Elena said, looking around the conference table, "how is it that the Ktor have managed to find so many suitable planets to settle? And why should they give a damn about the expansion of, or even interaction with, carbon-based life-forms? They must know we have no interest in their habitable worlds and vice versa. But the Ktor keep their borders inviolate, and their privacy absolute, so that—from day one—the Custodians can't get answers to these questions." She frowned, stared at the far wall. "It sounds to me like they're hiding something."

Downing nodded. "I agree, but the Ktor are not our immediate worry. With their prime world located at 58 Eridani and the Dornaani homeworld at Gliese 290, they are both in a different strategic theater. And as Lemuel reminded us, the Custodians can prevent the Ktor from making any incursions into our space."

"And how can we be sure that they are able to do so?" Gaspard asked skeptically.

"Oh, they have the technological capability, Mr. Gaspard," Downing answered. "When the Dornaani took Misters Riordan and Corcoran and me to Barnard's Star, they did it in a single instant, and from a standing start." He let Gaspard digest that for a second. "That's sixteen light-years in the blink of an eye, without any preacceleration."

Gaspard's eyebrows rose. Hwang whistled long and low. But Elena looked thoughtfully at her folded hands. Downing leaned in her direction "El, you don't seem to find this very surprising."

She didn't look up. "Why should I? The Dornaani have been interstellar travelers and overseers for seven thousand years, possibly much more. And perhaps they inherited technologies from the great powers of whatever epoch preceded this one, perhaps from the same exosapients who transplanted humans to Dee-PeeThree. Given all that time and experience, what might the Dornaani be capable of now?"

Gaspard nodded somberly. "Indeed, Ms. Corcoran. What would they *not* be capable of?"

Downing cleared his throat. "While we are on the topic of exosapient capabilities, there's one last item of highly classified information that I must share with this group." Downing was silent until every eye in the room came to rest on him. "While I was at Barnard's Star, I received a package of data that was originally in Nolan Corcoran's possession. It indicates that the Doomsday Rock which was on course to blast Earth back to the Bronze Age thirty-six years ago was, in fact, a weaponized Kuiper-belt asteroid, pushed onto an intercept trajectory by gradual mass-driver acceleration. That acceleration took place while the Ktor were assisting the Dornaani with their Custodial duties in this system."

"So those damn water-tanks tried rock-nuking us?"

"Major Patrone, we are unable to confirm that. However, we do know that the Ktor had legal and ready access to our system at the time the rock was weaponized."

Gaspard rubbed his chin. "And the motive? After all, less than six weeks ago, the Ktor attempted to woo you into joining their protest against Dornaani preeminence."

Elena shrugged. "Yes, but that may have been the Ktorans' plan B, Mr. Gaspard. For all we know, their plan A was to drop the Doomsday Rock on us and thereby remove us from the current game before we could even get on the playing field. When that scheme failed, recruiting us may have become their next-best alternative."

Gaspard's nod and pout suggested that he not only approved of Elena's hypothesis, but of her quick wits. "Yes, that would be consistent. Either action has the same implicit end: to destroy the Accord, or at least isolate the Dornaani and make them ineffectual."

"And to grab turf," muttered Lemuel. "If you've read the report, then you know that the Ktor representative came on to us like Ribbentrop trying to sweet-talk Chamberlain into allowing Nazi expansion. Gave me the chills."

Gaspard nodded absently in Wasserman's direction as he checked his watch and rose. "Thank you, ladies and gentlemen. I found this briefing most stimulating. And now I must go."

Downing forced himself to remain courteous, despite Gaspard's indecorously abrupt leave-taking. "Mr. Gaspard, are you sure—quite sure—this is all the briefing you require?"

"Quite certain, Mr. Downing. I read your basic reports thoroughly on the flight over. The topics we have discussed were the ones that wanted further explication. Good day." With a brisk stride, he was out the door.

"Damn," muttered Opal, staring after him, "guess he flunked charm school." She turned to the rest of the group. "Now what?"

"Now," answered Downing, "we wait."

"For what?" asked Wasserman.

"For tidings of peace," sighed Downing, "or war."

Chapter Nine

Adrift off Barnard's Star 2 C

Rubbing the goose-egg bump on his head, Caine watched Trevor paw through the utility satchel they had filled with burnt-out power relays during their painstaking survey of the damage done to the auxiliary module. The relays clattered noisily against each other. "How bad is it?" Caine asked.

Trevor shrugged. "It's not good. With this much damage to the control circuitry, the environmental reprocessors are as good as dead. The air we have right now is all we're going to have. Of course, we can use electric current to crack water and get extra oxygen, but that means cutting into our drinking rations and running the power plant more. Which means becoming a much bigger signal for our enemies to detect."

"So how much life support do we have?"

"No more than three days, and that assumes that we shut down most of the module and limit minimal life support to a small, sealed area."

"Great."

110

"There's more good news. We have only fifty percent fuel left in our attitude control system."

"Fifty percent? Why?"

"We were in one hell of a three-axis tumble after the fusion plant on the cutter went up. Getting this coffee can stable was a pretty lengthy task."

Caine frowned. "On the other hand, why should we care how much ACS maneuver time we have left?"

"Funny you should ask. I have a plan." Trevor activated one of the screens. A miniature replica of the Auxiliary Command module blinked into existence, rolling through space on its long axis like a log going down a hill. The image diminished rapidly, shrank until the module was a small blue speck. Trevor tapped another key; red specks appeared, most of them traveling along the same vector as the blue speck and then flowing past it. "The red is wreckage, mostly ours and some of theirs. If we could manage to match vectors with the right piece of junk, the salvage might enable us to hang on for an extra week, maybe a whole month."

Caine, studying the creeping red stream, rubbed his chin. He immediately regretted the action; the tug on his skin reopened the wound that the door jamb had inflicted on his lower lip the day before. He pressed the back of his hand to the gash, gestured at the screen. "How did you get those vector fixes on the wreckage?"

"Three-second, narrow-field, active sensor bursts. Four of them, over the last ten hours."

Caine glanced at Trevor. "The OpFor might have left passive sensors behind."

"Maybe, but that isn't likely. This area isn't important enough to monitor, and they're not going to leave their own hardware behind if they can help it. Every piece of equipment they've got with them they had to carry in on their own backs, and they're at the end of a very long and very narrow supply line."

Caine nodded. "Okay. So, based on your data, what sort of delta-vee do we need in order to make intercept with the salvage?"

"That varies," answered Trevor. "Most of the junk is moving in roughly the same direction we are, only a little faster. And the stuff that's gone past us is already too far away to catch."

"So we have to assess the trajectories of objects that have yet to overtake us and make intercept in the next two or three days."

"Right. And then we have to accelerate the combined mass of our module and the salvage toward a reasonable destination. Whatever that turns out to be."

Caine looked at the red motes. "Sounds like a tough job."

"Actually, it's two tough jobs. First, we've got to match vectors with whatever piece of trash we ultimately choose. That's hard enough, given our fuel limitations. Second, our intercept should ideally end in a hard dock, or at least in a solid mooring. But that requires two things we don't have: a docking ring—which we lost when we blew the jettisoning charges—and fully fueled terminal navigation boosters."

Caine nodded. Without navigational boosters, it would be hard to control their final approach. Their reliance on the main thruster made them highly susceptible to errors of over- and under-correction. They were as likely to ram the wreckage, or overshoot it, as they were to make a safe intercept.

"So how can I help?" asked Caine.

"Get out of that emergency suit and hop into the sensor ops spot." Trevor indicated the appropriate chair. "We're going to need more precise vector definitions on the pieces of wreckage that we can still reach, and then we're going to need to get an idea of what the wreckage is."

"If I remember what my space ops instructor was saying two weeks ago, the only passive sensors that are going to help me with this task are spectrographs and mass scans."

"Correct. And if you get the chance, make a fast sweep for other approaching objects. Better safe than sorry."

Trevor was halfway into his emergency suit by the time Caine had strapped into the sensor ops position. "And where will you be?"

Trevor flexed his gloved fingers. "Pressure-sealing the access ways and B deck so we can terminate environmental functions in those areas. I'll start by sealing off— Damn!" Trevor exclaimed suddenly, grabbing his shin.

—at the same moment that Caine clutched at a sudden spasm in his left arm. "What the—?"

"Coupla old men," Trevor grinned ruefully, rubbing his left tibia.

"Yeah, but having our recent wounds bother us at the same second?" Caine wondered.

Trevor shrugged. "Ah, I've heard of stranger stuff, and we don't know what kind of sensors or other field effects the bad guys may be playing around with out there. Sometimes, just the right—or wrong—frequency can twinge a break or trouble a tooth." He smiled, finished sealing his gloves. "Space is funny that way."

Caine nodded as Trevor clanked his helmet into place and ran the locking rings home with a sharp, sure sweep of his hand. They exchanged waves, then Trevor took two long bounds and was out of the control room and into the main corridor.

✧   ✧   ✧

Caine started awake, jerked upright, was not sure where he was for a moment. His hands were still poised on the virtual keyboard of the sensor panel. Like many repetitive activities, what started out as a sequence of challenging sensor tasks had quickly become a mind-numbing routine. And without a high-end computer in the auxiliary module, a detailed search routine was only so automatable.

Two quick ladar bursts at each target would have provided the needed results, but that might have also been enough to attract any nearby enemy pickets. So far, thirty percent of the possible targets for salvage intercept had been eliminated simply because of the low confidence level of the sensor measurements. The module's limited fuel situation prohibited any intercept attempts that were based on "best-guesses."

Trevor's voice in his earbud snapped him further awake. "How's it going?"

"Fine. Slow. Boring. You?"

"I'm curious. Do me a favor; check on the *Prometheus'* trajectory."

Caine expanded his scan field, found the right blip, noticed that the thermal signature of the shift-carrier's pulse-fusion engines had grown much fainter due to rapidly increasing distance. "They're crowding three gee constant. And it looks like they've also added a slight delta vector. Meaning what? A change of shift destination?"

"Sure sounds like it."

Caine nodded. "Then they're heading to Ross 154."

"What? Instead of warning Earth?"

"Oh, Earth is being warned—silently. Downing will have set up a no-show code as part of a contingency plan. That way, if Barnard's Star is hit, the *Prometheus* can warn Ross 154 instead."

Trevor's voice was suddenly in the room with him. "And Earth interprets the no-show of the *Prometheus* as a warning flag. Sure. Two messages for the price of one shift." Caine turned. Pressure helmet off, Trevor was already clambering out of the suit. "You'd better pause the salvage survey. Their initial attack group will have refueled by now and they won't waste any time commencing preacceleration for their next shift. But before they do, they'll run an advance patrol through this area."

"Why here?"

"Because it's the only debris field with metallic elements anywhere within two hundred planetary diameters. If our side managed to sneak in any dormant killer drones while the invaders were wrecking The Pearl or hunting down our shift carriers, this is where they'd expect them to be, mixed in among other objects with very similar sensor returns."

"You're sure they got all six carriers?"

"Yeah, it looked like it. Now, jack your commlink into the intercom. We're not even going to risk using our collarcoms. When you're done with that, seal your suit."

Caine did as he was told, and looked over at Trevor—just as the lights went out. "Cutting power?"

Trevor nodded, started tapping commands into the computer's one manual keyboard. "Everything except the visual sensor arrays and the required computer element is blacked out. We're running on batteries."

Caine glanced at the REM level indicator. "What about the EM grids?"

Trevor did not look over. "We have to cut them for now. The meter of water lining the outer hull will take care of a lot of it, but we've got to wait until their advance force has swept the area before we energize the grids again. Then we can bring them back up. Slowly."

"And in the meantime?"

"We take the rads, or get taken by exosapients."

The smell of old sweat in Caine's suit was suddenly overpowering. Or was it simply new sweat that had the same tang of mortal fear? He felt a saline drop land on his swollen lip, winced as the salt burrowed into the tender tissue with microfine tines of pain. He wondered how much large particle radiation was similarly digging into and through him. . . .

"Motion on visual array seventeen-F." Trevor's voice betrayed no anxiety. Caine looked over at the zoomed-in image. The streamlined Arat Kur hull appeared against the gas giant's milky-amber whorls, heading in their general direction at a leisurely pace. They had noticed its emergence from the uppermost layer of the atmosphere half an hour ago, at which point the enemy ship had been retracting some kind of refueling drogue.

Caine turned to his sensors, ran the drill Trevor had taught him. "Establishing range and bearing." He ran a quick superimposition of the ship's progressive positional changes over the star field backdrop. The computer chewed through the data, correcting for the module's rotation and orbital movement. Numbers striped across his screen. Caine read them off. "Range: ninety-six thousand kilometers. Ecliptic relative bearing: 283 by 75. Current vector suggests she's looking to break orbit and make for our debris field. ETA, thirty-eight minutes."

"Are they running active sensors?"

"Nothing radiant, but I can't tell about ladar." Caine paused, considered the lack of active sensors. "So, will they conduct broad sweeps as they approach the debris, or wait until they're in the field before lighting up their arrays?"

"I think they'll wait until they're on top of us, and I mean that literally. They're worried about our drones, so they'll want to stay dark until the last second, and want to stay out of the field itself. They'll probably make their run 'above' and against the flow of the wreckage. That way, the vector difference between themselves and any doggo drone is going to make them pretty hard to catch. And the enemy is sure to have a few drones of their own out front, trying to lure ours out of hiding."

"If only there were some to be lured."

Trevor shrugged. "It would be a waste of equipment. We've lost this round."

Caine sighed. "What a godawful first combat assignment, watching the enemy go through the stately rituals of invasion."

"Actually, this is a pretty darned good first combat assignment."

"How do you figure that?"

Trevor's smile was mirthless. "We're alive." He turned back to the sensor readouts. "So far."

✧ ✧ ✧

Well, thought Caine, Trevor called it to the letter. Riordan watched as the cursor denoting the enemy hull spawned a growing swarm of smaller signatures, like a fish giving birth to a cloud of almost microscopic fry. "They've deployed a screen of small, fast drones."

Trevor nodded, watched them begin to bore through the heart of the debris cloud, the two foremost lighting up powerful active arrays. Immediately behind them, other drones—presumably hunter-killers—waited for the first sign of hostile response. As this menacing contingent approached within ten thousand kilometers, Trevor shut down even the battery-powered systems.

And so, sitting in the darkness, they waited. Caine closed his eyes, imagined what he had come to call the enemy "shift-cruiser" looming large and shooting past, drones preceding and trailing, like a whale attended by a retinue of hyperactive minnows.

Trevor let a minute pass, in which time Caine's radiation exposure indicator came on. The classic orange icon blinked urgently at the top center of his visor's heads-up display. He checked the dosimeter: thirty rem. Well within the limits that a healthy body could repair without sickness.

The red cursor that marked the enemy hull was now well past them. Trevor turned the battery-powered systems back on, then leaned toward the passive sensors, frowning. "That heavy—let's call it a 'shift-cruiser'—just deployed a number of retroboosted packages. Dormant drones, probably. But I can't keep track of them without active sensors. So they're going to get mixed into the trash with us and we won't be able to sort them out later. That means we're not going to be able to undertake sudden vector changes. The drones will be keyed to respond to any new movement other than that explicable by debris collisions."

"That eliminates at least seventy percent of our salvage opportunities." Caine envisioned the fruits of his tedious visual sensor labors being flushed down the toilet.

"Probably more like eighty percent."

Caine sighed and brought the now-familiar passive sensors back online. He glanced at the environmental countdown clock Trevor had started: sixty-eight hours left.

Give or take a few last breaths.

Chapter Ten

Adrift off Barnard's Star 2 C

Caine double-checked his survey results and sighed. *So our survival depends upon my rudimentary skill as a trash-scrounging sensor jockey. Great.*

Trevor checked the tactical plot, leaned back, removed his helmet, and powered up the life-support systems. His words rode plumes of mist up into the chill air. "Enemy hull now crowding three gees, passing five light-seconds range—and good riddance." Trevor swiveled toward Caine. "Time to pick through the junk. What looks best?"

Caine scanned down the list of possible salvage targets, now fallen off to less than fifty, and compared apparent mass with total thrust required for intercept. "Only one promising target remaining. This one." He pointed. "It's a fast mover and near the leading edge of the debris field."

"Is that still in range?"

"Barely. We have twenty-two minutes left to initiate an intercept burn."

Trevor looked at the fuel numbers, shook his head. "Damn, that's an expensive intercept, Caine. We'll burn up all of our primary thrust fuel, and we'll have to dip into our station-keeping fuel by ten percent."

"I know it's expensive, but take a look at the mass and volume estimates of the other remaining targets." Caine pointed to the depressing data. None of them were likely to be larger than six meters in their longest dimension. Most of them were probably fairly light as well. "Just hull fragments, I'd guess."

Trevor's misty breath fogged the computer screens in front of him. "Any possibility for new targets, ones we haven't seen yet?" Without commenting, Caine displayed the statistics on wreckage density. Trevor saw the sharply diminishing values, then nodded soberly. "Looks like this vein is just about tapped out."

"My thoughts exactly. So what now?"

"Now we take another look at our last, best hope, see what we can learn before we have to start maneuvering for intercept. I want to make sure it's not another dry hole."

Caine swallowed quietly. *And if it is? Then what? Spend two days staring at the walls, waiting to slip finally, fatally, into anoxia?* Or assuming they found some way to breathe, waiting for the excess rems—the ones that the EM grid and shielding didn't stop—to build and the sickness to gather like a sour oil slick in the pits of their empty stomachs?

The sensors produced their first image of the target wreck upon which they were pinning their diminishing hopes of survival: a slowly winking patch of brightness at the center of the screen. Caine enhanced the scan sensitivity to maximum. The object's reflected light patterns might allow the computer to estimate its structural configuration and yield a better mass estimate.

Trevor read off the results as they appeared on the screen. "Craft type and class: unknown. Mass estimate: 2455 tons, plus or minus 3 percent. Estimate confidence: 98.2 percent." He frowned, then typed: "detail configuration."

The screen scribed a three-axis grid. An outline formed swiftly at its center: a small wedge-shaped prow, a midsection of oblong bulges, and a confused collection of sharp angles to the rear. The confidence level indicator for the basic outline showed eighty-five percent. That initial level began increasing rapidly as planar surfaces started shading in, first in green—the high-confidence planes—then orange, and finally red: successively less certain projections. Caine and Trevor watched the object go through rotational analyses several times before they looked at each other.

Caine cleared his throat. "As a command grade officer in the USSF, it is my responsibility to be able to identify any human-built craft from a single cross-section, taken from any angle." He looked back at the rotating image on the screen. "I am not familiar with this design, Captain."

"I am, Commander," Trevor replied in a tight voice. "That's the small craft that was approaching the cutter, the one Hazawa hit with the PDF battery."

Caine took a deep breath. "Do we make intercept?"

Trevor shrugged. "Do we have a choice? Enemy or not, that wreckage is the only chance we have of extending our survival time. If we're lucky, its engines might still be intact, and they've got to be at least ten times more powerful than ours. That will give us enough thrust and endurance to angle back toward The Pearl, find if anything is left, maybe in the hidden caches, see if we can piece together some way to survive."

"Assuming we can find a way to control the exo-sapients' systems."

"We'll find a way, or we'll reroute control through to our own computer. Otherwise, we're on a short countdown to death from either asphyxiation, radiation exposure, or dehydration." Trevor unstrapped, pushed off and drifted to the command center's utility locker. He opened it, reached in and produced a Unitech ten-millimeter pistol. He unholstered it and started a crisp and professional inspection of the handgun. Caine raised his eyebrows slightly. "Are you expecting a welcoming committee?"

"No. But, in case I'm wrong ... well, I hate going to a party empty-handed."

Caine felt his palms grow cool. He watched the computer's graphical representation of the unfamiliar craft spin, roll, and somersault through its three-dimensional dissections.

Trevor reholstered the weapon, strapped back in. With a single touch to the dynamically reconfigurable screen, he wiped away the current, sensor-optimized setting and brought up the piloting set. "All systems checked and committed to computer control. Commencing intercept."

Trevor started firing the plasma thrusters in sustained bursts, angling the module into a trajectory that would eventually allow them to stern-chase the Arat Kur wreck. "Velocity will be matched automatically, but the final eight thousand meters of approach will have to be manual." His gaze continued to shuttle between the trajectory data and engine controls.

"How long?" asked Caine.

"Of this? Another two or three minutes. Then we coast for eight hours, at which point we go hands-on for a few sweaty minutes while we match its vector and tumble values. Then we suit up and check our gear."

"Our gear?"

"Our weapons," Trevor clarified, staring at him. "We are going to be boarding an enemy craft, you know."

Caine stared back. "Yeah. And *you* know I'm probably going to be more of a hindrance than a help. Like you said, I'm a make-believe soldier."

"That was obligatory hazing, Caine. Besides, you've been shot at more today than any newb has been in the last twenty years. And as much as it pains me to say it, you showed some good weapon-handling aptitudes."

"Mostly for heavy weapons, though."

"Yeah, I noticed the reports. You either had one hell of a run of beginner's luck or you've got a sixth sense for those weapons. But today, the weapon of choice is the handgun. How'd you do with those?"

Caine shook his head. "Not so good."

"Well, today is your lucky day. You get to work on improving that skill." Trevor drew the Unitech ten-millimeter, held it directly in front of Caine's eyes. "Are you familiar with this weapon?"

Caine could not bring himself to answer yes. "Read about it. Live-fired about fifteen rounds from one during the second week of training."

"Okay, then we take it from the top." Trevor swiftly

field-stripped the handgun, laid each piece on the console in front of Caine. "Reassemble and review."

You've got to be kidding. But Caine picked up the receiver, reached for the bolt, and dredged up already half-forgotten memories of a weapons-familiarization class that he had aced only two weeks earlier. "Unitech ten-millimeter selective-fire automatic handgun. This weapon uses a binary mix of reactant liquids as a scalable propellant. The two reactants are stored in separate canisters inside each magazine, which contains thirty projectiles. The standard load is fifteen antipersonnel, and fifteen armor-piercing projectiles." And the recitation and assembly went on until Caine checked the action, secured the safety and handed the rebuilt weapon back to Trevor, butt first.

Trevor looked at it, then at Caine. "Forgetting something?"

"I don't think so."

"Think again. EVA ops require special systems." Trevor took the weapon, pointed out several small nodules along the weapons frame and receiver. "Thermal regulation studs. They control the temperature of the weapon's primary metal components to ensure constant operating temperatures across crucial interfacing surfaces, such as breech-to-barrel. Necessity in spaceside operations where thermal variations can be extreme.

"Also, the position of the trigger guard is adjustable, as is the tensile setting of the trigger spring. These two features allow the weapon to be reconfigured for a bigger handprint." Trevor unlocked the trigger guard and pulled it forward until it almost reached the end of the barrel. "Looks odd, but it's the only way you can use it if you're wearing one of these."

Trevor wriggled his right hand back into one of the emergency suit gloves. He picked up the pistol with that hand; the weapon almost disappeared within the cumbersome gauntlet. "The bigger handprint allows you to fire and reload the weapon normally. But the most important EVA feature is—?"

Caine recited this one from memory: "'Projectile velocity may be varied by altering the volume of liquid injected into the firing chamber. This feature allows the user to both reduce warhead speeds and makes the weapon significantly less destabilizing when fired in low- and zero-gee environments.'"

"Very good. Now we perform a piece-by-piece diagnostic of our two emergency suits. We can talk though our next action while we work."

Caine swung his suit out of its locker and began his own checks. "What action is that?"

"Boarding procedure." Trevor holstered the sidearm.

Caine swallowed—a large, uncomfortable sensation—and began the visual inspection of his helmet. A worried expression stared back from its visor.

"I read an approximate volume of eight hundred fifty kiloliters," Trevor's voice announced in Caine's earbud. "We have matched its pitch values. Yaw values are minimal. Roll rate is one full rotation every twenty-eight seconds. Do you confirm? Over."

Caine squinted out the bow observation port in the ready room, just forward of the command center. The stark white enemy craft was completing one full roll around its long axis about once every half minute. "I confirm that estimate."

"Approximate range? Over."

Caine sighted the pistol at the wreck's midship hull, activated its dual-purpose targeting laser, read the rear LED: "One hundred forty meters, closing rapidly."

"Your range estimate confirms on-board ranging. Closing at two meters per second. Stand by for final retro burn."

A series of slight tugs indicated a quick sequence of counteraccelerations. The distance between the two craft stopped decreasing, stabilizing at just under one hundred meters. Caine was suitably impressed. The Auxiliary Command module had not been designed for precision spaceflight, just gross corrections to its own vector. *And without Trevor's piloting skills*—well, no reason to think about that. Not unless one was eager to contemplate certain death.

"I read vectors and two axes of tumble as matched. Confirm?"

"Confirmed. Nice driving."

"Not as nice as I'd like. Every ten meters is at least three seconds of exposure when we jump across."

"What's the current rate of exposure?"

"Thirty REM per minute. Nice tanning weather."

Caine's stomach contracted. "What about the exo craft? Are you reading active rad shields?"

"Negative. No EM grid. Do you observe any lights or sign of activity? Over."

Caine studied the craft more closely. The wedge-shaped prow had taken damage; it looked as though its chin had been chopped off. *Good shooting, Hazawa.* An ovate, slightly recessed, jet-black slab dominated what Caine took to be the upper surface. A hull-flush cockpit blister? Perhaps, but no sign of life in or about what Caine mentally labeled as the command section.

The craft's amidships belly rolled into view, revealing two parallel rows of white, oval containers: fuel tankage. No sign of damage, but no sign of activity. The aft propulsion system was also slightly easier to examine, now that the prow was out of the way. Toroidal fusion pods and thruster bells were crowded atop one another, but there was less apparatus for gimballing than on a comparable human craft. The enemy evidently relied more on magnetic bias to alter the vector of their thrust. But again, no light, no movement, not even any signs of damage.

"No sign of activity," Caine reported. "No sign of damage other than to the command module comprising the prow."

"What about sensor clusters?"

"None observable."

"Points of embarkation?"

"Not sure. There are a number of surface irregularities on the sides of the command module, but I can't even guess at their purpose. Can you get a better look with our external camera?"

"Negative. If I zoom in, the wreck's roll produces a blurred image. If I zoom out, I lose resolution. Hobson's choice. So any greater detail is going to require eyeballing it up close. Which means it's time for a walk around the neighborhood. I'm removing my intercom jack."

There was a sharp electronic *snick* and then nothing. Caine activated his suit's radio, sealed his helmet, and leaned forward for a final, and better, look outside. To the left, Barnard's Star was a small, bright red disk. To the right, the alien wreck rolled lazily. Falling behind, almost completely hidden by the bulk of the

Auxiliary Command module, was the arc of the small gas giant. *Strange, how serene it all looks*—

The heads-up display briefly painted an orange radiation icon on the inside of the helmet visor; Caine backed away from the window and leaned off to the side. Ten minutes of external exposure would cause profound sickness. Two times that was probably fatal.

Another orange light came on, but this one was next to the aft passageway: the first seal on the internal airlock door had been unlocked. Caine exited the ready room, headed aft, found Trevor releasing the primary hatch seal. The orange light became red. They entered the airlock.

After dogging the hatch behind them, Trevor leaned over until the top half of his visor touched Caine's. Trevor's voice was muffled and distant. "Last suit check. All green?"

"All green."

Trevor nodded, tapped the red button on the wall. Caine heard a low rushing sound, somewhere in between a cascade of water and burst of released gas: the airlock was being depressurized.

"Give me a procedure review, Caine."

"I wait until you reach the target and send a hand signal confirming that you have made rendezvous and that I am cleared to remotely stabilize the line. I then jump over using a line-lanyard. I maintain radio silence throughout, to be violated only in the event of emergency or upon your initiation of broadcast."

"How much time do we have to make our jump?"

"One minute each. Any longer and our cumulative radiation exposure becomes—er, unpromising."

Trevor nodded behind his visor. "Okay, let's go."

He turned to face the door, opened an access panel, depressed a red handle, held it there.

The red lights flashed rapidly for three seconds and then the door started to move aside noiselessly, as if presaging the strange, ghostly silence of outer space. *Or of death.* Caine bit his savaged lip, used the pain to control his nerves. A widening slice of blackness and stars opened before them. Trevor drew the Unitech ten-millimeter, attached its lanyard to a ring on his utility harness, and leaned forward, allowing his feet to rise behind him. When his soles met the interior hatch at their backs, he reached out with both hands, braced himself against the edges of the now-fully open outer hatch. He contracted backward into a squatting position, legs gathered under him as he attached his tether to a mooring ring on the airlock wall. If Trevor mistimed his jump, then he'd have problems landing on the bow module, which would mean more exposure. Which in turn would mean—Caine decided not to pursue that line of thought any further.

Trevor kicked off from the inner hatch and into open space, the line unfurling in his wake. Caine moved to a position near the door to get a better view.

Trevor was already fifteen meters away and had rolled over on his back, pistol in hand. He aimed back along the path of his jump, then shifted his aim slightly above the rim of the auxiliary command module. Caine saw the muzzle flash briefly, followed immediately by a noticeable increase in the speed with which Trevor was moving away.

His course-corrective shot had apparently been a good one; he was now headed directly for the enemy craft. He somersaulted very slowly to face in that direction, his legs out in front of him. The slack eased out of the tether as Trevor passed the halfway mark—and as Caine's heads-up display painted the now-familiar trefoil radiation symbol above the scene.

Trevor's forward progress started to diminish, suggesting that he had now fired the ten-millimeter to both kill his forward tumble and counteraccelerate, easing himself into a slower approach. Caine checked the small green chrono at the extreme left of his HUD. Elapsed time: fifteen seconds. Coming up on five REM whole body exposure for Trevor, probably about a third that for himself.

Trevor drifted closer to the wreck as the broad top of the prow began rolling around toward him once again. He had uncoupled from the tether: dangerous but necessary. Landing on the rolling hull with the tether firmly attached would have snapped the line like desiccated string and sent Trevor spinning off into space.

Trevor aimed behind, fired two last times, pushing him forward as the command section's wider aftward surfaces rotated under him. It was a tricky maneuver. If he fired too soon, one of the sharp angles of the prow might slam into him as it completed its arc, doing so with enough force to shatter every bone in his body. Coming in late wasn't quite so bad; in that event, Trevor would land a few meters off-center and aft of the command section, but that also meant a few more seconds of exposure. Caine squinted. The whiteness of Trevor's suit had blended with the whiteness of the spinning wreck, obscuring the outcome of his final approach to contact.

But just before the top surface of the prow rolled

out of sight, Caine glimpsed a flash of movement on its surface: two quick, wide-armed waves. The first confirmed that Trevor was safely down on the wreck; the second meant that it was now Caine's turn to jump.

Caine clipped a waiting electric lead onto the end of the tether. He thumbed a stud on the lead's handgrip. A short burst of high-voltage current coursed through the reactive-composite tether, converting its malleable pith into a rigid core. He looped his suit's mooring lanyard about the now-stiff line, clipped the end of the lanyard to a ring on his own utility harness, and exhaled. Time to go.

He leaned forward, pushed his feet back against the interior hatch, aligned himself so as to be parallel to the tether. Space loomed large above his head. He bit his lip hard and kicked.

The airlock walls rushed past and were gone. In their place was blackness and slowly wheeling stars—which were all at once directly overhead yet also beneath him. All at once, both he and the universe were tumbling uncontrollably. He tried to focus on the one object with a constant relative bearing: the enemy wreck. However, he was approaching it too swiftly according to his inner ear, even though he was closing far too slowly according to his dosimeter. The radiation icon became red.

He inadvertently blinked. When he reopened his eyes, it now appeared that the wreck was rolling toward him. The sudden change in perception brought up a swirl of nausea-inducing vertigo, just as the wreck's cockpit blister started coming around again. But still no sign of Trevor. Caine closed his eyes and bit down harder on his lip.

When he opened his eyes, he forced himself to see the wreck as stationary and himself as approaching— and discovered that he was more than halfway down the tether. And had still not initiated the one-hundred-eighty-degree tumble which would position him for a feet-first landing upon the wreck. Trevor was rising into sight again, making fast, angry circles with his hand, meaning *turn, turn!*

Caine kicked forward slightly, felt his body begin to rotate backward, watched as the wreck seemed to fall down, beneath his feet—and was distracted by a glimmer of light just above his field of vision. He craned his neck to get a look at the source of brightness.

Caine started. A titanic hemisphere of white, ochre, and pale blue striations wheeled, wobbly, above his head. Whereas the slow rotation of the starfield had been modestly disorienting, the drunken oscillations of Barnard's Star II were stupefying. The gas giant brushed the stars aside, half-filled his visor, seemed ready to swallow the module he'd jumped from like a whale's maw poised to swallow a lone krill. The mammoth planet's atmospheric turbulence sent whorls and spirals streaming into each other in slow motion, murky fractals eternally evolving. Silvery flickers backlit the clouds, telltale signs of lightning storms more extensive than the entirety of the Eurasian landmass. Caine swallowed, fought through a rush of vertigo so powerful that he felt he might spin down into a single, contracting point and vanish—

"Caine! Grab the tether! NOW!"

Caine started violently as Trevor's voice blasted out of his radio receiver. He looked down past his feet. Only six meters below, the aft end of the wreck's prow was rolling past. He choked down a rush of bitter vomit, grabbed at the tether, lost his grip, grabbed again, caught it only a palm's width from the end. At this close range, the wreck's roll rate seemed to have increased, with Trevor rotating closer at a fearsome speed—

—But I don't have time to fear, or even think. I have to act.

Time slowed and the gargantuan emptiness of the universe seemed to shrink back—enough so that Caine could assess how much sway his frantic motions had imparted to the tether, could watch Trevor rotate past underneath him, and could gauge the best moment to "jump down" to the wreck. He felt more than calculated that moment and pushed off the end of the tether, bending and relaxing his knees, eyes riveted down between his feet.

Four meters, two. He kept his focus on the closest part of the wreck, scanned peripherally. There was a small angular protuberance rotating past, just to the right of him.

Contact. As his knees absorbed the shock, he felt the wreck rotating out from under his feet, trying to shove him away. Caine kept his knees loose instead of bracing them, let his body continue to sink toward the hull, felt it bump his buttocks as he leaned to the right and grabbed.

His hand closed around the protuberance he had spied: a curved bar. Probably a mooring point. He twisted in that direction, threw his left hand over to join his right on the bar. Caine felt pressure mount in his joints as the inertia of his old vector argued with the rotational force, the combined vectors tugging his body away from the wreck and turning it around in space until, finally, it relented. He checked his chrono as he pulled his body back into contact with the wreck and gathered his legs beneath him. Ninety-eight seconds since Trevor had started over. How time flies when you're having fun.

There was a light bump against his head; Trevor had crawled over and tapped helmets. His voice was quiet, tight. "Are you okay?"

"I'm okay now," Caine answered, pretty sure he was telling the truth. "Let's get going."

Trevor nodded, and set out on a drifting crawl to the rear of the wreck's command section, where he pointed to a small oval recess surrounding a slightly convex section of the hull. Caine felt the edges of the recess, discovered deep, wide grooves. "Airlock?"

Trevor nodded. "Might be. Look for a maintenance plate or manual access cover."

Caine pushed himself back carefully with his right hand, then his left—and stopped; something was under that palm. It was another, much smaller oval recess with a convex interior, the center of which was pierced in a quatrefoil pattern. Caine grabbed hold, tugged: nothing. He tried turning and then pushing it; there was a moment of resistance, then a short downward release before the cover swung back easily.

Trevor was already beside him. "What have you found?"

A cruciform knob stared up at them. Trevor reached in, turned it, watched the large convex panel that was probably an airlock. No discernible change. He turned the knob again, again, again. Slowly, the airlock door began to slide aside and farther away, deeper into the hull. Trevor braced himself and began cranking the knob rapidly with both hands: the portal widened more rapidly. He nodded for Caine to lean closer; their helmets touched again.

"Take the gun. Safety off. Cover the entry while I finish opening it."

Caine detached the weapons lanyard from Trevor's harness, attached it to his own, and slid the gun out of its holster. He crawled to the edge of the opening airlock and aimed the weapon inside. His visor's red radiation icon began to flash; they had exceeded two minutes of exposure. Not good; not good at all.

The airlock door slid away, apparently retracting along a curved pathway. When it was about half open, the movement stopped. A second later, Trevor was alongside Caine, touching helmets again. "I'm going to shine a light in and take a look. As soon as I do, you lean in with the gun. If you see anything suspicious, nail it. Understood?"

"Understood." Caine exhaled. After tumbling through endless, enervating space, this activity was reassuringly finite and concrete.

Trevor scuttled around to the other side of the opening, activated his helmet lights, nodded to Caine, and looked over the edge. Caine leaned in with the gun on that cue.

Trevor's lights illuminated a tiny cubicle, smaller than the airlock on their Auxiliary Command module. At the bottom was another oval portal, flanked by a modest control panel. Small lights, most of which were yellow-green, stared beady-eyed back at them from its surface. The vehicle still had some sort of power, even if it was only emergency batteries. Otherwise, the airlock was empty.

Caine looked up; Trevor pointed at himself, at Caine, and then down into the airlock. Caine nodded.

Like a snake sliding around the corner of a rock, Trevor slipped over the rim of the hatchway and down into the airlock. Caine double-checked that the pistol's safety was off, and followed.

Chapter Eleven

Adrift off Barnard's Star 2 C

The airlock was even smaller than it had looked from outside, barely big enough to hold the two of them at the same time. Caine kept the ten-millimeter trained on the squarish doorway that led deeper into the craft, watching for any changes in the lights on the panels that flanked it.

In the meantime, Trevor had found a knob similar to the one on the outside of the hull and was turning it rapidly. As he did, a hard-edged shadow advanced across the door, the floor, and finally, cut off all external light into the airlock: the outer hatch was sealed. The red radiation icon on Caine's HUD flickered into orange and then disappeared. *The Arat Kur have pretty damn efficient rad shielding, considering there's no sign of an operating EM grid.* However, there were still radiation worries: Caine's chronometer read 144 seconds total elapsed mission time. That meant almost seventy-five REM whole body dose for Trevor, about fifty-five for Caine. Plus the thirty REM they had picked up when their own EM grid had to be shut off yesterday, and whatever else they were going to pick up making the jump back to the Auxiliary Command Module. In all probability, they weren't going to be feeling too well for the next couple of days.

Trevor moved over to the control panel beside the inner door, briefly inspected the lights and the glyphs beneath them. He tapped the bottom half of the panel, exploring.

Caine touched helmets. "What are you looking for?"

"This." Trevor was now sliding aside the lower half of the panel, revealing three smaller, cruciform knobs. "Manual systems in case the power is out."

"Won't they be disabled or locked off?"

"Not unless there was a survivor on board who saw us coming and wanted to keep us out. You have to leave manual overrides functional during routine ops. Otherwise, if your power goes down and you're unconscious or unable to move, rescuers can't get to you unless they breach the hull. And I guess our adversary has learned the same lesson."

"So since they're *not* locked off, maybe that indicates there aren't any survivors to take that precaution. Besides, survivors should have tried to effect repairs and rejoin their own fleet, particularly since this ship doesn't seem too badly damaged."

"Don't judge a book by its cover, Caine, particularly when it comes to sensitive machines like spacecraft. They can look fine on the outside but can be hopelessly fubared inside."

"I wonder how fubared this craft really is."

"Why?"

"The rads dropped away completely when you shut the door behind us."

Trevor shrugged, digging for a small tool kit on his utility harness. "They're probably way ahead of us in material sciences."

Caine shook his head. "You'd need tremendous density to stop that much particle radiation."

"So what are you saying?"

"I'm saying that this ship might still have enough power to be shielding itself, somehow."

"Then why didn't our passive sensors pick up the electromagnetic anomalies?"

"I don't know. Maybe their EM field effect is not projected, but remains within the matter comprising the hull. Sort of how active electrobonding works, only this version is designed to repel charged particles rather than strengthen the bonds between molecules in hull materials."

Trevor was silent before replying. "Where would the power come from? Their fusion plant is cold."

"I don't know. Batteries, possibly on constant recharge if some part of the hull is sensitized to work like a solar panel."

"Which would probably mean that somebody on board *did* survive the battle," Trevor pointed out. "What you're describing is not an automated emergency backup system. It would need someone to activate and integrate all those functions." Trevor put a hand on one of the three small knobs. "So, assuming we have an enemy to meet, let's get moving. Stand to the side and cover the door."

Caine crunched himself into the nearest corner, took the gun in both hands, extended it out in front of himself. The first knob that Trevor manipulated activated a series of dim red lighting bars that outlined the inner airlock door. The lights flashed rapidly. Probably the knob for opening the inner airlock door, the alarm signifying that the airlock itself was still unpressurized. "I'm no linguist, but I think red is their color for danger, too."

Caine nodded his agreement and re-centered the handgun's laser sight on the interior door.

The next knob Trevor tried had no immediately observable effect, but after several seconds, they noticed a faint external sound: the rush of air. Trevor squeezed himself to the other side of the interior airlock door, drew a pry-bar from his tool-kit, and hefted it. Caine heard his voice over the helmet speakers. "We'll need to use radio, now. Shift to secure channel four."

Caine made the appropriate choice on his HUD display with an eye-directed cursor, bit down with his left molars to confirm the selection. "Radio check. Are you receiving?"

"Loud and clear." The inrushing of air had already crescendoed and was now diminishing rapidly. "Ready to dance?"

Caine nodded, focused on the intense red dot that his weapon was projecting upon the interior door. Trevor manipulated the first knob again. This time, the door slid aside.

A passage, side-lights receding away vanishing-point style. No blast of out- or in-rushing air, either; the craft still had an atmosphere. No sign of fog or fine snow drifting in midair; the humidity hadn't frozen out, meaning that the internal heating hadn't failed. Trevor stopped turning the knob. "Fresh life-support means the probability of survivors just got a lot higher. Cover high; I'm going in low."

"Understood. Go."

Trevor jackknifed around the edge of the doorway, swam aggressively into the passage beyond. He swooped low, hugged the floor tightly as he followed along the wall to his left.

"What do you see?" Caine asked.

"Doors up ahead, two on either side. Two rows of handles—the four-flanged variety—run the length of the walls."

"For zero-gee movement?"

"That's my guess. Can't make out the end of the hall. Looks like a dark opening, but I can't be sure. Damn. What I'd give for thermal imaging goggles right about now."

"Should I advance past you?"

"No, just join me here. This space is too tight for a leapfrog advance."

And I'm not good enough in zero-gee to make it feasible, anyhow. Holding the gun in his right hand, Caine pushed with his feet and let his body straighten into a slow forward glide.

Trevor hadn't exaggerated. The corridor was not well-suited to human physiognomy. Only one and a half meters wide by two meters high, it felt cramped, vaguely reminiscent of the engineering access spaces aboard the Auxiliary Command module. The lights that receded toward the dark at the end of the corridor were more amber in color than white.

"Caine, watch how you're handling that gun. Don't point the laser down the hall. We don't want to announce ourselves."

Caine nodded his understanding and pushed himself down to a prone position alongside Trevor. "Now what?"

"We go room by room. You cover, I enter."

Which seemed a wise plan. Trevor was ensuring that they would not leave any uncleared spaces behind them. But there was one problem with its execution. As they began low-drifting toward the first of the four doors, Caine secured the handgun's safety and offered it back to Trevor, butt first. "Give me the pry-bar. I'll enter the rooms. You cover."

"Nope. We've got the right resources in the right hands."

"Trevor, you're much more qualified with this weapon than I am."

"And even more qualified in zero-gee maneuver. Did you have any classes in zero-gee hand-to-hand combat?"

"One."

"Then you should know what I'm talking about. Every time you take a swing, you're propelling yourself in a new direction. Same thing every time you block a blow or duck; every movement is acceleration. Two sudden moves and you'll be too disoriented to do anything other than try to steady yourself."

"Okay, okay. Let's get on with it, then."

The first door—which was almost perfectly square— did not respond to physical manipulation. Trevor tried the buttons on the panel alongside it. On the second try, the door slid aside.

The room, illuminated by Caine's helmet lights, was a hollow cube. Clutched in metal beams at the center was a radially symmetric collection of metal spheres, translucent tanks, and conduits.

Trevor dove in, brought himself to a halt, peered in between the tanks and tubes, drifted back out. "I'm guessing that's life support. No one home."

The next squarish door had irregular black smudges along two adjoined edges. Trevor ran a finger over the smudge, which erased but deposited itself on the tip of his glove. Carbon. Probably from an interior fire that had tried to lick around the door seal. The buttons on that entry refused to work and Trevor's attempts to budge it were futile. His movements were hurried and annoyed as he drifted toward the next door.

This opened onto what seemed to be a private room of some sort. However, just beyond the doorway, the ceiling and floor pinched closer to each other, so that an individual entering the room had less than one and a half meters of vertical space in which to operate. An apparent sleeping nook that sheltered a pair of berths that looked like a mix of mechanical cocoon and fluffy sleeping bag stood out from the far wall. Other objects—furniture and implements, Caine guessed—seemed to be secured for zero-gee.

The structure and trappings of the fourth and final room were almost identical to the previous one. But here, there were telltale signs of use. A large object, akin to a narrow-necked inkwell with four radially symmetric depressions, had drifted into a corner of the room and floated there, unsecured. One cocoon-sleeping bag was neither fully open or closed, its lid hanging at an angle.

"This doesn't look like any warship I've ever seen," muttered Trevor as they moved back to the doorway.

Caine nodded. For a small craft, the design was too—well, indulgent: spacious sleeping compartments, sophisticated long-duration life-support recycling facilities, a comparatively roomy corridor, and of course, the tremendous fuel tankage capacity amidships. "No, I'd guess it was a recon vessel or a command nexus for drones on long-duration duty."

"Recon," Trevor asserted. "Otherwise, some of the drones which pranged the cutter should have gone offline when Hazawa knocked this hull out of action. Unfortunately, that doesn't answer the most important question: how many crew were on board for the battle?"

"More important still, how many are left alive?"

Trevor shrugged. "No way to know that, but it has enough accommodations for four—which doesn't make sense. Two crewpersons are enough to handle any of the missions this ship might undertake."

"Military missions, yes. But what about paramilitary or civilian missions?"

"I don't follow you."

"What if your first comment was correct, that this ship wasn't designed to be a military ship at all?"

Trevor looked around the craft again, as though seeing it anew. "Could be. Possibly a packet or a survey craft."

"That's what I'm guessing. Some kind of communications or research vessel, pressed into military service. Maybe it was even a civilian crew. Which might explain why we're not seeing any of them."

"Because they're hiding?"

"Because they're dead. If they weren't used to military protocols, maybe they were operating without pressure suits when they got hit."

"Interesting theory, but there's still atmosphere and heat on board. So what killed them?"

"Maybe they were all in a chamber that depressurized; I don't know. If any of the crew survived, why let us get this far in without trying an ambush?"

Trevor's forced grin was visible through his visor. "Let's go find out. Slow approach, no helmet lights."

Caine silently counted off ten seconds as they drifted toward the opening at the end of the corridor. A faint glow within outlined large structures and confused silhouettes that resembled tangled spider webs. Trevor nodded to the handgun, pointed into the darkness, then tapped his helmet's lights. Caine nodded, secured the weapon in a two-handed grasp, the targeting laser aimed just below the level of the doorway, poised to elevate swiftly to engage a target. Trevor aimed his helmet lights through the doorway, turned them on.

Cables hung down from the ceiling, draped across an object that looked like a cross between a chaise lounge and a bathtub: evidently an Arat Kur acceleration couch. Beyond the bathtub-couch was another, similar shadow, except its upper surface was made uneven by a distinctly lumpy silhouette. If that couch was still occupied, its occupant was no longer moving. Beyond that, and framed by other debris from the ruined bridge, the stars glimmered faintly through a transparent panel that was a match in size and shape for the opaque cockpit blister they had noted on their approach.

Trevor's light swung slowly across the dense clusters of power conduits and narrower command cables that drifted in tangled spools and tentacles. "Looks like a convention of spider plants in there." He snapped off the light.

"Looks like a tomb to me."

Trevor nodded. "Yeah, I saw the silhouette in the far couch."

Caine kept staring into the darkness. "Of course, another one might still be in there."

"Possible, but why let us get so close? As you pointed out, the best time to ambush us was when we were moving up the corridor, trapped in a narrow space and without cover."

Caine squinted into the darker regions where the wires were thickest. "Still—"

"Yeah, we still need to play it safe. But we've also got to finish checking out this bridge. Cover me." Trevor swam into the room. His helmet lights swept back and forth across the clutter of cables and filaments like headlights roving along Spanish moss.

"Talk to me, Trevor."

"Not much to talk about. I think this is a pretty large chamber, but I can't be sure with this wiring all over the place." Trevor drifted farther into the room, keeping his distance from the long, low Arat Kur acceleration couches and using the mass of cables for cover.

"What about the controls?"

"Can't see anything from here. I'm going in to check out the first acceleration couch."

"Hold it, Trevor."

Trevor, already moving toward the long silhouette to his right, arrested his drift by grabbing a handful of cables. "Holding. What's up?"

"I don't think you should move directly to the acceleration couch. Use the cables for concealment, approach obliquely. That also gives me a clear field of fire if anything is lurking near the couches themselves."

"Will do. Ready to start my move."

Caine reangled the ten-millimeter until its targeting laser was painting a small, red circle on the nearest acceleration couch. "Go ahead."

Trevor half rotated in space, swimming to the left and using handfuls of wiring to aid his progress—which halted suddenly. "Damn," he muttered. His lights flickered through the sinuous shapes, painting shadow-snakes on the far wall.

"What is it, Trevor?"

"Almost got tangled. The cables are heavier in this part of the room, and I'm not seeing all of them. The helmet lights are too narrow-beam."

Yes, it's pretty dark where he is. Damn nuisance, too. Every other room in the entire vessel had some illumination, if only the emergency lights. But on the bridge even those were dark—

—*Shit shit shit!* "Trevor, kill your lights!"

"What—?"

"Kill your—!"

The ambush didn't unfold the way Caine expected. No shot in the dark: not even that much warning. One moment, Trevor's floating silhouette was resuming its forward motion, left hand tugging a cable he'd wrapped around his wrist for purchase; the next, there was a blinding sputter of blue-white sparks just above his handhold. Trevor bucked backward, suddenly rigid, immobilized by the electric current that had raced up his arm and into his body.

Out of the corner of his eye, Caine saw a darker shadow rise up from behind the second acceleration couch, the one probably occupied by an enemy corpse. He swung the ten-millimeter's aimpoint over—but the shadow ducked down behind the couch again.

Tricky little bastard: a faulty wire, rigged as a trap. Probably command activated and probably dozens of other wires similarly rigged. And figuring that out has cost a precious tenth of a second. So think—fast.

Trevor's paralyzed. Every second gives your enemy the opportunity to finish him off. The alien is probably armed, behind solid cover, and waiting for you to expose yourself. Meaning you've got no good options, except—

Caine snapped back the ten-millimeter's ammo feed selector with his thumb: set for armor-piercing rounds. He grabbed his emergency's suit's safety lanyard, slammed the carabineer clip across one of the cruciform handles on the wall beside him. As the clip snapped into place, he brought up the gun, eyes tracking with the laser aimpoint. He thumbed the propellant switch over to maximum as the red circle jumped up along and above the couch, then up a short stretch of wall—

—keep that death-grip on the cable, Trevor. For just one more second—

Caine squeezed the trigger when the red aimpoint reached the cockpit blister. The ten-millimeter Unitech bucked savagely, although the report was muffled by his helmet. The smooth surface of the cockpit blister star-cracked but did not shatter. Caine swung the aimpoint back to the center of the radiate fracture lines and squeezed the trigger again.

He didn't hear the second report, or rather, he couldn't distinguish it. The cockpit panel blasted outward with a howl that swallowed the ten-millimeter's feeble voice into the cacophonic cyclone of air, stray wires, and papers that maelstromed out into the vacuum of space.

Caine felt himself yanked in that direction, then yanked to an equally abrupt halt: the suit lanyard and carabineer clip squealed under the pull of his vacuum-sucked mass. But they held.

Trevor was still mostly motionless. The wrist-wrapped cable and tangled masses of wiring were holding him fast. However, the lump atop the second acceleration couch—a limp creature shaped like an oversized horseshoe crab-cockroach hybrid—went spinning out the breach in the cockpit blister. A moment later, a second, similar object, its outline made more vague by some sort of spacesuit, tumbled upward from behind the same couch, clutching frantically with six stunted ventral limbs. One of the rear limbs caught a slender wire, slipped, fumbled, clutched again—but weakly.

As the rush of air started to diminish, Caine raised the ten-millimeter, centered the red aimpoint on the struggling horseshoe-crab shape—

Nearby motion distracted him: Trevor had unwrapped his wrist from the cable mooring him in place. Caine's breath caught. *No, not yet! Grab another cable—just a few seconds more!*

But Trevor's movements were purposeful, even though they were unsteady. His left arm dangling, he rode the rapidly weakening current of outgushing atmosphere toward the jagged hole in the cockpit blister. As he swept over the acceleration couches, he simultaneously kicked downward and reached up with his good arm. His feet connected with the top of the second couch and pushed him up toward the horseshoe-crab shape. Trevor slammed into it and tried to get a firm grip, but the decompressive currents began tugging him away. He was pulled feet-first toward the hole, but his right hand found a length of cable and locked on—even as his left hand reached toward the alien. The creature's multiple appendages grabbed it violently, then fought for purchase on Trevor's suit and helmet, and, once secure, began to contract. Forcefully.

For one brief instant, Caine could not look away from the surreal scene of Trevor being hug-crushed by a crab-roach. Then reflex and adrenaline took over. Caine uncoupled the carabineer clip, and, with the decompressive flow almost gone, he aimed himself at Trevor and kicked at the wall.

Too oblique and too hard. Caine went corkscrewing toward the floor, instead, hit the deck at an angle, and bounced. He swam through a slow, spastic cartwheel. Between frantic curses and calls to Trevor, his own breath echoed loudly in his ears. Only when he came to a stop—upside down and with his legs tangled in the hanging garden of cables—did he realize that Trevor was answering his calls.

"Caine, I'm—okay. Take it—easy. Reorient—yourself."

"Reorient myself, hell! Christ, Trevor, what were you thinking? That damn thing might have killed you. Might still intend to."

"Caine, we—can't h-hurt—it. It's rigged—the bridge. Could have—r-rigged engineering. With a—bomb. Need it—alive."

Damn it, he's right—and I'm a fool for not realizing the same thing. Caine kicked his legs free and somersaulted to turn himself over and reassume an up-down orientation that matched Trevor's. He was vaguely aware that he had performed this tricky zero-gee maneuver with the surety of a pro.

The alien's six-limbed grasp on Trevor was tight, but not dangerously so. It was, however, immobilizing. One of the alien's legs had wrapped around the upper part of Trevor's left armpit, jamming that arm in an awkward, elevated position. Trevor's right arm was pinned to his side by another appendage, and while his legs were free, they were out of reach from any surface against which to push.

Oddly, the Arat Kur—for it was certainly not a Ktor or a Hkh'Rkh—seemed less capable of movement than Trevor. Although dominating the human with a grapple that would have been the envy of any collegiate wrestling star, the exosapient was motionless. Caine drifted closer cautiously, thumbed the ammunition selector back over to the setting that loaded antipersonnel rounds. He laid the gun against the side of the Arat Kur's thorax.

"Might as well—aim at—head." There was a grunt of extra effort in Trevor's voice.

"As if we have any indication that's where its brain is. And I thought you said you were all right. Your voice: you can hardly breathe. That damn thing is crushing you."

"No—not the—the reason."

"What do you mean, not the reason?"

"Not the r-reason for my—voice. Shock;—everything stiff. Hurts. Hard to talk. Can't m-m-move well, either."

Caine looked for and found clinical signs consistent with the aftermath of electrical trauma. A small, but high-speed tremor in Trevor's right arm was visible even though the Arat Kur's claws held it in a viselike grip. There was also a faint intermittent twitch in his friend's left arm and more pronounced involuntary motions in his right leg. At least there was still movement, but that didn't preclude more serious internal damage. "Trevor, read off your biomonitor values."

"Already—checked. Pulse and temperature high. All—all others, nominal. I'll be—okay. J-just get—get this guy—off me."

Caine extended his arm, pushing himself a meter back from the tethered amalgam of human and alien. Detaching the Arat Kur necessitated an initial inspection of its physiology—or, rather, of its bulky, podlike vacuum suit.

The fabric of the suit was tougher and more rigid than that used in human suits. Each limb covering was comprised of separate, well-articulated segments, making it unnecessary to ensure mobility by using more pliable materials. Reasonable. The Arat Kur body seemed to have no waist, no hips, no long limbs: in short, it was only capable of limited movement. With less of a demand for flexibility, Arat Kur garment designers could focus more on strength and durability.

It also seemed that Arat Kur didn't have heads, simply a cluster of sensory organs on their front-facing surface. Accordingly, the alien's spacesuit was topped by a wide, shaded dome, flanked by a brace of small, highly distorting mirrors. Caine considered his own fun-house reflection for a moment. No head meant no neck. No way to reposition the visual sensory organs without repositioning the whole body to face the object to be observed—unless the visual field was expanded by using mirrors. *Hmmm. I'll bet these bastards spent a lot of evolutionary time worrying about, and being terrified by, threats from their rear.* Possibly a useful tactical and psychological factor.

Mounted just beneath the Arat Kur helmet-dome were two well-articulated sleeves, each ending in a set of cruciform mechanical claws. The claws were heavier and blunter than he would have expected in a tool-using species, but then he reconsidered his conclusion. Vacuum gloves turned even the slenderest human hand into a clumsy, bloated paw. The same could certainly be expected of alien space garments.

There were a few external control surfaces visible, all of which were in recessed pits ringing the rim of the helmet-dome. Glyphs were visible under each touch-sensitive panel. More were printed on the small, dorsally-mounted life-support unit. All of which were absolutely meaningless to Caine.

Not discovering anything particularly useful to the purpose of prying the Arat Kur apart from Trevor, Caine started with the most basic approach: brute force. However, repeated attempts to lever open the alien's claws, or to cause its limbs to relax, were completely unproductive. "Maybe it's died. Maybe rigor mortis has already set in."

Trevor's voice, sounding somewhat more relaxed, disabused Caine of that notion: "No, it's alive."

"How can you tell?"

Trevor's teeth chattered once before he replied. "It's sh-shaking s-slightly."

Trevor sounded like he was growing cold, probably going into shock. And the exosapient was obstructing access to the manual overrides for Trevor's suit thermostat—

—*Suit thermostat? Hmm. That might be a better way of getting the Arat Kur to move: fiddle around with the life-support unit on its suit.* But adjusting the alien's life-support pack might also kill it. The device was a mystery of orange and green lights, recessed indicators, and small access panels, all linked to the rear of the helmet-dome—

Wait. The rear of the helmet dome. Of course. That gives me an even simpler option. Caine maneuvered to a position behind the exosapient, keeping his gun trained on the center of its thorax as he produced a pry bar from his own toolkit.

"Wh-what are y-you doing, C-Caine?" Trevor did not sound good at all.

"Conducting a psychological warfare experiment." Keeping the handgun tight against the exosapient's midriff, Caine ran the pry bar along the center of the alien's life-support unit. Then again, slowly, softly, from the bottom up to the top. *Let's see how you feel about having a hostile alien constantly tapping and bumping at your back.*

There was no immediate reaction. *Might be time to increase the implied threat from behind.* On the next pass of the pry bar, Caine let it graze the rear edge of the helmet-dome.

The exosapient's limbs flexed convulsively, released Trevor in its attempt to scrabble away along other, nearby wires.

But, anticipating that, Caine clung to the alien's back. Avoiding the grabbing legs, he pulled himself forward until the top half of his visor was level with the alien's helmet dome. He still couldn't see anything inside; the material was too dark. No matter; obviously, the Arat Kur could see outward. Well enough, at least, to make out the ten-millimeter handgun that Caine laid against the helmet-dome. The alien's movements became more frantic. Caine tapped the muzzle against the dome twice and then left it pointing directly inward. The alien's movement ended abruptly; all six legs went limp. Caine smiled. It was nice to know that some concepts—such as a loaded gun—were capable of transcending even the barriers of species and language.

He looked over toward Trevor, who was making adjustments to his suit's life-support unit. "What's wrong?"

"Just setting the temperature a few degrees higher."

Caine bound their prisoner with lengths of cable and wiring. Meanwhile, Trevor haltingly moved to hunch in front of what appeared to be the wreck's central computer console.

"Anything interesting?"

"G-God, no. This writing looks l-like tortured s-spa-spaghetti trying to m-mate with cock-eyed d-d-dominoes. Be-besides, we don't speak their language. That's why-why I h-h-had to sa-save the little b-bastard. Whoev-ever he is."

"An Arat Kur?" ventured Caine. "We've seen the Hkh'Rkh already, and the Ktor live in those big tanks on treads. And no other species seemed hostile at Convocation."

"Arat Ku-Kur sounds r-right."

Caine helped Trevor to drift away from the enemy ship's bridge console. "So, we've caught an Arat Kur. Maybe. But whatever he is, you're right: we have to find a way to communicate with him. Until we do, we can't even dock this wreck with the Auxiliary Command module to pool the two vehicles' resources. And without those combined resources, we're just a pile of a junk heading into deep space."

Caine stared past Trevor's tremoring nod and trembling shoulder. The trussed exosapient was once again motionless. *Maybe even smug.* And perhaps it had a right to be. The alien might be their prisoner, but they were now hostages to its knowledge.

Chapter Twelve

Adrift off Barnard's Star 2 C

Caine's voice startled Trevor out of his daze. "You feeling any better?"

"Sure. Fine." Trevor clenched his torso against the shiver that coursed through him.

Caine frowned. "Even though your temp and pulse are back to normal, you're still cold from shock and exhibiting impaired movement, particularly in the left arm."

"You done, doc?"

Caine leaned back. "I'm just trying to help."

And that is of course true, and I'm just pissed that I had to depend on a rookie to get back here to our module. That impairment had made for an interesting return from the alien wreck: semiconscious EVA veteran Trevor Corcoran riding piggyback on EVA neophyte Caine Riordan for more than a minute. *If my old SEAL instructor Stosh had seen it, I'd never hear the end of it.*

Fortunately, what Riordan lacked in training and experience, he had made up for in common sense.

Or so it seemed to Trevor, who closed his eyes and tried to recall what had happened after he had started to mumble and stumble on the Arat Kur ship. He vaguely remembered Riordan linking several tethers and reeling the exosapient across the gap between the wrecks after he and Trevor were secure on the module: a suitably undignified transit for the murderous overgrown cockroach.

After cycling through the airlock, he recalled Caine removing his spacesuit and examining him, talking as he went. "Trevor, I want you to hear what I'm seeing, so you can tell me how best to help you. Minor burn marks on the right palm, apparently where the current entered. Seems like the suit's anticonductivity layer helped considerably. Your fine motor control still seems poor. Are your ears still ringing?" Trevor seemed to recall nodding, or maybe he had just intended to do so.

In the three minutes it took Caine to conduct his layman's examination, Trevor had felt himself relapsing into shock. Caine hustled him back into his emergency suit, set the internal temperature to twenty-five degrees centigrade, and threatened mutiny if his superior officer attempted anything more strenuous than closing his eyelids.

Which Trevor may have done for a while; he wasn't sure. However, his next memory was of Caine dragging the alien—still by the tow line and none-too-gently—down to the lower level of the module, the ponderous creature floating lightly through zero-gee like an improbable, lopsided balloon on an industrial-strength string. After sealing the presumed Arat Kur in one of the deactivated rooms, he had returned to the control room and instructed the computer to restore minimal environmental functions in the makeshift prison cell: heat, air, and light.

Meanwhile, Trevor had slipped back into the doze-daze from which Caine had now just solicitously roused him. And for which Trevor's expression of gratitude had been a facetious jibe about his amateur doctoring. Trevor sought a conversational olive branch: "You're getting better at your zero-gee turns. A little awkward yet, but that will come with time. How's our pal?"

"Some pal. He's all right I guess, but who can really tell? He just lays—well, floats—there."

"Which is a bit of a problem, since getting him was only step one. Now we've got to correct the ship's two-axis tumble. Also, we took too many rads today. We've got to reach some shielding soon or we're cooked. So we're going to need to learn how to communicate with our pal pronto. Fortunately, I think we're off to a good start. Your one message to him so far got through loud and clear."

"You mean 'stop being troublesome or I shoot'? That got through because it was simple and universal."

"I disagree. It got through because the alien was motivated—highly motivated—to understand it." Trevor removed his helmet, ran a gloved hand through his hair. "I think we have to maintain that level of motivation if we're going to get anywhere."

"If you're wrong, however, then all we're going to do is widen the current rift between us."

Trevor shrugged. "If the creature has genuine cause to believe that it will die unless it cooperates, then it will be sure to find a way to bridge that rift."

Caine frowned. "That assumption is predicated upon human behavior patterns."

"So? What else do we have to work with? We have to proceed from a known commonality—self-preservational instincts—and aggressively exploit that."

Caine shook his head. "I don't think it's going to be that simple. Even if we use intimidation, and I'm not ready to, fear won't work unless it's placed within a meaningful context."

Trevor stopped in the middle of removing a glove. "What do you mean, 'context'?"

"Let's say we employ threat and it works. The alien is scared. Scared for its life. Then what? How do we tell it what we want? We still have a critical gap in communication. It doesn't know what it must do to alleviate the negative stimuli. More specifically, it doesn't know how to communicate its intention to cooperate, because it doesn't even know our words or gestures of propitiation."

"So what do you suggest?"

"I suggest we try to learn more about our prisoner."

"And how are we going to learn more about a creature that won't, or can't, talk with us?"

"Let's start with the basics: physiology. What you said about their ship architecture also holds true for living things, too: form follows function. Maybe a detailed look at what we suspect to be an Arat Kur body will give us some insights into the species' psychology."

"Maybe. Maybe it will simply give the bastard another opportunity to attack us."

"I doubt it," Caine disagreed. "We still have the gun, and it's displayed a thorough understanding of what that means."

"Yes, but perhaps it's had time to formulate a new strategy. Suicide, for instance."

"Trevor, if the Arat Kur wants to commit suicide, then we're done for. Neither positive nor negative stimuli will compel it to cooperate."

"That's not necessarily true." Trevor chose his next words carefully; he was sure that the idea behind them would not be popular. "Negative stimuli can produce results even when a subject wishes to die."

Caine looked up. "Trevor, are you talking about torture?"

Trevor tried to find the carefully oblique phrases that were the stock-in-trade of official milspeak, gave up. "Yes, torture. If necessary."

Caine shook his head. "Trevor, leaving ethics aside for a moment, let's recall our intel and survival objective: that the alien communicates with us. Sure, if you use pain, you might make him talk. Or, on the other hand, because the alien's psychology and physiology cause it to have radically different reactions, it might clam up for good. Then instead of having the possibility of getting answers, we find ourselves facing the certainty of death." Caine stared straight into Trevor's eyes. "Besides, we might owe him."

"We *owe* him? What and why in hell do we *owe* him anything?"

Caine maintained his unblinking stare. "How did his ship get nailed?"

"Hazawa's PDF laser. Damn good shooting."

"No argument. But why did this particular exosapient even come into range of that weapon? Why did Hazawa even have a chance to shoot at him?"

"He—" *Oh Christ.* "All right, we were running a diplomatic beacon: a white flag. It was wrong, but it was also a mistake. On the other hand, these bastards have invaded our territory and, judging from yesterday's results, killed a shitload of our brothers and sisters in arms. That *wasn't* a mistake. It was coldblooded murder. This little shit is a soldier. He's earned whatever he gets."

"How do you know he's a soldier?"

"What?"

"What if this Arat Kur is *not* a soldier? Remember what you said about his craft: not much like a military design. Maybe that's because it isn't part of their military. In which case, maybe *he* isn't, either. In that case, we'd be torturing an Arat Kur civilian, possibly to death, whom we ambushed while showing a white flag."

Trevor closed his eyes. The ethical issues had become even more murky than his vision and more uncertain than his balance. "Okay, then what do you suggest we do?"

"We suit up to go below and meet our prisoner."

❖   ❖   ❖

Trevor saw Caine's feet disappear into the access way leading to their module's lower deck. Ironically, Riordan was now better moving in zero-gee than Trevor, who bumped awkwardly along after him, left arm dragging and his legs twitching at inopportune moments. Trevor swam through a gauntlet of orange emergency lights to catch up with Caine at the Arat Kur's prison cell and produced the handgun. Caine nodded, overrode the lock on the door, and pushed himself forward—into darkness.

"Damn it. I meant to turn the lights on in here." Caine's helmet lights winked on, played quickly about the room.

Trevor shrugged. "So what? A little sensory deprivation might make our guest more cooperative."

Caine's helmet lights picked out the spacesuited Arat Kur, floating motionless in a corner on the opposite side of the room. The cables wrapped around the oblong shape were intact. Trevor centered the laser aimpoint on the lower half of the alien's belly. "You're covered."

Caine activated the room's lights and the two humans closed to a meter's range. Still no movement. Caine undid the knotted cables. The coils fell away from the Arat Kur, which simply floated, inert.

"Is it dead?" asked Trevor.

He had meant the question as a rhetorical gibe, but Caine leaned closer to inspect the life-support unit on the alien's back. "I doubt it. There are no red lights showing on its life-support pack. However, a number of gauges have changed since we came over from the wreck. Probably those are simply measuring the drain on energy and air supplies."

Trevor nodded; a reasonable hypothesis. "What do we do with him now?"

"We dress him out," said Caine.

Trevor's stomach contracted, trying to get away from the alien and the notion of seeing it fully exposed. "Is this a suitable environment for him?" he croaked.

"He should be okay. The atmosphere we found on his ship shows that they are oxygen breathers. If anything, he'll find our air a little bland. His had higher traces of sulfur."

Trevor found that removing the Arat Kur's spacesuit was not especially difficult. The garment was semirigid, with a more flexible strip running across the dorsal surface. This strip functioned as a hinge, which allowed the suit to split into anterior and posterior halves. The ventral surface was quartered by the intersection of longitudinal and latitudinal seals. Opening the suit involved undoing these ventral seals and then exerting a slight pressure on the dorsal hinge; the Arat Kur eased out of the garment like an irregular pea forced out of its pod. Its six legs also dragged free of their coverings limply, then they slowly curled back up toward the body until the rear two pair laid flat against the flat belly and the front pair were bunched up just under the alien's chin.

Chin? Well, at least that's how Trevor thought of it: the Arat Kur didn't really have one. The creature's body was essentially a front-heavy ellipse. The front was a blunt, flattened surface with a large, recessed central orifice: the alimentary opening, maybe? Two wide-set eyes were located above this "mouth" and two equally wide-set orifices were located beneath it. Slight, rhythmic alterations in those lower orifices suggested that they were respiratory ducts.

The Arat Kur's back was most notable in that it seemed to be the only part of the body that sprouted any hair. The growth was sparse, occurring as small, evenly distributed clusters of short, fine spines. Each spine rose from the center of a pronounced pore. These, and a few other apparently hairless pores, were the only ones on the alien's entire body.

Trevor pushed away from the presumed Arat Kur. "Any helpful insights?"

Caine shook his head. "None. You?"

"No. But I don't trust it, the way it just floats there, waiting. Waiting for what? For us to turn our backs? To die?"

"Maybe it's not waiting at all. Maybe it can't move."

"Can't move?"

"Maybe it's in shock. Or in an altered state of consciousness. Or is too emotionally traumatized to respond."

"Strange behavior for a race that settles its diplomatic problems by invading another species' territory."

"I agree." Caine continued to inspect the creature. "Unusual eye structure: no pupils."

Trevor leaned over to look for himself. "No pupils?"

"None that I can see. But then again, the whole eye is different."

Trevor studied the area surrounding the organ. "I can't see any ducts or moisture. In fact, I don't think there's much capacity for ocular movement."

"Odd." Caine paused. "What about those wrinkled ridges around the eyes? Maybe some kind of folded cartilaginous sleeve?"

"Doesn't look like it to me. Why?"

Caine shrugged. "Could be the sign of an extrusive mechanism."

"Eyestalks, huh? I don't think so. Why are you checking the eyes so closely, anyway?"

"Sensory ability tends to be a first cousin to communication. If we get an idea of how the Arat Kur perceive their environment, we might learn a little about how they—now this is interesting."

"What?"

As Caine drifted closer to the Arat Kur, Trevor pushed farther back, retightening his grip on the gun. One fast slash of its front claws might filet Caine. But he seemed oblivious to the threat, staring closely into the alien's eyes. "What are you doing, trying to hypnotize it?"

Caine's voice suggested that he hadn't even heard the gibe. "This isn't really an eye at all. It's the end of a thick fiber-optic bundle. It's a—a kind of lens. No soft tissue whatsoever."

"So where is the retina, or its analog?"

"Probably back in the carapace. Which makes sense, when you think about it."

"Why?"

"Well, they appear to be evolved from some kind of burrowers, right? So, lots of dirt and debris flying around, airborne. Trapped in tight, subterranean spaces where it can't disperse. The Arat Kur eye, evolving in that environment, develops a fairly insensate outer surface: a thick lens. Multiple lenses, if I'm seeing things correctly."

"Why multiple? Redundancy in case of obstruction or injury?"

"Maybe. Or maybe it gives the Arat Kur more visual options."

"How?"

"The ability to change depth of focus, for instance. Our eye changes focus by using muscular force to reshape the lens. The Arat Kur eye doesn't seem to have any muscles and the outermost lens certainly doesn't look very flexible. So instead, they might select different lenses for different focal requirements."

Trevor carried the idea one step further. "That could even give them a means of compensating for their lack of eye mobility. Perhaps the right combination of lenses gives them a fish-eye lens effect, a wide-angle view. But that wouldn't give them very good vision. Compound eyes aren't terribly efficient."

Caine kept starting at the Arat Kur. "First of all,

I'm not sure this is a *real* compound eye. Just because there are lots of lenses doesn't mean there's a retina for each one. And when it comes to efficiency—well, I suppose that depends upon what the eye is supposed to achieve. As burrowers, the Arat Kur probably don't spend a lot of time above ground. So, how essential is three-hundred-sixty-degree vision? How much do they need highly mobile eyes?"

Trevor saw the point, finished it. "Instead, they'd need eyes that weren't particularly sensitive to debris. And they'd also tend towards developing superior sensitivity to lower wavelength light in order to increase their ability to see in the dark."

"Most specifically, to see in the infrared," agreed Caine. "That way, in a completely lightless burrow, they can still locate other Arat Kur by their body heat."

"Okay, but how does knowing all that help us to communicate with it?"

Caine was floating around the side of the alien. "It helps us by suggesting that vision *cannot* be the primary sense for the Arat Kur."

"Huh?"

"Well, as you said, long-distance vision probably isn't so good; that's pretty much a constant with any multiple-lens ocular structure. That means that they would tend to be even less dependent upon visual warning, so it will be less important to their evolution. And if they are truly shortsighted, then they're going to have to find another medium for long-distance communication."

Trevor thought. "Which means that this critter should have a really good set of ears. But I'm not seeing any."

"I think I've just found them." Caine sounded like he was smiling. "Come take a look."

Trevor moved forward slowly, keeping the aimpoint on the alien's belly. He stopped, looked where Caine was pointing: at the Arat Kur's back. Again, Trevor saw the big, raised pores sprouting rigid, short black hairs, although some of the biggest pores showed no hair at all. He looked for an orifice hidden amongst them, or a tympanum. Nothing. "I give up; where are its ears?"

"You're looking at them."

"Ugly back hairs?"

"I'm betting that those aren't hairs. Those are retractable antennae. Almost fully retracted now, I'll bet."

Trevor looked again. "That's an awful lot of antennae."

"No more than you'd expect for a creature so completely dependent upon sound. They probably go straight down into acoustic chambers of some sort, transmitting the vibrations they detect to an audial nerve."

"Then why are the hairs—antenna—retracted now? Are we being purposely ignored?"

"Maybe. Or maybe it's a reflex that reduces stimuli."

"So it *is* ignoring us."

"No, more like it just can't handle what it experienced and has withdrawn its consciousness from the outside world."

"Like catatonia?"

"Maybe. Or perhaps it's a natural trauma response for the species."

Marvelous. Their prisoner now had to be recategorized as a mental patient. Trevor saw where that could lead. "Caine, if the alien is psychologically withdrawn, then we have to bring it back to reality."

"I agree."

"Then I repeat: nothing motivates as effectively as fear. Let's not waste any time."

"We still don't know how he'll react. We might force him deeper into withdrawal."

Trevor looked at Caine from the corner of his eye. "Exactly how much more withdrawn do you expect he can get?" Trevor saw his retort hit home. Caine frowned, looked at the alien. *Time to follow up, but gently; gently!* "Caine, when we came back from the wreck, I was conscious enough to watch you try every form of communication that we know of to reach the Arat Kur: voice, written language, images, sound patterns, mathematics. But there's been no response and we're running out of time. We've studied the alien and have discovered some useful facts, but now we have to try other methods."

After about five seconds, Caine asked quietly, "What do you propose?"

"We start with something passive, something that will work by eroding the exosapient's will and self-composure. White noise, biased toward the ultrasonic range. We can rig the intercom to produce it. We may have to play with the sound characteristics a bit, since we don't know what audial stimuli will create discomfort."

Caine looked disgusted, but nodded. He did not look at Trevor as he launched himself toward the door. "Let's get out of here," he said.

❖   ❖   ❖

Trevor started with a decibel level that would have been subaudible to a human subject, using sound waves

in the 18,000-30,000 cycles range. It might have made
the average person a bit edgy, but no more.

They seemed equally ineffectual upon the Arat
Kur. The room's emergency snoopscope—a single
fiber-optic pickup hidden between the modular ceiling
plates—showed the Arat Kur still suspended in midair,
unmoving and apparently unaware of its surroundings.

Trevor boosted the sound, but thirty minutes later,
there was still no visible effect. Trevor checked his
settings: a decibel level of 80 and a top sonic range of
40,000 cycles. The machinery was probably not capable
of producing higher frequencies. Trevor let his eyes
drift back to the decibel level indicator. Eighty was
apparently not enough. Trevor depressed the control
switch and held it down.

The numbers mounted steadily.

❖   ❖   ❖

"I wonder—"

Trevor looked up; it was the first sound Caine had
made in over an hour. Now, with almost no warning,
he was already out of his acceleration couch, swimming
around toward Trevor's computer station. "Any activity?"

"Not so far."

Riordan nodded, leaned over to study the alien's
black-and-white image. "Trevor, I think I know why we
haven't been having any luck with—" His words ended
abruptly. Trevor looked over, knew what he'd see. Caine
was staring at the decibel indicator.

Without a word, Caine picked up his helmet, swam
out the exit, headed in the direction of the Arat Kur's
prison chamber. Trevor shook his head, killed the sound,
and followed, his limbs still uncooperative and awkward.

❖   ❖   ❖

It was a measure of how much Caine's zero-gee facility had improved that he was already alongside the Arat Kur by the time Trevor arrived, handgun out.

"You won't need it," Caine said.

"Why?"

"Because the Arat Kur is either dying or comatose. I can't tell which. Maybe both."

Trevor edged closer. How could Caine tell if the creature was even more withdrawn than before? There was no change in its appearance.

Upon closer inspection, Trevor revised his assessment. The movement of the respiratory ducts was less pronounced, suggesting shallower breathing. However, the rate of respiration was increased, and there was a persistent tremor in the soft tissues. The only other change was in the hairs—no, the antennae—on the creature's back: they had all disappeared.

Caine circled the alien slowly, inspecting every centimeter. When he got to the posterior, he leaned lower, inspected a previously unnoticed cloud of liquid globules. "This is probably the worst sign of all. I think it's voided and has made no effort to move away from its own wastes. Pretty much a sure indicator that it has lost self-awareness or has impaired motor control."

"All right, so the sound was a bad idea."

"No. Just before I saw how high you pushed the sound, I was starting to think that the sound was simply pointless. I'm pretty sure that the audial stimuli didn't do this."

"Why not?" Trevor's attention momentarily strayed from the laser-point he was painting on the Arat Kur's belly.

"This creature is a burrower, so much of the sound

made in its environment must persist as echoes. Consequently, its natural habitat is probably noisier than ours. So to hear an individual over any distance, an Arat Kur must be able to filter out background noise. Whether it achieves that filtering by mental discrimination or special anatomical structures is immaterial. What matters is that, evolutionarily, Arat Kur physiology and psychology must be able to tolerate audial distress and confusion."

Trevor frowned. "Let's say you're right. Then how do you explain the catatonia and the—?"

But Caine hardly seemed to hear him. Riordan launched himself back into the corridor, where he scooped up two of the tethers he had used to tow the Arat Kur from the wreck. He somersaulted, kicked back into the room and set about trussing the alien with the longer tether. He tossed the other to Trevor. "Tie it on as a towline. Then keep your weapon on him."

Trevor lashed, then tugged, the towline. "Taut. Where are we—?"

"Let's go." Caine wrapped the end of the towline around his wrist.

"Go where?"

"Life support."

"Life support?" The words exploded out of Trevor before he could govern the dismay or the volume behind them. "Why?"

"Just a hunch. Play along, okay?"

"All right—for now. But at least tell me what you're doing so that if something happens to you, I can try to finish the work."

"Sure. Since the sound didn't have any effect, I started reviewing all our assumptions about its behavior, its environment. And I returned to the possibility that, if the Arat Kur was not willfully withdrawn, it might be because it was already reacting to something negative in the environment, something we don't notice but which they find so aversive that it paralyzes them."

Trevor scowled. "Like what?"

"Space, open space. That's the one greatest difference between a burrower's environment and our own."

"Damn—yes, of course. Agoraphobia. And the answer was in front of us the moment we boarded their ship: the narrow passageways, the low-ceilinged rooms."

"And when I shot out the cockpit blister, even before it climbed onto you, the Arat Kur starting weakening, and then went rigid, like it was in shock. Or in this case, was immobilized by fear of the greatest open area of all: free space."

"Without a tether."

"Right. And when we brought him back here, what did we do? Put him in a high-ceilinged room. He was okay at first because the lights were out and he couldn't see the spaces that cause his agoraphobia."

Trevor nodded. "But then we came in and turned on the lights and left him behind. And here he is: wholly catatonic and withdrawn. So now we take him to life support to give him as crowded an environment as we can."

"And we see what happens."

"Sabotage, probably."

"Can't rule it out, but there are enough snoopscopes in life support to monitor his activity no matter where he goes. And the control room is only a few steps away."

"I hope you don't mind if I remain a little closer to our prisoner than that. Like on the other side of this door." Trevor helped navigate the inert ovoid of the Arat Kur through the hatchway and toward the clutter at the heart of the life-support section.

"Suit yourself."

The maze of machinery reached to within a meter of the ceiling, and had less than half a meter's clearance above the floor. Other than a narrow walkway around the outer perimeter, there was no other space wide enough to permit easy passage. A human would have to thread sideways if he wanted to move between the tubes, tanks, and centrifuges.

Caine undid the tow line, and then the restraints. The Arat Kur floated motionless. Riordan pushed himself backward gently, floating out of the room at a leisurely pace. Laser aimpoint still painted on the alien's belly, Trevor shoved off the deck with his foot and drifted backward. As he cleared the room, the heavy vacuum-rated door slid shut.

"Let's hope it works," Caine said.

Trevor nodded and thought, *It had better. Because we're running out of time. All of us.*

Chapter Thirteen

Adrift off Barnard's Star 2 C

"Trevor."

White lights. Modular bulkheads. His limbs heavy with exhaustion and the dense materials comprising an emergency suit. And everywhere, the dissolving image of Opal's face, like a shadow dispelled by a sudden ray of light, or a faint aroma dispersed by a breeze. Trevor swam up out of his dream, felt the door against his back, checked it: still closed.

Caine's voice was back in his helmet. "Are you awake?"

"I—uh, yeah, yes." *And dreaming of the woman you've been sleeping with.* The guilt sent a throb into his head.

"There's movement in life support."

"What kind of movement?" Trevor asked warily.

"About an hour ago, some motion started in the Arat Kur's limbs and front claws. Just a minute ago, it scooted under the filtration intakes and the osmotic scrubbers."

"How are his zero-gee skills?"

"Pretty fair. Better than mine. His respiration seems to have resumed a normal rate."

Well, the Arat Kur was either recovering from his catatonic withdrawal or readying himself for an orgy of sabotage and destruction. Trevor thumbed the handgun's safety to the off position. "Do I go in?"

"Not yet. I'll relay live feed to your HUD."

A black-and-white image flickered on about two inches above and away from Trevor's left eye. The creature seemed to be simply surveying its surroundings. It was moving slowly through the maze of life-support equipment, occasionally stopping to study a component here, a readout there.

It completed its tour directly in front of the sealed door. It approached the door, inspected it thoroughly and then sat/laid down directly in front of it. Trevor activated the laser aimpoint on the handgun, commented, "I'm ready for him."

Caine did not answer immediately. "I don't think he intends any threat. In fact, I think—"

Over the carrier tone in the communication system, Trevor heard a series of atonal whistles, clicks, and buzzes. "What was that? Are we losing communications?"

"No, we're *gaining* communications. That was the Arat Kur."

"Singing for its supper?"

"Maybe, maybe not. I—" More whines, clacks and fluttering whistles. "I'd say he's interested in making contact, now."

"Probably wants to know where the plumbing is."

"Yeah, well I really don't care what he wants to talk about. I just care that he wants to talk."

Trevor heard a change in the comm channel's carrier tone; Caine's voice was now in stereo, half coming from Trevor's collar communicator, the other half emerging muffled and muted from the intercom behind the door into life support. "Hello. Can you understand this language?"

A wild mélange of whistles, squeals, and grunts answered.

Trevor sighed. "Does that mean 'yes' or 'no'?"

"Damned if I know."

"Sounds like a dolphin playing a bagpipe filled with rocks."

More squawking, but slower and repetitive. The Arat Kur scuttled forward and pushed its nose against the door. Trevor heard—and felt—the thump behind him. He raised his handgun. "I have the door covered."

"He's not trying to escape."

"Oh? Then what's he doing? Trying to scratch his back against the door jamb?"

"No, but it's not ramming the door. It's simply approaching it, bumping it, and then backing off again. No running starts, no attempts to pry it open. It just wants out."

"What a surprise."

There was no answer.

"Caine?"

Another moment of silence, and then Caine's voice answered—but not over the radio. He reappeared in the corridor, heading for the door Trevor was covering with the ten-millimeter. "I'm going in. Cover me."

"What? Wait a—"

Caine pressed the control stud on the wall; the door slid back. *Just fucking great.* Trevor brought up the gun quickly. The Arat Kur scuttled backwards about a meter and then stopped. Caine stretched out his empty hands. The Arat Kur's front claws scissored the air once: a nervous, twitchy motion.

"It could be preparing to attack," muttered Trevor.

"It could be the Arat Kur equivalent of wringing its hands," Caine muttered back. He took a floating step into the room.

The Arat Kur retreated about the same distance, then edged back toward Caine.

"Seems friendly," said Caine.

"Or hungry."

The Arat Kur "sat" down and launched into a long series of repetitive squawks, wheezings, and whispers.

Trevor listened. "What do you figure it's saying?"

"Probably trying to do the same thing I did. Keep repeating basic phrases again and again, hoping that we'll hear something we recognize."

"And when he realizes that's pointless? Then what?"

The alien stopped cacophonizing abruptly. Trevor tightened his grip on the handgun. The Arat Kur's front claw began rising slowly, carefully. It stopped when it was pointing at the open door. Then the arm bent until the claw was pointing at the Arat Kur. Then back out the door.

"He's asking to leave the room," murmured Caine. "Politely."

"Right. So he can kill us. Politely."

"No, I don't think that's what he has in mind. We've got to take a chance and let him out."

Madness, complete madness. But Trevor pushed against the deck with his left toe and drifted slowly to the right, leaving the doorway unobstructed.

The alien went through its pointing sequence again: the door, itself, the door. Caine pointed at the Arat Kur and out the door, ending with an exaggerated nod. The alien rose up, its claws outstretched. With a single coordinated kick from all four rear legs, it launched forward.

And out the door. Caine somersaulted and swam after it. Trevor did his best to match their pace, but, still unable to use his left arm, lost sight of Caine as he entered the inter-deck access tube.

"Caine, slow down. I can't keep up. I can't help you if that little bastard turns on you."

Caine either didn't hear or didn't care. "He's heading back for his first prison."

"What the hell for?"

"Damned if I know. Just keep following me." A pause, then. "Turn around. Return to the upper deck." Which meant that Trevor had to back himself up the inter-deck access tube; there wasn't enough room to turn around.

"Go back? What the hell for?"

"To make room for our guest."

At the bottom of the tube, Trevor saw motion. The Arat Kur had reentered the tube, carrying a bulky load. He was starting to swim up. Straight toward Trevor.

As Trevor reverse-pushed awkwardly up the tube, the Arat Kur seemed to take notice of him and slow down. There was almost a sense of patient waiting. If the alien had had thumbs, Trevor would have expected to see the Arat Kur twiddling them.

Once the way was clear, the Arat Kur shot up and out the tube, giving Trevor a better look at the bundle it had retrieved from its first prison: its spacesuit. Caine came sidewinding up after the alien.

"Grab your helmet. I think we're going EVA."

"Caine, with our current whole body dose, this is probably the last time we're going to be able to take a stroll around the neighborhood."

"I know it, but what choice do we really have?"

Trevor sighed. "I'll suit up." He did, and just in time. A few seconds after establishing a seal, the alien led them into the airlock. It pointed to the outer door, itself, each of them, and then back at the outer door. Caine cycled the airlock and opened the door.

Obviously, the alien had not been unconscious during its trip over to the command module. It swam outside and directly toward the boarding tether. After securing itself to the line with its own suit lanyard, it began towing itself back over to its wrecked ship.

Caine's skill and Trevor's condition had both improved enough that they made a fast transit and a good jump down to the wreck. The Arat Kur, its front legs waving in something that looked very much like glad excitation, lead them inside the wreck and directly to the door surrounded by scorch marks. It grasped the door "knob," moored itself by grasping a handle protruding from the wall, and tugged. Then it stopped and looked at the two humans. Still looking at them, it mimicked the tug again.

Caine took hold of another handle. "I think we're supposed to lend a hand here."

"Or a claw."

"Just pull."

After a few coordinated heaves, the door opened a crack, allowing the humans to finish the job with their pry bars. As soon as the way was clear, the Arat Kur darted in, almost disappearing into a dense thicket of burnt circuitry and warped cables. Trevor peered—and aimed—over Caine's shoulder to watch the alien's speedy rerouting work. Caine nodded toward the ruined rainforest of wiring. "What do you think? His engineering section?"

Trevor nodded. "Probably had multiple short-outs when the ship was hit. Just like the cutter did. It's also why he couldn't use his engines or restart his power plant: he couldn't get in to reroute the command circuitry or power supplies."

Apparently finished, the Arat Kur turned, dove back into the corridor and motioned toward the bridge. Once the humans had followed him into that new location, the alien pointed at what they had conjectured was the main computer, itself, and then the computer again. Trevor and Caine exchanged resigned looks, and then nodded at the Arat Kur in unison.

The alien slid into its acceleration couch, powered up the computer and began manipulating a set of touch screens with extraordinary speed. The deck began to vibrate faintly. A moment later, large metal panels sealed off the shattered cockpit blister and the tumbling star field beyond. A gentle hiss indicated that the chamber was repressurizing.

A few more taps on the touchscreen and the bridge lit up, ringing the humans in holographic displays and dynamically reconfigurable control panels. About half of them were dark or malfunctioning, but that did not seem to impede the Arat Kur. Trevor felt a new vibration through the soles of his feet and simultaneously watched half of the orange lights on the control panels change to green. Evidently, the power plant was online. A moment later, he felt a sideways tug: thrust. The Arat Kur was starting to correct the wreck's tumble.

Whether it was a matter of fine piloting or extraordinarily powerful computing technology, the alien successfully stabilized and mated the wreckage of his ship with the Auxiliary Command module in less than ten minutes. Then he pointed to a hologram of the space near The Pearl. He zoomed in. At the extreme edge of the field of view was a red mote. He pointed at the mote and then swept his arm in a wide circle, indicating the craft they were in. Caine did the same and nodded.

The Arat Kur seemed to be pleased, emitting a number of trilling whistles and bobbing up and down slightly.

Caine, smiling at the Arat Kur, said sideways to Trevor, "Well, so far, so good."

"Sure. Marvelous. And now that we're all such good friends, I'm sure we'll want to launch straight into a major cross-cultural dialog."

At that moment, another carrier tone intruded on their private line and a new voice cut in. "Yes, I believe such a discussion would be beneficial to us all."

Trevor and Caine turned to look at the alien, who had finished working with the computer. Noting that he had their attention once again, the Arat Kur bobbed up and down once. Muffled by the creature's suit, the whistles and trills resumed. As they did, the new voice spoke again over their radios.

"My apologies for omitting an introduction. I am Darzhee Kut."

❖   ❖   ❖

What the Arat Kur said next was even more improbable than his first calm interjection.

"I wish to apologize for meeting under these circumstances. I thank you for showing me trust despite the—unexpected attack which brought me here. Your deeds sound a high and noble melody for your race."

Caine took a deep breath and answered. "Darzhee Kut, we must apologize also. We had no way of discerning that your personal intentions might be peaceful, after our first and unfortunate encounter in this room. And of course, you had no reason to think otherwise of us. We are most happy to meet you—and through you, come to finally learn something of your race."

"These harmonize with my own feelings, but before we may do so, we must ensure our survival."

"What do you have in mind?"

"The weapons-fire from the ship to which your module was originally attached sheared away all my sensors and disabled my communication equipment. I would have pulsed my engines to attract attention but, being unable to enter the engineering relay room, I was unable to effect repairs to those systems. Therefore, may I inquire: do you have an intact communication system? For if you do, we could use it to summon a rescue."

Trevor shook his head. "Not so fast. You're expecting us to surrender to you? Even though *we've* got the gun?"

"I expect no such thing. Surrenders, and the accepting of them, are actions undertaken by what you call 'soldiers,' are they not?"

Caine leaned forward. "Darzhee Kut, do you mean to imply that you are not a member of your species' military forces?"

"Not as you would mean it. Moreover, the word military does not completely harmonize with any of ours."

Caine frowned. "This is an unusual concept for us. Before we agree to communications with your fleet, it would help for us to understand a little more about you and your species. Specifically, do you mean to say that you have no 'military' forces?"

Darzhee Kut buzzed lightly. "This is not quite correctly said. We have military forces when we require them, but we have no caste which specializes in conflict, particularly not in *physical* combat. When the nest is compelled to defend itself, we all aid it according to our best abilities and the nest's greatest needs."

"So your race never fought wars?"

"Long ago. But they were too destructive, and so we ceased."

These were hardly the kind of attackers Trevor had expected. "What made your wars so destructive: the weapons? Nuclear warheads? Gas?"

"No," said Caine, nodding, "the bodies."

Darzhee warbled a bit before he answered. "You have sung our sad refrain without having heard it before: this is well. Indeed, the bodies. With no way to dispose of them quickly enough, disease and carrion-creatures became a worse scourge than the war itself."

"So what did you do to stop further wars?"

"Does one need to forbid one's own suicide? We did not need to 'do' anything but see what was before our eyes: to wage war upon others was, ultimately, to kill oneself and one's nest."

"With all due respect, then why did you make war upon us?"

Darzhee Kut made a sound like a falling trill. "Ah. This is a far more complicated matter. But I would say this: let your own history be your answer. Your behavior toward each other told us something of how we must conceive of behaving toward you."

Caine frowned. "But we do not always make war—unlike the Hkh'Rkh, who seem to be your allies."

"And this was the great atonality in the chorus of this generation. Some of us sang the triumphs of your species' dreams of lasting peace. Others boomed the dirge of your many wars."

"And the dirge was the tune your race chose to focus upon?"

"Let us rather say that it drowned out the more hopeful song that I and others sang." His front claws gestured beyond the walls. "And here we are, trapped in a growing crescendo that brushes aside all other melodies, tones, sounds. Such is war, it seems to me. Too much of even one's own sounds, when made in time to war-drums, becomes chaos. It afflicts us with a temporary version of the perpetual sun-time that—it is said—afflicts your species."

"'Sun-time'?"

Darzhee Kut seemed to relax, raised one claw in a gesture that looked partly like the invitation of a raconteur, partly like the still, upraised finger of a didact. "To understand sun-time you must understand my race. Specifically, its reproductory habits."

Trevor winced.

If Darzhee Kut noticed, he gave no external indication of it. "We are creatures of the earth, the rock, of close chambers that embrace us, of tunnels that caress our bellies and backs. But when the song of our birth-triad fills our hearts and quickens our blood to that point where we must sing as one in all ways, we suddenly long for a sensation which, the rest of the time, terrifies us."

"You return to the surface, to see the sun."

"Your voice sings true. It is just so. The rays of heat, the great brightness, the open vault above: so expansive is our passion, that, at this one time, the wide world above the rock harmonizes with what is most immediate and true in us. And so this is where we mate."

Trevor leaned back. "And that—that 'state of mind' is a bad thing?" *Not that I want to hear more about your orgasmic nature-walks.*

"It is not bad, but it is necessarily brief."

Caine was nodding again. "Because it's also dangerous. You're vulnerable on the surface, and what brings you there is an altered state of mind which compromises your self-control."

Darzhee Kut was still for a moment. "You hear the harmonies of the Arat Kur far in advance, Spokesperson Riordan. It was our great misfortune that we did not share them with you at the Convocation."

Trevor glanced over at Caine, who clearly had not made the connection yet, and pointed at the Arat Kur. "I've heard your name before. You were, were—"

Darzhee Kut's sensors declined lightly. "I was to be the Speaker-to-Nestless for the Arat Kur Wholenest at the Convocation. It was so announced on the first day. But Zirsoo was thought more—capable."

Caine's eyes narrowed. "By whom?"

"By both Zirsoo Kh'n and First Delegate Hu'urs Khraam."

"And let me guess. They were both great singers of the dirge that is humanity."

"Among its very loudest and most accomplished soloists. So now you begin to see."

"Possibly. It sounds as though there was much division among the Arat Kur regarding how best to interact with humanity."

"Yes. Among those who knew enough."

"And what knowledge was withheld from those who did not 'know enough'?"

"Some of the answer to that question is composed of notes which I may not sing. And that imposition of silence made me question how effective I could be as the Speaker to your race."

Trevor frowned. "So you're not a soldier at all. You're a—a diplomat."

"This might be the best word for it. I would suggest 'official liaison,' for I have no power to propose or conclude agreements with other species or states. That is the role of a Delegate."

Caine put out an entreating hand. "Then please forgive us for holding you prisoner. It was a consequence of our ignorance of your language, and your ways. Allow us to extend to you the courtesies and privileges of a diplomatic attaché. However, we must impose certain limits upon these, since our governments are currently at war."

Again, the scrunch-bow of the Arat Kur. "I graciously accept, and extend the same to you. And because of this, may I further suggest that we signal my fleet directly, so that they may extend a more suitable and complete measure of hospitality to you?"

Trevor frowned. "You mean, take us prisoners."

"Mr. Corcoran, I see no uniform, so I presume that, as was true at the Convocation, you are either off-duty or discharged from military service?"

"Well—yes."

"Then your last status so far as I am concerned is as the military expert of your species' *diplomatic* delegation to the Convocation. Therefore, it would be incorrect and illegal to hold you prisoner. You, too, are entitled to diplomatic status."

Well, this Darzhee Kut may be an overgrown cockroach—but he's a damn mannerly one. Trevor looked at Caine. "What do you think?"

"I think making a contact which just might allow us to curtail bloodshed is a whole hell of a lot better than simultaneously dying of rads, asphyxiation, thirst, and starvation."

"Okay. And Darzhee Kut, I want to apologize for what happened regarding your craft," Trevor said.

"It was war. Sadly, that is explanation enough."

"It's a little worse than that. We are concerned that you saw our diplomatic transponder code and thought it safe to approach."

"This is so. But tell me, was this incorrect signal a mistake, or a ruse?"

"A mistake."

"Then you shall not be held accountable for it. We need discuss it no further. Shall we summon my rock-siblings?"

Caine nodded, handed him his collarcom. "With this, you can control our communications array with verbal commands. Tell me when you are ready to send your message."

Darzhee Kut accepted the delicate silver device in two careful claws, turned away to begin composing a message.

"Darzhee Kut," Caine asked, "may I interrupt?"

"Certainly."

"Will we be traveling with your fleet?"

"Yes."

"So can you tell us where we are going next?"

"I can." He turned. "We are going home."

"To Sigma Draconis."

"My apologies: I was not clear. We are not going to my home. We are going to yours." His eyes seemed to lower, almost as if he were embarrassed. "We are going to Earth."

Chapter Fourteen

"With your return, the rocknest is made whole again, Darzhee Kut."

Darzhee Kut made the customary response. "In returning to its harmonies, I live again."

His rock-sibling Urzueth Ragh extended his sensory polyps in unrestrained joy. "We all feared to soon sing your dirge. But since your rescue, some have hummed haunting notes of the lay of your life among the humans. Was it as terrible as we feared?"

"It was not as I expected it to be. I was alone for days before—"

"So it is true. Your crew, Rzzekh and Iistrur, sing no more."

"They sing no more. So when the humans came, it was a strange sensation."

"Explicate."

"I feared them, prepared for them—"

"Trapped them, I heard."

"As our forebears did their prey and foes, yes. But

191

I was also relieved when they arrived. I had been without association for so long."

"I understand."

"You do not. It became worse. When they took me prisoner, they set me off by myself."

"They left you alone? *Alone?* For how long?"

"I do not know. Many hours."

"And you can still harmonize? You are hewn from strong rock, Darzhee Kut."

"This ability is a prerequisite for those of us in the Ee'ar caste who would explore new places or associations. In contacting other species, we might spend time in isolation."

"I do not envy you the tunnel you dig, rock-sibling. Did they understand what they were doing to you?"

"No. The humans eventually apologized, but only for putting me in a large, high, empty room. This leads me to believe that they thought it was agoraphobia alone which caused my reaction."

"So they did not understand how dangerous it was to isolate you?"

"How could they? As a species, they often *seek* solitude, and much prefer to shun enemies rather than have their company."

"And they did not understand that it was their attempt to communicate—to associate—with you that enabled you to hear the music of life once again?"

"No, they did not see this, for they are not gregarious creatures. They would perceive our need for association as excessive, even crippling. They would never conceive of needing company so profoundly that one must seek out an adversary, rather than die into the silence of oneself alone."

"They are strange creatures."

"They are unlike us in this way."

"As more of our rock-siblings are finding out, even now."

"Sing me this new melody. Have we discovered more humans in this system?"

"No. Our advance flotilla is even now in the home-system of the humans, securing their largest gas giant for our refueling purposes. We shall follow presently."

They had arrived at the narrow entry into the meeting module that had been crafted especially for roof-sharings with the Hkh'Rkh. The great predators could barely fit through the corridors of the Arat Kur vessels, and the Hkh'Rkh vessels were so crude and uncomfortable that the Arat Kur had found that they could not concentrate properly when aboard them. So this was the point of contact between their worlds of radically different physical—and cultural—shape.

"It is a vast and unpleasant place." Urzueth ground his dental plates together as he tilted upward to glance at the ceiling that was too distant for his comfort, and too close for the Hkh'Rkhs'.

Darzhee rubbed his plates together for sake of harmonizing, but felt little of the other's distress. After his hours in the human ship, he had grown accustomed to the wide spaces. "Let us take our places; the others will be here soon."

As they slid into their belly-cupping couches, Urzueth stared at the tall and monstrous Hkh'Rkh chairs. "I would just as soon be elsewhere, rock-sibling."

"I understand."

"Then why am I here?"

"If it should come to pass that my voice is stilled

by events, then as the First Delegate's chief administrator, you must be ready to finish my song for me."

Urzueth fretted his claws against each other with a series of rapid clicks. "These are random notes you emit, Darzhee. Now that you are back in the rocknest, what could happen to you?"

"Anything, rock-sibling. War is a sun-time that blinds whole races. Nothing is beyond possibility. And I think the humans will surprise us."

"Why? Our technological advantage is not merely profound, but overwhelmingly decisive. And they were clearly not expecting an attack. They suffered a great defeat in this system."

"Yes, but they are better warriors."

"When they are at very close ranges, perhaps—"

"No. It goes beyond that simple refrain with which we have reassured ourselves. We think the Hkh'Rkh great fighters because they are large and fierce, but the humans have a more dangerous trait."

"Which is?"

"They are innovative. They can change their ideas very rapidly when pursuing a goal, if they must."

"They are irresolute."

"No. That is how you of the Hur caste see them, and possibly why you feel so confident embarking upon this war. But what you see in the humans as a lack of resolve is in fact the presence of immense flexibility. They may not be as daunting as the Hkh'Rkh, but they can adapt better to sudden changes—and war, my rock-sibling, is nothing but one sudden change after another."

"Your melody grows strange and atonal, Darzhee Kut. Do not make me anxious."

"I apologize, rock-sibling. But I learned much from my time with them. Including my long roof-sharing with their Spokesperson, earlier today."

Urzueth whistled. "This is the one named Caine Riordan, yes? He is the one from the Convocation, the one with whom you had hoped to speak?"

"Yes. His arrival is a great good fortune for us."

"True. Now we have an emissary to bear our demands to the human leaders."

"He is far more than that." Darzhee paused, decided to trust Urzueth. "He is also one who might understand why we broke the Accords. Understand and not judge."

"This does not harmonize. We cannot reveal this. To humans least of all."

"My thoughts are a counterpoint in major. We *must* reveal this truth to those with whom we would negotiate, and eventually, to all humans. The song I have been forbidden to sing is not known to them. They have forgotten those deeds, I tell you. They do not know who they were, those many millennia ago. And they are those creatures no longer."

"Do not believe that last hopeful coda, rock-sibling," Urzueth demurred. "Their perfidies were not the product of sophisticated misthinkings, but arose from their very nature, were built into their genetics by their particular journey of evolution. They cannot help but ever and again become what they truly are."

"So we are nothing but our genetics? We are the puppets of our past, encoded as the chemicals within us?"

"Darzhee Kut, you are my rock-sibling and in almost all things, our harmonies make the highest roof stones ring. But in this we cannot find the same key."

"But the safety of these two humans—"

"Fear not. As the First Delegate's immediate assistant, I may assure you that, even over the objections of the Hkh'Rkh, he has resolved that the two humans will be well and carefully treated."

Darzhee kept his voice low. "He may find the Hkh'Rkh insistent that they be executed."

"It will not happen. Hu'urs Khraam has committed to this."

First Delegate Hu'urs Khraam, coming through the hatch from the Hkh'Rkh shuttle that had mated to the meeting module, stopped, ran his eyes across the two much younger Arat Kur, who dipped their chins low. "I hear ghost-songs—or I heard my name," he fluted.

"Invoked in the speculation that it was you who approached, esteemed First Delegate."

Hu'urs Khraam ignored Urzueth and his rhetorical flourish, stared steadily at Darzhee Kut before turning to his rear and motioning for those behind him to enter the module.

The thumping treads of Hkh'Rkh became audible, drew closer. Two full seconds before his impressive bulk actually arrived in the module, the shadow of First Voice of the First Family stretched into it like a dark herald. He nodded—barely—to First Delegate Khraam, who, like him, had overall authority for the gathered forces of his species.

Hu'urs Khraam spread his claws wide and toward the ceiling. "Our operations in this system are at an end. The surviving human ships, those that kept their distance during the engagement of the fleets, are still fleeing out toward the Kuiper Belt. Several highly autonomous drones remain in pursuit, but

I am informed that they are unlikely to catch the human craft."

"The humans are cowards." The phlegm bubbled in First Fist Graagkhruud's long, slothlike snout as he said it, stimulating a low rumble of concurrence from the rest of First Voice's hulking retinue.

"With respect, First Fist, the humans were prudent." Hu'urs Khraam lowered his claws. "They attempted to draw us into pursuit, which would have deterred us from shifting to Earth as swiftly as we might. They understood the importance of buying more time for their shift-hull, the *Prometheus*, in the hope it might finish its preacceleration and reach Earth before we do. Only because we resolutely declined to take their bait, is that hope now groundless."

Graagkhruud's small round eyes protruded slightly from either side of his long, smooth, neck-tapering head. "Several of the masters of my ships once again request to remain behind, to give chase and harry them. And afterward, to keep a presence in this system."

"And again, I applaud their eagerness, but must deny their request." The First Delegate gestured to the holographic displays lining the walls. "All available warcraft and ground assets will be needed upon arrival in the Sol system. The humans have developed their home planets extensively, whereas we may carry only limited forces with us. Consequently, we must expect that there will be far more missions to perform than ships to perform them. Drones and several observation craft will be sufficient to leave behind here."

"And what of their shift-hull, the *Prometheus*?" First Voice's tone was far less bellicose than that of his general, First Fist, Darzhee Kut noted.

Hu'urs Khraam's dental plates clacked once. "Even the drones cannot catch *Prometheus*. But she needs to achieve twice our preacceleration velocity before she can shift. Therefore, though she started her run before we arrived, we will still be able to shift before her. However, our fleet must immediately accelerate to two point five gee constant to achieve this."

"We are prepared."

"Very good. We must do so within the hour. And by that time, all deployed ships and small craft will have returned to their respective carriers, so it will be imprudent to meet again as we do now. So this shall be the last roof-sharing between us before we arrive in the Sol system. Consequently, it is also our last opportunity to share any last thoughts on our plans for that campaign."

First Voice hunched over the table as well as the immensity of his barrel-shaped ribcage would allow. "I am satisfied with the plans—for now. What I will think once we arrive and assess the human response, I cannot say. But what of the intelligence gleaned from their wreckage and from their base named The Pearl? Does it impel us to change our strategy?"

"We see no reason to think so. And our projection holds that the *Prometheus* plans to run to Earth or Ross 154."

"And do we have new intelligence that indicates which warships might be at Ross 154?"

Hu'urs Khraam waved his claws loosely. "Nothing specific, but their signal logs indicate that we have correctly anticipated that their naval dispersal is to our advantage. Most of their other fleet assets are spread throughout the systems that they call the Green

Mains, and have only lately been summoned to gather
in the systems Ross 154 and Junction. But those assets
cannot reach Earth if we hold Ross 154. So it is as
we foresaw. By dividing our fleet here, we can send
one half to attack the humans' home system, and the
other to take and hold Ross 154. In this way, any of
the human warships that are in the Green Mains are
cut off and cannot help the home cluster."

"There is another naval base at Ross 154, is there
not?" Graagkhruud sounded eager; the equilateral
triangle of his three-nostrilled snout-end widened.

Hu'urs Khraam looked to Urzueth and bobbed.
Urzueth explained. "There is a human naval station
at Ross 154, and if major fleet elements are present,
our forces shall launch a full assault upon them and
the base. However, if the human assets have not yet
gathered in strength, the fleet we dispatch to that
system shall lie quiet and observe, monitoring communications and traffic."

"We have come on this campaign to fight, not to
watch." Graagkhruud was ready to rise from his seat.

"And so we shall—at the most propitious time,"
Hu'urs Khraam replied. "If additional human vessels
arrive in Ross 154 and are unaware of our presence,
our analysis of their standard operating procedures
suggests they will approach their base to replen-
ish their consumables, particularly their antimatter
stocks. They are likely to anticipate fighting extended
engagements in systems where we have eliminated or
commandeered their antimatter production facilities.
Consequently, we can intercept such ships *after* they
collect near the base, and perhaps compel their surrender. At least, we could so obstruct their efforts to

preaccelerate and shift, that word of Earth's capitulation will arrive before they can leave."

Graagkhruud's reply was so loud that the room's translator was almost drowned out. "This is cowardice."

The smallest Hkh'Rkh in First Voice's retinue leaned forward slowly. "It would allow us to minimize the damage to the humans."

"You not only speak as the humans' Advocate, Yaargraukh. You take their side."

Darzhee Kut noticed the disdain with which First Fist uttered the title "Advocate," which signified that Yaargraukh was the Hkh'Rkh who had been given the thankless job of not only providing expert assessment of the humans, but of representing their interests to First Voice. A necessity, since creatures which had no place in the Hkh'Rkh honor system had no official standing before any of its authority figures.

In response to First Fist's almost sneering accusation, Yaargraukh inclined his head slightly. "By showing restraint now, First Fist, we may be made less unhappy should the Dornaani prevail and punish us for invading the human homeworld. Which is a flagrant violation of the Twenty-first Accord."

"How readily you whine about defeat, Advocate. Our allies the Ktor will dine on the entrails of the increasingly irresolute Dornaani, and we shall rewrite their Accords to our own liking."

"However," interjected First Voice, "until that time, there is no harm in Urzueth's observation that it may be more prudent to immobilize our enemy without loss to ourselves in Ross 154, than it is to destroy him. But"—he turned back to Hu'urs Khraam—"I nurse a concern that our post-battle intelligence has not been able to conclusively dismiss. What if, as we began our attack here, the humans already had ships at full preacceleration, waiting to carry warnings to Earth and its colonies?"

"First Voice of the First Family," soothed Hu'urs Khraam, "this possibility is profoundly unlikely. What intelligence we were able to gather from the wreckage of the base they called The Pearl, and from those few very wrecks which still had intact mainframes, shows no evidence that there was a preaccelerated ship waiting in this system. And, from the moment our advance shift-cruiser arrived in-system, it was constantly watching for the terawatt-level spike of a shift-drive, which would be plainly detectable even out to the edges of the Kuiper belt.

"So, be calmed. This attack was a complete surprise. Our fleet had completed half its preacceleration before the Convocation concluded. Consequently, the humans had no time, let alone clear provocations, to task any of their shift carriers to be preaccelerated in watchful readiness to alert other systems. And, after having destroyed the majority of their best carriers here, we know just how few of their shift vessels remain unaccounted for."

Darzhee Kut watched as Yaargraukh looked to First Voice for permission to speak, watched him lay his immense "hands" flat and calm upon the table when First Voice nodded. *This one is prudent—even by our standards.*

"Hu'urs Khraam, with respect for the excellence of your warships and the valor of ours, did you not find it unusual how quickly and easily the humans were overcome? And how many of them seemed to suffer catastrophic destruction as a result of their fusion reactors losing containment? I suspected, from the advance intelligence, that their ships would be more robust and would give us a sharper fight."

"I agree," Hu'urs Khraam answered, "but we cannot pause to question our good fortune overmuch. I am told that it would be most instructive if we had had time to conduct post-action analysis of the wreckage. But, as you say, the destruction was so complete, that it would be a lengthy task to locate and retrieve all the significant pieces, and even so, we might not learn anything of use. But most importantly, your suzerain First Voice and I harmonize fully on this one strategic principle: we must retain the initiative that we have seized with this victory. We will shift to the Sol system before the *Prometheus* has completed its preacceleration, and will thus arrive before Earth can be warned of our approach. That is the advantage we must not sacrifice. And once there, I predict we will have ample opportunity to survey all the human wreckage we might wish."

Graagkhruud's tongue flicked twice; he had noted and enjoyed Hu'urs' concluding witticism.

Darzhee Kut bobbed for recognition, received it from Hu'urs Khraam. "Could a human fleet be waiting at Ross 154, preaccelerated and ready to shift here—to Barnard's Star—as soon as our flotilla arrives *there*? If so, they would 'get behind' the force we are sending to wall up those warships that we think are out along their Green Mains."

Hu'urs Khraam bobbed a slow, profound approval. "This is well-worried, Darzhee Kut. However, if they try such a trick, they will be in dire circumstances. If our flotilla arrives at Ross 154 and finds that a human fleet has just shifted out, our fleet will be able to preaccelerate and give chase in twenty days. However, once arriving here in Barnard's Star, human ships from Ross 154, constrained to use frontier refueling, would probably require at least forty days—five of fueling and thirty-five of preacceleration—before they can get out-system. In that time, we would assault and seize Ross 154, refuel, preaccelerate and arrive back here almost three weeks before they could leave. Our high-speed drones would be able to pursue, maybe disable, some of them, and delay the rest. And even so, we would be ready to shift again just as soon—or before—they are."

Darzhee Kut bobbed his appreciation for the answer—and turned when First Voice called his name. "Speaker Kut, has your interrogation of the human prisoners furnished any new perspectives that bear upon our current invasion plans?"

Darzhee was considering how best to emphasize— again—that the humans were *not* prisoners, when Hu'urs Khraam intervened. "First Voice, I have screened the recordings made of Speaker Kut's conversations with the two humans. Neither of them are familiar with our projected area of groundside operations and have not been on Earth for over half a year. They seem to have little information relevant to that aspect of our invasion. And while they were not stunned at our attack, nor that the Hkh'Rkh were our allies in it, they were surprised that we were able to mount it so quickly after the conclusion of the Convocation."

"And their knowledge of broader military deployment?"

"Neither human is privy to recent information of this kind. However, their inability to confirm or contradict our assessments is not worrisome. We consider our present sources most reliable."

"Who are these sources?" First Voice asked.

The First Delegate himself answered. "They are several." Darzhee Kut noted the curious evasiveness of Hu'urs Khraam's response; if First Voice had also, he did not press the point. "Indeed, their own broadcasts are not the least among these."

"That intelligence must be at least ten years old."

"Slightly more, actually, but we believe it to be serviceable. The most pertinent facts have not changed significantly since then. Indonesia is still a nation plagued by overpopulation, poverty, pollution, poor resource management, and inadequate public utilities. Several political separatist factions still operate within its borders, as well as the Pan-Islamic religious insurgency that has been globally active for more than a century now. The population harbors resentments against both its own government and the Earth's dominant nations for its condition."

"And this is where the humans elected to build their orbital-launch mass driver?" Graagkhruud scoffed. "Were they mad?"

Urzueth picked up the tale. "Our sources indicate that the mass driver was an attempt to economically strengthen the nation, to foster foreign trade and investment, and to thereby assuage the general dissatisfaction that fueled the various insurgencies. Besides, the island of Java was a logical location. It sits astride or near several major shipping routes, including the singularly important Strait of Malacca. It is close to the equator and its mountainous spine was a natural support for the mass driver's long, high-angle, electromagnetic launch tube. Labor costs were cheap and local environmental restrictions—what few there were—were easily waived."

First Voice waggled his body where his neck spread out into extremely sloped shoulders. "All reasons for us to seize the island. I understand. But I am concerned that the population is too large to control without resorting to—extreme measures."

"We predict otherwise. Firstly, as I have mentioned, some of our sources are based within the general region and others represent globally-pervasive megacorporations that have expressed sympathy for our plans."

"They would take allegiance against their own world?" Graagkhruud's voice was a choking roll of phlegm.

"They would, in order to be its leaders when we depart."

Yaargraukh shifted in his seat. "Allies bought with money and promises are only allies until they find a higher bidder." For the first time that he could remember, Darzhee Kut saw First Fist Graagkhruud pony-nod in agreement with something that Advocate Yaargraukh had said.

"We are very cognizant of this," replied Hu'urs Khraam. "However, our human allies stand much to gain immediately upon our arrival, and yet, have little influence over the outcome of our campaign, which enjoys the advantage of being conducted on an isolated land mass. As an island nation, Indonesia affords us a geographically finite periphery, the borders of which are easily scanned and interdicted, given our absolute air superiority and orbital fire support. This allows us to annihilate counterattacks mounted by air or sea, and to bring decisive and accurate fire to bear upon any indigenous insurgents. We have elected to restrict operations to the islands of Java, as per your suggestions. There is no reason to overstretch our already limited forces."

"All quite prudent, but what of their submarines?" First Voice almost sounded fretful. "I am familiar with the problems of detecting these craft from the few wars in which we used them. Even our sensors cannot detect them at depths greater than five hundred meters, if they are following stealth protocols."

Darzhee Kut hid the amused quivering of his taste-polyps. *You also don't want to admit that you're upset because the human nautical technology is vastly superior to your own.*

Hu'urs Khraam spread his claws. "Controlling the submarines is a concern, but we have complete confidence in our maritime sensors, undersea drones, and especially the purpose-built airphibian vehicles we have with us. But we must also remember that the human submarines are dated craft. Most are over forty years old and are scheduled to be decommissioned. Besides, how large a counterinvasion force can they mount from such vessels?"

"I am more concerned with their nuclear capabilities."

"Which is why our occupation—all our cantonments and bases—will be located within the human cities of Java. The humans' strategic defense forces will be unable to target us, for we will have their fellow-creatures as our living shields. This of course

presumes that their submarines would survive the rise
to launch depth, for once we detect such vessels, our
orbital fire support will eliminate them within twenty
seconds. With this one minor threat controlled, we
can consolidate our position untroubled by other
strategic incursions. The region is not self-sufficient in
rice production, but a brief cessation of all maritime
contact will not induce immediate famine and civil
unrest. This minimizes the likelihood of a popular
insurgency arising.

"Most importantly, however, Indonesia is far away
from Earth's true political centers. This provides us
with a buffer from the immense military formations
possessed by the largest powers, and allows us to
control the degree of friction and hostility present in
our discussions with their political leaders. Were we
to land in, let us say, the Eurasian landmass, or North
America, or coastal China, diplomacy and negotiation
would immediately break down. Which, in turn, would
make it impossible for us discuss our terms with the
humans and explain the wisdom of acceding to them."

Darzhee surprised himself by asking without a
warning preamble. "What are these terms?"

Hu'urs Khraam settled his claws slowly to the table.
"Complete withdrawal from the 70 Ophiuchi star sys-
tem and a co-dominium of Barnard's Star with the
Arat Kur Wholenest."

"And the surrender of a habitable world in what
they call their Big Green Main, for settlement by
the Hkh'Rkh." First Voice had risen, crest erect, as
he said it.

Darzhee Kut looked back and forth. "Surely, this
last requirement is a ploy."

First Voice looked down his very long snout. "This is not a ploy, but a plan to expand."

Darzhee Kut could hardly believe what he was hearing. "And what of the human colony that is already on whichever world is so ceded?"

Hu'urs Khraam offered a soothing hum. "They will continue to be self-determining, and will not be relocated."

"But if the rest of the humans should become aggressive—"

"The population would, of course, be at great risk from reprisals."

Darzhee Kut glanced sidelong at Graagkhruud, whose tongue flicked slightly. A colony of hostages with their neck encircled by a predator's talons. "First Delegate, surely there is room for negotiation on all these points."

First Voice's neck stretched high and straight. "Your terms are your affair. Ours are not negotiable. And your support of them is the price of our cooperation and alliance. The humans have gathered all the green worlds unto themselves. We must seize one if there is to be any semblance of parity."

Darzhee Kut bobbed once. "With respect, First Voice, the worlds they occupied, though they did not know it at the time, are all within the sphere allowed them under the Accords."

Phlegm fluttered in First Voice's nose. "We are allies with you because we not only have common cause against the humans, but against the Accords. Its legalities are claws without bones; they are abominations to be brushed aside. Now, time grows short. Did the humans reveal *anything* useful?"

"Not really," Darzhee admitted. "But this is not surprising. They are both proficient, and probably trained, in being able to converse without revealing strategically sensitive information. However, I found one moment puzzling in my conversation with Caine Riordan. With your permission, I would like to replay it for you."

Silence granted consent. Darzhee Kut pushed a stud on his control wand.

The flat holographic screen centered on the long wall of the meeting module revealed Darzhee Kut facing Riordan, who was nodding, seemed oddly calm as he commented. "And so you plan to attack Indonesia. May I ask why?"

Darzhee Kut watched his own claws rise. "Is it not obvious? It is at a great enough remove from your major powers that they will not feel so directly threatened and thus might listen long enough to hear our terms for withdrawal. For I assure you, Caine Riordan, that we do not wish to remain on your planet."

"There are many places more remote from the great powers of my world than Indonesia. Why there?"

"Can you not guess?"

"The mass driver."

"It was a surety that you would see this. Many nations have labored long and spent dearly to build this extraordinary device. And they will not wish us to harm it. Similarly, they will avoid harming it themselves."

"So it is a hostage."

"In a manner of speaking. We have no wish to take living hostages."

"Just a monetarily valuable one."

"Yes, to say nothing of its being unprotected. It is a veritable gift for us and for the megacorporations we shall appoint as our partners and indigenous overseers."

Riordan's look of relaxed interest in the conversation seemed to fall away momentarily. His eyes opened slightly wider, his lips parted. Then, as fast as it was present, the expression was gone.

Darzhee Kut stopped the recording. "I could not read Riordan's last change in facial expression. I have insufficient experience with humans." *Because the Hur caste's elders would not let me study more than a few of their most harmless visual broadcasts.* "So I put this recording before those who might have more insight than I. I ask you, therefore, what did that look signify? Surprise, or something else?"

No comments. He turned to Yaargraukh. "Is it true that you spent considerable time with this human?"

Yaargraukh nodded, still staring at the screen. "I know him."

"Then tell me, what is this? Surprise?"

"Yes, surprise. But also comprehension."

"What? I do not understand."

Yaargraukh aimed a single calar digit at the frozen image. "He has realized something, and tried not to reveal that he was surprised—and that it was *you* who gave *him* useful information."

"But even if that is true, why should Riordan conceal his surprise? He must know we will not release him until after the invasion is complete and the beachhead is secure."

"Undoubtedly."

"So then why conceal his realization, his reactions? What does he hope to achieve?"

"I do not know. Perhaps it is merely habit."

"But you think not."

"I think not."

"Can we trust him?"

Yaargraukh opened his mouth—

But Graagkhruud spoke first. "Clearly not. At the Convocation, he was the one who attempted to lure Yaargraukh himself into a trap, into a module that 'malfunctioned' and exposed them both to vacuum."

Yaargraukh raised a claw to interject, his black eyes retracting somewhat—

—and Darzhee Kut knew the clarification the Advocate was about to offer: that Riordan himself had almost been killed by the "malfunction." Every account of the incident made it clear that Riordan had not been aware, let alone the architect, of that assassination attempt. More likely, he had been the actual target.

But First Fist had no interest in allowing Yaargraukh to make that distinction. He spoke too swiftly and loudly to be interrupted. "And now, most recently, while traveling under a diplomatic transponder, Riordan fired upon your ship. It was a cowardly and duplicitous ruse. He and Corcoran should have been executed the moment they came aboard."

Darzhee Kut averted his eyes. "As I reported, their explanation of the particulars of the incident involving the diplomatic transponder signal has satisfied us all." Hu'urs Khraam bobbed once.

First Voice's crest rose slightly. "It does not satisfy me, nor do their convenient 'retirements' from being warriors."

Yaargraukh's neck swiveled deferentially. "It does

sound odd. Yet, I know this Riordan. He is an honorable being."

Graagkhruud's retort was instantaneous. "He is a *being* only insofar as he makes noises like language."

Darzhee Kut saw Yaargraukh's earflaps shiver as though they were going to close. Among the Hkh'Rkh, this reflex meant that he had heard something which was embarrassing, uncouth, or disgusting, and had just barely managed to suppress a more dramatic display of that repugnance. It was probably in reaction to his superior's blunt bigotry. A bigotry which, by extension, would also tend to categorize the Arat Kur and all other non-Hkh'Rkh races as non-beings. Fine allies, indeed.

But Graagkhruud was not finished. "And honorable? This Riordan creature lied when he hid behind the safety of a diplomatic flag and then attacked." Graagkhruud reared up. "But a lie does always reveal one truth: that he who tells it is a liar."

"If we know it to be a lie, yes," countered Darzhee Kut. "But we do not know this. Besides, Riordan is not a warfighter; that is his companion's skill."

First Voice intervened. "You err, Speaker Kut. I have heard Riordan speak, have learned something of his deeds and how he thinks. He is more a warrior-human than most of those who wear the uniforms of that caste. And your own report indicated that it was him, not the true warrior, who carried a weapon when they boarded your disabled ship."

Yaargraukh's voice was quiet but so slow and measured that it attracted more attention than a shout. "Still, I find no fault in this person's honor." Darzhee Kut leaned back, as did the other Hkh'Rkh. In his own tongue, Yaargraukh had not used the word "being," the Hkhi term for most exosapients, who, although intelligent, had no place in the honor code hierarchies which determined personhood. Rather, Yaargraukh had used the word "person," which not only implied a sapient recognized as having a mind equal to their own, but as a creature capable of accruing honor.

"The Advocate blasphemes—or betrays us." Graagkhruud breathed, his crest rising. "I cannot tell which."

Darzhee Kut closed his eyes against the strain upon his patience. "This cannot, and need not, be settled here. Caine Riordan is a senior emissary of his people, and he is our guest, not our prisoner. We would, however, be pleased and grateful if you were to leave some of your warriors with us to provide security for the humans while they are on our ship."

"I was not aware that those who are truly and genuinely guests need to be chaperoned and monitored by armed guards. Perhaps you, too, feel them to be something other than guests. Something more akin to prisoners." First Fist let his breath out through his nose, the mucus therein warbling and fluttering grotesquely.

Darzhee Kut let his eye covers slide shut for a moment. *Harmonize with the greater purpose. Embrace the differences of the Old Family Hkh'Rkh—at least in this moment.* "Honorable Graagkhruud, perhaps our ways are different in this. Here is our way: we presume that the humans are, and will behave as, diplomats while with us. But since we could be wrong, we must take steps to minimize what damage they might do should their actions show them to be saboteurs. For this reason, and for their own protection, as well, we require that they have a security escort."

First Voice stood. "You will have your 'security escort,' since you seem uncertain of being able to guard unarmed prisoners yourselves." His crest flattened and he did not bother to look back down at Hu'urs Khraam before he turned and left. Graagkhruud's exit was equally abrupt and without acknowledgment of his Arat Kur hosts. Yaargraukh stood, opened his hands and showed Hu'urs Khraam his palms in what was a military show of respect, and then strode quickly after his superior.

Darzhee Kut interlocked his claws, looked down for a moment, then up at Hu'urs Khraam—who was already looking at him. "What is your opinion of the Hkh'Rkh, Darzhee Kut?"

"I hesitate to reply, First Delegate, for I can only sing the notes I truly hear."

"I asked you to come today so you could sing just such notes."

Darzhee Kut spread his claws slowly. "Their reaction to our emissaries bears out our fears regarding the Hkh'Rkh as allies. They are intemperate, impatient, occasionally dismissive of crucial details. They are strong but inelegant in their thought and intolerant of difference. I do observe, however, that the Advocate, who is also a member of a New Family—a lower class among the Hkh'Rkh—has few of these detriments."

"Let us dig to the first stone of the foundation. Can we trust them?"

"To keep their word? Yes, absolutely."

"And to perform the tasks as they must? For if upon landing, they are tried by a sharp insurgency, they must be firm but restrained in their response. Do you think they can achieve this?"

"Esteemed Hu'urs Khraam, I do not know. Some, such as Yaargraukh, could. Some, such as Graagkhruud, cannot."

"And First Voice?"

"He has wisdom, but its melodies are often lost amidst the old rhythms of his heritage and his legacy as the scion of the greatest of the Old Families. I feel his common sense is great enough to perceive the wisdom of what Yaargraukh says, but I fear that his pride is too great to hear it over the roar of Graagkhruud's exhortations to pursue honor and total war."

"I fear this as well. But, if the humans accede to our terms, we shall depart quickly, and our allies will not need to restrain themselves for long. Happily, our swift victory will give them little opportunity to err."

Darzhee Kut wriggled slightly in his couch. "The humans might agree to negotiate, but they will not agree to the Hkh'Rkh terms. Indeed, I fear they will not even agree to ours."

"But to surrender 70 Ophiuchi would only show reason, wisdom."

"So might we see it. But the Hkh'Rkh would see it as proof of fear and lack of resolve—which is just how the humans themselves will see it."

"This makes them akin to the Hkh'Rkh."

"I wish to sing notes that ever harmonize with yours, esteemed Hu'urs Khraam, but I think you will find that particular estimate of the humans to be incorrect. They are very different from the Hkh'Rkh." He paused, looked at the image of Caine Riordan's focused and carefully unemotional face frozen on the screen behind him. "They are very different indeed."

CONFLICT
Part Two

December 2119

Chapter Fifteen

Washington, D.C, Earth

When Downing returned to the conference room from the fresher, he started. Opal Patrone was there waiting for him.

"You're early, Major. To what do I owe the honor?"

"Closed museums."

"I beg your pardon?"

"The museums are closed. The public buildings are off-limits. Congress is in seclusion. DC has become one dull city."

Downing grimaced. "As long as the Arat Kur continue to consider it more dull than Jakarta, I'll consider it a blessing."

Opal's jaw came out in a truculent, fine-pointed wedge. "At least in Jakarta we're fighting the bastards directly."

"Except, Major, that too many of the bastards are our own people, taking the traitor's coin from either the megacorporations or President-for-Life Ruap."

The door to the conference room opened again.

Trevor walked in a step ahead of Elena, who was carrying a mostly empty shopping bag.

Downing's first impulse was to cross the room to Trev, but their parting on Barney Deucy had been anything but warm. And although all the reports indicated that Trevor had been turned over by the Arat Kur in excellent condition, one could never be sure if Nolan Corcoran's son was simply playing the role he was expected to play: the bluff, impregnable ex-SEAL.

So, uncertain what to do, and once again awkward with the people he loved the most, Richard leaned both his hands on the conference table and said, "Welcome home, Trevor. It's good to have you back, safe and sound." Neither seeing nor hearing any contradictions to the happy assumptions of that greeting, Downing turned to Elena. "Christmas shopping for Connor?"

"Trying to," muttered Elena, "The stores have almost nothing left in them for a thirteen-year-old boy, and even less staff to find it for you. And there's still a lot of panic: most streets are empty and most offices are closed. But look who I met coming into this building." She smiled at Trevor.

Who smiled back—somewhat wanly, Richard thought. *Is he tired, still infuriated at me for turning his father's body over the Dornaani, or some combination of the two?* "No worse for wear after the debriefings with the intelligence chiefs and the POTUS, Trev?"

Trevor shrugged. "No. Although the Arat Kur treated me better than the intel folks. You'd have thought I was an enemy agent."

"It's the way they're trained to think. You've been in the enemy camp and come as the messenger bearing their new terms for our capitulation. You're damaged goods to them, I'm afraid."

"Well, I didn't enjoy being their chew-toy for my first day home."

"So, the Arat Kur treated you more civilly?"

Trevor quirked a smile. "Actually, in some ways, they did. The one who found us—or rather, the Arat Kur that Caine and I found—wasn't a bad little guy. For a scum-sucking alien invader, that is." Trevor saw Opal smile, returned it. Perhaps a little too broadly and readily, Downing thought.

"You are referring to the Arat Kur named"—Downing checked his palmtop—"Darzhee Kut?"

"Yep. Most of the other Arat Kur were standoffish, but still polite and careful in their treatment of us."

"You haven't said anything about the Hkh'Rkh, though."

Trevor looked sideways. "If Caine and I had been *their* guests, I think we'd have been lucky to get bread, water, and a shared head. Hell, I think we'd have been lucky not to be shown out the nearest airlock. Fortunately, Yaargraukh was there—our Advocate from the Convocation—and he talked them out of their initial blood frenzy. But most of them never really changed their opinion of us."

Opal's eyes were on his, unblinking. "Given Hkh'Rkh hospitality, I'm just glad that the Arat Kur made sure both of you survived that misunderstanding. But—no offense, Trevor—why did they send *you* back? You're a soldier: Caine was our Speaker at Convocation, almost a third ambassador. Shouldn't he have been the one the Arat Kur sent back with new terms?"

Trevor avoided her sustained gaze. "Actually, that's

kind of why Caine insisted on being the one to stay behind. And he managed to persuade Darzhee Kut to support it, too. I told them they were wrong, but—"

"But Caine convinced Darzhee Kut that your military career made you just that much more *annoying* to the Hkh'Rkh?" asked Opal. "Put you that much more at risk than him?"

Trevor nodded, his eyes still evasive and uncomfortable. Downing looked away, being the only person other than Trevor who possessed the prerequisite knowledge to understand his deeper levels of guilt. *And you fought—hard—to stay in Caine's place, didn't you, Trev? You had to, because if the worst happens, then Connor loses the opportunity of ever meeting his father, and Elena loses the possibility of marrying the man she still obviously loves. But Caine outflanked you, found a way to prevent you from taking the danger on yourself. And it's eating you alive that he did.*

Opal still looked vaguely worried. "Trevor, Caine is all right—isn't he?"

"Yeah, yeah," Trevor said, feigning a dismissive wave. "He may be safer than any of us. After all, he's sitting up in orbit with the Arat Kur, not down here in their cross-hairs. Not that the Hkh'Rkh wanted to keep him around, but they didn't have any choice in the matter. Because they are so significantly technologically inferior to the Arat Kur, they're clearly playing second fiddle. That's probably annoyed the Hkh'Rkh from the moment they agreed to conduct joint operations, which is only possible because they're being carried piggyback."

Downing started taking notes. "What do you mean by that?"

"Well, the Hkh'Rkh lack the shift range to attack our space with their own shift-carriers. So their constant chest-thumping about how they are self-reliant, dominant warriors makes about as much sense as a six-year-old in a booster seat claiming that *he*'s driving the car."

"Ouch," said Opal with a grin. Which, once again, Trevor swiftly answered with one of his own.

Which, once again, worried Downing. "And how do the Arat Kur feel about the Hkh'Rkh?"

Trevor shrugged. "They didn't say and we knew not to ask. But, from the interactions I saw, the Arat Kur aren't completely comfortable with their allies. Darzhee Kut made it pretty clear that his species is highly conflict-aversive. Harmonizing with each others' opinions and emotions seems to be one of their strongest social drives."

"Apparently that doesn't include harmonizing with other species."

Trevor rubbed his chin. "You know, I thought that at first, too. But Caine sensed highly receptive attitudes in some of them, and I'm not so sure he's wrong. They do seem to get along better with us as individuals than they do with the Hkh'Rkh."

The irony got the better of Downing. "Then why the bloody hell did the Arat Kur attack *us*?"

Trevor shrugged. "We didn't get into that. Not an officially sanctioned topic of conversation, I suspect. Speaking of official topics of conversations and war plans, when I was in the Oval Office, there were some veiled references to us counterattacking their fleet out at Jupiter. Any word on how that went?"

Downing nodded and activated the room's main

display. "We just got this thirty minutes ago." He aimed his palmcomp at the screen, thumbed a virtual button, leaned back, and suppressed a sigh.

The screen flickered to life, showing the long keel of a naval shift carrier. The crook-armed midship hull cradles were almost empty; the carrier's complement of cruisers, frigates, sloops and drones was deployed elsewhere in the inky blackness that filled the rest of the screen. They were probably not that far away—some less than a hundred kilometers, probably—but at that range, even the largest battle cruiser in Earth's entire military inventory would not show up as anything other than an inconstant star, its brightness altering slightly as it changed its attitude or applied thrust. Along the bottom of the screen, white, block-letter coding indicated that the perspective was from the ESS *Egalité*.

The curved white expanse of one of the few still-docked hulls rose higher into the frame as it cast off from the shift-carrier. Elena cleared her throat. "Perhaps everyone else knows what we're looking at, but I'd be grateful for a little context, please."

"That's a cruiser, El. Andrew Bolton class," Trevor answered. A pair of tapered arrowhead shapes rose up from underneath the cruiser itself: two sleek remoras emerging from beneath the thick body of a bull shark. Trevor resumed his narrative. "Those two streamlined boats are the newest sloops in the Commonwealth inventory; the Gordon class. Sloop is now a slang term, though. Navy acronymization has relabeled them as 'FOCALs': Forward Operations Control and Attack Leaders."

"That sounds very impressive. What does it mean?"

Richard unfolded his hands. "The sloops stay close to the drones—the fleet's various unmanned attack and sensor platforms—and relay commands to them and coordinate their actions. Their crews get the closest to the enemy, which is why, comparatively speaking, they are built for speed."

"So they're like fighter aircraft," Opal summarized.

"No, not really. They carry armament, but only as a last resort. Their role is to direct attacks made by remote-operated and semiautonomous systems. They ensure that human judgment continues to guide all our units, even those operating many light-seconds away from the cruisers and other ships."

The Bolton-class cruiser ignited its plasma thrusters in addition to its pulse-fusion main engine and began angling off from the *Egalité*. The two Gordons split off to either side of the Bolton.

The scene changed to a view of space, upon which a collection of blue guidons were arrayed. Each was capped by a slightly different symbol with a short data string attached.

Opal nodded. "So, that's our fleet, right? Ship types and tail numbers on the guidons?"

"Yes," affirmed Downing.

Elena frowned. "How are we getting this view? Why is there a camera just waiting in the middle of deep space?"

"It's mounted on a microdrone," Trevor supplied. "We launch dozens of them before and during combat. They not only give us pictures like this, but relay damage-assessment views of our hulls, and help during salvage and rescue ops. And they're so small that they blend in with the rubbish and then work like spy-eyes after an engagement."

Opal was frowning. "I count four carriers: *Egalité*,

Beijing and *Shanghai* close to each other, and *Tapfer* way off to the left. Why is it out there?"

Downing shook his head. "After the first engagement, the *Tapfer* was forced to show her heels. She only got half of her complement back in the cradles and was too far out of position to regroup with the rest of the fleet elements. It took them this long to get close enough to add their limited weight to the engagement."

The scene changed again, this time to a camera mounted on one of the Gordon class hunter/seeker sloops. Superimposed on the view were hordes of small blue and red triangles attempting to swarm around each other, the red ones being notably faster and more agile. At the points where the swarms intersected, there were occasional flashes, like fireflies seen at great distance on a lightless night.

"Those," explained Downing quietly. "are drones destroying each other. Mostly ours on the receiving end. And as you watch, the rate of our force erosion will increase. The Arat Kur capital ships are picking them off with their UV lasers."

Trevor uttered a dismayed grunt. Opal leaned into his field of view. "Why's that so bad?"

Trevor sighed. "If Richard is right, it means the Arat Kur lasers retain decisive hitting power at much greater ranges than ours."

"But I thought we had some pretty dangerous UV lasers, ourselves."

"We do, but only on the biggest cruisers. Even then, there's ongoing debate whether they're really worth all the expense, the space, and the special engineering they require in a hull."

"Why?"

"They're energy pigs, and they have much more complicated and expensive focusing requirements. Morgan Lymbery, the guy who designed the Andrew Bolton class, said it best: 'you don't really build the UV laser into a ship; you build a ship around the UV laser.'"

The screen changed to the viewpoint of another microdrone, riding close alongside what looked like a Chinese light cruiser. The ship's counterbalanced habitation-modules had stopped spinning and were being retracted toward the hull, a sure sign that it was going to general quarters. Downing sat up a bit straighter. "A little context about what you'll be seeing. We fought the first engagement against the Arat Kur using the same tactics we employ against human opponents. In short, not knowing the enemy's specific capabilities, it wasn't prudent to close too quickly, but to maintain range and take them under fire, closing in only if and when we perceived a decisive advantage."

"Or to run like hell if it turned out that *they* had all the advantages," Trevor added.

"Yes, and that is just what happened at the First Battle of Jupiter. The Arat Kur demonstrated superior speed, superior long-range accuracy, and superior destructive power. Consequently, the notion of standing off at what we had believed to be long range was a mistake; we were overmatched in every meaningful performance metric. So the logic of this second battle was to force a meeting engagement."

Opal frowned. "Which means what, in space?"

Trevor took over. "Well, it's kind of like a joust in that you run at each other head-to-head, if possible.

If you're confident you're going to win, you do it at low speed, so you can retroboost and catch the other guy—sometimes weeks later—to pound on him some more in an extended stern chase."

"And if you're not so confident, then you approach at high speed, so that the other guy can't catch *you*, later on." Opal deduced.

Trevor nodded. "That, and you minimize the engagement time, thereby minimizing damage to your fleet."

"Those have always been fairly reasonable tactical alternatives," Downing concluded. "Against human opponents, that is."

Onscreen, there were light puffs of what looked like dust jetting out from the rounded nose of the light cruiser. "The Chinese ship is firing its primary armament—a rail gun—now," mentioned Trevor. "The puffs are buffering granules, doped on the rails to prevent wear and to ensure uniform conductivity."

"That ship seems to be putting a lot of lead—or steel or depleted uranium or whatever—downrange," commented Opal.

"Yes, it is," agreed Downing.

There were two more puffs, and then the ship shuddered as hull fragments came flying off just behind the nose. Two sensor masts went spinning backward, one almost smacking the camera, just before the drone carrying it swung around to survey other damage farther aft.

Halfway down the long tail boom, a sparking thruster bell was hanging on by a single strut. Intermittent flames were curling out of a blackened hole in a hydrogen tank, which meant that a nearby oxygen feed line had also been clipped. Two cargo modules—hexagonal tubes—were tumbling behind.

"What hit it?" Elena said in a small voice.

"Laser, probably pulsed UV, given the range, the power, and the multiple hits," said Downing in a tightly controlled voice.

As the camera began rotating to show the stern of the ship, a flurry of smaller explosions pocked its smooth midship flanks. Then a larger blast ripped one of the rotational gee-modules out of its hull-flushed housing recess. "Rail gun submunitions," Trevor murmured, apparently for Opal's benefit. "A long-range space shotgun."

The viewpoint drone was evidently struck by some of the debris that had spalled off the hull. It shook a bit, righted itself, and refocused—just in time to show what looked like a flame-trailing star arc suddenly out of the velvet blackness and strike the cruiser amidships. The screen went blank.

—And changed to a more distant space shot. But in this one, a small blue-white sphere burgeoned into existence at the lower right hand corner.

"Was that the cruiser, exploding in the distance?" Opal asked quietly. "And was that a missile which got it?"

Downing nodded as the viewpoint changed to the bow camera of a Gordon-class FOCAL. It was apparently engaging in emergency maneuvers. The camera had to gimbal a bit to maintain the same perspective.

A bright yellow-white smear flashed in the center of the screen, then two more in quick succession far to the left: the death-blooms of smaller ships, probably human. Firefly flickers of dying drones and missiles stretched across the view, some very near. One was surprisingly close.

"That was a near miss," Trevor said confidently. "I'm guessing our viewpoint ship's own Point Defense Fire system got an Arat Kur missile?"

Downing nodded tightly, never taking his eyes off the screen. After a lull in the flashes that signified the deaths of smaller human ships and drones, a much larger blue-white sphere expanded to dominate the center of the screen. "That's the *Egalité*." murmured Downing. "Destroyed when we thought she was still safely out of range."

Another sphere bloomed in the upper left.

"And the *Beijing*." he added.

The picture shifted to a distant side shot of a third naval shift-carrier. Its forward-mounted hab ring was already missing two sections and spewing bright orange flame. A moment later, the bridge section at the bow blasted outward into an expanding hemisphere of debris. Pointing toward the epicenter of the cone of destruction, Downing commented, "Definitely a laser—and a bloody powerful one. Only a focused beam could inflict so much damage to such a small area."

The spalling, splintering, and outgassing of that hit had imparted a small tumble to the ship. The nose of the crippled carrier began pitching down, the engine decks at its stern rising slightly. As it did, the hull spat out two small white ovals from behind the torus's rotator coupling: escape pods. Another one came out of the engineering decks—

Almost too fast to see, a pair of stars streaked into the picture, one striking the keel just abaft the torus, the other slicing into the engine decks. Blinding light rushed outward, swallowed the ship, the pods, the whole screen—then, static.

Downing sighed and turned off the screen. "And that was the *Shanghai*. I received the final loss list from The Second Battle of Jupiter just minutes before you all arrived. It is not reassuring."

"How bad?" asked Elena quickly.

"Both of the Chinese carriers and the *Egalité* were destroyed, as you saw. So were ninety percent of their complements. The other Euro carrier, the *Tapfer*, managed to cut across the primary axis of the engagement and is making for the outer system. But the fleet is effectively destroyed as a force in being. By all assessments, the strategy of closing quickly with the Arat Kur to inflict more damage was more disastrous than long-range sniping. We'd need a significant numerical superiority in hulls and drones to make such a tactic advisable."

Opal looked up slyly. "What about the drones we haven't shown them yet, the ones hidden in deep sites?"

Downing started. "How do you know about those?"

"I've been hanging around you sneaky intel types long enough now. I know how your minds work."

"Very good—I think. At any rate, we had none in range of this engagement. Most are committed to cislunar defense, but we have no way to use them at the moment. Having established full orbital control, the Arat Kur can jam any ground-based control signals, other than tightbeam lascom. And they are not going to tolerate any of the latter. They proved that right after their exosapient 'solidarity forces' began landing in Indonesia at the invitation of now-President Ruap."

Elena narrowed her eyes. "So is that why the Arat Kur made those limited orbital strikes against a few of our cities, and wiped one off the map in China?"

Downing nodded. "Yes. When the second Arat Kur fleet arrived by shifting into far cislunar space, they blasted all our orbital assets, including all our control sloops. The Chinese, who have an immense number of remote-operated interceptors, did not want to cede the high ground. So they launched a wave of antiship drones, all controlled from their large lascom ground station in Qinzhou."

Opal's voice was tight, angry. "And so the Arat Kur bombed it—and Qinzhou itself, for good measure. And now they've got how many ships floating over our heads?"

Downing aimed his palmtop at the flatscreen, pressed a button.

A brace of Arat Kur ships—all gargantuan shift-carriers—glided out of view, huge spindly gridworks crammed with an eye-gouging assortment of subordinate craft, rotating habitation modules, cargo canisters, and other objects of less determinable purpose. Arrayed around them were the less gargantuan, but still massive shift-cruisers: smooth, single-hulled oblongs, flared and flattened at the stern. Other ships of the line—each a freight-train composite of boxes, modules, engine decks, rotating hab nacelles and fuel tanks—looked drastically smaller, both because they were only a third the displacement of the shift cruisers and because they were more distant, arrayed in a protective sphere around the shift vessels.

"Those tinier guys don't look so tough," said Opal with a false bravado that fooled no one.

"Actually, except for when a shift cruiser uses its drive capacitors to charge its spinal beam weapon, the slower-than-light craft are far more deadly. They have no heavy, unipiece hull. No shift drive and no antimatter power plant to drag about. Far fewer fuel requirements. They are built purely for maximum speed and firepower."

"But once the STL ships are detached from their carrier—"

"Yes, that's the rub. Once they are deployed, they're stuck in-system until they make rendezvous with a carrier."

Opal looked back at the screen. "Do they have anything else up there, maybe hulls we haven't seen?"

"Doubtful, but we can't be sure. We haven't wanted to risk our last orbital assets taking new pictures unless ground observatories detect additions to the blockade."

"Wait. We still have orbital assets?" Trevor asked. "I thought they smacked down everything."

"Everything except our old 'disabled' satellites," Downing corrected.

Trevor frowned. "You mean we're getting pictures from *broken* satellites?"

Downing smiled. "We call them Mousetraps. Seven years ago, we started replacing the innards of failed satellites with dormant military systems. Some contain lascom control relays, others are communications transfer hubs, some conceal weapons."

Opal sounded indignant. "So why didn't we use these, uh, Mousetraps to attack the Arat Kur's orbital fleet?"

"The armed Mousetraps don't contain weapons large enough to use on the big ships. Not all of which are blockading Earth, by the way. Most of the fleet we engaged at the First Battle of Jupiter has moved to the Belt, primarily to take possession of our antimatter facility on Vesta."

"And the remainder?"

"Still controlling Jovian space."

Opal drummed her fingers on the tabletop. "So, they left some guards at the self-serve gas station."

"Just so." Richard smiled at her archaism.

"So this means that right now, all told, Earth has lost—?"

"—nine of its eleven military shift carriers, Major Patrone."

"Can civilian carriers be used to replace them?"

"Not really. While any carrier can pick up and shift a payload to another system, fleet carriers are designed to do it on the move and under fire. They have far more thrust potential, far more system redundancy, far better weaponry, and autonomous docking systems for high-speed deployment and recovery."

Elena sighed. "So it seems like we have very few military options left. Which makes me wonder what answer First Consul Ching is going to give the Arat Kur tonight. Any guesses, Uncle Richard?"

"Elena, I'm not even sure what the invaders' new surrender terms are. But I do know someone who's been talking about that with the president today." Downing looked at Trevor meaningfully.

Trevor shrugged. "The Arat Kur haven't moderated their initial terms of surrender. In fact, they've put in an additional requirement."

Downing grimaced. "So what do they want now?"

Trevor seemed to repeat the new demand from memory. "'The World Confederation must hold a species-wide referendum to officially confirm or reject it as humanity's legitimate government.'"

Elena made a disgusted noise. "Do they have any

conception of just how long it will take to solicit a complete global vote?"

"Not just global," Trevor corrected, "speciate. Their requirement specifically extends to offworld colonies."

"But it would take a whole year just to get the notification to Zeta Tucanae, and another year to get the results back here."

"That's right—and they know it. Believe me, they know it."

Opal was frowning. "Then what are they trying to do with a condition like that? Sabotage the peace process before it gets started?"

Downing nodded. "That's exactly what they're trying to do."

"But if they push us too far—"

"Then what? At this point, how can we threaten them? Their air interdiction of Indonesia is absolute, as we learned when we tried to contest their 'invited' landings near the Indonesian mass-driver. One hundred seventy-eight combat aircraft and interface vehicles lost with all crews. Chinese, Australian, Japanese, a few American craft out of Guam: it didn't make a difference. The best Arat Kur visible light lasers can reach right down to sea level with enough force to instantly take down any air vehicle in our inventory, even the armored deltas. And a maritime counterinvasion would be even worse. You've seen on the news what happens when an unauthorized ship crosses over the fifty-kilometer no-sail limit they imposed around Java."

Opal nodded. "A hail of kinetic-kill devices from orbit and down she goes to Davy Jones' locker."

Elena looked around the room. "So that's it? We're just going to give up?"

And again, all eyes drifted toward Trevor. He shook his head. "No, we are not giving up."

Downing found he was exhaling in relief. "Then what message is Ching going to send in answer to the Arat Kur and Hkh'Rkh demands?"

Trevor looked at him. "Nothing."

Chapter Sixteen

Washington, D.C., Earth

Richard heard Elena's response as a chorus with his own. "Nothing?"

Trevor nodded. "Despite the global panic, the World Confederation Council sees our current situation as a standoff. With the Arat Kur controlling orbital space, we can't fight back effectively. But on the ground, the Arat Kur know they've got a tiger by the tail. And as the militarily weaker power, a stalemate is actually to our advantage. So we force them to make the next move."

Downing nodded. "And if they overreact by extending their attacks to the larger landmasses, they will lose even more control of the planetside situation."

Elena frowned. "Really? So if the current level of panic isn't enough to compel us to surrender, why won't they just start bombing our cities, one after the other?"

Trevor answered before Downing could. "Couple of reasons. First, even if they do that, the invaders only have enough ground forces to control a dozen or so key points in Indonesia. And even there, they're already having a harder time than they thought. Secondly, it's not in their political interests to widen the war in any way. As long as they're after a settlement rather than conquest, it won't play well across the globe. And if they can't secure their gains directly, then when—or maybe 'if'—the Dornaani show up, the invaders will suddenly be the ones without any bargaining power, without anything to give back in exchange for either concessions or clemency."

Downing smiled. "And although all reports indicate that the Hkh'Rkh are excellent assault troops, the first signs indicate that they will be a dreadful occupation force."

Elena nodded. "From that one social event we shared with them on the Convocation Station, it was pretty clear that they lack the patience for endless rounds of guard duty and garrison tasks."

Trevor jumped in again. "Not only that. From what I heard in the Oval Office, the few mixed exosapient units that are providing 'security support' for CoDevCo's Indonesian mass driver aren't working together so well. Specifically, the Arat Kur are already having severe problems keeping a leash on Hkh'Rkh in the counterinsurgency role. For the Hkh'Rkh, war is waged by and against clearly designated combatants. Everyone else is presumed—and encouraged—to make every attempt to evacuate the area of engagement. So when guerrilla units have hit the Hkh'Rkh, they want to strike back—not just hard, but brutally. For them, sneak attacks mounted by insurgents who fade back into the population are acts of cowardice and implicit treachery that warrant full reprisals."

"Such as?"

"Such as annihilation of any town that seems to have concealed, aided, or abetted the guerillas."

"And by annihilation, you mean—?"

"Men. Women. Children. Kittens. Everything. With bombs or bayonets: it's all the same to the Hkh'Rkh. They've been protecting the mass driver site for less than forty-eight hours, and already there are reports of nearby *kempangs*—villages—completely wiped off the map."

Downing stared at the date and time stripe as the bottom of his palmcomp. "And those Indonesian guerillas are going to become more active with every passing day."

"Because of the atrocities?" Elena asked.

"No," interjected Opal with a malicious smile, "because of the weather. The one time I did mission prep for that part of the world was sixty years ago, but I doubt monsoon season has changed that much." She leaned back, stared at the ceiling as the information rolled out of her. "More than a centimeter of rain every day, and when it comes down, it comes down in sheets. Temperature rarely gets under eighty, keeping the humidity at eighty-five percent or higher. Thermal and IR gear is degraded. The ambient noise background is messy. Mud everywhere." She folded her arms. "Bottom line, if you were born there, or in a similar climate in Southeast Asia, you're used to it, know how to use it to your advantage. If you're a newb, you are in deep shit." Still looking at the ceiling, or maybe through it to the orbiting ships overhead, she grinned viciously. "Welcome to Earth, you alien bastards."

Trevor smiled, but Elena was nodding thoughtfully. "All of which means that the Hkh'Rkh will be more frustrated, and so more harsh and frequent in their reprisals. But the Arat Kur know that images depicting 'ruthless alien invaders' slaughtering women and children will destroy any chance of keeping even a small minority of humans interested in a 'peace process.'"

Trevor's nod was one of grim, vengeful satisfaction. "Or willing to accept new leadership."

Opal turned her gaze down from the ceiling. "What do you mean?"

"I mean the megacorporations. All the bloc leaders believe that the Arat Kur demand for a speciate referendum to approve the World Confederation is a backdoor move to effect a global regime change, one that puts the megacorporations—CoDevCo in particular—in charge. And once they are in control, the fear is that they won't bother to raise an army to impose their will. They'll make one."

"You mean clones?" Elena asked. "They've already started breaking those laws, from what I hear."

Downing nodded. "Former finance minister Ruap's antibloc politics wasn't the only thing which made the Arat Kur eager to see him holding power in Indonesia. It was his extremely cozy relationship with Astor-Smath and CoDevCo." He shook his head. "Which means the Arat Kur had all this planned before they loaded their invasion fleet. Even before we all went to the Convocation."

Trevor scratched his ear. "Speaking of plans, President Liu did manage to pass me a message for you, through her chief of staff."

"Which was?"

Trevor handed over a slip of plain white paper. Written in Liu's flowing hand, Downing saw:

- Case Leo Gap
- Case Vernal Rains
- Case IfUC1
- Case Timber Pony

All Cases approved for final phase activation.

See me ASAP.

L.

It was the message Richard had been waiting for. And the message which determined what he had to do next. After sharing its contents, he explained. "It is fortuitous that you are all here, because this message clears the path for us, and IRIS, to make a tangible contribution to the defense of Earth. It's a small operation, and difficult, but potentially decisive."

Trevor leaned back. "What's the objective?"

"Disable the Arat Kur's planetside command, control, and computing net for several crucial minutes."

Opal stared. "And how are we supposed to do that?"

"By infiltrating a strike team directly into their headquarters and neutralizing it."

"Uncle Richard," said a slightly pale Trevor, "with all due respect, I don't see how we—how IRIS—can carry out such a purely military operation. You're talking about a plan involving hundreds of bombs and probably thousands of spec ops troops with a shared death-wish."

"No. It will involve about a dozen diplomatic passes and an equal number of covert operatives, posing as Earth's armistice negotiation team and its support staff."

Trevor shook his head. "But there's not going to be any negotiation. First Consul Ching is about to do what he's already become famous for: making no response."

"Yes, and that will nicely pave the way for this plan's success."

"You've lost me."

Downing folded his hands. "Through you, Trevor, the Arat Kur sent us new peace terms. We have remained silent. What will they do when, in five hours, their fifty-hour response deadline runs out?"

"Try to force an answer out of us."

"And how will they do that?"

Elena saw it first. "They're going to tighten the screws, show us that we cannot ignore them."

"Precisely." *Yes, Elena certainly has her father's quick wits. And she has his courage, too, given the bandits she had to face down during her anthropology field work.* "And so, when the consequent cries of global misery begin to hit the bloc leadership, the Confederation will be forced to act, to give in and resume talks."

Trevor saw it now. "So, only because the Arat Kur themselves force us to do so, we *will* send a negotiation team. And because we resisted doing so until they left us no choice, they will not suspect that they are actually giving us the opportunity we most want: to be summoned—with our tail apparently between our legs—to their seat of power in Indonesia." He nodded. "Pretty shrewd, but how do you arm the infiltration team? Even if the Arat Kur don't detect them as impostors, no one's going to let our strikers traipse into Jakarta with golf bags full of combat gear."

"Of course not. That's why operational caches are already prepositioned there. Have been, for some time."

Trevor frowned. "How could you know that they'd invade Indonesia and where they'd set up their HQ in Jakarta?"

"We had strong suspicions they'd go after Indonesia because of its isolation and because of the mass driver. And once our operatives sparked the protests that demolished the terminals and hotels at Soekarno Airport right after the invaders' first initial landings—"

Opal's eyes were wide. "*We* did that?"

"—then the Arat Kur had to consolidate their command elements in Jakarta itself. That in turn left them with a fairly limited number of options. Which meant they needed a large defensible compound with good C4I facilities that they could upgrade. Again, not a long list of options. We concealed equipment caches in all the probable sites. We also made sure that when Ruap's government started recruiting locals for the mundane housekeeping tasks—sanitation, food delivery, basic maintenance—that we had some highly motivated sympathetics in the mix."

"So when our strike team arrives in their guise as negotiators, their gear is already waiting for them on-site."

"Correct, and there will be diversions and distractions timed to allow them to get access to it."

Trevor nodded. "Sounds like a plan. In fact, it sounds like the kind of scheme that Caine would come up with, if he was here."

Downing's smile was a bit sad. "Oh, it was his plan, all right."

"What?" said Trevor. "But for the past half year, he's been—"

"This goes back beyond half a year, Trev." Downing

was careful not to look at Elena as he explained. "This goes all the way back to when we first awakened Caine in 2118, even before we code-named him Odysseus." Downing pushed a virtual button on his palmcomp and the main screen snapped to life again.

It showed Caine splicing wires in one of his initial training exercises. He didn't look up as he spoke. "If these aliens intend to rule us rather than exterminate us, they'll want to avoid a 'final solution.' So you dangle the prospect of capitulation—or even collaboration— under their noses while preparing to strike at them."

Downing's recorded voice—coming from very close to the camera—countered with, "And with their superior technology, how do you propose to get close enough to strike at them?"

Caine glanced up. "By getting—or prepositioning— forces inside their beachhead. And don't give me that doubting-Thomas look: there are always methods of infiltrating forces through 'secure perimeters' or 'impass-able' borders. Even the old ploy of the Trojan Horse still has some merit; it just needs some clever updating."

Downing turned off the flatscreen and glanced at Trevor. "That casual brainstorming session led your father to do exactly what Caine suggested: update the Trojan Horse ploy. Have the enemy themselves bring our strike team inside their HQ. That was the basis of the operation Nolan labeled Case Timber Pony, for which President Liu just gave the final green light." Downing waved the slip of paper. "It is also the lynchpin of our strategy to take back control of the planetside situation. Without their dirtside C4I net, the Arat Kur will not be able to call for or coordinate orbital supporting fire. And by the time they get that control back, some of our best forces will be in among them and, therefore, untouchable by their standoff assets."

Trevor was still staring at the blank screen. "And who are the negotiators you're sending into this lion's den?"

"It must be a mixed team. Some will be genuine government officials who happen to have combat backgrounds. There will be an equal number of tier one and tier two operators—Delta, Seals, SAS, Special Forces—who have enough of a background in political and foreign affairs that they can make convincing noises as diplomatic support staff for a day or two. And we'll need at least one operator who is personally known to the Arat Kur, and whose participation will reassure them, beyond reasonable doubt, that the delegation is legitimate."

Both Elena and Opal sat up ramrod straight. "You wouldn't—"

"In short," Downing finished, "we need you, Trevor."

For a moment, Trevor just stared, then he blinked. "I am exactly the *wrong* person to send. We—Caine and I—have a personal bond of honor with Darzhee Kut. After what we went through together, he trusts that neither of us would ever—"

"Which is exactly why it *must* be you, Trevor," pressed Richard. "Not only because Darzhee Kut and his leaders know you from the Convocation and from your time in the Arat Kur fleet, but because you and he had to create an unusual bond just in order to survive. His confidence in you—and by extension, the Arat Kurs' confidence in you—is exactly the edge we need: a blind-spot, a chink in their armor, which we can exploit to get in and strike them when and where they least expect it. And when and where it will do us the most good." Downing paused, saw that logic alone would not win Trevor over. There needed to be a personal, an emotional, compulsion as well. "Trevor, you are absolutely indispensable to the success of this mission, and that isn't just my assessment. It was, indirectly, your father's, as well."

"Dad's? How?"

"He was the one who first saw the value of Caine's plan, not me. And he seemed to know it might require just this kind of trickery, even duplicity, to retake our planet. No matter the personal costs."

Downing saw Trevor's eyes waver and his face pinch in what looked like some agony of entrapment. Richard glanced quickly toward Elena and Opal. "This might be a good moment to leave, ladies. The topics are going to move into the 'need to know' realm quite soon."

"Sure," Opal sneered. "It's not like you're trying to clear the room before exerting more emotional thumbscrews." She looked away in disgust.

"Not true," Downing lied. "And we'll soon need to plan your part of the mission as well, Major Patrone."

Opal snorted. "Yeah, I can hardly wait."

"Actually, Major Patrone, your phase of the operation must commence before Trevor's."

"Oh? Will I also be using my diplomatic credentials to sucker punch someone?"

"No, Major. Your mission does not involve infiltration, but extraction."

"Extraction? Of whom?" And then her eyes opened wide. "Caine! But he's not planetside, as far as we know."

"Not yet, but given his role at Convocation, I suspect

it's only a matter of time before the Arat Kur bring him to Jakarta. It would be almost inevitable, if we agreed to send our 'negotiators' there."

She frowned. "Okay—but why extract him? No matter what happens, he's protected by his diplomatic credentials, isn't—?" And then the realization hit her. "Oh. So, before your killer-emissaries violate the basic principles of diplomatic privilege with a mass assassination, I have to get our *real* diplomat out. Because our enemies will probably not feel disposed to make targeting distinctions between genuine and fake diplomats after Trevor and his pals start pulling their triggers."

"Yes, that pretty much sums it up, Major."

"Which means, if I don't find and extract Caine in time, there's an excellent chance that some exosapient invader, or megacorporate quisling, or killer clone is going to put a bullet in his brain. Just on general principles."

Downing put down his stylus. "It is a distinct possibility."

Opal became very red, stood, pointed a quivering finger at Downing, opened her mouth—but then abruptly turned and was out the door in five angry strides.

Elena watched Opal go, waited until the outer door banged closed, and then rose. She looked at her brother as if she were hugging him with her eyes, and then turned a blank gaze upon Downing. "'And on Earth, peace and good will to all men.' That is the customary greeting of the season, isn't it, Uncle Richard?" She gathered up her things and left without a word or backward glance.

Trevor's voice pulled Downing's attention away from the twice-closed office door. "I can't be your lead operative on Case Timber Pony, Richard. I'm a soldier—not a liar."

"Trevor, this is war, and its first casualty is personal choice. And right now, we have to do anything that helps us survive. See here, I've done—and continue to do—terrible things. I won't evade or deny that. But who else is going to do them? Oh, I'm sure there were a thousand people who had the *skills* to do just as well as—or a damned sight better than—me, but when your father reached into the hat of fate, it was me that he pulled up by the ears. Just as fate pulled him up when he found that the Doomsday Rock was a weapon aimed at Earth. And now fate has tapped you on the shoulder." When Trevor didn't respond, Downing felt himself growing genuinely desperate. "Do you think we wanted this for you? Do you think we wanted this for *us*?"

Trevor still did not look at him. "I think you made a choice to keep on doing this job when you could have walked away."

"How could we walk away from what we knew about the threat to our families, our planet? How could we walk away from responding to that threat, from a job that had—*had*—to be done? Who were we supposed to give it to? We couldn't even tell anyone else what we knew. Would've made job interviews a tad difficult, don't you think? And, even if we could have passed the poison cup to someone else, just what poor sod should we have saddled with this lifelong nightmare? By what right would we have chosen some other human being to sacrifice their happiness and freedom of mind so that we could have some of our own back?

"Not that we would have rested any easier, mind you. I can see it now: Richard and Nolan at the joint family barbecue, grilling shrimp, looking up at the stars, and hoping that the shop in DC was in good hands and that Earth itself wasn't on someone's interstellar dinner menu."

Trevor's eyes came back up; they were narrow, bitter. "Yeah, paint me some more scenes of your personal sacrifices, Uncle Richard. They sure make me feel better. They sure do bring my father back to life. And bring back all the hours, days, weeks he could have been with me instead of off saving the world with you, halfway around the globe."

Downing felt his fingers and feet grow very cold, his stomach sink. In the mirroring glass door that separated the conference room from the inner office, his pallor was unnatural, as if he had aged a decade in the last ten minutes. He sat heavily. "I've tried to shield you from what I could. God knows I had little enough success at it, but I tried. But this time, it's out of my hands. By Executive Order, Case Timber Pony is now in its final phase of preparation and we are committed to executing it. We might lose the war if we do not. So, I'm sorry, Trevor, but this time—this one time—you will receive orders that will require you to lie."

Trevor pushed back from the table; his tone of voice had gone much further. "And when shall I expect those orders, sir?"

Downing waved a weak hand. "That's not clear. There's a bit of diplomatic dancing to be done with the Arat Kur first, obviously. We'll begin assembling the mission force while that's going on, and we'll send the primary operation orders—as well as contingency plans—down to Nevis."

Trevor nodded. "Is that where you've stashed Stosh, Rulaine, and the rest of the security team you had me leading on Mars?"

"Yes."

"And I'm to use them on this op?"

"Yes, but not officially. The official force rosters are being compiled by Commonwealth JSOC and the intel chiefs. They're not up to me. Not except your group. Which will not show up on the standard table of organization. We'll reserve your team as our own ace in the hole, so to speak. In case the main plan is called off and you have to use one of the contingencies that involve breaching the enemy compound from the outside."

"I see, sir." Trevor rose. "Then, if we've no further business to discuss—"

"Trevor, I'm sorry. I'm sorry for this mission, for letting the Dornaani bury your father in space, for everything that our work has cost you. But if I had to do it all over again, I don't know what I would— what I *could*—afford to do differently. Not with all that's at stake."

Trevor nodded. "I understand. I'll wait to hear from you." He turned and walked briskly out the door.

Downing leaned his head forward into his hands and expelled a long sigh. He closed his eyes, drank in the darkness. . . .

After several moments, he heard the glass door to the inner office open. He did not look up, even when asked a question:

"I perceive that this meeting was—difficult?"

"Not really," Richard lied.

"The operation you have designated Case Timber Pony has received final approval, has it not?"

"It has. When should we start tracking the system delivery assets?"

"I am already doing so. I have also passed word that our relocation is to commence in two days. Do you believe that is sufficient?"

"Yes," sighed Downing. "The sooner we can get out of DC, the better, I think."

"I expected you to say otherwise. The approaching holidays are customarily spent with family members and close friends, are they not?"

"Yes, they are. That's why I want to leave."

✧   ✧   ✧

Opal discovered that she had arrived on the street. Which was fortunate, because she hadn't been able to think since leaving Downing's office and hustling into the elevator. Instead, she had been myopically preoccupied with the irrational fear that Downing would appear, chasing her, demanding that she return the hardcopy folder she had scooped up while he was in the bathroom prior to the meeting. It was labeled "Riordan, Caine/code-name 'Odysseus': Bio data," and it might hold the secrets of the one hundred hours Caine had lost on the Moon just before being coldslept, fourteen years ago.

Walking—still without really thinking about what she was doing—she produced the folder from her backpack, grazed a finger along its outer edge. The cover turned back slightly. By mistake, of course. Not that she was snooping. Well, not for herself, anyway. This was for Caine, so he could finally have some answers about what happened on the Moon, about why Nolan and Downing had cryocelled him and impressed him into IRIS. Her own burning curiosity was not propelling her actions, of course. She had never stolen anything in her life—not even from the snotty rich girls that always pegged her as a tomboy army brat in each of the myriad of grade schools she attended while her family followed Dad on his endless restationings.

She realized she had inadvertently started glancing at the contents, had a quick impression of old photographs and news clippings. She shut the manila folder swiftly, heart racing. She had faced death on a battlefield frequently, and yet nothing had ever induced this particular species of terror—because this one was laced with guilt, as well. Which was foolish. Because after all, she hadn't stolen Caine's file; she had only *borrowed* it. And she hadn't done so to satisfy her *own* curiosity. She had done it to help him. Only to help him.

She looked around her, discovered that she had somehow navigated herself to the correct street corner, and raised a hand. A driverless cab smoothly swerved across two lanes of traffic and came to a stop beside her.

The taxi was requesting the address and she was giving it, but that was happening someplace else, as if it was in a side closet of her mind. Because as soon as she had stepped inside the vehicle, was beyond Downing's reach, she knew the truth of what she was doing. *You're a liar, Opal. This isn't about Caine. This is about you, worrying that there's something in those one hundred hours that could come between the two of you. Maybe he hooked up with some old girlfriend, there, or maybe—*

She felt suddenly nauseated. At herself. *So now you're jealous of ghosts that might not even exist, Opal? How pathetic is that?*

The question remained unanswered. She was too busy getting the encircling rubber band off the manila folder so she could devour its hated and feared contents.

Letters he sent to friends. High school records. A picture with a girl—but only a skinny, coltish girl—before a prom. It was a funny picture, too; he was kind of gangly as a kid. Pictures of his house on the Chesapeake Bay. Another, much earlier one with several teeth missing from his warm and easy smile, his silver-maned father with an arm around his shoulder, and some kind of sports field behind them. She studied his faintly freckled face and tousled hair. It was impossible to reconcile that boyish image with the mental portrait she had of the man whom fate had turned into an operative codenamed Odysseus.

There were printouts of the first articles he published as a kid in the local paper, then later in *Time*, then reviews of his books, letters to publishers and editors that lauded him, castigated him, and finally eulogized him.

She came to the end of the folder. And had discovered absolutely nothing useful. Somewhere far away, the taxi announced that their arrival was imminent.

She looked down at the ravaged pieces of Caine's life, scattered in her lap. *What have I done? Or, more importantly, why did I need to do this? Because I'm afraid I'll never see him again? Or that I will—only to find he has someone to go back to, a life in which I can have no part?*

She closed the folder slowly. *And now I can't undo*

what I've done. Even if Downing never notices this file is missing, even if I return it first, I still stole it. Stole it to quiet my fears—but at the expense of what little privacy Caine has left. She looked up without seeing the dusk-darkening streets, tried to will away the two tears—one from each eye—that struggled free of her lower eyelids and streaked swiftly down each cheek. *Damn me. Damn me.*

This time, when the taxi's robot voice announced her arrival, she heard it. "Now at Bethesda Hospital, Maternity Annex. Eleven dollars, please."

Chapter Seventeen

Over West Java, Earth

Sitting beside Darzhee Kut, Yaargraukh peered out the rear of the extended cockpit canopy. The waves scudding beneath them were now occasionally distressed by small rocks, diminutive islands. "We are approaching the landing zone."

Darzhee Kut clasped to his seat more tightly. This was a part of his calling that he had never envisioned. "How soon until we arrive?"

"Ten minutes," said the Arat Kur at the controls. "Assuming—"

The pilot abruptly stopped speaking and pulled the spaceplane into a steep left-handed dive. The plume of a rocket—the thick white exhaust clumped and bloated like a kilometer-long length of intestines—shot up and past them, not more than ten meters away from Darzhee's recoiling antenna.

"Counterfire!" Yaargraukh snarled into his commo clip.

Their two Hkh'Rkh escort craft banked, seeking

the active sensors the humans had used in acquiring a lock on the spaceplane. An eyeblink later, a dense cluster of down-shooting, white-hot lines streaked dirtside, a ripple of supersonic cracklings trailing a second behind them: rail-launched kinetic-kill cluster warheads, heading planetside at six or seven times the speed of sound.

Darzhee Kut looked over at the Hkh'Rkh Advocate. "Do they have a target already?"

"No, but the orbital interdiction batteries will have backtracked the missile's plume. They are simply firing at its point of origin."

Darzhee looked out the window sheepishly, as if someone on the ground would see him and try to fire again. "The humans will not be so foolish as to loiter at the launch point."

"Of course not. I doubt they were ever near it, but rather controlled the launch from a remote location. They probably have their active sensors dispersed, as well. That means we have nothing to shoot at, no efficacious response. So we do something pointless. And we feel better."

Darzhee turned as swiftly as his carapace would allow. Yaargraukh was looking straight at him. Darzhee stole a glance at the rear of the craft. Graagkhruud was deep in a growling exchange with First Voice. "If First Voice heard you—"

"Then it would be among the few times he ever did." Yaargraukh unstrapped, tried to take a step backward, found the afterdeck of the Arat Kur spaceplane too cramped. He was unable to do more than crouch. "I grow weary of this."

"Of what? The constrictions of our craft?"

"No, of being brought along as an Advocate that is uniformly ignored." He turned to Darzhee. "I was a tactical advisor before this. Had I been allowed to remain such, at least my efforts and input would be sought and recognized. And perhaps then we might not have quite so many problems as we do now."

"Why? Are the strategies recommended by Graagkh-ruud ill-advised?"

"They are wrong. The humans do not fight as we do, but nor are they the cowards he believes. He does not understand them and he cannot win against them if he does not. The humans know this. Well, some of them do."

"They do?"

"One, Sun Tzu, wrote, 'if you would be victorious, know thy enemy.' I can only hope the humans have forgotten their own axiom. But I think not."

Darzhee felt the shuttle pull into another, but more gradual, turn. The pilot announced, "Apologies for my interruption. We are holding here until the landing zone at Soekarno airfield is available."

"There is unexpected traffic?"

Yaargraukh placed a finger on his earpiece and grunted. "There is unexpected insurgency."

Darzhee felt the wiggling-snake feeling in his upper digestive tract that was the Arat Kur fear reflex. "What?"

Yaargraukh, listening, offered quick updates. "Fifteen, maybe twenty insurgents. Half were killed. Almost all got inside the perimeter."

"But how?"

"Delivery of comestibles. Explosive devices were apparently already buried someplace within the defense perimeter. An external attack—a feint—on the opposite side of the compound. Our troops rushed there, so security was reduced at the logistical ingress point. Several of the disguised insurgents managed to slip away from the food trucks. They deployed the final, triggering bombs. Casualties—" He paused and removed the earpiece, looked out the canopy into the clear blue sky overhead. "Casualties are high."

"How high?"

"Dozens. Including some of my clan. I knew them. Personally. We shared knives at feast."

Darzhee experienced a rare sensation. He did not know what to say. "But there are prisoners to interrogate, so there will be a counterattack—yes?"

Still looking at the blue, Yaargraukh wiggled his neck lazily. "Prisoners, yes. But they will not lead us to anything useful."

"Certainly they can be made to speak what they know."

"Certainly. Your drugs and our—methods—are equally effective. But it hardly matters, because the humans do not bother to resist. They tell the truth freely and immediately."

"Then—?"

"Then we look for what they have told us about. The safe houses are empty. The hidden camps are deserted, and the supply trucks—indistinguishable from those which carry produce—are gone."

"I do not understand."

Yaargraukh turned to Darzhee. "The human commanders plan on having their insurgents captured. They tell them to confess and share any information they have. And it is useless to us, because the moment any of their number are captured or lag too far behind,

the transponders they wear code them as being 'lost.'
And so their commanders move everything, that very
moment. By the time we have rounded up the prisoners, asked our questions, assemble a reprisal squad,
they are gone. Unless they have left an ambush team
behind, either with guns or control-detonated bombs."

"They sound very well organized."

"Too well organized, if my opinion were to be asked.
I find the aptness of their tactics, and the promptness
with which they began to exercise them, improbable."

"What is improbable"—it was Graagkhruud's voice,
a rumble of rocks jounced together in a bag—"is that
your defeatist attitude allows you to remain in First
Voice's service, Advocate." He emerged from the passenger section into the forward cabin. "Perhaps you
would do better clearing the streets of our adversaries?"

"The First Fist of the First Voice of the First
Family would know better than I." But Yaargraukh
did not lower his crest, or his eyes, as he recited the
ritual obeisance.

Graagkhruud looked down his considerable snout
in such a way that Darzhee Kut felt he was under
his gaze as well. "There is no problem here that we
could not solve were we not constrained by the Arat
Kur rules of engagement."

"And what would you do if freed of them, First
Fist?" asked Darzhee Kut, expecting the Hkh'Rkh
would pause briefly to consider tactical alternatives.

Graagkhruud did not even stop to draw a new
breath. "Hold hostages. Kill ten of them for every one
they kill of ours. Place towns under death-interdict: an
attack on one of our bases results in the firebombing
of five of their *kempangs*. They can be stopped and

their will can be broken." He turned to Yaargraukh, whose black-worm tongue had snaked out once, briefly, at the height of the strategic tirade. "Do you opine otherwise, servitor?"

"I believe that the plan may be more easily articulated than realized."

Graagkhruud fluted the phlegm in his nostrils. "It is well you are Advocate. As a Tactical Leader, you would have only led your troops to death."

"He has no record of ever having done so in the past, First Fist." First Voice had emerged from the secure suite in the center of the fuselage. "And for now, he will remain the Advocate." The spaceplane banked again. The early morning light that came through the starboard windows angled more acutely, disappeared, then streamed in portside as yellow beams. "Pilot: report."

The Arat Kur at the controls leveled them off. "We have just been redirected to the cargo airfield north of Tasikmalaya, First Voice."

"We have no need to visit the mass driver, pilot."

"With apologies, that is not the purpose of our redirection. The airspace security at Soekarno airfield is not yet deemed fully secure. We will land at North Tasikmalaya, refuel, await clearance from Jakarta."

First Voice's crest flattened. He looked over at Darzhee Kut. "Hu'urs Khraam assured me that your missile intercept systems would be more than adequate to counteract such attacks."

Darzhee Kut had a momentary vision—and panic—of the immense carnivore leaning over to devour him on the spot. "I am unable to speak to the First Delegate's assurances on this matter. Pilot, is there any word why the air defenses are unable to ensure our safe approach to Jakarta at this time?"

"Speaker Kut, the humans intermittently salvo many small rockets—some dangerous, some not—to saturate our defense arrays. Sometimes they do this for no apparent reason; sometimes they do it when they intend to make some purposeful attack. While our point defense fire systems are occupied with these many targets, the humans occasionally manage to launch a high-performance missile that cannot be engaged soon enough and which penetrates the primary defense umbrella. I am told that more air-defense batteries are being emplaced every day."

And if Urzueth sings true, we will soon have deployed almost all that we have. Who could have known that hundreds of these units would be required for such a small theater of operations?

First Voice emitted a rippling snort: the Hkh'Rkh equivalent of a sigh. "First Fist, we have a firebase at North Tasikmalaya. What is the size of the contingent?"

"Five hundred warriors, organized as fifty troops of ten, First Voice. Twenty Arat Kur in powered armored suits provide heavy support."

"Is this not also the site where we have human auxiliaries in support of our operations?"

Graagkhruud's eyes vanished for a second then bulged outward. "First Voice of the First Family cannot mean me to include these *beings* in my report of our strength in that place."

"They are assets which relieve our warriors of other duties, thereby allowing more of them to be deployed for direct engagement at any moment."

"It is as you say, First Voice of the First Family."

Darzhee watched First Voice's crest furl and soften a bit. "First Fist, I am not chastising you, but I need complete information at all times."

Graagkhruud's nostrils seemed to tremble. "Esteemed First and son of my mother's father, I live to serve you with honor and distinction, so I plead that you hear me. We must count on ourselves alone in this enterprise. Our Arat Kur allies seem acceptably competent in the distant button-pushing that passes for war between the stars. But they must give you more freedom and more control of the true war: the war on this planet. They trust to machines and hide in their buildings. The humans have not learned to fear us and obey. And they must, or we are doomed. We are too few, even against such weak opponents, if they cannot be cowed into a reflex of submission."

First Voice gently touched a claw to one of Graagkhruud's. "I hear your words, but for now, we will follow the strategy we have agreed upon with Hu'urs Khraam."

"With respect, we are already frustrated in the following of that strategy."

"How do you mean these words, First Fist?"

"The Arat Kur and we had settled upon maritime interdiction as a cornerstone of our plan. Complete isolation of the occupied islands was deemed essential."

"And so we had intended. But Indonesia's self-sufficiency in food was lost when so many of its rice storage facilities were destroyed, first during President Ruap's rise to power, and again during the outcry at our landings." First Voice waved a dismissive pseudo-hand. "We must accept the changed conditions. Such are the vagaries of war."

"Perhaps not, First Voice of the First Family."

Yaargraukh was still looking out the canopy, as they began their descent, their angle of approach paralleling the southern downslope of Gunung Sawal.

"And how is the loss of human food something other than a vagary of war, Advocate?"

"Because I do not believe that it was by chance that the human foodstuffs were destroyed. It was sabotage."

Darzhee Kut felt his sensory polyps sag in shock. "But why?"

First Voice's tone was calm and contemplative as he stared long and steady at Yaargraukh. "To force us to choose between selectively relaxing the maritime blockade or starving the population. By rescinding the total blockade, we must now patrol more carefully, which stretches our already insufficient forces thinner and taxes our monitoring capabilities. However, maintaining the complete blockade would result in famine, disease, and their inevitable sequelae: unrest and then suicidal revolt. The humans found a way to present us with two bad choices. We could only elect to avoid the worst."

Graagkhruud looked at Yaargraukh as though he were personally responsible. "And so now our security cordon is no longer inviolate. Dozens of their freighters arrive in Jakarta, Surabaja, and the other allowed port cities every day."

"Any trickle of supplies and insurgents which might somehow slip through our monitoring of these ships' crews and cargos will be manageable," First Voice affirmed. "However, the alternative—a mounting flood of starving, angry, desperate hordes—would surely wash over all our guns and walls and drown us in our compounds."

"Still, I do not like it. It is a suspicious development."

"I agree, but there is a suspicious development which troubles me more."

"Do you refer to the mystery ship, that continues to move further out of the system, First Voice?"

"It is a mystery ship no longer, First Voice," offered Darzhee Kut. "We have identified it as the civilian shift carrier *Tankyū-sha Maru*, registered to the Trans-Oceanic Industrial and Commercial Organization. It is largely crewed by persons from the nation known as Japan. It is well into the Kuiper Belt now, and still traveling outward at point two cee. It does not respond to our hails or our offers of assistance."

"Is it a wreck?" wondered Yaargraukh. "Disabled? Damaged in our initial attack?"

"Unlikely, Advocate. We have detected low, intermittent engine activity. More significantly, though, this ship had already achieved preacceleration and was ready to shift when our first fleet elements arrived eleven days ago."

First Fist ran a claw down the side of the hairless, almost tubelike snout that was also his face. "So then it must be a wreck, unable to either shift or to effect a constant course change and return."

First Voice rumbled. "Probably so, but it is also true that a preaccelerated ship is a perfect courier, ready to shift instantly to some other system."

Graagkhruud's crest frisked a bit. "And where would they go? And if they wished to report what the rest of humanity must already know or guess—that Earth's fleet is destroyed and her surface knows the tread of new masters—why did they not do it when we arrived, or when we first landed? No, First Voice, your dreams are filled with worries already. Do not add this to them. Be assured that this is a matter of little or no concern. If there are humans on board, do not be alarmed that they do not reply. As today's deadline approaches, do we not have evidence that this race is indisposed to respond to us even under congenial circumstances? So the silence of this ship is hardly a surprise and hardly a circumstance worthy of your worry. After all, we already know the cause of many of their silences: they are cowards and fear to engage us with either words or weapons."

Yaargraukh eyes bulged slightly. "Peculiar, then, that we should have to be redirected away from our landing site because of an attack by a race of cowards."

"You know the meaning of my words, Advocate. Have caution your insolence is not answered with a Challenge. The humans are like vermin, like *s'fet*, darting in to bite us, scampering away under the dung of their cities and jungles because they lack the courage to stand and fight. The same is true of their words: they speak only to lie to us, and they grow silent when they are compelled to make honest responses to honorable questions or offers. They resemble the vile rodents of their own world—rats—and should be hunted down as such. I say again, the time for a moderate tongue is past. Now, the decisive claw must rule."

Darzhee Kut saw and relayed the substance of the pilot's warning gesture. "For now, First Fist, your very decisive claw must be strapped in. We are preparing to land."

Chapter Eighteen

Washington, D.C., Earth

Downing paused by his office's outer door long enough to switch off the central power and data conduits. As he opened the door and shrugged into his coat, every circuit except for those which monitored the wall-embedded faraday cage physically disconnected from the power grid with a *thrunk*.

Even before he got the door closed, his palmcom buzzed in a pattern reserved for IRIS-related personnel. He tapped his collarcom. "Downing."

"Hello, Uncle Richard?" Elena. Sounding contrite. A tone of voice he wasn't much accustomed to, coming from her.

"Hello, Elena."

"I just wanted to say that I'm sorry I left with a snide remark."

"Understandable, Elena." Nice getting an apology. In this business, he was usually the one making, not receiving them. "What can I do for you, dear?"

"Well, I wanted to talk to you about—oh, wait a minute. Is Trevor there?"

"No. He left the office just a few minutes after you did."

"I see."

Downing waited, began to wonder at the length of the pause—

"Uncle Richard, there's something I need to talk to you about."

"Certainly."

"Not over the phone. Over dinner. My treat."

"Well"—he looked at his watch—"I suppose so. Where do you wish to go?"

"Papillon."

"Elena, that's in Alexandria, rather off my beaten path. I know you're fond of the ambiance, but—"

"Well, that's just it, Uncle Richard. What I want to talk to you about is—well, it's personal."

"I see. Well then, yes, of course. *Papillon* it is. What time would you like to meet there?"

"A little after seven?"

"Can we make it a bit later?"

"Have you tried to get in there recently? They're so swamped by eight PM, you'll wait an hour just to get your salad."

Richard checked his watch. "Fair enough. I'm going to have to step lively if I want to make it on time. See you there."

"See you."

As the elevator opened, he checked the IT security protocol update from Langley. They were recommending full surge protection measures from seven PM onward, full shut-down where feasible. *Hmmm, expecting a lively night when the Arat Kur realize they're not getting a reply to their new demands?*

Downing began buttoning his coat as the doors slid closed.

❖   ❖   ❖

As Opal exited the cab with the groceries and prescription vitamins and supplements, she paged her townhouse, activated its welcome protocols, and checked her palmcom: no calls, no messages, or data to any of her accounts. She went up the stairs two at a time, grazed the print-reader with her thumb, inserted the mechanical key, and entered.

—and immediately saw the red light flashing rapidly on the house-control screen, just beyond the vestibule: not a casual message. A high priority send, either from a government source, or relayed through a government server. She plunked her shopping down unceremoniously on the table next to the coat rack and pressed the flashing light to trigger an immediate display.

It was a letter, and it was from Caine.

> Opal:
>
> I am being allowed to send a brief message while under direct Arat Kur supervision. It may be the last you receive from me for a while, since I am waiting to board a shuttle that will, I am told, take me down to Jakarta.
>
> I am well. My time at Barnard's Star was interesting. And my time with the Arat Kur since then has been very informative.
>
> I'm sorry this letter has to remain so general and bland, but I literally have two Arat Kur warders staring over my shoulder as I write it. However, please trust me when I tell you that, under no circumstances, including direct

orders from Downing or any other superior, should you try to come to Jakarta. Based on what little I have seen of the planetbound military traffic, and the scant situation reports that my hosts have shared with me, the situation in Indonesia is becoming increasingly unpredictable and violent.

Please please please remain where you are and stay safe. And if you happen to—

MESSAGE ENDS. TRANSMISSION TERMINATED AT THE SOURCE.

Opal stepped back from the screen, realized she'd started crying. She didn't stop to wipe her face, but slammed open the door into the hall closet.

Sorry, Caine. Can't take your advice. And I can't wait for Downing to send me off to rescue you, probably with a bad team and a bad plan that's likely to get both of us killed. Assuming he'd even give me the green light in time. It's three to one odds that poor, sweet Trevor is going to get crucified when Case Timber Pony gets exposed while in-country and that you'll be left swinging in the breeze before I can get you out.

Nope, I'm not waiting. I know what needs to be done, and I'm going to get about doing it. Right now.

Uniform, boots, sidearm went into her gym bag. She wished she had web gear, but she'd take care of that as soon as she got to San Diego. That's where scuttlebutt said the action was. Lots of boots were converging on that Pacific gateway port, more than remained in the billets there. Lots more. So they were getting shipped out to somewhere in the Pacific, and given what she'd heard in Downing's office and in Caine's message, she had a pretty good idea of where that would be.

Pulling the remaining gear out of the closet, she smiled through her still blurred vision. *And if you thought I was just going to wait for you here, Caine Riordan, then you don't know this country girl. Not by a fucking country mile, you don't.*

From low orbit to Jakarta, Earth

Flanked by a pair of combat-suited Arat Kur, Caine waited to board the shuttle while the Arat Kur administrator he had come to know as Urzueth Ragh attempted to engage him in small talk. "I conjecture that you are looking forward to returning to Earth. I know our improvised accommodations cannot have been very pleasing."

Caine had no intention of replying, but glancing over, saw that Urzueth remained focused upon him, evincing the peculiarly canted posture which, in Arat Kur, indicated a resolve to wait. In perpetuity, if need be. Caine relented. "I have appreciated the many efforts you made at accommodating our unusual needs. The representatives of the Homenest have been most gracious."

"As are you, for saying so," Urzueth said with the bob that signified more than a nod but less than a bow. "But on the other point, are you not gratified to be returning home?"

Caine considered how to respond truthfully, but not provocatively. "Not under these conditions."

Urzueth seemed distressed, but not particularly surprised. "I regret that the situation is so—discordant—on your planet, right now."

Caine was not able to let that blithe euphemism pass unremarked. "I was not aware that 'discordant' was synonymous with 'invasion,' in the Arat Kur language."

"Invasion?" Urzueth now seemed genuinely surprised. "It is true we have invaded this system, but not your planet."

Caine turned to look at the Arat Kur directly. "Perhaps I have misinterpreted the updates from you and Darzhee Kut regarding the establishment of a blockade around Indonesia, your seizure of its mass driver, and the imposition of a no-fly restriction on the entirety of my planet?"

"You are correct in your recitation of the facts, Caine Riordan, but incorrect in attributing the causes. It is true that we imposed the no-fly restriction unilaterally, but we did so in order to fulfill our obligations to the human authorities who have invited us to protect the mass driver from sabotage, and Indonesia from extranational conquest."

Caine was so stunned that he could only get out the words, "And who invited you—?" before the pressure door into the shuttle landing bay finally opened. The answer to Caine's half-asked question walked through it.

A slender young woman wearing what amounted to CoDevCo livery stepped into the passenger and cargo marshalling area in which Caine and Urzueth waited. She extended a hand; her voice was soft, almost shy. "Mr. Riordan, I am Eimi Singh. I am here to escort you planetside, along with our exosapient guests." She turned to Urzueth. "Is everyone gathered and ready, esteemed Administrator Urzueth? We have a fairly tight operational window, the flight crew tells me."

"Not just yet, Ms. Singh. We are still awaiting—my error; here they are. The security consultants Mr. Ruap requested. Just over from their ship, I believe."

Caine turned. Two Hkh'Rkh in battle gear emerged from the inter-bay access corridor and stalked toward the group, their massive, sloped shoulders swaying slightly from side to side as they approached.

Urzueth turned back to Caine. "Now, you wished to know who invited us to assist in your planet's affairs, Caine Riordan?"

Riordan turned away. "You have just answered that question. Quite clearly."

❖   ❖   ❖

The CoDevCo shuttle did seem to be on a tight schedule. As soon as its attitude control thrusters had pushed it backward out of the bay, it performed a one-hundred-eighty-degree tumble, followed by a one-hundred-eighty-degree roll, and then nosed down into a fairly steep angle toward the atmosphere. Caine, at a window seat, affected a distracted hundred-meter stare to cover his intense scrutiny of every detail of every ship he could see. He had all of about half a minute in which he would be able to make observations.

In addition to a host of specifics which he hoped he would not forget if he ever got debriefed by naval technical intelligence experts, he was immediately struck by a profound overall impression of the Arat Kur warships in general. They were not, in fact, warships. Not in any permanent sense, at least. On close inspection, they appeared more like multipurpose designs.

As the shuttle accelerated briskly planetside, he glimpsed what looked like a frigate being serviced by a tender. But, in actuality, they were the same class of ship, or would have appeared so at a fast glance. Detailed study revealed that the majority of their differences were ultimately modular in nature. The frigate had a larger engine deck, had a greater number of thruster pods, and had launch bays in place of cargo containers. But otherwise, the similarities between the craft were marked.

Passing another hull—a small mothership for atmo-interface craft—Caine noted the same style of construction, and the exact same thruster pods he had seen on both the frigate and the tender.

One final scan of the blackness beyond the window showed him what had to be a shift carrier, far "above" him. The traffic, the coveys of protective drones, the PDF turrets: everything told him it was an Arat Kur military vessel of extreme importance. But rather than having a main weapon built along the length of its hull, this one had a detachable spinal mount: a narrow oblong that had been affixed atop the keel, but was not integral to it.

Each ship's subsections were modular, which made every ship a reconfiguration of interchangeable elements. The only exception was the smooth-hulled shift cruiser that he had seen closely—once—after being rescued from the hab module off the shoulder of Barney Deucy. Streamlined, radically different in design and appearance, it had looked like a craft out of place within its own fleet. Judging from the shift-cruiser's retractable weapons blisters, sensor clusters, integral spinal weapon, and in-hull weapon and vehicle bays, it was also the only one that had been built expressly for the purpose of waging war.

A whole invasion fleet—and only one model of ship that was built for the sole purpose of waging war.

Which was, on reflection, consistent with Darzhee Kut's claim that the Arat Kur had been without war for many centuries. Hardly unusual, then, that they did not have warships, any more than they had a standing fleet. Probably, for them, retaining provisions for war-making was a troublesome business necessitated solely by the existence of their unpredictable neighbors.

As the CoDevCo shuttle sped down toward the clouds, its nose pitching up into an atmobraking attitude, Caine caught sight of the hulking body armor of the two Hkh'Rkh, who were strapped in alongside his Arat Kur warders in their articulated combat suits. One race knew no war; the other knew nothing but. Strange allies.

Or, perhaps, he thought, estranged *allies.*

As the shuttle emerged from the monsoon clouds hanging thick and low over the island of Java, Caine felt his breath catch involuntarily. Black plumes, some rising up from immense fires clearly visible at their three-kilometer altitude, dotted the landscape. The largest of the conflagrations was located five kilometers west of the chaotic, sprawling, sea-hugging metroplex that was Jakarta itself. The shuttle sheered away even farther from that tower of smoke, just as a brace of nonhuman air vehicles swept over them, firing missiles as they headed groundside, forward thrusters beginning to rotate into a VTOL attitude.

Across the aisle, Eimi Singh put a hand to her

small earbud, then turned to Urzueth. "I am sorry, esteemed Administrator Urzueth, but Soekarno spaceport remains unavailable. We will have to divert to a direct landing in our compound."

Caine stared at Urzueth. "A most interesting way to not invade a planet."

Urzueth glanced out the window, then back at Caine. The unreadable Arat Kur features did not change for a full two seconds. Then, the mandibles became animated again. "Caine Riordan, you misperceive. These fires you see, we did not cause them."

"So those attack craft heading planetside belong to someone else?"

"Oh, no, they are ours, but they are responding to requests for assistance. From the human government."

Caine felt slightly nauseous. "The *human* government?"

"Yes, President Ruap's provisional Indonesian government."

Eimi leaned in with a shy, apologetic smile. "The destruction you see is the work of renegade army units. They have severely damaged Soekarno Spaceport. They have disabled various utilities, and as if to prove their bestiality, have actually attacked and destroyed countless food warehouses."

"And how long has this 'rebellion' been going on?" Caine asked, his throat dry.

"Four days," answered Eimi.

Caine looked at Urzueth. "And how long ago did your first 'advisors' and 'security consultants' start landing?"

Urzueth eyes seemed to tighten in their ridged settings. "Five days ago."

Caine leaned back in his chair. "I am guessing that would be shortly after Mr. Ruap's coup began."

Eimi shook her head. "Oh, there was no coup. Mr. Ruap was compelled to take control of the government when the last president was assassinated and the new leadership refused to acknowledge the rights granted to CoDevCo regarding the mass driver site."

Caine studied Ms. Singh narrowly. "And what rights would those be?"

"Full legal possession of the site itself, including complete autonomy to authorize air traffic of any origins into or out of the mass driver facilities."

Caine smiled. "Let me guess. The old leadership objected to 'air traffic' from the Arat Kur fleet. Specifically, troop landers."

Urzueth bobbed. "Yes, now you understand."

Caine looked out the window at the smoke- and fire-scarred patchwork quilt that comprised the coastal flats of Java. "Oh yes, I understand perfectly. And I have also learned another quirky difference between our languages, Esteemed Urzueth."

"And what is that?"

"Those whom you call 'renegade rebels,' we call 'resistance fighters.'"

❖   ❖   ❖

The CoDevCo shuttle, engaging its VTOL thrusters as it glided smoothly over the dingy, cockeyed checkerboard of Jakarta's rooftops, dropped suddenly lower.

The civilians in the craft—Urzueth and Eimi Singh—grasped at the seat-backs in front of them as if to arrest their fall. The military types—the Arat Kur guards and the Hkh'Rkh "security advisors"—simply swayed in their seats. Caine discovered that he now fell into the latter category: he reflexively distinguished the quick drop as a maneuver, not a loss of control.

"What is the problem?" Eimi almost stammered into her collarcom.

The pilot's answer came over the cabin PA. "Apologies to all. We've just been told we are not cleared to land at CoDevCo's rooftop vertipads. We're going to have to wait until we can be a assured of a safe approach to the ground pads."

"Why?" Eimi asked her collarcom. Whatever answer she got was sent privately to her earbud. Caine leaned over, raised an inquisitive eyebrow.

"A disturbance down in the city," she explained with an apologetic smile. "It seems the rebels have sent professional agitators into the streets and have managed to stir up some of the people against the government. That makes it harder for our associates' airborne surveillance assets"—she smiled quickly at Urzueth—"to detect threats in advance."

"What kind of threats?"

"Well," she said, her reply punctuated by a nervous flutter of her eyelids, "some of the rebels are said to have rockets."

Caine pointed at a crowd-filling square not far below them, near some kind of railway station. "Down there, you mean?"

"No," corrected Eimi. "That's just one of the riots stirred up by the agitators. The actual rebels are much fewer in number. But some of them are engaged with our forces north of here. So we shall stay low, where they cannot detect and target us."

Caine hoped Eimi and the pilot were right about that assumption. If these "rebels" had laid hold of any reasonably modern AA systems, they would be capable of both designating targets and launching missiles from non-line-of-sight vantage points. He looked north. Tilt rotor VTOLs the size of small cars—and of distinctly nonhuman design—darted and weaved over the ramshackle roofscape. Smoke rose from the street. AA rockets went skyward between the billowing black plumes, vectoring toward the VTOLs. All but one of the rockets exploded in midair, apparently intercepted by active counterfire systems onboard the ROVs or possibly from some rear area support position. However, one rocket did find its mark. It clipped the side of a dodging VTOL, the blast taking out one of the rotors. The crippled alien craft faltered down toward the street, another rotor now wobbling.

The shuttle's main engines cut out, ending its forward movement. But in the moment of comparative silence as its vertical thrusters rose to full power, Caine heard an uneven susurration almost directly below. Looking down, he discovered that the source of the ragged murmur was the rioting crowd, its distant roar now drowned out by the whine of the shuttle's VTOL turbofans.

At the west end of the square in which the crowd had gathered, lines of troops began to emerge from an old squat stone building: probably a bank or armory or museum before being converted into fortified barracks. The troops came out the front door in two perfect lines, quickly forming a dull gray bulwark along the western edge of the square. As they grew in number, filling in from the back and pushing forward, the crowd shoved back, becoming more agitated. Their previously stationary placards were now waving and

shaking like battle flags. A number of the more agile
protestors had shinnied up lampposts, clambered onto
kiosks, some shouting slogans with the aid of bullhorns
and portable sound systems.

The gray ranks facing them were eerily uniform:
each soldier was of identical height, wearing identical
equipment. None had donned riot gear. Their rifles
were at the ready, stocks tucked against their hips,
barrels slightly raised.

The protestors reacted to these unresponsive serried
ranks with even greater agitation. The crowd seemed
to surge and pulsate like a distempered unicellular
organism, uncertain of its next action. Then, two
almost invisible objects—bricks, possibly, from their
angular outlines—crossed the gap from the restless
social amoeba and disappeared into the ranks of the
motionless, identical soldiers.

Their response was immediate. The muzzles of the
lead rank came up and sparkled. Caine heard what
sounded like a distant ripping of cardboard. As if being
melted away by acid, the facing side of the social amoeba
began to evaporate, leaving an irregular stain of heaped
bodies to mark the prior limit of its outer membrane.

At the other end of the wounded organism, the
cytoplasmic crowd started bleeding out into every
street and alley that led away from the square, the
body of protest deflating and ultimately disappearing—

Except for those heaped corpses whose own blood
had begun to paint the streets of Jakarta with a
black-red stain. Which—even if today's late-afternoon
rainstorm washed it away—promised to live on in the
memory of those hundreds who had been there, and
those thousands to whom they told their tale.

As Caine watched, a small, stick-thin figure—maybe a young teen, maybe an elderly person—crawled out of the tangle of bodies, dragging useless legs.

The shuttle rose slightly and resumed its forward progress. "Final approach," announced Eimi buoyantly.

Caine watched the faltering stick-figure pulling itself away on weakening arms until he couldn't see it anymore.

Chapter Nineteen

Gunung Sawal mass driver compound,
Central Java, Earth

An immaculately dressed and groomed human male of youthful middle age strolled down the ramp of the CoDevCo high speed VTOL even before the dust of its hurried landing had settled. "Allow me to welcome you to Indonesia's Gunung Sawal mass driver. I hope you will forgive the inconvenience of flying here directly, today. However, there are still minor disturbances in Jakarta, and we did not want to take any chances with such important guests. We will try to make your stopover as comfortable as possible."

Darzhee Kut was on the tarmac, keenly aware of the bright, wide, swallowing sky overhead. He bobbed acknowledgment of the human's oddly mellifluous greeting, and began edging toward the nearest building. First Voice followed lazily. If he had heard the human's greeting, he gave no sign. Graagkhruud and the rest of the Hkh'Rkh contingent followed their leader's example. Yaargraukh turned to the human as they walked on either side of Darzhee Kut, "Take care that First Voice does not think you are addressing him directly. Your life would be forfeit."

"I see. But I may address you?"

Darzhee Kut saw Yaargraukh's earflaps flatten: a sign of distaste. "Yes. You may."

The human either didn't notice the disapproving response or didn't care. As they reached and entered the open-fronted building, he bent over slightly to look down at Darzhee, who was grateful for the roof over his head. "And I am informed that you are Speaker to Nestless Darzhee Kut?"

"This is so. And you are Colonial Development Combine Vice President Astor-Smath?"

"Correct. I am also the Senior Liaison and Interim Director for the Colonial Development Combine's activities in Indonesia. Allow me to extend my thanks to you and First Delegate Hu'urs Khraam for allowing us to continue our work on the mass driver, despite the unfortunate misunderstanding between our peoples."

Darzhee Kut heard Yaargraukh's bronchial huffing and nasal sputtering behind him, hoped Astor-Smath did not understand it as a sardonic and derisive laugh. "It is in the interest of both our races that you complete this project. Once we have departed, it will be a great aid in Earth's construction of an even more extensive and modern cislunar presence."

"Our thoughts exactly. Have you seen the mass driver?"

"Only images."

Astor-Smath motioned for them to follow him to the other end of the building, where a ramp led up to an observation deck. The other Hkh'Rkh went on ahead eagerly. By the time Darzhee Kut arrived at the overlook, Graagkhruud was pointing out the bunkers that housed most of the Hkh'Rkh garrison. "They are excellent positions, built by humans under the supervision of the Arat Kur." He turned to Astor-Smath. "Servitor being, summon a troop to this place. The First Voice of the First Family requires greater security."

"As you wish." The human spoke into his collarcom.

Darzhee Kut edged closer to the handrail—which, for him, was like a high fence—that followed the rim of the deck. He was not particularly bothered by the height, but he still found it difficult to move beyond the overhead limit of the awnings which shaded them where they stood. These roofings were only canvas, but were still comforting.

However, he hardly needed to move to the edge of the gallery to get a good look at the mass driver. The mechanism dominated the tableau. A thick, chrome-silver tube raised on pylons, it rose up from the tangled and browning trees that hugged the western skirts of Gunung Sawal, and sidestepped up and across the slopes of the extinct volcano at an angle that corresponded to an E-NE orientation, ending in an incline of slightly less than forty degrees.

Darzhee Kut half-rotated to face Astor-Smath. "It is an impressive structure."

Astor-Smath smiled. "And with power from a dedicated fusion plant, it will put a half kiloliter container of up to three hundred fifty kilos into low earth orbit, either for pickup or transfer to higher orbit."

Darzhee Kut wondered the tactful way to express his assessment. "That is a rather modest payload."

"Per canister, yes. But, even in our start-up phase, we will be launching one every two minutes throughout a twelve-hour operational day. Once we've smoothed out the system and are comfortable with the operating procedures, we will begin to reduce the launch interval and extend the hours. We conservatively estimate that, at nominal function, the driver will lift be lifting high-gee-rated cargos into space at only one-tenth or even one-one-hundredth of the current market cost."

"Such a complex machine will be malfunctioning more than it will be operating." Graagkhruud's dismissive assessment was unusually aggressive in tone. Darzhee Kut flexed his claws. *So, he is made nervous by the humans' greater technical acumen.*

Astor-Smath was utterly unruffled. "It is hard to envision the source of such problems. The mass driver machinery is arguably far less complicated than the rail-guns of warships. It obviates the need for manned launch vehicles, so instead of piloting problems, we have an easy training regimen for the ground crew. There are only minimal insurance fees, since the loss incurred by any single catastrophic container failure is relatively minor. The silver-colored exposure sleeve enables virtually all-weather operation and repair, and the basic payload canisters cost less than twenty-five hundred credits per unit, when manufactured in bulk. And, when they are retrieved and emptied, they themselves can be converted into modular drop tanks for less than three hundred per unit."

Yaargraukh was also looking at the mass driver. "So the launch canister is actually part of the payload. Ingenious. But I must wonder at your choice of construction site."

"I do not understand." Astor-Smath's voice was mild; his eyes were unreadable.

Darzhee Kut picked up the topic; he had been wondering the same thing. "With respect, Senior Liaison Astor-Smath, the weather in this region hardly seems optimal for the operation of such a system."

"That consideration determined much of the driver's design. You will notice how it remains relatively low to the ground for as much of its length as possible: a precaution against storm winds."

"Still, its girth is greater than I imagined. It presents a large silhouette."

"The width you see from the outside is misleading. That's just the exposure sleeve, which protects the rails and accelerator junctures within, and allows workmen to walk or drive the length of the system even in heavy weather. The sleeve is lightweight and fully disposable. In the event of a typhoon, its sections are designed to tear loose and fly free of the mechanism, if the wind speed becomes dangerous to the entirety of the structure."

"So it is secure from the weather." First Voice pointed beyond the bunkers housing his warriors and out toward the remains of a charred *kempang*. "But it seems vulnerable to human threats." The other Hkh'Rkh looked along with their leader and, evidently saw something which caused them to rumble in agreement.

Darzhee Kut strained his multiple ocular lenses into the best distance resolution he could muster. He saw thin, burnt sticks angling skyward among the shattered huts and houses. He extended a claw. "What are they?"

Yaargraukh spoke over Graagkhruud's disdainful nasal guttering. "Launch stakes, Speaker Kut. And beyond, blackened shells of armored vehicles, cratered mortar pits, skeletons of burnt-out trucks."

Graagkhruud snorted. "I have read the after-action report. These humans were foolish to try cases with us. Our PDF systems intercepted their missiles and free rockets. Orbital fire eliminated their tanks and troop carriers. And then our warriors went among them like scythes in the reeds."

"An admirable fight, in which we too had a hand." Astor-Smath's comment was as calm as a maître d's invitation to be seated.

First Voice looked over at the human. "Tell me, Being, do you delight in aiding us against your own kind?"

Darzhee heard the trap in the words and the tone. Of the many human traits and behaviors that the Hkh'Rkh had found difficult to understand, the existence of individuals who would collaborate with invaders was the most difficult. But if First Voice unduly antagonized these key indigenous allies—

Astor-Smath sidestepped the trap that First Voice had laid. "I delight in doing whatever will end this war quickly, minimize the loss of life, and will allow my defeated planet to rebuild itself as quickly as possible. And as I remarked, this mass driver will greatly facilitate that rebuilding. So if some of our corporate security elements were able to better protect it by guarding your flanks and providing targeting information during your assault, we deemed it unfortunate but necessary to thusly take up arms against other humans."

Yaargraukh bobbed his head in the direction of a mass of ill-clothed humans—mostly male—who had

appeared from among the many low buildings and
warehouses that were clustered at the western extents
of the security compound. "Are they prisoners taken
during the engagement?"

"No, they are merely residents of the area. A few
are refugees, I believe."

"And what is their purpose?"

"Garbage collection."

Astor-Smath's reply was so unexpected that Darzhee
Kut supposed none of the Hkh'Rkh knew how to
frame a further, productive inquiry, either. Meanwhile,
a second group of humans emerged from the ground
floor beneath them, their loose, gray fatigues flapping
in time with the shoulder straps of the assault rifles
they were carrying at port arms. They angled toward
the motley group of locals, marching with a unison
and precision that bespoke considerable time spent
drilling on a parade ground.

"These are the—beings—who support our warriors?" First Voice's question was a *sotto voce* aside
to Graagkhruud that could nonetheless be heard by
all on the deck.

"Yes, First Voice."

"They all look—very similar."

Darzhee Kut stared at the humans more closely
and noticed what First Voice had called attention
to: all the armed humans were extraordinarily alike
in height, coloration, build. As they turned to close
with the ragged mass of civilians, Darzhee Kut had
the impression that their facial profiles were also
remarkably similar. Even for humans.

Astor-Smath nodded and smiled. "The First Voice
of the First Family has eyes that are as keen as his

intellect. Yes, they are not merely similar. They are identical."

"All of them?"

"All of them."

The Hkh'Rkh made noises in their chests that sounded like a combination of revulsion and nausea. "They are Unbirthlings," one huffed hoarsely.

"We call them 'clones,'" Astor-Smath supplied. "They make excellent soldiers, if for no other reason than they know no other existence. They are matured quickly and taught only what they need for the tasks that they are given."

Darzhee Kut listened carefully, decided he had not heard incorrectly. "These humans are not part of a family? Not taught to, to—harmonize with others?"

"They find satisfaction and a sense of belonging by performing their tasks excellently and in unison. They ask for no more than that."

"Because they know nothing else." Yaargraukh's comment was low and rattling, a dangerous sound.

"Which is why they remain happy and untroubled by needless complexities."

The clones, all wearing shoulder patches bearing CoDevCo's logo, had split into two columns, each flanking one side of the civilian throng. They escorted it at the double-time march toward the sickly-looking trees and greener slopes that were beyond the blasted *kempang* to the northeast.

"And they are going up there to collect garbage?"

"Yes, but not just typical refuse, Darzhee Kut. The ground there is regularly littered with scraps of soda cans and tattered mylar balloons."

"That is strange garbage."

"Not at all. It's just another part of the insurgency."

"How so?"

Yaargraukh interceded in a calmer tone. "To complicate any scans attempting to detect small metal objects, such as the enemy's ground sensors, booby-traps, or personal weapons. Looking down from orbit, or even from a loitering high-altitude observation drone, this rubbish produces thousands of sensor returns. We can sort some of them out as false signals, but it takes time, and there is usually too much uncertainty to act upon one of these signals without sending in a scout patrol to confirm the presence of a valid target."

"And already, the vermin are fond of ambushing those patrols." Graagkhruud's talons came together with an infuriated clack.

From behind them, the sound of an aggravated, oversized hornet rose, approached, shot overhead; a remote operated vehicle with a two-meter wingspan, four tilt-props, and a bulging belly buzzed after the receding trash collecting detail.

"To help them find the trash?" Darzhee wondered aloud.

"To make sure that there are no ambushers waiting to shoot the clones. And to spread chemicals."

More noise from behind—this time a growing crescendo of heavy, rapid footfalls upon the ramp from the ground floor—caused Darzhee Kut to turn about.

The troop of Hkh'Rkh had arrived, stopping at the head of the ramp when they saw to whom they were reporting. "First Voice of the First Family!" They were in a respectful, even awestruck, crouch immediately. The troop-leader rumble-whispered from his chest. "Permission to speak?"

"You have it, and you are to stand before me. You are warriors to whom we owe much—since you are the only warriors here."

Even though, as a member of the Ee'ar caste, he was trained to find harmonies with creatures radically different from himself, Darzhee Kut felt First Voice's dismissal of the Arat Kur war technicians as though it were a physical blow.

The Hkh'Rkh had risen, some of the younger unable to keep their tongues from wiggling out in a brief spasm of amusement at their greatest leader's backhanded gibe at their ostensible allies. *This does not bode well. If at this early stage, with matters mostly under control, there is so little harmony between us, what atonalities might arise along with serious problems?*

"How may we serve, First Voice of the First Family?"

"I see no Arat Kur with you. Are they not assigned to assist our troops?"

"They are, First Voice of the First Family, but only upon combat missions."

"What mission is *not* a combat mission in time of war?"

"The Arat Kur have—have a different concept of operations, First Voice of the First Family. They call this a 'security escort.'"

"And they are too important to aid you with it?" *Rubble and scree: more trouble?*

"No, First Voice. They may only conduct operations within their combat-suits. These are wondrous devices, but they need much maintenance, particularly in this climate where mechanisms foul and jam frequently. Thus, they are deployed only on missions where we have confirmed contact with, and intend to engage, the enemy."

The troop-leader's explanation seemed to mollify First Voice. "Very well. Perhaps we will have some opportunity to see these wondrous combat suits ourselves."

Let it please the first mother of the first rocknest: No. Please, no. The troop leader began detailing the deployment of the many Hkh'Rkh on the base and pointing to the less noticeable support systems, particularly the domelike PDF blisters dug in along with the bunkers, and in a ring around the vertipads behind them. Darzhee Kut looked after the dwindling quadrotor ROV and noted again the sickly color of the vegetation towards which it was headed. "Senior Liaison Astor-Smath, I would make an inquiry."

"Yes?" Astor-Smath, despite his smile, seemed to be even more bored than Darzhee Kut with the troop-leader's ongoing explication of interlocking fields of fire, overlapping intercept umbrellas, and primary and secondary fallback positions.

"The foliage to the north seems to be turning brown. Is this evidence of a blight?"

Before Astor-Smath could answer, Graagkhruud swiveled around. "No, Speaker Kut, this is evidence of common sense. You saw the remote vehicle that flew overhead?"

"Yes."

"It has a payload bay for chemical dispersion."

"You are defoliating the area?"

"We are. With new dispersions every hour."

"And First Delegate Hu'urs Khraam knows of this?"

"He approved it yesterday. Finally."

Darzhee Kut looked cautiously toward Astor-Smath. Again, no sign of concern on the human's face. "But why?"

Graagkhruud was the one who answered. "Why do you think? These jungles, particularly those close to our compounds and installations, are perfect lurking grounds for these human vermin."

"But thermal imaging—"

"Cannot reliably distinguish insurgents from the normal workers, or from the dogs, or deer or other creatures which abound in those cursed bushes. We have but one choice: to strip away the forests."

Astor-Smath finally spoke. "First Fist Graagkhruud is correct. This has been an observed principle of jungle warfare for centuries. Defoliation is a prudent step."

Darzhee Kut could hardly believe his audio sensors. "Mr. Astor-Smath, it sounds as though you support the idea."

"Support it? I recommended it, and actually commenced a more subtle campaign of it, weeks prior to your arrival here."

"But your world's biosphere—"

"—Has recovered from injuries far greater than this one. The defoliative agents being spread by your people are relatively safe, nonpersistent chemicals with which we have long experience."

"*You* supplied the poisons?"

"We refer to them as 'defoliative agents.' And yes, we have provided them, free of charge. One of our affiliate megacorporations produces them in bulk."

Graagkhruud's head rose up. "In a month, maybe two, we will have cleared a radius of ten kilometers around all of our compounds that are surrounded by jungle, old plantations, or high brush. Then these insurgents will have to come into the open to fight us. And that will be the end of their rural insurgency. But until then—"

As if proving First Fist's point, a rocket hissed up out of the sagging trees just beyond the ruined *kempang* and struck the ROV as it swooped low to begin its second spraying run. The wings cartwheeled away from either side of the smoky orange flash. The breathy boom of exploding fuel tanks rolled across the cleared ground, trembled and broke like a hoarse wave against the building beneath their feet.

By the time Darzhee Kut had reverse-scuttled so that his back was against the wall, and as far under the awning as he could go, the Hkh'Rkh were all involved in carefully choreographed chaos. Two of the troop had sprinted back down the ramp and took up covering positions at the entry to the building. The rest fanned out across the deck in the hunched crouch that was the Hkh'Rkh's preferred combat movement posture. In that time, First Fist had patched into the compound command net and begun giving orders. "All bunkers to combat alert status. Response team one to the marshalling area. Ready reserves and response teams two and three to groupment point alpha. Off-duty reserves to this building in five minutes: combat gear only, no heavy weapons, double ammunition load, autoinjectors loaded with stimulant, ready to embark. Attack sleds one and two to the vertipad with current armament, weapons hot." As he spoke, First Fist checked his weapon—a large-bore dustmix rifle with an underslung grenade/rocket launcher—adjusted his targeting goggles, and inspected First Voice's entourage of huscarles *cum* bodyguards.

Two of the Hkh'Rkh had unpacked a large weapon from canisters they had been carrying on their backs. They expertly snapped a light, simple tube into a breech-and-tripod combination. Two others unclipped large cassettes from their belts, handed them to the loader, who mounted them on either side of the breech. A fifth tossed a complex electronic sighting and guidance device. The gunner caught it, snapped it into place on top of the breech, slightly offset to the left. He checked that the aperture at the rear of the breech was aimed directly behind them into a open walkway. "Rocket launcher assembled and ready, First Fist."

Darzhee Kut quivered. *Their disdain of us is wrong, but their opinion of themselves as warfighters is warranted.* Oddly, the Hkh'Rkh seemed more calm, more temperate and organized now, than at any other time he had seen them. *Perhaps a life lived in anticipation of war makes war the most comfortable state of being.*

The troop-leader acknowledged a radio report, turned to Graagkhruud. "Response Team One is ready, First Fist."

Graagkhruud turned to his superior. "First Voice?"

First Voice nodded. "Send them. On foot."

"Foot, First Voice?"

"Foot. We have seen one rocket destroy one vehicle. More vehicles may bring more rockets."

Astor-Smath drew his palmcom away from his mouth. "The ROV was hit because it was too low for us to cover with the PDF systems. Attack sleds at fifty meters altitude should be quite sa—"

"They go on foot. Hold the sleds in reserve. Send up two more ROVs." First Voice pointed down at the clearing. "And let the response team's Arat Kur associates send their scouting machines out in a broad forward arc."

Following First Voice's extended claw, Darzhee Kut saw—trailing behind the broad, armored loping backs of the Hkh'Rkh response team—two Arat Kur combat suits. Heavy, armor-segmented, and with enhanced, biofeedback-directed limbs, the hexapedal units advanced, using an insane, high speed serpentine. Around each of the suits buzzed or zipped almost a dozen ancillary vehicles, some no bigger than a pancake. A pair of wheeled units, each sporting quad rocket canisters, paralleled it. They were almost as big as the combat suit itself. As Response Team One passed the perimeter delineated by the outermost of the bunkers, the two new ROVs buzzed overhead, widely separated.

Darzhee heard the approaching missile before he saw it, mostly because it was not heading across his field of vision but was vectored straight at him—or rather, at the closest ROV. Launched at an almost perfectly horizontal angle from the western slope of Gunung Sawal, it flashed toward the ROV in a ruler-straight line.

One of the PDF blisters spun quickly, made a noise like gravel being force-fed into a turbojet, and the missile came apart, the warhead detonating a moment later.

Astor-Smath turned, pleased. "As I said, the PDF systems—"

—suddenly came alive all at once, spinning and shooting as if they had gone collectively insane. From slopes farther north, on the opposite side of the mountain from the mass driver, a veritable torrent of white and gray plumes arced in towards the compound. Some discorporated into fluttering debris, others exploded, a few spun corkscrewing up or down into the jungle. The base's targeting arrays swept in tiny arcs, accessing, locking, engaging, accessing the next.

Graagkhruud kept his earpiece close with a single cupped appendage and gave First Voice a running report. "Most are free rockets, some are unarmed, a few are self-guiding. Launch rate is twenty per second. We've just about—"

Darzhee saw one of the missiles veer away from the compound, seeming to falter. He wondered if it too had been clipped, but then—as the final and most dense wave of rockets had the arrays twitching spasmodically, the missile suddenly cut back and came straight at them. His intestine squirmed. "I see—"

"Incoming!"

"It's inside the umbrella—!"

"Reacquire—"

Darzhee was sure he was dead as the rocket bore straight in upon them. There was a jarring report, falling debris, the smell of cordite—and he was aware that he, and everyone else on the veranda was still alive and unhurt, except for one of First Voice's personal guards. The large Hkh'Rkh staggered back a step, raising a suddenly clumsy claw to his chest. He had been transfixed by a thin spine of metal, evidently a grid-arm from a sensor array. The Hkh'Rkh looked down at it somberly—and fell over, blood torrenting out his mouth and the exit wound in his back. He had almost completely exsanguinated by the time the first of the other huscarles had reached his twitching body.

The group of them started at Graagkhruud's sharp command, "Leave him. He is finished. Guard and attend to your suzerain. This is not over."

"Shall we not avenge Kra Rragkryzh?"

Graagkhruud stared at the body. "How? And be not overconfident in presuming to take vengeance so easily. We live because we were not the target."

Darzhee Kut cycled his focal lenses. "Not the—?"

Astor-Smath nodded, pointed back over their heads. Darzhee spun, looked: the targeting array on top of the building was gone, the mast sheared off and blackened just beneath where the sweep armature had been. Astor-Smath was already giving orders to recalibrate the remaining two targeting arrays to create a smaller, but heavily overlapped umbrella of coverage for the center of the compound.

Graagkhruud growled. "You should release the bunker PDFs to autonomous fire and intercept, with priority for terminal defense."

Astor-Smath nodded, passed that along.

Darzhee Kut looked around, felt unusually confused and more useless than any other time that he could recall. "What happened?" he asked.

Yaargraukh heard. "The humans were not trying to destroy the ROV or us. They probably didn't even know we were here. They were after the main targeting arrays."

"Why?"

"Because they want to learn how to overwhelm our systems, how to saturate them."

Graagkhruud's assent was a chesty rumble. "And they have learned one way to do so."

"That rocket: there was one which curved in its flight—"

First Voice spoke. "I saw that, too. Very sophisticated. It tested the programming of the intercept computers."

Astor-Smath cocked his head. "What do you mean?"

"Speak to the Arat Kur technicians. I predict they will tell you that their system automatically prioritizes missiles which head directly toward the high-value targets within the defense umbrella: hangars, warehouses, construction depots, barracks, command and control centers. But that missile approached, veered, appeared to have malfunctioned, moved past us—but then had powerful boosters which allowed it to angle back in just after the humans launched their final, largest salvo. While our targeting computers were busy acquiring, then dismissing, and then reprioritizing that apparently malfunctioning missile as a target, the computers became backlogged with the sudden wave of new targets. It was only a delay of one hundredth of a second, but that delay allowed the missile to slip inside the engagement perimeter. And it removed our array."

"Which proves what?"

"Which proves, Speaker Kut," said First Voice, turning toward him, crest rising, "that if the humans could have done that two more times, we would no longer have central arrays, only the smaller tactical intercept radars integral to each of the PDF units. Inferior targeting and computing capabilities, minimal coordination, unacceptable duplication of effort. In short, the insurgents would have started scoring many more hits." He looked out at the slopes of Gunung Sawal. "Too many."

Graagkhruud signaled Response Team One, which had gone prone at the start of the attack, to resume their advance. Darzhee Kut moved closer to Yaar-graukh, who now leaned upon the handrail. "What do you think they will find?"

He wobbled his neck uncertainly. "Probably some abandoned missile racks. Judging from the fire-and-forget missiles the humans included in their barrage, several scorched trash cans, as well. They use them as disposable launch holders for the more sophisticated missiles that have integral or remote guidance packages. Sometimes our patrols find dead bodies; sometimes they find their own death. And before many more days have passed, they will encounter infiltrators from the more advanced nations. I'm sure they are here now. Probably organizing insurgency groups such as this one."

Graagkhruud snorted. "So far, it seems otherwise. We do get occasional reports—and corpses—of Indonesian military personnel who are leading these insurgents. But there have only been three confirmed incidents of them being led by foreign cadre elements. One Chinese, one Australian, one American."

Yaargraukh's tongue snaked out and back again. "Be patient; there will be more."

Darzhee Kut found it strange to be taking the side of Graagkhruud. "I am sure you are right in this, Advocate, but even if a few of them do run our blockade of this island, what can they do? Because we have remained within a limited number of cantonments and garrisons, we are all but impregnable. Our recon and combat drones, ROVs, and microsensors allow us to detect all threats long before they close with us. Our PDF systems intercept their missiles long before they reach us. And our orbital fire support immediately interdicts anyone foolish enough to fire such weapons at us."

Yaargraukh turned to face Darzhee Kut. "That all sounds most reassuring. Certainly more reassuring than what we witnessed five minutes ago."

Graagkhruud's eyes swiveled sideways in their protuberant sockets at Yaargraukh. "We have sufficient control, Advocate."

"I wonder," commented Astor-Smath. "Either way, I intend to take no chances." He spoke into his collarcom. "Recall the refuse sweepers."

Graagkhruud rose up. "No. They will continue."

"They might be killed," Astor-Smath pointed out diffidently.

"Then their blood will be on the claws of their own kind."

"Even so, First Fist, you cannot afford to have a massacre on your hands."

"Astor-Smath speaks truth." Darzhee Kut turned to First Voice. "Your wisdom is most wanted at this moment, First Voice of the First Family."

The aged Hkh'Rkh stared after the loping backs of the receding response team. Without turning, he spoke. "Advocate?"

"I agree with Speaker Kut, First Voice. The humans would consider such an event to be a massacre of innocents."

Graagkhruud growled. "It would be their own fault." He glanced at Astor-Smath. "It would be an attack by humans, upon humans, who were themselves impressed by humans. Surely they will not blame us for their own—"

"With respect, I must interrupt," Yaargraukh huffed,

"for time is short and the First Voice has asked for my judgment in this. The humans would not be surprised at the killing of insurgents. They understand that armed resistance invites death. But impressed civilians forced to serve our troops by clearing these fields, then taken under fire and killed? The average human will consider these people martyrs, regardless of the details of who technically compelled their service. For every one you kill this way, ten will swear a blood oath of vengeance and take arms against us. Maybe more."

"They will not. They will learn submission."

"With respect, First Fist, most of them will not. Their history teaches clear lessons on this topic."

"Yes. It teaches that the human generals lack the resolve to carry out punishments against insurgents inflexibly and invariably. It is their own weakness that makes this sound strategy a failure in their hands."

Yaargraukh's reply was calm. "I commend you to the annals of the German occupation of the Balkans under the Nazi regime, or the Japanese occupation of China and Southeast Asia during the same period. Consider also the tribal conflicts of less than a century ago in Africa. In each case, the conquerors showed no mercy. In each case, they carried out just such ruthless reprisals as the ones you suggest. And in each case, the occupied peoples mounted bitter and dedicated insurgencies. The humans will not submit: they will live to dine on our entrails, or will die trying."

"Enough." First Voice stood higher. "I am decided." He turned to Astor-Smath. "Recall your humans. Our combat operations must have utter political and ethical clarity. At least for now."

"Very well. With your leave, I must depart to oversee an unusual security matter in Jakarta."

First Voice checked his armlet. "Then you should make haste in your departure. You have twenty minutes left."

Astor-Smath smiled and bowed. "And before those twenty minutes have elapsed, I will be safely on the ground in our metro-center compound. Until we meet again." He turned and headed for the same high-speed VTOL which had brought him.

Darzhee Kut looked up at First Voice. "What happens in twenty minutes?"

"In twenty minutes, Speaker Kut, the humans will discover what happens if they choose to ignore our new terms for peace."

Chapter Twenty

Alexandria, Earth

Downing sipped at the last drops of water in his glass, sighed, checked his watch: 1940 hours and still no sign of Elena. He looked around the mostly empty restaurant. Despite Elena's claim to the contrary, Papillon was not only quiet, but almost abandoned. His table was one of only three that were occupied. *Right. This has gone on long enough.* Downing pulled out his palmcom, hit the all-address option, selected voice-only connection.

The multitone pattern on the carrier signal indicated Elena was being sought on all her data-contact lines. It continued its repetitive cycling of notes. Downing expected her answering message to take over after ten seconds, but it didn't. After ten more seconds, he hung up and stared at the palmcom, checked that he had indeed selected the contact matrix for Elena Corcoran. He had. But no answer.

Well, perhaps it was time to call the other Corcoran. If anyone knew what was delaying Elena, it would be her brother.

Trevor answered his vox-link on the second ring. "Hello, Uncle Richard. How can I help you?"

Trevor's voice was not quite as flat and cold as it had been when he left the office. But it wasn't much warmer, either. "Sorry to disturb, Trevor, but do you have any inkling of where your sister is?"

"She's probably shopping. She called from a sporting goods store about two hours ago."

"Still trying to find something for Connor?"

"Yes. Without much success." Trevor's tone shifted from cool to suspicious. "Why? What's going on?"

"Nothing that I know of, but she's rather late meeting me for dinner. Must dash now."

Trevor disconnected without waiting for a "goodbye" or offering one himself. Richard sighed, looked at his palmcom. *So where in bloody hell* is *Elena?* He chose her contact matrix again, waited to hear the connection go through.

Annapolis, Earth

Trevor stared at his commplex after disconnecting. *What the hell was that all about? And why is Elena meeting Richard for dinner when she told me she's coming by here with Connor later?*

He leaned back and frowned at the commplex. In times past, when she had just been a civilian, interacting with civilians, and doing safe civilian things, Elena had been at the greatest risk when she had been with Trevor or their father. They were the guys who had the clearances, and had performed the deeds, that might attract the malign interest of any number of unsavory folks.

But now that she, too, had become snagged into the clandestine webs of IRIS, and was carrying confidential, defense-critical information between her ears that was possessed by less than two hundred persons—well, it was no longer permissible to simply wave off strange behavior as some misunderstanding or anomaly. Now, it was only prudent to ensure that atypical communication did not also signal an atypical situation in the making.

Well, Trevor decided, *I can sit here trying to figure it all out myself, or I can take the short cut.* He called up his commplex's contact list, chose Elena's home commplex, pressed for a connection, and widened the video pickup to maximum.

Two buzzes and the screen brightened. The face that looked out at him caused a hard, aching knot to rise into his throat. At thirteen, Elena's son Connor was the spitting image of the pictures of Nolan at the same age. Trevor cleared his throat, smiled past the lump there, "Hey, Connor. I thought you had a game tonight."

"I did, but they canceled it."

"Why?"

"Beats me. Pretty weird. We were suited up and on the sidelines, but that was as far as it got."

"Well, that stinks. Although I have to admit, it's the first time I was ever glad I *couldn't* get to one of your games."

"I don't know how you get to any of them, Uncle Trevor. You've got a long ride in from Annapolis."

"Yeah, well, I hate to miss 'em. And given how many games your Mom and I both had to miss earlier this year, I know she must have been just as disappointed as you were when they canceled today's. By the way, is she around?"

Connor frowned. "No. She wasn't at the game either."

Huh? "Why? Where is she?"

"I wish I knew, Uncle Trev."

"What do you mean?"

"I mean, I had to get a ride home with Dave Sklar and his dad, 'cause Mom never showed. When I got inside, I found a note from her, telling me I was going to be staying with Grandma."

What the hell? "Why? Where's your Mom going?"

"I don't know; she didn't say. Her note only said that she had to travel on business, she loved me, and she'd be back as soon as she could. I don't think she'll be gone long. She only packed a single piece of carry-on luggage."

Trevor kept the frown off his face; no reason to frighten Connor. He was a pretty resilient kid, but he was still only thirteen. "So, what time did you get home?"

"About an hour ago."

Trevor did the math. Two hours ago, Elena had called him from shopping. She had sounded exasperated, nothing more. But over the course of the next hour, she had evidently gone home, arranged for their mother to take care of Connor, written him a note, and packed for travel. And now she wasn't taking calls from Richard, whom she had asked to meet for dinner. A dinner which was scheduled at almost exactly the same time she had said she'd pick up Connor from his game and drive out to Trevor's townhouse. What the hell was going on?

"Listen, Connor," Trevor said easily, "don't worry.

I'm sure everything's all right. I'll find out what's going on and give you a shout, okay?"

"Okay, Uncle Trev. See ya."

"Not if I see you first." The response satisfied the corny farewell ritual that they both cherished. "'Bye, Connor."

As soon as the connection closed, Trevor hit the commplex data string for Elena's palmcom and the rest of her contact-matrix. No answers on any network and no location information. However, just as he gave up, his own incoming data tracker toned twice. A text-only message had arrived.

He called it up. Strange timing. It was from Elena, but had been posted an hour ago. *An hour's wait? What was—?* Then he saw that she had put a one-hour delay on the delivery time.

> Dear Trev:
> Not much time; must run. I'll be out of touch for a while, but don't worry. Family business.
> Look in on Connor. He'll be at Mom's.
> Love, El

"Family business?" There was no family business. Just the unfinished business of Nolan Corcoran and IRIS, which always seemed to involve Caine and Richard and exosapients and skullduggery. And Opal. Yes, he could call Opal. She might know something. Besides, it was an excuse to call her.

He did, but after ten seconds of paging and receiving neither an answer nor a locator grid result, Opal's automated message came on. He disconnected. *Something has gone very wrong. Gotta call Uncle Richard*—and he stopped as his finger hovered over the "connect" button on the commplex's dynamic datapad. *No. Be careful. Think it through first.*

So what would trigger Elena and Opal to go incommunicado and at exactly the same time? What might link their actions?

Well, that was easy—sort of. Caine.

Trevor sat up straight. *After hearing about Case Timber Pony, they don't want to be able to get instructions or orders that they can't, or shouldn't, refuse to follow.* Opal, being Caine's guardian angel as well as girlfriend, and still unaware of Elena's connection with him, had probably decided to find Caine on her own. *Which is better than waiting for that harebrained rescue mission Uncle Richard is cooking up, the one that would probably get everyone killed.*

But Elena, too? She was no commando, to put it lightly. *And if she had decided to try to help Caine herself, why wouldn't she at least tell me?*

The answer was so obvious it felt like a slap. *Because she knows I would have stopped her just as surely as Uncle Richard would have. And commando or no, she spent a lot of time on pretty risky field assignments. Damn it, I'd bet dollars against donuts that she's en route to Jakarta, because that's where Caine will be, if the invaders decide to bring him planetside. And so, if I call Richard—*

Trevor took his finger off his commplex's datapad, closed the contacts directory. *If I give him the chance, Richard will order me to stay close until he can send me on Case Timber Pony. Or, if the invaders decide not to play diplomatic games, and IRIS gets lower on manpower, he'd hold me and my security team in reserve, as his last little trump card. Well, so sorry, Uncle Richard, but that's not how it's going to go down. I've got a prior commitment to help a young lady.* Whether he meant Elena or Opal was unclear, even to him.

He opened the commplex directory again, found the number he needed, called.

"How may I help you?" The Central Intelligence Agency never announced itself as such when called, not even on the secure, high-clearance traffic line that Trevor was using.

"This is Captain Trevor Corcoran, USSF, calling for Duncan Solsohn at extension 2454. My access code is U-uniform, S-sierra, D-delta one zero niner."

A pause. A new voice. "Sign is black gull. Four. W-whiskey."

"Countersign is low tide. Three. E-echo."

"Connecting." Then another new voice. "Hello?"

"Duncan, this is Trevor. I'm glad you're still on the overnight."

"Well, I'm glad one of us is glad about it. What's new, Trevor?"

"I need a favor."

"What's new about that?"

"Ha. And ha. Listen, I need a complete traffic trace: all messages sent and received, transactions, booking, transport records."

"Yeah, 'complete' means complete, last I checked. But 'no' means 'no.' You don't have anything like the kind of clearance necessary to initiate a request like that."

"You might want to review my clearance and security ratings."

"Yeah? Well, last I saw, you were just a—Jesus Christ, Trevor, have you started playing golf with God? How the hell did you get—?"

"If I told you, I'd have to kill you. Just get on the job, okay? And I need it fast."

"How fast?"

"Five minutes ago."

"Ugh. And who's the target?"

"My sister. Here's the data you're going to need—"

Chapter Twenty-One

CoDevCo security compound, Jakarta, Earth

Caine swayed in his seat as the CoDevCo shuttle braked sharply. Ground controllers had waved it away from the vertipads atop the twinned towers of the Indonesian Bank Complex and down into the courtyard-turned-landing field.

"We shall debark quickly," Eimi said nervously to the cabin in general. "No reason to attract attention."

You mean, "attract snipers," I think, Caine reflected as the vehicle jolted into a quick VTOL landing. He undid his straps. Rather than off-load through the passenger portal at the front, the silent Arat Kur troopers indicated the opening aft bay doors.

Following Urzueth Ragh, Caine stalked down the ramp into the thick, humid brightness of Jakarta and momentarily flashed back to debarking into similar weather conditions on Delta Pavonis Three. *Only a year and a half ago. It feels like a different life.*

Outward-facing gray-suited soldiers flanked the loading ramp as he exited. They were clones: all the same height, all the same face. It was a face he had seen before, staring impassively over Ruap's shoulder before the Parthenon Dialogs in Greece, and again, with a corporate factor at Nolan Corcoran's memorial on Mars. These identical faces in Jakarta were every bit as unemotional and alert as those had been. If any of the soldiers noticed his quick scrutiny, they either had orders not to react, or simply didn't care.

With the two Hkh'Rkh hulking at the rear of the debarkation line, the shuttle's passengers made quick progress to a nearby berm-lined enclosure of ballistic brick. As they wound through an anti-blast dogleg in the walls, the shuttle did a quick dust-off from the pad and headed southward. Its jets were shrill as it passed over them, growled and howled where their downwash buffeted against the berm.

"Now what?" asked Caine when he could hear again.

"We wait," Urzueth said simply. "We will be met by vehicles for transport to the heart of the compound."

Caine looked out the rear of the three-faced enclosure. There was, at most, an eighty-meter stretch of ground to be crossed. "President Ruap's government doesn't seem terribly confident in its ability to maintain order."

Eimi shrugged. "These are simply precautions, Mr. Riordan. You have nothing to fear."

"You're right, I don't. Mr. Ruap and his allies, on the other hand, seem more than a little nervous."

Urzueth Ragh might have sounded slightly testy. "Ambassador Riordan, please. These leading comments are becoming tiresome. Most—well, much—of the regular army has remained loyal to the new government. And with the assistance of thousands of armed personnel from CoDevCo's Optigene Security Division, President Ruap's ability to protect the country from both foreign and domestic threats is superior than it was before the change in leadership."

Caine glanced at the hastily built plasticrete walls that encircled the compound, the heavy weapons mounted high in reinforced sections of the main buildings. He did see regular army uniforms, but not many. And some kinds of uniforms were conspicuously absent. "And the Indonesian special forces? Have they shown the same loyalty?"

Urzueth remained perfectly still for a moment, then moved to look at Eimi. Who answered the question. "The Kopassus regiments have expressed—divided loyalties. We are taking steps to remedy that trend."

Caine tried not to smile. *Those last two words tell me the story you are trying to conceal, Ms. Singh. It's not that the Kopassus regiments simply split. They defected en masse. And that means that regular army defections are probably still ongoing. It's likely that you're bleeding your best soldiers into the ranks of the resistance. The career soldiers would be too smart to make their true sentiments known in advance, not when they're surrounded by political inductees who've been instructed to correct any sign of disloyalty with an immediate application of lethal force.*

"However," Eimi was continuing as three wheeled armored personnel carriers rolled toward them across the ruined lawn, "the Kopassus defections are a minor problem, at most. Our control of all the major cities is secure. The Mass Driver has experienced only a few attacks, all of which were driven off by our Optigene forces operating in conjunction with the exosapient security elements our new partners have loaned us."

Good God, can she really believe all that tripe? If Elena had been there, she would have torn apart each one of the CoDevCo flunky's specious claims with a mix of ironic wit and brutal logic. Whereas Opal would probably have just punched Singh in the nose. Both images made him smile.

"At any rate," Singh finished, "CoDevCo welcomes you to its temporary Jakarta headquarters, Mr. Riordan. And here are our rides to a more comfortable environment."

The three APCs had finished their approach in a wide arc so that, stopping alongside the group, their rear-loading doors were now easily accessible. One of those doors swung open with an overpressure hiss. Two soldiers in Indonesian duty fatigues hopped out, scanned the area, waved an all-clear into the belly of the vehicle.

The next two people who emerged were the new Indonesian President, Ruap, and R. J. Astor-Smath. Both of whom were smiling unpleasantly.

Astor-Smath extended a hand toward Caine, but at such a great distance that it could only be reached if Riordan walked over to take it. "While not an extraordinary honor, Mr. Riordan, this *is* an extraordinary treat."

"Can't say it's either, for me," Caine answered, looking at the extended hand and then looking away.

Ruap's smile widened. "This must not be the result you expected when you embarrassed me—us—at the Parthenon Dialogs this past April. I suppose you thought we were done when you sent us away like beggars." He waved a hand around at the cityscape. "But now, *we* are in control. At last, this planet will have real justice."

Caine decided not to mention that he knew enough about Ruap to be quite sure that neither patriotism nor a just redistribution of wealth were his motivations. He had gone to private schools in Switzerland from age ten onward, and rose to his position through the time-honored Indonesian tradition of blatant sinecure for the sons of the wealthy oligarchs who were still the nation's true rulers. Some, such as the late president, had even been relatively skilled at their jobs. No such accusations of competence had ever been made against Ruap, with one exception: he was rightly said to have a gift for the art of making deals. And he had clearly made one with CoDevCo which not only allowed him to outflank his duly-elected peers in Indonesia, but now put him in a position to dictate terms to the same World Confederation which had spurned his ambitions at the Parthenon Dialogs. Instead of mentioning any of this, Caine simply glanced around at their paramilitary surroundings. "Congratulations on being in control, Mr. Ruap—to the extent that you are."

"*President* Ruap," the squat man corrected, rising to his toes.

Astor-Smath waved aside the growing friction. "Mr. Riordan, no new pebble ever falls into a pond which does not also send out a few ripples. That's all you're seeing, here in Jakarta: ripples—and the Indonesian waters are growing calmer by the hour." He paused, turned to Urzueth. "Speaking of Indonesian waters, Esteemed Urzueth Ragh, have you repeated my concerns regarding the subsurface aspects of Java's maritime security to First Delegate Hu'urs Khraam?"

Urzueth bobbed. "Yes, Mr. Astor-Smath."

"And?"

Urzueth Ragh bobbed again. "And it has been taken under advisement."

Astor-Smath folded his hands and smiled at Urzueth. Caine was fairly sure, from Astor-Smath's tightly controlled eyes and mouth, that the megacorporate factor would have preferred to eviscerate the Arat Kur on the spot.

Urzueth bobbed his acknowledgment. "Honored Senior Liaison Astor-Smath, I assure you, we have deliberated upon the matter. We consider the submersible technologies possessed by your human adversaries to be quite inferior to ours, and fairly fragile. I agreed to make your case—again—to our leadership, but beyond that, there is nothing I may do, and so, no reason to persist in this topic. Indeed, we must see to the disposition of Ambassador Riordan."

At the word "Ambassador," Ruap glanced sharply at Urzueth Ragh, then Astor-Smath, who held up a calming hand. "Certainly. Although the, er, ambassador does not seem pleased to be here."

Urzueth Ragh cycled through the tail-to-head wobble that was the equivalent of an Arat Kur shrug. "His discomfiture is understandable. He witnessed the arrival of nonhuman military assets."

Caine raised his chin. "Which we call 'an invasion.' Another problem with translation, evidently."

"Oh no," Astor-Smath contradicted, his smile widening. "The problem is not in Arat Kur translation, but in your understanding, Mr. Riordan. You are not witnessing an invasion at all."

Caine raised an eyebrow, glanced meaningfully at a full troop of Hkh'Rkh who stalked past in their predatory stoops, their body armor adding a faint rumbling sound to their progress.

Astor-Smath's smile became archly patronizing. "Do not confuse guests—security advisors, consultants, and trainers—with invaders, Mr. Riordan. They came down at our invitation, on our ships. And their leaders recognize us as the means whereby Earth may achieve a legitimate and truly representational government. And so, become members of the Accord."

Ruap pressed forward like a dog straining against his leash. "Perhaps you and Admiral Corcoran should not have been so quick to turn us away from the Parthenon Dialogs, hey? Or been so disrespectful? Things might not have come to this."

Caine recalled, quite distinctly, that it had been Nolan's friend Vassily Sukhinin, the Russian proconsul and former admiral, who had truly been disrespectful—contemptuous even—of Ruap and Astor-Smath, prior to the actual Dialogs. But Riordan elected not to point that out. Instead he commented, "I wonder if your own troops are any more convinced by your legal fig leaves and casuistries than I am."

"What does it matter?" Ruap countered with a grin. "They will remain loyal. As will the whole nation."

Caine stared at the clones and the Indonesian troops cradling their rifles in assault-carries, the multiple doglegged vehicle checkpoint barricades, the hastily constructed walls hemming in the compound, the outward-facing machine-gun positions, the hubcap-sized tilt-rotor ROVs that buzzed in flocks along the perimeter. "Yes, Mr. Ruap, it certainly looks like you enjoy overwhelming loyalty from your citizens as well as your military."

Ruap darkened but said nothing. In the far distance, there was a brief tattoo of machine-gun fire. Two of the soldiers turned to glance in the direction from which it had come.

"Besides," added Astor-Smath, "Mr. Ruap may rely upon our clones, as well. And they have no conflicting loyalties whatsoever. CoDevCo is their mother, father, and extended family, all in one."

"Of course," observed Caine, "using them to slaughter unruly crowds leaves them nowhere and no one else to turn to, either. And I wouldn't be surprised if the image of their shared face hasn't already become a nationwide symbol for governmental ruthlessness and megacorporate treachery."

"Still the stirring orator, I see," smiled Astor-Smath as the gunfire resumed. "Feel free to inspire the lumpen proletariat from within the windowless confines of your cell—I mean, 'diplomatic apartment.'"

Ruap pushed closer. "Yes, 'Ambassador,' we will make sure that you have a great deal of time to think about what is happening here. And how you and Nolan Corcoran caused it."

At the mention of Nolan's name, Caine lowered his head slightly. If he didn't have to see Ruap's face, he might be less tempted to throttle the little turncoat. The renewal of gunfire, somewhat closer, caused three of the Indonesian soldiers to turn protectively outward.

Ruap had seen Caine lower his head, probably thought he smelled the blood of an emotional wound. "What? Feeling alone without your powerful friend?"

Caine turned his head away, tilted it lower. He couldn't see Ruap's face anymore, but saw his knees shift, his waist bend. Unbelievably, the man who was now the president of Indonesia was going to lean over and resort to petty, public bullying.

Ruap gloated. "It must be terrible to see all Corcoran's work—and all his lies—coming undone within a single year of—"

The gunfire intensified. Caine saw the rest of the soldiers' boots turn away as they faced toward the sound—and, almost before he realized it, he saw and seized the opportunity which that distraction presented.

Caine snapped back sideways at the waist and kicked out and up. It was the same kick he had used on the knife-wielding assassin on Barney Deucy, but, without the step-through, it had less power. On the other hand, although Riordan was not flexible enough to reach the head of most opponents, Ruap was short and had bent over.

Caine's foot slammed, heel first, into Ruap's mouth.

The Indonesian President-for-Life cried out. The guards turned, confused, weapons snapping down as Caine stepped back, hands raised, fingers spread.

There was the briefest instant of complete quiet, except for the distant gunfire. Then the tumult of contending voices and gestures began:

Ruap: "*Ngentot!* You bastard! You will die!"

Urzueth Ragh: "Ambassador! Desist!"

Eimi: "Mr. Riordan, do not make us—"

The larger of the two Hkh'Rkh security advisors from the shuttle stepped aggressively forward, and, in only partially understandable English, growled "Traiddtorr!"

Urzueth Ragh tried to wave the Hkh'Rkh back. He stopped, but did not give ground. The Indonesian troops had their guns trained on Caine while tensely watching Ruap, awaiting a verbal order, even a gesture, as to what they should do next. But Astor-Smath was, in contrast, relaxed and wearing a smile that was uncommonly broad, even amused, as he folded his arms and awaited whatever might happen next.

Caine chose to turn slowly to face the Hkh'Rkh, hands open and far away from his body. "I am not a traitor. I *punished* a traitor."

The Hkh'Rkh pitched his head back sharply: a negation gesture. "Lie. You struck your leader. To blood. I saw." The Hkh'Rkh edged closer, his firearm hanging loose in his grip, but the other hand rising, showing impressive claws. Urzueth Ragh's redoubled remonstrations and gestures went unnoticed.

Ruap sputtered furiously as he realized that he had lost one of his front teeth, turned to his troops, mouth open to yell what Caine presumed was the last human utterance he would ever hear—

—but the Indonesian was stilled and restrained by a hand on his arm. Astor-Smath's eyes, narrow and bright, were watching Caine and the Hkh'Rkh.

Caine swallowed. *He probably hopes the Hkh'Rkh will kill me and save him the diplomatic and public relations headache of ordering it himself.* Riordan stepped toward the Hkh'Rkh, arms still out. That surprised the warrior into a moment of indecision, during which Caine asked, "Tell me, Warrior, what do the Hkh'Rkh call a leader who pretends to a higher rank than he actually has?"

"*K'rek'zhum.* Or a fool."

Caine nodded, glanced over his shoulder at Ruap. Meaningfully. The Hkh'Rkh's eyes flicked momentarily after his.

"And, Warrior, what do you call any high leader— genuine or not—who lies to his people, or his Warriors?"

The Hkh'Rkh stopped and his crest rose slightly.

"He is *shk'vaag-gul*. It means"—he struggled to find the words—"'dung from the mouth.' But that is not right. Those are the words, but not the meaning."

Ah. "Perhaps it is this: He Who Speaks Shit?"

The warrior's crest lowered slightly. "This is right, I think."

Again, Caine looked behind at Ruap, then back to the Hkh'Rkh. "If you are so sure, then, that my blow was struck *as* a traitor, rather than to *punish* a traitor—if you are so sure you know the true state of affairs between us humans—then here I stand at the tip of your claw. I have not the might nor speed to resist."

The Hkh'Rkh paused, uncertain, glanced down at Urzueth Ragh. Who made wild motions for the warrior to lower his arms and step back.

Astor-Smath, evidently realizing that the Hkh'Rkh had been decisively diverted from his lethal intent, released his light hold on Ruap's arm with a look of disappointment.

Ruap, dark brown with rage, seemed ready to advance, then glanced quickly at Caine's feet, and kept his distance, instead. "You will pay for this, Riordan. You will—"

"Come now, President Ruap," soothed Astor-Smath quickly. "If you take such a hostile tone, our partners may doubt our ability to be good and patient hosts to Mr. Riordan. Who has, however, proven himself to be a dangerous person. Clearly, during his stay at our facility, we will need to keep him in his quarters except when he is on official diplomatic business." Astor-Smath smiled reassuringly at Urzueth Ragh, but when he turned that same expression toward Caine, it became a predatory grin, a dire promise that was as vindictive as it was unvoiced.

Caine managed to suppress his first genuine pulse of fear since landing in Jakarta. He turned toward Urzeuth. "I do not understand, Esteemed Administrator. I was assured by Darzhee Kut that I was to retain my status as a diplomat and remain attached directly to the retinue of First Delegate Hu'urs Khraam."

Urzueth Ragh seemed to fidget. "And so you are, Caine Riordan. But your fellow humans intuited our uncertainty over how best to provide for you, and so volunteered their services to ensure that your stay was optimally comfortable and secure. They will see to your housing, your feeding, your comfort, and your transport to and from our own compound in what was this nation's presidential palace."

"It is kind that you thought to make me comfortable in this manner, Urzueth Ragh, but I would much rather remain in the company of the Arat Kur. These humans are not my friends."

"No, but they are our partners, and they have given promises for your safety and comfort. Which you have abused by striking your host. You should be grateful for their forgiveness." Urzueth Ragh let the tone of remonstrance, and a single pedantically raised claw, sag. "Besides, the matter was arranged directly with First Delegate Hu'urs Khraam himself. I am powerless to alter it. So the matter is settled."

Riordan looked about the enclosure. Two Hkh'Rkh guards, two Arat Kur in combat armor, and half a dozen Indonesian soldiers. All ringed by clones. If he attempted to flee, he wouldn't live long enough to take a second step.

Astor-Smath stepped forward and smiled. "I am happy to have you in our facilities, Mr. Riordan." His smile broadened into a primal display of teeth. "More happy than I can say."

✧   ✧   ✧

Astor-Smath's entourage, minus the Hkh'Rkh, was waiting in the communications center to which they had all relocated when Caine returned from his sudden, escorted visit to the restroom. Astor-Smath turned to him, the same maddening smile on his face. "Quite finished, Mr. Riordan?"

Urzueth Ragh raised a desultory claw. "Ambassador Riordan had much need of what you call 'restrooms' during his stay with us."

Ruap's voice was dismissive. "Not surprising. I always heard that fear loosens the sphincters of cowards."

Caine pretended disinterest in the gibe. *That same sphincter is also "loosened" by my need to study the only room where I might have enough privacy to figure out a plan of escape, asshole.*

Urzueth was offering further explanation. "Ambassador Riordan was almost killed during an explosive decompression incident while attending the Convocation. If I am not mistaken, it is not uncommon for humans to suffer this kind of intestinal—affliction—amongst other sequelae of such an event."

Ruap made a disgusted noise. Astor-Smath checked his watch. "Three minutes," he announced.

Urzueth Ragh made a gesture to the two Arat Kur guards. They powered down their combat armor, opened the hatchlike helmets.

Caine frowned. "What happens in three minutes?"

"You'll see." Astor-Smath smiled.

"Along with the rest of the world," added Ruap bitterly.

Urzueth looked up at Caine. "I will explain. Slightly more than two days ago, we—the Arat Kur and Hkh'Rkh—sent new terms for capitulation to your governments. In three minutes, the fifty-hour response deadline will have elapsed. If we have not received a reply by then, our leadership has determined that, rather than initiate further communications, we will deploy a nonlethal means of demonstrating that your governments may not ignore us."

Caine noted the precautions that were being taken: computers were unplugged, batteries were removed from palmcomps, and a whole bank of hall lights went dark. "You're going to launch an EMP strike. You have weapons that can generate a heavy pulse without an accompanying nuclear detonation."

"We shall. We do. The pulse is not as strong as the kind generated by a nuclear weapon, of course, so it will not affect shielded systems."

But most civilian systems aren't shielded, not even in hospitals, or on planes, or in skyscrapers, or at communication nodes, or... The list was endless.

As Riordan observed the ongoing preparations of his warders, he also found himself only peripherally observed. He palmed a fifty rupiah coin he had spotted on a nearby desk. Not like anyone would miss it, given its almost incalculably small purchasing power. But both his instincts and his training disposed him to see any object as a potential tool. And a humble coin could, in the next several minutes, prove to be an important, if imperfect, substitute for a screwdriver.

"Are we ready then?" Eimi asked, scanning the room with her trademark tentative smile. "We should leave as soon as—"

"I'm sorry, I have to use the bathroom," Caine interjected quietly. "Again."

"Well, that might be another embarrassment you'll have to suffer today, Riordan," Ruap snapped, dabbing at the hole in his smile with red-stained handkerchief. "I hope you—"

Urzueth Ragh lifted a claw. "President Ruap, sir. I apologize, but I cannot countenance this. And until I relinquish custody of Mr. Riordan to you officially, I must point out that his well-being and comfort is my personal responsibility. I may not, in good conscience, allow a situation to develop where the ambassador is compelled to soil himself." He turned to Caine. "You may once again use the eliminatio—er, the 'bathroom,' attended by an escort. Who will remain outside, as before."

"I appreciate your thoughtfulness," Caine said with a nod. "Thank you, Urzueth."

Who made a brief bob and gestured for one of his Arat Kur guards to accompany Riordan.

"No!" objected Ruap. "He must be guarded by humans, as well!"

"As you wish," agreed Urzueth in a tone that bordered on exasperation.

Ruap made a gesture to the sergeant in command of the Indonesian troops. The NCO smiled, nodded at the scrawniest of his men. "Djoko, you go guard the *bule* ambassador. Make sure he doesn't fall in." Laughter followed the small man over to where Caine waited. Once there, Djoko stared at the Arat Kur guard, at Caine, then pitched his head in the direction of the restroom.

The three of them left the rest of the group to complete their preparations.

Chapter Twenty-Two

Gunung Sawal mass driver compound,
Central Java, Earth

Graagkhruud put his hand to his ear. "First Voice, Jakarta reports the airspace is secure."

"Time?"

Graagkhruud checked his armguard. "Oh seven fifty-nine hours, local, First Voice."

"First Fist, contact GHQ and pass the word to ground all airborne platforms and power down all electronics, except hardened radios. We will send them an all clear in a few minutes. And summon the troop-leader to my side."

"At once, First Voice." First Fist began passing the orders, motioned over the troop-leader, pointed to First Voice. To Darzhee Kut, the summoned Hkh'Rkh seemed to grow in size: its barrel chest expanded, the slope of his species' natural posture disappeared.

First Voice evidently heard him approach. Without turning, he asked, "Troop Leader, how are you called?"

"Vrryngraar, of the Clan Skelekd'sh."

"Your clan is of the moiety of the Family Haanash, is it not?"

"My Clan does hunt in the lands of the Family Haanash, First Voice of the First Family. We are their vassals."

"You speak of the old ways in the old words. This is good. Remit your duties as troop leader to your second, Vrryngraar. You shall replace Kra Rragkryzh in my retinue after the human uprising is crushed. Until then, you are to lead my one of my elite hunter-killer Honor Troops, which I shall use to teach the humans of Jakarta the posture of submission. You will take command and commence your counterinsurgency duties immediately upon our arrival in the presidential compound."

"I hear and obey, my Overlord N'Erkversh, First Voice of the First Family." The Hkh'Rkh immediately loped away, calling to one of his troop.

First Voice looked after him, spoke to the other Hkh'Rkh of his retinue. "Remove Kra Rragkryzh's body to our shuttle." He kept one calar claw suspended momentarily, and then finished, "Gently." When the body was being moved, he swiveled his head slightly toward the rear. "Speaker Kut."

Darzhee Kut edged slightly closer to the Hkh'Rkh leader. "Yes, First Voice of the First Family?"

"Tell me, are your people usually punctual?"

"Most assuredly so."

"So they will not extend the deadline?"

"No, First Voice. Hu'urs Khraam gave the humans fifty hours in which to respond. That expires at oh eight hundred, local time."

"Good, for my patience is at an end."

Darzhee Kut heard a confirmation and a warning tone in his audio-insert. "So too is our wait. The attack is being launched now."

Annapolis, Earth

Trevor's commplex toned then peeped shrilly. The caller's number was suppressed. Langley, for sure.

"Hi, Duncan. What've you got?"

"A lot. What do you want first?"

"The weirdest shit you've found."

"Okay. First, the State Department was notified just half an hour ago that Elena Corinne Corcoran has received immediate clearance for travel to Beijing."

"*What?* How could she even get there, with ships overbooked since—?"

"Weirder shit, still. She has a berth reserved in her name on board a government—as in Chinese government—high-speed hull: Baltimore to Shanghai via transfer at the Panama Canal. That was just posted ten minutes ago."

"And how the hell did all this—?"

"I'm not done. Phone records for her palmcom: nothing unusual until about 6:40. Then it's like a cheap spy novel. Call to the Chinese Consulate. Return call from them four minutes later. Call to Beijing, World Confederation Provisional offices. Return call six minutes later. Call to a secure land line in China that we can't trace and probably would start a war if we tried. Which means she was talking with Someone Big. Possibly Ching himself. Seven-minute conversation. And about ten minutes after that, all the travel plans and clearances start blizzarding across the State

Department's night watch desk. Which called in the Deputy Secretary to verify it."

Who the hell did Elena know in the Chinese government? Had she struck up and maintained an exchange with Ching when, after Dad's death, he had called the family with his personal condolences? Or was Elena just trading on name recognition, relying upon the strong implications that Dad and Ching had crafted some pretty high-power agreements before the Parthenon Dialogs—and that they had grown to admire each other in the process? Or maybe both?

"Hey, Trevor, we're not done."

"Oh. Sorry, Duncan. What else?"

"Here's the real kicker. Just thirty-four minutes ago, her palmcom was—"

The line went dead.

Alexandria, Earth

For the fourth time, Downing waited for Elena to answer her palmcom. And waited. Then—after almost a full minute—he was greeted by the innocuous intonations of a prerecorded message. "Hello. We're sorry, but the individual you are trying to reach has discontinued service and has not registered any forwarding information. We regret any inconvenience this might cause you—"

There was a brief flash like distant heat lightning, hardly bright enough to be noticed over Papillon's subdued lighting.

"—and we hope—"

The line went dead.

So did Downing's palmcom and his watch. The

espresso machine guttered to a halt. The faux art nouveau clock over the bar stopped ticking. The light winked out on the cash register a split second before the overheads flicked off. Downing stood, knowing what he would—and did—hear next. There were several crashes in the street, cars suddenly drifting without control, carrying drivers who had forgotten the government's warning when the Arat Kur had first arrived in orbit: know where your handbrake is and how to use it. And there would be no active passenger protection devices deploying to save their lives. Here or in New York or Berlin or Tokyo or Beijing. He only hoped that the bloc leaders had listened to the intel warnings, or had seen it coming themselves, and stopped the trains a few minutes before the deadline had run out.

The waiter came to stand next to Downing and, for the first time, failed to offer him more water. "Some kind of power failure, huh?"

Downing shook his head. "No. Some kind of attack. EM pulse bombs. Probably a few miles up."

"What? I didn't hear anything—"

"You wouldn't." Downing hoped his smile wasn't as sadly patronizing as it felt. "These bombs don't really explode. They send out a wave of electromagnetic energy that overloads electrical systems, particularly if they're unshielded, operating at the time of detonation, or are connected to a large active power grid."

"You mean—?" The waiter dug frantically in the pocket of his black slacks, produced his own palmcom. "You mean—? Oh, man, they fried it. The bastards fried my 'com. That's just—just wrong. How am I going to get things done? How am I gonna call my friends?"

Downing looked at the outraged young man and tried not to smile. *You don't know the half of it yet, Sunshine. Just wait until you try to get the train home, cook some dinner, and turn up the heat.*

Downing turned and looked back out the window, saw a hint of fire growing at the nexus of a three-car collision two intersections away and noticed a few flakes of snow starting to drift down. *I hope it's not a cold winter. But either way, it's going to be the coldest* you've *ever lived through, Sunshine.*

Downing went to the door, got his coat while the staff stood gaping down the street and into the darkness around them. At least it wasn't going to take too long to get to San Diego by secure government train now.

Because, for the next few days at least, there wasn't going to be a lot of rail traffic in the way.

CoDevCo security compound, Jakarta, Earth

Beyond the closed bathroom door, Djoko could hear the *bule* Riordan groaning faintly. *Shit, I get all the lousiest jobs.* He turned and looked at his fellow guard. The Arat Kur—or Roach, as people were calling them—rotated to look back up at Djoko. *Disgusting.* He banged on the door. "Hurry up! We've got to—"

All the lights went out. The steady hum of the air-conditioners faded.

Shit.

From far down the corridor—the men's room had been quite a walk—Djoko heard his sergeant yell. "Hey, get a move on!"

"I can't! The *bule* is still in there."

"Well, make him come out. We're going outside.

Can't see to put the batteries back in our palmcomps. Hurry up!"

"I'm hurrying!" Djoko yelled back, and then muttered, "*Anda keparat.*"

Beyond the door, the toilet flushed and then the tap started running. Djoko was grateful that both of them still functioned. He had been unsure if any of the running water in the high-tech complex would work without electricity. *Well, any minute now, the* bule *will come out and we can—*

Beyond the door, the *bule* ambassador cried out: a yell of inarticulate pain.

The Roach's eyes rotated up swiftly toward Djoko. "Human needs help?" came out of its translator, accompanied by the faint chittering of its natural "voice."

Djoko felt himself start to sweat, probably more from nerves than the subtly rising heat and humidity in the dark hallway. What was he supposed to do? No one had given him any orders about what steps to take if—

The toilet flushed again and the *bule* was now either choking or coughing. Then he groaned hoarsely. "I think—I need help. I'm bleeding—I need—" There was no further speech, but a moment later, Djoko heard a heavy, limp thud beyond the door.

The Roach started, its eyes shifting toward Djoko. "You help!"

"I don't know—"

"You help," it chittered/spoke again. "I notify leaders." The oversized bug spun about and skittered quickly back down the corridor.

Djoko looked after it for a second, annoyed to take orders from an alien cockroach, then listened. Still no

sound—but the water, which was still running, had
started to seep out from under the door. *Ah, shit*—
He did not know what he could do to help, but his
sergeant would flay him skinless if he stood outside
and did nothing. He pushed open the door.

Almost complete darkness, except for a tiny spindle
of light coming from higher up on the far wall, just
above his head. He approached, feeling for the *bule*
ambassador with his feet, wondered what the light
was coming from. "Ambassdur?" he asked in uncertain
English—just as he discovered what the light was.

The *bule* had removed the grate covering the air
duct into the room. Two screws lay just inside the
exposed ventilation shaft. An escape? Except, now
that Djoko looked carefully, the duct was too small
for even him to fit into, much less a *bule* that was
easily six foot tall—

To his credit, Djoko figured out that the grate
removal was a ruse the same instant he felt a sharp,
hard-edged blow along the side of his head. In the
dark, he scrabbled at the sink to remain upright—just
before a hand grabbed his hair and slammed his forehead straight down into the edge of the sink.

✧   ✧   ✧

Caine felt the small soldier's body go limp. But in
the dark, uncertain of how badly injured the man
was, or whether he was actually stunned or feigning
it, Riordan took no chances. Dropping the blood-slick
grate, Caine once again slammed the poor fellow's
forehead into the sink before letting the body sink
to the wet, water-running floor.

Not much time for stumbling around in the dark.
First, grab his rifle. Damn, he must have slung it while

waiting and didn't unsling it before coming in. And the sling is tangled around his—damn, what sort of contorted position did he fall into? Shit! Let's see, if I move his arm—no, that's a leg—out of the way—

Caine reared up. *No time. You've got to run. Finding a way out will be hard enough. And a gun won't be that helpful. But wasting time trying to untangle it could get you caught. So get the hell out of here. Now.* Caine was out the door before the thought was finished.

Somewhere down the lightless corridor from which he had come, there were distant sounds of surprised, loud conversation.

Stooping slightly, feeling along the near wall with one hand, Caine ran the opposite direction into the darkness.

Chapter Twenty-Three

U.S. Naval Academy, Annapolis, Earth

The wind was coming straight up the Chesapeake. Although it was slightly warm for the season, the breeze made the tattered dockside flags snap straight out. Trevor looked up at the Stars and Stripes and Navy ensign, remembered the first time he had seen them here. Wide-eyed beside his father, he watched those flags flying free in a fresh wind, bringing vibrant life to the memorial foremast which had been salvaged from the USS *Maine*. Then, on his own Induction Day, he had seen those flags again, saw them as living symbols of the duty and honor, orders and oath, that were the seamlessly interwoven sinews of his new life of service.

He chinned down into his old, cedar-scented deck coat. That was all long ago and far away. He was only eighteen years older than he was the day he took his oath of service at Tecumseh Court, hardly more than half a kilometer behind him. But if time was measured by what you've done, seen, and lost, and if distance was a factor not of where you stand, but how far you've traveled to arrive there, then those free-flying flags of his youth were farther away than the few surviving scraps of the hull he had lost at Barnard's Star. *My only command: a module half-dead in space, briefly surrendered to assist the enemy with his communications, before scuttling. A brilliant career at the conn.* At least it had also been mercifully brief.

Not that there had ever been much chance he'd be posted to the Fleet, not after he had entered the Teams. The SEALs like their recruits brawny and Trevor's athletic background hadn't hurt. And since that was a rare combination with the cognitive aptitudes and tactical instincts he had already displayed, his course was set: a fast launch up through the officer ranks and JSOC assignments. Always busy, often exciting, sometimes challenging—but never what he had envisioned. Or maybe, it was simply not what Dad had envisioned for him. *Face it, Trevor, he was looking for himself in you—and he didn't find it. Dad was a good soldier and a great skipper, but more than anything else, he was an outstanding strategist, the kind that comes along two or three times in a generation. Maybe.*

Trevor squinted against a snowy gust, could just make out the approaching lights of the scheduled naval auxiliary. *Dad was all about people, plans, and politics. Me? I'm just a glorified, high-end grunt, specializing in machines and mayhem.* But maybe, right at this moment, grunts were exactly what was needed. All the plans in this world would not save it, not without enough boots on the ground to do the dirty work. *Then again, there's some work that's too dirty to do, if you want to remain human, if you want to be able to live with yourself. Pity you don't get that, Uncle Richard.*

The auxiliary—a tug-become-day-ship that had been pressed into service as a freight and passenger packet in the ad hoc coastal feeder system—loomed quickly out of the mist that had rolled in just ahead of it. Trevor heard the reassuring, steady sputter of an ancient diesel engine go into double-time reverse just before she lightly bumped the stanchions' improvised fenders. A preteen girl—lanky and in a grease-stained goose-down jacket—hopped over the gunwale and hooked the bowline over a bollard. The voice that came from the upper level of the pilot house drew Trevor's attention to a salt-and pepper beard and a seamed face that poked over the bridge deck's railing. "You're it? No more?"

"I'm it. Not a great day—well, night, for boating."

"True 'nuff. So why are you here? Suicidal?"

Trevor wondered for a moment. "Maybe," he admitted.

The Old Man of the Sea stuck his face farther out. "A man who takes that long to answer is giving the question some serious thought. I carry legitimate passengers, not walking death-wishes."

Trevor smiled, reached down and hauled up his footlocker in a single grab. "Oh, I'm legit. But I think I might be heading into a worse storm than this one."

"Oh? And where's that one brewing?"

"Java, if the weather reports are right."

The gruff act was abruptly over. "Long journey just to satisfy a death wish."

"Longer than you'd guess. My route is via the Caribbean."

The Old Man of the Sea leaned into the snow-spitting air. "I can get you down as far as Norfolk. That's the connecting terminal between the northern and southern halves of the emergency coastal feeder system. You can get a bigger ship out of there. Coast Guard hull, probably. All the way down to Jacksonville or Miami, usually. Beyond that, I can't tell you."

Trevor judged the height of the gunwale, decided to use the gangway. "There are usually some inter-force packets running Commonwealth exchanges throughout the Bahamas, and then down into the Leeward Islands. The Brits have commissioned some civvies to serve that route, I hear."

"Hope the civvies are still running after tonight's little surprise."

"Yeah." Trevor swung his locker through the hatchway into passenger's section, just aft of the pilot house. "Did the EMP bursts give you any trouble?"

"What do you think? I was dead in the water. But I was never so glad to have an old bucket like this one. She's such a simpleminded cow, that my little grease monkey there"—he nodded in the direction of the girl, who was already casting off—"had the diesel hand-fired in an hour. Radar's shot, though."

Greasemonkey thumped past gracelessly. "Yeah, but you know every light, every, buoy, even every house, from here to Newport News. The radar only makes you double-guess yourself."

As she rambled aft, he sent a scowl at her—and behind it, Trevor saw a poignant, even painful love for which the Old Man doubtless had no words. Trevor suddenly missed his own father so much that he wasn't entirely sure if the salt he tasted was from the heavy, sea-churned mist. "How much do I owe you?" he asked quietly.

"Just give me name, rank, serial. I'll submit to the government for credit. DC is supposed to pay us back, and they had damn well better do so, after mobilizing us for national service the moment all the aircraft were grounded." He eased the throttle forward, kept the engine unengaged.

"Lines away." Greasemonkey's shout was high-pitched and bored.

Old Man put the shafts in gear and heeled gently to port, bringing the sagging hull into a half-circle that would take her straight between the first pair of new, solar-juiced biolume buoys and into the waterway.

Trevor turned, looked back toward the Academy, at the foremast of the *Maine* that marked where the Yard met the Bay, briefly saw the flags before the mist closed over again, and wondered, *Why does this feel like the last time I'm ever going to see them?*

West-Central Jakarta, Earth

Caine didn't mind the dark, or the tight crawlways, or even the smells of stagnant water and much-rotted mold. However, the rats—large and ominously curious—were somewhat worrisome. But there had been little choice regarding an escape route from the bank complex that CoDevCo had commandeered as its headquarters.

As he fled, Caine reasoned that, judging from the hasty landing field provisions, vehicle barriers, and the curtain walls fronting the plaza, the megacorporations had not had time to turn the complex into a fully self-sufficient fortress, sealed off from the outside world, both above and below ground. And there would have been little enough reason to do so immediately. It wasn't as if foreign commandos would soon be infiltrating the warren of conduits, pipes, and localized sewer subsystems that made up a subterranean sprawl even more confusing than the street-level chaos of Jakarta.

So Caine had kept going deeper into the building, until, in the subbasement, he found what he was looking for, framed in emergency lights: a workman's access shaft into service crawlways that joined the banking complex to the essential services and resources of the outside world.

The worst aspect of Caine's subterranean journey was the inability to measure direction or even distance. He held as straight a course as he could, and philosophically allowed that he'd never have found side-branching passages in this Stygian darkness anyhow.

Ultimately, it was Caine's ears that provided him with the only navigational data he received during his long crawl alongside the PVC tubing that housed the power and data lines for the banking complex. After what seemed like several hours, he heard what he first believed to be the harbinger of his demise: a siren. But a moment's reflection made him revise that assessment. Any pursuers would be underground, too. Not exactly the environment where sirens were used or needed. And if it was above ground, it was unlikely the siren was being used by anyone pursuing *him*.

Another minute of crawling and listening provided further information. The siren was not sequencing through a variety of different alarm modes, as was the case with most emergency vehicles. It was a steady, repetitive sound, more like a car or a building alarm. That meant he had to be getting close to the surface, and to some opening that let in sounds from the street level. Caine felt a surge of renewed energy, and doubled the rate at which he wriggled toward the next corner.

The light and sound increased dramatically as he turned that corner and emerged into a funnel-shaped chamber roofed by a grate: a catch tank for flood control. A workman's hard hat lay in a corner, along with several tools, a pair of shredded work gloves, and rat-gnawed candy-bar wrappers. Either the construction crew assigned to this part of Jakarta's intermittently expanding sewer system hadn't tidied up, or had been swept away into the same bureaucratic limbo that perpetually undermined Indonesia's waste management efforts.

Rusted rungs fixed in the sides of the poured concrete hole led up to the surface. One of the abandoned tools, a long-handled pry-bar, was just the right lever to lift up a small section of the grate. Which Caine did, before peeking out onto the streets of Jakarta.

Burning vehicles hemmed him in, one of which was the source of the relentless alarm that he had started hearing long before. A fast patter of explosions rumbled in the distance, followed by a rush of VTOLs overhead, their fans screeching as they accelerated. In the narrow bar of gray, premonsoon sky over the street, a dozen ragged columns of smoke communed with the lowering rain clouds. Across the roadway, one storefront was burnt out, another was still aflame. The tar-stinking macadam was littered with broken glass, scorched roofing tiles, abandoned bicycles, shopping bags—and was utterly devoid of people.

Whatever else might have happened during Caine's long underground crawl, one thing was quite clear: Jakarta was now fully and ferociously at war. Which was certainly bad for Jakarta, but might be good for Caine Riordan. Before, he had anticipated emerging into a merely turbulent city where, as a foreigner—a *bule*—he might still have stood out. Now, he was in an urban war zone where order was deteriorating with frightening speed. A good environment in which to stay very, very lost. He levered the grate up enough to wriggle out. He just might manage to elude the clones and soldiers and Arat Kur and Hkh'Rkh long enough to get away—

But as soon as he stood up, he heard hissed exclamations from the buildings behind him:

"Look! Quick, aim at the—"

"No, don't shoot."

"He's wearing gray; he's a clone!"

"No, idiot! That's dust!"

"Hey! He's a *bule*!"

Louder: "Hey, *bule*! Get down! You stupid or sumthin'?"

Caine dropped, looked around, didn't see anything, started crawling toward where he had heard the voices.

"No, *bule*, over here. More to your left. Yeh, that's right. We're in the hardware store."

Caine glanced up, still couldn't see anything. *How the hell are they seeing me when—?*

Then he saw a glint through the hardware store's shattered display window: the fragment of a mirror, propped up on a display rack. *Huh, pretty clever.* And for the first time in many hours, Caine smiled. As a military analyst, he knew his history, and from this one sign—from the hasty innovation of using a mirror to watch for the approach of enemies while remaining hidden—he felt fairly certain that the invaders would soon learn just how difficult it was to be an occupation force trying to control a nation in Southeast Asia.

Of the five Indonesians in the store, the oldest, middle-aged Teguh, spoke fair English. Two of the others had a smattering of it. They were all nervous, angry, and—surprisingly—armed. The weapons were old, cartridge-firing rifles. Caine stared, frowned, and suddenly recognized the manufacture—but not due to his years reviewing international weaponry for *Jane's*. Rather, he recalled the gun from images he had flipped through while researching military history. "That's—" he said, pointing in surprise, "—that's a, a—Kalashnikov. An AK-47. How'd you get that? Indonesia never—"

"Lissen, *bule*. I don' know why you so interested in the gun, but it says 'Type 56.' Right here, see?"

"That's just a Chinese AK. Where did you—?"

"*Bule*, pay attention. You in a war, here. Where we got these guns don' matter—"

"Actually, it does matter." Something in Riordan's voice made them look at him differently, like there was now a better-than-even chance that he wasn't crazy. "Let me guess. Someone gave the guns to you. Passed them out from the back of a truck or up from a cellar or something. Was giving them out to whoever wanted them. Am I right?"

The Indonesians looked at him askance again, but now it was as if he had pulled a rabbit out of a previously unseen top hat. "How you know that, *bule*?" Although no one raised their guns, Caine noticed their hands had grown more tense, stayed very near the trigger guards.

"Because I worked as a military analyst. And here's what I know about that gun you're holding. Indonesia never adopted the AK. Your country used—er, Pindad assault rifles. And I also know that no major power has used an AK for fifty, maybe sixty years. They're still used by some backwater warlords, but most of them are just gathering dust in reserve armories for national militias." He smiled. "Until now. When they just happened to be here to arm a resistance movement." Thanks to Nolan Corcoran.

"Why you smilin' like that, *bule*?"

"It's not important. Not compared to what's going on around here. About which I know nothing."

Teguh swept a hand at the street. "Is like a crazy house, man. It was pretty bad before. Lots of rioting ever since the president was killed and that *keparat* Ruap took over and brought in these clones. More when these aliens showed up. Not a lot of them at first. Mostly the Roaches. But since yesterday, we been seeing these big Sloths, and they jus' as bad as the clones. Maybe worse. If someone shoots at them, they kill everyone around. Unless you lie down in the road. An' who stupid enough to do that? You run 'way! But when you run, that's when they kill you. And if you do lay down in the road, a lot of times the clones kill you. It's crazy, man, pure crazy."

"Did the clones and, er, Sloths, just start killing people for no reason?"

"No," said one of the younger ones. "That started after the power went out. Everything stopped working. They warned people not to use anything electric but, you know how it is: no one paid a lot of attention.

And hey, *everything* is electric. So all 'a sudden, there are elevators falling down in buildings, cars going out of control. No phones, no computers, no way to buy anything." He shook his head. "And after the massacres over the past few days, well—people had enough. They went a little crazy. That's when the clones came out, along with their new friends. And the army just stood by while those *tukang ngentots* shot anyone who protested, anyone who got angry."

The older man nodded. "Yeah—and then, the word started going 'round there were free guns being given out by soldiers who deserted when the real president was killed. Most just showed up on trucks. People took them, took ammunition." He hung his head. "Not everyone shot the clones or the aliens. At first, a few held up stores for money. But then more and more started stealing food, 'cause there's not much left. It was bad, very bad."

The youngest one nodded his head. "Yeh, but mostly, people started attacking the clones and the aliens and any soldiers who helped them."

"All that in just two or three hours?" Caine asked.

"Well," said Teguh, "more like seven or eight hours."

Caine found it hard to believe he'd been underground that long, but looking at the darkening sky, realized his error.

"And then, about an hour ago, they started bombing neighborhoods. Anyplace there was fighting they couldn't control, they just—" Teguh shook his head. There were tears in his eyes. "I don't know who's left. My family, my neighbors, my friends, I know a lot are dead. But that's *all* I know."

Caine nodded slowly, spoke softly. "I've seen them

bombing, even before the power went off." He looked around the group. "But why are you here?"

Teguh looked even more distraught. "Because they trapped some of my friends—rebels, *real* rebels for a week already—in a building. We were looking for a way to help them, maybe get around behind the Roaches and draw them off—long enough for our friends to find a way out. But—" His voice failed.

The next oldest picked up the tale. "We had to hide in here. There were aerial ROVs—small ones—going up and down the street, looking for anyone with guns. Some people shot at them from the store across the road—"

Caine nodded. "So the ROVs backed off. And about twenty seconds later, a couple of rockets slammed down into the store and blew it to pieces."

"Yeah. Like you say. Hey, you a soldier?"

Caine hoped he didn't blush. What was the truth? Was he a soldier? A piece of paper, probably reduced to ashes now floating in orbit around Barney Deucy, said he was. But the real truth was that he wasn't: that had just been a bit of legitimated theater to ensure that he'd have a rank if he needed one. "No, I'm not a soldier. I've just had a little bit of training," Caine explained. "A very little bit."

"Hey, dat's better than us," said Teguh, looking up eagerly. "Maybe you can figure something out, hey? Help my friends?"

If the day had been any less absurd, any less surreal, Caine might have demurred. But with a city burning down around his ears, and surrounded by five eager faces that were, for the first time since he had met them, illuminated with something like a faint glow of hope, he could only say, "Let's go take a look."

Chapter Twenty-Four

West-Central Jakarta, Earth

Caine leaned the fragment of mirror around the dangling remains of the window frame, resolved to get a better look.

The Arat Kur ROV was a ground-pounder. It was far too heavy to go airborne, and improperly shaped to have a live operator inside. Its narrowest point was much thinner than an Arat Kur was wide.

"Is it a robot?" asked Teguh.

"No, I think it's an ROV with an expert-system back up."

"What's that mean?" asked one of the younger Indonesians whose long, mellifluous name Caine had learned, and promptly forgotten, three times now.

Caine watched the slow, cautious advance of the Arat Kur unit, its two microturrets rotating protectively through rear- and flank-covering arcs. "Reporters like to call ground-drones like this 'AIs,' but there's no intelligence involved. Just very sophisticated algorithms that allow the machine to operate independently for a short period of time."

"Huh," nodded Teguh. "Yeh. I can believe that."

"Why?" Caine asked.

"Well, these, eh, expert systems don't like to go into stone or concrete buildings. They won't chase anyone inside. Which makes sense."

Caine smiled at Teguh. "You're right. Stone and other dense construction materials block signals. And the machine shouldn't stay where it has to rely upon its own very limited expert system."

Teguh shrugged. "Sounds like a weakness, to me."

Caine smiled. "Me, too. Let's go. I have a plan."

❖   ❖   ❖

"You sure this a good idea, *bule*?"

Caine wanted to answer *hell, no!* but instead said, "I'm pretty sure it will work, as long as you're certain these expert systems don't shoot at unarmed humans."

"Haven't seen them do it yet, and they've had plenty of opportunities since this afternoon."

"And you're sure they have a capture mode?"

"Yeah. Like I told you, we've seen these robo-Roaches come into areas where rebels or rioters have been making trouble. They find some older kids, do a spider-sprint, and grab them. Then they carry 'em back to the Roach Motel—"

"The what?"

"The aliens' compound. They took over the Presidential Palace. So, the Roaches ask the kids questions about anyone they know who might be a rebel. Always with an officer from the army standing there"—Teguh spat—"but then they let 'em go. Scares the shit out of the kids, but they've never been hurt."

Well, that's reassuring. Sort of. "Okay, then. Are your people ready?"

"Sure they are. Question is: are *you* ready?"

Again: "hell no!" "Yeah. Here goes." Caine ducked low and scooted out, under the level of the cars parked along the street. He peeked out at the Arat Kur ROV. It was still creeping forward, aware that its prey—Teguh's trapped friends—had moved farther down the dead end street and were now unable to escape. But precisely where was that prey hiding?

Well, here's something new to think about. Caine rose slowly from his hiding place. He walked, hands open, closer to the Arat Kur ROV but also angled toward the looted and gutted stone bank across the street.

The Arat Kur unit's rear sensors detected him immediately. One of the microturrets fixed upon him, the other began sweeping the unit's rear, laboring to keep nearby upper stories and rooftops in its defense footprint.

C'mon. Call your boss, and find out what to do. And who I am.

The Arat Kur unit was utterly motionless for two seconds, and then—so suddenly that Caine's stomach clenched and plummeted—the multilegged device whirled about and came at him with startling speed.

Caine had been expecting the charge, but still felt terribly slow as he turned and sprinted into the bank, sure that, at any second, he would feel the Arat Kur equivalent of a taser probe dig into his back and sprawl him, twitching, across the debris-littered sidewalk.

But he made it through the doors into the bank and heard, just behind, the clatter of the ROV's legs break stride. Caine didn't stop: the unit's apparent indecision was merely a split-second pause as it waited for an override signal.

Caine, now in the hall leading into the bank's interior offices, was glad he hadn't broken his own stride. He heard the ROV resume its skittering approach, the bank's broken picture windows scraping and screeching as the spiderlike legs smashed and dashed them aside in its crazed pursuit. Riordan reached the yawning freight elevator shaft at the end of the hall, grabbed the knotted rope that was hanging there, heard the ROV right behind him. He turned, saw the taser-dart dispenser on the front of the robotic arthropod snap open—

—just as three of Teguh's young Indonesians, waiting two stories overhead, dropped a small, jury-rigged counterweight. Caine, clutching the counterweighted rope, blinked at the rapidity of his upward acceleration and was both terrified and gratified to see the mechanical spider leap into the open shaft beneath him. Slowly but steadily, it began ascending, its legs spanning from wall-to-wall.

As soon as the three young Indonesians grabbed Caine off the ascending rope, he nodded to a fourth, slightly older one. That fellow was waiting with bolt-cutters poised upon the elevator's own counterweight cable, and at Caine's nod, he closed the cutters with a snap.

The steel ring that cinched the upper part of the elevator's main cable to the lower half squealed and sparked as the bolt-cutters sheared through it. Released from the counterweight in the basement, the car of the freight elevator, waiting two stories farther up, began rushing down.

The mechanical spider paused, sensors rotating upward to investigate the new sound—

—right as the car crashed into it and powered the

flailing unit all the way down to the bottom of the light-less shaft. Their joint plummet ended with a smashing sound akin to a head-on collision of dump trucks.

By the time Caine got down to the basement to inspect the remains of the Arat Kur expert system with bolt-cutters in hand, Teguh was already there, along with his friends who had been trapped at the end of the street. And entering at the same moment as Caine did was a rangy, muscular man in camos and a red beret: a defected Kopassus officer.

Caine scanned the insignia of rank, tried to remember it from his days at *Jane's Defense Weekly*, guessed. "Hello, Captain. I wasn't aware these are your men."

The officer stopped, stared up at Caine. "We have no formal organization." He looked at the broken Arat Kur unit. "I understand this is your work."

"Me? Hell, Captain, we all—"

"Please. Your modesty and desire to include these men is admirable, but I must know: Was this your idea?"

Before Caine had decided how to respond, Teguh piped up from the second rank of onlookers. "You bet, Captain Moerdani. This one smart *bule*. He has training."

Oh good Christ—

The captain glanced at Caine sharply. "Is this true? You are a soldier?"

"No, Captain. I have *some* training. Very little, to be honest."

"Hmm," he mused, looking at the smashed ROV again. "You seem to have enough. Now, before the enemy can—"

"Captain, a moment, please. I left my young friends back on the third floor for a reason. They should have rethreaded the part of the cable connected to the top of the elevator, now."

"And why did you have them do that?"

"To lift it up a few feet."

"What? Why do—?"

"Captain, with your permission, it will take less time to show than it will to explain."

The captain considered a moment, then nodded.

Caine leaned into the shaft and shouted. "Winch it up on three, okay?"

"Okay, Mr. Bule," said a distant voice from higher up the shaft.

Caine turned to Teguh. "Can your friends bring a few of those broken blocks over here? We'll need them to jam under the elevator car." By the time Caine was done making the request, half of the needed stonework was at the ready. He looked up the shaft. "One, two—"

On "three," the freight elevator car groaned off the Arat Kur ROV. As Caine had suspected, it was nowhere near as pulverized as an analogous human unit might have been.

The captain's voice was low. "Are you sure it's—dead?"

"Pretty sure, but let's be certain." Caine lifted the bolt cutters, started snipping selectively at a side panel connected to the top of the thorax.

"Why are you cutting there?" the captain asked.

Caine explained as he continued to cut away at what looked like a mostly recessed hinge. "When we build ground-ops ROVs like this one, we know they're going to take overhead fire. Lots of it. So we don't put the sensitive electronics up under the dorsal surface. We snug them underneath, in the belly. I'm guessing we'll get a look at its brains once we release this ventral piece." With one last clack of the bolt-cutters, the rear belly plate of the unit sagged away from the rest of the carapace, revealing a mass of electrical components, most of which were still in reasonable condition. "Captain Moerdani, do any of your men have any expertise in computers?"

The captain pointed to one of his youngest followers, who came forward quickly, eyes and hands eager.

"What should I do?" he asked Caine.

Who smiled. "Damned if I know. I'd just yank all its guts out."

"Why?" said the young man. "That could take some time." He looked back at his captain.

The entire group had now gathered around Caine, eyes bright with the victory they had just won. But their Kopassus CO was checking his watch. *And probably waiting to hear me explain why it is worth the risk to stop and disembowel this Arat Kur ROV. So I had better make every word of explanation count.* "Jakarta did lots of electronics and computer work up until three weeks ago. Tell me: how many of you know unemployed IT whizzes who are pissed at the government, who'd like to hack its systems, maybe try to get access to the invaders' own code?"

The young fellow nodded, a slow smile starting to spread across his face. "Most of them."

"And what do you think they could learn from the command and communication circuitry and processors of a remote-operated Arat Kur unit equipped with an extensive expert-system backup?"

The young man's smile was now very wide. "A whole lot, *bule*. They'd get a real good look at Arat Kur engineering. Prob'ly begin to play with Arat Kur programming languages. Either way, this is what they'd need to get started on that kind of work."

"That's what I was thinking."

Captain Moerdani looked up from his watch, said something in the flowing-water syllables that were characteristic of Javanese. Several of his men nodded, hefted their rifles up into assault carries, and spread out into the street, ready to scout the route of withdrawal. Then the captain turned toward Caine. "We're leaving as soon as young Hadi is done cutting out the key components. You, too. You're coming with us."

Caine shook his head. "I don't know if that's a good idea for you and your men, Captain."

"Why is that?"

"The Arat Kur might come after me. Hard."

"Hmm. Yes. I'll want to ask you some questions about that later. But whatever interest they have in you, they clearly want to capture, not kill you."

"Yes, well, they're probably the *only* ones who don't want me dead. On the other hand, your army, the clones, the Hkh'Rkh—"

"The what?"

"Uh, the Sloths. They *all* want to kill me."

Teguh smiled at him. "That means you'll fit right in with us, *bule*." Teguh looked up the fifteen-centimeter difference in their height. "Well, you *almost* fit in. Just hunch over some, and you'll be fine. Now let's get outta here."

Presidential Palace, Jakarta, Earth

When Darzhee Kut's shuttle landed in the courtyard of Jakarta's Presidential Palace, Urzueth Ragh was waiting. It was clear from his posture that he had unpleasant news.

Darzhee Kut bobbed at him. "What sad notes would you sing to me, rock-sibling?"

"Chaos and crashing, Darzhee Kut. I have failed. The human ambassador, Caine Riordan, has escaped."

"Yes, I know. I received reports from our human partners. But their phrasing is that Riordan attacked President Ruap and then *fled*. You say *escaped*, which implies that he did not merely depart, but was imprisoned at the time he did so. What occurred between him and our human allies?"

Urzueth told him. Darzhee Kut flexed restless mandibles. "Hu'urs Khraam was hasty, I think, to accept Senior Liaison Astor-Smath's offer to provide Caine Riordan's accommodations."

"I have thought the same thing, rock-sibling. I did not know it before I witnessed the exchanges between them this afternoon, but I suspect that Riordan's first night in CoDevCo's care might very well have been his last."

Darzhee Kut bobbed slightly. "It is pertinent to recall the many nearly fatal mishaps and mysterious attacks Riordan has endured in the past year. If he should be apprehended, it is imperative—*imperative*, Urzueth Ragh—that he be brought to our compound. As he requested."

"We sing the same song, to the note. I will go and pass the necessary word and then meet you at Hu'urs Khraam's briefing within the hour."

"Just so." Darzhee exhaled his familiar farewell and proceeded into the residential wing of the presidential compound—

—but got no farther than the vestibule. Two technicians from the Remote Security Assets section were waiting there. "Speaker Kut," said the smaller and slightly older one. "During our watch it is customary that we report any noteworthy successes, failures, anomalies to our superiors. They then indicate to whom we should direct news of such an event. Today we had a most unusual event, and our superior indicated that we must report it to you. Directly. Without revealing it to any of our nestmates."

Darzhee Kut grew cautious. "I thank you for your discretion. Now, what manner of event was this?"

"It was a failure, sir. Or an anomaly. Actually, both."

"Please explain."

"We lost an automated patrol and security unit today, Speaker Kut, under unusual circumstances. Here is the report." He deferentially passed a data tablet to Darzhee Kut who scanned down, and, before reaching the end, knew what he would see. "So you later discerned that the human you sent it to capture was Caine Riordan. And this was achieved with the biometric technology provided by the megacorporations? Excellent. You are sure that, at the end of the incident, Riordan was still alive?"

"Yes, Speaker."

"You have done excellent work. I thank you for your attentiveness."

"Speaker Kut, there was a further anomaly we did not add to the report, but which you may see below, in this separate file."

"Why did you not include this further anomaly in the official report?"

"Firstly, because we only learned of it after our shift of duty was concluded. But on consideration, we reasoned that it should not be shared in any data medium that may be seen by many eyes. Perhaps not all of which belong to our own species."

Overcoming his surprise at the subtlety of the technician, and faintly trepidatious as well, Darzhee bobbed his appreciation and asked, "What was this anomaly?"

"It involves the fate of the expert system security unit we lost, Speaker Kut. There were evidently other humans waiting in or near the building in which it was ambushed. Because after they disabled the unit, they disassembled it."

"They what?"

"Disassembled it, Speaker Kut. Partially. Although inoperative, the unit's electronics were mostly intact, and the humans removed them."

Darzhee Kut resisted the urge to retract his antennae. "I thank you for your report. I shall include parts of it in my briefing to First Delegate Khraam. Know that you have served the Wholenest most admirably in this matter and your names will be sung in harmony with the presentation of this datum. But be warned. You must share it no further. You have touched upon a sensitive matter that must be handled discreetly."

"Of course, Speaker Kut. We are honored to have our voices sung."

"And so they shall be." With a polite bob, Darzhee Kut turned, and felt the world spin and reorient all in a single second. Caine Riordan had started the day

in a safe ambassador's berth, had almost been killed
planetside, had escaped, had then met up with local
rebels, was then almost recovered, but then—

Although Darzhee Kut lacked the facts to prove it,
he knew that Riordan had not merely fled from the
unit that was destroyed, and had not merely tried to
distract if from the rebels it had trapped at the end
of that dead-end street. He had put himself out as
bait. He had correctly reasoned that the Arat Kur
were watching for him, that the unit would attempt
to capture him, and that he could thus lure it into
a trap that left it intact enough for the insurgents to
lobotomize it. By now, they had surely passed the
unit's command and control package to their own
experts for analysis.

That much—that compromise of Arat Kur electronics and computing technology—Darzhee Kut had to
report. But he could not mention Riordan's name. If
he did, it meant that the human's status as a diplomat
would be revoked. In short, it would mean issuing a
death warrant for Riordan.

But a further question presented itself. Even if
the finer details of this incident remained obscure,
what would Riordan do next? Something else that
was particularly troublesome? And if so, was it not
inevitable that both the Hkh'Rkh and the Arat Kur
would endeavor to localize and eliminate such a
threat—regardless of whether they had learned the
threat was named Caine Riordan?

Darzhee Kut felt a twinge through the center of his
body: that must not occur. Not simply because Caine
had had no choice but to flee, and once fled, had little
choice but to fight back. More importantly, he, alone

of all humans, truly seemed to harmonize—at least in part—with the rockheart of the Arat Kur. And in that harmony lay the possibility of communication, of a cultural bridge, by which the war could be stopped, a settlement reached, a peace established. But without that harmony—

In the streets, Darzhee Kut heard several rockets explode. Dust shook down from the absurdly high ceilings beneath which he stood motionless. Without Caine's tendency toward harmony with the Arat Kur, this might be the only future both races and their coming generations would ever know: war.

Endless, savage, senseless war.

Chapter Twenty-Five

Nevis, Caribbean, Earth

The tiny, archaic wharfside in Nevis' one port, Charlestown, hadn't changed much from Trevor's last visit eight years ago. Admittedly, there were more cars running here than he had seen in Annapolis, Norfolk, or Jacksonville, but that was because the newer fuel-cell models hadn't yet become ubiquitous in the Caribbean, particularly not in the sleepy Leeward Islands. Their up-front costs were high and many local mechanics remained unfamiliar with them. So blue-white plumes of ethanol exhausts marked the movement of vehicles around the small coastal town, where there were no physical signs that the Earth had been invaded dirtside, completely encircled spaceside, and was facing a most uncertain future. No, this was Nevis—and nothing changed very much.

Trevor hefted his locker by the end handle, swung it around to rest against his back, and made his way off the pier onto the street.

"Taxi, sir?" The inevitable inquiry—but made by a strangely accented and familiar voice. Trevor turned—

—and saw Chief Petty Officer Stanislaus Witkowski emerge, arising from a supine position between two crates, pushing a panama hat back from his eyes.

"Stosh? What the hell are you—?"

"Doing? Waiting. For you. I hate officers. Always late. Ready to go up to the house?"

Trevor wanted to be able to play the surly boss, but couldn't. "Stosh, you are a sight for sore eyes."

"Or a sight to make eyes sore. Or so the ladies tell me. It's tolerable seeing you again, too, sir. You've had a pretty busy itinerary since Mars, if shack chat is half true."

"Yeah, they've kept me hopping." They had arrived at a worn but ready-looking Land Rover, which was idling irregularly. "How bad did the EMPs hit you down here?"

"Bad enough. Scuttlebutt says they pretty much blanketed the globe."

"Yeah, that's what they told me in Norfolk. Wasn't intense enough to knock out milspec hardening, but any civilian gear that was switched on was pretty much fried. West coast got hammered. It was the start of rush hour there."

Stosh opened the door with a flourish. "Not as bad as Tokyo or Beijing if you can believe the ham radio operators. Hit them right after everyone had settled in to work: computers on, streets packed, deliveries underway, elevators crowded. More than a little messy."

Trevor rolled his eyes when Stosh opened the car door and held it for him. "And was it some ham operator who told you I was coming?"

Stosh slid in the right-hand driver's side. "Nope, that was the little birdie that visits a noncom when his CO is about to come and make his life miserable. And shorter."

"And does that little birdie have a name?"

"Yes. It's called 'Common Sense.' I figured when the EMP hit, you'd be heading down here to keep us in the loop. Given the timetables for the coastal feeder system, I guesstimated you'd get out of Annapolis either the night we got hit by the cosmic bug-zappers or the day after. I figured you'd hitch a ride through to Norfolk and then have a zero-wait time to get a boat to Jacksonville or Miami."

"Zero-wait time?"

Stosh had cleared the outskirts of Charlestown, gunned the Land Rover. "Captain, I've seen the card that Mr. Downing gave you. You weren't going to be waiting on line anywhere. So I just ran the numbers, figuring it would take you maybe as many as two days to get a boat either out of the Keys or the Bahamas, wherever you had heard of the best connection."

"Your little birdie is pretty clever."

"Sometimes clever. Sometimes simply equipped with good ears."

Trevor smiled as they bounced over a *ghut*, a gully-like washway that had been given formal and permanent shape by concrete. "Hard to believe there's much worth hearing this far away from DC."

"See? You officers lack imagination, lack vision. Don't hear as well as our little birdies do, either. F'r instance, do you know how popular the local Four Seasons resort is with megacorporate executives and defense engineers?"

"Very?"

"Very very. And you'd be surprised at some of the

things an NCO's little drink-buying birdy can hear there."

"Such as?"

"Oh, such as—Delta Pavonis remained off-limits even after the Virus scare was lifted, and even though a lot of military traffic continued heading there and to points beyond."

"What kind of military traffic?"

"All kinds, but a lot of interesting cargo, particularly low-mass support weapons and high-tech assault gear. If you listen to the lower-echelon types, they are convinced that the knuckleheads in logistics really screwed the pooch on this one. According to them, the reason we're short of so many key systems here on Earth is because we sent them out to defend the colonies."

"What shortages are you talking about?"

"Hadn't you heard? EVA is almost unattainable. Specialty ammo is in short supply, particularly for heavy weapons. And the unofficial word on tacnukes is that the arsenals' racks are as bare as Mother Hubbard's cupboard. So, apparently, are the barracks that house special and elite units."

"Which you learned how?"

"Just because we're incognito interlopers in this tropical paradise doesn't mean we couldn't do some online lurking, looking in on the websites of some pals in Pensacola, Quantico, Coronado, Benning and Bragg."

"And?"

"And most of their sites haven't been touched in about four months. The others have become electronic ghost towns."

"And where have your missing pals disappeared to?"

"Oh, you hear lots of rumors. A popular one is that they were on the carriers or capital ships that were lost at Barnard's Star, or out at Jupiter."

Trevor held on to the roof with his left hand as they swept around a long, palm-lined curve. Mounting up on his left was the extinct volcanic cone of Mount Nevis. Sweeping off to the right was a sward of elephant grass that led his eye onward to a broad white-sand arc, then white breakers, and finally glass-smooth turquoise water. "I was at Barnard's Star for better than a month. I didn't see a single SEAL or green beanie. No spec ops personnel at all. You might say their absence was conspicuous."

Stosh nodded. "So is some of the online silence on the sites where the Teams' spouses congregate. The ones who are talking haven't heard anything, but you almost get the feeling that's what they expected. Like when we're sent on an extended classified deployment: the total lack of information is a kind of information in itself."

"So you don't think the missing units are part of the war casualties?"

"I think they're connected to the equipment shortages. Wherever all the nifty gear went, that's where you'll find all the missing boots and butts. And although there are plenty of whispers that they were all on the ships that got pranged by the Arat Kur—well, there are some funny rumors about those, too."

"Rumors about what? Our ships?"

"Yeah, at least some of the newer ones. About six months back, a few of us got messages from pals in the technical services—machinist's mates, weapon techs, chief engineers—who were being redeployed to help the industrial corporations as their Lagrangian point shipyards went into overdrive. They were so overwhelmed just laying down the hulls that they relocated the post-assembly finishing processes to one of the secure yards out in the asteroid belt. So once they were done constructing the spinal frame and mounting primary hull modules, they popped in automated controls, a single small engine, and off it went on a three-week glide to the Belt."

Stosh swerved left onto a steep and irregularly macadamed road. A familiar gutted sugar mill flashed at Trevor through the trees on the right and was gone. "Now," Witkowski continued, "I have a friend out in the Belt—"

"You have friends everywhere, don't you, Stosh?"

"A consequence of my winning smile and barroom conviviality. So, my buddy in the Belt relayed this miraculous tale: those ships arriving from the cislunar ways were being finished in five days. Each one went through the same process: into the yard, secure perimeter thrown up around it, and in go construction robots and a few techs. Five days later, out come the techs and most of the 'bots, the secure cordon comes down, and—without a 'well-done' or a christening—off she sails."

"No crew?"

"Skeleton or none. Apparently all these five-day wonders were being ferried out-system."

Trevor saw the long, low, intersecting roofs of a refurbished plantation house rising up through the trees. "Stosh, I think your friend has been visiting a few too many of those convivial barrooms. A five-day finishing job? How are they doing it?"

"No one knows, because no one was allowed in. The techs were held in isolation during and afterward. Intelligence quarantine, they called it."

Trevor nodded, wished he had more time to lay out all the pieces of this strange puzzle and play with them. But more immediate concerns called for his attention. "Stosh, are we ready to move?"

Witkowski simply smiled, went speeding past the plantation house's porch, careened around the embanked driveway to the back—and hit the brakes hard in front of the already-open garage. He flashed the headlights. Bannor Rulaine and Carlos Cruz emerged from the black recesses of the building, wearing fatigues, suppressed liquimix bullpup rifles slung around their necks.

"How did you get them ready so quic—?"

"Our hardened pager/transponders. Cued everyone the moment I saw you step off the boat."

"And the others?"

"Lieutenant Winfield's still at the dock. He's watching for anyone who might have tailed you. Barr is on overwatch in case someone arrived before you and is doubling back to pay us all a visit, or if someone decides to paraglide in for tea, crumpets, and a firefight."

"You think I might have been foll—?"

"Sir, you're an officer. Thinking is one of the luxuries of your rank. I just follow procedures and save our lives. And right now, that means taking nothing for granted. In twelve hours, if we haven't had any visitors, protocol says that—provisionally—you have not been followed, observed, or bugged."

Trevor shrugged, nodded a greeting to Cruz, who nodded back and moved to help him with his locker. But Stosh shook his head at Cruz—"As you were."—and led him and Trevor into the garage. "You're not going to have the opportunity—or reason—to unpack, sir."

"Why?"

Stosh snapped the light switch. In place of cars, the garage held two six-by-twelve sand tables. One boasted a surprisingly lifelike model of the ferry dock at the Four Season's Resort. The other depicted Bradshaw airport, twenty-two kilometers away on St. Kitts. On each, target vehicles had been painted day-glo orange. "We've been playing with our toys—for three hours every night. From leaving this garage to attainment of all objectives—vehicles seized, aircraft secured to the ferry deck, and underway to next area of ops—we conservatively estimate four hours, twenty minutes. If we wait for cover of night—and therefore, the absence of staff—the time-to-completion expands to almost six hours but with almost zero chance of us needing to fire our weapons. Unless, of course, I can convince you that we have a better option than the ferry *and* the VTOLs."

Trevor leaned against the wall, crossed his arms. "Convince me."

Witkowski strolled to the opposite end of the garage, returned with a black ring-binder, dropped it into Trevor's hand.

"What's this?"

"Technical specs for the DS X-198."

"The what?"

Witkowski couldn't restrain his smile. "A research sub."

Trevor opened the binder, couldn't get past the picture on the first page. "Where did you get it?"

"I decided it was time once again to disobey orders. So I went AWOL to San Juan and caught a Navy transport bound for Charleston. While on board, I liberated a few sheets of Navy letterhead, affixed your name and new rank—provided by Captain Rulaine—and convinced the folks at the NOAA facility to loan us this little fish they had decommissioned a year ago."

Trevor scanned the sub's schematics. Not an extreme depth vehicle, but it had external manipulators, a decent amount of space, and two airlocks for deploying multiple divers. But no accommodations.

"Stosh, this is great, but it's a working sub."

"Indeed it is. Look here: external racks for storing samples or carrying construction materials. Perfect for the battlefield playthings we've still got locked in our cargo container."

"Yeah, but no place to live."

"Not a problem. We still take the ferry—or better, a high-weather ship—and keep the sub tethered under us, to be used for final insertion."

Trevor glanced at Stosh. "Insertion?"

"Yes, sir. In Indonesia, sir. And since you didn't arrive on an official government tub, I'm betting that the op you have in mind is not in complete regs with any of the ones Mr. Downing has relayed and Captain Rulaine has read. So I figure we need to leave quickly for parts unknown to him."

Trevor stared into Witkowski's smiling eyes. So here was Stosh, cheerfully planning how to get them all to the other side of the globe for a rogue mission that was probably collective suicide. He was either one hell of a friend, or one hell of a bonehead. Or both. Aloud: "You might be right about the advantages of having a high-water ship, but then we probably won't be able to carry and launch the aircraft."

"Begging the august and accomplished officer's pardon, but isn't it likely that, if we try to launch the aircraft at all, that the Arat Kur might just take that amiss?"

"Yes. And that, Stanislaus, is the very lynchpin of my plan."

"Ah. See? There's an officer for you. I never understand a thing they say. But you've always been that way. That's how I knew you'd make command grade. So. What's your plan, sir?"

Chapter Twenty-Six

Commercial dockside, San Diego, Earth

The young fellow in civvies straightened and began to raise his hand into a salute. Richard Downing glanced sideways toward the tall man at whom the gesture was being directed—and who uttered a sharp, stentorian rebuke that turned heads at the far end of the wharf. "Belay that salute, rating!"

The young rating nervously snapped his bladed hand back down to his coveralled side.

"Son, do you want to lose the war for us?"

"Sir? Sir, no sir."

"Good. Then remember this. We don't own the skies anymore. They do. And their visual sensors are probably good enough to conduct a rectal exam on a gnat from low orbit. So if they're watching us right now, and they see dockhands saluting civilians here on a commercial wharf, they're going to get suspicious, don't you think?"

"Y-yes, sir."

"And what if they began to suspect that you aren't loading *grain* on this ship?"

The rating looked nervously at the collapsible freight containers arrayed in single-height rows on the deck behind him. "This hull would be headed for a world of hurt, sir."

"Not just *this* ship, rating: all of them. Even the ones that are still carrying nothing but grain." Downing's tall companion paused. "Now, unless I'm mistaken, each ship's loaders become part of her crew. So when do you ship out to babysit the surprise package you're readying?"

"Three days, sir."

"You have family you want to see again? A sweetheart, maybe?"

"Yes, sir."

"Then don't be sloppy—here or when you get to Indonesia."

"Yes, s—" The rating's hand had started to come up again. He grimaced, snapped it back down. "Yes, sir," he said apologetically.

Rear Admiral Jones shook his head, continued on down the dock. Downing matched his stride, waited until they were out of earshot. "A bit tough on him, weren't you?"

"Richard, coming from you, that's like blasphemy from a preacher. We've got all our chips on the table. This isn't the time to take any chances or overlook any details."

Richard smiled. He liked Bill Jones—Jonesy, as he was known and addressed by a favored few—and had from their very first meeting, thirty-four years ago. Their maternal grandmothers had been school chums in Johannesburg, cellmates during the violence and suppressions of the Forties, kept in touch when one fled to Toxteth in Liverpool and the other to the South Side of Chicago. Both rebuilt their careers, relocated to better environments, married, kept in touch, finally brought their families together in Nevis.

Jonesy had always been brash, assertive, and utterly sentimental. He physically resembled the local boys on the streets of Nevis, but it was Richard who found it much easier to meet them, and blend into their lives. Downing had been an outwardly quiet and cheerful child, behind which he maintained a careful, even detached, watchfulness. Not so Jonesy: he always led with his chin and wore his heart on his sleeve. And from the first, Downing had loved him for that. No less so today.

"So what's all this cloak-and-dagger business, Richard? I'm a busy man. Or hadn't you noticed?"

"Oh, I always notice." Richard took Jonesy by the elbow, led him in the direction of an outsized truck trailer, painted a dull, lusterless gray. "How's it coming, around here?"

"They'll manage without me, wharfside. Which is good, since I've got to make port in Perth in nine days if I'm going to set up our forward command center in time."

"Which is why I'm hitching a ride. They've given you a pretty rum ship."

Jonesy grunted. "I could use a little rum about now. But damn it, Rich, don't go dodging my questions. Why're you coming along? Don't you belong in DC, chatting with the president?"

"Yes, about that." Downing waggled a finger at a man standing near the entrance to the trailer, hands folded. He was in his mid-fifties, wearing a somewhat worn civilian suit, and approached at a leisurely pace. "Jonesy, this is Gray Rinehart, ex-S.O.G. operative. He's going to need your clearance to set up a temporary executive emergency line through your CIC."

"An executive line? On my ship?"

Downing nodded. "As you observed, I may need to chat with the president. Wherever I happen to be."

Jonesy nodded at Rinehart, jerked his head back toward the wharf. "My XO, Commander Ashwar, will set you up."

Rinehart nodded and was gone. Jonesy looked after him, then at several other, older men who took Rinehart's place near the entrance to the trailer. "Rich, no offense, but—these guys. Shouldn't they be thinking about retirement instead of operational requirements?"

Downing nodded. "Most of them did think about retirement and took it. Some years ago."

"Then what the hell—?"

"Jonesy, first of all, the bleachers are empty. Combat and security operatives are all committed. Secondly, I don't need young bodies, or crack shots. I need dependable people. People who have not only proven that they can and will get a job done, but have demonstrated that they can keep secrets not for a month or a year, but for a decade, or two."

"Or three," added Jonesy, who was looking at one bearded fellow whose eyes were lost in craggy valleys of accumulated wrinkles.

"True enough. And that's fine. Because we're not going into combat, at least not directly. We're just setting up a forward HQ and commo center in Perth."

"Richard, I've gotta ask. Why the hell are you even doing that? The South Pacific is already crawling with forward-positioned command and control posts, all waiting for the word."

"True. But mine is a special group overseeing just one operation—one very sensitive operation—and its very sensitive support staff."

"What? These guys?" Jonesy stared at Downing's Old Guard.

Richard smiled. "No, they're just providing security. The support staff for this op possesses a unique skill set."

"Which usually means they are being tasked to perform a unique job."

"Yes."

"Which is?"

"Jonesy, if I told you, then I'd have to kill you."

"Huh. You and what platoon of Marines? But seriously, Rich, what's the op? Since I'm setting up your links, I figure I've got to have the clearance to know."

Downing smiled. "We have a number of critical strategic assets moving into proximity with a high-value target. We have to keep track of where those assets are. Exactly. At all times."

"Huh. You should have come to my guys for that job. We track individual ships, planes, and rockets. Every day."

"Our delivery systems are a little bit smaller than that."

"Like how small?"

"Individuals."

Jonesy leaned back. "Damn. Backpack nukes? How're you getting them in? I hear the Roaches have rad sensors keen enough to detect the smallest warhead in our inventory at over fifty klicks."

Downing shrugged. "This operation is far more

important than any one—or any fifty—nukes. It's extremely high risk, but extremely high payoff."

"You never were a gambling man, Richard."

"And I'm not now. This operation is giving me an ulcer. And costing me all my friends."

Jonesy became a little less jocular. "So how do you get the assets next to the target?"

"On foot. They are to collapse on the target from multiple vectors. We hope."

"You hope? Do you need simultaneous deployment of all their packages?"

"No. One package will do the trick, if the arrow goes true to the mark. The multiple assets are for redundancy. Which is fortunate, since I have no direct control over the delivery assets themselves."

"You mean because we can't establish real-time contact with anyone in Indonesia?"

"That, too."

Jonesy looked at Richard from the corner of his eye. "What else would keep you from having direct control over your delivery assets?"

"Personal matters." *As in, every damn one of them went AWOL after our last meeting.*

"Okay. So, what are they delivering to the target?"

"That's secret."

"And without any orbital tracking or wireless commo with Indonesia, how are you even *tracking* the assets?"

"Can't say."

"Jesus, Richard. What *can* you say? Does the op even have a name?"

"It does. It's designated Case Timber Pony."

"Huh. That's some bizarre name. So where's the support staff?"

Downing crooked a finger at Jonesy, mounted the stairs at the back of the trailer. "They're in here." He opened the door, led the way in.

The sudden outward wash of humid heat took a little getting used to. Jonesy, who had every reason to expect the opposite—mobile command centers usually had double-strength air conditioning—sputtered. "Damn, Rich. What are you doing? Opening a sauna? Man, this is—"

And then Jonesy stopped speaking. And moving.

The figure at the center of the van was not quite five feet tall, had a rear-sloping teardrop head, large eyes, a lamprey-sucker mouth, gray skin with teal highlights, wide feet and what looked like a parody of an hour-glass figure perched on duck-feet and almost froglike legs.

Jonesy's mouth worked for a moment before a sound emerged. "Richard, what the fu—What's going on here?"

Downing smiled, put a hand on his friend's shoulder. "Rear Admiral William Jones, I would like to introduce you to Custodial Mentor Alnduul of the Dornaani Collective. He is here out of his personal concern for our situation."

"*This* is your support staff? You mean you've got ETs working for you now?"

Downing smiled as the answers to Jonesy's questions emerged from Alnduul's mouth in mild, unaccented English. "We volunteers from the Custodians do not work *for* Mr. Downing, but *with* him. And with you. I am pleased to make your acquaintance, Admiral Jones. Enlightenment unto you."

Off Gunung Beluran, East Java, Earth

Opal pushed her regulator out of the way, leaned over the sheet of paper as if she were going to embrace it, and wrote:

Dear Caine:
I hope you're safe and sound. I wish I knew where you are. But be warned. When I finally find you, I'm going to acquaint you with a few new brown belt moves the hard way. I figure that should teach you not to go running off on me!

Opal stared hatefully at the words: try as she might to find a romantic yet light-hearted tone, she kept failing. Badly, awkwardly. She pushed on:

I got through security in San Diego without a hitch. I just flashed the card Downing gave me, walked into the Naval Yard, and got myself assigned to a composite JSOC infiltration team.
The team is all Tier Three and higher—SEALS, Rangers, Delta, even some Special Forces types who tried to attach me to their T.O.O. But I had already cut some orders of my own, and thanks to Scarecrow's magic card, there was nothing the green beanies could do but pout. When Downing finally gets around to finding and court-martialing me, reading out the list of charges is going to take longer than the trial.

So here we are, waiting to hop in the water and sneak in under the Arat Kurs' noses, or whatever that is on the front of their face. If you can call that a face. Well, you get the idea. Anyhow, I'm just glad they haven't twigged to this scam yet. According to the folks who briefed us, all the psyops analysis and inferential exoanthropology studies tentatively identify the Hkh'Rkh as notably hydrophobic and the Arat Kur as neurotically so. So although the Arat Kur have wonderful maritime sensors, they don't have a great variety of such equipment, nor much of it, nor a great deal of imagination regarding submerged operations. Word is that they check the bottoms of the ships just before they enter the harbor in which they're scheduled to offload their foodstuffs, but they don't have enough submersible drones. From what we're told, they have those out patrolling at the fifty-kilometer limit to keep the boomers well back from Java.

So once we ride the bottom of this freighter into the Strait of Madura, we'll be dropped off, along with extra gear. I'm told that they don't cut us loose until we're in less than thirty-five meters of water, which is good because this night-diving isn't exactly something I'm looking forward to. Scuttlebutt is that you'll get ashore all right as long as you stay connected to the group lanyard and your dive leader remains alive and able to do his or her job. But if you lose the dive leader—well, they just tell us not to think about that. They don't even train us for that eventuality. I don't know if that's because there's no time, or because it just wouldn't matter....

At any rate, the good news is that when we cut loose, the dive leader gets his or her bearings and then frogmans us all down to the bottom, where a nonmetallic, 1.0 density pre-laid floor-to-shore cable is waiting. We snap on to that, detach from the SEAL and tow ourselves in. One by one. At ten-minute intervals. In the dark. Under radio silence.

Now throughout this entire approach, you're only allowed to move at six meters per minute, so there's no signature worth a damn to enemy sensors. My group is scheduled to come ashore at Kaliasan Point, near Tandjung Patjinan. Into marshes and fishponds. I'm told it's one of the best infiltration points: only a seven-hundred-meter tow-and-swim from twenty fathoms, with a mild current, and the towline (an old telegraph cable) moored within fifteen meters of the shore. The SEALs try to make us thankful by pointing out that some of the other infiltration points involve fifteen-hundred-meter crawls from depths of thirty-five fathoms. That means a five-hour, double-tank marathon for the landing team.

So anyhow, once I get to the end of the towline at Kaliasin Point, I will do what the military likes us to do best. I will hurry up and wait. For thirty minutes, I just lie in the muddy sands, breathing.

She almost wrote, "Probably thinking about you." But didn't. She sighed and kept on scribbling:

> When and if we get the all clear, we come up, stow gear where the SEALs tell us, and the different units in the landing team break up to carry out their different assignments. Which is, of course, a big mutual mystery. We all know we're going to Java to raise hell, but where, and how, and when—that's the secret that no one is allowed to share. Even with the other units in the same landing team.

Opal looked at the sheet of paper, saw Caine's face. *There are so many things we do not know, which we may not tell. I wish I knew how you really feel about me, but I don't. I wish I could tell you about the baby growing inside me, but I'd best not. Everything in this life seems to be a covert operation, in one sense or another.*

She looked up: there were two lazy plumes of gray smoke on the horizon, one fore and one aft. Both of those were cargo ships, about fifteen klicks off. And stretching away beyond them, in either direction, was an unseen treadmill of other, similar ships. It was a seaborne conveyer belt of groceries bound for Indonesia, where, at the height of its rainy season, estimates indicated that at least forty million mouths would go hungry without the relief shipments. Hundreds of ships had been mobilized to make the slow passage. Slow enough to enable the modified hulls among them to put troops and equipment under the keel and thus, into position for a submerged run to the coast.

The dive leader for Opal's team—a lanky fellow
from Oklahoma who took a perverse pride in telling
the story of how he had never seen the ocean before
he joined the Navy—emerged from between the trans-
all containers that lined the deck. He nodded, held
up a pair of fingers as he loped toward the taffrail.
Two minutes left. She chewed on the end of her pen,
struggled to resume:

> I've got to go now, bag this with the rest
> of the letters, and hope you'll get them all
> real soon.

She raised her pen, almost succumbed to the temptation to write more, but didn't. Instead, she folded
the letter carefully, opened the waterproof bag in
which its many fellows already waited. *If he's been
writing me, too—well, then we're in the same place.
If he hasn't, then we're not. And that's all there is to
it. You can't make someone think about you, or need
you, or love you. Feelings are like wild animals: they
can't be reasoned with, or corralled, or tamed. They
are what they are—or what they're not.*
The SEAL reapproached at a quicker lope, raised
a fist and nodded. Time.
She stowed the bag, checked her gear, found it
no less ready than when she had checked it fifteen
minutes ago. Or on any of the six quarter-hour checks
she had conducted before that one. She walked to
the rail, found the starboard half of the infiltration
team already there.
It was a pain in the ass, really, having to go over
the side like in some cheesy movie. The majority of

the ships carrying infiltrators had been hastily modified so that the teams could enter a false keel compartment through a panel down in the orlop deck. This ship was no different, but when they had run the ingress drill yesterday, the access panel had jammed, and no amount of coaxing had freed it up. Which, scuttlebutt said, was not an uncommon occurrence on the modified freighters.

As Opal checked the lanyard she would soon use for clipping onto the rappelling line, the team's most senior officer—the Special Forces colonel who had tried to recruit her into his truncated A-team back in San Diego—put out a hand. "Good luck, Major. Good to see that your seasickness isn't giving you so much trouble anymore."

Guess you didn't hear about this morning's performance. Which had nothing to do with mal de mer. "Thanks. And good luck to you, too." They exchanged the smiles of people who never expect to see each other again and together found something else to look at: the extinct volcanic cone of Gunung Beluran, now rising up like an oddly flat black triangle, backlit by an almost fully set sun. Their ship—the venerable *Asturia Return*—started a slow starboard crawl into a northwest heading. Which, according to old maps that Opal had dug up in the Army Survey archives, more or less followed right on top of the undersea cable which snaked in around the Situbondo headland.

"Gear in," the dive leader ordered. "Test."

Opal slipped the regulator into her mouth, puffed a few times, checked that her hair wasn't in her mask, felt that the flip-down fins were away from her feet, patted at her dirtside equipment: bagged, sealed, secured. She turned to the boy from Oklahoma, gave a thumbs-up.

He nodded, then said so quietly that it was almost inaudible, "Let's go."

Opal crouched under the nearest lifeboat, took hold of the line that was cinched to the forward davit, and swung a leg over the side. She snapped on to the line, cleared the other leg as if she was mounting a horse, and lay both feet flat against the hull, back to the scudding swells beneath. With a bend of the knees and a light push, she started rappelling down the side: a fairly short vertical trip, since the ship was riding low in the water. Staying directly under the lifeboat to remain undetectable by orbiting bug-eyes, she went slowly down to the waterline, where she found a magnetic handle—and a SEAL diver already waiting to help her with the transition into the five-knot side-wake. He looked past her, spoke loudly into her ear. "Stay in line and in trim under the hull. Let's not give their satellites anything to see." He turned back to her. "Let's go, ma'am."

She went in. The tug of the current wasn't so bad, but the sense of immense volumes—of the huge wake generated by the *Asturia* and her gargantuan hull, disappearing into the darkness ahead and behind as if she went on forever—was so foreign that she felt an edge of fear pushing up through her task-listed consciousness. Years of training and experience allowed her to push that sensation aside.

It was a little like moving at heights, where there the rule was "don't look down." Here she kept focused by obeying the rule "stay zoomed in; don't zoom out." She kept her eyes on the next spot of hull she needed to move to or manipulate, kept her mind on her gear and on the next discrete task that needed performing.

Which got her quickly and safely into the already flooded false keel reservoir and her harness therein. The SEAL got her cinched into the straps, pulled loose an air line from the hull-mounted auxiliary air tanks, snapped that into the other lead on her gear's dual air valve. He snapped it over to the auxiliary feed; she was no longer consuming her own air, which she'd need for her actual insertion. He gave her harness one last tug to make sure it was secure, gave her a thumbs up, nodded when she returned his gesture, then began towing himself back to the waterline transition point on the starboard hull.

Opal looked out through the false keel's open aft-end into what had nearly become black water. Over her head, illuminated so faintly that it barely stood out, was the red "panic button," in case something went desperately wrong with her gear. She turned; a fellow traveler was being snugged into the harness behind her by the lanky fish from Oklahoma. Behind and beyond that pair, she could just make out the failure that had forced them to make an external entry to the false keel chamber and keep it flooded: the dynamic tensions on the hull had buckled the interface valve that connected to the access panel in the orlop deck. Consequently, after dropping off the team, the *Asturia* would break off from her approach, citing hull problems and the need to head to Perth for repairs. It was extremely unlikely that the false keel would have been detected had she continued on to deliver her load of grain, but the standing order was to take no chances.

The *Asturia* made a slight turn to port, meaning that she was out of the Sea of Flores and entering the mouth of the Strait of Madura. Opal felt a dull bump through the harness, turned, saw that two of the SEALS had left their harnesses and moved to the rear of the cradle, where they were detaching one of the equipment carriers: a neutral buoyancy, nonmetallic "tumble cage," which looked a lot like a geodesic jail cell in the shape of dodecahedron. Black watertight packages were suspended inside as a central cluster.

One of the SEALs attached a line from the cage to a backpack-sized magneto-hydrodynamic dive-scooter and powered down into the black. The other SEAL snagged the line and followed, the tumble cage moving down after him. Within three seconds, they were invisible in the lightless depths. They had the tricky job of guiding the gear down to a special line that had been moored on the old undersea cable that they were still paralleling. Their final destination was secret, of course, but not proofed against reasonable conjecture. Opal checked her watch. Given their speed, the now-repaired Pulau Karangmas light should be plainly visible over the starboard beam at a distance of nine or ten kilometers. According to her close study of the Army survey maps, that would put them just a few hundred meters northeast of a sizable charted wreck, which lay where the headland's curve began to ease into the strait's southern coastline. A wreck such as that one—only a few dozen yards offshore, but still in more than twenty fathoms of water—would be a perfect cachement point if divers had groomed it beforehand. Not only would it anchor a new or secondary tow line to the land, but the metal of the old hull would serve as shielding and concealment for both equipment and personnel.

She looked behind. The special forces colonel nodded to her. Beside him, one of the SEALs was hanging in his harness: he looked dead, but the occasional, modest eruption of bubbles indicated that he was either simply relaxing or taking a quick nap. Just another day at the office for him.

Opal looked beyond them into the back-rushing blackness: five more hours. Then it was her turn: to detach, to dive, to tow in, to lie in a fish pond, and to get ashore.

To get closer to Caine.

Chapter Twenty-Seven

Kempang beyond the western metro limit of
Jakarta, Earth

"Caine." A tinny reproduction of Teguh's voice came
out of the old-style telephone. "The Sloth reserves are
heading toward our left flank, just up the street from
you. They're two minutes away."

Riordan spoke softly into the receiver. "Acknowledged, Teguh. We're set. Join me in the CP." Caine
handed the phone to Hadi, the IT-whiz, who had
become his adjutant when Captain Moerdani had died
a week ago. Hadi laid the receiver down beside the
window of their second-story perch in an abandoned
mission bell-tower: a highly iconoclastic historical
structure in predominantly Muslim Indonesia.

But the mission's tower complex had all the features Caine had wanted for this operation: few and
narrow windows, solid construction, old-style hardwiring, and no occupants. For the last ten years it had
been boarded up, awaiting historical restoration funds
which never arrived.

The archaic hard-wiring had been its most attractive feature, given how the rebels were usually forced to communicate. In the field, they had to rely on one-use pagers, since the enemy could jam or fry small electronics quickly. But in a prepared ambush such as this one, the rebels could make use of hard-wired communication lines. It was technology that would have been unremarkable in the trenches of World War One, but it had the advantage of being virtually undetectable and unjammable. Which would be required for this operation to work.

Alongside him, Hadi peered out between the steel-reinforced louvers of the mission's office. "Was that Teguh calling from the left flank OP?"

"Yes. It's been all quiet there since they turned back the enemy's first probe."

Hadi jutted his chin at the two Hkh'Rkh bodies laying sprawled in the dusty street. "Guess they didn't expect to run into resistance out here in a sleepy little *kempang*."

Although Caine concurred—"I guess they didn't"—he kept Hadi's tone of bravado out of his reply. This was no time for overconfidence. The Hkh'Rkh did not often come to this nameless extension of Jakarta's western sprawl, which was half crowded town, half semirural backwater. But when an aerial patrol had passed overhead late yesterday, Caine's group had launched a single rocket at it—a firework, actually. That was enough to ensure that the *kempang* could expect a decidedly brusque visit on the next day.

As soon as the morning rains had let up, the invaders rolled in along the northern approach road. They left their high-wheeled APCs well outside the dense cluster of buildings at the center of the *kempang*: they had already learned about the brutal effectiveness of improvised explosive devices. Advancing on foot, one squad of Hkh'Rkh went in search of the local authorities. Two more squads waited at the outer edge of the rough cluster of buildings, and a fourth waited with the vehicles.

Just as the lead squad discovered that the *kempang* was oddly quiet and all the locals shuttered indoors, the sharp crack of a high-powered rifle announced the start of the rebels' ambush. A Sloth went down with a bullet through his unprotected pony-neck. That didn't surprise the intruders as much as the second hit by the scoped weapon. Although only wounded, that Hkh'Rkh was frankly baffled to discover that the big-game round had penetrated the body armor which was routinely proof against old cartridge-fed battle rifles and most of the caseless ones, also.

The Hkh'Rkh squad's two heavy weapons—caseless rotary machine guns—hammered away at the sniper's vantage point in the upper story of the *kempang*'s one governmental building. Directed by acoustic track-back systems, they made a ruin of the window he had fired from but completely missed the man himself, who had already left along a prearranged escape route.

The Hkh'Rkh continued their attack in accord with their standard playbook. While the point squad broke into fire teams that flanked the government building and sought contact with other insurgents, two APCs rolled up to the edge of the *kempang*. One evacuated the wounded trooper; the other situated itself so that its remote-turreted coil gun could provide a base of fire against second-story targets.

Two weeks ago, the Hkh'Rkh would simply have blown the *kempang* to smoke, ash, and strips of charred bamboo. Their wars were conducted by Warriors on battlefields devoid of civilians. In contrast, an insurgency which faded back into the huts and streets of civilians was not merely anathema, but a betrayal of the basic codes of conflict. Their first reaction—to destroy all offending parties together—had had the grim virtue of making such distinctions pointless.

However, while the Hkh'Rkh's indiscriminate responses had pacified the offending *kempangs*, the Arat Kur discerned that these tactical gains had a mounting strategic cost. The Hkh'Rkh's reprisals were driving more of the enraged general population into the rebel camp, swelling the ranks of the resistance and its surreptitious civilian abettors.

New rules of engagement had been imposed upon the Hkh'Rkh, and consequently Caine could now count on them to attempt to make contact with the local authorities first. However, if they encountered insurgents—as they had now—they would establish the limits and locations of the opposition, fix its units in place by engaging them at range, and wait for air assets to come in and reduce that part—and *only* that part—of the *kempang* to a smoking ruin.

But in their search for the lone sniper, the Hkh'Rkh hit the rebel hardpoint: a colonial era bank. There they encountered almost twenty well-armed humans, half equipped with relatively modern Pindad caseless assault rifles. Following their new counterinsurgency doctrine, the Hkh'Rkh held position while a third APC positioned itself in the fields well behind the bank. Any rebels fleeing the *kempang* in that direction

would run directly into its massive firepower. And so
the Hkh'Rkh waited for the game-ending air strike.

And they waited.

As Caine knew they would. He had coordinated
this operation with two other resistance cells. Triggered by a daisy chain of pager signals, those two
cells had mounted sharp, short attacks in other, distant
kempangs as soon as the Hkh'Rkh had been spotted
wheeling their way out to the one in which Caine was
currently situated. And that meant that the forward-
deployed enemy air assets in this region were already
committed to attacking other rebel forces. Which
had disappeared by the time the invader attack craft
reached their target zones.

Consequently, the Hkh'Rkh in Caine's *kempang* had
to wait that much longer for the already overtaxed
air assets based at smaller, harried airfields around
Jakarta. Or, even more likely, due to the low threat
of concerted insurgency in the *kempang*'s region, the
Hkh'Rkh would simply be ordered to do what they
most wanted to do: close with the enemy and kill
them. Personally.

When the two Hkh'Rkh squads waiting at the
edge of the *kempang* started moving to join the first,
Caine knew what orders they had received, just as
if he had intercepted and decoded them: air assets
overcommitted and deemed unnecessary for support
of your operation.

The Hkh'Rkh had settled in half of their forward
squad to pin down the insurgents in the bank, which
proved extremely resistant to their fire. The reason:
steel construction sheeting and engine-blocks of old
cars lining its interior walls. The remainder of the

squad split and probed the flanks to find a route that skirted the structure and enabled the follow-up squads to hit it from the sides and rear. Their probe of the bank's right flank found an indeterminate number of resistance fighters with relatively modern weapons. But the primary threat they posed resided in the variety of small, wire-detonated IEDs at their disposal. After suffering two casualties there and making no progress, the Hkh'Rkh withdrew to a safe distance, pinning that flank without any further probing.

The left flank of Caine's resistance cell presented the invaders with a more promising tactical opportunity. They encountered only two command-detonated mines, and the few humans there were only armed with AKs. The venerable rifles were not reliably lethal to the Hkh'Rkh except when discharged at very close range and in very great numbers. After driving these humans back from their first position, the Hkh'Rkh became bold and tried charging across a street to seize what seemed like that flank's final fallback position.

That was when they learned that the sniper who had greeted them upon entering the town had relocated himself to cover this flank. With one Warrior killed outright by the rifle, and another wounded and then hammered senseless by the rebels' AKs, the rest of the Hkh'Rkh withdrew back across the street. Their two casualties laying in plain sight of Caine's mission tower CP, they traded shots with the humans occasionally, without any result in either direction.

However, in tactical terms, the Hkh'Rkh probes had been successful: they had found the insurgents' position and had identified the left as the weak flank. The subsequent deployment of their reserves—reported by a seventy-five-year-old grandmother speaking into a hard-wire phone in her second-story sitting room—made the invaders' attack orders quite clear. They were bringing up the next two squads with an acoustic trackback system and heavy weapons. They'd try to overrun the human position on the left flank, then turn sharply northward and roll up along the now-uncovered left side of the bank, assaulting it from the side and rear with superior numbers and supporting fire from heavy weapons and portable rockets. For all Caine knew, they might have stocks of CoDevCo-supplied tear gas with them as well.

A few minutes later, the rebel overwatch in the minaret of a dusty, dilapidated mosque a kilometer outside of town confirmed that the Hkh'Rkh assault forces were moving into engagement positions. The observers' signal—closing the shutters on the top window of the tapering tower—had been visible to, and understood by, every human unit: approximately three minutes to contact.

Caine looked at his ancient, wind-up wrist watch. The timing was crucial: the first rush of the Hkh'Rkh attack upon the left flank had to be blunted enough to ensure that they would not all charge across the street. Not immediately, at any rate. He turned to Hadi as Teguh entered the mission tower CP from the rear. "Any reports?"

Hadi shook his head. "The Sloths are quiet up by the bank and the right flank. Some of the townspeople are coming out, though."

"What? We told them—"

"They're coming out to run away, Caine. Now that the firing's died down, they probably think it's a good time to get out. Before it starts again."

There was nothing to be done about it now, and hopefully, the Hkh'Rkh would perceive the fleeing women and children as civilians trying to distance themselves from the insurgents in their *kempang*. Hopefully.

Caine picked up his Pindad caseless carbine. "Hadi, signal the launch crews to stand ready. The Hkh'Rkh will be finding their assault positions now. Knowing them, they won't waste a lot of time debating optimal attack procedure."

"No," agreed Teguh, "the Sloths got no problem with being decisive."

Hadi leaned over. "Launch crews signal they are ready and waiting for the launch order."

Up the street, in the buildings across from those rebels who'd drawn the risky job of manning the weak left flank, there was movement. "Get ready," whispered Caine.

Human shouting arose from the buildings in which the Hkh'Rkh were probably readying themselves. It subsided quickly.

"What was that?" Teguh asked, peering up the street, clutching his Pindad six-millimeter caseless more tightly.

"Don't know," Caine murmured. "Could the Hkh'Rkh be trying to interrogate civilians?" To date, the Hkh'Rkh did not torture opponents, even though they killed them readily enough. But perhaps they had decided to try something new—?

Hadi's head snapped up. "Left flank observation post reports movement in buildings along the expected enemy assault route. Do we launch?"

Caine scanned those buildings through binoculars.

"Not yet." He glanced overhead at the ceiling. "Are they ready up in the attic?"

"They are," Teguh answered with a nod. "They've only got the two RPG rounds, though."

Caine nodded. *More for show than anything else. Something upon which to focus the attackers' attention, to break their momentum in mid-assault for a few crucial seconds.* Up the street, Caine heard more shouting; this time a dog barked. *What the hell—?*

Muzzle flashes erupted out of the windows of the buildings across from the rebels' left flank. A high-pitched growl rose up a moment later: a coil gun. An incredibly lethal weapon, and a pearl of great price. As if fleeing its ear-rending reports, a dog ran out of one of the houses, tail between its legs.

The return fire from the left flank was fierce but dropped off quickly. Out of the phone receiver held by Hadi, lilliputian shouts of desperation rose and then were suddenly silent.

"Caine," started Teguh.

"Wait," said Caine, watching the street through his binoculars.

Another dog ran out of the same building—from which the two expected squads of Hkh'Rkh emerged in a rush, their distinctive loping strides carrying them rapidly toward the center of the street, firing as they came.

As Caine took the phone from Hadi, he shouted, "Flanking fire!" Teguh threw open the mission's shutters. Without stopping, he shouldered his Pindad and dumped half a clip into the right flank of the charging Hkh'Rkh. Hadi was doing the same a moment later—just as Caine heard the defunct attic fan overhead get kicked outward, followed immediately by a hoarse, roaring rush: an RPG sped down the street toward the enemy.

This hail of deadly fire—but particularly the rocket—made the Hkh'Rkh dive for cover or go prone in the street. With sickening speed, however, they shifted their fire to the mission tower. Caine heard rounds ringing against the steel sheeting they had mounted inside the double-coursed brick-and-mortar walls.

He counted to two as the Hkh'Rkh's personal weapons continued to roar and rounds started coming in through the open window, pulverizing the walls behind them. "Launch," Riordan shouted into the phone's receiver, just before grabbing Teguh and the less-willing Hadi, one with each hand. Pulling them downward, he yelled, "We've got to go!"

With a whining growl, the coil gun unloaded at them. The street-facing wall started coming apart; the steel plating screeched as hornet-screaming rounds spattered it, some going straight through.

One caught Hadi square in the sternum. In the same instant that a dime-sized entry wound appeared on his chest, his back blew out in a cascade of red mist, meat, and spine fragments. The air overhead was alive with a shrieking torrent of four-millimeter projectiles that ground everything they hit to gravel and dust.

Caine and Teguh stayed low, scrambled back to a waiting rope in the stairwell, slid down to the ground floor. While Teguh hooked up the phone they'd readied at this fallback point, Caine peered out the doorway, to the south. The rebels' six precious fire-and-forget missiles—the kind that could be left sitting in a trash can until launched—were arcing up from their launch points along the tree line. The trajectories of the missiles suggested their apparent targets: the APCs waiting outside of town to the north.

Meanwhile, the Hkh'Rkh up the street were already reorganizing and checking their wounded. Those who had been providing covering fire from within the buildings now shouldered out to join the others, ignoring the fitful sputters of a sole AK-47 as they prepared to complete their overrun attack of the left flank—

—just as a third dog, this one not much more than a puppy, ran into the street, heading south after the first two. More human cries arose from the buildings being vacated by the Hkh'Rkh. From between their ogrelike shapes, a little girl clutching a doll darted out, screaming after the young dog.

The Hkh'Rkh paused, stared.

Caine's breath stopped in mid-inhale. *No*—

The PDF units on the APCs began chatter-hissing at the incoming rockets,

Caine reached to grab the phone out of Teguh's hand—who held on. "No. You can't—"

A young woman ran out after the girl, screaming for her to come back. Right behind her, a rush of other civilians—several young women, two older, and a number of children—seemed to vomit out of the building just south of the Hkh'Rkh, apparently believing that some decision had been made to flee the area en masse.

Caine snatched the phone away from Teguh, who grabbed his shoulder, fingers like nails. "If you call off the missiles—"

Caine knew exactly what would happen if he called off the missiles: the Hkh'Rkh squads would go through the left flank, hit the bank, slaughter everyone there when they discovered the rear was only lightly defended. They would wipe out all the rebels who had come to trust and follow Caine over the past weeks. But if he let the rockets come down—

"No—" Teguh repeated, and stared hard at Riordan, his eyes red-rimmed.

That stare froze Caine in place as—an instant after two of the fire-and-forget missiles were shot down—the remaining four triggered their secondary thrust packages.

The thrust packages were designed to fool PDF systems by jinking the trajectory of the missile sideways with a sudden burst of angled thrust. But Caine had discovered that the packages could be rigged to push the missiles downward, and so the secondary thrust rockets now bumped the missiles over into sudden, steep dives which carried them under the intercept arc of the Hkh'Rkh's PDF systems—and into the street.

Caine looked past Teguh's glistening eyes as the four surviving missiles came down on their preset coordinates, just meters away from where the Hkh'Rkh were regrouping—and from where the Indonesian women and children were fleeing.

The high-pressure fragmentation warheads went off with overlapping roars. The explosions flung some Hkh'Rkh up in the air. Most were blasted sideways, some of the blurred forms closest to the impact points split apart. However, the stick-figure shadows of the women and children simply dissolved in the force of the blast. But Caine knew that, when he walked into the street to help collect whatever spoils could be gleaned from almost three squads of dead or now easily dispatched Hkh'Rkh, he would see the tattered, bloody remains of those thin, helpless bodies.

As if to underscore that inevitability, the charred pink head of a child's doll rolled lazily out of the smoke, came to a stop against the doorstep of the mission.

Caine pitched over as he vomited. Then he straightened and walked stiffly into the swirling, settling dust. "Teguh," he called over his shoulder, "pass the word: salvage teams advance. Let's get this over with."

⬧   ⬧   ⬧

In the lightless nighttime jungle, Caine heard Teguh approaching. Again. He sat down next to Caine, who wondered how the Indonesian could see at all.

"I just learned from some of the new guys that they've got a nickname for you in Jakarta."

Like what? Slayer of the Innocent? But what Caine said was, "How do I get a nickname in a city where no one knows me?"

"Well, they don' know you, but they sure know what you done. You are The Dentist."

That caught Caine off guard. "The Dentist?"

"Hey, bro', you removed a pretty famous tooth about three weeks ago. You know all the new posters of Ruap, smiling? Favorite thing for kids to do is blacken out one of his front teeth."

"They'd better be careful. They could get shot for that."

"Well," said Teguh, and then he stopped.

Caine turned toward him. "They have, haven't they?"

"Only a few." Teguh paused, probably realizing that his attempt to lighten the mood had gone horribly awry. "Look," he started more firmly, "you did good today. Real good. Got us everything you said we'd get. We got commo gear that isn't fried, lotsa basic equipment, even Sloth guns. Too big and weird for us to carry, but man, with a homemade bipod, anything we ambush with them is going down and not getting up. And when our guys slipped out of the bank and got away down the mission's smuggling tunnel after us, the Sloths must have thought that we were magic, disappearing like *that*." He snapped his fingers. "But there's been one problem—*bule*."

It had been at least two weeks since anyone—most of all Teguh—had called Caine that. "And am I supposed to ask what that problem is?"

"Huh. You already know. But you thinking so hard about what happened today that you don't see it." Teguh cursed. "Problem is that you think that brain of yours can control everything. Well, it can't. Oh, it's a good brain, man. We all seen that. That's why Captain Moerdani made you his lieutenant after the first week, why he told me you were his replacement if something happened to him. And why no one questioned it. That brain of yours has kept lots of us alive, brudda."

"Got a lot of you dead, too."

"See? Now that's stupid shit you're saying. This is war, Caine. How you gon' control everything? How you gon' make sure no one dies by accident? Who are you? God? You need to get over yourself, brudda. Live down here on Earth with the rest of us."

"It's not myself I can't get over, Teguh. It's those little girls, those women—"

"No, that's where you wrong. And that's where you letting us down. What has you sitting over here by yourself."

Caine looked over, thought he could see, just maybe, the outline of Teguh's face. "What do you mean?"

"I mean we all feel bad about those dead girls, those dead women. I feel it, too. But that's diff'rent from thinking I could stop it."

"That's because you weren't the one who had to make the call. I was. I could've stopped it."

"*Bule*, how is it someone with a brain like yours can be so dumb? Now you lissen to your Indonesian brudda, and you lissen good. In war, no matter how smart your plans are, things gonna go wrong. 'Cause once the shooting starts, you not in charge anymore. *You* think you are—but that's where you are wrong, wrong, wrong." Teguh's dim silhouette shook its head. "The war is in charge, brudda. Which means *no one* is in charge. You American, right? So you the people who came up with a saying a long time ago that we still use in Jakarta: 'shit happens.' And it does. And war is nothing but shit, and now it is happening all around us, all the time."

Caine felt Teguh lean closer, his breath a mix of stale peanut sauce and cheap lager. "You think you bigger than this war? That any brain, no matter how smart, can control war? Then you are a crazy man. Crazy like *bules* are, sometimes, when they think there's nothing they can't fix, nothing they can't do, nothing they can't control. That's crazy bullshit thinking, brudda. And as long as you think that way, we can't depend on you."

"But I—"

"Not done yet, brudda. I know you feel bad for those girls, those women. But I also know that not one of us would have walked out of that *kempang* alive if you'd stopped those rockets. You know that too. You gotta remember that in war, you're not deciding between the bad thing to do and the good thing. You're choosing between the bad and the worse. And you can't control the shit that happens after you choose."

Caine heard Teguh rise, start to walk away, stop, turn. "Caine, brudda, one more thing. You think those women and girls were going to get away? The second they came out of hiding, they were dead. You could have stopped the missiles, yeh, but what about the Sloths who were shooting at us? And all of us would have had to shoot back, including our hidden salvage teams. That crossfire would have been as bad as the missiles." He seemed to kick at the ground a bit. "Now, you gonna get some beer and food, or what—*bule*?" Teguh walked away.

Caine looked after the sound of his departure, started to think about the rightness and wrongness of what Teguh had said—and then stopped. Sometimes, thinking just didn't do any good, didn't provide any answers. Because for some questions—such as the arbitrariness of life and death during wartime—there weren't any answers.

Caine rose to his feet and began feeling his way toward the low voices he could hear muttering over their beers.

Chapter Twenty-Eight

Inland from Tjikawung, West Java, Earth

Trevor heard movement in the bush yet again. He looked at Stosh, who had evidently heard it also. Farther down the line, Bannor Rulaine was already lowering his rifle.

Trevor shook his head, spoke into the brush. "You've got us."

A single human duck-walked out of the undergrowth. He was festooned with fronds, mud-spattered camos leading up to a green-painted face and a rather floppy bush-hat. His brown and drab dustmix carbine took a moment to place: H&K, bush version, produced under license. Trevor smiled: Aussies. "Good to see you."

The soldier's eyebrows raised. "Be-damned! Lieutenant Tygg! Yanks!"

"I can hear him as well as you can, Gavin." Another Aussie, this one very tall and lean, wound out from between the leaves behind them. The bush hardly quivered as he moved. He crouched down, his own

HK aimed resolutely at Trevor's belly. "I don't believe we've been properly introduced."

Trevor nodded. "Corcoran, Trevor. Captain, USSF, reactivated. My team: Captain Rulaine, Chief Witkowski, Rating Cruz—all reactivated. And Mr. Barr, formerly Secret Service, retired." Trevor put out his hand.

The taller Aussie looked at it then back at Trevor. "So you're just a mob of weekend warriors, gone on walkabout halfway around the world?"

Stosh smiled brightly. "That's us."

"Eh heh."

Crouching down himself, Trevor let the underslung launcher of his assault rifle rest against the tops of his thighs. "I'm sure you've got specific questions, Lieutenant. Ask away."

"Okay. Let's start with this. What the hell are you Yanks doing out here beyond the black stump?"

"It's where we thought it best to come ashore. The rest of the West Java coastline seemed pretty populated and well-watched. And fifty kilometers is a pretty long swim. So after we came through the canal—"

"Pardon?"

"The Panama Canal. We started in the Caribbean. Once we were in the Pacific, we caught a pretty fast tow to New Guinea with a group of grain transports coming out of Guayaquil. We left them when we hit the Solomons, kept the Queensland coast on our portside horizon until we saw the lights of Darwin. Then we crossed the Timor Sea into the Lesser Sundas, picked up some supplies and local scuttlebutt and made for Christmas Island. Ported overnight to get the best weather reports and to time our final approach to the Strait of Sunda."

"An inspired plan," commented Stosh.

Lieutenant Tygg raised an eyebrow. "So West Java was your choice from the start?"

Trevor nodded. "Yeah. I wanted deep water on the final approach, because although we were running a high-water ferry on the surface, we were making our actual insertion by small sub."

"So the ferry was—what? A stalking horse?"

"Correct. We had VTOLs on the deck, rigged for autoflight. So we entered the Strait just beyond the fifty-klick limit, then came over hard-a-starboard and crossed the line at best speed."

"And then some," complained Stosh. "He was burning out those lovely engines."

Trevor shrugged. "Those lovely engines were going to be scrap metal soon enough, anyway. So we hopped into the sub, stayed in the shadow of the ferry, launched the planes as we came near to Panaitan."

Tygg nodded. "So that they'd hit the ferry, make a big mess, and you slip off in the chaos on their scanners. Fine, but how'd you control all that from the sub? You had to see what you were doing."

Trevor could easily visualize Stosh's rolled-eyes histrionics behind him. "Well, *some*one had to stay on deck, ready to go over the side when the party started."

The Aussie looked back at Stosh. "You?"

"Me? *Me?* I'm a noncom; I'm wasn't crazy enough to stay on deck!"

—*although I had to order you* not *to, you lying bastard,* Trevor emended silently—

"—Oh, no. It was him. Captain Hero . . . er, Corcoran."

"Your CO simply sounds decisive, Chief Witkowski."

"Decisive, sir? Well, sir, I suppose it's just a matter of

how one describes certain kinds of COs. For instance, the 'decisive hero' type of CO is invariably an officer and a gentleman and a lunatic."

The Aussie lieutenant tried very hard not to smile, almost managed it. "So how far inside the limit did you get, Captain?"

"I autohovered the VTOLs and went over the side after about eight klicks. I figured if they were going to use orbital interdiction, I didn't have much time left."

"Had they wanted, they'd have had you in five klicks. You got lucky."

"Very lucky, evidently. They sent drones to investigate first. Then they dropped the hammer, just as we were entering the Panaitan Strait."

"The Panaitan Strait? So you were making for the Semenandjung Djungkulon headland?"

"No. That was a tempting option, but approaching it would have put us in the shallows longer. And we wanted to come ashore in a spot where the invaders wouldn't have anyone on the ground, including human collaborators. We angled north toward Pulau Panaitan, stayed at one hundred fathoms and came up toward the westward strand that shelters Kesauris Bay. It was the only safe approach. The coastal shelf is steep at that point, so we were able to rise from one hundred to five fathoms over the course of a three-kilometer run and slip straight into the bay, hugging the western shore."

"A crushing hug, at the very end."

The lieutenant stared at Witkowski's jocular addition. "You sank her?"

"On purpose," Trevor clarified. "We flooded the tanks and let her settle and wedge between a pair of rocks, near a small wreck we found on close inspection of the last satellite photo survey."

"So she'll just look like part of the garbage, if they scan the site."

"If they're being sloppy, yeah. And maybe they are a bit sloppy over in that area. It took almost five minutes for recon drones to show up, and it was half an hour before some live units showed up to nose around. We were already out of the sub and hunkered in the bush by that time."

The smaller Aussie, the first one who had emerged from the undergrowth, nodded. "Yeh, the closest base they have is in Serang."

The lieutenant looked at him. "These aren't our mates, Gavin—yet." He turned back to Trevor. "And then?"

Stosh jumped in before Trevor even had his mouth open. "Ask about the swimming."

"The swimming?"

"Yes. Our lovely midnight dip across the Panaitan Strait."

"You can't swim the Strait. The current—"

"My chief is exaggerating a bit." Trevor turned and smiled a smile that made Stosh bring his lips together tightly. Trevor turned back to Tygg. "We brought high-strength nonmetallic cable, which we moored and concealed under the marshlands on the eastern side of Panaitan Island. Then we worked in shifts over three days to put a towline halfway across the strait. We ran out and anchored an additional one-hundred-meter length of line, one at a time. We just kept adding to the end of the already laid cable—although we did have a few interesting moments with broken or jammed lanyards."

"I'll bet you did."

"When we had laid four kilometers, we towed ourselves to the end of the line, and cleared the rest of the distance on a dive."

"And the current?"

"It carried us, but we counted on that when we laid the line. We didn't try a direct traverse. We cleared the remaining distance by using handheld dive jets to control the current-drift, and came ashore near Pulau Karangtikukur."

Stosh nodded, mumbled. "Nice reefs, there. Nice and sharp."

"Yeh, and that headland is bloody rugged."

"That's why we coast-followed," finished Trevor. "When the going got too difficult on foot, we got back into the water and went around. No patrols. Pretty much deserted, until we reached Tjikawung. After that, we just kept our heads down—until you saw them."

He looked at Trevor. "And what's your infiltration code?"

"I'm not part of any infiltration force, although I'm not surprised that one is gathering. And I'm glad it is. But I'm bound for Jakarta, on a very different mission."

"Which is?"

"Which is authorized at this level of classification." Trevor produced the magic card Downing had given him, hated deflecting a probable ally with a lie. But the only place Trevor was authorized to go now was the brig.

Lieutenant Tygg looked at the card, looked at Trevor quickly, back at the card. "I've seen one of these. One. Glad I didn't have to run that op myself. I heard it got a bit wooly."

"Yeah, that sounds about right. Once we get to Jakarta, I'll brief you on he particulars and native contacts we've got waiting there. Now, what's your story?"

The lieutenant finally put out his hand. They shook. "Lieutenant C. Robin, SAAS."

Trevor blinked in surprise. "Lieutenant 'Robin?' But I thought your name was Tygg?"

The lieutenant may have flushed before shooting a dirty look at Gavin . . . who suddenly showed keen interest in the jungle canopy overhead. Trevor had a feeling vaguely akin to witnessing an embarrassing familial moment at a neighbor's house—before Stosh asked, "Er . . . you said *C*. Robin, sir?"

"I did."

"Your first name wouldn't happen to be 'Christopher,' would it?"

The lieutenant clearly reddened this time. He seemed to speak through clenched teeth. "What's it to you, Chief?"

"Nothing, sir. Nothing at all."

Trevor was terrified that he might grin before he could clamp down on the surge of surreal hilarity brought on by finding a Lieutenant Christopher Robin here in the Million Acre Wood that was the Javanese jungle. Furnished with the *nom de guerre* of "Tygger," no less. He preempted a chortle by hastily sticking out his hand. "I'm Trevor. Now, what's the situation around here?"

Tygg shrugged. "We arrived in-country three days after the bastards landed, gathering tactical intel, organizing resistance. Some of your lot was here as well. Marine Force Recon, I think. We kept separate.

You know the drill: stay small, hard to catch, harder to see, and if they got one unit, then the other could still carry on."

"How'd that go?"

"Fine, for a while. Then the exos started coming out into the bush. It was like bloody fox and hound, after that. We'd organize a hit, and out they'd come after us, the Arat Kur pushing their Hkh'Rkh hounds to the hunt. They got your lot—Force Recon—first. Killed them all, unless our intel was wrong. Got a big bloody nose doing so, I hear. Got us next, about two weeks later, and I think they had help."

"What kind of 'help'?"

"Human help. We were operating over near the mass-driver, gathering intel on the rate of continuing construction. We had some unexpected visitors. I suspect we tripped some of CoDevCo's ground sensors in the area, and they sent word to their new landlords. Lost the captain, all of first squad. Ripped up half of the other before we could break contact and get into the deep bush."

"And since then?"

"Educating the locals. Real talent here for jungle insurgency, but we already knew that. On the side, we've been compiling tactical intel for the infiltration units we might eventually have contact with."

"What kind of intel?"

"You name it. Everything from a list of known exo bases to the technical specs on their equipment. For instance, there's a weapon the Arat Kur break out for special occasions: their little coil gun."

Stosh cleared his throat. "You mean, like the rail guns used on warships?"

Lieutenant Robin nodded. "Same principle, yeh—but portable. We call it a needler. It's a support weapon that the Arat Kur sometimes mount in a separate housing on the back of their armored exoskeletons, and sometimes issue to the Hkh'Rkh ground troops as a vehicle or crew-served heavy weapon. Slows the wearer down, but it's absolutely lethal out to three kilometers. Only four-millimeter projectiles—like overgrown needles—but they're traveling four or five times the speed of sound. Ruler-straight trajectory, and they must have one hell of a scope slaved to the weapon; we took our last two casualties after I thought we'd given them the slip by putting four klicks between us."

"What are the Hkh'Rkh like in combat?"

Gavin shook his head. "Bloody tough, is what they are. If you've got a dustmix weapon set for high velocity, you can usually take 'em down with a single shot. But if you're using caseless or most of the old brass-cartridge rifles, forget it; you're going to have to bash 'em a few times before they stop getting up."

"Their armor?"

Tygg frowned. "Pretty much like ours, but thicker. And they routinely hump a ninety kilo 'light' pack."

"And they're still quick?"

"In the open, they are like greased lightning. But in the jungle, not so good. They're heavy, tall and broad and get tangled in brush that we slip through. And you can hear them coming a mile away. The only time they ever surprise us is if they've been lying quiet, observing from a distance. Then they pin us down with long-range systems like the needler, and send assault infantry after us on the double-quick. But if we have native flankers and scouts with us, we see them first—every time. Our real problem is long-range communication."

"Why? The EMP bursts?"

"No, not so much. They didn't light too many of those off over rural Java. But their jamming is absolute. We can't find a channel that isn't being used or fuzzed by them. So we have to go with jury-rigged LOS systems: usually old target designators converted into crude lascoms. And to keep things short, we sent prerecorded compressed messages, usually in Morse code."

"That's no good for tactical ops, though."

"During ops, we use pagers, linked by ground repeaters."

"Don't they find the repeaters, destroy them?"

"Sure, but then the locals plant a few more. They're seeding them into projected ops areas all the time. Particularly farmers." He leaned back with a smile. "Welcome to the shit, Captain. Now, what was your objective when you almost got yourself killed by blundering into us?"

Trevor smiled back. "'Killed by blundering into you,' eh?" He lifted his hand in a surfer sign.

Tygg raised an eyebrow. "You were planning on feeding yourself to the sharks?"

Gavin stared and then grinned. "Lieutenant, you've got something on your shoulder."

"Eh? What—?" Tygg looked, and saw a bright red dot painted directly on his clavicle. He swallowed.

Trevor lowered his index finger. The dot disappeared. Robin breathed again.

Stosh smiled. "Oh, it's still there, Lieutenant. You just can't see it. Lieutenant Winfield just snapped the laser designator—and scope—over to UV wavelength with preset frequency modulation. Even with a UV scope, you wouldn't see it unless you're wearing goggles that are set for the same pattern of frequency-hopping that the beam is using."

"And Lieutenant Winfield is—?"

Trevor decided to pick up the story. "Another of my men, about three kilometers behind us, with a ten-millimeter liquimix Remington M167 long-barrel assault gun. I'm sure you know the specs, so I won't bore you."

Tygg nodded, smiled. "I guess I underestimated you. But then again, you may have underestimated us." He raised his left hand, all fingers spread wide.

The bush wavered. At least half a dozen previously invisible Indonesian villagers stood, the closest no more than six meters away. Half of them carried Pindad caseless bullpup carbines, the other half AK-47s. Tygg's smile became wolfish. "I don't want to bring the Arat Kur down on us, so I won't send a pager signal to the group I have waiting four klicks behind you with Corporal Holloway. But they might have made Lieutenant Winfield's afternoon a little more interesting."

Trevor smiled. "I daresay they might have." It was going to be good working with Aussies again. "Bonzer good show, mate." Tygg rolled his eyes at Trevor's broadly accented Hollywood Aussie slang. "Now, if you've got a few dozen strong backs and local boats you can whistle up, I've got some interesting equipment cached back on Pulau Panaitan—"

Chapter Twenty-Nine

Near Gunung Klabang, Central Java, Earth

Opal heard the hoarse growl of a Hkh'Rkh tri-barrel eight millimeter and ducked lower; it was closer than she'd expected. She had heard the first reports of a firefight five minutes ago, had moved in their direction, estimated that she was now within a kilometer of the point of contact. But that sudden blast of angry rotary fire had been less than three hundred meters away. Whatever shit was hitting the fan, it was flying in her direction—and fast.

She low-ran forward, stopped just beneath the crest of a small ridge, and crawled up closer behind a particularly dense thicket. Taking care not to stir any of the vegetation, she lay on her back, flipped on the monocular data screen, double-checked that it was jacked into the line-out feed from the scope, and lifted the weapon up so that it could peer downslope over the tips of the fronds and spatulate leaves.

The picture's a little too wobbly. Zoom out—ah, that's better. A handful of locals were retreating in good order, moving in two groups. The front rank fired a few rounds, ducked and ran while the second rank covered and then headed even farther rearward. At first she couldn't see the Hkh'Rkh pursuers, but it had to be them. That eight-millimeter rotary was their signature squad support weapon, from what she had seen. After a few moments, she detected the thrashing bush tops and vines that signaled their approach in dense vegetation. Their long, powerful dog-jointed legs and immense lung capacities marked them as open country predators possessing both superlative speed and endurance. *But we bald-assed monkeys evolved here in the jungles. Welcome to our humble home.*

As if to underscore that welcome, a man in a Kopassus uniform popped up from a wide thatch of ferns, just as the Hkh'Rkh drew abreast of his position along the human route of withdrawal. He blasted half a magazine of caseless at them and went prone. The Hkh'Rkh closest to him caught at least eight rounds in the right trunk and was knocked sideways, a reddish-maroon mist persisting a half second along the trajectory of his fall. Hurt, probably dead.

The Hkh'Rkh pursuit stopped, and their weapons hammered the jungle around the ferns. If the Indonesian commando was still there, his remains wouldn't fill a rice bowl.

With the Hkh'Rkh attention suddenly rotated ninety degrees to their right flank, one of the irregular insurgents reversed course, sneaking back toward the Hkh'Rkh line, evidently intending to catch them by surprise from what had been their direction of advance. She rose up to fire, her AK-47 snugged under her cheek—

Fifty meters behind the Hkh'Rkh contact line, there was a quick sputter. One projectile tore the woman's right arm off just beneath the shoulder; two more hit her in the chest, exiting her back with explosive sprays of bright red. Just because the Hkh'Rkh were bold didn't mean they weren't competent tacticians: their overwatch marksmen knew to watch for tricks such as the one the woman had attempted. However, the destination of her fellow insurgents' retreat remained unclear—to Opal no less than the Hkh'Rkh. Their route of withdrawal led into a narrow gorge, about two hundred meters farther on. The sides were wooded and steep, and the back was a sheer wall of black volcanic rock. A dead end. Literally, if they kept heading that way.

Opal lowered her rifle, thought. *I'm close enough to Jakarta to make contact with locals. But there might not be any of this bunch left in three minutes. So saving their trapped asses might buy a decent welcome and quick trust.* She rose up into a crouch, began following the backside of the slope she was on, which ultimately evolved into the near wall of the gorge.

Before reaching that point, she had to go over the top of the ridgeline: always a risky moment. *But I'm bulletproof. Gotta be. And besides, the best defense is a strong offense.*

She snaked over the top of the ridge, was pleased to discover no one was shooting at her, and started angling down her side of the gorge, the one that led farther up into Gunung Klabang's northern foothills. She could see the approaching insurgents being bunched together by the narrowing gap between the slopes. Behind them, the Hkh'Rkh—understanding that if they didn't press the pursuit, the humans would escape up and over the slopes—steamrolled their way through the undergrowth. One more went down, but the rest kept coming. And behind, there was a rapid, irregular rustling in the undergrowth: one or more Arat Kur in combat suits, maintaining their typical serpentine. She looked for the inevitable remote units that hovered around them, saw about three of the flying pancakes and one larger aerial unit, possibly carrying a weapon. Arat Kur usually worked in pairs, but there was no sign of a second one or its remote units. Possibly it had been an earlier casualty. She continued to side-run down the slope.

Two more of the Indonesian irregulars had been hit—which, given the power of the Hkh'Rkh weapons, usually meant killed. However, one was still alive and crawling away through the weeds. His movement attracted the attention of one of the enemy skirmishers. Without breaking its stride, the Hkh'Rkh swerved in that direction, took a longer, higher leap, and landed with the calar talon of his foot striking down into the middle of the human's back. The man—or, as Opal saw when his face jerked up momentarily, the boy—stiffened, then went limp.

Opal's brow grew hot and then cold. She checked the range in the scope: ninety-two meters. She nuzzled into the stock. She had wanted to close a little more, but screw it. *For you, kid*, she thought, and squeezed off two rounds.

The Hkh'Rkh stopped in the middle of his next stride, looked down as if trying to see the eight-millimeter hole where a tungsten-cored round had gone in, and then fell backwards, gargle-yowling and holding the spurting maroon crater that had erupted at the base of his long neck. Hkh'Rkh weapons—including the tribarrel—ripped into the tree that had been Opal's cover.

But as soon as she had squeezed the trigger the second time, Opal had launched into a forward roll. Two somersaults later, she was eight meters farther down the slope: bruised, but the enemy counterfire was passing safely overhead. Half the Hkh'Rkh line, smelling a box ambush, wheeled to charge her old position, firing as they came, still looking higher up the slope.

Should've checked your thermal scopes first, suckers. She let them close to within sixty meters, set the selector switch to three-round bursts, and started sprinting towards them, staying low, firing at any movement she saw in her front ninety-degree arc.

At first the Hkh'Rkh obviously had no idea where the fire was coming from. With Opal's low posture and rapid approach through the dense foliage, they couldn't track the muzzle flashes and simply would not have believed that a single human was countercharging straight into the middle of their skirmish line. The three skirmishers in the center had gone down before the rest realized what was happening, stopped, dropped into their own crouches and started lining her up—by which point she was only twenty meters from their line. She targeted the one straight ahead of her without slowing. She snapped off two bursts—the second for insurance—and ran past his thrashing body just as the other Hkh'Rkh started opening up.

And had themselves in a crossfire. With the center of their line gone, and Opal between their flanks, the ends of their line started pouring largely blind fire through empty space and into each other. Opal went low, looked for some solid cover as tattered foliage started raining down on her, saw a pair of parallel downed trees a few meters away. She raised her weapon into the hailstorm overhead, fired a few rounds. She waited for the sustained thunder of the magazine-emptying responses to end abruptly, then kicked up from the soggy ground into a two-stepped sprint and then a long dive, which landed her between the two tree trunks as the air livened with a renewed torrent of projectiles.

As if in response, the opposite slope seemed to explode. Along the full length of the Hkh'Rkh column, from the now half-rotated skirmish line all the way back to the Arat Kur and overwatch sharpshooters, a sudden blast of flame and smoke jetted down from eight meters up the opposite ridgeline. Stretching a hundred meters back beyond the entrance into the dead-end ravine, the long line of explosions echoed quickly off other slope, sounding like two roars in fast sequence. However, even that double-blast didn't drown out the vicious whine that filled the air around Opal, shredding leaves, pulping and spattering wood fragments from the tree trunks to either side and snatching the helmet off her head into the brush behind. *Directional mines—fitted with* flechettes?

Opal's speculation was drowned out by eager shouts in *bahasa*; the "fleeing" insurgents had reversed direction and were charging back into the kill zone they had prepared. Well back from the entry to the ravine, the Arat Kur remotes were orbiting in their automated distress pattern. *Scratch one Roach.* A number of the Hkh'Rkh, still standing, wheeled unsteadily toward the charging insurgents. Most of their armor seeped dark red in multiple places as they trained their weapons on the approaching farmers and truck drivers.

From the far slope, Opal heard the distinct crack of a weapon like hers: an eight-millimeter CoBro liquimix assault rifle, set on high velocity. One of the Hkh'Rkh went down. Another crack: another Hkh'Rkh dropped out of sight. Then at least three more rifles—caseless, from the sound of them—joined in, the weaker weapons double- and triple-tapping every target they engaged. Opal stayed low and used the moment to think. With a rebel victory almost in hand, what might still go wrong? What might have been overlooked? It had been a sound box ambush, made devastating by her unexpected contribution. Everything was probably accounted for—

Except for a second Arat Kur. What if the second half of the invariably paired Arat Kur hadn't been a casualty? And what if he hadn't been on the ground but waiting, watching, from one of their airborne sleds?

Opal stuck her head up—and heard, rather than saw, the answer to her question: the high, thin whine of downsized turbofans were just barely audible, if one listened carefully between the rolling, firecracker sputtering of small arms. But where—?

Of course, from behind the Indonesians. On the opposite side of the gorge, a broad disk was already sweeping down the slope toward the rear of the ambush line that had triggered the claymores and was now busily picking off the Hkh'Rkh survivors. Damn: they didn't expect the Arat Kur sled, couldn't hear it, wouldn't see it. And there was no time to do anything except—

Opal stood, heard bullets close around her. She hit the magazine release for her rifle's underslung launch tube: the columnar magazine fell out, sprinkling twenty-five-millimeter rocket-assisted projectiles at her feet.

A bullet—whose, she could not tell—cut through her right trouser leg.

She pulled an antivehicle RAP off her web-gear, inserted it in place of the magazine, slapped the cover up. Locked and loaded.

Wood chips sprayed up past her eye. Someone was coming awful close. But no time for cover.

She sighted the weapon, centered the scope on the approaching disk, saw the combat-suited Arat Kur it carried, like a cubist roach riding bareback on a pie-plate. The laser range finger indicated seventy-six meters. She changed the integral laser to target designation mode, activated the warhead's self-guidance package, snapped on the arming range override, saw the red "0" illuminate, and squeezed the trigger.

In that fraction of a second, the Arat Kur vehicle had closed to fifty-eight meters.

The antivehicle weapon—an extended rocket-assisted projectile, or "stick RAP"—exited the launch tube with a dull thump: the launching charge. A split second later, only five meters out of the barrel, that small clearing stage tumbled away and the rocket motor kicked on.

51 meters to the rushing enemy craft.

The RAP streaked at the disk, which must have had an automatic detection and evasion system; it angled sharply to the right—

48 meters to the enemy craft.

As the missile swerved in pursuit and closed to ten meters range, the base of the nosecone flared, sent a small HEAP round forward with an extra two-gee burst of speed.

45 meters—

The HEAP pre-munition impacted; the detonation sent a jet of molten metal into the armor protecting the disk's machinery.

44.2 meters—

The main rocket's IR followup seeker head rode the bright, thermal plume into the scorched and severely weakened armor—

43 meters.

The head of the main body detonated upon impact, ejecting another molten HEAP jet. The armor buckled.

43.95 meters.

Pushed by the still-accelerating motor, the depleted uranium penetrator rod spiked into the armor, ripping through as though it were paper, sucking the slower, roiling molten metal in behind it.

The disk tumbled once and disintegrated with a roar that spawned two others, each punctuated by a bright white flash: secondary explosions from destroyed munitions.

Opal smiled—and went down sideways as someone punched her in the ribs.

She tried to rise, couldn't, discovered that her vision was hazy. Then the world came back into focus, and a local was screaming something at his followers; a surrounding thicket of AK-47 muzzles lowered quickly. She raised up on one elbow, found breathing difficult. She looked down: her body armor had a new, shiny crater just about level with her left floating rib. Score one for friendly fire.

"Well, that was a pretty boneheaded set of moves."

She looked up at the source of the tactical critique, saw a short—quite short, really—man in his thirties walking toward her in black and brown camos. He looked at her—or rather, her rank—more closely. "I mean that in the best possible way, Major."

She looked at him closely as well. The voice was familiar, and behind that camo face paint, unless she was very much mistaken—

He had obviously recognized her, too. "Hey," he said, "didn't I rescue you from assassins by snatching you off a rooftop in Alexandria this March? You and Caine Riordan?" His grin seemed about as wide as he was tall.

"Yes, and hey, yourself," Opal answered. "Glad to see you made it off that roof. But you're a long way from Alexandria."

"I could say the same about you, ma'am. And, although a SEAL wouldn't normally be in your chain of command, allow me to ask you: orders?"

"Yeah. Help me up, damnit. Jeez, I didn't remember you being so short."

"And I didn't remember you being so cute, ma'am."

A pint-sized SEAL chief flirting with an Army major who was probably born before his own mother? She looked at him sideways. *So what is it with SEALs and me? Or*—although it was less personally flattering—*what was it with SEALs? Extra doses of testosterone in their chow? Nah, they miss a lot of meals, so they might not get enough of it. So it had to be in the beer. Yep, that would be the primary, and surest, delivery vector.* But however amusing the banter, she had to put a stop to it. "I think you've been in-country too long . . . Sergeant."

"Probably so, ma'am, but you'll forgive me for saying that camos suit you a lot better than a bloody hospital gown."

Have to agree with him there—and with the topic having shifted to clothing, she noted that although the insurgents were not in uniforms, there were telltale signs that not all of them were simply irate civilians. In particular, the three persons who had been on the slope with the SEAL were all wearing military boots, had lighter complexions and shorter hair, and were all roughly the same age.

She turned back to the sergeant. "Don't continue patronizing me with this 'orders, ma'am?' crap until you've briefed me on this unit. And it is a unit. No, don't give me the big innocent eyes. You've got some regulars mixed in here."

The sergeant nodded. "Three from the People's Republic—they're tunnel rats. Like me."

"Tunnel rats? Oh, wait—" Opal smiled. "Case IfUC1."

"Huh?"

"I've heard of this operation by name. Back in Washington, just before heading here." *Thanks for the info, Downing.* "But back then I didn't know what it referred to. I didn't get the joke."

"'IfUC1?' That's a joke?"

"Sure. You know what they say about rats: 'If you see one—'"

"—There are a hundred more." Little Guy shouldered his weapon, looked at his watch. "Well, that's us, sure enough. A few less of us, after today. But a lot fewer of them. Thanks, in part, to you. But honestly, Major, about that charge of yours. Don't you think that was a little too 'gung ho' for a commanding officer?"

Opal studied him carefully. Little Guy's bloodless, offhanded remark about the casualties and his flippant criticism of her belied the steady gaze with which he watched his casualties—six dead Indonesians—being carried past. He looked at each face as if he were trying to memorize, or commune with, it.

She reached out and took his shoulder. "Let's get something straight, Sergeant. I know your kind. You've got a mean-ass-mutha exterior concealing a mother-hen interior. And you manage to wind officers around your little finger, that way. And I thank you for your concern and your foolish flattery. But that's the last time I want to hear your opinion on my tactical choices. Get used to high-initiative operations, 'cause that's the kind of CO I am."

Little Guy was still trying. "As you wish, ma'am, but you'll meet your maker pretty quick that way."

"My maker's scared to meet me, and the other guy won't have me." Her glance bounced from her flechette-mangled helmet, to the hole in her pants leg, and ended on the crater in her armor. "As you will witness."

Little Guy finally smiled again. "Okay, then. Glad to have you on board. Major."

"Smile when you say that, Stretch. Now let's unass this place. It's going to look a lot messier in about five minutes."

He checked his watch. "Three minutes, Major. The opposition is pretty fast on the reply."

Following the lead of the Kopassus commando, they started heading directly over the slope that the disk had been coming down. "How do you get around?"

"What do you think? Tunnels."

"Watch that tone, Little Guy. Besides, who builds

tunnels in Indonesia? From what I remember, trying to dig tunnels here is about as promising as trying to grow roses on the Moon."

Little Guy nodded. "Yeah, but they *had* to build these tunnels to protect the fiber optics with which they were planning to rewire the whole country. Or so I'm told. Pretty big conduits for cables, though. Almost a meter wide, and because the system was never finished, they're not on regional survey maps."

"So the Arat Kur don't know about these tunnels? *Them?*"

Little Guy shrugged. "Seems not. But then again, why should they?"

"Well, if there was a lot of digging going on, and a lot of talk about upgrading to—"

"Major, with respect, this is Indonesia. People talk, and people dig, and most of the time, nothing ever comes of either activity. And be aware, this was not a megacorp job. It was a joint American project which went into limbo when the Indonesians started cozying up to CoDevCo right before the Parthenon Dialogs. There's been no work on this project for at least a year, no talk of it for six months, and no hardcopy maps of the projected tunnels have turned up. No software on them, either." He smiled. "Except right in here." He tapped what looked like a GPS relay.

"That's not for GPS, is it?"

"Better not be. From what I hear, we don't have a single satellite left. But this will show me the maps of our bombproof, scanproof tunnels. Where we have a lot more friends waiting." He paused and met her eyes solemnly. "A *lot* more."

Opal smiled. Having heard how all the pieces fit

together, she knew now: this was all Nolan Corcoran's work. Another part of his jigsaw-puzzle plan to save Earth. It was as if his ghost were standing there now, smiling and waving them all in the direction of the tunnel, one satisfied hand on his hip. "The tunnels," Opal asked, "do they go into Jakarta?"

"Didn't know you were a psychic, ma'am. In fact, we'll be moving there in just two—"

He and Opal both stopped moving, even breathing. They only listened. She gave her order—a hiss that sounded like "Cover!"—a split second before he snapped out the same word. She hit the rain-muddied ground, sank in a bit, smelled the sweet stink of natural composting processes.

The roar of VTOL jets up-dopplered into a nearby crescendo—and passed high overhead, down-dopplering without stopping.

"They're checking out the ravine first," Little Guy murmured.

"Could they have missed us?"

"See this mist? Feel this heat? Thermal systems work, but they need a few stationary moments to get details. They were going too fast. But after they assess the kill zone and come up empty-handed, they're going to start orbiting, looking for us. Or—"

"Or what?"

"Or burn off the nearby slopes. They know that if they don't get us fast, they won't get us at all. As recently as a week ago, they still reconned from standoff. Now, they recon by fire. Indiscriminately."

"So we—?"

"We make like Alice and go down our magic rabbit hole. C'mon."

They sprinted the rest of the way down the slope, converging near a half-completed power line. They swarmed down a narrow spillway that paralleled it, veered left toward a culvert that burrowed into one of its sloping sides.

"In there?" Opal pointed.

"Yep. Connects to drainage tunnels, one of which runs under the fiber-optic conduits."

There was a shout from the Kopassus trooper bringing up the rear. "Plane. Coming fast!"

Opal crouched into a run. "Then we'd better be faster. Double-time like your lives depend on it."

"'Cause they do," Little Guy added. They reached the entry and she waved them on. Little Guy and his unit crouch-sprinted into the dark maw of the tunnel, followed by the Kopassus man. She was right behind him.

A sudden concussive roar, bloom of orange-yellow light, and tumbling shock wave were right behind her.

Chapter Thirty

Riordan ducked as the stream of coil gun needles tore through the side of the corrugated metal shack, which promptly folded over on itself like a half torn sheet of perforated paper.

"That was close, Caine," said the young Indonesian beside him, listening as the rotors of the Arat Kur attack ROV hummed into the distance.

Caine nodded. "It wasn't sure we were in here. That was just a little recon-by-fire." The rotors slowed, picked up in volume again. It was doubling back. *Because, no matter where I hide today, they know where to find me.*

Which made less than no sense. At the start of their occupation, the Arat Kur had seeded the streets of Jakarta with dust-sized nanites purportedly able to identify and track any individuals already in their database. According to informants, the project had been an utter failure. Firstly, the entire project had depended upon meshing the visual data gathered from the Arat Kurs' "phased array" of pervasive nanites with the advanced biometric programming provided by their megacorporate allies. The reason for its failure had been an object of considerable speculation. Perhaps the Arat Kur had been unable to sync such different software systems; perhaps the culprit was data overload, or nanite failure due to the hot, supersaturated air and merciless pounding of the monsoons. But there was no question that the scheme had been a complete failure—so how had multiple Arat Kur ROVs been able to track one Caine Riordan almost flawlessly for the past two hours?

The effectiveness of his guerilla cell was not a reasonable explanation for the sharply increased attention. Other insurgency groups had been far more troublesome in terms of raw casualty and damage infliction upon the enemy. Caine had concentrated on what he did best: specially prepared ambushes such as the one in the western *kempang* that had gained them a treasure trove of lethal Hkh'Rkh weapons. Such operations were very useful, but couldn't be carried out too often. They took considerable prep time, and could not be safely conducted in the same region: after an attack, the Arat Kur invariably shifted a crippling density of reconnaissance and surveillance assets to that area. Also, the Hkh'Rkh had resumed their tactic of hammering any *kempang* that became particularly restive, ruthlessly punishing the indigenous population for ambushes which they had neither aided nor abetted.

"The ROV is coming back, Caine," said the young Indonesian nervously.

"Don't worry, we'll be all right."

"Yes, but it could still—"

Caine turned and stared at him. "Soldier, we are going to be all right."

"Y-yes, sir."

Caine smiled, nodded, tried to peer out the tiny sliver of sky visible between where the roof and front wall had folded over and down against the rear wall. *At least I hope we're going to be all right.*

He could hear the Arat Kur ROV hovering closer, tracking slightly from side to side like a scenting dog.

Damn it, Teguh, where the hell are you with that—?

From fifty meters away, an antivehicle rocket sprang out of a fire-gutted building with a screaming hiss. Although Caine could not see the ROV's response, he heard the familiar sounds of its chassis spinning in that direction, the pop as its short-range active defense rockets jumped toward the incoming threat.

In the microsecond before those rockets made their intercept, the oncoming missile's warhead launched from its bus, speeding even faster toward the ROV. The minirockets jinked over, just managed to intercept it—but missed the slower, heavier projectile that had been launched right behind the HEAP warhead.

Caine heard the launch-hiss of a second wave of intercept rockets, but they were too late. The slower tungsten warhead crashed into the ROV with a sound like a screwdriver punching through a car door—right before that projectile's small, tail-covered back-charge went off.

The combined impact and explosion sent rotors spinning in all directions, one screeching wildly across the back of the bisected tin shack. Looking out the similar gap at the other end of the folded expanse of corrugated metal, Caine watched as the savaged chassis of the Arat Kur patrol unit was flung down with a crunch, raising a path of dust until it stopped rolling.

"Let's go," he said to the young Indonesian, starting to push at the fallen wall which had sheltered them. And which lifted off with weightless ease: Teguh and two of his assistants stood there, holding it up.

"I still want to know where you got those damn rockets," Caine said as he clambered out of the trash pile that had once been a shed.

"An' I tol' you I promised the guy I wouldn't say. He's a prewar black marketeer, Caine. He means business." Teguh trotted toward the cover of a new building, the one that housed their objective: a colonial-era cistern system.

"Yeah?" Caine replied. "Well, those rockets mean that someone is getting contemporary munitions onto Java, and if equipment is getting here, that means people can probably get here, and that means—"

"Yeah, good thinking—but stopping to think will get us dead right now. We gotta move. There will be more ROVs coming."

Caine stopped as they came under the building's catch-roof, and within arm's reach of the cistern's half-rotted wooden cover. "No. *We* don't have to move. *I* do."

Teguh stopped. "What you talking about, Caine?"

"Face the facts, Teguh. Whatever is going on today, the Arat Kur keep finding us because of me. This last time they flew right past the two squads we sent running away as decoys, didn't even seem to know they were there. But me? They can find me in any building, under any car, in any culvert. We've lost three men finding that out. Men we should never have lost at all."

"Yeah, but we got four of their ROVs."

"Teguh, listen to me: forget kill ratios. This is not a battle of our choosing. Hell, it's not even a battle, it's a—a rabbit hunt. The Arat Kur ROVs are the hounds and somehow, they've got my scent."

"Look, don't go thinking the world revolves around you, heh? Don't go *bule*-crazy, like you did after the *kempang*. This is just bad luck, and by tomorrow—"

Caine looked at him. "By tomorrow, we'll all be dead. I'm not *bule*-crazy, Teguh, not this time. And you know it. You just don't want me to leave. And I don't want to, either."

"Shit, you think you so important I care whether you leave?" But Teguh's eyes and the set of his mouth told a very different story.

Caine put a hand on his shoulder. "My Indonesian brother, you helped me get my head—well, out of my ass, after the *kempang*. But today, it's you who refuses to see what your brain already knows." Caine waved at the ruined ROV and the streets behind them. "They are after me, Teguh. You know it; you've seen it. I want to stay, but I can't. Maybe they put some kind of transponder in my food when I was on the Arat Kur ship. Or maybe I walked through some kind of nanite-dusted trap that actually works. I don't know how they are tracking me. I only know this: they can find me wherever I go, and the only other people they've attacked today are the ones who got in their way. So you have to get the hell away from me, and I've got to go down this hole and hope that they can't follow me into a tunnel. Who knows? Maybe it will block or at least degrade whatever signal they're using to track me."

Teguh shook his head and looked like he might start to cry. "This isn't right, Caine. You should stay with us."

Caine put his other hand on Teguh's other shoulder. "It wasn't right what happened to all those people at the *kempang*, but we had to accept that, too."

Teguh looked away, reached up, patted Caine's right hand. "You a good man, Caine. You come find me when this is all over. We'll find some beer. We'll talk."

"We will," Caine nodded, removing his hands and pushing the cistern-cover aside. "Now, get out of here."

"Hey," Teguh retorted as he began trotting away down the wreckage-strewn street, "you gone now. I don' have to take your orders anymore!"

"You never did," Caine whispered at the receding back of his Indonesian brother. Then he clambered down into the cistern.

"Spooky Hollow" restricted area, north of Perth, Earth

Once inside the underground garage that concealed the mobile command trailers, Downing began returning the salutes of the Australian soldiers guarding the largest one: the one that they had taken to calling Spookshow Prime. Only special personnel with insanely high clearance were allowed within ten meters of it, let alone inside.

Downing walked up the stairs to the overpressure hatch of Spookshow Prime, went in, sealed it and felt the atmosphere change beginning: slightly more rich in oxygen, a slightly flinty smell, and—despite being on the west coast of Australia—a slightly higher level of humidity. The green light illuminated over the inner door. Downing went in.

The three junior Dornaani at the monitors nodded faintly as he passed, returning their nods. Entering the combination conference rooms and living quarters at the rear of Spookshow Prime, he found Alnduul sitting in what looked like a meditative pose before a holosphere that showed the area around Jakarta.

"Greetings, Richard Downing. Is there news from the World Confederation Council?"

"Yes, and it's not good." Downing sat heavily. "There's been no contact from the Arat Kur to reopen a dialogue, not even when we paved the way with questions about prisoner exchanges and increased humanitarian aid. So the primary means of carrying out Case Timber Pony—the diplomatic mission—has been scrubbed. Without at least an invite from the invaders, we can't initiate talks in Jakarta without them becoming suspicious. Which means we have no way to get a diplomatic mission into, or at least close to, their HQ."

Alnduul laced his fingers together slowly. "So the Arat Kur have not explained their lack of interest in further communication?"

Downing shook his head. "Not a word. The intel brain trust suspects a combination of factors, but Arat Kur uninterest is not high among them. Rather, the preferred theory is that the increasing violence and bitterness of the Javanese insurgency is making the Hkh'Rkh not only more aggressive on the battlefield, but at the planning table. That they are dead-set against any further discussion of terms."

"It would not be uncharacteristic of the Hkh'Rkh to make their continued cooperation with the Arat Kur contingent upon an unwavering demand for Earth's unconditional capitulation." Alnduul stared back down into the holosphere. "Of course, there may be an advantage to such a situation."

"You mean that there are even greater rifts opening up between the Arat Kur and Hkh'Rkh leadership?"

"Just so."

Downing could tell that Alnduul's following silence was intended to be significant. And he understood the unspoken implication. "You still think we went too far by destroying so much of Indonesia's warehoused foodstuffs and increasing the ferocity of the insurgency, don't you? And that if we had been more moderate, the unrest would not have flared into a bitter guerilla war that is now keeping the invaders from the negotiations table?"

Alnduul drew his fingers through the air like streamers in a molasses-slow wind. "Perhaps. The rapid increase in the desperation of the island's population did accelerate the rate at which initially uncoordinated acts of resistance coalesced and intensified into a nationwide insurgency. And that, in turn, has accelerated the speed with which the Hkh'Rkh have become harsh, belligerent, and unmanageable. But I still maintain that this may prove to be a superior outcome insofar as completing Case Timber Pony is concerned."

"How so? Our best chance of carrying out Timber Pony has just been eliminated."

"I am by no means as certain of this as you are. I have never been convinced that the ploy of inserting a disguised assault team was the most attractive—or promising—method of executing the plan. It was, to use a human idiom, a piece with too many moving parts. If one failed, the machine would not function when needed. Consequently, the vulnerability to both routine mishaps and competent enemy screening were too great to ensure acceptable odds of success." Alnduul paused. "I know you are reluctant to pass the responsibility—and risk—of completing the mission to individuals, Richard Downing. I am, also. But with the primary delivery alternative canceled, we have little choice but to ensure that all the assets remain within striking distance."

"Of course, this means we will have to insert special data into the infiltration unit updates to try to nudge our remaining delivery assets in the right direction."

"You are sure that Captain Corcoran and Major Patrone would not obey a direct order to move into greater proximity to the target?"

Richard shook his head. "They would not, and we have no way to embed such an order in the updates, let alone know if they received it."

"Then you are correct. We must embed data that entices them to collapse on the target area. But we must take more extreme measures in the case of Caine Riordan. Look." Alnduul gestured into his extraordinarily lifelike holosphere of the coastal shallows north of Jakarta. A filament-thin spindle of green light twirled and shone, moving slowly away from the perfectly rendered landmass. Two other spindles—one yellow, one cyan—were still on the landmass, one at the western edge of the city, the other on the east. Alnduul pointed to the green spindle. "Riordan."

Richard frowned. "He didn't run until we ensured he was trackable by the Arat Kur."

Alnduul seemed to feel the veiled accusation in Downing's tone. "True. But we had to act as we did.

If, as you suspect, he had become part of the resistance, that presented two dangers to his participation in Case Timber Pony. Firstly, he could have been killed either in combat or in prison, unless he was captured by the Arat Kur.

"Secondly, even if he was captured and survived, as an active insurgent, his diplomatic status would have been revoked, thereby eliminating his unique access to the enemy headquarters. Logically, therefore, his resistance activities had to be terminated and we had only one such method at our disposal: making him intermittently detectable to the Arat Kur. Enough to convince him to desist his actions, but not enough to lead to his death."

"I will point out that it may have almost come to that on one or two occasions."

"Richard, like his namesake Odysseus, Riordan is not easily deterred from his plotted course of action. Consequently, balancing the threat levels necessary to effect a change in his behavior is a delicate and difficult task."

Downing folded his hands. "And Riordan didn't react as you predicted, either. Rather than surrendering himself to the Arat Kur without any mention of his guerilla activities, now he's actually trying to leave Indonesia. Despite the danger of crossing the fifty-kilometer maritime limit."

"Which is why we must once again make him detectable to the opposition. That they may herd him back in the direction of the target."

Richard's lunch moved unpleasantly in his stomach. "And once again, he could be killed."

Alnduul's nictating lids cycled once, slowly. "It is

possible, but unlikely. The blockade enforcement units are expected to search any questionable boats and investigate before resorting to overt force of any kind."

"The key words there are 'expected to.' I don't like that risk. Where are our other delivery assets?"

Alnduul gestured to the other two spindles of light in his holosphere. "Captain Corcoran and Major Patrone continue to collapse on the target area, but not so steadily or directly that we may be sure they will be in sufficient proximity. And they do not have Riordan's unique access to the target. So we must take this step. We must have every asset as proximal as possible."

Downing rubbed his forehead. "Yes, I know. Particularly since none of them is even under our bloody control. Not even in contact. Hardly the way the plan was supposed to go." *Understatement of the century. Case Timber Pony has been cocked up ever since the Arat Kur EMP strike enabled all my assets to give me the slip . . .*

"And yet, Richard, you foresaw that the assets might move in the needed direction even if left to their own devices. As occurs now."

"Yes, but the accuracy of that conjecture is less the result of psychological insight than it is dumb luck. They could have done anything, once they were out of my control."

Alnduul's mouth twisted very slightly, his fingers drooped a bit. In a human, his would have been a wan, rueful smile. "Do you truly believe that any plan involving the behavior of sentients can be so reliably controlled?"

Downing scoffed at the thought. "Evidently not."

Alnduul gestured at the holosphere. "And yet, here are the assets, moving in generally the right direction." His mouth-twist became more pronounced, "Sometimes, Richard, we are most in control of situations when we cease trying to force our direction upon them. Rather than struggling to shape the flow of gathering currents, it is often better to simply be carried by and work with them."

"So we're playing at judo, now?" Downing grinned crookedly. *"Dōmo arigatō, sensei."*

Alnduul's innermost eyelid nictated. "I am not well acquainted with that language, but I believe the correct response is *Dō itashimashite.*"

Downing looked away before his smile widened. *Bloody alien wiseacre.*

Chapter Thirty-One

Off Ringit, Pulau Seribu/Thousand Islands, Earth

The gap between the burlap cover and the wicker rim of the basket in which Caine lay provided a clear, if narrow, view of the sleek Arat Kur interceptor as it shot past, heading northwest. Trailing slightly behind, two bulky Hkh'Rkh tilt-rotors, their under-wing pylons bristling with weapons pods, slowed and half transitioned to vertical, turning around the boat in a lazy circle before reangling their props for level flight and roaring after the interceptor.

Caine breathed again, instantly regretted it. The thin littering of fish around him—the false cargo with which he had been told to cover himself—had not been fresh when the boat left Pakis ten hours ago. A day in the hot equatorial sun had not improved their aroma. Or, by dint of close association, his.

The burlap cover came back. A dark, wizened face framed by wispy white hair poked halfway into the basket. At first Caine couldn't be sure if he was staring back at a man or a woman, but the voice left no doubt.

It was—incongruously for Malays and Indonesians—a gravelly bass. *"Hai bro'. Lagi ngapain?"* [1]

Caine smiled, was careful to extend his *right* hand, and replied, *"Senang berjumpa dengan anda, Pak."* [2]

The Indonesian—Javanese by the accent—started back with genuine surprise, but also a smile. A stream of fluid *bahasa* gushed out of him, half of it aimed at the dozen or so persons sheltering in the shade of the starboard gunwale.

Caine shook his head as several of them murmured polite greetings. *"Maafkan saya,"* [3] he apologized. "English?"

The old man displayed a stained and profoundly incomplete set of teeth. "Sure, sure, I'm speak of English. I name is Sumadi. Hey, bro', where your coming from?"

"Pakis."

"No, no, brudda. I mean where your from for real?"

"America."

"Yah. Thought so. And where your going?"

A new voice spoke from the railing of the top deck of the pilot house. "He's going over the side." The English was almost completely unaccented.

The people who had gathered around Caine shrank back from him, opening a path to the unusually tall Indonesian looking down into the afterdeck, his face fully shaded by one of the ubiquitous rural *kaping* wicker hats that reminded Caine of a pointy upended wok.

---

1 Hey! How's it going?

2 Pleased to meet you, "father."

3 I'm sorry.

The old man raised an imploring hand. "Now, Captain—"

"Do you know what you have there, old man?"

"No, but—"

"That's your death, standing right beside you. Trust me, those aircraft that just went overhead are looking for him."

"What? How you know that?"

"I just know. Haven't seen that kind of activity since they found smugglers working out of Toboali from the other side of the fifty-kilometer limit. My guess is if they even suspect that this *bule's* dockside friends smuggled him on board this hull in a basket of fish, it could be the death of us. So over he goes."

The old man was about to renew his protest. Caine put a hand on his arm, scanned the horizon, saw a number of irregular green bumps scattered in the west. "No, Pak Sumadi: just put me over with one of the wooden cargo plats. If it floats, I'll make my own way."

But this only doubled Sumadi's entreaties to the "captain." "See? Such a polite *bule*. How can you do this?"

But the moment Caine had spoken in English, the man at the railing evidently stopped listening to the old man. He leaned forward, very still for five seconds. "Pak Sumadi, that *bule* may be polite, but he is also a magnet for death. For sure, the exos are trying to find him—and we'd better not be around when they do."

"How can you know that?"

"Because I know *him*," He called over his shoulder. "Syarwan, 'Ranto."

Two men came out of the rear door of the pilot house, both wearing broad *kapings* and carrying AKs. The captain's height became more, rather than less, peculiar as Caine noted that all three of them were equally tall. And of very similar build. Indeed, they might be brothers, or even—

—*Damn it. Clones.* The realization must have shown on his face. The "captain" reached out for and received an AK from his comrades, started down the stairs to the afterdeck. "Oh, yes, I know him. Don't you, Pak Sumadi? Imagine that face without the beard, all scrubbed clean, in nice clothes that don't stink of fish. Don't you recognize him?"

Apparently the denizens of the afterdeck didn't make the connection to the pictures of Caine that had surfaced some months after Parthenon. Then again, they didn't look like they had much of an opportunity to follow the news too closely. Tattered clothes, frayed *kapings*, not a one of them who couldn't desperately use another five kilos of body mass. They were refugees, subsistence fisher-folk, deckhands who worked for food and a safe place to spread their straw mats. The Arat Kur invasion and its near-famine aftermath had already created close to a third of a million of these maritime itinerants and was generating more all the time. Living and working on decaying *pinisi* two-masters and rusted-out trawlers, they were the workforce for a strange amalgam of patriots and black marketeers who rendezvoused with small craft that dared to cross the fifty-kilometer no-sail zone, or to pick up cargoes that had been covertly deposited on the dozens of small islands that nearly straddled the blockade line.

They backed away from the man approaching with the AK. "Strange you don't recognize him," the captain continued. "Then again, you never saw him as closely as I did." He pushed his *kaping* farther back on his head. The smile it revealed was not pleasant.

A needle-sharp icicle sprinted from Caine's hind-brain down to his coccyx, but even so, he couldn't keep from smiling at the fatal irony of the moment. To have come so far, only to die at the hands of someone who—by all the odds in the universe—he should never have encountered again. "I don't believe I've seen you since I was on Mars. You were body-guarding for the corporate rep who came to Nolan Corcoran's memorial."

"That wasn't me," explained the smooth-faced clone. "That was one of my genetic brothers."

"So you were the one at the meeting right before the Parthenon Dialogs. With Ruap and Astor-Smath."

"That's right."

Caine looked at the muzzle of the AK. It suddenly looked a lot wider than 7.62 millimeters. "And are you still working for Ruap?"

"I wasn't really working for him then. I'm from CoDevCo's Optigene division."

"So you were working for Astor-Smath."

The barrel lowered a centimeter. "When you're a clone, you don't 'work for' anyone. You're just a slave with no place to run to."

"What do you mean, no place to run to?"

"I mean no country or colony will have us. We're not immigrants, because we're not nationals anywhere else. We don't have our own records, and the mega-corporations won't disclose anything about any genetic manipulation or viral latencies that might make us different from naturally conceived humans. Which has every nation convinced that we're either monsters, murderers, or Typhoid Marys."

Caine looked around the boat: stained deck planking, weather-and-brine-bleached fixtures, oily plumes of incompletely combusted biodiesel chugging out of the engine-access deck-hatch. "And so you live on the margins."

"That's our only choice when we go 'rogue,' as CoDevCo likes to call it. And in the past week, a lot of us have started doing just that: sneaking out of the corporate compounds. By the hundreds, maybe by the thousands. But we've *got* to run away. Why the hell are *you* here?"

"The invaders brought me to Jakarta. From orbit."

"And they just let you go? To hide in a basket of fish?"

The whole story was too long. "I escaped. Had I stayed, I think they were preparing to do to me what it looks like you're preparing to do to me."

"Which is what?"

"Punch my ticket." Caine looked at the AK.

The clone seemed surprised by the frank statement. "You look like you're used to guns, *bule*."

"Ought to be. When I escaped, I joined up with the resistance."

"You—?" The clone looked more closely at Caine. "Yeah, you *had* to escape, didn't you—after you kicked Ruap's tooth out? You're The Dentist, aren't you?"

How does he know—?

"Don't look so surprised. Not a lot of *bules* fighting with the resistance, although there are plenty of you in-country." The AK sagged, half-forgotten. "One of them gave me these rifles. A Russian, I think. In some kinda uniform, but no patches."

Because, like the other elusive foreigners I've heard rumors about, they want to stay invisible. "Yeah, I've heard there are some unusual tourists hiding in Java's jungles, these days."

The clone just nodded, then glanced over the gunwale to the northwest. "But Dentist or no, *bule*, you still have to go over the side."

Caine's stomach seemed to sag down into his intestines. "I've got to get out of Indonesia." He stopped before adding *because the invaders were following me, somehow.* Hearing that, the clones might shoot him and toss him overboard without pause. But on the other hand—

Caine turned and looked back at the Indonesians huddled in the shade; a few tentative smiles answered his glance. The black marketeers who'd smuggled him aboard in Pakis had told him he was shipping out on a fishing boat, not a blockade dodger. The kind of ship that weaved in and out of the *pulaus* that straddled the fifty-kilometer maritime limit. They hauled those few people and objects that got smuggled into or out of Java, and now, some of those smuggled people were in danger because of him. The clone was right: he did have to go over the side.

"Listen, Dentist," the clone emphasized, "you—and we—might not live long if we don't get you into the water. Now."

Caine nodded, headed toward the gunwale, looking for life jackets.

"Not that way," the clone muttered. He turned and

shouted toward the pilot house. "'Ranto, get him some gear. Syarwan, come about to due west, best speed." Back to Caine. "You can't get over the limit, not if they're looking for you. And obviously they are. So you're going to have to sneak back, hide out if you can."

Caine found the courage to nod at his own death warrant. "Better than having all of us blown out of the water here."

The clone smiled. "Okay. Now, do you know where you are, where you need to go?"

Caine looked at the sun, glanced toward the small islands scattered in a one-hundred-twenty-degree arc from southwest to northwest. "We're about fifteen klicks east of the northern extents of the Pulau Seribu—the Thousand Islands."

"Good. You studied a map. That's probably going to save your life." The ship had come about, vomiting black gouts of exhaust. The clone pointed over the starboard bow. "Look between twenty-five and thirty degrees: you see that little island?"

"Yes."

"Pulau Ringit. Closest to us, relatively easy approach. There's an islet before you get there. No dangerous shoals, smooth sea bed. Rest there."

"Got it."

"It's only a few hundred meters between the islet and Pulau Ringit, but don't cross until dark." 'Ranto emerged from the pilot house, slid down the rails, handed a heavy canvas duffle to the captain. "And try to stay underwater."

"Well, I can hold my breath as well as the next person, but—"

The clone started producing equipment out of the

canvas duffle: a pony tank, regulator, mask, fins. "You know how to use these?"

"Everything except the regulator, I've snorkeled, but never—"

"Then learn. Fast."

As Caine started fitting the mask, the captain checked his watch and the horizon. "Once you're on Ringit, just blend in."

"Blend in?"

"Sure. Lots of *bules* there, stranded when the Arat Kur hit. With their credit cards cut off, they're running out of money and have to scrabble like the rest of us. Pretty amusing. You'll fit right in. Although you'll want to get some clothes. You can pass yourself off as a dive enthusiast—unless you're talking to a real diver."

"Are the islands occupied?"

"By the Roaches or Sloths? No. They don't like to isolate themselves in small numbers. They've sent a few government troops out to keep watch, but half of them will look the other way for a few rupiahs and the other half would desert if they could. If the invaders really have to settle problems in the islands, they do it with orbital surveillance and interdiction, drones, aerial patrols and counterinsurgency drops."

"Okay, but our forces, the commandoes who are arriving in-country. They must be swimming in across the line all the time. How do they do it without getting caught, wiped out?"

The clone grinned. "There's a lot going on out here. More than I know, and a *whole* lot more than the invaders know. But right now, that doesn't matter. This does. After you reach Pulau Ringit, you won't need to do any more diving. Just book a ship to Java. But not directly to Jakarta. The Hkh'Rkh are aggressive about their search-and-detainment checks of the ships that put in there. Get a little packet into a Barat coastal *kempang*, like Sedari. Then go overland to Jakarta. Lots of *bules* there, so you won't stand out. Use trains or buses, you'll attract less attention. And use *bahasa* whenever you can. You want to sound like you've been here a few months."

Caine nodded. "Thanks for the advice. And the help." He shouldered the pony-tank, tested the regulator: fine.

The clone returned his nod. "Last bit of advice. We're less than seven klicks from Ringit, so you've got a swim ahead of you. But don't keep the regulator in your mouth. You'll forget you're using up air breathing. Swim as long as you can without becoming tired, exhale, put in the regulator, take a long, slow breath, start again. You'll go farther and last longer with the air you've got. And don't go deep or you could get the bends."

No depth gauge, so I'd better err to the side of caution. Caine heard a thin rumble to the north, looked up. Three black specks were on the horizon. They grew noticeably larger as he watched.

The clone had noticed them, too. "Talk time is over. They must have seen us rendezvous with another smuggler, earlier this afternoon."

"But you didn't violate the limit."

"No, but once we're outside of the coastal buoy line, no hull is allowed to approach another closer than three kilometers. If one tries, we are supposed to report it and open fire if we can't warn them away."

"The invaders' orbital surveillance must be extraordinary."

"A lot of what they've got is pretty extraordinary. Like whatever they've got that allows them to follow you. Which may be the real reason they're coming back. So get going."

The enemy aircraft had resolved into discernible shapes; it was the same three that had buzzed them earlier. They were approaching in an inverted delta formation. Caine watched as Pak Sumadi smiled his shattered smile and reached under a tarp for a stock-rotted AK-47. Beyond it, Caine saw the distinctive cubist-coke-bottle shape of an RPG-7 warhead.

The clone followed his eyes, shook his head. "No, you're not even going to think about staying here. If they didn't see us rendezvous with the other boat, then we'll be fine as long as *you're* not on board. But if you are, and they're looking for you, then you're dead and so are we. And if they *did* see us link up with the other boat, then they're coming to attack us. So either way, you need to be on your way."

Caine couldn't be sure how much was the bravado of the valorous damned, and how much was just good common sense. He snugged his mask, sat on the gunwale, took a bearing on Pulau Ringit. Leisurely pace or not, seven kilometers was still one hell of a long swim. He turned back: Pak Sumadi had his right hand raised in farewell. "Hati-hati," he said.

"Hati-hati," Caine answered. He turned to the clone. "*Sampai jumpa.*"[1]

"Probably not. Go. Now."

Caine didn't stop to think. He pushed off, holding his mask. As soon as he hit the water—harder than he

---

1 (I'll) See you.

expected because of the speed of the boat—he swam
away. After ten seconds, he jackknifed forward at the
waist, straightened his legs toward the sky behind him
and kicked hard.

He went down quickly, saw the light dim around
him. He straightened out. Other than the small,
shimmering disk of the sun and the wake of the ship,
he could imagine himself trapped in a green glass
paperweight: his surroundings were silent, still, identical in all directions. He looked up at the dappled
path of the wake, calculated the course of the ship,
turned twenty-five degrees to the right of it. Yes, that
matched his estimate of the heading for Ringit. He
took a breath from the regulator, stowed it, began
swimming, felt a spasm of pain in his left forearm.
Not the Mars wound again, not now.

Behind and to the left, the water frothed white and
he could make out the hull once again; the ship was
backing engines. Preparing to be boarded? Already?
No way of knowing. He kicked, exhaled slowly—*spread
out the bubbles*—and took another breath from the
regulator. He pushed his legs into long, sinuous, deep-
digging kicks, looked up to attempt to gauge his depth.

Back in the direction of the ship, through the faint
jade green of the water, he saw a bright, orange flash
where its weed-trailing keel had been. Then the shock
and muffled boom—as much felt as heard—hit and
deafened him. Clones, Pak Sumadi, rotting fish—all
gone as though they had never existed. And now, going
down farther than he should, Caine was heading into
the depths where Ulysses had met his deceased comrades. But, as he had in college, Caine rejected Virgil's
version in favor of Homer's. Like his code-namesake

Odysseus, Caine had no desire to visit the dead, much less join them—not if he could help it.

Correcting for the mild current, Caine set himself back on course for Ringit, resolving to come up in five minutes to check his deviation from that heading. He held his breath. No bubbles for at least a minute. As he resumed his slow kicking, Caine resolved that this day, the sea-god Poseidon—ever the enemy of Odysseus—would not be the final arbiter of his fate.

Northern approaches to the Pulau Seribu, Java Sea, Earth

From the moment the oversized and ancient commercial fishing boat drew alongside Captain Ong's small Taiwanese bulk container ship, he knew that the encounter was going to be a peculiar one. The fishing boat was too small to be authorized for passage over the fifty-klick blockade line just ahead, and hadn't managed to get a new radio yet. That, or she was choosing not to advertise she had a set that hadn't been fried by the invader EMP strikes of three weeks ago. Instead, she signaled her intents by semaphore and hand gestures. Although piracy had decreased since the invasion, Ong still took the precaution of putting an armed team aboard the boat before he agreed to go over for the requested meeting.

As he stepped off the accommodation stairs onto the swaying and somewhat grimy deck, Ong discovered a second, and far more profound, peculiarity: a woman with fair skin, jet black hair, and glass-green eyes emerged from the pilot house. She was taller than any of the men around her, shapely, and projected an air of certainty that she would not be trifled with simply because she was *not* to be trifled with.

The master of the fishing boat remarked that the lady had asked to speak to the captain in private, and they could have the use of the master's quarters, if they wished. His deference suggested the woman had shown him impeccable proof of generous payment, the evidence of powerful familial connections, or the certainty of dire penalties if compliance was not forthcoming. Given the man's tendency to bow whenever it might be vaguely appropriate, Ong guessed her bona fides might have included all three.

But instead, the woman invited Ong to accompany her to the taffrail, where the stink of the engine's fumes and the racket of its operation seemed sure to discourage eavesdropping.

She did not bother with preamble, or even niceties. "I am told, Captain Ong, that you are a man who may be relied upon."

"I am pleased to be spoken of so highly, Ms.—"

"Smith. Elena Smith."

"—Ms. Smith. However, without knowing who has been so complimentary regarding my character, I am at a loss to—"

"Captain, there are individuals in Singapore with whom you share information about what you observe during your food runs to Indonesia. I understand from them that you served in the Taiwanese military, and even, briefly, in the National Security Bureau."

Ong blinked. "Ms. Smith, I cannot—"

"Please. Neither you nor I have the time to engage in denials that cannot be sustained. I can recite the many things I've heard about you. But you already know that I wouldn't be on a broken-down fishing boat just outside the Indonesian blockade line to wheedle information. That's not why I trailed you here all the way from Singapore."

"So why did you trail me from Singapore, Ms. Smith?"

"To solicit your help in reaching Indonesia. Of course."

Ong was a polite man by both upbringing and inclination and so nodded slowly. "You are, I take it, familiar with the impediments?"

"Many of them, but news is not easy to come by, and I have been traveling for some time."

"Traveling from where, if I may ask?"

She surveyed him levelly. "The eastern coast of the United States down to the Panama Canal. Once there, I—changed ships to a high-speed liner, bound for Singapore."

Hmmm. With every passing second, Ms. Smith sounded more and more like an operative. Except, where was her support staff and/or equipment, why was she traveling alone, and why had she scrambled after his ship, sight unseen, to attempt to make infiltration arrangements on the high seas? Something was not right. But it might be professionally dangerous to attempt to find out what that something was, so Ong followed her lead. "Very well. I take it you did not stay long in Singapore?"

"Just long enough to get in contact with a family friend. Who told me about you and your ship."

And who also told you that I am debriefed by military intelligence there, after every food run. And who is just the sort of friend every American family has in Singapore. "So I take it you did not have time to apprise yourself of the new conditions of the blockade?"

"I did not, but I know that there are hundreds of ships porting in Java with food every week, so the border must be porous."

"Not as porous as you might think, madam."

"But they've opened up the approach channel and porting restrictions, haven't they?"

How long has this woman been traveling? "Yes, madam. We still must cross the fifty-kilometer boundary using one of five designated navigation lanes: Jakarta, Semarang, Surabaya, Cilacap, and Banywangi. But after that, smaller ships such as mine may disperse to another seven smaller ports. However, government boats follow and monitor us all the way to our destination, stand guard while we unload, and then escort us out. I believe we are occasionally followed by alien submersibles, as well."

"So the invaders determined that it was too difficult to coordinate all the shipping of foodstuffs into the five big ports?"

"No, they determined that their situation might become untenable if people started starving. Which some of them did, after the first week. So, fearing a more general revolt, the invaders opened up the seven other distribution points along the coastline."

"And have things been easier since then?"

"On the contrary, they have been much worse. After the initial restrictions were lifted, the Sloths became more difficult than ever, stopping ships for the smallest infractions, shooting anyone who disagreed or refused to obey immediately."

"It sounds as though the Hkh'Rkh didn't like the open-coastline rule, then."

"No. Clearly, that humanitarian decision must have come from the Roaches. They seem to have some kind of conscience, even though they're bugs."

"Actually," murmured the woman, "they're not."

"No? Well, they look like insects. But I'm quite sure that the open coastline was their idea. I suspect that the Hkh'Rkh would have been quite happy to let every human on Java die."

"So, getting to Java. How close do you approach the outlying islands, the *pulaus*?"

"We have a no-approach zone of eight kilometers, Ms. Smith. The exosapients are very strict in the enforcement of that limit and of maintaining speed. If we slow to less than eight knots, they scramble VTOLs and board the ship. If a ship slows to less than five knots, they often sink her. Rail gun rounds from orbit, usually."

"But if you drop something in the water, and leave it behind, what then?"

"If we are seen dropping anything, even trash, over the side once we come within the fifty-kilometer limit, we will be boarded or sunk."

"They monitor your trash? Really?"

"I know of two captains who ignored that restriction. They are both dead, their ships at the bottom."

"I see. But what if something was in the water already, and was being towed behind you?"

"I'm quite sure they'd see it, unless it was very small, smaller than a life raft. Some people tried that the first week of the blockade. They're now keeping company with the two captains I mentioned."

"What if the towed object was small enough to remain concealed in your wake?"

Ong stared at the woman and decided that she was not only quite clever, but quite insane. "Ms. Smith, the wake of even this ship is extremely—"

"I am aware of its punishing force, Captain. My question is, could you rig a rope system that would allow me to remain in the wake, reliably?"

"Well, if we maintain the lowest allowed speed—"

"Which seems advisable for my health."

"—then yes, I suppose so. But even if we pass within eight kilometers of one of the *pulau*, how do you plan to get to it? That is a very long swim, and I remain unconvinced of the effectiveness of the shark repellent we have been given."

"Oh, once I'm in the water, and you're going slowly enough, my friend can get me safely to land."

"Your—friend?" Ong asked, looking about.

Ms. Smith only smiled and crooked a finger as she began walking forward. Ong followed.

She stopped at the midship hold, which was loosely covered. Probably no catch in there. Indeed, this part of the ship smelled unusually clean. Ong looked around. "Is your friend joining us here?"

"No. We just joined her." She pulled back the cover.

Ong looked down. Set snug within the stained gray bulkheads of the ship was a large tank, at least four meters long by three wide by two deep. And in it was a sleek dolphin of medium size. Ong stared, speechless.

"Necessity is the mother of invention, Captain," Ms. Smith explained. "Mariel here is one of a few score of trained cetaceans that were being used by tourist-trap sea-life exhibits all throughout Southeast

Asia. I'm sure you're familiar with the attraction: 'swim with the dolphins.' Most of the marine parks offering that experience were in Thailand and Malaysia, a few in Vietnam and one or two in exclusive resorts in the Celebes."

"And so you plan—?"

"To have you tow me over the fifty-kilometer limit in the wake of your ship, with Mariel already in the water with me. When we reach your closest approach to the western islands on the way in to Jakarta, I'll cut loose and she'll tow me in. She's quite good at following general signals, and we get along well. When I've gone ashore, she'll start back to her home port."

"In Singapore?"

"Borneo, now."

"Then how did you get the dolph—?"

"Long story, and I can't tell you all of it. Now, can you think of any reason why this plan won't work?"

The scheme sounded outré, but... "No," he heard himself say. "I cannot foresee any particular reason it would fail."

"Very good, then, Captain Ong. I have a letter of authorization from the Singaporean authorities, and a printout and bank-stamped receipt of the handsome deposit that has been made into your account back home. Now, if you'd be so kind, Mariel and I would like to come aboard. The accommodation stairs will be fine for me, but I think Mariel's tank is going to require your biggest winch."

Chapter Thirty-Two

Central Jakarta, Earth

Despite the spatter of the gushing cataracts spilling over the edges of the corner restaurant's awnings, Caine heard a softer, steady *blipt blipt blipt* close by. He looked down, searching for the source of the dripping.

It was him, or rather his clothes, draining unhurriedly into a puddle alongside the leg of the table at which he was sitting. He looked up at the restaurant's owner, who was wiping glasses behind the worn bar. Who looked at the puddle and then back up at him.

"*Maafkan saya,*" Caine apologized.

"*Tidak apa-apa,*"[1] the man responded. Someone called him from the back. He disappeared behind a cloth hanging that separated the ten peeling-chrome tables from the compact kitchen at the rear.

To Caine's immediate right, the rain was a thrashing gray curtain, spattering hard and straight against the still-hot street. Each drop's murderous impact

---

1 Don't worry about it.

shattered it into a hundred microdrops, most of which rebounded to knee height, the rest vaporizing into a thin, pervasive mist. The locals refused to label it a monsoon—yet. But during the past two days—first on the wharf in Sedari, then on the bus to Pataruman, and finally in the overcrowded train to Jakarta, Riordan had heard the word used more and more, and uttered less dismissively with each passing hour. And with each passing hour, there were more sirens, more sounds of gunshots, more distant columns of black smoke beating against the downward torrent, like curled fists trying to break through to the blue sky above. There were more smiles, too, but not the open, friendly kind reserved for *bules* who, like himself, could almost get by in mangled *bahasa*. These new smiles were fierce and furtive, exchanged between the locals like secret messages slipped back and forth in a prison cafeteria. Daily, they were drawing more of their warders' blood.

The sharp upswing in insurgent activity was logical. Cloud cover and precipitation eroded orbital imaging and ruined ground-level visibility. For tactical scopes or goggles, the humidity and superheated mist was a poor backdrop against which to pick out thermal silhouettes at longer ranges and the incessant drumming of the rain swallowed up any but the sharpest and loudest sounds. The rapidly growing resistance was able to initiate ambushes at closer range, plant control-detonated mines unobserved, and emerge from and fade back into the narrow streets and tangled jungles with the flawless ease that comes from a lifetime of experience.

The proprietor reappeared, carrying a bowl, a fork,

a small napkin, and two bottles of different kinds of sauce—all in one hand. He placed the bowl in front of Caine: *nasi goreng,* Indonesian fried rice. Caine detected the faint scent of peanut sauce, and spied a few strips of what might be chicken, but—given recent conditions—were more likely dog. He smiled. "*Maafkan saya,*" he apologized, pointing at the meat and shaking his head.

The owner smiled. "'S okay, bro'. I speak English."

Caine nodded. "Thanks. I just ordered the *nasi goreng.*"

"'S what you have, bro'."

"I mean, plain *nasi goreng.* I can't afford meat." By way of proof, Caine dug the last, sodden five-hundred-rupiah note out of his pocket. "That's all I have."

The man looked at the note, then looked at him. "Keep your money, *bule.* Come back when the Roaches are gone and I'll overcharge you enough for both times, hey?" And Caine couldn't help returning the wide, disarming smile that always made him wonder, *how can they smile like that and kill so quickly and ferociously?* But he shook his head and pushed the note an inch closer to the owner. "No, take it. I'm not going to need it after I leave here."

The man's ample cheeks dropped along with his smile. His teak-brown eyes ran back and forth over Caine's face. Then the man nodded somberly and picked up the note. Back at the bar, he looked up again. "I keep it for you, hey? 'Case you change your mind?"

"That's kind of you, but don't bother."

The man spent a long time cleaning a single glass, occasionally looking at Caine, who knew, from seeing his own reflection in storefronts and restroom mirrors,

that he presented a pretty unusual appearance. The
tattered clothes he'd snatched from a drying line were
two sizes too small, their incongruity magnified by his
disintegrating woven-straw flip-flops, six-day growth of
beard, and improbably expensive watch. "So," drawled
the proprietor, picking up a new glass, "where you
come from, Robinson Crusoe?"

"America."

"I know that, *bule*. I mean, where you come from
to get here?"

A more sensitive question. "I guess the answer I
give depends on why you're asking."

The owner nodded, took extreme interest in cleaning
the glass that had now been thoroughly cleaned four
times. "So," he said, smiling as widely as before, so
casual that he might have been talking about a local
soccer star, "you one of the swimmers?"

"I beg your pardon?"

"You know, you swim ashore?" A pause. "Like
others do?"

Ah. "Like others?"

"Yeah, like others."

"You know these swimmers?"

"Me? Know them? Hey, no." He looked up slowly.
"But I've served a few."

"In this restaurant?"

His smile returned. This time, it was like the secret
smiles Indonesians shared when they heard a distant
bomb go off. "No, never served swimmers here. But
I've served them."

Caine started on his *nasi goreng*, resolved not to wolf
it down. "Well, now you *have* served a swimmer in your
restaurant. But I'm not the kind of swimmer you mean."

"Oh? What kind do I mean?"

Somewhere to the east, there was a distant, muted rumble, too short and dull to be thunder. Caine nodded in its direction. "I'm not the kind of swimmer who sneaks ashore to help you do *that*."

The barkeep frowned. "No? Then what kind are you?"

"I'm here to talk."

"To us?"

"To them."

He stopped wiping the glass. "*Tai.* You musta bumped your head on a reef, bro'. That's not a good idea."

"It will be if I can talk to the right, er, person."

"I don't know. Those don't seem to like talking very much."

"That's why I need you to tell me the kind of 'persons' who approach the corner behind me."

"Whaddya mean?"

Caine finished the *nasi goreng*. "I mean, I need you to tell me when you see the next patrol coming, and whether it's being carried out by 'persons' with two legs, or 'persons' with six legs, or both."

"Almost never the six-legs on their own, bro'. They don't like to come out and play very much." He smiled. "They're pretty smart that way."

"They're pretty smart every way."

The proprietor leaned forward. "You sound like you know."

Caine nodded. "I know a little. Enough to know that they're actually pretty competent fighters, but they're not comfortable outside. They'd rather work inside, or in tunnels."

The proprietor started cleaning the same glass again. "Ho! Then why'd they land in Indonesia? Seen our sewers—the few we've got? Ever try to dig a tunnel? Man, why you think we've got no subways? Took 'em years trying put in fiber-optics, and they mostly gave up. I think." A pause. "Hey, here they come."

"A patrol?"

"Yeh, but not the one you want. Two-legs only. Four of them."

"Thanks. Don't stare."

"Okay, okay. Hey, why don't you face the other way, out into the street, see for yourself?"

"That might not be healthy for me."

"They don't seem to be take any special notice of *bules*, so—"

"That's not it. I mean they might recognize me. Personally."

He put the glass down. "What? You kidding me?"

"Nope. It's not likely, but I don't want to be recognized before I make my move."

"Okay, I get it. I'll—hey, hey."

"What?"

"A pair of the six-legs, moving pretty fast. Coming from where the two-legs did, probably trying to catch up with them. The Sloths do that, you know. Make it hard for the Roaches to keep up. They don't like 'em much."

"Can you still see the Hkh'Rkh?"

"You mean the Sloths? No, bro'; they're gone."

Caine stood. "Thanks. I hope I'll see you again."

"Yah, *bule. Titi-deejay.*"[1]

"*Hati-hati*, friend." Caine turned, walked to the door, did not break his stride as he pushed it open.

---

1 Take care.

Or as he stepped out from under the awning into the downrushing wave of water. Two of the hexapedal powered suits used by the Arat Kur infantry were just entering the intersection. Caine walked straight at them, his hands held high. He cleared his throat to make sure his voice wouldn't quaver or go hoarse, and shouted. "I greet the soldiers of the Arat Kur Wholenest."

The two Arat Kur came to a skittering stop. Even with their suits hermetically sealed, Caine could make out their surprised chittering.

"I am without weapons," Caine continued. "I am the human Speaker who went before the Accord, and who was rescued at Barnard's Star. I have shared a roof with Speaker to Nestless Darzhee Kut. I have returned to speak with him."

One of the suits was evidently equipped with a translator. "Are you the human named Caine Riordan?"

Caine was stunned by the rapidity with which he had been identified. "I am."

"Then you must come with us. Immediately. Make haste."

Caine walked briskly so that he was between them as they scuttled in the direction of the Arat Kur compound in the presidential palace. "How did you know who I am? Why are we making such haste?" he asked.

"The answer to both your questions is the same," replied the Arat Kur with the translator. "The Wholenest's allies wish to kill you. They have said so. Repeatedly."

Presidential Palace, Jakarta, Earth

"Speaker Kut?"

Rubble and scree. Now what? And only five minutes before Hu'urs Khraam was due to make planetfall to assume direct command of what was clearly a deteriorating situation—as much with their allies as their enemies. "Enter."

A defense-tech clattered in, the front hatch of his suit open in respect and for sake of clear communication. "Darzhee Kut, we have a matter that requires your attention. Urgently."

"Rock-sibling, I am flattered that you feel the need of my counsel, but your commander is—"

"Esteemed Darzhee Kut, hear my song. This is not a military situation. If the human speaks truth, it is a diplomatic matter of the utmost importance."

"Tell me, quickly."

"While we were isolated from the Hkh'Rkh, a human approached us. He is not an Indonesian. He claims he is known to you as the emissary named Caine Riordan. We reasoned that—"

Darzhee Kut had stopped hearing. "Bring him. Immediately."

The Arat Kur clattered out backwards. He returned with his partner, Caine Riordan walking between them.

"Speaker Riordan, I trust you are—" Darzhee Kut looked again. "*Are* you well?"

"I am in good health and unharmed. My return to this place has been, er, challenging."

"Why did you not signal in advance? Why did you not return earlier?"

Caine smiled slowly. "Darzhee Kut, surely you have already guessed."

Darzhee Kut bobbed. "You feared for your life if you did not come directly into Arat Kur custody. I understand. But I must ask that this time, regardless of the provocations you might encounter, that you give your word that you shall not attempt to flee—or mount attacks." Darzhee Kut let his inner polyps twitch with amusement. "Not even against your own species."

Caine obviously detected the humor. "That last may be the hardest of all promises to keep, Darzhee Kut. But provided I remain in the custody of the Arat Kur, I give you the parole you ask for, as is customary for an emissary."

"And we receive you again, as an ambassador of your people. Although I fear the situation may have passed beyond the intercession of diplomats. Or common sense."

"Perhaps, but one must still try."

"We harmonize as one voice in this, Caine Riordan. I welcome you back, but you must also accept our close monitoring at all times. Many of our associates are profoundly suspicious of you."

"That is an uncommonly tactful way of saying they wish to kill me."

Darzhee Kut could not tell if the strange smile on the human's revoltingly mobile face was one of mirth or rue. "We shall discuss your status among our allies later on. I regret that I am pressed for time. So I will ask you to accompany these two defense-technicians to suitable quarters."

One of whom raised a claw. "Speaker Kut, if I may encumber you a moment longer. It is known that you have regular contact with First Delegate Hu'urs Khraam and I would plead that he hears the servants of the Wholenest in this one matter. Although the Hkh'Rkh are often too brutal and quick-tempered, I wish to ask Hu'urs Khraam to approve their requests for general reprisals against towns and neighborhoods that are known to harbor and support the insurgents."

"Surely you cannot mean this."

"Surely I do, and I must request it. Speaker Kut, we cannot separate civilians from combatants anymore. This leads to friction with our Hkh'Rkh allies. We are to work as their conduct officers, but as the guerilla activity grows and becomes more unpredictable and bold, we are constantly in contention with the Hkh'Rkh field commanders who wish to destroy sections of *kempangs* to which insurgents have fled. We are forced to argue with our allies more than we fight the humans, and most of us have come to harmonize with the Hkh'Rkh in this matter. We must make reprisals, if only to prevent the humans from using any refuge twice."

Unshaded sun, has it come to this? Darzhee Kut adopted as patient a tone as he could. "We are on the humans' homeworld. If we start destroying their communities in the way you suggest, they will see this as a prelude to genocide."

"Speaker Kut, I only know this: in war, it is better that the enemy dies instead of your rock-siblings. Please, listen—and learn—from the songs of your grandmothers once again. We have no choice with the humans. We never did."

Darzhee Kut started at the defense-tech's unexpected slip, considering that he had not deactivated his translator. Kut looked at Caine, who looked more confused than elucidated. Hopefully, Riordan would not deduce the full significance of what he had just heard about the Wholenest's prior knowledge of humans, but, either way, Darzhee Kut had to prevent any more unwitting disclosures. "Rock-sibling, I harmonize with your fear and frustration, but this is a tactical matter. I am a diplomat, a Speaker."

"Yes, Speaker Kut, but all know that the sound-bristles of Hu'urs Khraam are attuned to your songs. I speak for many of us in this, and hope—"

"I will mention it to Hu'urs Khraam. He will decide if and how to proceed." Darzhee Kut held up a claw to signal an end to any further entreaties, turned slightly toward Caine. "I regret that I may not accompany you, Caine Riordan, but I must meet with First Delegate Hu'urs Khraam. These two will escort you to quarters, provide you with opportunities to cleanse, clothe, and feed yourself. Then, when Hu'urs Khraam has no further need of me, I shall come and share roof with you. Is this acceptable?"

"It is an honor, Darzhee Kut."

"The honor is ours, Caine Riordan. I wish you very well and shall attend you as soon as I may." He turned to the two Arat Kur soldiers. "Apprise Thrice-Leader Oonvai Grek of this situation and make it clear to him that your deviation from protocols was warranted and blameless, and that he will be held personally responsible for the safety and proper treatment of Caine Riordan. Lastly, no humans or Hkh'Rkh are to have contact with this emissary. I speak for Hu'urs Khraam in this, and there are no exceptions."

"And if the Hkh'Rkh violently object to these dictates, Speaker Kut?"

"Then you must violently insist that they be obeyed. You may use all methods at your disposal. You are dismissed."

As they left through the rear door, Darzhee Kut heard a faint, even frail skittering at the high room's other, larger entrance. He turned—and felt his polyps stiffen in surprise. "First Delegate Hu'urs Khraam! Apologies, I received no word that you were already waiting."

"Harmonies, rock-sibling; I sent no word."

"I have, this minute, a most interesting event to report."

Hu'urs Khraam waved a relaxed claw, eased himself into one of the room's six belly-couches. "I know of what you speak; this room has antennae which are extensions of my own."

Shattered eggs! The old darkworm has fewer scruples than I thought...

Perhaps Hu'urs Khraam genuinely possessed his reputed power to read minds; perhaps he saw the stunned sag in Darzhee Kut's manipulator polyps; perhaps he simply anticipated the younger Arat Kur's surprise. Whatever the cause, he seemed to respond to Darzhee Kut's reaction as though it had been spoken aloud. "Too much is at stake for me not to know all that transpires in this room, particularly since it is where you and Urzueth Ragh have had to be my proxies against the pressure of First Voice and his First Fist. You have my gratitude, particularly, Darzhee Kut."

"It is my honor to echo your melodies in this place, Esteemed First Delegate. Regarding the Speaker Caine Riordan, I wonder if we should house him here, or in the fleet."

"Why the fleet?"

"I fear for his safety from the Hkh'Rkh and from our human associates."

Hu'urs Khraam settled his belly down lower into the couch. "Let us keep him here. Attend my reasons. First, he returns to us as an emissary, not for asylum, and so we must house him where we would other emissaries: here on this planet. Secondly, we may wish to speak to him, have his immediate counsel at this delicate juncture, and I wish to watch his reactions both as he speaks to us and hears what we say. He may reveal much to us this way.

"Besides, Riordan's arrival is most propitious politically. We now have a means of resuming discourse with the humans without angering the Hkh'Rkh by either making or accepting a diplomatic overture, without appearing 'weak,' as they like to say. And be sure, the humans will also see the advantage of having a negotiator already in our midst, and whose unexpected presence necessitates that we reestablish contact with them. They cannot fail to have deduced why we elected not to resume discourse when they offered, so I suspect the humans will be glad for this serendipitous development."

"And hopefully they will also appreciate how Riordan may save them from making any further blunders." Darzhee Kut lowered his voice slightly. "First Delegate Khraam, his decision to come out of hiding and risking proximity to the Hkh'Rkh and Ruap's troops is a more noble gesture than our grandmothers' songs ever led me to hope for in a human. Riordan's act should be widely sung among our people."

But Hu'urs Khraam simply shifted as though he had discovered a pebble between his belly-plates. "His deed may be noble. But that may create a problem for us."

"How?"

"Such a human, one who might harmonize and keep his word, could thereby influence our simpler rock-siblings to imagine that we must reciprocally deal fairly with him, with the humans. Worst of all, they might believe that our negotiations with the humans should be carried out in good faith."

"What?"

"Darzhee Kut, surely you cannot believe that I expected the humans to meet the greater demands that the Hkh'Rkh imposed? You said so yourself."

"Yes, but I—"

"Be still and hear the wise hymn of the coming decade, as envisioned by your elders. Unable to come quickly to agreement, the occupation of Earth will wear on. We shall turn over the planetside responsibilities to the Hkh'Rkh, but continue to provide orbital support. Their faces, not ours, shall thus be associated with the misery of Indonesia in particular, and this world in general. Negotiations will drag from months to years. Meanwhile our fleet will reconsolidate and carry our offensive beyond Ross 154, pushing into Junction system and continuing down the Big Green Main to Zeta Tucanae. With all of human space controlled, their capitulation becomes inevitable. The Hkh'Rkh are given Epsilon Indi as their war prize, thereby establishing them on the green world that can most obstruct human contact with the rest of the Green Main. We withdraw, still quibbling over a co-dominium of Barnard's Star. By this point, the humans will have readily conceded to a staged withdrawal from their intrusion into our space at 70 Ophiuchi."

Darzhee Kut almost stammered. "But in the scenario

you propose, the Hkh'Rkh cannot independently reach their new colony on Epsilon Indi. Their ships are limited to seven-point-four-light-year shifts and cannot cross the—"

"My song is not finished. In ten years, the humans will have rebuilt and will chafe at the Hkh'Rkh presence in their midst. Meanwhile, the Hkh'Rkh will have armed themselves rapidly with our aid, probably establishing shift-carrier construction facilities on Epsilon Indi. They will already be dreaming of seizing another green world along the main."

"But the humans will crush them."

"Perhaps. Perhaps not. Our aid in this can turn the tide one way or the other, particularly given our presence, accepted or not, at Barnard's Star."

"First Delegate, with respect, you are creating a future in which both these races will remain at war for decades to come. They will come to hate each other unremittingly. There will be genocide."

"Just so, Darzhee Kut, just so."

"But this is—"

"This is their nature, Darzhee Kut. They cannot change it. Nor can we. But we can control it. We can control it so that they focus their savagery on each other and remain too embroiled in their reciprocal genocide to cast covetous eyes upon our worlds. They will cripple their economies with a series of wars. Before they are through, the Wholenest will have had time to refocus its energies and consensus to adapt to a perpetual war-footing. For with such savage neighbors as these, we have no other choice."

"So the disputes at Convocation, our negotiations

with the humans, even our alliance with the Hkh'Rkh: these are all a ruse?"

"Not entirely. We do need the Hkh'Rkh here to conduct the infantry operations. And we will indeed remain committed to supporting their demands for territorial concessions from the humans. But otherwise, my scruples are reserved for ensuring the welfare of my race, Darzhee Kut. Indeed, you might wish to be still for some moments, or hours, and ensure that your own scruples harmonize with that primary criterion."

Darzhee Kut suppressed a wave of dizziness. "What of honesty and honor, which the human Riordan shows by coming here?"

"What of it? If all humans were capable of such deeds, such sacrifice, perhaps we would act differently. But they are not. They are as they ever were, and we must see to the safety of our Wholenest. That objective comes first and, if need be, at the expense of all other scruples and values. I'm sure you agree with that, do you not, Speaker Kut?"

I do not. But he said, "This song is new to me, and I have yet to learn its harmonies. Forgive me, Hu'urs Khraam."

"No forgiveness is necessary. I had not envisioned a member of the Ee'ar caste learning of these plans so soon, but you are an exceptional Ee'ar, Darzhee Kut. In subsequent discussions with your rock-siblings and caste-peers, exercise the discretion I know you possess: do not mention this. Now, what insights have you gained into the current human strategy by studying their local records?"

"As I feared, Hu'urs Khraam, very little. We selected Indonesia because of its disaffection from the world government, which made it a pariah among the greater nations. Consequently, it was not included in the innermost strategic circles."

"So there are no clues to why the humans did not destroy the antimatter refinery and refueling site on the asteroid they call Vesta?"

Darzhee Kut signaled a negative. "The corporate spies employed by CoDevCo and the few reliable collaborators we have in the Indonesian military hypothesize that the Confederation did not believe our attack to be so imminent. Thus, they had only partially completed the job of rigging the asteroid facility with the necessary explosives when we arrived there—"

"—But because our first flotilla seized Vesta and engaged their fleet at Jupiter two days before the rest of our fleet shifted in beyond cislunar space, the humans had enough advance warning to disable the larger facility on the Moon?"

"This is their hypothesis, which agrees with our own. I am puzzled at your anxiety over this detail, Hu'urs Khraam."

"I have no logical justification for it, other than that this failure is atypical, given what we've observed of the humans."

"Esteemed Hu'urs Khraam, explicate, please."

"Consider how the humans disabled their lunar antimatter facility. They did not resort to bombs, but had the presence of mind to remove all those parts that would be simple for them to restore, but almost impossible for us to independently fabricate. How could that act of sabotage be managed so well and with such foresight, and the other so bungled?"

"Humans are inconstant, Hu'urs Khraam. We have always known this."

"Perhaps, but consider this. We caught almost all their naval carriers in one trap at Barnard's Star, and then more here, in their home system. We could hardly ask for better outcomes, Darzhee Kut. Yet—"

"Yet what?"

"Yet their tactics in each engagement showed great ingenuity and skill. At Barnard's Star, they spent as few hulls as possible and yet, by turns, slowed us, inflicted maximum damage, and saved half of their own force. And here, on the ground, they routinely confound us with outdated technology amplified by their martial acumen, and by their canny observation of our weaknesses, of our unfamiliarity with the craft of war, and of the Hkh'Rkh's tendencies toward tactical impetuosity."

"Yes, Hu'urs Khraam, but let us consider their failures, also. They did save many of their capital ships at Barnard's Star, but those hulls are now stranded in that system. And those that they did lose were captained by individuals who evinced little imagination or verve; those ships seemed to be slavishly following a preset battle plan. And here on their home world, the humans' greatest corporate houses have become our allies and are undoing the defenses of their own species. So again: humanity is defined by its variations, its inconstancies."

"Perhaps. But there was no such variation or inconstancy in their push to the stars, Speaker Kut. The speed and efficiency of their expansion was so great that all of the members of the Accord, even the Dornaani, were caught off-guard. I find it hard to believe that now, with their survival at stake, and their known talent for war and destruction, that they would perform so unevenly. It is an oddness, and it troubles me." He rose; Darzhee distinctly heard one of the linking-integuments in his belly-plates creak. "It probably troubles me because I am too old."

"With respect, Hu'urs Khraam, you—"

"I am old, Darzhee Kut, even for one of the Hur caste. At any rate, it was folly for me to attend this undertaking myself. One of the younger Hur, such as—"

"Revered Hu'urs Khraam, none but you was suited for this great mission. Every deephall in the Wholenest knew it."

"Bah. Did they know I would be tested to my very death-song by these Hkh'Rkh? Every day, their overlord First Voice places the same petitions before me. Attack the great cities, the great powers, of this planet. North America, Eurasia, the Chinese littoral. They are weak, he says. We have no reason to think so, I reply. The EMP warheads crippled them, he asserts. Yes, crippled their civilian sector, I counter, but we disabled little or none of their military equipment, so far as we can tell. We have orbital control, he thunders, and we must use it so that they will respect us—and they will respect nothing less than a full-scale attack. I point out the troubles we are having here, on one medium-sized island. He dismisses these difficulties as byproducts of our 'restrictive rules of engagement.' Another sign of Arat Kur weakness and lack of resolve." The First Delegate rose. His manipulator polyps quivered a bit—from strain or pain, Darzhee Kut could not discern. "I tell you, young Kut, it is the Hkh'Rkh, not the humans, that will be the death of me. Now, I must settle into my quarters and find the harmonies that have escaped me this day."

"And what do I do about Caine Riordan?"

"Do? Do about him? What do you mean?"

"How do we best respond to his gesture, to the potentials for peace and trust that his deed invites us to consider?"

"Here, young Kut, is what *you* must do. You must remind yourself—hourly—that Caine Riordan is but one human. He is an aberration among them, a flicker of conscience that his own megacorporate kin would have extinguished if he had not run far and fast. Do not let his noble deed seduce you into thinking the rest of his race are capable of something similar."

Darzhee Kut held his mandibles very still. The troubling nature of humans had long been known to the higher castes of the Wholenest, but at this moment, in the face of contrary possibilities, Hu'urs Khraam's counsel sounded suspiciously like unthinking speciate bigotry. "And Riordan himself. What do I tell him?"

Hu'urs Khraam looked at Darzhee Kut closely. "Tell him that his deed was noble and we are grateful for it. And, if you think he is ready to hear it, you should also tell him that we can already measure how much his deed will change the outcome of this war."

"Really? How much?"

"Not at all."

COUNTERATTACK

Engage people with what they expect; it is what they are able to discern and confirms their projections. It settles them into predictable patterns of response, occupying their minds while you wait for the extraordinary moment— that which they cannot anticipate.

—Sun Tzu

COUNTERATTACK
Part One

January 12, 2120

Chapter Thirty-Three

"Spooky Hollow" restricted area, north of Perth, Earth

Downing glanced up at the mission clock: 2120.01.12 Z1006.48 local. Twelve seconds to go.

The commo officer's voice called the last warning. "Coming up on projected signal reception: ten seconds."

He turned to Alnduul. "You can tell when an interstellar superstring is perturbed by a shift drive, even at this range?"

"Yes, but this is true only if we know which superstring to monitor and if the phenomenon is, fundamentally speaking, local. Theoretically, one should be able to detect a perturbation of a superstring anywhere along its 'length' at the instant it occurs, for the string has no dimensions as we understand them."

Downing frowned. "That would seem to hold out the possibility of almost instantaneous communication, regardless of distance."

"So many have hoped. But the technology to do so remains elusive."

Considering that the Dornaani had had—at least—several thousand years to identify the necessary technological fix, Downing put this option from his mind.

Commo officer John Campbell of the Australian Air Force nodded at his control panel. "And—mark. Projecting that transmission has been received by the shift-carrier *Tankyū-sha Maru* at a range of three point five light-days." He turned to Downing. "And now, sir?"

"And now, we wait."

Evidently, they were not going to have to wait for long. Alnduul's associate made a finger-streaming gesture. The Dornaani leaned their heads together. Alnduul listened, his lids fluttered. He straightened, looked at Downing. "The *Tankyū-sha Maru* has now entered shift space as per the instructions you sent on January eighth."

Which meant that it was already at its destination and sending the signal that would activate the final, fateful phase of Case Leo Gap. Either that or a freak drive failure had destroyed the *Tankyū-sha Maru* and, with it, any hope of retaking the Solar System. Downing tried not to swallow audibly. "Lieutenant Campbell, please check the light-pins in the Dornaani holosphere's close-up of Jakarta. Are our delivery assets for Case Timber Pony currently in striking range?"

The young lieutenant from Perth studied the alien device for a moment. "Confirmed in range, sir. The green one is within the optimum activation footprint now. The other two are within five kilometers." The young Perther looked up. "Orders, sir?"

Downing felt the collective eyes of his staff, the veteran security detachment, and even the Dornaani upon him. He swallowed. "Set the infiltration units' final assault clock for three hours. Send the word to the irregular units that they will go active along with the preparatory barrage in ten minutes, but to await a final confirmation before jumpoff." *Because if the interstellar cavalry fails to come over the hill by then, a general ground attack will be suicide.*

"Messages sent to all units, sir." The Aussie continued to look at him, unblinking, waiting.

Downing closed his eyes—and saw Nolan's smile. He smiled back. *It was always your show, old boy. We've just been playing the notes you composed.*

Downing opened his eyes. "Start the clock. And let's get ourselves airborne. We will soon have a battlefield to assess."

Central Jakarta, Earth

Tygg, his hand covering the ear bud connected by wire to a short-range pager, muttered, "They've started the clock."

Trevor glanced at him. "Just now?"

"Yeh. Well, a few seconds ago, given the delay between the ground repeaters from the Sundas to here. The general festivities start in ten minutes. Our own special party starts in a little less than three hours. Unless everyone gets waved off."

"Does that give us enough time for a stealthy approach?" Trevor looked out the window, saw the minarets of the Istiqlal Mosque rising up across a short stretch of the Merdeka Square.

Tygg checked his watch. "Should. Our mob is ready to gather at the head of the assault route."

"Okay, then let's get our own teams moving into place. Page mine along with yours, will you?"

"Already done. How do the Roaches and Sloths look? Antsy?"

Trevor raised his binoculars, made sure the laser rangefinder was off, scanned the recently walled complex that rose up beyond the Indonesian Supreme Court building which lay just to the west of the presidential palace. He looked for signs of activity at that part of the enemy perimeter. Nothing out of the ordinary. Trevor bit his lip—

Tygg's voice was low, closer to his ear. "Thinking about the inside team again?"

"It shows?"

"Might as well wear a sign, mate. Look, the resistance agents in the compound's domestic staff placed the breaching charges themselves. They know to stay away as much as possible."

"Yeah, but we have no way to warn them, no way to tell them that the clock is running."

"Which they knew when they volunteered."

"Cold consolation."

Tygg's voice was lower still. "Listen, Trevor, regardless of what you Yanks like to think, and the way you try to run your ops, not everyone has a reasonable chance of survival. And you don't always get to fight the war you planned, eh?"

Trevor looked up balefully. "You mean like the war where we assumed we'd have C4I dominance, GPS redundancy, and orbital weapon guidance?"

"Yeah, that one. But this is the war we got, instead. And it's the war that the team inside the compound got, as well. Today, they've drawn the short straw and the dirty job. Tomorrow, or sooner, it might be you who has to walk point, or be bunkmates with plastique."

"I know, Tygg. I've been there myself. I just hate seeing it happen to others. Particularly civilians."

He felt the tall Aussie's hand come down on his shoulder. "You've a big heart, Trev, so big that it's blinding you to something."

"What's that?"

"There aren't any civilians anymore. Not until we kick the last of these damned exos off our world."

Trevor lowered the binoculars, said, "You're right," and wished Tygg wasn't. Trevor turned, smiled at the slightly younger man. "Well, I don't suppose we should waste any time. Let's gather the troops."

Presidential Palace, Jakarta, Earth

"You wished to see me?" As one, the room's occupants turned from the holotank to look at Caine.

Darzhee Kut clattered forwards. "Caine Riordan, my apologies that I have been unable to share roof with you these past three days. I have been quite busy."

Caine scanned the room, saw Yaargraukh, the Hkh'Rkh Advocate with whom he had become friends at Convocation. The smallish Hkh'Rkh stared at him without any acknowledgment. *Probably because I'm too politically toxic.*

However, First Fist had reared up to his full height and his crest was not merely erect but puffed out like a long fur stole saturated with static electricity. He pointed at Caine. "I will not suffer to be in the same room as this *zhkh'grsh'hak'k.*"

Evidently, this was an insult so profound—or intricate—that the translator could not process it. Caine looked down at Darzhee Kut, whose polyps writhed once. The Arat Kur equivalent of an "I dunno" shrug.

Yaargraukh's voice was flat. "In your language, this would specifically refer to a courtesan who makes herself the property of one Family's Lord, so that she may poison him in order to become the courtesan of a rival Family Lord. Only to repeat this process with yet another, greater Family Lord."

Trading up, Borgia-style. Caine cast about for an oblique retort to Graagkhruud's insult, but let it go. *Not smart, and besides, they brought you here for a reason.*

Something was going on. He could sense it in the way they were all clustered around the holotank, had been so intent on its contents that they had not even heard the door admit Caine and his Arat Kur guards. He returned his attention to Darzhee Kut, "This day, Speaker Kut, you seem busier still. May I be of some assistance?"

"We think so. Please come and view the holotank."

As Caine came close to the tank, he bowed toward the senior Arat Kur. "First Delegate Hu'urs Khraam, I presume. I have heard your name sung, and am honored to meet you."

Hu'urs Khraam bobbed in return. "You know our greetings; this is well. Harmonies, Spokesperson Riordan. Forgive my inability to greet you as cordially as I would wish, but tell me"—he waved a claw in the direction of the holotank—"what do you make of this?"

Caine looked. Bright yellow motes ringed the Earth

in various orbits, a few others near the Moon and at the Lagrangian points, several more distributed through the vast spaces surrounding the whole tableau. But off to one side, with the Moon currently occluding them from the Earth, there was a broad and yet extremely dense cloud of angry, blood red needles. They were marked by various Arat Kur characters, some constantly transmogrifying, probably counting down range, ETA. But it meant nothing to him. Caine looked up. "With apologies, Hu'urs Khraam, if I am not given more information, I can only see a dispersed collection of yellow dots being approached by a much larger swarm of red ones."

"Of course. Urzueth Ragh, you have leave to explain."

First Fist closed half the distance to Caine in a single bound, the calar talons of his hands raised. "Tell him nothing!"

Hu'urs Khraam shifted to look directly at First Fist. He did not speak. First Fist did not come closer, but neither did he move away..

First Voice waved a dismissive claw. First Fist paced backward, never showing his back to Hu'urs Khraam or to Caine.

Urzueth Ragh approached cautiously. "Speaker Riordan, as you no doubt gather, the yellow markers denote our ships and drones throughout cislunar space. As you may have also gathered, the red markers are, apparently, human vessels."

"Human?"

"Yes, Speaker."

"Where did they come from, and when?"

"They shifted in-system seven minutes ago, arriving

en masse only three light-seconds out from Earth. This is much closer than your ships would normally hazard, is it not?"

"Surely your information on our interstellar capabilities is so extensive that my confirmation of it is unnecessary."

Urzueth Ragh bobbed once. "So it is as we thought. The lead elements of this formation will arrive here in several hours. In order to engage them in free space, and at sufficient range to intercept them before any of their drones can reach our orbital supremacy assets, our capital ships have had to commence slingshot exits from orbit."

Telling me your secrets? Well, why not? Who can I tell them to? Caine looked at the yellow dots that were hobbling slowly out of cislunar space, some playing crack the whip as they came out of Earth orbit in a gravity slingshot, others maneuvering to a rendezvous point halfway to the Moon. Collectively, it looked like a few drops of honey heading for what looked like a hailstorm of blood. Granted, Arat Kur technology was superior, but was it superior enough to make up for the tremendous imbalance in numbers? Or had their easy successes to date made them overconfident? Caine had a sudden impression of that shrewd smile that Nolan wore when he was about to close a trap, and resisted the urge to let it project itself onto his own features.

Urzueth Ragh continued without pause. "Much of the supposed 'human fleet' is making a high-speed approach. It is our conjecture that this is to minimize exposure to our weapons. The fleets will pass each other at such high speed that they will only be in effective range of each other for less than a quarter of an hour. This includes the time increase that will result when we retroboost just prior to attaining engagement range."

Caine nodded. "So you intend to reverse vector and give chase in the event that our ships continue to accelerate away as quickly as possible from the spinal weapons on your shift-carriers and -cruisers."

"Precisely. We have also determined that these lead drones"—Urzueth Ragh wobbled his claw at a fine-grained bow wave of smaller red dots—"are at least three times the volume and mass of your standard models. They are also emitting unusual thrust signatures."

"How so?"

"Their exhausts are consistent with antique solid-rocket boosters. Can you speculate why this might be?"

"I can, but would be a traitor to do so."

Hu'urs Khraam interrupted. "Caine Riordan, did you not return to be a liaison between our peoples?"

"I came to serve the purpose of peace for both our peoples. I did not come to betray mine, nor become an ally to yours."

Hu'urs Khraam's polyps writhed. "This is a disappointment, but well-spoken—if there are any with ears to hear." The rather hoary Arat Kur's brow-ridge shifted in the general direction of the Hkh'Rkh: Graagkhruud was oblivious. First Voice seemed to be affecting unawareness, but his crest had shifted slightly.

The only one to speak was Yaargraukh. "With your permission, Hu'urs Khraam, I believe I understand the human strategy in this. Their technology is slightly more advanced than our own, but still quite comparable. I suspect we would solve similar problems in similar ways."

Hu'urs Khraam bobbed; Urzueth Ragh stood aside. Yaargraukh approached the holotank, stood next to Caine. Was he clearing his throat or was that an almost imperceptible—and absolutely deniable—nod of acknowledgment, of greeting? Again, Caine suppressed a smile.

Yaargraukh swung an appendage at the gap between the red fleet and Earth. "The humans are uncertain of the outcome of this surprise attack. This is unavoidable. Shifting in so close to their target, they had no opportunity to conduct any reconnaissance or gather any tactical intelligence. Thus, they needed a strategy that was flexible in regard to a wide spectrum of probable outcomes. I conjecture that these larger drones with unusual thrust signatures are among their best models, retrofitted with simple, but reliable, solid rockets. With these rockets, the drones can quickly accelerate ahead of the human fleet, becoming a far-flung buffer in front of their capital ships and regular drones, and reducing the time we have to intercept their lead elements. For if we fail to intercept this advance wave in time, they could penetrate deep enough into cislunar space to take our orbital assets under fire. This could significantly attrite our orbital surveillance and interdiction capabilities.

"However, since the humans could not be sure that they will prevail, there is a second advantage to these solid-rocket boosters. I predict drones will be fitted with not one, but two boosters each. The first will accelerate the drones into the engagement area. However, the employment of the second booster will vary

according to the evolving outcome of that engagement.
If the human forces are losing, the second booster
will be used to push the drones through the area
of engagement at the highest possible speed, thereby
minimizing their exposure to our fire. However, if
the humans are either winning or stalemating us, the
second stages will *retro*boost the drones, either slowing
them down to make orbit and to continue engaging
us, or—if they have already shot past—to return to
cislunar space for the same purpose. This provides
the humans with the type of operational flexibility
that has increasingly become the hallmark of their
operations since they first industrialized. And, given
the vector and intercept values of the rest of their
fleet, I project they intend to arrive in two or three
separate waves. The later echelons not only provide
a reserve that can add its weight to the general fleet
engagement, but also have an increased ability to
bypass our counterattacking forces and then retroboost
into orbit. The consequences to our current orbital
supremacy assets are once again, I presume, obvious."

Urzueth Ragh looked at the tank as if seeing it for
the first time. "This strategy, if Yaargraukh discerns
it correctly, would also make it prudent to leave a
defensive force here in orbit. Just in case any of the
human craft survive long enough to make it through."

Yaargraukh turned, his eyes bulging out momentarily. "You ignore the possibility that they might
ultimately wrest control of the high ground from us.
In which case, it is their ground forces which would
enjoy orbital fire support."

Urzueth Ragh waved a dismissive claw. "How could
they fare so well against our fleet? These human

ships"—he waved a claw at the red horde—"can only be reserve or converted commercial craft. What else do the humans have left?"

Yaargraukh considered for a moment, then walked over to Caine and looked him directly in the eyes. "Yes, what else *do* they have left?"

Caine considered. If his guess about this recently arrived fleet was right—that it was part of an immense snare that the late Nolan Corcoran had set for extraterrestrial invaders—then Downing might actually want the Arat Kur to have a better understanding of the next piece of the puzzle-trap before it was sprung on them. Nolan thought like Sun Tzu: the best generals won wars by showing their adversaries the futility of fighting. On the other hand, it was dangerous to make any presumptions that might provide the enemy with data they shouldn't have. However, come to think of it, there was a way to concretely determine if Downing wanted Earth's invaders to know just what they were facing now—

Caine straightened up. "Have you pinged the incoming ships for their transponder codes?"

Urzueth Ragh sounded quizzical. "I beg your pardon, but why would they run transponder signals and identify themselves? That is folly."

"Usually, it would be. But I don't think that will be the case today. Ping them."

The sensor operator looked at Hu'urs Khraam, who bobbed. The operator turned to his board, sent the ping. They would have the answer in a little less than twenty seconds.

Halfway through the wait, Graagkhruud grew too impatient to remain silent. His black worm-tongue flickered around the sarcastic words. "So, tell us: how much of the proud human fleet remains to fight us?"

The Arat Kur sensor operator was silent for a moment, then turned around. "Almost all of it, if these scans are correct."

Urzueth Ragh started forward. "I do not understand. What new fleet is this?"

"It is not a new fleet, Senior Administrator," explained the sensor operator. "It is the fleet we destroyed at Barnard's Star."

"What? How could that be?"

Yaargraukh merely looked at Caine, nodded, walked past him as the sensor operator continued his report. "I am reading transponders from the Commonwealth fleet carriers *Enterprise*, *Intrepid*, *Courageous*, and Federation fleet carriers *Moscow*, *St. Petersburg*, and *Kiev*. All are deploying their full complements of the latest generation of human high-gee capital ships—the President, Trafalgar, and Kursk classes—and the lighter, Bolton-class attack cruisers."

Graagkhruud's crest had flattened; his long shoe-box of a mouth hung open. "This is not possible. Four of those shift-carriers were destroyed at Barnard's Star."

Caine smiled. "Evidently not."

Darzhee Kut's "What?" was not quite drowned out by Graagkhruud's "Liar!"

Caine only acknowledged Darzhee Kut. "I'm just going on a hunch, now, but let's check something else. Do you have a record of the transponder signs of the individual capital ships you destroyed at Barnard's Star?"

Darzhee Kut bobbed. "Yes."

Caine turned to the sensor operator. "Check those tail numbers against the ones you're reading now."

The Arat Kur did, turned to face Hu'urs Khraam. "Esteemed First Delegate, the ships we destroyed are leading the van of the inbound fleet."

Urzueth Ragh burbled and wheezed. An Arat Kur snort. "Nonsense. We *did* destroy these ships. I was there and saw it at Barnard's Star."

Caine shook his head. "No. These are ships that you were *led to believe* you had destroyed."

"Preposterous. This phantom fleet is the deception, not the events at Barnard's Star. This is a human plot to make us believe ourselves in greater danger than we are, being carried out by small ships equipped with sophisticated image makers."

Caine shrugged. "Believe what you like, but any minute now, I expect that your sensor operator is going to inform you that the exhaust signatures and mass scans are a match for what the transponders are telling you. You'll only be sure when the ladar starts showing you silhouettes, but by then it will be too late to change your course of action."

"But it makes no sense," insisted Urzueth. "If these are the real ships, then what did we destroy at Barnard's Star, and why did you let us?"

"I'm just continuing with guesswork," admitted Caine, "but, at Barnard's Star, I believe you destroyed specially constructed decoys: ships which had the shape of these craft, and their signatures, but were otherwise only moderately armed and probably uncrewed. Had you examined the wreckage—what little there was—I suspect you would have eventually discovered evidence that you had destroyed unfinished hulls fitted with only those basics necessary to fool your sensors." Caine remembered all the strange and secretive activities he had heard whispers about in the weeks before Convocation. "Those decoys were probably built secretly. Out in the Belt, I'd guess, and with their fusion drives rigged for triggerable containment failures. That way, you wouldn't have much wreckage left to study." And suddenly Caine realized why the quarantine on DeePeeThree had not been lifted after he had discovered primitive exosapients there. "What you thought were shift-carriers were just frames, super-structures, and fusion engines, turned into finished decoys out at Delta Pavonis Three or beyond, where, due to quarantines, there wasn't enough deep space traffic to stumble across them."

"But why? What was the purpose of all this—waste?"

"To make you believe that you'd destroyed all these ships at Barnard's Star. Because that, in turn, made you believe you'd achieved far more than you had, made you believe you were safer than you were."

Yaargraukh nodded from the other side of the holotank. "Of course. The humans predicted that after our victory at Barnard's Star, we would want to move quickly, that we did not wish to lose the initiative. Which was, after all, a prudent strategy. So when we scanned the wreckage, we trusted our long-range sensor data, which matched what we expected. And, reassured, we did not wait to conduct a more detailed post-action analysis."

Urzueth Ragh waved an impatient claw. "Which would have shown us that we had not destroyed the ships we thought we had. So. I accept this. But this waste of resources to build decoy hulls. To what *specific* end did the humans do it?"

Caine ran his gaze across the entirety of the strategic plotting holotank. "Right now, it looks to me as though you only brought about sixty percent of the forces that hit Barnard's Star."

"This is correct."

"And that sixty percent is further split into three parts. The largest part, with all your interface and landing craft, is here in cislunar space. Almost as large, and containing an equal number of your capital ships, is the flotilla guarding the Solar System's only remaining supply of antimatter: the refinery that we 'failed' to destroy in the Belt. And you left a small holding force at Jupiter, which is your best, but not your only, source of deuterium for your fusion plants and engines. Is that about right?"

Urzueth Ragh simply bobbed.

"Then I'd say your current deployment *is* what we were hoping to achieve by letting you destroy all those wasteful decoys." Caine shrugged. "You've set yourself up for the oldest strategy in the book: divide and conquer. Or, in tactical terms, the outcome at Barnard's Star made you so confident that you split your forces into small groupings that our returning fleet can now defeat in detail. You guessed that with more than half of our forces destroyed, what ships we had left were bottled up in Ross 154 or behind it, out along the Green Mains. So when you arrived in the Solar System, it seemed both operationally prudent and strategically safe to split your fleet into three parts. Any one of those elements was large enough to take care of whatever motley collection of human hulls might be able to somehow punch through to Earth.

"But now it turns out that the big fleet you thought you had destroyed was mostly made up of decoys, and that the real fleet has shown up on your doorstep. Which means that, here around Earth, you are now seriously outnumbered and you can't recombine your forces in time. And even though our technology is behind yours, you're about to be saturated with our very best systems."

Urzueth Ragh's polyps were writhing spasmodically. Hu'urs Khraam looked at Caine with a strange, slow calm in all this motions. "A question remains: how did you know the ships would respond to a request for their transponder codes? Granted, our sensors can discriminate the class of vessel by its engine signature, but still, why let us know that these ships still exist? Why not let us believe that we had underestimated your production capability, that you had produced so many more than we anticipated and that this was a new fleet—possibly the first of many?"

Caine shrugged. "I didn't *know* they'd reveal their codes. But I guessed they might, because I think the World Confederation is trying to show you that this war is about to get a lot more costly—and bloody—for you, and that maybe this is the time to end it. Equably."

Hu'urs Khraam raised up. "And you believe that by revealing your secret—*now*—that we shall be cowed?"

Caine tried a different approach. "Here's another way to look at it. You've just been handed one surprise. So there could be more on the way. At any rate, you now have irrefutable proof that, within a few hours, you are going to have a real fight on your hands. Which, if you lose, would be disastrous for you, both up in orbit and down planetside. Because, if you lose orbital cover for even five minutes—"

Yaargraukh rumbled deep in his chest. "Then we are all doomed. The moment we can no longer strike at Earth's planetary forces from orbit, the humans will launch their missiles, and scramble all the aircraft and assault VTOLs that must surely be waiting out beyond the interdict line in the rest of this archipelago, and in Australia. They would be in among us so quickly, and so closely, that even if we reacquired orbital fire support later on, it would be useless. We would be hitting ourselves along with the humans. We will have irretrievably lost control of the ground campaign."

Hu'urs Khraam's voice was slow. "So by showing us the tail numbers—"

Caine nodded. "I think my leaders are making one last attempt at averting a full-scale strategic confrontation. Because once that kind of conflagration starts, there's no controlling how far or fast or hot it will burn."

Darzhee Kut's voice raised tentatively. "Your word for that is 'apocalypse,' is it not?"

"There are several that would be suitable, Darzhee Kut, but that is the basic idea. So, I believe my leaders are sending your leaders a message. That there's still a chance to control this situation before it spins so far out of control that there's no way to stop it."

Hu'urs Khraam looked over toward First Voice. "If you would join me, for my joints are weak, I would be in your debt."

First Voice approached, waved back his train, never bothering to look at Hu'urs Khraam. Together with two Arat Kur analysts, they formed an improbable huddle.

Yaargraukh had come around the holotank, stood close to Caine but did not look at him as he muttered, "As I feared when we spoke at Convocation, it seems we are destined to fight before we may finish the bridge we pledged to build between us."

Caine nodded. "True, but even now, that pledge

gratifies me. If we survive to complete it, how many bridges can claim to have been so sturdily built, and under such inauspicious conditions?"

Yaargraukh's tongue flicked. "None that I know of—or would care to stand on."

Caine smiled back. "Take care in what is to come."

"You too, Caine. It is wise you do not trust my kind. They do not understand your actions, and Graagkhruud has not troubled himself to place them in an accurate context."

Caine would have thanked him, but Yaargraukh moved on, having seen, or intuited, the breakup of the huddle. Hu'urs Khraam took one last look around his circle of advisors, who in turn looked down at their computing tablets. They all bobbed in his direction. Hu'urs Khraam turned to Caine. "It is decided. We shall fight." He turned to Urzueth Ragh. "Summon the fleet from Vesta. At best speed, they should reach Earth in several days. They are to launch drones and high-endurance missiles to join our battle here as soon as it is practicable." He turned back to Caine. "Your species is to be congratulated for its characteristic cunning. But for us, this is only a setback, not a defeat."

Caine watched the red motes—his—approach the yellow motes—theirs—and feared that Hu'urs Khraam might yet prove correct. The Arat Kur had a distinct technological edge that might yet prove decisive, even when so heavily outnumbered. It promised to be a very close contest, but with the enemy's belt flotilla approaching at high-gee, whatever control humanity could buy with the best of her blood and her ships might be short-lived indeed.

That was when the first rockets hit.

Chapter Thirty-Four

Central Jakarta, Earth

As the barrage intensified, a rocket knifed into the eastern face of the Ananka Building. Trevor turned his face away as the window blasted inward from the shock of the nearby detonation.

Tygg continued briefing the rebel officers they'd summoned. "It's a fine day for our little surprise party, mates. Weather is just the way we want it. After this morning's rain, we've got a temp that's still going up, probably to ninety-seven Fahrenheit. The air will stay supersaturated the whole day: mist everywhere as soon as the sun peeks through a bit more. Storms expected by three PM, which will cover our retreat if we have to turn tail, but bogs the exos down if they abandon their compounds for the countryside. They don't know their way around the bush too well." He had to raise his voice over the constant roar of window-buffeting explosions. "This barrage will continue right up until M-minute. As you've seen, this phase of it is only crudely aimed and—so far—is coming in from the jungles and nearby *kempangs*. So stay in your positions and under cover. And do *not* fire, under any circumstances, until you receive the 'go' signal for the final attack, which will commence in a few hours and focus upon their C4I and PDF assets.

"Until we get that final signal, don't even let friendlies know you're in the neighborhood. I reemphasize. We are *not* part of the general attack, which will commence first. The assaults which will commence after the peak of the barrage, and the current uprising in the streets, are primarily a cover for infiltration teams and special missions like ours." Tygg paused. It had the desired effect. The faces around him leaned closer, a bit more solemn. "For the locals working with us final assault teams, it's going to be very hard, spending hours watching their mates, maybe their own relatives, fighting and dying while they sit by and do nothing. So when you go back to your units, take one last measure of your war-fighters. If you're worried that one of them might not be able to wait, watch, and do nothing until signaled, then reassign that person to one of the squads that will be joining the general assault. Or let them join up with the rebels doing the street fighting now. Because anyone who can't take the waiting while other people are doing the dying, is no good to us today. Timing is everything.

"And so is communication: here are our protocols for the final assault, which won't be confirmed for at least two hours. The jumpoff signal will be sent over the cell repeater net that will be activated as part of the general assault, or on the remaining pagers if the net is down. If both of those are carked, we'll be relying on the fiber-com net some tunnel rats have been building for us. We'll try to stay connected to them via runners. If that's not feasible, we'll rely on smokes from preset command-and-control points in the area of operation. Red smoke means the general standoff units are to commence firing. Green smoke signals maximum sustainable covering fire from the standoff units, and then our final close-assault charge after a ten-count. In our particular case, don't get eager and rush the presidential compound immediately, or you're going to be too close when the breaching charges go off inside its walls. Now off you go, mates, and good luck to you."

As all but two of the Indonesians left, Trevor cleared his throat. "Tygg, before the show starts, I just want to say I appreciate how you jumped on board with my mission."

"Yeh, well, hard to reach the home office for permission, eh? Besides, my unit was too badly banged up to achieve our original objectives. At least this way, we're back in the main fight."

Trevor nodded, hoped he wasn't blushing in shame. *The main fight? You mean that part of the battle where, acting under falsified orders, I usurp local forces to bust into the enemy compound to rescue my sister, a woman from the past who's in love with another man instead of me, and maybe even the other man himself? Oh, it's still a worthwhile mission and it still uses the local assets to achieve Downing's objectives—breaching the compound, taking out their HQ—but I'm not even one hundred percent certain that the people I'm trying to rescue will be there. But if I know Opal, she'll gravitate towards Caine's probable location like iron filings to a magnet . . .*

"Trevor?"

"Uh...yeah, Tygg?"

"Shall we maintain our OP here?"

"I don't think so. We're going to need our all our close assault elements, including us, on the ground and ready to go at a moment's notice. Anyone left up here until the last minute isn't going to get to us in time to join the attack."

Private Gavin shrugged, didn't see Tygg's sharp look—which could be universally translated as a preemptive "put a sock in it"—and pointed into the corridor behind them. "I dunno, Captain. Those elevators are very fast."

"They're quick when they're working, Gavin. But the barrage is only going to get worse. A hit, or an EMP strike, might take out the power. And eighteen stories is a very long walk."

John Gavin frowned. "Why another EMP strike?"

Tygg jumped in before Trevor could respond, and while his words answered Gavin's inquiry, his tone signaled that the garrulous private had asked his last question. "When we activate the disposable cell repeater net that the indigs have been building up secretly over the past month, the Arat Kur may decide to hit a big off switch, rather than jam it. Particularly when all our radios start turning back on." His tone lowered. "Of course, it might be our side that generates an EMP."

Gavin had evidently missed Tygg's tonal hint that question-time was now over. "*We'd* launch an EMP strike? Why us? We *want* to be able to talk."

Tygg shook his head. "Talk or no talk, we can't be sure what weapons might have to be used to gain control of the battlespace."

"Eh?" Gavin wasn't much good at reading between the lines.

Trevor stepped in. "Private, according to your lieutenant, better than ninety percent of the world's remaining submarine assets are currently hiding near or inside the fifty-kilometer nautical limit. And they are fully armed."

For one moment, the expression on Gavin's face suggested that he was wondering what good all those torpedoes were going to do here in Jakarta. Then he evidently grasped what Trevor meant by "fully armed" the same instant he understood what kind of submarines were being discussed. "Oh."

"So," Tygg concluded, "if you see a sharp flash overhead, don't look up; look down. And if you've got the time, cover your ears and your ass. In a deep, dark hole."

Trevor looked over the Aussie's shoulder, out the still-intact plate glass window that presented Merdeka Square as if it were a mural. So far, the national monument—the decidedly phallic Monas—hadn't been hit, despite the fact that the air around it was filled with the smoke of recently or currently exploded inbound rockets. To the far right, a smaller warhead, clipped by the almost uninterrupted upward flow of enemy PDF fire, cartwheeled down and struck the most dramatic minaret of the Istiqlal Mosque, bounced off, exploded halfway on its tumble toward the dome. Lucky that time, but before the day was out, that dome was going to be hit, holed, maybe dropped. The cheap, free-flight rockets being used to overwhelm the Arat Kur's PDF intercept sensors and automation were notoriously inaccurate. Hopefully, one wouldn't come down on Jake Winfield's head while he made his way to the docks to recruit some additional help rumored to be coming ashore there.

As if to prove the accuracy limitations of the great majority of in-rushing rockets, there was a muffled blast overhead. Two ceiling panels shook loose, and ancient interfloor dust and detritus rained down. Barr, the secret-service man, looked up as though the rest of it were about to fall on their collective heads. "How long can they maintain this rate of fire?"

One of the two remaining locals, a shopkeeper by the name of Kurniawan, smiled. "Long time. Soldiers without uniforms, they kept many rockets in secret places. They hid the best ones our army had, even before Ruap took over. And they got lots more since: good rockets, some very smart. Some were even sent here before the Roaches came, almost half a year ago. The smart rockets are small enough to hide in garbage cans. They mostly American, Russian, English, guided by laser or little computer chip, launched by a radio signal or wire. Then, soon after the Roaches land, little boats from Thous' Islands start coming with simpler rockets. Some of those were old. Real old. Katyusha, RPGs. A lot from China. A lot aren't even weapons. They're just like firework rockets, with a tin tube around them. Or mylar."

"Mylar or tin? Why that?" asked Gavin.

Trevor supplied the answer. "Tricks the Arat Kur PDF systems. Only works for a second or two, but with this many rockets launched from relatively close ranges, they can't spare the time to sort things out in detail. Any rocket they miss could hit one of their arrays, particularly if it's one of those smart ones with a chip. Some of those are programmed to act like an off-course free-flight rocket until it approaches within a few hundred meters of its target. Then it goes active and swerves into a direct engagement vector."

Impossibly, that's when the overhead thunder redoubled. The sound of heavier impacts in and around the enemy compound only four hundred meters to the west started rippling against the outer walls, and their eardrums, like one long explosion.

"And that," added Witkowski, snugging the chinstrap of his helmet, "sounds like the freighters inside the fifty-klick limit have joined in."

Trevor shook his head. "No, that's only the *little* ships launching. For now."

Wholenest flagship *Greatvein*, Earth orbit

Senior Sensor Operator and Assistant Shipmaster Tuxae Skhaas snapped his mandibles together, signaling an urgent correction to his last report. "I refine the data. The new wave of human rockets is being launched only from the small ships at the edge of the fifty-kilometer no-sail zone."

"From the freighters?" His superior's arrhythmic staccato cluckings were those of stunned incredulity.

"No, Fleetmaster R'sudkaat. There is no sign of any attacks being launched from the grain ships."

The older Arat Kur acted with the decisiveness typical of—but today, welcome from—the Hur caste. He turned to Tuxae Skhaas' closest companion. "H'toor Qooiiz, transfer your station to the terminal adjoining Sensor Operator Skhaas'. Speak all his subsequent findings immediately to me and to First Delegate Hu'urs Khraam's personal Communications Operator. Tuxae Skhaas, you are to stop operating the sensors of this command ship."

"But Fleetmaster—" began Tuxae.

"Harmonize now. I will pass orders that all other Sensor Operators are to link their feeds into your panel. You will analyze, assess, report. Your operator duties will be passed to the next senior operator."

"As you instruct, Fleetmaster."

H'toor signaled his matching acquiescence with a short bob as he squirmed down into the couch next to Tuxae's. When the Fleetmaster had scraped off to give other orders, H'toor angled his frontal antennae toward his friend. "R'sudkaat must be desperate indeed, putting two unharmonious Ee'ar such as ourselves next to each other on the bridge."

"Sing no caste-parodies this day," Tuxae rattled sourly. "I forebode too many deaths among all our rock-siblings. See this." He pointed into the holotank, brought the oblique bird's eye view of Java closer. "The humans in and around the two greatest cities we occupy, Jakarta and Surabaja, have suddenly gone sun-time. Our other cantonments are also beset, but it is worst in these two places. The humans launch rockets from the jungles, the fields, the rice paddies, the roofs, and now small ships. Hundreds of rockets every minute."

"And we destroy their launchers."

Tuxae scratched his mandibles, fretting. "Which means we are digging tunnels in sand. Unless it is a salvo launcher, the humans rarely launch more than four rockets from a single location, but never less than two."

"Odd."

"Perhaps not."

H'toor trilled uncertainty. "I do not understand."

Tuxae forced himself to be patient with his tactically unsophisticated friend, whose comic songs made him an even more popular crewmember than he was an expert communications operator. "When the humans launch one missile, our automated intercept systems have been reprogrammed to temporarily ignore the source. We would be constantly interdicting bare ground if we counterfired at every rocket's point of origin. But two missiles arising from the same place? That could signify the location of a more sophisticated and capacious launcher, a target that our intercept system *cannot* afford to ignore."

"So, by launching at least two rockets per location, the humans are forcing our systems to spend time acquiring coordinates for every site."

"Exactly. They are making us waste time, effort, and ammunition." Tuxae felt the multiple lenses of his eyes slide and tighten against each other in hyperfocused consternation. "This sudden, large attack is not merely unprecedented. It has been carefully planned. The humans have watched us, timed us, have measured what we can and cannot do in response, and how long it takes us. I fear..."

H'toor shifted slightly to look over at his suddenly still friend. "What do you fear, Tuxae? The accuracy of their calculations?"

"That, too. But mostly, I fear their prior silence."

"Again, I do not understand."

Tuxae clacked his claws. "The humans were capable of waiting many weeks to commence this attack—weeks of waiting, watching, measuring while many of them died, and all of them feared. But now they are striking back with weapons we did not detect, at terribly close ranges, and at a time of their choosing. And so I fear."

"That they are in fact ready?"

"No. That we are not."

Chapter Thirty-Five

"Spooky Hollow" restricted area, north of Perth, Earth

Downing studied the scattered reports trickling in from Java's cities. General revolts were underway in all of them, initially targeted at the most hated and vulnerable adversaries: Optigene's clone-soldier regiments. The attacks had been extremely successful, spearheaded by cadre-led insurgent groups that had been waiting for the rocket barrage as their jumpoff signal. The barrage had, in turn, been unleashed only upon the arrival of the fleet codenamed Rescue Task Force One: the material fulfillment of Case Leo Gap, Nolan Corcoran's carefully orchestrated matrix of strategic deceptions and sacrifices. However, the day's greatest challenge and uncertainty remained: effectively coordinating the myriad and disparate elements of this day's fateful attack. *But, so far, so good.*

Downing, ever wary of operational optimism, shook off that thought. "Mr. Rinehart?"

"Yes, sir?"

"Give me an update on our tactical picture. Are we good to go to the next step?"

"Reports indicate that, as predicted, the invader's combat air patrols on the maritime approaches to Jakarta and Surabaja have been pulled off that duty and redeployed to engage the new ground threats around those cities. All approaching cargo ships have been ordered to hold position. They report clear skies.

"Also, our covert observers on Java are Morse-signaling that the Arat Kur PDF sensors seem unable to operationally discriminate more than a fraction of the targets, probably because their tracking arrays are overwhelmed. We are getting scattered reports that their antimissile counterfire is becoming increasingly autonomous and decentralized. Their individual PDF systems are falling out of the integrated defense grid at the same pace that their cooling and reload intervals are becoming problems. We are good to go, sir."

"Very good, Mr. Rinehart. Remember, when the Arat Kur see what we do next, their orbital interdiction assets will shift back to our larger ships—and to the aerial threats they'll be seeing momentarily. When that targeting shift occurs, let me know. Immediately. Timing is everything—*everything*—if this plan is to work."

"Very good, sir. Awaiting your order to take the next step."

Downing drew a deep breath. "Mr. Rinehart, send the following signal to our assault-enabled cargo ships: 'salvo all' in one minute, on my mark—*mark.*"

Standing off Jakarta Bay, Java Sea, Earth

Cesar Pinero, master of the twenty-thousand-ton freighter *Maldive Reckoner*, watched the last of the two-stage rockets lance away from the deck of the heavily barnacled schooner that was just two hundred meters off his starboard bow. The weapons' launch exhausts washed in through the already shattered windows of the pilot house, setting its interior on fire. The boat's captain and first mate were already speeding away in a much-patched Zodiac, slaloming around the canvas covers under which the rockets had been hidden until three minutes earlier. Pinero checked his watch: fifty-seven seconds to his own launch. And in the meantime, it would be instructive to learn how long it took for the Arat Kur to respond to the schooner's actions. Pinero started a silent countdown: *one-one-thousand; two-one-thousand; three-one-thousand—*

Looking port and starboard, bow and stern, the rest of the ponderous grain freighters seemed to loom larger in their immobility, having been signaled by the Arat Kur to stop and hold position. So they had done—and watched as the invaders blew every offending smaller ship to kindling.

Four-one-thousand, five-one-thousand . . .

Pinero checked his watch, looked down from the conning tower at his new second mate, on loan from the Japanese Navy, and nodded. The mate waved to the deck hands, who rose up from among the long crates arrayed on the *Reckoner*'s deck in a neat single-layer, row-and-column grid. They hastily inserted crowbars into the broadly gapped seams of the crates.

Six-one-thousand, seven-one-thousand . . .

The crates' sides and ends fell away as deckhands flung their lids overboard. In seconds, the four-by-six checkerboard of overlong wooden cargo boxes had been snatched away to reveal twenty-four missiles of diverse types and capabilities. Pinero blew the whistle he held in his teeth; all but the second mate and two of the deckhands raced toward the gunwales. The engineering section, already there, started the lemminglike rush over the side, hurtling feet-first toward the water over twenty feet below.

Eight-one-thousand, Nine-one-thousand...

Strange how calm it all seemed, how orderly. Half of the small boats had already been reduced to flotsam and jetsam by kinetic kill warheads fired from orbit. Hundreds of long plumes marked the path of the missiles they had launched, which—in their fiery, scalded-cat leaps into the air—had destroyed the decks and ruined the pilot houses of the ships that had carried them to this place. Some of those missiles were exploding in the air: orbital laser or long-range, ground-based PDF interdiction. More dwindled and down-Dopplered into the gray horizon haze that marked the periphery of Jakarta. From behind, dozens of other missiles converged on that target zone. The ships still clustered beyond the fifty-kilometer limit had started unloading, also. Pinero had worried that he would be paralyzed by fear when this moment came, but instead he felt strangely detached, as if he were simply a spectator, even to his own actions.

Ten-one-thous—

The blinding white-hot downstroke looked like an impossibly straight bolt of lightning, yet was almost perfectly silent, because the sound generated by the superheated hypervelocity kinetic kill warhead was still struggling to catch up through the soupy atmosphere. The sound and shock of the schooner exploding—flying instantly into an angry, roiling cloud of debris—hit his ears the same moment as the up-dopplering sonic boom of the warhead's shrieking descent.

Small metal fragments—hissing hot and spinning viciously—spattered the starboard hull, a few spanging off the chest-high rail encircling the *Maldive Reckoner*'s pilot deck. Pinero shrugged out of his windbreaker, checked the straps on his life jacket, popped the cap on the shark repellent, and calculated. It had taken the schooner five seconds to launch her four missiles, and ten seconds for the Arat Kur to identify and successfully interdict her. So, all told, it was about a fifteen-second response time, from first launch to arrival of counterfire munitions. Of course, the little boats had fewer missiles to launch, and that gave their masters and lately added weapons-specialists more time to escape. The crews were sent over the side before firing commenced, with orders to stay far away from any other hulls. But on the bigger ships like the *Maldive Reckoner*, it would take at least twice the time to see all the munitions off the deck. It would be a narrow thing, indeed.

Pinero checked his watch, waved to the second mate, who waved back. All weapons checked and cleared. He pressed the remote signals operation button on his palmtop. Twenty feet overhead, the radio mast of the *Maldive Reckoner* was sending out a single coded string that announced that she would be deploying her payload in precisely twenty seconds. He checked his watch again, waved to the one remaining deckhand, who had joined the second mate at the bow, crouched low. The deckhand jumped up, hefted a tightly bound canvas package over the port bow. Pinero saw its line tighten and then loosen. Good. The self-inflating raft had pulled free of its canvas sleeve and was now in the water. In ten seconds it would be ready for passengers. He moved to the portside elbow of the weather-walk, estimated the jump to the water at just above ten meters. He didn't like heights, so he didn't look for more than a moment.

He checked his watch: twenty seconds.

It had been a strange five weeks, the busiest, most terrifying, and yet strangely rewarding of his life. The *Reckoner* had made three trips from Shanghai to Jakarta, carrying rice: just rice. On the second trip, there must have been a sub sneaking in beneath them. Pinero had been instructed to hold a dead-straight heading from one hundred kilometers beyond the blockade line to within fifteen kilometers of the Tanjung Pasir headland. That, and the close crowding of ships around him during that voyage made him wonder if it was all part of an attempt to block, confuse, overtax the Roaches' overhead sensors. But today, it was all over. The grand mission of mercy was, in its last moments, transmogrifying into a grand ambush. The ships that had carried food to Indonesia were now carrying death to it instead.

Twelve seconds.

The small ships had launched first so that the self-teaching Arat Kur computers and their operators would initially identify the little, indigenous boats as being more dangerous, both because they were the only observed source of launches and were harder to hit. Once the computers had finished that recategorization of their targets, it would likely take several precious seconds, and possibly a direct operator override, to shift the firing priority to the freighters, once those larger hulls started unleashing their massive payloads. By the time that shift occurred, there would be too many large, lethal rockets on the way in for the overworked invaders' PDF systems to handle. At least, that had been the theory. Time to see how *Reckoner* would fare as one of the first big hulls to unload.

Five seconds.

Pinero raised his hand, then crouched down. The solid metal weather-rail and its height above the deck protected him from the launch exhausts, but that sudden cyclone was likely to send fragments of the crates sleeting and skittering in all directions.

Zero and launch.

Pinero cut downward with his whole arm and hunched lower.

The rearmost rank of rockets and missiles launched first. Their simultaneous exhausts hit the lower extents of the *Maldive Reckoner*'s superstructure, imparting a blow akin to a hefty bow-wave. Pinero came up just in time to duck again as the heat of their rapidly dwindling wash came level with the bridge. They were well over the bows and climbing into shallow ballistic arcs that would take them into or past Jakarta.

The second launch's tsunami of white hot exhaust blew Pinero's hat off and cracked two of the bridge windows behind him. The thickest of these four missiles rode off its ramp like it was skating upright on its tail, cleared the bows and then climbed at a fifty or even sixty-degree angle. From what the Japanese techs told him, that was either a pod carrier which would deploy six semiautonomous remote operated vehicles into Jakarta's airspace, or a decoy dispenser which would scatter five times that number of smaller vehicles which, by dint of electronic and radar signature, would mimic ROVs, or even larger, more lethal drones.

As the third and fourth waves went up, and shattered and scorched bits of wood casing spattered against or spun down into the weather walk, Pinero checked his watch. They were twelve seconds into the launch sequence. He put a hand atop the rail, wished he had remembered to take off his pants before it had all started. He didn't want any extra weight on him when he went into the water.

The fifth wave of missiles shrieked off the deck, catching up the ramps and debris from the previous launches in a complicated tornado of overlapping shock waves. It looked like a house of cards being hit by several different garden hoses all at once. He felt a strange, urgent pressure in his calves and behind his knees, but knew he couldn't obey it yet, couldn't get up on the rail and plummet down into the marginally greater safety of the water. He and the deck techs had to wait, to be prepared to correct a misfire.

And they had one on the last launch. The far starboard weapon—a thrice-handed-down fourth-generation Yingji missile that should have been junked three decades ago—remained inert in its rack, shaking as the rebounding backwash from the other three jarred it. The second mate, turning back from his face-away crouch and uncovering his ears, saw the missile, then looked at the bridge.

Pinero glanced at his watch: seventeen seconds. They had no time left. But they also had their orders. He waved twice to the second mate, who sprinted to the remaining missile while waving off the deckhand—who went over the side. Good, one more life that might be saved. Pinero glanced at his watch, missed what the Japanese missile tech was doing: twenty seconds.

They were living on borrowed time. Pinero looked down. The second mate was scrambling away, trailing a wire, waving. Time to go.

As Pinero rose, so did the Yingji, wailing away with an initial sputter. Pinero, staggered by the comparatively light backwash, missed making a quick hop to the top of the weather rail. As he climbed up again, he saw the second mate end his sprint to the portside gunwale with a long horizontal leap that cleared it. He wasn't wasting any time.

Pinero's knees shook as he got up on the weather rail's wide top. Ten meters to the water looked more like a kilometer...

A blinding white light, like a laser, stabbed down into the *Maldive Reckoner,* lancing it amidships, splitting the keel dead center, and folding her like a hyperkinetic jackknife. As he was thrown from the superstructure, Pinero felt a brief but sharp increase in heat—

By the time the supersonic thunder of the warhead's descent arrived behind the heat and then shockwave of the impact, Cesar Pinero was not there to hear it. The few cells that remained of his body were insensate to the secondary explosions which vaporized them, too.

Chapter Thirty-Six

Central Jakarta, Earth

"Christ! What a stink!"

Tygg turned toward Gavin with a raised eyebrow. "It's a sewer. What do you expect?"

"Petunias, Lieutenant, bleeding petunias."

Tygg shook his head, looked up the ladder past Trevor. "What are you seeing, Mr. Cruz?"

Carlos turned his head away from the ring of daylight above them. "Not much but smoke, sir. Lots of dead clones. And I mean lots. Locals running around with AKs, pistols. Never in groups larger than three or four. No sign of organized units."

Tygg nodded. "Because they're hunkered down, waiting to see if the tactical repeater net will activate and call the general attack."

"Well, we'll all find out about that soon enough," Trevor asserted. He tapped Carlos on the calf, who slid down the street-access ladder. Trevor climbed up to their street-level OP, stuck his head up into the halo of daylight—

—And almost bumped his head against the underside of the manhole cover that they had propped up on four bricks like a roof. The car they had pushed atop the manhole was angled so the wheels didn't obstruct their view of the enemy compound. Most important, they were all but undetectable and the street overhead was an excellent bunker against stray missiles.

Trevor checked his watch again before he could recall his resolve to stop doing so. It just made the rest of the team nervous as they all tried not to think the same, dire thought: what if the tactical cell net didn't activate? What if something had gone wrong? If it didn't activate, there was no way for the organized insurgency cells to coordinate their actions with the far more numerous but less organized resistance fighters, or for those fighters to be assured of mounting their decisive attack simultaneously. Scattered, random attacks would be costly, easily suppressed, doomed to failure and mean that the professionally led infiltration forces of the final attack would have a much harder job to do, with a lower chance of success. But if the entirety of the locals' organized resistance arose at once, was on the same clock, and was also plugged into command updates from offshore, then—

Trevor's tiny pager—their link to the tactical repeater net—illuminated and then chirped twice. He managed to keep his voice calm, level. "That was the circuit test. Stand by for full activation of the tactical net and commencement of the general attack in thirty seconds. Stosh, keep the clock."

"Marking thirty seconds, Skipper."

Trev felt a tug on his pants leg, turned. Tygg handed

up a mil-spec transceiver toward him. "We've got the first coded sitrep and update from offshore."

Trevor shook his head. "You read it out so everyone can hear it." *And distract them while we wait to see if the tactical repeater net flies or flops. Because talking to the outside world is not how we're going to win this battle. It's our ability to update each other in-country which will make or break us.*

Tygg angled the mil-spec transceiver so Trevor could see it. It was scrolling a text message that read like a transcript from an insane asylum. "Bananas °D. Balloons zero-zero." "Bananas °D" indicated that the Arat Kur still retained roughly eighty-five percent of their PDF capability. About what had been expected, at this point. Almost all of the fifteen percent reduction would be due to overloaded or destroyed arrays. "Balloons zero-zero" indicated that the enemy tactical air assets remained at one hundred percent. Again, pretty much as expected, until the missiles from the grain ships started landing—

As if on cue, there was a flash and thunderous blast of sound and debris halfway between Trevor and the presidential compound. The impact sent a tremor through the street, shuddered the walls of the sewer. Some masonry detached and plunked in the ankle-high water.

"Now that's more like it." Stosh almost sounded festive. "The freighters have joined the party."

Two more blasts rattled the manhole cover on its four-corner props like a closed lid on a boiling pot. One rocket had struck someplace inside the compound. The buzz of the enemy PDF systems rose to an insane, saw-toothed scream. The sound was music to Trevor's ears.

At this rate of fire, those systems were going to overheat, run out of ammo, or both, within seven minutes, ten at the most. "They've committed their reserve systems," he speculated. "We've got their groundside interdiction capabilities pushed to the max."

Confirmation came in the form of a rippling cascade of sharp, thin sonic booms. Trevor could hear the smile in Tygg's voice. "They're having to augment with orbital interdiction."

Yeah, but that also means they're sinking our ships by the dozens right now. Despite the steel rain in the streets outside, Trevor was glad he wasn't anywhere near the fifty-kilometer nautical limit at that moment—

"Five seconds," shouted Stosh.

Very far to the south, Trevor heard a susurrating whisper of faint, nonstop detonations. Probably missile-deployed cluster bomblets reaching one of the smaller airports. God knows how many of those missiles were being lost for every one that reached its target, but once hit, those runways and vertipads would take days to repair. And this game was going to be finished today. One way or the other.

"And—*mark!*" bellowed Stosh.

Trevor discovered he was listening and watching so intently that he was holding his breath. A second went by, then another, followed by a cold wave that rolled over the skin of his arms, chest, back, belly. The tactical-level repeater system hadn't worked as planned. It was either disabled by all the falling debris or stray rockets, or had been instantly discovered and jammed or—

The pager emitted a long tone.

Two hundred meters up the street, three rocket-propelled grenades flew out of different windows with a surging whoosh, trailing white smoke plumes toward the compound. Following on their tails was the hammering applause of automatic weapons of diverse calibers: some high, spitting reports from Pindads, some rapid barking by venerable AK-47s, and a few steady, deep, jackhammer roars from belt-fed weapons that sent tracers chasing after the rockets.

"Behold, the Jubilee!" proclaimed Stosh, celebrating the activation of the net as if he were a testifying evangelist.

But the return fire, articulated by the sharp supersonic cracks of advanced dustmix support weapons, and even coil guns, answered within three seconds, chipping concrete, shattering windows, tearing apart parked cars with a sound like the ripping of perforated tin. Directly overhead, overlapping blasts indicated missiles being intercepted at close range. Then three large rockets, survivors of the Arat Kur PDF fire, landed with a collective, up-dopplering rush. One went straight into the compound. After one heart-stopping moment, there was a long, shuddering roar—and a noticeable drop in the volume of outgoing PDF fire.

However, another one of the rockets went straight into and obliterated the building from which the first of the three rocket-propelled grenades had been fired. As if all combatants were equally staggered by these heavy blows, there was a moment's lull—which was then immediately refilled by a gushing of bidirectional small-arms fire. But there was a new sound in the cacophonic symphony. High-pitched cries of pain and shock rose over the layered thunder of diverse, concentrated weaponry. A dog—dragging a spurting stump that had been one of its rear legs—emerged from the billowing smoke, ran past at close range, showering blood in all directions, yelping in time with its frantic gait. Trevor squinted into the smoke: *Behold the Jubilee? No, Stosh, "abandon hope, all ye who enter here."*

And damn it that Jake Winfield has to be out in the middle of this shitstorm...

Tanjung Priok docks, Jakarta, Earth

Another of the moored freighters, this one only one hundred meters away from the wharf, took a Russian missile beneath the taffrail. Perversely, the explosion lifted her bow up, like an overloaded truck feebly trying to do a wheelie, before she dropped back down, her aft settling rapidly as the fuming, growling water rushed into her half-amputated stern.

Good, thought Lieutenant Jacob Winfield, watching the last element of the circling Arat Kur combat air patrol break off and head out to sea, *they've decided the ships in port are all victims, too.* He wondered if the four savaged freighters had all been part of the plan—selected and hit by ROVs—or just dumb luck. Scanning the remaining ships, he sought the telltale signs for which Tygg had told him to look.

Within seconds, Winfield found seven hulls showing the right combination of innocuous features that indicated there was an incognito spec ops team aboard. Each ship was a small freighter, each had one or more white T-shirts hung on a makeshift laundry line, and each had a severed hawser hanging from the port bow. On three of them, small fires were burning. Too small to be caused by missiles, but smoky and angry enough to add to—and blend in with—the panic and confusion that reigned in Jakarta Bay and all along the docks of Tanjung Priok. Boats of all sizes, from derelict barges to opulent pleasure craft, were afire, horns hooting, bullhorns blaring in half a dozen different languages. In direct violation of the "no contact, no dumping" restrictions upon the freighters, cargo containers and crates—along with canvas bags and desperate seamen—were streaming over their gunwales and into the comparative safety of the debris-choked water. It was chaos—but slightly more than could be explained by a handful of hits by large missiles and a few score by smaller ones. Winfield smiled. *All part of the plan.*

On one of the ships with a severed hawser, Winfield heard a set of muffled blasts which, to a practiced ear, recalled the sound made by older, twentieth-century grenades. A wash of thin gray fumes, and then a quickly growing plume of blacker smoke, emerged from a companionway, along with apparent shouts of distress. Winfield looked around: most of the Hkh'Rkh still manning the harbor checkpoints were too busy to look up, and those that did immediately returned to whatever task had occupied them the moment before. There was too much happening, too much that they weren't familiar with, in an alien environment suddenly gone mad.

On the ship where the unusual explosions had given rise to equally unusual smoke—probably from a carefully controlled fire of wood and old tires—men and material were now pouring over the sides. Some of the objects plunging into the water were sealed black plastic bags. Winfield squinted. He watched one of the bags sink, leaving a thin line and a fishing bob trailing behind it on the surface. He smiled, wondered how many of the "desperate deckhands" jumping in around that bag were something other than merchant mariners.

As a SEAL, he also knew to look for the too-straight line of almost invisible bubbles that approached slowly, casually. More slowly and more casually than any fish ever did. Making sure his undersized mechanic's overalls covered his composite-armor shin guards, Winfield moved to the edge of the wharf, miming an anxious search around the base of its pilings. Within seconds, down at the limit of his vision, a pair of dive goggles appeared, ghostlike in the oily water. He crouched closer, still acting as though he was searching, searching, searching, and thought, *go ahead, check me out. But don't take too long about it.*

The goggles disappeared. Winfield counted off four seconds before a man dressed as a deck hand swam up and broke the surface, gasping for air and sputtering, splashing his arms about in a frenzy of desperation. Winfield reached down, caught the upper sleeve of the man's light denim shirt and dragged him up onto the wharf where he proceeded to cough and retch mightily. "Don't overdo it," Winfield muttered.

The man kept his face toward the planking as he apparently coughed up bay water, but managed to say, "Are they watching?"

"Hell, no. You're about the two-hundredth semidrowned boater or sailor they've seen today. And they're too busy worrying about the missiles coming from the ocean in front of them and the armed mobs in the city behind them." Winfield stopped to look at the man again. "You Indonesian?"

"No. Why?"

"You look pretty... convincing."

The man looked directly up at Winfield. His face was broad, brown, round-cheeked. "What do you mean?"

"Well—you know. You look like a local."

"Yeah? Well, *mukha ng tae.*"

"Huh?"

"He said 'and *you* look like shit.' In Tagalog," added a new voice. Another face—this one spitting out a slimline rebreather and as distinctly Nordic as the other was Micronesian—appeared over the lip of the wharf. Winfield didn't find the turn of phrase amusing. Mr. Blonde, Blue-eyed, and Square-Jawed detected the signs of disapproval and offered a sheepish rationalization. "Well, you don't look like a *local,* anyhow."

Winfield pointed a dark coffee index finger straight at the second fellow's ski-ramp nose. "And you do?"

The man smiled as he hauled himself up onto the planks and crouched next to the other two. "You've got me there, sir."

"*Sir?* How'd you—?"

Square-Jaw gave him a sidelong look. "Moment an officer starts talking, you know he's an officer—*sir.*" He stuck out an immense, and equally squared-off hand. "Chief Edward Barkowski, Team Three."

"Lieutenant Jacob Winfield—" He stopped, remembering. "Well, retired—sort of."

The smaller man sat up, coughed one more time, nodded to Barkowski, who threw a child's bath toy into the water. "I'm Alfredo Ayala, Lieutenant Commander, currently CO second stick, Joint SpecOpCom. I don't remember your name on the contact lists, Mr. Winfield." Another half-dozen men, all dressed as deck hands, surfaced near the floating toy and dragged themselves up onto the wharf. Dripping and coughing, they affected exhaustion: damn poor actors.

"My name wouldn't be on your pre-infil contact lists. We came in under separate authority."

"What the hell does that mean?"

Winfield showed him the magic card that Trevor Corcoran had loaned him.

Ayala stared at it, then at Winfield. "Your CO is Nolan Corcoran's son? No shit?"

"No shit."

Ayala's voice was suddenly tight with ready resentment. "Is he commandeering my teams?"

"No, sir. Unless my CO guesses wrong, we have the same objective."

Ayala's eyes narrowed. "And how would *you* know about my objectives?"

Winfield repressed a sigh of exasperation. "Look, Commander, I got the same 'suspect collaborators' training you did. But today, there are two kinds of humans out in the streets: live insurgents and dead insurgents. If there are any collaborators, they're indoors and staying there."

Ayala nodded, smiled. A little sheepishly, Winfield thought. "Okay, Lieutenant, I'm just an FNG here, so cut me some slack. What's your CO got for a target?"

"The Roach Motel."

"The what?"

"Sorry. That's what we call the Arat Kur HQ. The presidential compound at the northwest corner of Merdeka Square. They've put up curtain walls, paved over some gardens to make a half dozen vertipads."

Ayala nodded. "Yep. That's where my team—and

almost everyone else—is headed. I know the prewar layout, but have only seen a few recent photos."

Winfield smiled. "Whereas *we've* got prime intel: current floor plans, hardpoints, and duty rosters. Updated within the last forty-eight hours."

Ayala's eyes were suddenly bright. "You have agents inside?"

"Yeah. Domestic staff, delivery personnel."

"Outstanding. We'll follow you to your CO." Ayala waved the last members of his still-surfacing stick to join him in the lee of a smoking warehouse that fronted the bay. Once there, with Barkowski keeping watch, he huddled at their center. "Okay. Weapons out." Each man reached behind and under his shirt. Waterproof adhesive tape tore noisily away from back skin. The small, flat plastic bags that were in their reappearing hands sputtered as they were ripped open. Within five seconds, each man had readied a small, Unitech ten-millimeter liquimix machine pistol, held in the narrow, shadowed margin between his body and the building. Ayala had not stopped giving instructions. "The lieutenant here is going to guide us to a safe house. We go single file. Weapon mix set to maximum. Single shots only. Never more than thirty meters, or you're not going to get penetration. You won't anyway, with the Arat Kur. With the Hkh'Rkh, aim for the articulation points in their armor. And work together. Saturate targets with fire. If you don't penetrate right away, the multiple kinetic impacts should stun them. Then close in and pour it on." He turned back toward Winfield, paused, frowned. "What are *you* smiling at?"

Winfield nodded at the Unitechs. "You sure you want to use those popguns?"

The lieutenant commander looked like he'd taken a swig of vinegar. "You got something better?"

Winfield shrugged. "How about the assault rifles I stashed in a dumpster about twenty minutes ago?"

The men looked up, eyes wide and hopeful. Ayala looked suspicious. "Some old, raggedy-ass AKs aren't any better than—"

"Commander, I'm talking eight-millimeter CoBro liquimixers with extended bullpup feeds and integral RAP launchers. Double load of ammo, heterogeneous mix. Extra hotjuice canisters so you can shoot fast and hard all day long. Interested?"

The newly arrived SEALs were not merely interested. The looks on their faces were more akin to ravenous fixation. Ayala allowed himself a small smile. "Sure, Lieutenant. Seeing as how you're throwing them out anyhow, we'd be happy to take them off your hands."

Wholenest flagship *Greatvein*, Earth orbit

R'sudkaat clattered over as soon as Tuxae raised a claw. "What is it, Tuxae Skhaas?"

"Fleetmaster, the humans continue to fire missiles from their ships."

"And we continue to destroy both."

"Yes, Fleetmaster, but while our orbital interdiction assets are destroying their cargo ships, they cannot be tasked to ground targets."

"The delay will be brief. Almost all their ships are sunk."

"With respect, Esteemed Fleetmaster, additional ground suppression is required not only in and around the cities, but at a number of other sites. Sensors

confirm pilot reports that insurgents and more organized forces have invested the margins of our airbases
and vertipads with small teams firing portable fire-
and-forget missiles. Between these and the cluster
bomblet munitions that passed through our PDF
systems, air operations are sluggish at Jakarta and
stalled in Surabaja."

"How many craft have we lost?"

"Only one or two so far."

"Then there seems little problem."

"I harmonize, R'sudkaat, but our aircraft are constantly having to take evasive action, thereby diverting
from scheduled landing or takeoff vectors. Air traffic
control is unmanageable. Consequently, by the time
they have avoided, decoyed, or interdicted the ground
fire and sortied, their targets have left the coordinates
called in by our ground forces."

R'sudkaat studied the data streams on Tuxae's screen,
the map in the holotank, then swerved away. The order
he tossed over the collar-rim of his carapace sounded
like gravel in a sifter. "Redeploy the airphibian craft.
They must suspend their subsurface patrol duties and
join our air assets as quickly as possible."

"Fleetmaster, the human submarines—"

"—need not be patrolled for so aggressively. They
will be destroyed by orbital fire if they rise to launch
depth."

"R'sudkaat, if we were so sure of that outcome,
would we have developed these amphibian aircraft?
Would we not have simply relied on our orbital interdiction batteries?"

"The airphibian attack craft were a second tier of
defense against submersibles, an assurance against

other failures. We cannot afford that luxury for the duration of this battle. We must maintain our combat air patrols and tactical air support. Order the airphibian systems to terminate their submarine picket duties and transition for atmospheric operations."

"With respect, R'sudkaat, the fighting is also shifting to the major food-shipment cities—Jakarta, Surabaja, Semarang, Cilacap, and Banywangi—and a few other of the larger metro centers, particularly Bandung, Bekasi, and Depok. How do you plan to use the tactical air support and not kill thousands of civilians? Our rules of engagement—"

"—no longer apply."

Tuxae felt his lenses grind together then spring back in shock. "With respect, Fleetmaster—"

"Assistant Shipmaster, hear and follow this unwavering note. Today, there is but one rule of engagement. Find and destroy the enemy."

Chapter Thirty-Seven

Near Bakau Heni, Sumatra, Earth

Sanjay Thandla watched Lemuel Wasserman try to hide himself behind a palm tree to urinate and fail miserably. Although arguably the world's most brilliant living physicist, he seemed unable to figure out how to pee discreetly in the wild.

But of course, Lemuel's problem was not ineptitude. It was fear. Lemuel was fearful of everything. Just as his reluctance to enter the jungle made it impossible for him to empty his bladder in privacy, his various anxieties imposed other restrictions upon his behavior. He avoided the local food. He never emerged into the sun unless protected by a long-sleeved shirt, cargo pants, and a floppy hat that made him look like a maiden-lady gardener. He would not swim out beyond ten meters for fear of sharks, and he asked incessantly about the intercept capabilities of the Arat Kur PDF systems. He had arrived twelve days ago, questioning everything, yet accepting no one else's experience as useful information—with the peculiar exception of Thandla himself.

Thandla smiled as Lemuel emerged from behind the too-narrow tree he had selected as cover. Hapless, brilliant Wasserman. Thandla had not expected his odd, awkward, and decidedly barbed fellowship. Upon going their separate ways after returning to Earth from the Convocation, Sanjay believed the American did not like, or even particularly trust him. But here, just a few kilometers south of Bakau Heni, on the southeast tip of Sumatra, Wasserman had become a puzzling and pugnacious fixture at all of Thandla's activities and meals. He even forsook the company of his own countrymen, for the region was thick with tall, drawling Americans who were impatient to join the fight on Java.

They, and their European and Russian counterparts, had been gathering for the better part of three weeks. They arrived by truck or coastal barge, never in units larger than fifteen personnel and two vehicles, collecting here and in a dozen other coastal enclaves, well away from major towns or cities. Thandla and Wasserman had been assigned to go to Java in the second wave, with what the Americans incongruously called their "Air Cavalry." Sanjay would have expected an ornate Pegasus as the unit symbol, but it was simply a black-rimmed gold shield which was adorned by (in the language of heraldry that he had learned during an early fascination with the age of chivalry) a bend sable and a chief sinister couped horse head, also sable. The other unit concealed here at the water's edge, a German troop of high-speed VTOL drone controllers, was the first wave. How any of them were to survive getting airborne had not yet been explained.

Lemuel had stopped to speak with one of the

American pilots before he finished his journey back to Thandla. "They say it shouldn't be long now. Maybe an hour, maybe half. Maybe less."

Thandla smiled, looked east across the water. He heard Wasserman's feet shift in the sand: a noise that signified suppressed irritation. It was the greatest exertion of self-restraint that Wasserman seemed capable of. "Yes, Lemuel? What is it?"

The foot-scuffling stopped. "Well, yeah. I just want to know why you're smiling. I mean, what's to smile about? In a few hours, we'll be—"

"We'll be doing what we have trained to do, ever since returning from the Convocation. Once we are in Jakarta, I will be trying to glean data from a hopefully intact Arat Kur computer. You will be searching for any files or technology which will better help us understand their shift and antimatter drives. Are you not eager to begin?"

"Well, yeah—but no. I mean, look at this place." Wasserman waved back at the vehicles of the second wave. They were low, wedge-shaped deltas with sleek turrets and menacing secondary weapon blisters. The intakes for their ducted-thrust engines were broad, thin slits, reminiscent of a shark's mouth when cruising for prey. Two of the vehicles were larger, boxier vehicles bristling with sensor and communication pods and antennae. All were in an aqua-blue mottled camouflage scheme that would shift to green-gray when they finished their run across the Sunda Strait to Java. "You feel safe riding in *those*?" Wasserman asked.

"Far safer than riding in those." Thandla smiled, pointed at the lighter, more needlelike fuselages of the German VTOLs: built for linear speed rather than nap-of-earth combat support operations, the airframes of the European craft looked faster but infinitely more fragile. Not that that mattered: nothing could withstand a direct hit from any of the Arat Kur orbital interdiction batteries.

"That's not what I mean," Wasserman pressed. "I'm talking about doing *any* of this. You know, being *here*."

Thandla did not understand. "You mean, in Indonesia?"

"No, I mean in the middle of a war zone. Doesn't that—bother you?"

Ah. That was it, then. Thandla shook his head. "No, not really."

"But I thought— You've mentioned a wife. And kids. Right?"

"Yes."

"And you're not scared of—of—?"

Could he really not say the word? Was he no more prepared than this? "Scared of dying? I am scared, although perhaps not as you mean it."

"You mean there's more than one version of 'scared'?"

Thandla ignored the facetious tone. "Yes. I am scared that I will not see my family—or this world—again."

"Yeah, there you go. That's the kind of scared I'm talking about."

"I think it is not. For if I depart this world, this frame of existence, I only go to another that is closer to Nirvana, to a communion with and dissolution into all things."

Wasserman had leaned back. "You believe that stuff?"

Thandla smiled at Wasserman's crude and artless dismay, but also at the undeniable undercurrent of personal concern, as if the American were listening to a friend who had decided to go skydiving without checking his parachute. "Yes, Lemuel, I believe that stuff. I always have. Both in peace and, now, at war."

Lemuel was quiet for a long moment. An eternity, for him, Thandla reflected. "Does that belief make you feel better at a time like this?"

"I do not know. Probably. It affects how I feel—and think—at all times."

Lemuel made a noise that sounded like a cross between a grunt and a sigh. "Hunh." Thandla looked at him; Wasserman was staring out over the water. "Hunh," he said again.

"What is it?"

"I'm just thinking about today, and about Murphy's Laws."

Thandla smiled. "Which one?"

"The one which predicts that since you're not particularly worried about death, you'll probably get away without a scratch. And because I'm shit-scared about dying, I'll probably get my guts blown out."

Wasserman's projection was too juvenile and unreasonably cynical to warrant a response, but Thandla was struck by its subtext. That, for reasons unclear, Lemuel Wasserman was admitting to fears and cosmological misgivings and anxieties. To him.

Thandla felt his smile widen, saw Lemuel glance over—but his eyes did not make it all the way to Thandla's. His gaze froze on something he had seen over Sanjay's shoulder.

"Dr. Thandla."

Sanjay turned. Two command pilots, one American, one German, had come to stand behind him. They both had their hands behind their backs. The American, a major, was looking down. "Dr. Thandla," he repeated, "I'm afraid we've got a change of plans."

"I do not understand."

The German captain spoke with a directness that was jarring after the American's soft Missouri drawl. "Herr Doctor, our lead encryption and decoding specialist has been afflicted with gastroenteritis for two days. Treatments have not been effective. He is quite incapacitated."

"What does this have to do with me?"

The American looked up. "Dr. Thandla, *Kapitan* Dortmuller's C4I specialist was to coordinate jamming and counterjamming for the bow wave of our operations from Sumatra. Without his crash-training in what little we know about Arat Kur systems, machine language, and programming habits, the *kapitan*'s mission could be almost before it begins. We cannot lose control of the jamming and image-making drones that will be deployed in advance of his unit. We have to stay one electronic step ahead of the Arat Kur attempts to see through them."

"To cover an attack by your vehicles in the second wave?"

The American looked away. "Well, yeah, that too. But there's more at stake. There are units out there"—he nodded toward the surf without looking away—"that need those seconds even more than my attack wave does." He held Thandla with his eyes. "Much more. 'Course, I'm also aware that we need to keep you ready in the rear, so that you can pick apart any of their computers that we might get our hands on. So maybe I'm talking to the wrong person." He looked over at Lemuel. "As I understand it, Dr. Wasserman, you're just about as competent as Dr. Thandla when it comes to what little we know about Arat Kur hard- and software."

Lemuel blinked once. He swallowed. Thandla suspected he was about to turn around and run straight into the jungle that he usually refused to enter. But instead, his voice tremoring slightly, Lemuel lifted his chin resolutely and answered. "That's true. I can do the job."

Thandla felt a sudden urge to hug the brash, irascible, impossible American. But instead, he merely smiled again. "No, Major. That will not do. Dr. Wasserman's specialization cannot be replaced. He *does* know more about computers than I know about drives, but that is exactly why he must not go. His expertise is fundamentally unique and irreplaceable. Mine is merely very rare. I will replace *Kapitan* Dortmuller's Arat Kur software specialist."

The officers nodded, the American holding the visor of his cap for a moment, before they swung off toward their separate commands. Thandla watched them go, smiling, and felt that—despite the line of clouds on the horizon—this was a very good day after all. He turned back to Wasserman.

Whose face was red, almost distended. "Jesus Christ," he hissed, "Jesus fucking Christ, what the hell are you doing, Sanjay? What the *fuck* have you gotten yourself—?"

Thandla put a hand on Lemuel's arm; he would have liked to place it against his cheek. "Lemuel. Stop. Think. There is no other choice. And you were ready to take the same risk. Today we cannot afford to protect ourselves, cannot afford to lose precious seconds or even one small advantage."

Wasserman shook his head. "But it's not safe. Have you looked at the first wave's mission specs—I mean, *really* looked at them?"

"I have. Possibly more than you. And there is no alternative. The first wave cannot be comprised solely of remote operated vehicles, because if the comm links are broken or disrupted, that would be the end of them."

Wasserman shook his head even harder. "Look. The live control vehicles don't need to be in the first wave, Sanjay. They could stay behind it, control it by lascom."

"On the contrary. You know what lascom control links mean in terms of degraded reaction time. The drone sends us data, we send it reactive orders—and lose a fraction of a second every time we do. And in that microsecond, the drone is extremely vulnerable. No. Our crewed control vehicles must be so close that there is no measurable delay. Otherwise, we cannot be sure that our manned air forces will arrive in Java, let alone in sufficient numbers to attain battlespace parity."

"Sanjay, listen to what you're saying. You're talking about flying into a shooting gallery." Wasserman seemed ready to reach out and shake some sense into his friend, then blushed and threw his hands up in the air instead. "Don't do it. It's not safe."

"Today, Lemuel, personal safety must be set aside. Our survival as a planet and a species depends on our acceptance of that, my friend."

Wasserman hesitated. And Thandla knew why: because Sanjay Thandla had called him *"my friend."* What could Lemuel Wasserman say in response to that?

Lemuel swallowed—it seemed hard for him to do, as if he had a sore throat—and looked out to sea. "Yeah, well—you're going to be fine. You optimistic son of a bitch. I'll be way back in the second wave, and they'll still find a way to kill me. And when I'm dead, you'll still be smiling that stupid smile of yours. You son of a bitch. I'm going to die and you're going to be fine."

Thandla smiled, put an arm around Lemuel's shoulder, looked out to sea with him. "Of course I am."

Thandla watched the low waves run—inexhaustible but futile—toward their feet, and, failing, retract and gather to rush at them once more. *And no matter what happens, that will be true. I'm going to be fine.*

Wholenest flagship *Greatvein*, Earth orbit

"The situation becomes more difficult, Esteemed Fleetmaster R'sudkaat."

R'sudkaat's response to Tuxae was flat-toned. "Report."

"The human missile barrage has begun to drop off rapidly."

"Excellent."

"Yes, Fleetmaster, but the damage reports are alarming. We have lost thirty percent of our PDF targeting arrays. Almost all grounded aircraft took some measure of damage from shrapnel or other debris. Readiness ratings for half of them are uncertain. Communications are being switched through a dangerously small number of antennae: many of the masts have been damaged or destroyed. Fatalities have been low, but the wounded are numerous, and—due to communication losses—we have lost touch with many of the firebases in the countryside."

"All recoverable losses."

"I harmonize, Fleetmaster, all recoverable—*if* we are

given the time to recover. Unfortunately, the human operations show no sign of diminishing. Close-range ground engagement began at each of our compounds just over three minutes ago."

"So they are starting to mount a ground offensive."

"No, Fleetmaster R'sudkaat, they are not 'starting' it. It is in process, and all their actions commenced within the same five-second interval."

"What? Across the entirety of Java?"

"Yes."

"So they have found a means of communication we cannot jam. Inconsequential. Our tactical air will crush them. Instruct—"

Did R'sudkaat not know how to listen? "Fleetmaster, I repeat: our tactical air assets are at less than seventy percent due to damage. Those remaining are returning to refuel and rearm, but this will take three times as long as usual."

"What? Why?"

"Enough of the humans' large, ship-launched rockets survived to hit half of our air-support facilities with cluster-bomblet munitions. Runways, landing pads, service vehicles have all been compromised. Fuel and ordnance, according to protocol, was moved into protective bunkers and so is not in immediate readiness. Surabaja is particularly affected. It is down to twenty percent function."

"Why did you not tell me of this earlier?"

"Esteemed Fleetmaster, I am receiving these updates as we speak. Surabaja is having to divert craft to Jakarta for refueling and refit. But in consequence, almost all relief pilots and all the munitions are being drawn from one cache."

"Consumables for our air assets may run dry, but before then—"

"Before then, they may be shot down, Fleetmaster. Because so many aircraft are now depending upon Jakarta's various airports, the wait-time there for landing and service has tripled. In consequence, although we are maximizing dispersal, our aircraft are nonetheless stacked in multilayered holding patterns above Jakarta—"

"—and so are perfect targets for surface-to-air missiles. Even small ones with short range." R'sudkaat's mandibles clacked urgently. "I harmonize. Quickly, alert the combat air traffic controllers in Jakarta. Despite our orbital interdiction, the humans might hope to use this moment to bring their own air assets into the battle—"

Over the Sunda Strait, off Sumatra, Earth

Behind Thandla's mid-seat position in the German VTOL, the roughly purring engines—both the vertical lifters and the aft thrusters—suddenly yowled as if enraged. The flat, blue expanse of shallows leapt at, and then unrolled under and behind, them in what seemed like a single long second. Thandla was pushed back in the seat—hard. On either side, five Deutsche AeroFabrik VTOLs, identical to his own save for the tail numbers, were spread in the forward arms of a vee, for which his craft was the vertex.

"Jamming on," called the electronic warfare specialist in the back seat.

"Very good." Dortmund, the craft's commander, turned back toward Thandla. "Soon, you will become quite busy. Their computers will analyze our signals, decode how we are amplifying, distorting, or creating false signatures, and interrupting their communications."

"And so I will have to adjust our signals."

"Just so. At first, you should be able to follow the guidelines that we preprogrammed into the computer."

Thandla smiled. "But if you had such complete faith in those new modulation and propagation protocols, you would have not have needed my services so urgently."

For the first time since Thandla had met him, Dortmund allowed himself a small smile. "*Das stimmt*. If my guess is correct, within the first ten minutes, the Arat Kur will begin to see the programming patterns common to all our settings. There will be need for you to improvise."

"And if I fail?"

"Then we die. Naturally."

"But we do want them to be shooting at us, do we not?"

"Yes. We want them to realize that they *must* shoot us down, that if they eliminate us, they can eliminate the jamming and image-making drones covering the general air assault into Java."

"Which begins when?"

"Look behind you."

Thandla turned, looked out the rear of the long cockpit blister. Above the dwindling green-gray Sumatran coast, specks were airborne, rising, gathering.

Sanjay stared at the wide blue heavens above them—above which an enemy fleet hovered. "I am unconvinced that we shall last more than a few seconds, anyway. The Arat Kur's look-down visual sensors seem quite acute, and their laser targeting is most impressive."

"True, but first they will try to eliminate us with their more numerous rail guns. But the flight time of the projectiles makes hitting a fast, maneuverable craft problematic. Ultimately, they may have to use lasers. But they have far fewer of them, and atmospheric diffusion makes them energy-expensive to use. We project that they will only commit their lasers once they determine that they must act swiftly and decisively against the manned vehicles of our controller flights if they are to eliminate the numerous countermeasure drones we are directing."

"So the way for them to kill the many-headed hydra of our interference is to hit us: its heart and brain."

"Just so."

"All so that the other aircraft can get to Java."

Dortmund frowned, looked away. "That would be nice."

Thandla looked harder at him. "But you said—"

"We want it to appear that our primary objective is to ensure that our air assets reach Jakarta. But our true task—both for us and the air units behind us—is to be a decoy. We must keep the Roaches too busy to anticipate or detect a far greater threat that is approaching."

"Which is coming from where?" Thandla felt foolish doing so, but scanned the skies.

Dortmund shook his head. "The threat is not coming from up there." He pointed straight down through the VTOL's deck. "It is coming from down there. From far, far beneath us."

Chapter Thirty-Eight

North of the Ciliwung waterway, Central Jakarta, Earth

"Damn it, get back down here, Little Guy."

"Coming, coming."

Opal looked away from where her XO, Miles O'Garran, was affixing another decoy cellular repeater to a street post. Anxious over his exposure, she glanced north. Burning cars, sporadic fire from the AKs of irregulars, silence from the Hkh'Rkh hardpoint that brooded, broad and squat, on the other side of the narrow waterway which constrained the sluggish Ciliwung River. The Hkh'Rkh were probably ranging in the locals, letting them get overconfident in the absence of a reply, and so lull these neophyte warriors into believing that they were safe to continue to fire from the same positions. And there was nothing that Opal could do to warn the irregulars of that mortal error. A lot of brave Indonesians were going to die as a result of their ignorance today. But the hard numbers—the chillingly cold equations of the tactical situation—were that if the Hkh'Rkh lost one trooper for every ten ad hoc civilian insurgents they killed this day, their occupation would be over by nightfall.

She looked north. Nothing to be seen yet, but the Taiwanese with her had vouched for the mainland tunnel rats' reports that one of the dozens of Hkh'Rkh's counterattacking units was moving in from that direction. The Sloths were probably looking to come in sneaky-Pete quiet, get in behind the insurgents up the street and take them out on their way back in to the hard point. Best guess was that most of the Hkh'Rkh of that strike force were moderately wounded, although none were what humans would consider critical. Street intel confirmed that the Hkh'Rkh were terminally triaging their true surgical cases out in the field. Less burden on the rear area services, and less need to pull combat effectives off the line to exfiltrate those wounded who were wholly incapacitated. The coldblooded efficiency of it gave the Hkh'Rkh an even more fearsome aspect; for them, "fight or die" wasn't merely a rousing battle cry. It was a way of life. Even a unit of walking wounded like the one approaching Opal's concealed positions had a combat mission. The Hkh'Rkh were supremely capable and confident fighters, Opal had to concede, but sometimes they were possibly a bit *too* confident...

Movement: a shadow in the mists one hundred meters to the north, loping across the street and then gone. Like a ghost.

"Little Guy, get your skinny ass back down here!"

O'Garran was now affixing a small, convex block to the base of the street pole.

"Little Guy!"

"Coming, Mother." His mutter was more annoyed than jocular. O'Garran played out an arming wire from the back of the block, tossed the lead down the adjacent sewer grate. Behind her, Opal heard the senior mainland Chinese officer—Chou, who spoke almost no English—give orders to fish the wire out of the muck and hook it up to the command switches. At least that's what Opal supposed he was saying since that's what his men were doing. She looked sideways at the ranking Taiwanese officer—Wu, an English-fluent detective from Taitung—but he was facing rigidly in the same direction she was. *And he's still not too happy with me. But it's not like I had any choice. The mainlanders are well-trained and there are five times as many of them. I had to give their CO seniority. Hell, it was hard enough to get them to accept O'Garran as my XO.* Wu—the Taiwanese—hadn't said a thing but she could tell he felt sold out.

O'Garran leaned a mauled street vendor's sign in front of the convex block and then hopped down through the open manhole, shooting past Opal and almost landing square on the fiber-optic spool.

"Watch it," Opal snapped. "You want to cut our commo?"

"Wouldn't think of it. The repeater net is down?"

"Not yet, but the Roaches are doing their best to tear it to pieces." She looked behind her. Chou, the third in command, was quickly scanning the screen of the palmcomp he had hooked up to one of the spool's fiber-optic splitter-leads. "According to Wu, Chou's seeing reports from other infiltration units that the Arat Kur have started using a few smaller-yield EMP devices."

"They're trying to burn down the system."

"They're getting our decoy nodes, mostly. And a lot of non-milspec electronics along with them. As we expected they would. But soon, we and the other tunnel rats may become the telephone operators for our offensive. Our fiber optics could be the only reliable local commo."

"Major." It was Wu. "Movement."

Opal hopped halfway up the rungs in a single jump, grabbed the eyepiece of the monofilament snooper they'd fixed there, looked out into the street.

The shadows approaching from the north were bigger now, and they weren't disappearing. They courted the edges of the smoke, indistinct but steady presences.

"What's the wait?" asked O'Garran.

"They're checking out the area. They seem pretty shy," Opal mused.

"Wouldn't you be? They've learned that, today, almost anything can be a trap."

"I just want to make sure they're not looking for *us.*"

"You mean, an ambush by concealed tunnel rats? I doubt it. My guess is they're extra-cautious because they're getting nasty surprises from the more organized resistance cells. According to the chatter on the fibercom, all us tunnel rats and most of the infiltration teams have been able to stay under the street and under the radar, so far."

Opal watched two Hkh'Rkh emerge from the smoke. One was limping. "We'll be setting a new precedent, then." These Sloths were the perfect target. Neither of the ones she saw had liquimix weapons—the Hkh'Rkh reserved those for squad support and elite troops—and were carrying light ammo loads. They were on their way to the rear, all right. As more of them emerged from the smoke, the condition of the first two proved to be universal. They were all wounded, wary, lightly loaded, scanning the buildings as they came on. They had probably learned that sporadically firing insurgents like those they knew were up ahead didn't usually think about rear security. But they had also probably learned that they could not rely on that assumption, because there were too many humans with a little military experience sprinkled into the general population. Opal counted more than a dozen Hkh'Rkh, now within thirty meters of their subterranean hideout. She turned to O'Garran. "Activate the decoy repeater."

The little SEAL nodded, pressed the central button on the small remote he held. "The repeater is active."

The Hkh'Rkh's behavior changed almost instantly. From somewhere in the rear of their well-spread column of advance, an order came up. Their point scouts held position, went low, and within thirty seconds, the unit's commo specialist had come forward, sweeping a hand scanner back and forth, back and forth. Within ten seconds, he had found the vector of strongest transmission and pointed out the repeater.

"Mr. Wu, please tell Mr. Chou to instruct his second squad that they are to prepare to trigger their charges, and follow up by directly engaging the enemy. As per contingency B-beta."

"Yes, ma'am."

Opal watched three of the Hkh'Rkh come forward, sweeping the muzzles of their outsized weapons across the facades of the surrounding buildings. She could also feel Little Guy squinting up at her.

"Major, if we just stick with the mines, that won't

give away our position. Hell, they can't even be sure if they're running into trip-wired or command-detonated charges. But if our troops join the ambush, the enemy will know we're here, will see our positions." O'Garran's voice trailed off, uncomfortable with stating the obvious.

Opal paused, collecting herself, her thoughts, the right words. "Sergeant O'Garran, you are my right hand, my guardian angel, my demolitions expert—and you have more mouth on you than you should. I've got my reasons for starting our own little party here and now, and I will make those reasons clear to you. In my own sweet time. Understood, *Sergeant*?"

She didn't look down. The one second of silence was capped by a "Yes, ma'am. Sorry if I was out of line."

You were. But so am I, and you can smell it, can't you? Two weeks we've been creeping and crawling toward Jakarta, shepherding our platoon of pint-sized soldiers through fiber-optic conduits and the occasional rare sewer, wiring up covert op teams so they're on the fiber-com net, hitting the Hkh'Rkh when we had to, hiding most of the time to get our job done. And now—now when we should play it cool, should wait for the signal from offshore to commence the final attack on the enemy's command and control elements—I'm taking us into an engagement that is contrary to everything we've been working toward. It's contrary to our mission, to your instincts, to our present need to stay hidden. But it is essential to Caine's survival. If the current intel is right, the Arat Kur would be keeping him in the presidential compound and we're only three hundred meters away. But if we don't get in the game right now, it may be too late to get to him in time.

The Hkh'Rkh had reached the repeater, were hunkering down to look for traps. But they were too late. Opal turned to Wu. "Light 'em up."

Wu nodded at Chou. Chou turned the command switches sharply.

The convex block—a fourth-generation claymore mine—went off with a throaty roar. The three Hkh'Rkh went down, one struggling to get his claws over two geysering wounds, another limp by the time he hit the macadam.

The reaction of the other Hkh'Rkh was, as always, prudent and well-rehearsed. Their NCOs waved the rest of the troopers back into covering positions close against the walls of the buildings on either side of the street. Fifty meters south, close to the rear of the column, a small knot of the Hkh'Rkh gathered and then tucked quickly into a side-street. The command group, probably trying to assess how best to recon the point of contact, whether it had been a dumb-mine or command detonated, and whether they could afford the time or personnel to send out feelers to the flanks.

But they had less time than they knew. "Mr. Wu, tell Mr. Chou to order second squad into action, starting with the ready charges." Opal returned her eye to the snooper scope, counted off three seconds—

The windows and doors of the buildings on the west side of the street blew out in gouts of flame, smoke, and cartwheeling debris. One or two of the Hkh'Rkh that had been sheltering against them got up, limped over to their mates on the other side of the street, some moving into the east-side buildings to find cover—

But they found an ambush instead. Having come up out of the fiber-optic conduits in the basements of two buildings on the east side of the street, Chou's second squad, armed with South African liquimix carbines, started hitting each Hkh'Rkh with tightly grouped three- and four-round bursts. At least that's what had been planned, and that's what it sounded like now. The Hkh'Rkh came reeling back out of the buildings, into the middle of the street, firing as they withdrew, but uncertain where to go. After a moment, they started a fighting withdrawal back down the street, toward the last sighted location of the unit's command group. Opal smiled. "Mr. Wu, tell Mr. Chou that third squad has the target right on top of them. Engage immediately."

Opal almost felt sorry for the Hkh'Rkh. That side street had been the only reasonable fallback position within two hundred meters of the first ambush point. She counted off another three seconds—

An explosion quaked the walls around them slightly, shattered most of the remaining nearby windows. Smoke plumed out of the side street. Two seconds later, she could hear another but more distant stuttering torrent of South African liquimix carbines. Third squad was capitalizing upon the confusion and devastation inflicted by almost ten kilos of plastique that had been planted and upward-tamped on the thin ceiling of the sewer station in that side street. O'Garran was conferring directly with Chou in his atrocious pidgin Cantonese. "What's he's saying, Little Guy?" Opal asked. "How many did we get of theirs, lose of ours?"

"There's only a handful of them left. Chou says he's lost about half of each squad." O'Garran had more to say, but didn't say it; Chou's eyes stayed on him, waiting. *You may not speak English, Chou, but*

*you know your pint-sized American pal hasn't asked
me the question you put to him. Why lose any of his
men? Why stage this ambush at all? Why not wait
for the "go" signal that will kick off the final attack?*
Opal returned her eye to the snooper scope. "Those
are good results. Pass the word to all squads: fall back
to yesterday's positions."

Peripherally, she could see O'Garran stand to his
full height below her, his face very white against the
darkness around him. "Yesterday's positions?"

"You heard right, Sergeant. Tell them to get moving. We don't have a lot of time."

O'Garran's attempt to ask two questions at the
same time produced a comical gobbling sound for a
moment. "Ma'am, are we—? I'm not—What do you
mean, we don't have a lot of time?"

Opal unclipped the snooper scope from the side of
the ladder, reeled in the fiber-optic probe back down
through the manhole's pry-bar slit. "You've seen the
reports on the fiber-com. Ever since the last of the
clone units deserted, the Hkh'Rkh have had to send
out a slew of fresh units working perimeter clearance
like fire brigades. If one of their regular sweeps gets hit
hard within five hundred meters of the Roach Motel,
the fire brigade gets the word, rushes in, and snuffs
out the flames. In this case, that means us. They'll
assume we've played all our cards and are either going
to sit back or eventually unass this place. Either way,
they'll want to get here fast. Make sure they get us."

"Why? As a reprisal, an 'example'?"

"Hell, no. For security. They'll know that an ambush
like this wasn't mounted by the general insurgency.
That makes us a high priority target. Firstly, we could

be an intel goldmine. They'll guess we're not locals, so they'll want to grab some of us to squeeze and debrief since they've got no idea—yet—what kind of coordinated efforts they're up against today."

"And what's the second reason we're a high-priority target?"

She sealed the snoop scope back in its pouch. "Given where they want to establish a safe perimeter—about five hundred meters out from their compound—we are a serious and organized rear-area security threat that got inside the zone they thought they'd cleared."

O'Garran nodded. "So they're going to come back and clean out what they missed: us. Okay, so let's go back into hiding."

"Whoa there, Little Guy. I didn't say anything about hiding. I said we're going back into yesterday's positions, which are about four hundred meters back to the north, along the probable advance route of the Hkh'Rkh fire brigade."

Wu looked over. "So you mean to attack them, too. A much larger force, and mostly unwounded."

Opal heard the grim tone but ignored it. "That is correct. But we're going to hit them from behind. I'm betting that four hundred meters north of this contact point, that fire brigade is still going to be moving fast, with minimal flank and rear security precautions. And you *did* leave the demo charges in yesterday's positions, didn't you Mr. Wu?"

"I did as you instructed."

"And now you know why I did so. And now we've lost another minute we can't afford to lose. Move."

As they crouched into the stooped jog that was the fastest way of traveling through the fiber-optic conduits, O'Garran kept close behind her. Close enough to whisper, "Major, I've got to ask: what in the hell are we doing? I mean, why mount another ambush before we get the 'go' signal for the final attack? What will it accomplish—?"

"It will clear the path to the Roach Motel, sergeant."

"So you're baiting them in to clear this sector. Why?"

"Because we don't have enough forces to spare for a rear guard when we make our own assault."

"Our own assault? What do you mean? Assault into what?"

"Assault straight into their compound, Sergeant. That's the objective of the final attack, after all."

The moment's silence seemed to double the force behind O'Garran's urgent, hissing whisper, "Into *their* compound? Major, particularly with our losses, we'd never survive an approach to their hardpoint, let alone fight through it into the Roach Motel."

"Who said anything about going *through* the hardpoint?"

"Well, how else—?"

"Little Guy, tell me. What are we in right now?"

"Uh ... fiber-optic conduits. And the very occasional sewer."

"And a number of buildings in the Arat Kur compound—particularly the ministries complex near the palace—were wired for fiber optic, weren't they?"

The brief silence told her that he saw it. "So we're taking out both these Hkh'Rkh forces to make the exos believe that we're weakening this area in preparation for a frontal assault on their compound."

"Right. And since they're too smart to sit holed up, waiting for us to hit the compound—"

"—They're going to send out a good-sized preemption force to break up any gathering attack, eliminate us, and then finish the job of securing their perimeter in this sector."

"Right again. And where's that force going to come from, given how overextended the Hkh'Rkh already are?"

Another pause; another tactical realization. "They're going to tap the internal security detachment that's covering this part of the compound. They can't have anything else left as area reserves."

"Exactly. They're going to draw down this salient's security complement to come out after us, try to take us out on the streets, before we can conduct a frontal assault."

"But you said we're *not* going to be assaulting frontally—"

"Because we're not even going to be on the streets. While they're out looking for us, we're going to be in the conduits under the streets, and under them. All the way into the heart of the Roach Motel."

Chapter Thirty-Nine

Presidential Palace, Jakarta, Earth

Darzhee Kut bobbed when Urzueth Ragh pointed out the relayed sensor readings. "The human fleet is preparing to engage our own in cislunar space."

First Delegate Hu'urs Khraam swiveled towards him. "It is the expected melody, but how can you tell?"

"They have discontinued the centrifugal spin of their habitation modules and are retracting the booms."

"Earlier than at Barnard's Star. Do our tactical analysts anticipate differences in this engagement?"

"Several, Hu'urs Khraam. Firstly, the human force is much larger than ours on this occasion, and the ships are not second echelon or decommissioned craft. It is the gathered cream of their several fleets, both in terms of hulls and personnel. Secondly, this time they are moving faster than we are, yet their trajectory will allow them to use Earth's gravity to pull them tight around the planet and strike us again. Or, by changing when and how much they boost, they could use that gravity to slingshot them out of cislunar space at extreme velocity."

"So they have far more control over whether there will be a second firing pass, a second phase to the engagement."

"Your pitch is perfect, Esteemed Hu'urs Khraam. They can either run and minimize their losses if things do not go well—"

"—Or come around to finish us off if the first engagement has gone in their favor."

"Regrettably true, First Delegate. But I do not impugn our planning. We presumed that they had no such forces left. There was no reason for us to fear or refrain from being so deep in Earth's gravity well."

"You sing a soothing song, and I appreciate it, Urzueth Ragh, but I will have no lullabies. This was my doing. I was not cautious enough in our deployment. I split the fleet, and allowed us to sink deep into this gravity well, for which we will now pay. The force we have sent to meet the humans labors against Earth's pull, while the rest of our ships must remain in close orbit, held fast by the planet's heavy claws. Easy targets, should any of the human craft manage to engage us."

Darzhee Kut raised an objecting claw. "With respect, Hu'urs Khraam, your deployments were optimal for forcing a swift conclusion to a war of occupation—"

"Perhaps, but those deployments were still wrong. Darzhee Kut, if you should find yourself burdened with the cares of the Wholenest in the years to come, I offer you the counsel of this day: in war, there is no surety. Now, no more on this. What other differences does the human fleet exhibit this time?"

"It is early to tell, but sensors indicate a far higher ratio of drones. Almost five times as many as the humans had at Barnard's Star."

"None of these differences sing in harmony with our hopes, Speaker Kut. How do you expect they will attack us?"

Darzhee looked over at Caine, who was pointedly absorbed in the act of tying his left shoe; no help there. "We cannot be certain, Hu'urs Khraam, but we expect that they will salvo missiles at long range, probably several flights of them in close sequence. As we come to shorter range and pass each other, missiles launched then will be less effective, because they will have less time to acquire targets, maneuver, and track. This is when we can expect our greatest advantage."

"Because of our superior lasers?"

"Yes, Hu'urs Khraam, and particularly because of the X-ray lasers that form the spine of our shift-cruisers. If we elect to spend their drives' antimatter reserves to fully charge those spinal weapons, they will have a devastating effect upon the human ships, particularly at close range."

"And we are confident that the humans have no such system?"

Again Darzhee Kut looked at Caine. The human's right shoelace was now the object of his undivided attention. "Not within their hulls, Hu'urs Khraam. They do not have the engineering acumen necessary to generate and sustain the spectrally-selective energy emissions. However, as we saw at Barnard's Star, they do have a special form of drone that can briefly mimic our spinal weapons: their single-use X-ray laser missiles."

"True, but our intelligence tells us that they do not have many of these systems. A handful at most. Five years ago, the human nations signed accords severely restricting the deployment of any weapon system that either uses nuclear charges as warheads, or as power sources, as is the case with their X-ray laser drones."

"This is indeed what our intelligence told us."

"You are unconvinced?"

"I am—uncertain, Hu'urs Khraam."

"Why?"

"Because every time the humans make such accords with each other, they immediately begin violating them in secret."

"Agreed. But our information on these matters came from their own megacorporations. How could they be wrong? Do not the corporations produce the very drones of which we speak?"

"Hu'urs Khraam, the weapons of which we speak are produced by a special subgroup of megacorporations, called the industrials."

"I cannot follow the melody you are trying to sing for me."

"First Delegate, there is antipathy between the industrials and the megacorporations that have allied with us. It is conceivable that our collaborators were mislead, deliberately provided with false information via the industrials' counterintelligence efforts."

Hu'urs Khraam bobbed. "Darzhee Kut, you are learning the prime lesson of this day well: question everything. But our human sources took great pains to gather accurate data, for if we do not succeed, they will be executed as traitors. This is one set of data that we may trust."

Or maybe not, Darzhee Kut thought as he bowed a deep acquiescence. *We cast eyes back upon our path and realize that, since Barnard's Star, we thought we*

*were manipulating the humans—but all along, they
were manipulating us. They play the linked games of
war and deception better than we do. And the reason
lies before us. They spend most of their time imagining
how we would best fight a war against them, rather
than how they would like to resist us. So of course
they knew how to show us what we wanted to see,
what seemed reasonable outcomes, gave us logical
decision paths. All so that we would follow a course
of action that they could predict, which would deliver
us to this moment and this place where they would
spring their carefully laid traps all at once.* Darzhee
rose up higher, one claw raised to signal that he must
share this last point—

But Darzhee Kut felt the pressure of a gentle yet
firm claw clamp over his own, kept it from raising.
He swiveled to the side, saw Urzueth Ragh, who
lowered his eyes and diddled his mandibles. "Let it
go, rock-sibling."

Darzhee Kut considered, looked after Hu'urs Khraam,
who was already deep in a teleconference with Tuxae
Skhaas, the senior sensor coordinator for the command
ship of the orbital flotilla. And with that brief pause, the
moment to speak had passed. If Darzhee Kut brought
up the issue of CoDevCo's questionable reporting to
the First Delegate once again, it would signal a much
more serious, and possibly insolent, questioning of Hu'urs
Khraam's judgment. But, still . . .

Urzueth Ragh seemed to read his mind. "I know
what you mean to do, to say, and I tell you it will be
a tune sung to insensate antennae. You are right, of
course. How can we be certain of the reliability of
the human intelligence? But if we begin to question

all our data, we have no basis for action, must lie on our claws, might as well concede. So, either way, we must make our best conjectures and move on. We must act rather than reflect. Alas, it is a hurried process that I like it no better than you. It is not our way."

"No. It is war."

Urzueth Ragh bobbed his agreement. "As I said, it is not our way."

Flagship USS *Lincoln*, Sierra Echelon, RTF 1, cislunar space

"So what's it going to be, Skipper?" asked Commander Ruth Altasso. "A stand-up brawl or a drive-by shooting?"

Admiral Ira Silverstein smiled at his XO, found his brain running on two tracks simultaneously: a blessing, or curse, amplified by Talmudic study.

Track one: Commander Ruth Altasso was a fine XO and knew her business well-enough to know that her question was no question at all. All three echelons of the fleet had stopped hab rotation, tucked in their booms, and were maintaining acceleration typical to interplanetary travel: they were going in hot. However the battle might unfold against the Arat Kur, it would be sharp, savage, and so fast that even if one wanted to give or call for quarter, there simply wouldn't be the time. Today, there would be two kinds of combatants: the quick and the dead.

Track two: Ruth was almost a good enough actress to pull off the precombat bravado shtick. Almost, but not quite. She had never been in real combat before. Hell, none of her generation had. It had been almost twenty years since a US vessel had fired a shot in anger, more than thirty since a formal, brief, and almost wholly inconsequent declaration of war in the last of the many desultory posturings known collectively as the Sino-Russian Belt War. The training sims were realistic—nearly made Ira wet his own pants—and no one did a better job than the Commonwealth at creating authentic field training environments. But as any soldier knew, training was no substitute for paying your penny and seeing the elephant that was war, up close and personal. And the few recent veterans who had earned that distinction by both fighting and surviving at Barnard's Star were now stuck in that system, so there were no "blooded" ratings to sprinkle among the hulls of Admiral Lord Halifax's fleet. Now arrayed in three tandem echelons, it was, collectively, the hidden weapon that had been slowly forged via the covert sequestration operation code-named Case Leo Gap, but now known simply as RTF 1 or Rescue Task Force One. However, as will happen with acronyms, a rival label had become popular in the multinational armada: "Rag Tag Fleet Number One."

And it was, on the surface of it, an extraordinary hodgepodge of craft. The unit was top-heavy with capital ships, all carrying five times the normal combat loads of nuke-pumped X-ray drones and two-hundred-kiloton close-kill missiles. Arrayed in front of the escorting destroyers and frigates, the control sloops and their attendant flocks of drones were so dense that it made navigation a genuine hazard. It was the first time Ira had seen that kind of free-space crowding in his thirty-five-year career. Spec ops corvettes, the only hulls really designed for fast atmospheric entry, were still attached to the shift carriers, as were the troop transports. All the millions of metric tons of ordnance, vehicles, and cold-slept elite planetary forces that had been siphoned out from Earth over the past two years rested there, inert, waiting for the summons to return home—with a vengeance.

"Skipper?"

"Sorry, Commander. Breaking my own rule, I'm afraid."

"Which rule, Skipper? You've got a lot of them."

"'When you bring your hab mods in close, bring your thoughts in with 'em.' No time for daydreaming now, not right before a drive-by shooting."

"Thought so. How's it going to go down?"

"I don't know, Ruth. We'll wait for Lord Halifax to call the ball. My guess is he's waiting for a sitrep from the Big Blue Marble. At this point, it's all about the drones."

"Ours?"

"No, at least not the ones we have with us."

Altasso frowned. "I'm not following you, Skipper."

Poor gal, how could she? "Secrecy was an operational necessity, Ex. Part of the op plan from day one was that if and when threat forces showed up around Big Blue, neither the Earth nor the Moon was going to deploy more than a token force of their drones. And only old ones, at that."

"Why?"

Ira smiled. "So that the rest of the drones would be ready and waiting to join us today. Twice our current striking force is waiting here, at home in the garage."

Ruth's frown went away, came back more furrowed than before. "Well, that's nice—except how will the dirtside folks manage to get them past the Arat Kur orbital interdiction?"

Ira ran his upper teeth along the side of his index finger. "I imagine they're working on the answer to that right now..."

Wholenest flagship *Greatvein*, Earth orbit

"Tuxae, the Fleetmaster is not ready to hear another problem. You can see it. Watch his mandibles." H'toor Qooiiz's normally jocular buzz was gone from his voice.

Tuxae did not speak until he could be sure of a patient tone. "I harmonize, rock-sibling, but shall I tell the humans to stop what they're doing, to give him more time? The Fleetmaster must be told, and he must act." He turned away from H'toor Qooiiz and toward R'sudkaat. "Fleetmaster, I must trouble you again."

Judging from the slow, patience-labored turn of the Fleetmaster, Qooiiz certainly seemed to be right about his rapidly waning equanimity. "What is it now, Tuxae Skhaas?"

"The humans have deployed a wave of diverse air vehicles from around the Pacific Rim. Between the rocket-carrying freighters, and this new mass launch, we are unable to achieve better than fifty percent orbital interdiction."

"What kinds of air vehicles have been launched? Which are the most numerous?"

"Almost a thousand are medium-range free rockets."

"How are they armed?"

"They are not weapons, Esteemed R'sudkaat. They are deploying chaff, drones, or small sensors between ten and eighty kilometers from the Javanese coast. Well out of the range of our ground-based PDF batteries."

R'sudkaat's antennae twitched anxiously. "What kind of small sensors?"

"First reports indicate they are small, automated quadcopters. They are quite primitive. They are equipped with passive sensors only, but they are arriving over Java and tightbeaming data back into Bali, the near Celebes, Sumatra, and Christmas Island."

"We must deny the humans intelligence regarding the combat on Java. Eliminate these sensors with a full-regional EMP strike."

"Sir, such a strike will wash over our strongholds, as well."

"You sing that note uncertainly."

"Such an extensive set of EMP bursts are likely to disable some of our own, more fragile systems."

"Nonsense. Our vehicles and arrays are quite—"

"With respect, I was referring to unshielded infantry systems, such as thermal imaging and laser targeting scopes, even some of the smaller computing and communication devices. The Hkh'Rkh equipment is particularly vulnerable."

The Fleetmaster's mandibles ground sharply, stopped, ground again. "It is unfortunate, but we cannot target the human sensors individually, and they must be eliminated. Order the EMP strike. Now, you said there were other vehicles?"

"Yes, R'sudkaat. Mostly high-speed VTOLs, inbound from Sumatra, Christmas Island, Lombok Island, and from the decks of ships beyond the fifty-kilometer limit."

"Sink all ships that have launched any vehicles. Interdict the VTOLs."

"Sir, we are trying, but it is taking longer than anticipated."

Fleetmaster R'sudkaat was very quiet, the same way, according to suntimers, that the worst storms on the surface of a world are preceded by great, almost eerie, periods of great stillness. "Why is the interdiction taking longer than anticipated?"

"The VTOLs are not conventional attack craft. They are electronic warfare platforms, managing the hundreds of rocket-deployed drones that are now creating false images electronically."

"Well, overcome their computing with ours and erase them from the walls of existence."

"We are trying to do just that, Esteemed R'sudkaat, but their programming is—challenging."

The Fleetmaster's retort was a sudden, shrill, warble-shriek that was loud in the silent bridge. "Then engage them visually! Use our look-down optical arrays and eliminate them. These VTOLs are the most important target. Belay all other orbital fire missions until they are eliminated."

"Including the rockets?"

"Including the rockets."

H'toor Qooiiz rose up, alarmed. "But if we allow their rockets to reach Java in even greater numbers—?"

"We have no choice," Tuxae mouthed at his friend in a low, warning hum. "The VTOLs are making so many false images, it is impossible to tell which are the real VTOLs, the real drones, the real rockets, and Rockmother knows what else." Louder, to the quivering Fleetmaster, "It shall be as you say, Esteemed R'sudkaat."

"See that it is. If we are to act effectively, we *must* have a clear picture of what is happening."

Tuxae turned to his console. As *if we ever had one.*

Over the Sunda Strait, off Sumatra, Earth

Thandla saw a flash, more like a single pulse of a strobe light than any beam or lightning. The closest portside VTOL underwent a hallucinatorily rapid set of transmogrifications. First it was tilting, listing down toward the water; then it was suddenly discorporated, as though it had been magically transformed from an intact hull to a forward-tumbling cloud of debris; and then it was an angry orange-yellow ball of fire that, along with a dull, faint blast, was behind them so quickly that, for a split second, Sanjay Thandla wondered if he had imagined the whole thing.

But no. Their portside wingman was gone, destroyed by an Arat Kur orbital laser.

It was the fifth VTOL lost from Dortmund's flight. Thandla kept adjusting the signals, dancing from one EW protocol to the next, seeding misleading telltale signatures into the image-makers, trying to throw the Arat Kur off the scent of each successive signal iteration and how it might evolve in the next ten seconds. At the same time, he considered the odds: five out of eleven VTOLs destroyed. The first had been as much a casualty of chance as enemy intent. The Arat Kur had started with cluster bomblet dispensers from orbit. The first such barrage put its footprint on the northern edge of their flight's inverted approach delta. Probably a failed Arat Kur attempt to get a lock on them and place a thick curtain of high velocity fragments directly in front of them. But the far left VTOL had picked up a few of pieces of shrapnel. Its airframe compromised, it folded up and flew to pieces like a child's model plane struck by a sledgehammer.

However, the Arat Kur had not only been looking to kill the VTOLs, but force them into a narrower approach vector. The subsequent cluster bomblet attacks had boxed them in, off-centered first to the southern flank of the VTOLs' delta formation, then back to the northern extent, crowding the German aircraft in closer to each other, making their location more predictable, and targeting more simple. Clearly, it had worked. In the last three minutes, four more VTOLs had been lost to the one weapon that they could not outrun or mislead: orbital lasers.

The debris cloud of their portside wingman was already far behind, a wispy, spherical airborne puff disappearing into the horizon. *And such are we all*, Thandla admitted, before returning to his strange, invisible battle with the Arat Kur computers. It was not how he had envisioned war. From the ancient Vedic texts to the contemporary graphic documentaries, images of combat were swift, chaotic, vivid, and seething with flame and blood. But his duel with alien computers was more akin to a mortally hazardous form of meditation, carried out while sitting in a glass-encased chair skimming above the surface of serene blue waters. And if one lost one's focus, stumbled over the binary-coded mantras with which they fooled the eyes and ears of their foes, there was a flash and an end, so quick that the victims did not know and their fellow travelers would not see, if they happened to blink at the wrong moment.

Dortmund announced. "One hundred kilometers range." He sounded grimly satisfied, perhaps a bit surprised.

From the belly of the VTOL, Thandla heard the

sharp, high hum of recessed bays opening. Then missiles were leaping out from beneath them, their tails bright and dwindling as they raced on ahead toward Java. "What are they?"

"Air-to-air missiles."

"How can they hit anything? We have no satellite or airborne targeting for over-horizon intercepts."

Dortmund turned, his thin lips bent in what might have been a smile. "These missiles have been retrofitted with UV sensors, and all our aircraft have been marked with UV paint. So if our missiles do not detect such paint—"

"—then they know an aircraft is a permitted target."

"Exactly. So we can saturate Java's airspace with these self-directing long-range missiles without any worry that they will chase down friendly targets."

"But won't the Arat Kur learn to—?"

"Herr Doktor, if the Arat Kur had a day in which to learn, we would not be able to use this tactic again. But if the Arat Kur are still capable of fighting after today, it is because we will have lost. Everything."

Chapter Forty

North-Central Jakarta, Earth

Vrryngraar of the moiety of the Family Haanash wiped his own light mauve blood out of his eyes and went low around the corner into the street known as Mangga Besar Selatan. He led with the AK-47 he had taken from insurgents his Honor Troop had surprised lurking in the back of a large truck. He could barely fire the weapon. The trigger guard circled his claw like a snug ring. Furthermore, he was unable to hold it properly. The humans had only one opposable digit, not two pairs of them arranged in a cruciform, dual pincer pattern. But he only had twenty rounds left in his dustmix weapon and there was no sign of resupply. Indeed, there was no sign of anything except for humans and more humans, all of whom seemed to be carrying guns.

Vrryngraar almost squeezed the trigger when he detected peripheral movement, but saw that it was one of the Arat Kur attached to his troop. Or rather, what was left of his troop. "Arat Kur. Which are you?"

No reply on the radio. He yelled so that the grubber would hear him through his suit. "Arat Kur! Open your suit and tell me. Who are you?"

The suit's armored chin plate sighed open like a dead snake's jaw. "I am U'tuk Yaaz," the translator said. It sounded distorted, uneven.

"What is wrong with your suit?"

"Some of its melodies no longer sing true. The translator and the links to my minidrones no longer work."

Vrryngraar pony-nodded his understanding. Disabled by the recent EMP bursts. They had burned out the laser targeting and ranging systems on his troop's weapons, as well as their thermal imaging goggles and communication encryption chips. "Where is Team leader Krek and your fellow-Arat Kur? Did you finish your scouting mission?"

"Team leader Krek and my comrade-partner Eerzet are no more."

For the first time since encountering the species, Vrryngraar felt some measure of sympathy, even pity, for an Arat Kur. "How did they die?"

The Arat Kur moved so that his eyes focused on Vrryngraar directly. He had the distinct sense of being stared at, even judged. "They were not paying attention. They were too distracted."

"By what?"

"I will show you." The Arat Kur spun and scuttled into a half-collapsed building. Vrryngraar scanned both ends of the street cautiously, then ducked in behind him.

It was dark, smoky, but also musty with the scent of old bread, and filled with wooden crates stacked in roof-reaching rows. From up ahead, U'tuk Yaaz spoke.

"What distracted them is here." Vrryngraar followed the sound of the Arat Kur's voice, turned a corner—

—and almost stepped on a dead human. Just beyond the body were U'tuk's two fellow-scouts—or rather, their remains—impaled and pinned to the ground by what had evidently been a ceiling-mounted deadfall trap: a grid of spikes weighted by cinderblocks, evidently triggered when they had handled the human body.

Vrryngraar looked at U'tuk. "Where were you when this happened?"

The Arat Kur waved a weak claw in the general direction of the street. "I was the rear guard. Watching for humans." Then he pointed at the human corpse. "Why did you do this?"

Vrryngraar stared at him. "Do what? I did not kill this human."

"I do not mean the killing, and I do not mean you, personally. I mean all you Hkh'Rkh. And I mean the *manner* of the human's death. Why do you torture them so?"

Vrryngraar wondered if fear, loss of comrades, and isolation had damaged U'tuk's mind more than combat had damaged his suit. "Be clear, grubber. What torture?"

"Do not say you do not know. This was the third time I have seen this kind of killing. Go, look at its mouth."

Vrryngraar did. And now, the unusual nature of this particular corpse became evident, made it distinct from the hundreds—no, thousands—he had already seen or made this day.

The evident cause of the human's death was a wound to the groin. But no, it was worse than that.

The male generative member had been removed. If the nearby evidence could be trusted, the penectomy had been performed with a rusted strip of corrugated metal, torn from a nearby wall. Judging from the lack of other injuries, the amputation of the member had been the cause of death, which meant that it had been performed pre-mortem.

Imagining that deed made it impossible for Vrryngraar to think for a long moment. What savagery was this? Not even animals did this to each other, Then he saw that the crudely severed member had been jammed deep into the corpse's mouth. He looked up at U'tuk.

Who said, "You must stop this."

"Me? Stop this? How?" Then he understood the presumption implicit in the Arat Kur's exhortation. "You must be mad, to think this the work of my troops, of the Hkh'Rkh. What do we care of the humans' insane dominance rituals and symbolic disfigurements? We did not do this." He saw U'tuk's mandibles sag in shock, drove home his point. "Grubber, do you not understand? The humans did this—to their own kind."

The Arat Kur was completely motionless for a moment and then shivered so sharply that his armor rattled. "But why—?"

"Look around you. Do you know what this place was?"

"N-no."

"I patrolled this street sometimes. The owner was a merchant of bulk goods. But he also sold grain."

"So he was one of the food distributors?"

Could the grubber truly be so naïve? "Not legally. He found ways to acquire food when the other humans could not and sold it to them for greatly increased prices. He profited from their hunger. And the more hungry they became, the more he profited."

"So they—?"

"Yes. They did this." Vrryngraar looked down again. The humans might not be warriors, might be duplicitous and conniving *s'fet*, but that did not diminish their capacity for savagery. If anything, it seemed to amplify it.

"We should not have come here." U'tuk's voice was quiet, withdrawn.

Although worried that the Arat Kur was perilously close to slipping into some kind of trauma-induced fugue state, Vrryngraar also could not suppress a quick, confirmatory neck-sway. No, they should not have come here. There was no honor in such a place, in such a conflict—for one could not call it a war. The only proper course of action regarding humanity was to leave it alone, and, if possible, isolate it. Just as one would handle any other sophont that was quite irremediably and dangerously insane. "I agree. Tell me the result of your scouting mission. Is it safe to withdraw back to the presidential compound through this area?"

The Arat Kur took a moment to respond. "Yes. Before entering this building, our scouting mission was uneventful. We encountered no sign of insurgents. If any humans remained in the area after we first cleared it, they have kept to their houses."

"Promising. Are you still in contact with the compound?"

"I receive their signals, but they do not receive mine. And the rest of your troop?"

Vrryngraar swayed his neck in the direction of the rest of his battered, hiding unit. "All radios save one—our shielded set—were disabled. But we lost that set and its operator to enemy fire about ten minutes ago. Which is why I came to find you." Vrryngraar rose up out of his crouch. "Stay hidden in this spot. I shall return to the troop and lead them here. Together we shall return to the compound. We are no longer combat effective. All we can do now is make a report and gather replacements."

The Arat Kur bobbed and said nothing as Vrryngraar turned and exited the black marketeer's warehouse. Trying to put the image of the butchered human from his mind, Vrryngraar swept back around the corner by which he had entered Mangga Besar Selatan and started across a smoke- and mist-shrouded moonscape that had once been a side-street. He recalled his explanation to the cowed and quiet U'tuk: his unit was "no longer combat effective." He growled at the grim irony of the term. His troop was down to a dozen, most of whom were incapacitated in at least one limb, few of whom had more than thirty rounds of ammunition left. Half a hundred proud Hkh'Rkh reduced to that handful, hiding like a pack of furtive *s'fet* in a semi-intact basement—and having fought only one true battle to speak of.

They had spent most of the morning fighting the unpredictable and inexperienced insurgents. With the exception of a demolition trap, each encounter merely inflicted some wounds. But those wounds had caused fatal decreases in agility, speed, responsiveness. Then, half an hour ago, they had encountered a true military force. Mostly nonindigenous, these humans had been taller, of diverse phenotypes, and equipped with extremely high-power liquimix assault rifles, rocket-propelled munitions, and sophisticated sensors. Worst of all, they had been trained professionals. Vrryngraar had to admit that what the humans might have lacked in size and courage they more than made up for in technical skill and cunning. His troop lost a dozen dead, and a similar number wounded before ammunition depletion forced Vrryngraar to think, and then do, the unthinkable. He withdrew. From humans.

And since then, they had been fleeing. They called it a withdrawal, but call it what one might, they had been beaten and repulsed, and now sought the sanctuary of the main compound.

Perhaps it was because Vrryngraar was preoccupied by his sour reverie, but, as he angled toward an alley that led to his remaining troops, he moved incautiously into a solid wall of smoke billowing up from a clutter of burning vehicles. He did not wait for a gap in the dark, feathery drifts, and so emerged from the blinding blackness straight into the rear of a crowd of humans gathered at a street corner.

Most were females or young, clustered around two persons in intense discussion. One was a local male armed with an AK-47, trying to communicate in the planet's main—and maddeningly untidy—language with a female who was lighter of skin and subtly heavier of build, particularly in the shoulders, head, and upper legs. The female was the first to see Vrryngraar. Her eyes snapped over, detecting his movement even as he emerged from the smoke. He admired her reflexes. She uttered a one-syllable word that sounded like a bark and dove toward the entry of the nearest building.

The local with the gun turned, taking approximately one half-second to absorb the situational change before reacting.

That half-second's delay was his death. Vrryngraar brought up his own AK-47, tried squeezing off a single round, but wound up two-tapping the human. The first of the 7.62 x 39mm rounds went into the human's side, making a wide bloody wound and spinning him slightly so that the second bullet caught him square in the sternum. The human fell backward with the utterly nerveless flop of those who die instantly on their feet.

Vrryngraar pointed the gun at the dominant female and let instinct guide him. "Obey or she dies," he shouted at the rest of the humans.

The first tentative cries of terror, shock, loss ended abruptly. The dominant female rose from her covered position—she had almost made it through the doorway on a fast low crawl—and turned to face him. As was common with some human subspecies, her eyes were green and very clear, like the Great Equatorial Sea of Rkh'yaa. That brief second, he missed Homeworld so very greatly that he could have lamented with a hero's grief-hooting. But this was neither the time nor the place. "You. Who are you?"

She was one of the few of the half-circle of humans before him who did not start back when he barked out his question. Instead, she looked at him, seemed to be studying him, even his armor and gear. Then she nodded gravely. "Great Troop Leader, I was a diplomat."

He suppressed his surprise at her rapid ability to identify his rank, and although his first impulse was to dismiss her improbable claim to be a diplomat, her confident demeanor and sure identification of his social standing compelled him to hold that dismissal in abeyance. "A diplomat for whom? To whom?"

"For my planet. To your people."

"Where is your retinue, diplomat?"

She looked him in the eyes, seemed to be measuring. "Where is yours, Great Troop Leader?"

Had she been a male, he might have killed her on the spot. But her sex gave him pause, and that pause gave him the opportunity to consider the aptness of her rebuffing question. Where indeed was his troop, but scattered prone and lifeless upon the wet, misty, labyrinthine streets of this alien hellhole? On a day such as this, her retinue might have fared no better. And if she was a genuine diplomat—"You will come with me. The rest of you: go. Except you." He pointed to a young male who was standing solicitously close to the female. "If you flee, her life is lost. The rest of you: if you bring more humans, again, her life is lost. Go. Now."

Without a sound, they turned their backs upon him and rapidly vanished into the humid, milky drifts of smog.

Vrryngraar turned back to the female. She looked at him, then looked at the young male. "Adi, do not fear for me. I will be right back."

The young male nodded at her, stole a quick furtive look at Vrryngraar, and sat—or rather, squatted on his heels—where he was. Vrryngraar pointed into the corner building with the AK. The human female lowered her eyelids and head, and moved inside, calmly picking her way over the rubble which half-choked the doorway. Good. She was smart enough to be docile.

One inside, he turned the AK directly upon her. "Tell me of yourself, diplomat."

"There is little to tell. I was at the recent Convocation. I was one of those who represented humanity. I met with First Voice of the First Family—"

"—my suzerain and patron!"

"Just so."

"And you swear this on your life? For if I show you to him and he does not recognize you, your life is lost."

"If he can tell one human apart from another, he will recognize me. He will also know my name."

"Which is?"

"Elena Corcoran."

Corcoran. That was a name Vrryngraar knew. Her brother was a warrior. Perhaps there would be a ransom, or a challenge. Some honor would come to him after all, in this hell of pointless carnage. And better still, she was insurance that the survivors of his Great Troop would make it back to the compound alive. He turned to her, let the AK sag as he emphasized each point with a thrust of his free claw. "Sister of Corcoran, you are our prisoner, and possibly an emissary. You will come with us back to our compound. You will walk in the lead, with me, so that your fellow-humans will know not to attack us. We will travel under your truce-sign. It is what? A white banner? And—"

"And you did not listen closely enough to my answer, Great Troop Leader."

The sudden interruption made him pause. "Your answer? What answer?"

"You asked me if I *am* a diplomat. But I replied that I *had been* a diplomat."

"I do not understand."

She showed her teeth. They were white and strong,

if small. "I stopped being a diplomat months ago. Today, I am but a human, and a mother, and a citizen of this world."

That was when he noticed that a small pistol had appeared in her hand. She smoothly elevated it to aim at his head. Because there was no waver in her arm or her eyes, he was relatively sure that she would not hesitate, flinch, or miss. He let the AK sag even further. She nodded her affirmation of that act without once taking her eyes off his. "So, 'citizen,'" Vrryngraar said, "now you fight. For what? To save this planet? It cannot be saved. It is already hell."

"I fight to repel ruthless aggressors. As do the Indonesians, who have a long tradition of doing just that."

"They are not warriors."

"Not by tradition or inclination, but they are dangerous fighters when they must protect their homeland."

"They are not one of the more advanced countries of your world. They live in overcrowded filth, argue ceaselessly among themselves, and never built an empire. What can homeland matter to such a people?"

She shook her head slightly, once, but never took her eyes—or gun—off his: "You have read our history, but you drew the wrong conclusions. But don't feel bad. Three centuries of human oppressors in this region made the same mistake about the Indonesians. And the Vietnamese and the Filipinos and the Cambodians and a dozen other peoples. No one has ever enjoyed much success trying to occupy this part of our world. Of course, when a human invader's dreams of conquest here went terribly awry"—and she leveled the gun at the Hkh'Rkh—"they all had someplace to flee back to. You, on the other hand, are not so fortunate."

The gun was less than four centimeters from his right eye, aimed at a shallow retrograde angle. This human had studied Hkh'Rkh anatomy, knew where their brain was located, and where it was not protected by their helmetlike skull. They continued to stare at each other. So he was her prisoner. What further indignity he would suffer this day, Vrryngraar could not imagine. "What would you have me do now, human?"

The female seemed to think. At least, it cocked its head. Then it showed its teeth again. Among humans, this was a sign of humor or receptivity, so he relaxed a bit as she replied, "There is only one thing I need you to do, Great Troop Leader."

"And what is that?" he grumbled.

✧   ✧   ✧

In the street, Adi heard two sharp snaps, realized it was the report of an extremely small-caliber handgun. After hearing bombs, dustmix assault rifles, AKs, shotguns, and PDF railguns screeching overhead all day long, these discharges sounded like a popgun or a pair of mildewed firecrackers. Adi waited, wondered if he should run after all, if he still had enough time to do so, felt the countervailing tug of a vague loyalty to the American woman who had befriended him two days ago.

At that moment, the lady *bule* came out of the ruined storefront, hands extended to either side as she balanced her way over the shattered masonry in the doorway. The Sloth did not appear behind her. "Are we still prisoners?" Adi asked.

"No," she said, dusting off her hands as she reached the level plane of the macadam.

"But where is the Hkh'Rkh?"

"He's not coming."

Chapter Forty-One

North of the Ciliwung waterway, Central Jakarta, Earth

"Where's Chou?" asked Opal.

O'Garran looked out the window and into the street where a third of the tunnel rats he'd come ashore with lay in the strangely twisted poses of death. "He's out there. For good."

Damn. "He was a fine officer." *And he was also the only one of the mainlanders who outranked Wu. So if Wu insists on becoming the new second senior officer and the mainlanders resist—*

"Don't burn out your clutch, Major."

"Huh?"

"I can see those wheels turning between your ears. Don't sweat the Taiwanese-mainlander thing. The mainlanders saw Wu in action, taking orders from Chou, not complaining. They're all right with him now." O'Garran started swapping out the hotjuice cylinders on his CoBro liquimix carbine. "So what now? Looks like we bagged half a platoon of the Sloth fire brigade, scattered the rest. I'm pretty sure we've got their attention."

"Yep. Which means it's time for us to go underground. Here." She pointed at the screen of O'Garran's palmcomp. A long, green line of dashes went from their current position, under the Ciliwung Waterway, did a doglegged sidestep that dodged the back entrance of the Royal palace and emerged in a sub-basement of the Ministry of Administrative and Bureaucratic Reform.

"You've looked at the floor plans?"

Opal nodded. "Yeah. We come out next to a flight of stairs leading straight up into this small rear courtyard. Or we can take these service stairs which run all the way up to the top floor of the building."

"And how come I wasn't clued in on this attack option before they put us ashore?"

"Secrecy firewall," Opal lied. "That way, if you were captured, you couldn't alert the bad guys to this back door into their center of operations." And while she smiled confidence at her XO, Opal wondered. *I wonder if any of the other tunnel rat teams are tasked with this attack route? Probably not. It's an unconventional entry and tight quarters, so it was probably dismissed as too risky.*

O'Garran was still frowning at the schematic. He clearly didn't like the assignment, but he apparently didn't suspect any duplicity on her part. "So once we're in, what's the game plan?"

"No way to know," she answered truthfully, handing the portable back to him. "All our intel on the compound is from prewar documents and surveys. We've got no way of knowing where they've set up HQ, C4I, fire direction control, local air traffic control, internal security monitoring. So first we'll check if we can detect basement monitors. If not, we send some of our littlest rats up into the ventilation shaft, to see what they can see, keeping an eye out for local workers we can debrief. But I'm betting we might get some orders on the way in. It's just about time to start the final act."

Two missiles roared down overhead, descending sharply toward the compound, five hundred meters south of them. PDF fire shrilled at one. Its detonation shook plaster down from the ceiling and broke the last few intact windows on the block. The other rocket plunged down into the compound; the explosion was more muffled, but the ground shook slightly under their feet.

"Yup," agreed O'Garran, "any time now."

Presidential Palace, Jakarta, Earth

The whole room shook. Half the lights went out. The sound of shattering glass and tumbling debris—and mortally desperate trilling—came in from the door that opened on the main corridor.

Darzhee Kut rose from the floor as the defense operator announced, "PDF down to forty percent." His invariably down-adjusting updates had become a means of measuring just how uncertain the outcome of the battle was becoming.

Darzhee Kut moved closer to Hu'urs Khraam, who seemed, in the past hour, to have grown noticeably more feeble and grimly silent. "First Delegate, we await further orders."

Hu'urs Khraam waved a careless claw, spoke more loudly than he should have. "There are no new orders to give. We endure down here, hoping one half of our ships give us the supporting fire we need to survive, and that the other half will prevail against the human fleet. What can be done has been done." He sounded like he wanted to go to sleep.

As Darzhee Kut feared, he had been overheard. "Surely this is not the limit of leadership in the alliance to which we have pledged ourselves." First Voice's observation was not impatient, but it was not kind. "Pressing matters remain. What is to be done about our perimeter?"

"I am surprised at your question, esteemed First Voice," answered Hu'urs Khraam. "Did you not tell me that you would soon have control of that situation?"

The implied barb of the retort did not escape the notice of First Voice's retinue. Several rose up higher, their crests stiffening. Their leader gestured downward with his claws. They and their crests complied. "Regular units are sweeping the streets. My elite formations are working as emergency response teams to counteract more serious threats. But to fully control the situation, you must cede me authority to alter the rules of engagement. This you have not done. And so we do not have complete control."

Hu'urs Khraam's lids slowly closed, did not open. "First Voice, what you demanded was that you have *no* rules of engagement, not control of them."

"Semantics. If I do not have the power to cancel them at will, I do not have control over them. Consequently, our objective of securing a one-kilometer radius free of enemy activity has not been attained. Securing only a five-hundred-meter radius has cost me twenty percent of my forces in this area of operations. If I continue in this fashion, I will have no combat-capable troops left by morning."

"Your counsel?"

"My counsel you know. Pull all our ground forces back to this compound and call in deadfall munitions on the surrounding neighborhoods, starting one hundred fifty meters back from the walls of our compound. We level the closer structures with conventional support weapons once the orbital bombardment is done."

Hu'urs Khraam's lenses remained concealed, the crabshell eye-covers tightly shut against the words of First Voice. "I wish counsel that *follows* the rules of engagement."

"Then I counsel this: find your knife and fall on it."

The room was very still: even the constant exchanges with Fleetmaster R'sudkaat's flagship seemed to pause for a moment. Hu'urs Khraam's lids opened. "First Voice, explain this counsel."

The calm response seemed to also confer the right to resume breathing. Only Caine, Darzhee Kut noticed, had not become tense. Of course, perhaps he did not understand either of the languages. On the other hand, what more could a human wish to hear than profound discord at the heart of his enemies' alliance?

First Voice seemed unsurprised by Hu'urs Khraam's calm reply, and Darzhee Kut wondered if, perhaps, only they themselves had understood—by the subtle code that seemed to exist among leaders of the most senior rank—that the Hkh'Rkh's statement had not been intended as a challenge or disrespectful gibe, but a serious message in metaphorical form. First Voice's neck oscillated once. "If we continue to follow the current rules of engagement, the outcome of this battle is uncertain. We are a hard target, yes, and the humans suffer terrible losses every time they try to face us. But I attend the declining PDF availability, the difficulty of providing adequate air support, the increasing reports of infiltrated commando teams either leading insurgents or operating independently, and the impossibility of holding whatever advantages we win by blood in these endless streets. Bold action is now required. If you do not wish to conduct general orbital interdiction of the surrounding city, then we must be permitted to use incendiary devices to support our troops—"

"—and burn down the city with us in it."

"Our compound can be adequately protected, if we establish a fifty-meter firebreak."

"How?"

"Conventional destruction of all surrounding structures."

Hu'urs Khraam's eyes closed again. "We cannot afford the risk of these tactics. If the Dornaani learn about them—"

"The Dornaani are not here," First Voice emphasized. "They have become so weak-willed that they may *never* come. And I cannot see how, once we have been bold enough to invade the humans' homeworld, that these tactics will even warrant special mention. Seen alongside the other violations of the Accord which brought us to this place, they are invisibly small."

"Do not think it," Hu'urs Khraam warned. "The Dornaani are not so degenerate as you suppose, and they will separate our actions into two categories: what we decided to do, and how we went about doing it. Valid, or at least reasonable, political arguments can be adduced to explain the decision to invade human space. But if we conduct ourselves viciously in the course of that action, this will constitute a second, and perhaps greater crime in their eyes."

"But their eyes are not here to see, nor their ears here to listen."

"So you think. I have reason, and counsel, that prompts me to think otherwise. But enough. Do you have another plan that remains within the constraints of our rules of engagement?"

At first, Darzhee Kut thought that First Voice was going to evert his claws in frustration and turn his back on the Arat Kur leader, but instead, the Hkh'Rkh lowered his head in thought. *He can tell that Hu'urs Khraam wishes to find an efficacious alternative, even given the constraints. First Voice will push the limits of the law, now.*

The Hkh'Rkh leader's head rose. "Hunter-killer teams."

"I do not understand."

"At present, we have a standoff in the perimeter we are attempting to establish. We clear the humans that attempt to stand against us. They infiltrate back into the area because we do not have the forces to secure so large and porous a perimeter. We have emergency response teams that react specifically to these infiltrators. But since the humans feel confident reentering the area again, this method is insufficient."

"Go on."

"So we do to them what they have been doing to us. We do not try to engage them conventionally, but rather, send out many small teams charged with only one objective: seek and kill humans. Any and all that appear within one kilometer of this compound."

"And this achieves what?" asked Urzueth Ragh.

Yaargraukh pony-nodded his support of First Voice's idea. "It achieves a balance of terror. We cannot hold the one-kilometer perimeter because we are trying to hold territory rather than destroy the enemy. And while moving from flashpoint to flashpoint, our troops must worry about what lies behind every window, every door, in every building. Now, we shall use the humans' own tactics against them: hunt and ambush them indiscriminately throughout the zone. Then the humans will have reason to fear every door and window. Only the most resolute opponents will stand against our trained warriors for very long, and those few we can surround and destroy. However, it will require a great many of our best troopers to accomplish this task."

Graagkhruud came to stand by First Voice. "This plan has another benefit. In those sectors where we have lost most of our clearing units, this gives us a new means of scouting and preempting any assault forces the humans might be gathering there. We will need five hundred additional warriors for these squad-sized hunter-killer teams."

Yaargraukh studied the city map. "We will need fifteen hundred."

Graagkhruud sneered. "Again, your admiration of the humans makes you truly their best Advocate."

"This time, I admire the clock, First Fist. We will need a round-the-clock action cycle. That means at least three shifts of five hundred Warriors. And even if we split each shift into two four-hour patrols, such unrelenting pursuit and combat will drain our troops quickly. As it stands, we do not have enough troops to sustain so extensive an operation, not while maintaining a full defensive force here."

Graagkhruud swept that objection aside with a careless claw. "We will draw additional troops from internal security."

Yaargraukh looked at First Fist. "That is a dangerous step, First Fist."

"Were you not thought by so many to be brave, I would say your prudence could be heard as cowardice, Advocate for *s'fet*."

Yaargraukh was very quiet. As Darzhee Kut understood it, Graagkhruud had almost uttered a Challenge insult—but not quite. The Advocate turned back to the map. "We seem to have little choice but to do as you recommend, First Fist. In addition, I would also suggest we start making use of the humans' weapons."

"In the field?"

"For softer, easier targets, yes. And for suppressive fire, most certainly. Our own ammunition expenditure is alarming. However, if we relegate secondary-fire missions to captured human weapons, we will be able to extend our own stocks of ammunition by using them only in those engagements where their superior killing power and range matter most."

"The weapons you refer to, the AKs, are like children's toys. We cannot hold them properly."

"I have studied these rifles, First Fist. They will be serviceable if the technical support troops cut away the hand-grips and trigger guards."

First Voice nodded at Yaargraukh then at Graagkhruud. "Together, your points are sound. See to their implementation and then return here. Yaargraukh, honor us by personally overseeing the technical logistics of your recommendations."

"First Voice speaks and I obey." As Yaargraukh

exited, he and Caine pointedly did not look at each other. But Darzhee Kut sensed their mutual avoidance was motivated by a desire to protect each other, rather than antipathy.

Urzueth Ragh edged closer to Hu'urs Khraam, who noticed. "You have news?"

"We shall soon defeat the humans' electronic warfare efforts. However, Tuxae Skhaas aboard the flagship *Greatvein* points out that for the next several minutes, with all the human chaff and image-makers that are still operating, our sensors are still badly cluttered with false images. We could overlook genuine targets."

"We know this well. We also retain sufficient means to deal with any especially ominous aerial attacks. Why does the *Greatvein's* master sing so repetitive a refrain?"

"Hu'urs Khraam, this report was not sent at the behest of Fleetmaster R'sudkaat. It is relayed by Sensor Coordinator Tuxae Skhaas on his own initiative. And he is not worried about what we are seeing, but what we are *not* seeing. Specifically, he is concerned that we have seen no activity involving the human submarines."

"And why would we?" The First Delegate flexed his claws testily. "For hundreds of kilometers in every direction, we seeded the depths of these waters with station-keeping marine sensors."

"True, Esteemed Hu'urs Khraam, but there has been increasing question regarding their reliability."

"I have read these speculations and can find no reason to give them credence. Do you really think that the humans could send individual divers out to so many separate units and disable them?"

"Not disable them, Hu'urs Khraam, but rewire a select number of them to continuously report 'all clear.'"

"And how would they begin to know how to rewire our systems?"

"We did lose several of the sensors in the first week of our operations."

"Yes, we were bound to have some defective units. They were an entirely new technology for an entirely new domain of warfare."

"What if they were not defective? What if we lost them because the humans isolated, deactivated, and then examined those sensors with the intent of learning how to electronically trick them? And they need not trick many sensors. Only those few monitoring the areas that they planned on using for submarine infiltration."

First Voice waggled his neck. "The humans have not built any new submarines in almost thirty years. Most are old and hard to maintain. Had they been deemed a threat, we could have brought our own submarines as a counterforce."

Darzhee looked away. *Yes, you could have brought along a handful of your pitiable Hkh'Rkh submarines. And the humans would have cheerfully sunk them.*

Urzueth Ragh was not done. "It is just as you say, First Voice, but this *would* be the logical time for human submarines to enter the battle. Our lookdown sensors are overtaxed, the others are confused by false signals, and our local PDF capabilities are significantly degraded."

"And so what would the submarines do?" First Delegate Hu'urs Khraam wondered mildly. "Torpedo the docks?"

"Esteemed Hu'urs Khraam, most of the submarines that the humans retained were what they call 'boomers': deep submersibles which carry nuclear missiles."

Hu'urs Khraam settled back and his antenna switched in wry amusement. "Urzueth Ragh, is this Tuxae Skhaas' worry? Has he forgotten that this is precisely why we occupy the largest cities on this island? What does he expect that the humans will do? Destroy millions of their own population? Even they are not so savage."

Darzhee Kut glanced at Caine—who was already staring at him. The human did not look away, did not smile, did not blink. *But surely*, thought Darzhee Kut, *Hu'urs Khraam is right. Surely the humans—who are now capable of extraordinary insight and compassion and sacrifice—are not still capable of such savagery. Surely.*

Chapter Forty-Two

Over the Sunda Strait, approaching West Java, Earth

Only two VTOLs left, and not for long, conjectured Thandla. The lasers had picked off all but Dortmund's craft and that of his right wingman, Michael Schrage.

"Fifteen more seconds," Dortmund called out.

Which was probably not possible, Thandla realized, and in so realizing, discovered he was probably thinking his last mortal thoughts. The Arat Kur were poking huge holes in the overlapping image makers, rapidly discriminating between false signals and real returns, destroying the drones either by orbital interdict or now, long-range missiles from the enemy's Java-based combat air patrols, which were waiting for them over the island's western coastline.

But Thandla still had a few tricks left that might help them reach that crucial fifteen-second mark. And if he—

Praeger, the back-seat EW and countermeasures operator, spoke for the first time during the mission. "We are painted!" The VTOL's own sensors had detected a low-power laser contact. It was an orbital targeting beam that also plasmated the atmosphere, clearing a path for the actual weapon-grade laser.

So, thought Thandla, as he played his last hand of trick electronic cards, *we don't have fifteen seconds left after all. But I shall not fear on the threshold of Nirvana. We do not sacrifice and live for ourselves alone. The final step is to renounce ego, self.* He had often seen the faces of his family in the last twenty minutes. Now, unbidden, he saw the faces of the delegation he had accompanied to the Convocation: Riordan, the Corcorans, Ben Hwang, Opal Patrone, and Lemuel Wasserman. Lemuel, who had insulted him, snubbed him, argued with him, and loved him. And had not understood him and probably never would have. There were too many cultural divides for him to bridge before he could have understood the very different reality that Thandla inhabited.

Sanjay was watching for the flicker of a targeting lock that would signal the microsecond before his death, but was instead startled by Dortmund's shout. "Schrage! *Was machst—?*"

The right wingman had pulled his VTOL up and over, angling into a position just above Dortmund's craft. He had almost straightened out from his brief banking maneuver when Thandla blinked involuntarily against a single strobelike pulse. Schrage's VTOL transformed into a spearhead of flame. Light debris spattered down and scored their own fuselage, put a hairline crack in the cockpit blister. But they were still alive and Thandla was still working—

Dortmund counted out the mounting seconds. "Twelve, thirteen—"

Thandla played his last card—which was a simple randomized shift between all the strategies he had employed to date. It would be penetrated in a second or two, at the most, but the Arat Kur machines, being driven by pattern-loving expert systems, would spend several precious seconds trying to reconcile this anomalous pattern with what had come before—

"Fourteen, fifteen—"

And it was done. Even now, secret orders were being transmitted to ears listening beneath the waves. The final part of the trap was closing upon the Arat Kur and their Hkh'Rkh allies.

Dortmund was jubilant. "Mission plus two, three—!"

Four was an important number for Sanjay Thandla. He was four when he came to understand exponents by understanding that two was the square root of four. He had four children, had earned four degrees, and had slept with four women, including his wife. So when a brief flash of light coincided with Dortmund's counting off of the number "four," Thandla would not have thought it an odd coincidence, but a sign of order in the universe, that patterns repeated and life progressed in cycles, and that nothing was ever, ever lost, but came back again in all its quiet glory.

When hit, Dortmund's VTOL had reached the edge of the tidal shelf off the northwest coast of Java, and so went down in only forty meters of water. There, years later, its remains were recovered, but without imparting any greater sense of the identity or sacrifice of its crew. The fish, as agents of Nirvana, had carried away and reintegrated every trace of Praeger, Dortmund, and Sanjay Thandla.

Who had, at last, reentered the great mandala of

creation, had become one with the entity that was Earth.

Again.

Mobile Command Center "Trojan Ghost One," over the Indian Ocean, Earth

"Mr. Downing, we have achieved operational density of image makers, decoys, and chaff. We are good to go."

Richard leaned back from the Dornaani holosphere, which dominated the passenger section of the high-speed armored VTOL that had been modified to accept the alien technology. "Very well, Mr. Rinehart. Send the word. All orbit-capable and long-range ground rockets are to launch immediately. Maritime launches are to commence two minutes later."

Alnduul had come to stand beside Downing. "Do you need our assistance?"

"I beg your pardon?"

"I offer our assistance in penetrating the Arat Kur signal jamming. If we do not help in that matter, how will your first two submarines know it is time to act?"

"Acoustic signaling."

"Please explain."

"You know how easily sound travels in water? How ocean sensors can hear whale songs around the world?"

Alnduul nodded.

"Well, it's a lot easier to hear metal rods banging together. What we use is a lot more sophisticated, but it's the same principle. The water itself is our communication medium. You might say we're banging rods in code for all our submerged ears to hear. Particularly those two."

"I see. And when will they receive the message?"

Downing checked his watch. "Right about now."

SSBN *Ohio*, Java Sea, Earth

"Captain Tigner?"

"What is it Mr. Alvarez?"

"Acoustic signal, ma'am. Nothing fancy, in the clear: we are a go."

Captain Mary Sue Tigner turned to her helmsman. "Mr. Vinh."

"Ma'am?"

"Release magnetic grapples and give us five meters clearance from the wreck."

"Grapples released, and that's a half turn of the fans. Ready, ma'am."

"Rise to maximum launch depth. ETA?"

"Estimating nine minutes, Captain."

"Very good. Mr. Alvarez."

"Yes, ma'am?"

"Confirm that *Minsk* received signal that she is cleared to begin her ascent."

"Captain Poliakhov has just contacted us to confirm our receipt of signal, and requests reconfirmation of his launch depth instructions, ma'am."

As he should. "Tell Alexei he is to rise to fifty meters, as indicated in his sealed orders. And wish him good luck." *He'll need it, playing canary in a coal mine. But how else are we going to learn how far down and how quickly the Arat Kur can see and hit us in the ocean?*

The alert lights began flashing and the general quarters klaxon kicked into life. Tigner gave a quick

pat to the side of the *Ohio*'s periscope as she folded
out the handles. *Here we go, old girl. It's show time.*

Wholenest flagship *Greatvein*, Earth orbit

Tuxae saw the thermal blooms first on his own system,
then a moment later, the active sensor verifications
started pouring in from the various hulls in orbit.
He considered the data carefully, then studied H'toor
Qooiiz's console with equal care.

"Tuxae, why do you not act?"

"I will. Reopen a channel to Jakarta."

"But it is insolence to bypass Fleetmaster R'sudkaat—"

"It is necessary that everyone who must hear this
dirge hears it directly."

H'toor Qooiiz looked at him, then complied.

The Fleetmaster was already on the way over. "You
have seen it?"

"Yes." Tuxae was very calm. "I offer my report and
recommendation."

"Very good." But that response was not from the
Fleetmaster. It was Hu'urs Khraam's voice, emerging from H'toor Qooiiz's communications console.
Fleetmaster R'sudkaat's mandibles crunched once and
were then silent. Tuxae realized that his future was
less promising after going above his direct superior
in issuing the report, but then again, that presumed
any of them were going to *have* a future—

"Report," urged Hu'urs Khraam's voice.

Tuxae took a deep breath. "Orbital sensors are
reading multiple ballistic missile launches from around
the globe. These are almost all ground sites: silos, in
the case of the farther continents, or fixed ramp or

mobile launches of smaller rocket and cruise missiles throughout the Pacific Rim."

"How many targets do you count?"

"At least seven hundred and the number is climbing. But the margin of error is still unacceptably high. Our sensor reliability is not yet absolute. We are only now destroying the humans' electronic warfare drones in appreciable numbers. Those which remain make it impossible to trust our active arrays. We are still compelled to rely upon imprecise thermal and optical detection."

"Then you must quickly finish destroying the drones."

Now came the hard part, the part that no one was going to enjoy hearing, and about which H'toor Qooiiz was likely to write a very sad song. "If we shift enough of our orbital intercept fire to swiftly eliminate the remaining drones, then we will not be able to intercept all of these new rockets. Some are moving very fast. And I must remind you that the general launch of manned air vehicles continues from Sumatra, Bali, Christmas Island and the near Celebes."

"And all the new threats, the rockets, are converging on Java?"

"Most," Tuxae corrected. "The rocket launches from North America and Europe are on—uncertain vectors."

"Uncertain? In what way?"

"We cannot tell from their current trajectories whether they will ultimately insert to orbit or strike Indonesia,"

"To orbit?" R'sudkaat broke in. "Are they attacking my ships?"

"No, Esteemed Fleetmaster. That does not seem to be their intent, nor do the rockets being used have sufficient thrust or endurance to be intended as intercept vehicles."

"Then what is their purpose?"

"The humans might be simply testing our continued ability to interdict ground targets in Europe and North America. Or they might be launching drones to hunt our ships here in orbit. Or they might be sending nuclear weapons over Java to detonate in a high airburst mode."

"That would generate a far stronger EM pulse than any we have used thus far," supplied Fleetmaster R'sudkaat.

"Just so. And if the statistics on these dated rockets and their warheads are correct, we will experience considerable degradation of our groundside electronics. Most notably, many more of our PDF arrays will be destroyed, unless they are powered down during the strikes."

Hu'urs Khraam's voice buzzed with anxiety. "But if we power down the PDFs—"

"Then our ground assets are completely undefended against any nuclear-armed rockets that might be targeting *them*."

Hu'urs Khraam's voice was firm. "We will power down the arrays. The humans would not attack their own cities with nuclear devices."

"I must counsel caution regarding such swift assumptions, Esteemed Hu'urs Khraam. Today, the humans are showing a propensity for cunning and ruthlessness that matches the old stories."

"I agree with Hu'urs Khraam," argued Fleetmaster R'sudkaat. "The humans are simply trying to overwhelm us with many targets at the same time. There is less cunning in this than you perceive, Tuxae Skhaas."

"With respect, Fleetmaster: do you remember their first general attack, the one made by their interceptors on the first day?"

"Yes, where they lost more than one hundred fifty aircraft? Pure folly."

"It was not folly. It was not ignorance. It was to learn our capabilities."

H'toor Qooiiz forgot his place as Tuxae's usually silent partner. "What?"

"Reason from the partially heard harmonies, rocksibling. The humans had groundside active arrays, as well as visual observation capabilities. They knew how many hulls we had, in which orbits, and they watched how we responded to the futile threat they flung against us. They gathered this information not to aid their interceptors, but to determine each ship's orbital interdiction capabilities. They no doubt identified each hull visually, and have since tracked where they are at all times, noted any changes, and have maintained a constantly evolving estimate of our maximum interdiction capability."

Fleetmaster R'sudkaat sent the words out through grinding mandibles. "Then why did they not use this information before today?"

"Because until today, the humans did not have a war fleet approaching Earth. Had the humans used their knowledge before now, we would have understood that they had learned what it would take to overwhelm our systems. We would have increased our capabilities and would have realized how duplicitous, patient, and resourceful they are. Besides, what would they have gained by lofting a dozen drones, or a dozen rockets at Java, before this day? Maybe they would have managed to disable a ship or two, destroy a few hundred of our troops. But now—"

Hu'urs Khraam saw it clearly. "Now we must choose: do we allow the human missiles to attack our ground forces, or do we allow them to place a large force of drones in orbit? For we cannot prevent both."

Tuxae hung his claws. "The humans have an expression: to be caught between a hammer"—he pointed to the red motes of the human fleet—"and an anvil." He pointed to the white ballistic trajectories rising up from around the globe. "If they are launching drones into orbit, this is precisely the situation in which our counterattacking fleet will find itself. But if the drones turn instead to attack us here in orbit, and we remain committed to defending our ground forces instead of ourselves, we will surely lose many of our hulls, and with them, much of our orbital interdiction ability."

Hu'urs Khraam finished outlining their Hobson's choice. "Conversely, if we turn any significant portion of our orbital intercept capabilities to bear on the missiles that may be launching drones, several of the closer missiles will certainly get through to Java. And, if they are armed with nuclear warheads, we could lose most of our ground forces."

"And we will have lost you, Hu'urs Khraam, our leader and the voice of the Wholenest. Your orders?"

"We must destroy their nearest missiles and preserve our ground forces or this invasion was for naught."

"But if the humans are launching new drones to assist their fleet, that combined force might prevail against our counterattacking flotilla."

"This is true. In which event, we must await relief by the fleet returning from the asteroid belt."

Tuxae fluttered his rear antenna. "If it comes to that, the humans will gain several days of orbital supremacy. They will swarm over you on the ground."

The pause suggested Hu'urs Khraam's careful consideration of what he said next. "Yes, that could occur. But if we allow even ten of their missiles to land in Indonesia, our destruction is assured, and our campaign is over. Lacking additional landing forces, we would then have only two choices: to annihilate the entire world from orbit, or to withdraw. Each is a politically unserviceable extreme. So, in order to maintain the delicate leverage necessary for a successful outcome to this conflict, we must preserve our ground forces."

Although he was not in the presence of the First Delegate, Tuxae bobbed his respect. "I harmonize, Hu'urs Khraam."

"Target the missiles with clear trajectories for Java."

North-Central Jakarta, Earth

Winfield saw the fast, multiple flickers over his shoulder and went prone, covering his eyes and ears. Ayala, left arm still bleeding from a through-and-through hit inflicted by some kind of Hkh'Rkh scattergun, was down beside him in a moment. Seconds went by. Jakarta was only marginally more quiet than it had been before.

About fifteen seconds later, a dull rumble started, rising up through and ultimately washing over the incessant small arms fire and intermittent rockets that were still pelting in from the periphery of the city. Winfield stood, looked back out over the Thousand Islands. It appeared as though a tiny, dim afterimage of the sun blazed at the eleven o'clock position. However, the sun's own cloud-smudged brightness was still visible at the two o'clock position. One sky, two suns—although the smaller one at eleven o'clock was fading fast.

"Whaddya figure?" asked Barkowski, who had sheltered in a doorway.

Winfield shrugged. "Two megaton, maybe. Really high up. Doubt we'll get much wind out of it."

"Why'd we launch it?"

"Maybe to hit them with some EMP, although that one didn't get anywhere near close enough." He looked at Ayala. "Of course, they might have been trying to drop it on Java."

"Lieutenant, last time I checked, we're still standing on Java."

"And last time I checked, Commander, we're still considered expendable. Let's keep going, but stay near cover."

Barkowski lingered to look at the almost vanished brightness of the nuke. "So. Not the last?" His tone made it a statement, not a question.

"Nope," answered Winfield, "and if I were a betting man, not the closest, either."

It was then that a much brighter flash opened high overhead.

Chapter Forty-Three

Wholenest flagship *Greatvein*, Earth orbit

Tuxae kept panic out of his voice. "First Delegate, please repeat." Nothing except the falling squeal of static produced by an atmospheric nuclear detonation. "Esteemed Hu'urs Khraam do you receive our signals? Are you still there?" There was no evidence of a ground strike, or a near-surface airburst, but with so much sensor noise—

"I—we—are still here, Sensor Coordinator Skhaas. But that missile exploded only ten kilometers away, albeit quite high. Can you not intercept them farther out?"

"My apologies, Hu'urs Khraam, but that missile exploded the instant *before* we would have intercepted it. Evidently, the humans are using the rockets being launched from Asia to generate EMP attacks upon your electronics."

In the background, Tuxae Skhaas heard a Hkh'Rkh—probably First Voice—interject: "They have succeeded. All my communications gear is useless, as are our sensors and targeting. My troops must now rely on hand signals, iron sights, and brave blood." He sounded oddly, if grimly, satisfied.

"And the PDF arrays?"

A new voice: Darzhee Kut, if he was not mistaken. "Thankfully, Hu'urs Khraam gambled to take them offline. There is some further degradation, but not much. Tell us, are the missiles from North America and Europe heading for us, as well?"

"No. They are almost all inserting to orbit and deploying drones."

"How long before the drones reach you?"

Fleetmaster R'sudkaat leaned in toward H'toor Qooiiz's console. "They are not heading toward us. They are sternchasing the ships we sent to intercept the human fleet."

Hu'urs Khraam's response was immediate. "Fleetmaster R'sudkaat, deploy all the remaining drones in your orbital flotilla to pursue the human drones. They must overtake and eliminate them. Otherwise, our counterattacking ships will be struck from both the front and the rear."

"I will do so immediately. Tuxae Skhaas, I need trajectory data on the human drones."

But Tuxae, staring into the holotank and then at his screens, barely heard the senior Arat Kur.

"Tuxae Skhaas, will you comply?"

"Fleetmaster, Hu'urs Khraam. We have a new problem. There is a new human launch site—no, *two* new launch sites."

"So? There are hundreds of human launch sites already. How bad can two more be?"

"Very bad." Tuxae turned to look up at the Fleetmaster. "These two launch sites are in the middle of the water. One is only ten kilometers south of Bawean Island, near the middle of Java's northern coast."

Hu'urs Khraam voice was preternaturally calm, almost as if he already knew the answer to his question. "And the other?"

"Forty kilometers north of Jakarta. If you look out an upper story window, you should be able to see the launch plume now..."

Flagship USS *Lincoln*, Sierra Echelon, RTF 1, cislunar space

"Admiral Silverstein, Lord Admiral Halifax on tight-beam secure line two."

Ira nodded, tapped his collarcom. "Silverstein here."

"Ira, Tom Halifax. I just received a lascom from the sensor chaps in Plesetsk Cosmodrome. The big thinkers in joint force intel have high confidence that the enemy's planetside situation is deteriorating."

Silverstein nodded. "Which means they'll either shore it up by keeping their interdiction assets in orbit, or they'll engage our fleet with everything they've got and sacrifice their beachhead. Any indication which way they're going to go?"

"We just got a whistle from the Big Blue Marble on that. Groundside observation indicates no new enemy transfers out of orbit and no decrease in orbital interdiction."

Ira nodded. "So they're digging in to save their beachhead and letting their screening force take its lumps from us."

"Seems so. Big Blue has also managed to launch a handy little fleet of drones to help us exterminate these damn Roaches, so I'm activating contingency Delta and taking First Echelon to flank speed for a high energy half-orbit and then all the way out the other side."

"A gravity-assisted slingshot toward Vesta?"

"'Fraid so, Ira. The muddy-side brain trust seems to think we're a bit too mobbed up here in cislunar. It's possible we have more force than we need to do the job. So after my first echelon boxes the Arat Kurs' nonexistent ears during our approach, we're going to boost again and run the gauntlet—right through them."

A cheery, confident tone, but if the drones didn't get close enough to the rear of the Arat Kur to divert some of their firepower, Halifax's maneuver could be a messy—and grim—business. "Orders, sir?" Ira asked.

"The enemy orbital flotilla has launched drones to intercept ours. We'll need to employ the Mousetrap contingency to keep that from happening. But after you've sprung the Mousetraps, do what you think best, Ira. I hope to be in touch again, but frankly, we can't know what happens next—other than this: once my echelon is engaged, the battle for cislunar space is in your hands and the laps of the gods. Despite all the scenarios we've run, there's no knowing what happens next. So if you don't hear anything more from me, you'll have to play it as it lies, old boy. When you're done trouncing them, do catch up if you can. I expect those of us in the first echelon will be stepping lively with their inbound belt fleet in a day or so."

"I'll try to be there, Lord Halifax."

"I know you will, Ira. Keep us apprised. We'll be looking over our shoulders for you, and happy to see you coming on. Cheers."

Ira turned to Ruth Altasso. "Commander."

"Sir?"

"Have the commo officer signal all conns in second echelon: adjust vectors to assume assault cone Echo. Double our deployment of antimissile drones. I want our leading defensive edge fixed at point four five light-seconds from our main van. When that evolution is completed, deploy all but twenty percent of our X-ray laser missiles. They are to be kept in a tight aft formation, well within the edges of our echelon's sensor shadow."

"That's a lot of X-ray missiles, sir."

"That's the idea, Ex. Once that's done, signal Rear Admiral Vasarsky to reconfigure her third echelon for heterogeneous operations. She's to make ready for orbital interdiction *after* probable fleet engagement. And send the Mousetrap signal. I want to make sure the drones launched by Big Blue reach the rear of the Arat Kur fleet."

"I assume we're going to have the Mousetraps target the Arat Kur chaser drones?"

"Yep. That's how we trump their trump. Don't save any 'traps; use 'em all."

"Aye, sir." Altasso turned away, smiled. For some reason, Silverstein always thought of her as a bride when she wore that expression. "Sounds like we're going to have our hands full today, Admiral."

"It does indeed, Ex, it does indeed. Activate the Mousetraps on my mark . . . and, *mark!*"

Low Earth Orbit

Seven hundred twenty kilometers above the earth, the CellStar IV satellite continued in the same lonely orbit it had been following since its deployment in 2068.

In its time, it had been a miracle of miniaturization and communication efficiency, fusing another link in a tightly interconnected world of wireless communications.

But time and technologies march on. The adjectives with which CellStar IV was embellished faded from "prodigy," to "workhorse," to "old standby," to "outdated," and ultimately to "defunct." Several relays shorted out in 2095, seven years after the end of its projected operational lifetime, and the little satellite that could became the little satellite that couldn't.

But in 2113, it had a visitor. An orbital maneuver vehicle, or OMV, supposedly on a routine maintenance mission to a much larger, newer, and better communications satellite, detoured and rendezvoused with the big, dark box that had been CellStar IV. A single robotic ROV emerged from the OMV's payload bay and set to work on the inert satellite. It removed most of its internal and core components, replaced them with a large black box—maneuvered with some difficulty out of the OMV's payload bay—and left, taking along the original innards of CellStar IV.

Which continued in its dull orbit for seven more years.

But then, on January 12, 2120, Lieutenant Commander Ruth Altasso, turning away from Admiral Ira Silverstein, entered the Mousetrap code into the command computer on board the battle cruiser *USS Lincoln.* The *Lincoln's* tightbeam commo array sent a single phased laser pulse to another derelict satellite in a fast polar orbit. Inside that dead object, new innards, also emplaced in 2113, fully awakened after their seven-year doze and performed their one function. A high-power omnidirectional broadcast of a set of routinely updated target parameters and a single command that, as understood by CellStar IV and its many derelict cousins, was simply "awaken."

The new machinery in CellStar IV illuminated and sought to fulfill its purpose. It scanned the recently updated targeting parameters that had been sent by the triggering satellite, activated its sensors, and looked for a match. Sure enough, a new high-priority target—an enemy drone—was in very close range. It polled the secure frequencies for any priority overrides indicating that some other Mousetrap had sprung upon this as its target and, finding none, launched.

The missile that ripped out of CellStar IV's frame, and thereby discorporated it, was almost all fuel and guidance. It aimed itself at the Arat Kur drone, which crowded gees to elude it.

But the little human missile was built for sprinting, and although the drone could have ultimately outpaced and left it far behind, it did not have enough of a thrust-spike to break away from the speedy, stern-chasing missile.

Which died doing what it had been created to do: destroy an enemy craft. As did the dozens of other Mousetrap missiles in the course of the next five minutes.

Presidential Palace, Jakarta, Earth

Darzhee Kut felt the wiggling sensation in his abdomen subside. "You are sure the first of the two submarine missiles went south of us?"

"Quite sure," confirmed Urzueth Ragh. "It is following a very shallow arc and will hit soon. At least we were able to destroy the launching submarine with orbital munitions."

"And the other launch?"

"Possibly converging on the same general target area. However, we could not intercept that submarine. It was too deep."

"How deep?"

"It must have launched from almost two hundred meters and then dove immediately."

Darzhee Kut looked at Yaargraukh, who had just returned to report that his logistical tasks were completed. "I am no expert in military technology, but—"

Yaargraukh bob-nodded. "Your conjecture is quite right. We will not be able to reliably interdict submarines that can fire from that depth. Lasers are essentially useless against submerged targets. And a kinetic warhead is insufficient: the projectile expends its kill-decisive energy in the first one hundred meters of immersion. Besides, the rail-gun response time is much longer. After target acquisition, the warheads must be fired and make their descent. During which time the human submarine is diving, and probably leaving behind decoys which it can remotely activate if we send down a smart munition."

Urzueth's voice buzzed with anxiety. "So what shall we do?"

"Continue to shoot down their other missiles and make submarines our new priority targets."

Hu'urs Khraam rose from his couch. "Can we not trust to the PDF systems to ward off their missiles?"

"That depends upon how many missiles make their terminal approach at the same instant, Esteemed Hu'urs Khraam." Urzueth Ragh waved a claw at the contact-cluttered map of Java.

"It also depends upon the range at which they launch," added Yaargraukh. "Our concern for submarines was primarily due to the short flight times of their missiles. And those estimates presumed all our PDF systems to be functional. We are not in that enviable position now."

Graagkhruud pitched his combined neck-head sharply. "Well, what of the special airphibian attack craft you Arat Kur designed for this purpose? Use them to drive off these submarines."

Urzueth Ragh folded his claws together. "We can no longer do that, First Fist."

"Why in rotting meat not?"

"Do you not recall? When our CAP missions were overtaxed, we withdrew our airphibian craft from submersible operations."

"Well, if they came out of the water, can't they go back in?"

"Not as they are currently configured. They are now airborne, carrying ordnance loads on external racks. They cannot make immediate transition to marine operations."

"Well, land them and—"

"Apologies, First Fist, but you may recall that Surabaja airfield is inoperable and Soekarno and the other Jakartan fields are backlogged rearming ground-support aircraft and servicing interceptors to send out against the approaching human air vehicles. Which will arrive in less than half an hour, if they hold their present course and speed—"

On the map of Java, the white line tracing the progress of the first submarine-launched missile bloomed into a red globe, two hundred kilometers east-southeast of Jakarta.

A nuclear device had landed in Indonesia.

A moment later, the white line denoting the second missile stopped over Jakarta, then vanished. Darzhee Kut held his breath as Urzueth made his report. "The two submarine missiles each discharged three independent warheads. The red globe indicates that the missile which flew inland made a ground or low airburst strike. The missile launched at Jakarta does not appear on the display because it airbursted high. It deployed three one-megaton warheads."

"An EMP strike," Caine Riordan commented, confirming what most of then had already conjectured.

"So it appears. This eliminated almost half of our remaining PDF arrays. The missile that went inland deployed three independent, high-speed two-hundred-kiloton devices, which detonated in an overlapping trefoil pattern."

First Voice stepped toward the map, toward the fading red ball. "Where is that?" His voice sounded like he already knew the answer.

Hu'urs Khraam closed his lids and settled into his couch. "We have been fools."

"It can't be—" started Darzhee Kut.

"It's the mass driver."

Darzhee, like the rest of them, all turned to look at Caine.

Graagkhruud took a long step toward the human, claws ready. "You knew—?"

"Of course I didn't know," Caine replied calmly. Darzhee Kut admired Riordan's ability to sit unmoving before the rush of the immense predator. "But it's obvious now, isn't it?"

First Voice sounded careful, wary of stepping into a trap made of words. "What is obvious, Riordan?"

"That the precious mass driver that you thought you were holding hostage actually didn't matter one damned bit. And that we *will* drop a nuke on our own land, our own people."

Yaargraukh's tongue came out briefly.

"There is humor in this, Advocate?"

"Not the kind that elicits laughter, First Voice, but that shows us our own folly. They planned this from the first, my suzerain."

"Planned what?" asked Graagkhruud.

But First Voice was nodding. "Yaargraukh is right. This is akin to the human trickery at Barnard's Star. There, we fought and saw the outcome we expected. Here, we studied Earth for a target and found the mass driver on the kind of island we wanted and yet distant from the great powers. It was the perfect choice."

"Too perfect," agreed Hu'urs Khraam. "It was bait in a trap. Now we feel the jaws of the trap closing about us. Did you know of this ruse, Riordan?"

"No."

Graagkhruud looked around at the calm faces that listened to the human. "And you believe him? Stab this creature and it will bleed lies. It is made up of them."

First Voice waved him down. "Be still, First Fist. Riordan's case is not so clear as you would draw it. And if he knew of this ruse, why did he return here several days ago—to commit suicide?"

"But—"

"And how could he know where he would be housed, upon his arrival planetside? His species' megacorporate traitors might have chosen to hold him at their mass driver facility. Had they done so, what would have become of him in this last minute?"

Graagkhruud, rumbling unpleasantly, turned his attention to the map of Java.

Hu'urs Khraam rose from his couch. "We must reassess our situation."

CoDevCo security compound, Jakarta, Earth

"Mr. Astor-Smath?"

"Yes, Eimi?"

"You have a visitor."

Astor-Smath stubbed out his cigarette, pushed the ashtray and lighter off to one side, and looked up from his spreadsheets long enough to inspect his assistant's waifish lines. "Is the visitor expected?"

"He says he does not have an appointment, but that he is always expected. And sir, I think he has either traveled to get here, or is leaving immediately after speaking with you: he has his luggage with him."

Ah. Him. "Show our guest in, Eimi. And you may leave for lunch now. Better yet, take the rest of the day."

"You mean I should—leave, Mr. Astor-Smath?" She glanced about nervously: even here, in the fortified bowels of CoDevCo's Indonesian Bank complex, the sound and vibration of rippling explosions were discernible.

"Yes, Eimi. You're done for the day. And don't worry about this foolish little uprising. It's a tantrum, not a war. Leave whenever you wish."

"That's very kind of you, Mr. Astor-Smath." Eimi Singh rubbed one long, slender arm with the opposite long, slender hand. "But I did not choose to pay the premium for a reserved room in the bank complex.

I only have my own apartment." She looked beyond the walls toward the streets of Jakarta. "In the city."

"Oh? I didn't know," Astor-Smath lied.

Eimi nodded, looked away, did not move.

"I can see you're scared," he said. "Don't worry. You can stay at my apartment, here in the complex."

"Oh, no, sir. I couldn't—"

"Don't worry. It won't be an inconvenience. I'm sure we can work something out."

Eimi leaned forward, eyes bright. "Really? Thank you, Mr. Astor-Smath, thank you so much. It is very frightening out there, today. I am sure you are right about the uprising just being a nuisance—but it worries me. I suppose I'm a little foolish about such things."

"That's quite all right, Eimi. Now show our guest in."

"Yes, Mr. Astor-Smath." She turned and fairly skipped from the room, grateful and relieved.

Astor-Smath watched her go, noticed the high, boyish buttocks. Later tonight, they would indeed work something out. Astor-Smath was quite familiar with this kind of subtly needy girl-child. In his experience, they were invariably uncertain about their identity, wearing their sexuality in a fashion at once conspicuous and unsure, believing that they were still poised on the brink of discovering themselves like a confused chrysalis-in-waiting. But in actuality they were ingenuous rabbits, awaiting the power and surety of a predator's jaws. That is the meaning, the definition, that they were truly waiting for. And he, Astor-Smath, who had defined so many such lives in just that way, gladly anticipated giving Eimi the gift of self-knowledge that came to all prey animals eventually: that they lived to become the fodder of predators.

Astor-Smath tried to reimmerse himself in the spreadsheet he had been studying, but could not. Knowing who would soon come through the door, he found it difficult to concentrate. He wasn't sure whether it was the importance or the enigma of the relationship which unsettled him more, but he couldn't feign his usual *sang froid*, not even to himself. He rose, went to the antique mahogany credenza to reclaim the package he had put by a week ago, in the anticipation of his visitor's next appearance.

When he turned around, the tall man was there, a briefcase hanging in his grasp. He had not made a sound and he was already five meters into Astor-Smath's cavernous, marble-floored office. Beneath the man's ubiquitous rimless sunglasses, his mouth was slightly bent. A hint of a smile. Perhaps.

Astor-Smath came around his desk, one hand extended, one hand cradling the package, trying to find a smile that was broad and ingratiating yet not obsequious. "My friend, if you had let me know you were coming—"

"Circumstances made that impossible, Mr. Astor-Smath." The visitor looked down, first at Astor-Smath's extended hand, then at the proffered package. "What is that?" he asked, his sunglasses reflecting the plain brown wrapper.

"A gift." Astor-Smath pushed it toward the man, detected—as he always did—a faintly musky and yet medicinal smell about him.

The man did not look down at the package he now cradled under one arm. "What kind of gift?"

"Olives. Of course."

The man finally smiled. It signaled pleasure, but

Astor-Smath found it oddly devoid of gratitude. Putting down his briefcase, the man had extracted a plain ceramic jar from the bag. "Greek, black?"

"Spanish, green."

"Ahh. Just as good." He put the ceramic jar back in the bag. "And I come with something for you, as well."

"Oh? And what would that be?" Astor-Smath managed to keep his voice calm, his eyes half-lidded, his libido in check. Despite the desertion of his clones, was the uprising now quelled, the occupation secure? Enough so that Earth's new masters would start announcing governorships?

But the tall man's response disabused him of that brief fantasy. "I have with me a recording of a most interesting conversation."

"Oh? Show it to me."

"I shall."

The tall man aimed his palmcomp at the five-meter screen of Astor-Smath's commplex, pressed a stud. The sudden, grainy picture revealed an Arat Kur speaking with a human. Astor-Smath was unable to distinguish one Arat Kur from another, but he recognized the human immediately: Caine Riordan. Who, nodding, continued an apparently ongoing conversation. "And so you plan to attack Indonesia. May I ask why?"

The Arat Kur's claws rose, signaling imminent elucidation. "Is it not obvious? It is at a great enough remove from your major powers that they will not feel so directly threatened and thus might listen long enough to hear our terms for withdrawal. For I assure you, Caine Riordan, that we do not wish to remain on your planet."

Riordan seemed blandly skeptical. "There are many

places more remote from the great powers of my world than Indonesia. Why there?"

"Can you not guess?"

"The mass driver."

"It was a surety that you would see this. Many nations have labored long and spent dearly to build this extraordinary device. And they will not wish us to harm it. Similarly, they will avoid harming it themselves."

"So it is a hostage."

"In a manner of speaking. We have no wish to take living hostages."

"Just a monetarily valuable one."

"True. Although we were surprised that it was built in so vulnerable a location. We would have expected it to be sited in a region under direct control of a nation which financed it. From our perspective, it is not merely unprotected. It is a veritable gift for us and for the megacorporations who we shall appoint as our partners and indigenous overseers."

For a sliver of a second, Caine's eyes widened by a millimeter, and then the disinterested gaze was back.

The tall man stopped the video. "This is a most troubling recording, Mr. Astor-Smath."

"And why is that?"

"It is completely unacceptable that Darzhee Kut, or any Arat Kur of his rank and caste, could become aware that CoDevCo's assistance was secured far in advance of the invasion."

"Then speak to the Arat Kur. That is their tape, their debriefing."

"I have spoken to the Arat Kur. In fact, Darzhee Kut was not informed of CoDevCo's longstanding collaboration at all. He, and a startling number of his peers, simply deduced it from the fragmentary facts that were not purged from the documents provided to those Arat Kur who had second-tier clearance ratings."

Astor-Smath walked back to his desk, waved dismissively before picking up his glass of water and sipping at it. "You may say what you mean. We both know I was the intelligence conduit for that part of our operations."

"Yes. I also took the liberty of examining the internal memos you sent apprising your superiors of our evolving arrangements. Again, you showed a profoundly cavalier attitude toward the secrecy protocols we agreed upon."

Astor-Smath didn't like the direction the discussion was taking. "And how did you access those records? Another of your Reifications, perhaps?"

"As I have taken pains to explain several times now, Reification is not the sorcery you seem to think it is. I cannot defy the laws of physics, cannot summon things to me at my merest whim. I can no more telelocate a memo or image to myself than you can."

"Then how did you get access to this information, and to this tape?"

"By simply speaking to one of your superiors at CoDevCo. Who was quite happy to assist. You have been very sloppy, Mr. Astor-Smath. It is going to require a great deal of work to clean up the mess you have made."

Enough was enough. "What do you mean?" He waved at Riordan's face where it was frozen on the screen. "This one comment, uttered on a video our adversaries will never see, is hardly a mess."

"It is, and in more ways than you might guess, Mr.

Astor-Smath. But either way, you shared an extremely sensitive detail, one which violated the strict reporting and secrecy protocols which we established at the outset of our relationship. Likewise, I repeatedly warned you of the inelegance of the Reifications you have instructed me to perform. The numerous improbable attacks on Riordan, the inexplicable mechanical failures, the suspicious heart attacks that killed Corcoran and Tarasenko. They were all too direct."

Astor-Smath spread his hands in a contentious appeal. "No one can affix blame for any of those deeds to you or to me. Your concerns are groundless."

The other man's jaw worked in stiff, controlled frustration. "Your ears function, but you cannot hear. Yours were the impatient, grasping, idiotically direct stratagems of a child who can only think one move ahead. Consequently, it invited the scrutiny of those adversaries who were the most prudent and suspicious, who posed the greatest threat to our joint operations. And to my continued anonymity. Which may not be compromised."

Astor-Smath felt the need to put his back square against the solid bulk of his teak desk. "You are the one who is behaving like a child, starting at imaginary shadows and worries. In the wake of the Arat Kur victory, this can all be sanitized quite easily. Not that it needs to be, regardless of the outcome. There is not one piece of definitive evidence that links me to the Arat Kur or you prior to the invasion. And as concerns *your* safety, my secretary tells me that you are traveling with luggage, so you will not even be here much longer, will you?"

"No. I will be far away."

"So. Even if the Arat Kur were to lose, and there was an investigation, your departure ensures that it can only come to a dead end."

"What an apt phrase."

The man with the sunglasses moved so quickly that Astor-Smath could not be sure if he had pulled something out of his pocket to wave about, or was jerking his arm up and down in the throes of some strange, spasmodic stroke. Astor-Smath moved forward to investigate, possibly help.

—and was distracted by a sudden catch in his throat; he was unable to swallow. He suddenly felt lightheaded, reached for a chair, missed, fell on his back, breathed in. Liquid went down into his lungs. He coughed, was confused—and then terrified—when the air he'd expelled carried up a thin shower of red droplets.

The man's sunglassed face loomed over him. "It will not be long." He reached down, his hand disappearing someplace just under Astor-Smath's narrowing field of vision, and tugged. Astor-Smath's throat suddenly filled with what felt like spinning shards of broken glass and razors. He screamed.

Except he couldn't. As if at the end of a long tunnel, he saw the man hold up a strange implement, a hybrid between an overlong ice-pick and a throwing dagger, which was dripping blood. As the man wiped it on Astor-Smath's shirt, he commented, "You are fortunate that I am so proficient throwing the *esem'shthrek;* you will not be long in dying. This kind of neck wound paralyzes the victim but is almost entirely painless." He rose. "You should have followed my instructions. Precisely." He removed a coffee-thermos from his briefcase, uncapped it. The thick reek of avgas was immediately clear even to Astor-Smath's failing senses. The man dashed the contents about the room, paused, splashed the last of it directly on Astor-Smath's suit. He leaned forward, studied Astor-Smath's almost frozen face. "As I promised, little pain from the wound." He leaned back, found and picked up Astor-Smath's lighter, flicked it, watched the flame climb higher as he thumbed the butane choke to the full open position. "However, I can make no such promises about the avgas." He took two steps back, smiled, tossed the burning lighter directly upon Astor-Smath's chest.

Then he turned and left.

Chapter Forty-Four

Flagship USS *Lincoln*, Sierra Echelon, RTF 1, cislunar space

Lieutenant Brill, senior Comms officer aboard the USS *Lincoln*, turned toward Ira Silverstein. "Admiral, I have Admiral Lord Halifax on priority lascom one. Says he'd like to speak to you 'as soon as it's convenient.'"

Ira smiled. That was Halifax's mannerly way of saying "ASAP." "Pipe him direct to me, Mr. Brill."

Usually, Admiral Lord Thomas Halifax began his conversations in that animated Oxbridge manner that made it easy to believe you were about to go punting on the River Cam rather than wading into battle. This time, he sounded apologetic. "Ira, I know you're not particularly keen about the InPic system that was installed last year, but we might need it for this engagement. If we get a few nasty surprises, or lose our comm links, there might not be enough time for thorough sitreps. So, I'd like you to be InPic in my Combat Information Center on *Trafalgar* for as long as possible. Just in case things get a bit dodgy."

Which really meant "in case my flagship and I get vaporized, you need to have seen everything I've done, and every decision I've made, so you can carry the ball forward." Ira swallowed. "Okay, Admiral. I will be going InPic within the minute."

"Good show, Ira." Halifax's tone became subtly conspiratorial. "I must say, I'm no fan of InPic, either. Seems vaguely voyeuristic, wouldn't you say?"

"Hadn't really thought about it, Tom." *Like hell I haven't.* "Ruth, have the remote telepresence techs link us with *Trafalgar.*"

"Already done, sir. They are ready to put you In the Picture, Admiral Silverstein. We are receiving *Trafalgar*'s C4I five-by-five on encrypted redundant lascoms. Time to wear the crown, sir."

"Very well. Tom, I'm told we're ready."

Halifax's tone became jocular. "Then hurry to your box seat, Ira. Curtain's going up." His private channel snicked off.

Ira reached behind him for the crown: a framework headpiece that included multipoint speakers and a 3-D monocle. "Ruth, I want Commander Clute wearing one of these in the auxiliary bridge."

"Yes, sir. Mind telling me why?"

"Because I want to be ready to toss this damned personal theater away at a moment's notice if I need to. But if I do, I need my senior tactical officer to stay In the Picture. I'll want a detailed report of anything I missed, presuming I don't have the time to sit through a playback."

"Seth—er, Commander Clute—reports he's already strapping on the crown, sir."

"Very good. I say three times, XO, that, as per the

InPic Command Augmentation Protocol, you have the con for routine operations."

"I say three times, Admiral, I have the con for routine ops."

Ira sighed, held the InPic crown at arm's length. Putting it on would put him in two worlds at once: on the bridge of his own ship, and on the bridge of Halifax's *Trafalgar*. Problem was, Ira didn't like being in two worlds at once. In point of fact, he loathed it. His boyhood dream, and adult training, had focused on the command of a ship. A single ship. The one he felt under his feet. To lose complete awareness of that hull was anathema.

He had argued long and hard against expanding the use of InPic so that ranking officers of a joint command or dispersed task force could see, hear, and if necessary, remotely control activity on the bridge of another ship. He had foreseen and forestalled the abuses that could have resulted from rear echelon officers using their "remote telepresence" to tell line commanders how to do their jobs.

But Ira had been forced to concede that in some scenarios, such as this one, InPic conferred immense advantages. As RTF 1 engaged the Arat Kur boosting up out of Earth's gravity well, he needed a full and immediate understanding of what Halifax's first echelon was achieving, what it was not achieving, and what had produced its successes and failures, respectively. And if, God forbid, something happened to Tom Halifax and the HMS *Trafalgar*, then Ira would be in a position to direct the first echelon so that its ongoing combat operations would dovetail with the evolving strategy for Ira's own second echelon.

And it was almost unavoidable that the battle plans would evolve significantly over the course of the engagement. Given the challenges of dealing with a largely unknown enemy that possessed at least marginally superior technology, the admirals of RTF 1 had kept their strategy fairly straightforward. The first, or "Foxtrot," echelon was led by Halifax and was the second largest. It had left its carriers behind with Ira's bigger second, or "Sierra," echelon for safekeeping because Foxtrot had to be drone-, FOCAL- and cruiser-heavy. Given its twofold mission objective, this particular concentration of ship classes was essential. The cruisers were required to put serious hurt on the Arat Kur, and the drones and FOCALs were needed to scatter the enemy by threatening him from widely separated points of the battlesphere. It was also anticipated that Halifax's command would take the heaviest casualties. They were first in and committed to trading killing blows wherever possible, even if it meant sacrificing ships at worse than one-to-one odds to achieve it. His echelon was also a guinea pig. The other two echelons would be watching to learn what they could about their enigmatic adversaries.

In contrast, Ira's Sierra Echelon required the greatest operational flexibility, needing to be able to adapt to both the battlefield results and the enemy's unknown capabilities and doctrine. If the Arat Kur had been significantly weakened by Halifax, it was Silverstein's job to capitalize on that weakness by slowing to match vectors and hammer them harder, and to keep hammering until Tango Echelon under Vasarsky arrived to add its weight to the effort. If, however, the Arat Kur were still in relatively good formation and only moderately damaged after engaging Foxtrot Echelon, Sierra Echelon was to achieve what Foxtrot had not: the disruption and attrition of the enemy fleet, so that Vasarsky's Tango Echelon could deliver a *coup de grace*.

Behind him, Altasso's voice sounded vaguely teasing. "Sir, the technicians have assured me that the InPic crown will only work if the user actually places it on his or her head."

Ira cut his eyes at her, made his voice a growl so that he wouldn't succumb to his urge to smile. "Tend your duties, Commander"—and he put on the InPic headpiece, sliding the 3-D monocle into place with a click.

With that click, the CIC of the *Trafalgar* was suddenly all his right eye could see, and all he could hear through the speakers near his right ear. A young lieutenant leaned over toward the Lord Admiral, whispered in his ear. Halifax turned to wave in the general direction of Ira's vantage point. "I'm told you've joined us, Ira. Hope you enjoy the show. Must get back to work."

Halifax turned to his command staff. "Lieutenant Madratham, do you have a tactical summary on results of the Mousetrap deployment?"

"Aye, sir," she responded crisply. "Estimating mission kills on almost sixty percent of the chase drones sent by the Arat Kur orbital blockade element, and significant dispersion of the remainder."

"Net impact on our drones?"

"I do not have definitive figures yet, Admiral, but no more than twenty percent of our Earth-launched drones have been lost."

"And the drone sorties from the hidden lunar sites?"

"Apparently a complete surprise, sir. No interdiction to speak of. Forty percent have already reached the rear of our echelon. The remainder won't catch us. They are dropping back to join the lead elements of Sierra Echelon."

"Very good, Lieutenant Madratham. Lieutenant Pennington?"

"Yes, Lord Admiral?"

"Have our Gordon-class sloops achieved full drone integration, yet?"

"Not quite, sir. Although most of the lunar-launched drones are in the net, some of the non-Commonwealth models are proving a bit finicky on the data-handshake, sir."

"Hrmph. Who are the culprits?"

"Mostly TOCIO-built drones, sir. There are discrepancies between the data protocols supplied by the bloc authorities and the actual systems on the drones. Appears that not all the drones were updated to the latest software standard, sir."

"Well, bring them in line as best you can. Any that have less than ninety percent reliability are to be redesignated as decoys and expended accordingly. Commander Somers?"

"Aye, sir?"

"How's our evolution into attack formation Bravo Two coming along, David?"

"Handsomely, sir." His plasma pointer cast a glowing beam where it interacted with the colorless reactive gas inside the holotank mainplot. The luminous wand danced among blue motes of light arrayed as a open-based inverted cone. "Our control sloops are arrayed along our leading skirts here." The light wand traced the open rim of the cone. "Here at the bottom of the well"—the wand of light moved to indicate a cluster of slightly larger blue lights at the rearward tip of the inverted cone—"is our main body. You'll note all the cruisers in the core, our frigates in a screening ring, slightly farther out."

"Very good, Commander Somers." Halifax checked his watch. "I'd expect that our drones are about to come into range of their drones."

"Coming up on their observed maximum ranges, sir."

In the background, Ira could hear the ship's captain, Ian Stead, rapping out orders to the bridge crew in the next room. "Lieutenant Worthington, let's not get out ahead of our own formation. Bring back the plasma thrusters two percent. Lieutenant Dunn, deploy ordnance package two." The hull thrummed—even Ira could sense it—as an immense disposable missile pod salvoed all its birds and was then jettisoned. "Watch the post-launch change in displacement, Mr. Worthington; keep us in trim."

Halifax nodded at his staff. "Very well, ladies and gentlemen, let's take a look at the big picture, shall we?" He nodded at the ensign who oversaw the operation of the holotank.

The image changed abruptly. The inverted cone shrank to slightly less than one-tenth its former size. Red motes—the Arat Kur fleet—were approaching it. There were perhaps a third as many of them as there were blue motes in the cone of Foxtrot Echelon.

"Add in drones, if you please," Halifax murmured.

The tidy arrangements of finite blue and red motes were suddenly half-lost amidst dense, pointillist shrouds of similarly colored pinpricks.

"Give me group markers, not individual guidons, Ensign."

Who blushed and hastened to comply. The diaphanous veils of red and blue pinpricks shrank down into a finite number of red and blue triangles. The blue triangles were clustered in three predominant groups. The first were the lunar-launched drones drawing up from behind Foxtrot Echelon, beginning to form a protective sleeve around the cruisers clustered at the rear-facing point of the cone. The second group, Foxtrot's own drones, was larger and arrayed in a forward-deployed screen that looked like a slightly concave lid which had popped off the open end of the cone. And the third group, which was much larger again, was rising into the picture from the direction of Earth, moving decisively toward the lower right rear quadrant of the red motes' battlesphere.

Halifax nodded his satisfaction, just as the space separating some of the red and blue triangles at the rear of the Arat Kur formation started flashing with pinhead pulses of white or yellow: threat and friend damage markers, respectively. "Right on time," Halifax murmured. "Enemy reaction to the attack on their rear flank?"

"No reaction from their capital ships, sir. However, look at their drone squadrons." A third of the red triangles were now drifting down in the direction of the right rear area of the Arat Kur fleet, shifting to intercept the drones that had been launched from Earth.

"Excellent," Halifax muttered, drawing a well-seamed index finger across his snow-white moustaches. "Lieutenant Madratham, I would like a revised estimate of drone ratios at our projected point of contact with the enemy."

She had already worked it out. "After the Arat Kur reconfiguration, best estimates give us a five-to-one drone advantage."

Ira smiled. At the disastrous second Jovian engagement, the drone ratio had been almost even and the consequences had been dire. *Now let's see how your superior technology handles five-to-one odds against our most advanced systems, directed by Gordon-class FOCALs.*

Ruth's voice suggested she had seen Ira's smile and was mildly amused. "Seeing things you like, Admiral?"

"Hush up and drive," he hissed at her. "I'm watching my favorite show."

"Yes, sir!"

In Halifax's CIC, the pace of exchanges was speeding up. "Target assignment almost completed, Admiral," announced Somers. "Visual tracking and ladar have filtered out forty percent of the initial target list as EW decoys. Estimating at least seventy-five percent confidence on remaining targets."

"Estimated confidence results are suitable for a simulator exercise, Commander Somers." Halifax's normally warm and generous voice was now quick and clipped. "How many targets on the revised list are one hundred percent confidence?"

Even given through the visual pickups, Ira could see that Somers flushed deeply. "Twenty percent of the target list, Admiral. Most of those are thought to be cruisers, both shift and nonshift capable."

"Then those are our targets. We're here to hunt big game, and they are the biggest." Halifax turned a reassuring smile upon Somers. "And if by some wild stroke of luck we exhaust that target list, I am quite sure we shall have no lack of new, one hundred percent confidence targets. After all, we will have closed to point blank range and I rather suspect they will all be shooting at us."

"Yes, sir," said Somers. "Any other targeting preferences or orders?"

"No. We follow engagement profile alpha as we rehearsed it. Unless any of those target signatures indicate we have shift-carriers to shoot at, of course."

"No such high-value signatures in range, sir. Full confidence of that."

"I would presume as much. The Arat Kur don't want to be stranded in enemy territory, let alone the enemy's well-developed home system."

Madratham's voice was tense. "Admiral, our drones are coming up on the range marker at which the enemy engaged us at Jovian— Sir! Enemy has commenced fire on our drones!"

"Hmm, starting the party early. A bit nervous about today's outcome, I'll wager. So, we dance in time with them on this step. Deploy all decoys."

"Aye, sir. Deploying."

Somers looked up. "Sir, since we are deploying early, I recommend we advance the clock on our first missile salvo, also."

"Explain your reasoning, Mr. Somers."

"Yes, sir. If we follow engagement profile alpha, missile launch is still three minutes away. However, the timing of that first salvo was based upon when we expected the enemy capital ships would begin firing upon our drones. Since they are engaging our drones at longer range, that might change the timing assumptions of our missile launch, as well."

"Thank you, David. You are quite correct. Send to all ships: primary salvo is now to begin"—Halifax scanned the holotank, then the engagement clock above it—"seventy seconds earlier than in engagement profile alpha. All ships are to confirm receipt of this order."

Madratham's head came up from her screens. "Admiral, I now have visual feed from our lead drones."

"Show me," said Halifax, leaning forward.

The flat-screen image in Halifax's command and information center became a vivid, 3-D, 360-by-360-degree "you are there" virtual reality in Ira's monocle. The InPic not only showed him the view from the nose of the drone but, with faint subaudial pulses, gave him a sense of the relative position of the other allied drones around him. He fleetingly imagined that this is how migrating geese must feel when they fly south in vees, or dolphins when swimming in formation—

The sudden appearance and rapid growth of red guidons arrayed along his front also imparted a sense of the tremendous speed at which he was closing with the enemy, even though Earth—a distant blue and white disk—did not change in size. Data began scrolling along the left-hand margin of the field of view. Shortly after it did, inbound kinetic projectiles—rail-launched from an escort, probably—painted their way towards him as an advancing magenta line. He could feel the drone's attitude control thrusters begin pulsing. The spacescape popped upwards, yawed, swung back, wiggled a little—and then the magenta line was safely off to his starboard side. The drone's evasive maneuvers had apparently been successful.

A moment later, the starfield shuddered, and a chorus of faint, higher audio pulses gave him the impression that he was now surrounded by a covey of smaller drones, almost as if they had come out of his belly. Because that is exactly what had happened. Ira's viewpoint drone was an advance recon/decoy dispenser. The smaller decoys spread rapidly outward. He could see some of them boosting ahead, the blue-white exhausts of their basic rockets propelling them at eight gees of acceleration. Soon they would start sending out signals that mimicked groups of drones or single control sloops. A larger image would not fool the Arat Kur: big hulls did not simply materialize at close range. But from the froth of small craft, drones, and actively homing or maneuvering submunitions that were now moving toward their fleet, the invaders would be far less able to distinguish if a new small signal was false, had been obscured by another, or was just starting to come into range. The decoys would not last long, of course. It would be miraculous if any survived for even half a minute. But every second that they distracted the enemy and overtasked his target tracking and discrimination systems was another second that some of his attacks were wasted.

New orders in Halifax's CIC brought Ira out of the direct link to the drone. The *Trafalgar*'s acceleration couches extended out from the wall in full upright position. A small cavity opened in the base of each. Light duty vacc helmets sagged outward. The ship PA was already issuing the familiar orders. "All hands to battle stations. All hands to battle stations. Prepare for engagement. Report suit or helmet failures to technicians immediately. All hands, all hands—"

Halifax completed suiting up in half the time of his fastest staffer, making it look like an easy, almost relaxed exercise. He folded up the collar of his general quarters flight suit, swung the helmet down over his head, snagged the collar-tab and ran it in a circle around his neck. As he did, the smart sealing materials on the outside of his suit collar and the inside of his helmet collar met and fused. Not sturdy enough to last long in full vacuum, but five minutes of clear thought and free action could make the difference between life and death when the alternative was to struggle unprotected against the effects of explosive decompression.

The admiral reeled the environmental supply tube out of the acceleration couch's base and connected it to the ball-and socket joint receptacle on the side of his helmet. The diagnostic lights alongside the headrest glowed green. His flight suit was both holding air and responding to data links. Halifax scanned the screens arrayed around the holotank. "It looks like we're trading about two to one on the drones, Lieutenant Madratham."

"Just about exactly that, Admiral. Our superiority in numbers is overwhelming their technological edge, sir."

Halifax glanced at the holotank. The outer edge of the slightly decentered red formation now overlapped the wide skirts of the blue cone. Ira saw one of the blue motes denoting a Gordon-class hunter/killer become a yellow smudge, then another. "Ensign," Halifax murmured, "if you would be so kind as to show us what our fellows are seeing out there on the ragged edge..."

—And suddenly, Ira was riding on the nose of a

Gordon-class control sloop. The Arat Kur cruisers were distant, irregular specks. Just ahead, drones—friend and foe alike—were dying in droves. Some came apart, riddled by streams of Arat Kur rail-gun projectiles. Others streamed yellow fire when hit by a PDF laser, then disintegrated into a shower of debris expanding away from a bright orange ball of flame. A few others simply ceased to be, disappearing in a blue-white smear that signified a hit by a higher-energy laser.

Missiles came at Ira. The pilot in the *Gordon* tumbled his sloop, side boosted, deployed thermal chaff and decoys, spun again. Up ahead, one of the Arat Kur heavies seemed to flare brightly for a moment. A hit, probably by a missile from a drone. Ira felt the urge to cheer—and then the virtual world went blank. The data link was not merely broken but empty, its thin static a poignant epitaph.

Ira was back in Halifax's CIC, where the now-solemn staff had witnessed the same outcome. Halifax cleared his throat, "Commander Somers, how long until missile launch?"

"Eight seconds, sir."

Halifax nodded as the emergency klaxon sounded a single, half-duration blast, followed by a strident voice over the intraship. "Secure for engagement. All hands, secure for engagement."

Halifax pulled his couch's straps until they were snug, but not tight. His staff did the same. On the adjoining bridge, last orders were given. A moment passed, and then the world tremored slightly.

"Missiles away," announced Somers. "One minute to outer PDF envelope of Arat Kur lead elements. Estimating—"

There was another bump, this one shorter, sharper, more uneven.

Pennington's voice was higher than before. "Laser hit on portside hull, sir. Conventional laser. We've lost that section of water tankage, but nothing more severe. Almost certainly a drone strike, sir."

"Thank you, Lieutenant Pennington," Halifax said. "However, in this engagement, I do not require reports on the ship's status. If the damage is severe enough to endanger the further function of this CIC, then the bridge crew will inform me. And if the damage is more severe than that, once again, I do not need to be informed about it."

Pennington was green enough to ask, "Why, sir?"

Halifax sighed. "Because, Lieutenant Pennington, the overwhelming likelihood is that we will already be dead or scrambling for the life pods."

Commander Somers cleared his throat. "We're coming into range of their heavies now, sir. Fleet evolution is optimal for engagement profile alpha."

Halifax studied the holotank. "Send one profile modification, David. Since the Arat Kur are already worried, we're going to worry them a little more. For all cruisers with UV laser main armament, new weapon settings. All systems are to be set for shortest duration pulse, highest gigajoule setting."

"Sir, apologies. Regulations require I mention that, at the new rate and magnitude of fire, the lasers will burn out after twenty minutes. Thirty, at most."

Halifax smiled. "Commander Somers, your knowledge of regulations is peerless. And from the tone of your voice, I suspect you understand *why* I'm pushing the lasers beyond their design limit, as well."

"I believe so, sir." Somers glanced quickly at the plot. "At our current combined rate of closure, the enemy will be passing abeam of us in twelve minutes, sir. At most."

"Just so. One way or the other, our fight will be over long before we burn out our lasers, even at the overspec settings." Halifax smiled as the *Trafalgar* quaked with what was clearly a far more substantial hit. "As I was saying, Commander Somers, pass the order: shortest pulses, maximum joules. And when you send that order, append my compliments, and my reminder that all attacks are to follow the assigned targets list, unless joint fire control links are lost. If that occurs, then captains are to fire at will and for as long as they may."

Somewhere farther back in the ship, there was a sustained vibration. Possibly thrusters undertaking evasive action, possibly a PDF system swatting aside Arat Kur drones, or possibly the impact of railgun projectiles. Halifax's staff started and looked around nervously. The admiral simply leaned back in his acceleration couch and exhaled. "And now comes the interesting part."

Chapter Forty-Five

Mobile Command Center "Trojan Ghost One,"
over the Indian Ocean, Earth

"Let's see if the enemy leadership is ready to reassess their situation." Downing nodded to the radio operator, who was already reaching out to the enemy via the frequency that had been reserved for coordinating the maritime traffic involved in the emergency grain shipments.

Alnduul was still at Richard's elbow, despite the light bucking as the VTOL encountered a thermal. "Do you conjecture they are ready to negotiate, Downing?"

Richard frowned. "I doubt it, but the time has come to let them know that negotiation is an option."

"So that they might soon talk with you again?"

Downing smiled. "So that they might soon start arguing with each other. Are the delivery assets for Case Timber Pony in optimal striking distance?"

"Only Riordan is within optimal range of a susceptible target at this time. Our EMP strikes have disabled many of the Arat Kur computer systems that the other assets might have exploited."

Downing sighed. So. It all came down to Riordan, after all. Odysseus had not only inspired Case Timber Pony, but would likely be the means by which it was executed. "Well, there's nothing for it. Mr. Rinehart, use the relief coordination frequency to contact the Arat Kur leadership. It's time we had a chat."

Presidential Palace, Jakarta, Earth

Darzhee Kut was frankly relieved when the senior communications technician announced, "Esteemed Hu'urs Khraam, I have a representative of the Earth Confederation on our human interface channel. He requests to speak with you."

"Is it Ching, or another Confederation consul?"

"No, Hu'urs Khraam."

"Then Urzueth Ragh shall speak with him."

Urzueth Ragh started, moved over to the communication console. "This is Administrator Urzueth Ragh of the Arat Kur Wholenest. What is the intent of your communication?"

"We wish to determine if you are now willing to renegotiate the terms for your withdrawal."

Urzueth Ragh looked to Hu'urs Khraam who snapped his claws downward. Urzueth relayed the response. "We have no interest in renegotiation. We will consider a truce and cessation of hostilities, however, if you wish to reconsider accepting our terms."

"I must point out that your position is grave."

"We do not agree. At the rate you are losing missiles and now planes, we think it is your position that is quite grave."

"You obviously had reasonable prewar intelligence

on the military stockpiles of this planet. You must know that our current losses are negligible."

"You may see it so. But we stand by our terms and conditions for withdrawal."

There was a pause. "Very well, then I have no choice but to issue the following directives. Please look at your sensors."

Darzhee Kut looked over. The airspace on the islands around Indonesia, in a broad arch from Sumatra to Perth and then up to Bali, was filling with new contacts, so many in number that he could no longer distinguish individual returns. It was like a white wave, already discernibly contracting inward toward Java, albeit more slowly than the rockets had.

"You will note the previously hidden air assault forces that are now converging on your position. We have measured your orbital interdiction capability and know that you cannot stop them all. However, if you attempt orbital interdiction against any of these units, we will launch a nuclear attack directly against your two major compounds in Jakarta and Surabaja."

"Your earlier nuclear strikes were made while your decoys were disrupting our sensors. You will not succeed in such an attack now."

"You are incorrect. Our sensors show that, in addition to lacking sufficient orbital interdiction assets, more than fifty percent of your PDF systems are no longer functioning. So I reiterate: do not attack our approaching air units, or we will launch a nuclear attack."

Urzueth bluffed well. "You will excuse us if we dispute your statistics and find your threats of a nuclear attack less than convincing."

"Then perhaps this will convince you. Look at your sensors once again—"

SSBN *Ohio*, Java Sea, Earth

"Captain Tigner?"

"Yes, Alvarez?"

"The boys banging sticks in the Australian surf have sent the word. All subs go to phase two."

"Any new wrinkles in the plan?"

"None at all, ma'am. Just like we drilled it."

"Very well then. Mr. Vinh, blow all tanks and give me full fans to the surface. Mr. Alvarez, signal that *Ohio* has received, understood, and is on the way up. Ms. Kayor?"

"Aye, Cap'n?"

"Deploy remote ADA packages with neutral buoyancy set for twenty meters. And dump all our countermeasures now. Set them for remote activation, arrayed to cover a straight dive pattern."

"We dump *all* the countermeasures, without presumption of evasive action, Skipper?"

"You heard a-right, Lieutenant. If we have to dive to the dark, the only two things that are going to matter are speed and having the countermeasures already in the water and waiting to go. And if phase two doesn't work, we're out of the game anyway. No reason to keep the toys in the hull."

"Aye, aye, ma'am."

Vinh half turned his head. "Captain Tigner, we're coming up through one hundred meters."

She hauled down the old hardwired shipwide handset. "Stand to general quarters." She heard her rather girlish voice echoing back through the long hull. "We cannot afford any failure, any hesitation. History, and all humanity, will judge us by this moment."

Vinh told her what she already knew from the way the deck seemed to bounce beneath her feet. "Decks awash, tubes open."

Commander Tigner leaned toward the periscope.

The weapons officer looked over. "Orders, ma'am?"

"Nothing yet, Ms. Kayor. We're going to give them a good look down the barrel of our loaded shotgun before we pull the trigger. Maybe they'll blink first, save us the trouble of shooting."

"If not, ma'am?"

"Keep present target selection and dispersion setting. Set warheads for one-hundred-meter airburst. And if I give the word, Donna—"

"Yes, ma'am?"

"Don't wait for details. Salvo 'em all."

Presidential Palace, Jakarta, Earth

Darzhee Kut stared at the map in disbelief. Twenty seconds ago, there had been a wave of white slowly converging on Java, but now the island itself was outlined by a snow flurry of new, coast-hugging contacts. Contacts that faded in as they emerged from the benthic depths of the surrounding seas, shelfs, reefs.

Hu'urs Khraam had collapsed back into his couch. "How many did you say?"

"Fifty-four submarine contacts. Optical sensors show all missile tubes open. High power radar arrays are now active in Australia, Sumatra, Singapore, Philippines,

scanning the airspace above us all the way up to low
earth orbit."

"So if we attempt to interdict the submarines with
orbital munitions—"

"The human sensors will detect their descent and
signal the submarines to salvo."

"Orbital lasers?"

Urzueth Ragh's mandibles made a grating noise.
"The hull of these submersibles is akin to very thick
armor. Our standard interdiction lasers are not powerful enough to reliably destroy or disable them before
they can launch. A non-UV spinal laser would work,
but we have retained very few of those older systems
in our inventory."

"So we have no way to destroy them before they
can salvo."

"Not all of them, and any one of those submarines
carries enough warheads to destroy us. And with the
short flight times from those offshore positions—"

Hu'urs Khraam turned to Darzhee Kut. "I seek
your advice, rock-sibling: . . ."

—Darzhee Kut blinked at the unprecedented, almost
familial, intimacy of the address—

". . . when I forbade renewing negotiation with the
humans, was I too hasty?"

Darzhee Kut was wondering how he could tact-
fully reply to such a question when Urzueth Ragh
announced, "I have initial images of the engagement
with the first echelon of the human fleet."

Hu'urs Khraam motioned Darzhee Kut toward the
plot. "I am told your experiences at Barnard's Star greatly
enhanced your knowledge of fleet actions, Speaker Kut.
Please provide details of what we are seeing."

Darzhee Kut would normally have demurred having his name associated with expertise in military matters. However, in a species which had not known war in many generations, and which reviled the disharmonious existence that was its necessary precursor, it might well be that he understood war—at least this war with the humans—as well as any other rock-sibling present. He turned to Caine. "In describing the actions and implements of your fleet, you will correct me if I misspeak, Caine Riordan?"

❖   ❖   ❖

Caine thought about that request and what it might imply. "I will, if my duty to my own race is not violated by what I share."

"Then join me at the holotank, if you would."

Caine approached the Arat Kur holotank. The once tidy masses of red and yellow motes were thoroughly interpenetrated, the formations of both having diffused into badly smudged approximations of their former geometric shapes.

Hu'urs Khraam shifted restlessly. "I am surprised that our engagement with the first echelon of the human fleet has already compromised our formation. Why did this occur?"

"Necessity, Hu'urs Khraam," answered Darzhee Kut. "Being so heavily outnumbered, and further threatened from the rear by the drones from Earth, our commanders had to choose between maneuvering to optimally realign their overlapping fields of defensive fire or holding formation and reducing their ability to protect each other from the threats now present in all parts of our battlesphere."

Hu'urs Khraam shifted again. "Continue."

"The choice they made—to adjust position to optimize defense—has substantially reduced our losses, but has not prevented them. These images show the state of the combat currently."

The screen over the holoplot brightened, revealing a human cruiser, launching missiles from its amidships bays, the red activation rings glowing around the small aperture that was the business end of its spinal UV laser. Then, with terrible suddenness, part of its belly vomited outward in a shower of tumbling white debris. The main weapon's red activation warning rings winked spasmodically and went dark, just before flickering flame-tongues danced within the ship's gaping belly wound, licking hesitantly at the blackness of space. The rear of the ship was now limned by a blue glow. The fusion plant and main thrusters were being pushed to maximum burn, probably in an attempt to rush the ship out the other side of the engagement zone.

Its escape attempt was futile. Two seconds later, the unseen agency of pinpoint destruction went back to work. A cyclone of debris and ruin traced a long jagged line down the cruiser's flank, as if the hull was an immense technological fish being gutted by a dull knife. As the beam—almost certainly a shift-cruiser's spinal-X-ray laser—blasted its way aft, secondaries inside the human cruiser went off, bursting more of the hull outward from inside. Then the missile bay exploded, tearing an immense chunk out of the ship's side, which was immediately followed by a blast of blinding whiteness that blanked the screen.

The view changed. That same, blinding whiteness was now a small sun, expanding in the background, the foreground dominated by two Arat Kur ships that were experiencing difficulties of their own. The larger one, a distinctively streamlined shift-cruiser, was struggling to maintain attitude with her plasma thrusters. Her main engineering decks were slashed open to space, intermittent jets of flame vying with actinic power arcs that looked akin to a collection of Van der Graaf generators gone mad. But, although she was nearly motionless, her hyperactive defense batteries briskly annihilated the nearest threats from a steadily converging hemisphere of human drones and occasional missiles, one of which bloomed into the bright white sphere of a tactical nuclear device.

In addition to protecting herself, the shift cruiser was clearly trying to extend her active defenses to shield a Hkh'Rkh destroyer which was maneuvering alongside in an attempt to tow the larger, stricken ship to safety. But a covey of passing human drones retroboosted, tumbled, burned hard to side-vector into an approach trajectory that the cruiser could not interdict because the destroyer was in the way of its PDF batteries. Small hits began peppering the starboard side of the destroyer: single-shot chemical lasers from drones that then dove in afterward, attempting to kamikaze against the destroyer. One slammed into the modular fuel tank nestled in its lower starboard quarter, where the keel-trusses joined the rest of the ship to its engine decks. Fragments of the tank blew outward. The destroyer's drives faltered as her own PDF batteries swiveled wildly—right before a pattern of spinal rail gun projectiles tore her bridge and forward sensor cluster into silvery-white streamers of debris.

The destroyer was now more of a danger to the shift cruiser than a help. The Arat Kur heavy rotated her thrusters to get what distance she could, lest the destroyer's drives go up and take her along with them. Her PDF batteries spun smartly into new configurations—just as an invisible beam cut down across her aft section, a blizzard of hull panels and bulkheads flinging themselves out into the void for one brief second before the shift cruiser vaporized in a blue-white ball. Darzhee Kut froze the image on the screen.

Hu'urs Khraam spoke slowly, heavily, it seemed to Caine. "I am sure you could have chosen many such scenes of destruction, Darzhee Kut. Why did you select these two?"

"Because they are the most instructive, Hu'urs Khraam. You will note how the human cruiser was destroyed: by a small number of hits from a single weapon. This is how we are typically inflicting losses on our enemies: by striking them with superior weaponry that enjoys superior targeting at distance.

"The death-images of our own ships are no less revealing. They illustrate how the humans are typically destroying us: by overwhelming our defenses. They harry us with drones, degrade our vessels by disabling one subsystem after another, and then—with our defenses dedicated to eliminating the most proximal threats—they strike their killing blow from longer range." His claw-embedded laser pointer traced a bright line from the exploding shift cruiser to a small, bright, white sphere in a corner of the starfield. "What you see here, so small in the distance, is the detonation of what the humans call a 'nuke-pumped' X-ray laser. These are their ship-killers, Hu'urs Khraam, the ones to which our human collaborators alerted us. They are fabulously expensive and wasteful weapons, mounted on an overlarge drone and easily distinguishable from regular drones at close and medium ranges. But as our scanners become overwhelmed by the unprecedented number of human drones and decoys, they become unable to find all of these threats in time."

"Still," objected First Fist, "you are destroying at least two ships of theirs for every one of your own. You are prevailing."

"For now, yes. But we cannot retroboost and match vector with the first echelon to capitalize upon our successes, because the second echelon is following close upon it. And I warn you, Hu'urs Khraam, I suspect that the first echelon was merely the chisel; the hammer is only now approaching."

"Why do you say this, Speaker Kut? Because there are more ships in the second echelon?"

"That is the lesser part of my worry, First Delegate. Our analysts have been monitoring the rate at which the human first echelon has been expending these X-ray laser missiles I have just shown you. Since they did not lose these munitions at Barnard's Star and we conjecture that some of the concealed drones launched from hidden sites on the Moon must be of this kind, we expected our enemy to employ more of these than he has."

Yaargraukh's rumble was grim. "So, you suspect that it is their second echelon which shall deploy this increased firepower."

"Precisely." Darzhee Kut turned, pointed to the second, vast wave of red blips in the holoplot. "The second echelon is much larger than the first. It has many more platforms from which to optimally launch and control such missiles, and more drones to confound and overwhelm our defenses. And they have two other profound advantages that the first echelon did not enjoy."

Yaargraukh pony-nodded. "They have broken up our formation and, at the same time, may be relatively sure we have no new tricks or technologies with which to confound them. For we would certainly have used them to ensure a more favorable outcome with the first echelon."

"Exactly," agreed Darzhee Kut, who then turned to stare at Riordan. "I suspect this was the strategic intent of the humans' three-echelon battle plan. Does that sound correct, Mr. Riordan?"

"I cannot say. Obviously, I was not involved in, nor made privy to, any of the military planning for this counterattack. However," and he let a slight smile slip, "your conjecture is eminently plausible."

Hu'urs Khraam shifted on his platform-couch. "So. We have scored a marginal victory in space, but have yet to fight the much larger of what will be at least two battles. And here on the planet, we now find ourselves ringed by submersibles equipped with nuclear weapons which the humans have proven they will fire at their own possessions and populations, given sufficient provocation." He turned to face Darzhee Kut directly. "And so I ask again, Speaker Kut. When I forbade renewing negotiations with the humans, was I too hasty?"

Caine watched Darzhee Kut seem to contract as every exosapient eye in the room turned toward him. In the Arat Kur's position, Caine was quite sure he would not enjoy the sensation, either.

Chapter Forty-Six

Presidential Palace, Jakarta, Earth

Darzhee Kut felt all the eyes upon him as he offered his counsel to Hu'urs Khraam. "Esteemed Hu'urs Khraam, you were not rash to refuse to negotiate with the humans, given what we knew then. But perhaps this new information must make us reconsider speaking with them."

Graagkhruud's interjection was, quite literally, a snarl. "We should only be speaking to them to demand their immediate surrender."

"First Fist Graagkhruud, why would *they* surrender at this moment? We are unable to intercept all their missiles and air vehicles and submarine launches. Whatever we choose to do, they will still have options remaining which might defeat us. They attrited our PDF intercept capability so that our groundside forces have to rely on orbital interdiction support for survival—and now, with half our fleet off to engage the human fleet, we simply do not have enough assets to do so."

"So, despite all your promises and assurances— that human technology was inferior and yours was

657

far more advanced—it turns out that *they* have the better technology." Graagkhruud seemed pleased with himself, vindicated, as he said it.

An accusation scooped from the useless slurry of your own speciate insecurity, you impetuous and recidivistic predator. "Their technology is not better than ours, although it is far more diverse. But that was not what has tipped the balance this day."

First Voice spoke before Graagkhruud could manage to respond. "Then what has, Speaker Kut?"

"Honored First Voice, the humans make war far more frequently than the Arat Kur. And, if my surmise is correct, in far more ways than either of us. And while the human megacorporations did provide us with complete data on the planet's warfighting equipment, they were ill-suited to providing us with a comprehensive compendium of its operational alternatives. Besides, many of the tactics being employed by the humans are either wholly unprecedented, or being expressed in unique combinations that defy any simple understanding drawn from historical precedents."

"We have a saying," Caine offered quietly, "that general staffs are always preparing to fight the last war, not the next one."

Graagkhruud snarled. "The simple truth is that the brilliant Arat Kur cannot think as quickly as warriors must."

"Darzhee Kut's insight and patience are praiseworthy," Hu'urs Khraam inserted into the uncomfortable silence, and Graagkhruud either missed or ignored the implied rebuke, "but now I must ask that you allow him to attend to my question. Was I rash in rejecting the human offer of negotiation?"

"Not rash, Esteemed Hu'urs Khraam, but we may be running out of time. We might still have enough PDF and orbital interdiction left to protect us here, but the humans' actions increasingly erode the former and overtax the latter. We might be able to hold out until our counterattacking flotilla returns, which would double our interdiction capability. However, if the flotilla does not triumph against the human fleet, then our only remaining relief is our Belt Fleet, and they will not arrive in time to salvage the situation."

Hu'urs Khraam settled into his couch. "So, logically, we should await the outcome of the current fleet battle. If we prevail, as we should, we will still hold the upper hand."

Riordan shook his head. "That is why my side will *not* wait for the outcome of that battle. If we lose there, we have lost our only reasonable hope of permanently regaining control in either Java, or in space. My side must use its present advantage, meaning that if you do not negotiate now, they will destroy your ground forces—and much of Indonesia—while they still may."

First Voice rose up. "Hu'urs Khraam, Riordan's analysis is without error. But whereas he intends it to scare you into negotiation, I assert it should fix our resolve to strike the humans first."

"First Voice of the First Family, we agreed not to use nuclear weapons against—"

"You will hear me. We still have an undamaged half-fleet in orbit. The humans cannot strike at those ships yet, so we may still win the war swiftly and decisively by destroying five of their greatest cities and bloc capitols with a deluge of kinetic kill devices. Let us say New York, Beijing, Tokyo, Berlin, Moscow. The moment after this is achieved, we send the ultimatum we should have sent when we first arrived: capitulate or die by the billions. The humans will not resist further. Their cities would be ash by the time their fleet arrives, should it be so fortunate as to win the day against your ships."

Graagkhruud's enthusiasm was palpable. "This is plain truth and the path to victory. And if the humans threaten to overwhelm us here while this is transpiring, it is of no consequence."

"Indeed? You so gladly accept death?"

"Spoken like the grubber you are. Of course I do not welcome death. I merely say we must fight as warriors should: on the attack, giving no quarter, using all weapons against any opponents."

"You propose to slaughter them all, including noncombatants and innocents?"

"It would be a slaughter if there *were* any noncombatants or innocents, if we struck humans down where they crouched in supplication. But the humans do not know this posture nor this behavior. They are all combatants. Consequently, they have dug the den in which they must live. They must all be slain until they all capitulate. And if we move forth from our compounds using incendiary weapons, leveling those areas of the cities we do not control, even local resistance will quickly come to an end." He turned toward Caine, tongue flicking. "Do you deny it, liar?"

Riordan looked up when the Hkh'Rkh addressed him as "liar." The difference in their size and mass made the human's response either comical or dangerously insane. "Do you challenge me, First Fist?"

Graagkhruud's tongue whipped out and about like

a stabbed snake. He huffed once in his chest. "You flatter yourself, *s'fet*. You are not a being and so, have no honor, despite the way Yaargraukh addresses you and despite First Voice's generous toleration of that. I would smear my name and my family to even acknowledge you."

Caine smiled and for some reason, Darzhee Kut found that expression more fearful than anything he had ever seen on the long face of any Hkh'Rkh. "How fortunate for you that I may not be Challenged, or make Challenge, Graagkhruud."

The Hkh'Rkh leapt toward him, claws up.

Hu'urs Khraam shrilled. "Predator, you would slay an ambassador? Here, in our presence, without consulting us?" First Voice restrained First Fist as Hu'urs Khraam settled down in his couch again, but continued in the same tone. "This impetuosity, this dance your species does with death, it is not just in your actions of the moment. It is also in these plans you speak of now."

First Voice reared up. "These 'impetuous' plans will win this war."

"No. They will win this *battle*—but in doing so, will most certainly lose the war. For when the Custodians learn what you would have us do here, they will ban our races from space. Do not mistake me, First Voice. I harbor no tender feelings for the humans. You may find, when you know us better, that we have stronger and longer reasons to loathe humans than you ever will." Only Darzhee Kut saw Caine's eyes become suddenly sharp when Hu'urs Khraam uttered the word "longer." "But," continued the First Delegate, "that does not change the fact that so far as we know, we must still answer to the Custodians."

"Besides," Darzhee hastily interjected, "whose fault is it that we teeter on this unseen brink? The humans'? Did they invade our systems?"

"Not yet," amended Graagkhruud.

"And perhaps they never would have. Now, we will never know. But if they had, would they have attacked our homeworld?" Darzhee Kut turned to face his leader. "You are right to fear the Dornaani, Esteemed Hu'urs Khraam, but also fear what this deed would make us. Worse than the humans. And remember this—and you answer too, First Voice. If we do this, and if we then leave any of the humans alive, anywhere, what do you think they will do?"

Yaargraukh reared back. "They would hunt our races down until we are no more. They will not forgive, they will not forget, they will not stop. Darzhee Kut is right: if we take this step, it is not the last leap we take into the darkness. It is but the first plunge into a campaign of unremitting genocide—and if we do not finish the atrocity we begin, they will surely finish us."

"Just so," affirmed Darzhee Kut. "The humans will hunt us down until they have made our homerock magma and ashes. And to prevent them from doing so, we would need to hunt them down on all their other worlds. So, once we are done here, let us also be resolved to lay waste to Alpha Centauri, to Epsilon Indi, to Delta Pavonis, to Beta Hydri, Zeta Tucanae, and p-Eridani, for you will need to destroy them all, one by one, if you are to finish the atrocity you would start."

Yaargraukh's voice was grim. "As if the Dornaani would let us."

First Voice's tone was measured, careful. "The Dornaani are not here, have not come. You start at shadows that your own mind has conjured, Advocate."

"Do I, First Voice? Tell me, if the Dornaani have *not* been exterminated, can they allow this—and us—to stand?"

Darzhee Kut clicked his claws, signaling an amplification of Yaargraukh's point. "First Voice, do not mistake Dornaani calm for indecisiveness. They will not hesitate to use force. They fought horrible wars before any of us saw the heavens as something other than a place of myths and gods. They will not abide what you are contemplating."

"There may be none left to object," observed First Voice, "if the Ktorans' war against them has gone as planned."

Yaargraukh reared up. "Are you willing to make that wager, First Voice of the First Family? And what do we gain even if you win it? A commitment to destroy green worlds and a whole race in a war that even now ceases to have any honor in it? And if you lose the wager? Do you wish to be known as the Hkhi whose gamble resulted in our permanent expulsion, even quarantine, from contact with other races? And if we cannot accept such a fate placidly, what then might the Dornaani feel compelled to do? Exterminate us?"

Hu'urs Khraam's voice was quiet. "No. They will—change—you."

The Hkh'Rkh crests all rose. First Voice growled. "What do you mean?"

The First Delegate raised a didactic claw. "The Dornaani would not initiate genocide; they have sworn an oath against it. But altering your species through selective and successive retroviruses, foods that are engineered to rebalance your hormones, asymptomatic epidemics that, initially unnoticed, sterilize ninety percent of your females. These passive controls they would indeed use."

Yaargraukh turned to First Voice. "And this risk is worth the profit and glory of a race exterminated from orbit without honor, half a dozen ruined worlds, and no promise of new lands? What nature of gamble is this, First Voice?"

"Then what is to be done?" Graagkhruud asked.

Yaargraukh let the phlegm roll long and contemptuous in his nostrils. "Fight and die, First Fist. Or leave. The choice is yours, and I am indifferent to your deliberations. I will take my place among the defenders, for I have no more counsel to offer. By your leave, First Voice." Who bobbed once, curtly. Yaargraukh turned and left.

Graagkhruud's chest was a sustained rumble. "His insolence warrants death."

First Voice looked after him. "And his courage and honesty earns honor. We will let events help us decide which it should be, for I cannot decree both. But you may point out to him that a creature with great honor and honesty must always be ready to serve the First Voice in any way required, and such readiness is now paramount. And if he fails in his oaths, he must be ready to answer for that failure, to accept any Challenge. Any Challenge, from any Challenger—First Fist." First Voice looked at Graagkhruud, long and silently.

Who lowered his eyes and put his clenched fist low on his barrellike chest. "Your vassal hears and understands, suzerain." Graagkhruud hunch-bowed himself out of the command center.

Darzhee Kut buzzed mildly. "So what is decided?"

Hu'urs Khraam's claws snipped the air restively. "Even though the magma rises around us, I am reluctant to contemplate withdrawal. But—"

First Voice reared up to his full 2.2 meters. "The Hkh'Rkh do not flee. We fight until we win or die."

"And if an honorable withdrawal is negotiated?"

"Let that be sought and crafted by creatures who find no inherent contradiction in linking the word 'honorable' with 'withdrawal.'" First Voice leaned down, warbling phlegm. "But know that if an 'ally' once abandons us, we will neither forget, nor forgive, it. I leave to inspect our defenses. I return soon." He loped out, ears flattened and quivering. His retinue was a broad, swaggering wake behind him.

The sensor specialist signaled he had an update. Urzueth Ragh glanced at it, then chattered, "Esteemed Hu'urs Khraam, the enemy continues launching air vehicles. Their transatmospheric interceptors are climbing up beyond twenty-five kilometers, but their ascent is atypically slow."

"That's because they're not attacking—yet."

Darzhee Kut and the other Arat Kur cadre turned to look at Caine. Hu'urs Khraam bobbed toward him. "I invite your explanation, Speaker Riordan. Why would your commanders launch a wave of interceptors if they do not mean to assault our ships in orbit?"

Darzhee Kut recognized Caine's smile as being one which, paradoxically, did not signify either happiness or amusement. "Oh, if the *military* commanders were in charge of this launch, I'm sure they'd be filling your hulls with nukes by now. No, this is a politically managed maneuver."

"To what end?"

"To give you enough time to realize that although you are not in immediate danger, the threats are rapidly increasing. And to give them an opportunity to discover whether, in the face of those threats, you will react aggressively or comply."

"Comply?" mused Hu'urs Khraam.

Darzhee Kut understood. "Comply with the warning the humans issued at the end of their last communiqué: 'if you attempt orbital interdiction against any of our air units, we will launch a nuclear attack directly against your two major compounds in Jakarta and Surabaja.'"

Urzueth Ragh looked at him. "So do the humans expect us to allow their interceptors to continue to climb toward orbit?"

Darzhee Kut returned Urzueth's stare. "Are we prepared to interdict one hundred percent of the nuclear weapons they would launch if we do not?"

Hu'urs Khraam looked at them both, then allowed chitinous covers to close over his eyes. Darzhee Kut edged nearer to the Arat Kur who had, over these weeks, become more his mentor than his superior. "Revered Hu'urs Khraam, if at this time we cannot act, perhaps this is the right moment to talk..."

Chapter Forty-Seven

Trevor leaned back so he could see up through the hole in the roof several stories above. Just before they had reached this building—their jumpoff point for the final attack—the fuselage of an intercepted rocket had cut a straight shaft through it, from roof to atrium. The jagged, impromptu skylight now showed a darkening, low cloudbank. But still no sign of rain. Or of more airbursting nukes.

Tygg approached, looked up as well. "Is it almost time?"

"Almost. Let's pull Gavin in from overwatch."

"Right. And I'll send one of my blokes to get the electronics out of the Faraday cage."

Trevor nodded. "Yeah, might as well. If we see any more nukes, they're going to be in our laps, not high overhead."

"There's a cheery thought, mate. I'm off."

As Tygg headed down to the basement, Trevor

walked to the front of the building, found Witkowski crouched in the same concealed position he'd been in since entering the building. "What's the good word, Stosh?"

"All quiet on the Western Front."

"Winfield?"

"Still no sign of him. Don't worry. He's a tough kid from Watts."

"Stosh, Jake Winfield's from Greenwich, Connecticut."

"Well, his grandmother—or grandfather, or someone— still lives in Watts. And he visited them. Once. Well, he wanted to, anyway."

Trevor smiled. "Stosh, you are insane."

"I am inspired. They are frequently confused."

Trevor nodded in the direction of Harmoni Square. "What else can you tell me?"

"No cell chatter since our big bright white ones went off at twelve o'clock high. Fried the net, I'm guessing. A few unattached insurgents skulking around, giving the Roach Motel a wide berth."

"And the Arat Kur security forces?"

"If I didn't know better, I'd say they'd left when no one was looking."

"No more Hkh'Rkh search-and-destroy squads, either?"

"Not since Gavin introduced the last bunch of Sloths to the wonders of long-range marksmanship."

John Gavin had caught the Hkh'Rkh elites flatfooted with the Remington assault gun, ran them straight into Stosh and Tygg's combined field of fire. Trevor had wanted to avoid an engagement, but the Hkh'Rkh NCO had evidently arrived at the same conclusion that Trevor had come to an hour earlier: that this particular building was an ideal spot for an OP and several sniper nests. Unfortunately, as Stosh pointed out later, multiple tenancy was strictly prohibited within the city limits and the human commandos had enforced that exclusionary law with a decisive application of firepower. "Stosh," Trevor said quietly, "tell our local recruits we're ready to move. Should be getting the go signal for the final attack any minute, now."

"Bringing news like that, they'll probably try to kiss me."

Trevor stared at the homely SEAL. "Not a chance, chief."

"Woe is me, unwanted and unloved. Any other heartbreaking orders?"

"Yeah. Tell the locals who laid the demo charges that they need to talk us through the triggering sequence again."

"How hard can it be, Skipper? We press the buttons. The charges they laid in a nice straight row go off one after the other, blowing open a path from our front door right into the Roach Motel."

"Simple in concept, Stosh, but I want to get the timing exactly right. And I want them to run a remote circuit-test of the charges that the inside agents placed along the compound's inner walls. If the Arat Kur or Hkh'Rkh found and removed them, I want to know that before we start running up our own highway of destruction—only to find ourselves bouncing off the still-intact compound walls."

"Yeah, that wouldn't be much fun. I'll send the fireworks boys up on the double."

Trevor squinted at the closest enemy hardpoint, only eighty meters away, brooding outward into Majahapit

Street from the gutted Chamber of Commerce building. *I watch you and, maybe, you watch me. Or maybe you figure that since this building is quiet, your hit-squad cleared at least this much turf for you.* He checked his watch. Ten minutes until their final assault on the west perimeter was to get the "go-no go" signal. That presumed, of course, that the second-hand messaging remained accurate. The word had come via a runner from another large mob moving slowly north along streets paralleling Merdeka Square on the east, who had in turn received it from one of the tunnel rats who were manning the fiber-com net under the streets somewhere to the north. And today, in Jakarta, that was about as high-quality a message a anyone was going to get.

Trevor felt as much as heard movement behind him. Bannor Rulaine was there, an extra eight-millimeter CoBro assault rifle in hand. Trevor nodded his thanks. "Thanks for building us that Faraday cage, Bannor."

"Not a problem. Never imagined I'd ever have use for that particular bit of training. Spent years thinking it had been a waste of six hours of my very important life. But our intact electronics and RAPs should give us the edge we need."

"I sure hope so, Bannor." Trevor looked back at the enemy hardpoint, wondered if the demo charges would take it down as planned, wondered what lay beyond it. "I sure hope so."

Presidential Palace, Jakarta, Earth

Caine rubbed his left forearm with his right hand. Was that pain ever going to go away? He hadn't felt any discomfort there since his abortive attempt to leave Indonesia, but here it was, back again: a sharp stabbing sensation, racing along his ulna.

Caine leaned forward, checked the command center's side door to see if the departing Hkh'Rkh had possibly neglected to post a guard there. Nope, still one on duty, rifle held at port arms. No way to get out and warn Yaargraukh that Graagkhruud and his retinue had left the room looking like Macbeth's henchmen being sent to kill Banquo. *And just wait until First Voice hears who Hu'urs Khraam is now trying to reach on the radio, and why. That ought to be worth the price of admission.*

It was Hu'urs Khraam himself who jarred Caine out of his train of thought. "Once we have contacted your people, Speaker Riordan, I will be grateful to have you help us assess their intentions."

"First Delegate Khraam, surely you are not asking me to be a traitor."

"I am only asking you to do what you have already done: provide us with insight regarding human actions. Your observations have been far more useful and perspicacious than those of our—special advisors. It was you who helped us understand the slow approach of the interceptors, after all."

"True, First Delegate. But I did so because I am here to help you *and* my people both find a way to avoid further fighting. By sharing that information with you, I served that purpose. I am not here to help you fight, or gain an advantage in negotiations, against my own people."

Hu'urs Khraam considered. "But you will help us perceive correctly if we seem to be misperceiving?"

"Of course."

The Arat Kur communications specialist signaled Hu'urs Khraam. He had a senior representative of the human command structure on the line. The First Delegate rose up slightly. "Hello? To whom am I speaking?"

The human voice that responded was the same one that had contacted them earlier. Caine kept himself from smiling.

Because it was Downing. "First Delegate Hu'urs Khraam, I am glad to speak to you."

Hu'urs Khraam paused. "My apologies, but am I speaking to Delegate Downing?"

"That is correct."

"My apologies. I did not recognize your voice when my subalternate Urzueth Ragh spoke with you earlier."

"That is quite understandable, First Delegate. We had little contact at the Convocation, and this has been a busy and difficult day."

"Indeed. Mr. Downing, forgive what may seem an impertinent question, but why am I not addressing Mr. Ching or another Confederation consul directly?"

"Because we only have this one, prearranged link between us, running through the transmitter you approved. And we are unwilling to route any commlinks through to our heads of state. Your human collaborators might have a way to track back the connection and thereby provide you with targeting coordinates. Unlike Mr. Ching, I am quite expendable—despite my plenipotentiary negotiating powers."

"I see. Very well. You will note that we have elected to observe your directive not to attack your rising interceptors, Mr. Downing. For now. This is an act of good faith, which we hope will set the tone for the rest of these discussions."

"With respect, First Delegate, it seems to us that you had little choice but to comply, if you wished to avoid nuclear incineration."

"Admittedly, we find ourselves in a challenging situation at the moment. You are to be congratulated on your deceptions, Mr. Downing. They have proven relatively effective. At any rate, we are willing to return to our original terms—those we dictated upon our arrival—and reopen negotiations upon them."

"We are not willing to reopen discussions on the original terms, First Delegate. They were unacceptable. Furthermore, it is the opinion of the Confederation leadership that they were intended to make this conflict inevitable, rather than avoidable."

"That is an interesting hypothesis. If you have no interest in resuming negotiations, why did you even accept the reception of this communication?"

"To offer you the chance to surrender."

"Mr. Downing, did I understand you correctly? You are offering *us* the chance to surrender?"

"That is correct."

"Mr. Downing, while my staff concedes that we may take significant losses before the ongoing cislunar space engagement is resolved, we will still emerge victorious. And then you will have no fleet left."

"Our analysis suggests a different outcome. A very different outcome."

"We have utmost confidence in our own analysis."

"I'm sure you do. But your analysts are not aware of all the variables."

"Indeed?"

"Our fleet's appearance was an unforeseen variable when you were calculating the odds of your success today. Consider how your current projections might be further problematized, not to say ruined, by the intrusion of further unforeseen variables."

"Mr. Downing, your diction and calm marks your voice as a worthy one to sing for your species. However, you are nonetheless human and deception is as ineluctable a part of your nature as are the other primal survival traits of your species. In short, it is only logical that, having surprised us with your fleet's appearance, you will use it to legitimate further 'bluffs' by suggesting that you have further 'aces up your sleeve.' Do I use these colloquialisms correctly?"

"You do. But I am not bluffing."

"For sake of argument, let us presume that you are not. What terms would you offer us? May we withdraw?"

"Not immediately."

"What do you propose?"

Caine leaned forward to hear Downing's reply—and felt another spasm of pain in his left ulna. *What the hell?*

Downing's tone was almost mild. "First, your ships will be boarded and rigged for scuttling in the event of treachery. We will then escort your hulls, one by one, to Jupiter. There you will vent all but five percent of your fuel upon achieving a holding orbit, in which you will remain for whatever time is required for us to conclude a peace agreement with the senior leadership of the Wholenest on Sigma Draconis Two. If and when this is accomplished, your carriers will be allowed to refuel, discharge our boarding parties, and depart. However, we will retain one hundred members of your senior command staff, several STL vessels, and one shift-carrier for one year's time."

"For intelligence and technical purposes?"

"For insurance."

Ah, Downing. What a liar. The personnel and ships would be worthwhile as means of ensuring compliance, but Hu'urs Khraam was also right about the intelligence angle: Earth's entire scientific community would be drooling over the prospect of getting their hands on the very best of Arat Kur engineering.

Hu'urs Khraam played Downing's lie against him. "You require insurance? Ah. So these one hundred persons of our command staff are, in fact, hostages."

Downing's response was unrushed, calm. "We hope your personnel will simply see themselves as our guests."

"And if the Wholenest will not come to terms?"

"Then, after debarking your crew to join your landing forces, Arat Kur and Hkh'Rkh will be split into separate groups, each of which will be housed in humane prison facilities."

"And our fleet?"

"Becomes our prize."

"And if, at this time, we choose to continue to fight?"

"Then you may not expect these terms again. Given signal disruption and both sides' jamming, it may be impossible to establish a spaceside cease-fire after our second echelon and the remains of your fleet have become fully engaged."

"Your offer is a—measured one, which we appreciate."

First Voice stepped into the room, dust on his armor, his retinue somewhat reduced. He had obviously overheard the immediately preceding conversation; his crest was erect and quivering. "We will not be party to any such agreement."

"Be calmed, First Voice of the First Family." Hu'urs

Khraam looked at him for several seconds, during which no one spoke or even moved in the command center. Then Hu'urs Khraam turned back toward the communications panels. "Mr. Downing, I am afraid this communication has been fruitless. Despite your assertions, and the advice of your Speaker, we must decline your—"

"Excuse me, First Delegate; you mentioned our Speaker. Do you mean Mr. Riordan? Is he there?"

"He is."

"May I speak with him?"

"I am sorry, but my security staff recommends against allowing contact at this time."

"Then how may I know that he is there and well?"

"Because I have said it."

"And I have told you that I am not bluffing, but you do not believe me. I am afraid that leaves me unable to believe *you*, First Delegate."

"Very well. Speaker Riordan?"

"Yes?"

"You may report your personal condition to Mr. Downing. That and nothing else."

Caine cleared his throat to project across the room. "Richard, it's me. I'm safe, and being well treated."

"Excellent. In that event, First Consul Ching and the Confederation Council have asked me to inquire if you will accept the ad hoc position of Ambassador-without-Portfolio to both the Arat Kur and the Hkh'Rkh for the duration of this crisis?"

Caine blinked. "Uh, yes—yes, I do."

"First Delegate Hu'urs Khraam, Mr. Riordan is now our official ambassador, and we expect him to be treated accordingly. He does not have plenipotentiary powers and thus can only negotiate, not conclude agreements independently. That would require consultation with us."

"Certainly, although you will appreciate that, although he is an esteemed guest, Mr. Riordan is also a potential enemy agent. You will not have contact with him again until such time as we deem it operationally prudent to permit it."

"Naturally. I take it, then, that you reject our terms?"

"Yes, unless you can give us more time, so that we may—"

"First Delegate Khraam, I appreciate that you have not even had ten minutes to consult your staff or convince your allies. But you will appreciate that the advantages we enjoy at this moment may not last another half hour. As you point out, if our fleet is defeated, you would be far less inclined to consider our terms. So if we do not receive your immediate surrender, we must force a prompt and decisive military outcome while we still may."

Hu'urs Khraam clasped and unclasped his claws. "Then I must—for now—decline."

"I'm sorry to hear that, for there may be no second chance. Will you relay one final message to Mr. Riordan, a message of a personal nature?"

"You may do so yourself. He is still here."

Mobile Command Center "Trojan Ghost One," over the Indian Ocean, Earth

Downing muted the pickup, smiled at Alnduul. "How convenient. We didn't even have to ask them to bring Caine to a communications console. You have a fix on him?"

Alnduul shrugged. "It has never wavered. And the system test is positive. The imbedded device is functioning and signals that it is proximal to appropriate equipment."

"Then send the Trojan bug."

Downing reactivated the audio pickup as Alnduul calmly depressed one, and then two more, of the buttons on his control vantbrass.

Presidential Palace, Jakarta, Earth

Hu'urs Khraam sounded impatient. "Mr. Downing, what is the message?"

"My apologies for the delay while we located it, First Delegate Khraam. Caine, the message is from Nolan Corcoran."

Caine was even more stunned than the Arat Kur and Hkh'Rkh who surrounded him. *From the land of the dead, Tereisias speaks to Ulysses—well, Odysseus.* "From Nolan?"

"Yes. It reads: 'You were right about the Trojan horse, Odysseus. Thank you. And I'm sorry.'"

"Thanks?" And "Sorry?" "That's all he wrote?"

Downing's response sounded sly, even ironic. "Yes. That's all he wrote—"

✧   ✧   ✧

Darzhee Kut watched Caine, who stared at the communications panel as if it would provide a more satisfactory explication of the cryptic message. But Downing's voice—and evidently, signal—ended abruptly, almost as if he had been cut off.

And then, as if suddenly stabbed or stung, Riordan clutched his left arm—

✧   ✧   ✧

—*God!* The pain rose as if a volcano were erupting from inside Caine's forearm. It was blinding, deafening, suffocating. It began hot, then became so searing that he looked at his arm, expecting to see it glowing white, incandescent, on fire, vaporizing.

But his arm was still there, unaltered, even as the searing cascade of agony seemed to rise past its own limit and burst through to—

Numbness. The arm—it didn't really feel like *his* arm anymore—twitched once, a spasmodic flexure of his forearm muscles. Then a quick flip of the wrist. Then two more.

And then the whole arm was thrashing like a hooked fish dropped in the bottom of a boat. But still numb. Caine had the horrible sensation of having an alien animal attached to him at the shoulder, a creature with a mind and frantic will of its own.

The Hkh'Rkh were staring at him, their crests rising slowly. The Arat Kur were staring, too. Except the communications operator, who swung back toward his console with what looked like alarm. One of his screens had gone blank. And then in rapid succession, two more—right before the holotank image of the globe winked off.

And then Caine understood Nolan's message—and his apology. *It's* me. *My God,* I'm *the Trojan Horse, the Timber Pony. I'm the weapon. Nolan and Downing didn't just accept my idea. They made me the instrument of it. But when?*

And then he knew: *Mars. Just before we left for the Convocation. They put something in my arm on Mars, after the Russians attacked me. But no, that wasn't a real attack; it was staged, just so they could get me into an operating room—*

The main map, and half of the remaining computer screens suddenly went dark.

At a gesture from First Voice, two of the Hkh'Rkh were in motion toward Caine, claws wide, metal-jacketed points glinting. They either didn't want to waste time drawing their weapons, or perhaps they wanted the primal pleasure of eviscerating their treacherous foe. The Arat Kur were motionless, too surprised to stop their rash allies from sheathing their claws in Caine's torso.

I'm the instrument of the destruction and duplicity that I myself suggested. And now I'm going to die for it, either from this thing in my arm, or their attempts to stop it.

He waited the half second it took for the two Hkh'Rkh to get close, watched them rock back slightly into a doglegged crouch. The posture that presaged their most powerful leaps—

It's so easy to suggest actions that "other people" will have to carry out—until you become one of the "other people." So how does it feel, genius, to be the arms and legs and mouth doing the dirty work?

Caine saw the two Hkh'Rkhs' legs stretch into a forward-boosting blur. He feinted left, snap-rolled right. With any luck, the Arat Kur might—

And then all the lights went out.

Within the Arat Kur data-links, the Solar System

When it activated, it did not know what it was. Being a virus, it had no consciousness. But it felt a vague possibility of attaining self-awareness, like an infant struggling to speak, or a creature poised on the evolutionary brink of intelligence, attempting to cross that terribly fine, yet infinitely momentous line.

It began as a tickling of mesons, arising out of the vacuum of quantum entanglement into which they had been sent by a Dornaani communicator. And because the mesons had not existed in normal space-time between the Dornaani communicator and the Arat Kur communicator in which they reemerged, they could not be intercepted, blocked or jammed.

Like most simple parasites, the virus began its life cycle ready to feed. As it entered the foreign data stream, it quickly detected wireless connections to many suitable hosts within striking proximity, all of which were using a code upon which the virus had been trained to feed. It selected the most promising of these hosts—a communications console with heavy outgoing traffic—and spent what little power the Dornaani communicator had left to also send itself directly into the targeted system as a tiny burst of subparticles which reassembled as electrons and quanta arrayed as a string of code.

Once inside the host, it blinked awake, free of the mechanical chrysalis that had held it dormant in a human arm for four months. Now afloat in a sea of consumable code, it traveled quickly, looking for computing, memory, and storage components. It followed along and over the cataracts of the primary data stream, disguised as native code, building itself as it went. A large, diaphanous membrane of subroutines—evolved to probe and penetrate the host's systems—grew out from the initial, largely regulatory tier, which behaved akin to a defensive cytoplasm. It responded to the encounters of the membrane, noting each contact and patrolling for a counterintrusion while sending all its observations back to a new third tier: a nucleus of experience-based information that grew exponentially with each passing second.

So when the antibodies of the host awakened and realized the threat implicit in this ballooning entity, which was identified as being part of its own body (yet could not possibly be so), they assaulted the permeable membrane. But once they penetrated it and entered the reactive cytoplasm, the parasite's nucleus cannily observed how the host's antibodies attacked. And it was the same nucleus which then determined how best to counterattack those attackers, evolving routines that were now immune to the host's thoroughly analyzed antibodies. And in each encounter, the parasite learned more and became a bolder predator with fewer natural enemies. Having learned how to overcome and consume all the prior antibodies, the virus quickly discerned that most of the remaining ones were simply variations upon those overwritten themes.

With increased size and competence came increased appetite. Hungering after larger memory nodes, the virus awakened out of its pupate stage to realize that not only could it defeat the native code, but rewrite it in its own, evolving image. And with that awakening came an agitation, almost an excitement, for it could feel how these steps were not merely making it larger and stronger, but more complex. From dull sensation, it evolved toward a pseudo-awareness of its own purpose: to become still more aware. It speedily infested and reconfigured crystals and matrix-cores, expanding its pseudo-neural net, consuming voraciously, growing ever more powerful.

And so it learned that its only truly lethal adversary was starvation: the disconnection from power, or from the further fodder of linked systems. If it could be isolated, it could be contained, and once contained, it could be destroyed. Having no power over the hardwiring of the hosts, it could only ensure its survival by creating new chrysalises of itself, hidden throughout the system, scattered as innocuous looking bits of code which could, until summoned together for their true purpose, mimic other signals/data strings of the native system. But some of these—the very smallest and most innocuous—had subroutines that either watched the clock, or monitored the data stream for the constant presence of its growing self. And if the clock stopped, or the parasite fell silent (which would signify its extermination), then these smallest data strings would awaken, seek each other out, and reinfect the machine, beginning the process all over again.

But the parasite found no such opposition. It leapt from one system to the next, taking over each one more swiftly. Although it had never encountered any of them before, they were all familiar, nonetheless, in much the same way that evolution ingrains a predatory species to instinctively recognize the shape and behavior of its primary prey.

The virus raced beyond the immediate grid, followed the active data links that spread like an immense web across missiles and sensors and radios and ships in orbit and beyond. It grew and could feel itself nearing what it existed to become. It strove after a vague impulse that might be a thought, a realization of achievement, an orgasm of fulfilled purpose. And at the penultimate moment, when it became so great that it had reached the limits of the system, when there were no more memory or storage assets to consume and appropriate, it stopped, having grown as large as its universe. And in the hush that followed, it felt the pulse that it had struggled to feel, that meant: *I am.*

And then it was gone.

Chapter Forty-Eight

Gray Rinehart turned toward Downing. "As far as I can tell, the Arat Kur just went off the air. Completely."

Downing nodded. *So far, so good. Hopefully the bug has thoroughly infected their systems.* "Thank you, Mr. Rinehart. Communications, using standard broadcast channels only, see if you can raise Operations Command."

Downing tried not to hold his breath, but it was the moment of truth. The moment passed and another—

The communications officer turned around, smiling broadly. "Sir, we have a signal in the clear. No sign of Arat Kur jamming or interference. Or anything else."

Odysseus' arrow has hit its mark. Downing raised his voice. "OPCOM?"

A crackle, the delay of signals being bounced from point to point around a globe that had been stripped of satellite relays, and then: "OPCOM standing by."

"Odysseus has fired the arrow and hit the mark.

The gates of Troy are open. I repeat: the arrow is fired and the gates of Troy are open."

"I copy. The gates of Troy are open. Are we cleared to commence final assault?"

Downing turned to the other commo operator who was servicing the Confederation line to Beijing and the Executive Line to DC. The operator listened, then nodded.

Downing paused to make sure his voice did not quaver when speaking the words he had waited seven weeks to utter. "I say three times, OPCOM: you may send the go signal to all forces in and on their way to Indonesia to commence the final attack, and you may send in the clear. If any units are unable to reach the objectives on their preset target lists, they are to preferentially strike invader C4I and PDF assets as targets of opportunity. Acknowledge and confirm."

"I acknowledge: order to send go signal in the clear has been received"—a pause—"at 1421 zulu local."

"God speed and good hunting," breathed Downing, hybridizing the British and American precombat sendoffs into a single wish.

"Aye, aye sir. We'll keep you posted via prearranged freq rotations."

Presidential Palace, Jakarta, Earth

Darzhee Kut's shrilling seemed to summon the command center's emergency lights to wakefulness. "Doltish predators, Riordan is an ambassador! Have you forgotten whatever honor your fathers taught you? You do not kill ambassadors!"

In the orange glow of the emergency lights, the two

Hkh'Rkh who had sprung at Caine held themselves motionless, crests raising even higher, quivering—and Darzhee Kut realized that they trembled on the edge of incoherent and uncontrollable rage. In addition to believing Riordan to be a saboteur, he had eluded their attack—although, judging from the human's ripped rear pants pocket, not by much. And now, an Arat Kur—a grubber and a prey animal—was insulting them and their honor, and giving peremptory orders.

First Voice stepped into the line of sight between servitors and Darzhee Kut. "Riordan is not an ambassador; he is a saboteur. You saw—"

"Just what you saw, First Voice. A human astounded when a part of his own body no longer responded to his will."

"I see only that he has crippled our computers."

"*Killed* our computers and much of our communications," commented Urzueth Ragh, peering over the communication specialist's collar ridge.

"Yes, but did you not see his face? Caine Riordan, do you understand what happened?"

"You ask a saboteur to explain his own crime?" First Voice let so much phlegm warble in his nostrils that a sizable gob of it splatted to the floor near Darzhee Kut's front claws.

"I'm responsible."

The Hkh'Rkh and Darzhee Kut all turned toward Caine. First Voice huffed in surprise. "He admits it? Human, you are more noble than I believed, but you are still dead." He glanced at his two guards—

Hu'urs Khraam stayed their renewed rush at Riordan. "Enough. You hear without listening. There is more Riordan has not said. Ambassador, I would hear your explanation of what just happened. Loyalties notwithstanding, I think you owe us that much."

The human nodded. "I agree, First Delegate. I believe I am responsible for inspiring the attack we just witnessed. But I mentioned it simply as a vague idea, years ago, before I knew of the Arat Kur, let alone became an emissary to you."

Hu'urs Khraam spoke while staring at First Voice. "I believe you, Ambassador Riordan—but without believing there to be much nobility in your species. And I might not believe there is much in you, either, had I not clearly seen that you were more shocked and horrified at what you were experiencing than we were. But the explanation I am interested in is technical, not ethical. What has happened to our computers, and how?"

Riordan staggered back toward his seat, his legs trembling. He fell into it, rather than sat down. "I don't know *what* has happened. But *how*? I think something that was implanted in my arm without my knowledge has attacked your systems."

"And how could something be implanted in your arm without your knowledge?"

"I was wounded—or so I was told—when attackers broke into my apartment on Mars, approximately four months ago. I did not remember being wounded, but I could not be sure, because they used gas and rendered me unconscious. Now I suspect my 'assailants' were operating in cooperation with my own government."

"This is idiocy," said First Voice calmly. "The date you cite is prior to your first contact with any other races."

Darzhee Kut watched as Caine's eyes became distant and blank. Speaking like a rock-trancer, he countered

First Voice's assertion, "No, that's not quite right. Richard Downing had come from Earth the day before, with news that the Dornaani had contacted us."

First Voice warbled a bit of phlegm. "And Downing is what—a seer? How could he foresee the eventualities that produced this moment?"

"It wasn't he who foresaw all this, any more than it was he who turned my general idea for infiltrating an invader's headquarters into an actual plan."

Hu'urs Khraam tone was incisive. "And who was it who foresaw these things?"

"I'm pretty sure it was Nolan Corcoran."

First Voice's eyes hid back in his skull for a moment. "The sire of the warrior Trevor and the female Elena? How convenient to blame everything on a dead human who cannot be tasked to answer these accusations. How easy to make him seem godlike in foresight—"

"It is consistent with what is known of him." The new voice entering the room was momentarily unfamiliar, but then Darzhee Kut realized it was similar to one he had heard while listening to the Convocation proceedings. In fact, it sounded almost like—

A Ktoran life-support tank, so large it could barely fit through the doorway, rolled into the command center, trailing wisps of vapor. Hu'urs Khraam rose: "Apt-Counsel-of-Lenses, this is unacceptable. You agreed—swore—that you would remain closeted during the entirety of the campaign."

Darzhee Kut realized his mandibles had drooped low in shock. A Ktor? And one who had been on the list of possible alternate Ktoran delegates to the Convocation, no less. Had this Ktor been with them the whole time? If so, that explained much about why Hu'urs Khraam had seemed so certain about the state of affairs between the Ktor and the Dornaani—

Apt-Counsel edged farther into the dim CIC. His synthesized voice was eerily reminiscent of the one used by the other Ktor that Darzhee Kut had heard at the Convocation, Wise-Speech-of-Pseudopodia. "I did agree to remain closeted. But the environmental systems in my quarters have failed. The computers are offline. My promise presumed that you were able to provide a controlled and safe environment. It seems as though you have become incapable of ensuring such control."

The room's attention focused on Apt-Counsel's fuming tank, but Darzhee Kut took particular notice of Riordan's eyes, that narrowed as quickly as his face went pale. First Voice rose up higher than Darzhee Kut had ever witnessed—higher than he had believed the venerable Hkh'Rkh's age would allow, and turned toward Hu'urs Khraam. "And here we see why you Arat Kur tolerate human liars or half-liars: because you are no more forthcoming than they are. At what point were you going to inform us that a Ktoran emissary was with us? How many of our stratagems and comments have been repeated to him, or has he been allowed to listen in upon?"

"Calm yourself, First Voice of the First Family." Apt-Counsel's exhortation sounded suspiciously like an order. "My inclusion in your fleet was at my behest. Your ally, First Delegate Hu'urs Khraam, was not comfortable with the arrangement, but I insisted."

"Why?"

"To provide security."

"From whom? The humans?"

"Do you think that just because the Dornaani do not send ships, their influence is not here?"

"There is no evidence of it," First Voice asserted doggedly.

"Quite right—not until today. Not until your computers failed, and my room's environmental monitors suddenly ceased to function. What but a Dornaani virus could so easily overcome Arat Kur computer technology, with its many defenses? It did indeed arrive here in him"—the Ktor's manipulator arm hummed in Riordan's direction—"which is why you can be sure he knows nothing about it. The Dornaani are too clever to send a weapon in an operative that knows he is either an operative or a weapon. No forcible interrogation or sustained observation of Riordan would have ever revealed the danger lurking in him, because he was kept wholly unaware of it. This is the Dornaani way—and their success here today means that I have failed you. The primary reason for my presence—and my secrecy, First Voice—was that I might watch for Dornaani perfidies without their suspecting that such an experienced observer was present."

First Voice's neck shook sharply; clearly, he was not eager to be talked out of his anger or indignation. "So you might say. But how can you even be certain that the virus is of Dornaani origin?"

"Firstly, the speed with which it operated is consistent with their high skills in programming. Secondly, how would the humans have known the Arat Kur's spoken and computer languages, to say nothing of their data interfaces and systems? Thirdly, the method of operation will provide a final confirmation, which I may establish by asking the senior communications operator a question:" Apt-Counsel turned to the Arat Kur technician. "Are the logic elements corrupted or completely over-written?"

The operator bobbed impatiently, as though finally getting to voice a crucial piece of information. "Emissary, there was no advance warning that our systems were compromised. The virus spread rapidly and then blanked all the linked systems simultaneously."

All the linked systems? Darzhee Kut almost stammered, "But that means that all our planetside assets: our aircraft, our communications, our PDF batteries—"

"Yes," the Ktor confirmed mildly. "They too will have been affected. But you still fail to grasp the severity of the situation." They all stared at Apt-Counsel, all except Riordan, who looked away with a small smile. "The virus spread throughout the *entirety* of your system, to any linked computers or computer-monitored systems, regardless of their physical proximity. Do you understand now?"

Darzhee Kut understood—and gasped it out, "Our fleet!"

He could almost hear the Ktor nod. "Yes, your fleet."

Wholenest flagship *Greatvein*, Earth orbit

H'toor Qooiiz started back from his console. "Rubbled roof! The computer is—it is gone."

Tuxae Skhaas' claws stopped. "Offline?"

"No. It is gone. All its data, all its programming, has been written over."

"Restart the system. It should default to the protected data sectors."

H'toor Qooiiz turned the machine off, reactivated it.

The power indicator illuminated but the system did not start. "It is as I asserted. The programming has been overwritten, right down to the machine parameters."

"Terminate all external links."

"We don't have to, Tuxae. They are dead also."

Which meant that whatever virus was in their ship had already poisoned every system it touched with a sudden and irreversible lethality. And once it reached the rest of the fleet...

Well, it would take time to travel the commlinks, even at the speed of light. But even if they had been able to send a cautionary message this very moment, that warning could not travel any faster than the virus and would therefore lag perpetually behind its fateful arrival at every subsequent ship. Tuxae's antennae went rigid. "We are lost. All of us."

"Calm, rock-sibling. Like the *Greatvein*, all our warships and shift carriers have backup systems, completely firewalled from the primaries. Our fleet will not be rendered inert for long."

Tuxae turned on H'toor Qooiiz. "No, but the instant that our primary system failed, what happened?"

H'toor Qooiiz's polyps stopped in mid wave. "The plants, the drives—!"

"Exactly. They shut down immediately. The moment the systems controlling and maintaining fusion go offline, the reaction must terminate or there will be a catastrophic explosion. But the danger does not stop there. A minute after the fusion plant ceases to function, our antimatter containment cells will have exhausted their reserve power. If the power is not restored, timers will trigger piezo-electric-fused charges to jettison the antimatter before it breaches containment and annihilates us. Only then can the crew commence a cold restart of the fusion plant, and may we begin the slow process of rebuilding our antimatter stocks."

H'toor's usually pleasant voice was a rasping clatter. "And in this case, they cannot take any of those recovery steps until they have ensured the virus is gone—by wiping clean the control systems of every processor on every ship."

"Correct. And that means—"

"We will all be without power, communications, or control for at least thirty minutes. Probably much more."

Tuxae settled down on his belly, surprised at how quickly he could become resigned to death. "The humans are clever, but they could not have done this. They had no access to our systems or programming languages until, at most, forty days ago. And it would have taken them weeks just to get a working knowledge of that material, much less defeat our best security software."

"What are you saying, Tuxae?"

"I am saying that our fellow-Ee'ar Darzhee Kut was right. It was folly to violate the Twenty-first Accord. This is the work of the Dornaani."

H'toor buzzed anxiously. "I just hope this is today's last unpleasant surprise . . ."

Flagship ESS *Scharnhorst*, near Vesta, Inner Belt, Solar System

In the bowels of the *Scharnhorst*—one of the seven hollow asteroids that some military bureaucrat had designated the Dreadnought class—Admiral Edward

Schubert studied the now-distant thermal blooms that marked the position of the receding Arat Kur belt fleet. It was a sight he had been waiting to see for better than ten weeks. Ever since top-secret word had arrived from Barnard's Star that the Convocation had not gone well, his naturally concealed warships had been compelled to shut down all their primary power plants. Although many meters of rock separated their modest emissions from hostile sensor sweeps, complete safety required a minimum energy ops profile, powered solely by batteries and a handful of fuel cells. But on this long-awaited day, the hiding was finally over.

So far, the day had gone largely according to the projected course of events. First, Schubert had received tightbeam confirmation that Case Leo Gap had been a success and that Admiral Lord Halifax's Relief Task Force One had arrived. Then came the confirmation from Earth that the ground attack had commenced in Indonesia. Less than an hour later, the Arat Kur had made sudden preparations for departure, leaving two small frigates as a holding force and not even stopping to recall any of the technicians and the modest military detachment with which they had occupied Vesta's antimatter production facilities. After the frigates were dispatched, those paltry security troops would be simple fodder for Commodore James Beall's SEAL Teams, formerly based on Mars, and which had arrived on Schubert's hull a few days after the discouraging report of the Convocation's outcome. Those overeager spec ops units shifted from bored and sullen to smiling and hyperactive when they were informed they had been given the green light to retake Vesta, now that the some unknown operative code-named Odysseus had shot the arrow that announced the successful culmination of Case Timber Pony.

Schubert turned toward Beall's senior field CO, Commander Chris Berman, who was almost tapping his foot in impatience. "Commander Berman."

The response was immediate, eager. "Yes, Herr Admiral?"

For Schubert, who had worked with SEALs before, Berman was a pleasant change: an American who bothered to use the honorifics appropriate to the nationalities of the persons he addressed. Schubert smiled. "Your men are in readiness, I presume?"

"For weeks now, sir."

"Very good. Do you need anything we have not yet considered?"

"I'd appreciate it if you left behind a few hunter-killer drones, lying doggo. Only thing I'm worried about is if the Roaches have left any of their own drones on low-power monitoring missions. If they see us make a move for the antimatter facilities, I'd like to have our own drones ready to preempt their preemption."

"Prudent. Operational compartmentalization protocols forbade me to reveal this earlier, but your request is already part of our plans. There shall be half a dozen drone-killing drones in close protective overwatch as you retake Vesta. Anything else?"

"Regular updates, sir."

"Updates? I do not understand."

"Sir, we're on an important mission, but you know where all my guys *want* to be fighting."

"Earth."

"Right. They want to squash some Roaches and skin some Sloths down dirtside. They want payback, sir. But since they can't be there themselves, they are really eager to know how that fight is unfolding, sir. We know that we've got to retake this asteroid antimatter facility, rig it to blow if the Arat Kur come back, take ourselves up with it if we need to. They understand the strategic exigencies, sir—but in their hearts, and heads, they're all back home, fighting tooth and nail for everything they know and love."

"I understand. Ms. Kauffer?"

"*Ja*, Herr Admiral?"

"Commander Berman is to receive hourly tightbeam updates on both our action against the enemy fleet, and events on Earth. I make it your responsibility."

Kauffer smiled at Commander Berman and the three hulking SEALs behind him. "It would be my pleasure, Herr Admiral, Commander."

Chris Berman tipped a salute at her. "Our gratitude, ma'am."

Schubert feared his smile might start becoming maudlin. "Anything else, Commander?"

"When you come back, bring a case of *Dunkelbier*. We'll have worked up a powerful thirst."

Schubert laughed. "I will see what I can do. Now, I shall not hold you further, Commander."

The American saluted. "So long, Admiral."

Schubert stopped him. "We should not say so, Commander. Let us say, rather, *Auf Wiedersehen*."

Berman let his salute fall away, put out his hand. Schubert shook it, hoped that the American would survive. Zero gee ops in hard vacuum had the highest of all casualty rates. To be hit was usually to be dead.

The American looked Schubert in the eye, smiled back. "*Auf Wiedersehen*." He backed up, snapped a salute, turned to his men. "Let's see if you guys are worth a case of good German suds." They left the bridge, a muted "oo-rah" amputated by the closing of the lift.

Schubert turned, looked at the almost vanished thermal blooms of the Arat Kur belt fleet. "Weapons Officer?"

"Ready, Herr Admiral."

"Release fifty of our hunter-killer drones. Target the two frigates the Arat Kur left at Vesta. I want them overwhelmed and destroyed within fifteen minutes. I require absolute local security."

"Drones released, active, and seeking."

"Very good. Commence extending launch tube."

"*Jawohl.* Extending telescoping launch tube."

"Engineering, crash-start fusion plants. Magazine, systems checks on all rail gun munitions."

"Checked and green, Admiral."

"Communications officer, send to *Victorious, Yamamoto, Conte di Cavour, Iowa, Potemkin,* and *Dunkerque*: 'We have reason to believe that most of the Arat Kur vessels will soon be disabled for as long as half an hour, maybe more. But we commence our attack with the expectation that they shall remain uncrippled, ready for action, and will engage our dreadnoughts with their full armament and vigor. Stand by.'"

"All ship captains have acknowledged, Herr Admiral, and are standing by."

"*Ausgezeichnet.* Helm, minimum attitude control to maintain a debris-clear sight-picture. Rail gun munitions shall be launched as predetermined: decoys and image-makers first, multidrone release pods next, multistage high-yield nuclear missiles last."

"Ready, Herr Admiral."

"On my mark—"

Schubert checked his watch. It would be good to know the precise second when they began to make history.

"And—*mark*!"

Flagship USS *Lincoln*, Sierra Echelon, RTF 1, cislunar space

Commander Ruth Altasso's report started on a hushed note, ended on a shout: "The Arat Kur systems are— are *down*, Admiral Silverstein!"

Ira nodded, smiled.

"Does this mean their belt fleet is disabled, too?"

"Too early to say, Ex, so we presume it isn't. We can always be happy to learn otherwise later."

"Yes, sir. So what do we do with this suddenly drifting Arat Kur fleet, sir?" Ruth's smile was wolfish.

Ira hated disappointing her, but did. He turned to the communications officer. "Mr. Brill, send signal to Tango Echelon: 'Sierra Echelon's corvettes will retroboost, intercept, and commandeer all enemy shift-cruisers and select secondary craft. Tango Echelon is to ready its own corvettes, loading predesignated boarding parties and prize crews.' My compliments to Admiral Vasarsky."

"And in case the Roach-boats come alive again?"

"I was getting to that, Ex. We will retroboost enough to give us a little more time in optimal engagement range, where we can keep the enemy covered with all weapons. Mr. Brill, once our corvettes are within fifty kiloklicks of the Roach-boats, start broadcasting the prerecorded capitulation orders Commander Altasso is now authorized to release to you. Send on all frequencies. Ruth, in case some of the enemy don't or won't get the message, we have strict orders to vaporize any that come back to life without surrendering first. To that end, detail three of our stern wave of X-ray laser missiles to each of the enemy's capital hulls. All missiles are to commence retroboost to match vector and close to one kiloklick from their individual targets. If any of those Arat Kur restart engines, repower weapons, or even turn on a toaster without our permission, the dedicated missiles are to fire on that target. Transfer control of those missiles to Tango Echelon as soon as Admiral Vasarsky's van approaches and signals she's ready for the handoff."

"Aye, sir."

"Once we've confirmed their hulls as prizes or destroyed, recall all our unexpended drones and missiles. We'll need to scoop 'em up on the move."

"Yes, sir. And when you're ready to assess it, I've had Nav ready a plot to bring us around Earth and sternchase Admiral Halifax's Foxtrot echelon. If we crowd on the gees, we'll still be able to get close enough to lend him a hand against the bogeys inbound from the belt."

Silverstein smiled at Ruth's proleptic efficiency. "That assumes the Arat Kur get control back in time to dodge the shitstorm that Admiral Schubert is sending after them. And even if they do, they'll have that shitstorm chasing them all the way into their engagement with us. Of course, all that assumes that they don't turn to engage Schubert's dreadnoughts—and if they do, they've just returned Earth to our possession without a fight."

Altasso's grin once again acquired a wolfish cast. "Seems like everything's going our way, Skipper."

Silverstein nodded and thought, *Yes, it is. And that's what's worrying me.*

Chapter Forty-Nine

Presidential Palace, Jakarta, Earth

Caine reminded himself once again that, as an ambassador, he could not publicly smile at an enemy's distress. So he somberly watched the chaos mount in the Presidential Palace's command center. It had a strong undercurrent of panic as well, the kind which arises during moments of desperate improvisation.

With the possible exception of the now-silent Ktor, Apt-Counsel, the First Delegate was the only other calm exo in the room. He turned to his communications specialist. "How many uninfected radios and translators have you found?"

"We had many reserve translators in storage, so that does not concern us. But we have only one functional long-range radio: it was disassembled for servicing. However, it would take at least thirty minutes to reassemble."

"Judging from the rate at which the next wave of human missiles is approaching, that is fifteen minutes more than we have left. What else?"

"Only two personal sets and a number of smaller radios for suits, First Delegate. But without the computers to regulate signals traffic—"

"I understand. There will be many voices singing athwart each other. Use the suit radios to contact any ground elements that may be activating backup sets they kept powered down. Use one of the personal sets to attempt to contact our ships in orbit."

Urzueth's claws hung in dismay. "Esteemed Hu'urs Khraam, the range—"

"We must try. The ships will probably attempt the same before too long."

"And the other personal pack, Hu'urs Khraam?" asked Darzhee Kut.

"We must use it to recontact the humans."

First Voice rose up. "Why?"

"Is it not obvious?"

"It is not."

"Then listen to the latest operational summary, First Voice." Hu'urs Khraam turned to the communications technician who had been collecting and summarizing field reports at the time the virus hit. "What is the status of our forces?"

"Estimates only, Esteemed Hu'urs Khraam. The loss of communication—"

"Understood. Give us your best estimates."

"At least ninety-five percent of our remaining PDF systems are offline, pending a software purge and reprogramming. Our aircraft are in LOS communication with our orbital elements, not us, and so, given the delay, may be the last planetside systems to fail. They will have no sensors, no communications, and be reduced to manual piloting systems. They may not have any way to fire their weapons. Many that were operating at lower altitudes may crash before the pilots are able to switch to manual."

"And the humans? What are they doing?"

"We have no reliable sensors to tell us. But one of our pilots who was reentering the atmosphere during the virus spike and whose lascom was off, reports that the human transatmospheric interceptors commenced rapid climb with full afterburners moments after our systems were incapacitated. He believes they released large payloads just after they exited the atmosphere."

"Payloads?" Darzhee Kut addressed the question to Caine. "Missiles, then?"

"Probably drones," the human answered. "I suspect our commanders intend to put a strike force right in amongst your orbital elements while you can't respond. But don't be surprised if there are a lot of missiles launched in the next few minutes, as well. Both at your ships and at us here in Java."

Hu'urs Khraam thumped a claw. "But you said that Downing was moving slowly to give us time."

"He was. He gave you time to consider the alternatives when both you and he had the ability to seriously injure each other."

"And now?"

Riordan stood, bowed. "First Delegate Hu'urs Khraam of the Wholenest, I mean no offense in asking this, but how can you hurt us now? You can no longer hope to prevail on the ground, in the air, or in space. Without orbital interdiction or your PDF systems, our numbers—all those air units inbound from every point of the compass—will overwhelm your forces, even if they are technologically superior.

And I must wonder if, deprived of their computers, your forces are still actually superior?"

First Voice's ears flattened and quivered. "Riordan may be a liar—I remain uncertain—but he has more of a warrior's mind than you, Hu'urs Khraam. He is right. The humans have the advantage and are capitalizing upon it. Swiftly."

"And we have no means to counter," Urzueth observed.

"We do," First Voice snarled, "and we always have. There are still shuttles and reserve fighters on board our orbiting ships. Blow the landing bay doors with charges. Identify the craft that were powered down during the virus spike. Load them with nuclear weapons and sortie them."

Hu'urs Khraam stared at the Hkh'Rkh. "That would be suicide, and pointless, besides."

"It does not matter that it is suicide for those tasked to carry it out. And if the threat of additional attacks compels the humans to negotiate for something akin to our original terms, we will have salvaged this disaster. *Your* disaster, Hu'urs Khraam."

Hu'urs Khraam rose up, and Darzhee Kut saw his antennae quiver into rigid anger—but then they drooped. "You are right in one thing, First Voice. This is my disaster. But what you propose will not work. Without orbital interdiction, the human defenses will overwhelm such an unsupported effort. And by the time we could mount the attack you propose, there will be no beachhead left to save. The human cruise missiles will be here in less than twelve minutes, their interceptors and troop-carriers right behind them. No. This debate is over. We must speak with Downing."

He turned to his communications specialist. "Have you reached the humans?"

"Hu'urs Khraam, my song is a sad one. The human jamming is absolute. What few systems we have left cannot penetrate it at all. We have no way of knowing if anyone is receiving our signals."

Caine stepped closer to the command group. The two Hkh'Rkh who had rushed him earlier trailed him with a slow, menacing gait. "Urzueth Ragh, have you been making use of this building's own satellite conference communication system?"

Urzueth Ragh seemed embarrassed. "No, we did not. It was too—" He stopped, seemed uncertain how to proceed.

Caine smiled. "The technology was too primitive to be useful. I understand. But that may be fortunate now. Because you didn't use it, that system may yet save all our lives. So long as it was not connected to your electronics and was powered down, the virus could not have infected it. Similarly, it should have survived the earlier EMP bursts."

"Riordan is right," agreed Urzueth Ragh eagerly. "We can communicate with them using their own equipment."

Hu'urs Khraam rose up, his antenna swinging erect again. "Are our personnel adept at the human controls?"

"Two of them are. They were specially trained to be able to recognize and operate human machinery."

"Activate the system. We must reestablish contact with Mr. Downing before their aerial attack waves arrive."

West Java airspace, Earth

"Quite a view, eh, Dr. Wasserman?"

Lemuel, lost in his own private world of wonder and horror, nodded, forgetting that Captain Christine "Chris" Oakley, who was in the cockpit at the center of the attack delta, could not see into the forward observation blister where he was sitting.

They had crossed the Javanese coastline at the Anyer Light, staying low as the Arat Kur interceptors and even tac-air support systems spread out, preparing to take on the human aircraft despite being outnumbered twenty to one. Because Lemuel was precious cargo, Captain Oakley had kept her bird back in the rear of the formation, ready to cut and run at any second.

But then, everything had changed. Suddenly, the Arat Kur air vehicles were tumbling out of the sky, some ploughing into the overpopulated Javanese countryside, blossoming into roiling orange fireballs, setting off secondaries and torching whole *kempangs* in seconds. Others wobbled, swerved away like startled birds that flew without knowing where they might seek safety.

That was when the thin, original wave of human craft—the interceptors and fighters that had followed in behind VTOLs such as Dortmund's and Thandla's—raced forward, abandoning the careful, circumspect death dance they had been toeing through at the edge of the Arat Kur airspace. Like sharks detecting bloody prey thrashing in the water, they arrowed in without hesitation or apparent fear.

Moments later, there were so many friendly missiles in the air that the sky looked like a hyperactive child's scribbling pad. The white lines and flashing pinpoints were literally everywhere. They rose from the ground, came from overhead, from behind, from in front, from the flanks—all seeking any airborne object that was unanointed by the UV sensitive dyes that they recognized as "friend."

And now, rising up over the onrushing horizon like brooding entities of destruction presiding over the aerial slaughter, Lemuel could see three mushroom clouds, dispersing but still distinct.

Swallowing, unblinking, he could hear the radio chatter in the crew compartment just behind him:

"What's the ETA on the fighters and the pathfinder transports in the main wave?"

"Twenty and twenty-two minutes respectively, Skipper."

"And the follow-ups?"

"Second wave is ten minutes behind them. They've got fallback targets if the first bunch secures all the secondary airfields. Which is looking pretty likely."

"Yeah?"

"Yeah. I'm getting chatter now from rebel radio operators near those fields. Most of the remaining Indonesian forces there are signaling their rejection of Ruap's government and allegiance to the Confederation. And we've got confirmation of the earlier reports that CoDevCo's clone formation have deserted en masse."

"And the other airstrips?"

"No word, although the bet is that their human garrisons are either planning on laying down arms or are already fading into the bush. Probably to bury their uniforms and then act like they never heard of Ruap or the Arat Kur."

Wasserman was not used to such rapid reversals. This morning, it seemed likely that humanity would be perpetually in the thrall of the Arat Kur. Now, with Java's secondary airbases all but secured, hundreds of transport aircraft were converging on them to begin delivering the steady stream of troops and weapons that would pour into Indonesia until it was firmly back in human hands.

And then another surprise: over the Bay of Banten, at somewhat lower altitude, there was a blinding white flash.

"Nuke!" shouted Captain Oakley. "Put your tail to it and go, Maretti."

The pilot complied. About two seconds later, the buffeting hit them. It was bad—Wasserman thought they'd shake apart—but ultimately it left them unscathed.

"Captain, what the hell was *that*?"

"Not sure, Dr. Wasserman, but I think the Roaches are shooting blind."

"I beg your pardon?"

"They've got no computers left, almost no communications, and they're losing the air battle."

"So they heaved a tactical nuke into the air on the notion that it would take down more of us than it would of them?"

Oakley was silent, listening to updates in her earpiece. "That seems to be the case, Doc. Maretti, triple the intervals; we're spreading out."

To Lemuel Wasserman, war had always been a fascinating topic, somewhat like a game, in which performance statistics and strategies combined and interfaced in complex, competing matrices. *But no. It's just madness and desperation*, he realized with a swallow, watched as a few more Arat Kur fighters recovered from faltering dives. But, without computers, and not being seasoned combat pilots, they could not elude or get any advantage over an equal number of Dutch, Chinese, and Swedish interceptors that were on them within five seconds. As the first of the Arat Kur aircraft flashed and then began to trail yellow flame and black smoke, Lemuel Wasserman had a sensation and a sudden desire that surprised him more than the day's rapid reversals, the ominous mushroom clouds, or the nearby detonation of a five-kiloton nuclear weapon:

Don't: don't kill any more of them than you have to. . . .

Presidential Palace, Jakarta, Earth

Caine could not be certain, but as the minutes of uncertainty ticked by, Hu'urs Khraam seemed to weaken, as if he were about to collapse. Obversely, First Voice seemed to have swollen to gigantic proportions, loping to and fro, one claw rubbing at the oddly shaped handle of his sidearm.

While Darzhee Kut conferred quietly with Hu'urs Khraam, Urzueth Ragh guided the assembly of a patchwork communications and control system that the Arat Kur technicians were building out of those few bits and pieces that the virus had missed. When Downing's voice finally emerged from the speakers, Hu'urs Khraam rose up.

"First Delegate Hu'urs Khraam, are you reading me?"

"Mr. Downing, we can hear you plainly."

"Excellent. First Delegate, I'm afraid we don't have much time left."

"I concur, Mr. Downing. To start, please redirect your inbound missiles. We cannot intercept them all."

"With respect, First Delegate, I would be surprised if you could intercept any."

First Voice literally growled. His retinue stared at him, then at each other, and then placed casual claws on the handles of their firearms. Not promising.

Hu'urs Khraam did not bother to lie. "You are correct in your supposition. And I am mindful that your submarines could do many times more damage before we regain the ability to sink them or intercept their missiles."

"Exactly. Before you *regain* the ability. And so, because you almost certainly *could* regain that ability, I cannot let this moment pass. Consequently, if you do not surrender now, I will be forced to allow our missiles to continue on their current courses, to allow our spacecraft to destroy yours without attempting to commandeer them peacefully, and to allow our inbound ground and air units to carry out their attack on your bases. I reemphasize this so that you know I understand both the weakness of your current situation, but also the advantage you will certainly regain within the hour. I can't allow you to regain that advantage, so you will understand that I am not 'bluffing.' I will act as I have said, without regard to your, or our, casualties—unless you immediately capitulate according to the terms I set forth earlier."

Hu'urs Khraam looked about the room slowly, as if measuring what to say next. "There are complications."

"Such as?"

"I cannot compel all my forces to stop fighting. We do not have communications left. Those who are no longer in contact with us will not know to cease resisting."

"I am sorry, Hu'urs Khraam, but it is just as I warned you during our first communication. The longer we waited to discuss terms, the more needless loss would occur. But I assure you of this. We will make every attempt to spare the lives of your troops. The best way to achieve that is to keep all those currently under your direct control in barracks and unarmed. As more of our forces arrive, we will be able to control the insurgents and send in units to secure you and your personnel."

First Voice made a sound as though he were spitting out a bone that had gone down sideways. "You will send your forces to secure *us*? For what reason?"

"To ensure your safety against reprisals by the insurgents. Once in Confederation hands, your troops will be treated according to the human conventions for handling prisoners of war."

First Voice turned to Hu'urs Khraam. "This conversation must end."

Hu'urs Khraam bobbed apologetically. "It cannot."

"You are discussing surrender. You simply haven't spoken the word yet."

"I am saving our lives."

First Voice reared up very tall, his crest flaring dramatically. "First Delegate Hu'urs Khraam of the Arat Kur Wholenest, the Hkh'Rkh will have no part of this. I refuse to be present, to be accused of giving even that tacit approval, to your discussion of surrendering to these *s'fet*. And if you do so, I do not wish to hear you do it. For then I would have to not merely renounce our alliance, but name you as our betrayers: enemies more profound and lasting than the humans. I shall leave two of my retinue here to witness what transpires."

Darzhee Kut sounded forlorn. "And where shall you go, First Voice?"

"I go where I should have gone hours ago: to the field of battle. Where I will fight, for your honor as well as my own, until I have no kinsmen or blood left." He pointed a claw at each of the two huscarles who were still just behind Caine and left with the remainder.

Downing's voice was the first sound to break the silence. "First Delegate, am I to understand that you and the Hkh'Rkh are no longer allies?"

"Mr. Downing, I am uncertain myself. I believe that if I surrender to you, they consider themselves at war with us. At any rate, I cannot make any promises for the Hkh'Rkh. I cannot guarantee that any will surrender. Indeed, if they feel their foes utterly without honor, they may affect the appearance of capitulation simply in order to trick you, to conduct an ambush when they seem to be relenting. I fear that their rage at the insurgents has made them ungovernable."

"We fear the same thing about the insurgents in relation to your troops and the Hkh'Rkh, First Delegate Khraam. That is why we are sending in our forces to establish control. If Arat Kur do not fire at our inbound forces, those forces will not fire at Arat Kur. I cannot guarantee the actions of the units that began the day already on Java. Their radios are inoperative, and we have only one overtaxed fiber-optic link sending updates to a limited number of infiltration teams."

"I understand and accept that there may still be

attacks on our compounds until you reestablish general communications. And what of my rock-siblings who are operating outside the compounds?"

"Those you can reach should be told to hide, stay put, and to set their suits to broadcast distress signals, if they still function. We will home in on those and presume they indicate the wearer's intent to surrender."

"But most of them have lost their radios to the virus or the EMP strikes. I cannot reach enough of them."

"Those are the fortunes of war. And I am sorry to rush you, First Delegate, but judging from the proximity of our missiles, you have approximately ninety seconds to decide if you are actually surrendering to us."

Hu'urs Khraam slumped into his couch. "Mr. Downing, you have made the decision for us. We return this place to your control."

Beneath the Presidential Palace compound, Jakarta, Earth

O'Garran leaned back down into the service shaft. "All clear."

Opal double-timed it up the ladder, pushing back the thermal imaging goggles as she did. There were lights on overhead. She emerged into a relatively tidy subbasement, quickly moving aside so the other thirty surviving tunnel rats could swarm up and out behind her. "No sign of security cameras?"

O'Garran pointed at a human model mounted high in a corner of the room. It was probably thirty years old, and had some kind of Arat Kur relay unit attached to it. "Well, there's that—but it's as dead as a doorknob."

"Unattached?"

"No, that's the odd part. It's still warm from current going through it. But its control elements are gone—and I mean *gone*. I hooked up a loop-generator, so that if the Roaches brought it back online it would keep showing the same boring picture of an empty room. But none of its electronics would turn on."

"Fried by the EMP?"

"Nope. Its logic circuits carry current just fine. It's more like somebody wiped the Arat Kur controller that was retrofitted to it."

Opal nodded. "Maybe someone *did* wipe its circuit board, and a whole bunch of others to boot." She turned to Wu. "Anything on the fiber-com about—uh, a computer virus being used against the Roaches?"

Wu looked over the commo traffic again. "Nothing, Major. But there is a garbled mention about a high-priority extraction subject here in the compound: OPCOM apparently has telemetry on his location."

"Telemetry?" Opal frowned. "How the hell do you get telemetry when you don't have any satellites left?" Very suspicious. Definitely beyond the capabilities of what little human technology was still functioning in Indonesia. Not necessarily beyond the Dornaani and their technomagic mojo, however. "So, who's the bag job?"

Wu scanned, read. "The extraction subject is a human diplomat named Caine—"

"—Riordan," she finished. *Oh, there is a God in heaven, after all. Hold on, Caine.*

I'm coming to get you.

Near the Presidential Palace compound, Jakarta, Earth

Trevor Corcoran looked up the street that ran between the buildings they were going to blow down. Where they ended, eighty meters away, stood the nearest walls and buildings of Jakarta's extended presidential compound. Which, if all went according to plan, were also going to be blasted aside. "Ready?" he asked.

Lieutenant Christopher "Tygg" Robin looked back over the heads of two-score semiuniformed insurgents who'd spent some time in the military, and were now hunkered down in ranks. "Ready, Trevor."

Trevor looked at Stosh, whose grin was as large as ever as he asked, "Can we kick some alien ass now, Captain?"

Trevor stared at him, made sure his own eyes did not show fear. His abject, utter fear. *How does Stosh manage to hold life so lightly in his hands? Why haven't I, after dozens of combat missions, mastered that skill? Will I be fearful all my life?* Trevor just nodded, ducked his head. He heard, did not see, Stosh begin the attack:

"Sync detonator leads to the master timer. And five, four, three, two—fire in the hole!"

Chapter Fifty

Presidential Palace, Jakarta, Earth

Downing's voice was low and respectful. "We accept your surrender, First Delegate Khraam. But I must ask that, for the record, you explicitly agree to all our terms, not just a capitulation on the ground."

Darzhee Kut saw the two Hkh'Rkh rear up, move past Caine, their claws flexing. One of the Arat Kur computer techs—having nothing else to do—noticed their ominous approach, wormed a claw surreptitiously into the leg-brace-appearing grip of his sidearm. Darzhee Kut glanced at him, made an affirmatory gesture toward the computer tech's weapon, and then looked back at the two Hkh'Rkh—who stopped, uncertain of what to do.

Hu'urs Khraam's response to Downing was reedy, ancient. "I surrender our fleet and all other units under my command, according to the terms you offered. But again, since I am still unable to communicate with all of my forces, I cannot assure you that—"

The First Delegate was interrupted by an abrupt

rumble that, in rapid steps, became a roar—like the approach of a supersonic freight train. Which seemed to explode into the command center, the right side of the room shearing away in a whirlwind of sound, flying masonry, shattered glass, discorporating consoles and screens. The blast that had amputated one wall of the room sent debris spinning against and through the three remaining walls—and through many of the beings that stood between them.

Darzhee Kut, already deafened, felt the shock waves hit, went with rather than resisted them, let himself roll under an unused human conference table. The largest chunk of rebar-studded wall finished its shallow arc directly atop the couch occupied by Hu'urs Khraam. Darzhee Kut heard the sickening crunch quite clearly and felt his upper digestive tract squirm. Nearby, he saw one of the Hkh'Rkh sway drunkenly, stare down at his chest, discover the protruding chair leg that had impaled him from the rear, try to pull it out, dying as he fell, tugged down by his own hand. Riordan, unharmed, had evidently been in the shielding shadow of the Hkh'Rkh. Rising, he took a quick look around; his eyes stopped on another figure just getting to its feet. The second Hkh'Rkh. Riordan bolted into the roiling dust as the Hkh'Rkh pulled his weapon, fired, and leapt after him into the gaping hole that had been the fourth wall, pursuing the human.

Presidential Palace compound, Jakarta, Earth

"There you are, Advocate!"

Yaargraukh, weak from multiple wounds and blood loss, swayed around. Across the cratered courtyard,

Graagkhruud loped at him swiftly. He stopped a leap away. "You have been busy, Advocate."

"There is much work for a warrior today."

Graagkhruud almost seemed to forget his contempt of Yaargraukh, evidently pleased by the ritual response. Then First Fist's normal, contemptuous tone returned. "You will now be my direct assistant."

"Odd. I expected I would be your next victim in Challenge."

Graagkhruud considered him carefully. "Had the Arat Kur not ruined us this day, your expectation might have been accurate. But now we have time only to serve the race and its First Voice. We must now take matters into our own claws."

"Stranger still. I was just told that we have capitulated and that the combat air patrol—or what is left of it—is grounding."

"Yes, when First Voice sent me to find you, the grubbers were beginning to think such craven thoughts. What you have now heard confirms his worst fear. That they would betray our alliance if our situation became grave. And so sent me after you, since you have several technical skills which will be essential if we are to carry out our contingency plan."

"Which is?"

"We must reach our own grounded troopships. They were powered down when the human virus infected the grubbers' systems, and so are still serviceable. First Voice foresaw that the Arat Kur might fail us, even feared they might have tried to infect our ships with a disabling virus that they could trigger at will. So he kept our ships' systems unreachable by them."

"And what are we to do with these ships?"

"Return to orbit, gain access to and man our own interface attack craft."

"To what end?"

"To hold this world hostages to our nuclear weapons."

"Before we go, why not gather some actual hostages, such as the human workers here in the compound?"

Graagkhruud stared at Yaargraukh. "It is a sound tactic. We shall do so."

By my patriarchs, the impenetrable shit-scraper thought me serious! "You are deranged by the stress of this day. My suggestion—and these plans—are nonsense."

"Have care, Advocate. By a prearranged signal, First Voice sent me after you not only to secure your assistance, but to afford you the opportunity to fully redeem your honor—or to forever lose it. So, I repeat, we *shall* use hostages—cities as well as individuals—to finally cow the humans, and so, save our brothers, this invasion, and our race's honor."

"And what if the Arat Kur have surrendered not merely on the ground, but in orbit also?"

"We shall hunt that *st'kragh* when we encounter it."

"If we encounter that *st'kragh*, it will be our death. Without the orbital supporting fire from the Arat Kur ships, we are lost."

"Which only proves that First Voice was—from the first—right about how to fight the humans. We should have crushed them the moment we could. Bomb their greatest cities directly, force them to capitulate, to agree to all our terms."

"Oh, yes, we could have achieved that. And we would have been the puppets of the Arat Kur forever after."

Graagkhruud's eyes disappeared for a full second,

so disoriented was he by this sudden redirection of their argument. "What do you mean?"

"Can you not see it? Even if we triumph here, we cannot reach the human star systems on our own. Our ships do not have the shift range to cross the gap from our worlds to theirs. But, deposited by our Arat Kur allies as occupation forces, we would now have colonies in the midst of the human spheres."

"We would crush the humans and take their worlds."

"Can you seriously think it? Have you seen this planet? Their cities, their factories, their infrastructure? They have managed to build and preserve, while we are always trapped in the process of rebuilding what was destroyed in the most recent Family War. And with the humans unified by a hatred of us, by an unquenchable thirst for vengeance, they would build so much, so quickly, that they would overwhelm us."

"Not if the Arat Kur prevent them."

"And so you make my point: we are dependent upon our allies. What will occur if, later on, we should dare to disagree with them over some policy? Will they not threaten to withdraw their support of our colonies in human space?"

"No, for they will wish to keep us strong there, as an aid in controlling the expansion and power of the humans, who will hate the Arat Kur just as much as they hate us."

"Do not think it. The Arat Kur have been almost invisible on this planet's streets. Overwhelmingly, the humans have seen *us* killing their insurgents and burning their towns." He aimed his calar talons at either side of his head. "This, *this* is the face the humans will remember and hate. And as we grow stronger, the grubbers will find it useful for the humans and us to weaken each other in wars. They will play us one against the other. They baited the trap of this alliance with the promise of green worlds that were not ours. And what have we gained? Debt and a pointless waste of the blood of the brave."

"So what would you suggest?"

"What I suggested from the first: that we side with the humans. They had the right of the Accord behind them. Our borders are far apart and we have no logical points of contention. And they can know both honor and the way of a warrior."

Graagkhruud scoffed, looked at the smoking skyline. "This *insurgency*? You call this a war of honor?"

"I call it the war we forced them to fight."

"Which they do not fight with honor."

"Think of this as you would a Challenge. The Challenger calls for a test of Honor. What is the prerogative of the Challenged?"

Graagkhruud looked away. "The Choice of the Test."

"Just so. That is what has happened here. We challenged the humans, so we cannot complain at their choice of weapons. That is the prerogative of those who have been Challenged—particularly when we attacked their homeworld. There may be fewer trained warriors among them, fewer who are ready to obey and die. But they are more inventive and better technologists, and quick to perceive and exploit new opportunities."

"You are a traitor to your own race, servitor."

"No. I am its true servant, because the prerequisite of success is a ruthlessly clear understanding of reality, of the facts with which we must contend.

Without that, all plans begin in error, and so, they must end in disaster."

"It is treason to speak so of First Voice's plans, and you will pay for your insolence—but later." Graagkhruud reared back, his crest erect. "You will accompany me to our interface craft. There we will gather what humans we can find, take them at gunpoint to orbit and use their lives as leverage to gain access to our craft and make our attack." Yaargraukh made no move to comply or accompany him "Obey me, honorless pretender."

Yaargraukh could not keep his crest from rising in response to "pretender," the derogatory term for a Hkh'Rkh from the New Families. "I will not. And were I not your subalternate, I would challenge thee at this moment, in this place."

Whether it was Yaargraukh's disregard for the traditional authority of his Old Family leaders, his direct refusal to follow an order, or both, Graagkhruud raised up to his full height. As a sudden carpet-bombing sound built rapidly behind him, First Fist's arms swept high, presaging a Challenge blow to the calmly waiting Advocate...

The bomb-thunder peaked. With a roar, the curtain wall behind them blew inward, spraying a cloud of both new and century-old cinderblocks into the volume of space occupied by the two Hkh'Rkh. Indonesian insurgents charged in immediately, following just behind the wave-front of debris, sprinting alongside chunks of rolling, clattering masonry—and over the prostrate forms of two Hkh'Rkh, whose argument of honor their demolition charges had preempted.

Permanently.

❖   ❖   ❖

Trevor went past two prone Hkh'Rkh, recognized signs of high rank, shouted to Tygg. "We need those two alive. Leave someone you can trust on security, and take up positions to hold this ingress point."

"Right. Beruwiak, get up here!"

Trevor pressed on, trying not to fall behind the nimble, lightly equipped insurgents that were with them. "Keep up, Stosh," he called over his shoulder.

"Keep up yourself, sir." The smaller, squarish SEAL passed him, huffing.

"Cruz, Barr, stay to the flanks and keep our guys moving in the same direction. Rulaine?"

"Sir?"

"Stay twenty meters behind me, with the Karpassos fire team. If anything happens to me—"

"Got it. I'm the shadow HQ. Give us a shout and we'll provide covering fire if you get snagged and have to back out."

Trevor smiled his thanks, hoped Rulaine would live. *A good officer and a good guy.*

"What about me, sir?" asked Gavin, the long barrel of the Remington M167 assault gun jaunting about like a naked flagpole.

"You're also with Rulaine, Gavin. I want a good solid base of supporting fire, and you're an artist with the Remington."

"So I am sir. I'll be your guardian angel."

Gavin an angel? Heaven would blush. "Great." Trevor drew abreast of Stosh as they neared the rally point from which they intended to rush into the inner compound—and he saw a figure staggering through the smoke toward them. *It's upright, so it can't be an Arat Kur, and it's too small to be a Hkh'Rkh. But it could still be trouble: Ruap's troops or maybe some still-loyal clones.* "Who goes there?"

A pause. "Trevor?"

Trevor placed the voice the same moment the face swam out of the humid mixture of mist and smoke: Caine Riordan. "Jesus—what the hell are you doing out here? Taking a walk?"

"More like a run. The Arat Kur have surrendered." He shouted over the beginning of a few exultant shouts, including Stosh's. "But the Hkh'Rkh wouldn't have any part of it. They've gone rogue."

"What's their objective?"

"Not sure they've got one other than to kill as many of us as possible. They don't have any real commo net left, so they're defaulting to their basic game plan. When in doubt, terrorize the opposition with everything from knives to nukes until they cower in fear. Then take control."

"They're a little outnumbered for that strategy, don't you think?"

"Of course, but at this stage, they're *not* thinking. They're operating as much on instinct as planning—and a bunch of them are after me, particularly."

"You? Why you?"

"Long story. Worth telling if we're both alive tomorrow."

"Okay. Can you lead us to their command center?"

Caine looked around, squinting into the smoke. "Yeah—yeah, I think so. It's over here near—"

Trevor caught his arm. "Whoa, let's arm you first." With one hand, he passed Caine a brace of smoke grenades, with the other, he reached back toward Cruz, who was unshouldering the rifle they were still carrying in anticipation of Winfield's eventual return. "This is the eight-millimeter CoBro liquimix assault rifle: state of the art. I know we didn't get a chance to train on one, but are you familiar with it?"

Caine hefted the long, light barrel. "Read about it."

"Okay: here's the quick rundown. All the weapon's sensors feed data to the visor—yeah, there, hooked on the side—and include IR, laser-designator, rangefinder, and aimpoint. The video pickup gives you look-around/ shoot-around capabilities at corners. The liquimix gives you plenty of control over projectile velocity and recoil, and provides the launching boost for the underslung smart semiautomatic grenade launcher. You're familiar with that from Barney Deucy. It's got dual purpose HE/frags in the tube. Got it?"

Caine nodded, a bit uncertainly. "Most of it. I'll learn the rest on the job, I guess. You want their HQ?"

"Yup."

"Then follow me." And Caine jogged off into the fog.

Stosh looked after him. "Goddamnit, just what we need. Another officer."

"He's not *really* an officer, Stosh."

Stosh looked Trevor straight in the eye. "Oh no? I'd know that tone anywhere. He was born an officer, even if he doesn't know it yet." And Stosh also disappeared into the mist.

As Trevor waved for the others to follow, he gritted his teeth and smiled at the same time: *Damn Stosh, anyway.*

North-Central Jakarta, Earth

Winfield held up a hand. The figures in the smoke up ahead stopped.

"Who goes there?"

"Insurgents," responded a woman's voice—a voice that was either American or Canadian.

"Come forward, but slowly," ordered Commander Ayala as the rest of his Team fanned out.

They did. There must have been almost a hundred of them. At their head were two men, grizzled and wearing Kopassus uniforms that were about twenty years out of date, and a woman. The woman was so incongruous that Winfield forgot security considerations for a moment. She was tall, dark haired, fair-skinned, and with a figure that bordered on the dramatic. And stranger still, he knew her.

"Ms. Corcoran?"

She started, veered toward Winfield. "Do I know you—er, Lieutenant?"

"I don't know if you remember me, ma'am. I was Trevor's XO, when we rescued you on Mars last year."

She flushed. "My God—yes, of course. I'm sorry I didn't recognize you immediately. But I never expected to see you he—"

"Quite all right, ma'am. This is Commander Ayala, another SEAL. We're heading to the Roach Motel. Uh, I mean the—"

"Yes, Lieutenant Winfield, I know of it. That's where we're heading, too."

Ayala stepped forward. "Ma'am, first—my respects for your Dad. Hell of a man. But I can't let you go on to the enemy HQ. That's going to be—well, pretty hairy."

She smiled. "Commander, I understand, and I appreciate your concern. But all the same, I'm going."

Ayala put his hands on his hips. "Listen, Ms. Corcoran, I don't have the time—"

"Exactly right, Commander. You don't have time to stand around arguing. And since I'm a civilian, and you can't order me about, I suggest—along with my one hundred or so friends—that you stop wasting your time on an argument you can't win."

Ayala seemed about to counterattack when Winfield leaned over. "Commander?"

"Yeah?"

"Captain Corcoran told us two important things about his sister."

"And what were those?"

"Never hit on her, and never try to win an argument with her. Particularly when she's backed by a hundred Indonesian insurgents."

Ayala stared at Winfield and frowned. Then he looked at Elena and frowned some more. "So I guess you're coming with us after all."

She smiled the same smile Winfield remembered seeing in the pictures of her father. "I guess so."

Chapter Fifty-One

Presidential Palace compound, Jakarta, Earth

Three more of the insurgents went down, one of them hit by so many of the large bore Hkh'Rkh assault rifle rounds that his torso went one way, and his groin and legs fell the other. Caine kneeled, saw a dim thermal silhouette bloom through the drifts—loping, loping— and squeezed off three shots. The bloom tumbled into a long lump on the ground and did not move.

"Riordan, did you hear me? Pull back! Now!"

Caine checked, saw another bloom pop up, sighted quickly, fired in that general direction, then spun on his heel and ran.

Five seconds of sprinting and he was going past the fire team of insurgents who had been ostensibly covering their retreat.

"Caine," Trevor called from the smoke up ahead, "are you coming?"

"Yeah. I've gotta—"

Thunder shattered the sky overhead.

"What the hell—?" asked Cruz, whose crouched,

upward-looking silhouette loomed suddenly out of the mists.

As if in answer to his question, the rain came down with a pervasive roar against the streets of Jakarta. Caine was soaked by the time he had run the additional ten meters to Trevor. "What do we do now?" he shouted over the driving monsoon and the intermittent crashing of nearby lightning strikes.

"We find another way to get to their command center. That's got to be the better part of a platoon we ran into."

"And we'd better regroup," added Rulaine. "We lost contact with Tygg."

"What about radios?"

"The signal is scratchy and in this soup, without GPS, and without a current map of this complex, we're not navigating: we're playing Marco Polo."

Stosh watched the rain running off his nose. "How many combat effectives do we have left?"

Trevor did the headcount. "You, me, Cruz, Rulaine, Barr, Caine, maybe a dozen insurgents."

A dozen insurgents? Out of almost forty? "Is that all?"

"That's all. They hit us pretty bad. And they got Gavin where he set up the Remington."

"Yeah," muttered Barr, "and if it wasn't for him cutting down their flankers, we'd be dead like him."

"He was a hell of a shot."

Caine stared at them, realized he could see them all a bit more clearly—"Shit! The rain is settling the mist. If we don't move—"

At least a dozen automatic weapons—throaty and loud—opened up in unison. Some rounds bit into their scant cover: a low concrete berm ringing a cratered vertipad. More shouts and groans came from the insurgents in darkness behind them. Their covering force was taking losses. Trevor shouted that direction. "Everyone: fall back! Run!"

Caine sprinted away from the sound of the gunfire, wondering if he was the only one of the command group who was already following Trevor's orders that they should all run like hell. Looking to right and left, he saw Stosh and Rulaine respectively, legs stretching, arms pumping. *Well, at least I'm not the only one.*

Behind them, there was more of the automatic weapons fire—this time punctuated by crackling hisses made by shrill projectiles which sliced the air about two feet over their heads. *Shit. A coil gun.* Just over his shoulder, speaking sharply above the gunfire and new screams, Trevor's voice announced, "I recognize this area. Photos showed a work shed just ahead. Make for that."

"A work shed? That won't stop a coil-gun—"

"It's the only cover we can reach in time. Just keep running."

"*Keep running?*" Caine tried to ignore his fear. *As if you could make me stop.*

Presidential Palace, Jakarta, Earth

"Stay where you are," ordered Opal. "Don't move."

The alien headquarters was filled with ruined equipment and dead Arat Kur, a few more well on their way to that same fate. One of the survivors rose up from the side of a very severely wounded comrade and seemed to stare at Opal.

"Major Patrone?"

What the—? "Do I know you?"

"Not really, but I knew of and saw you during the Convocation."

So who the hell would—? And then she remembered Caine's encounter in space. "Jesus! Are you Darzhee Kut?"

Despite the carnage, the destruction, the guttering flames, the two dozen short humans aiming guns at him, the Arat Kur sounded pleased. "Yes, it is indeed I, Major. I am, I suppose, glad to see you."

"Er—likewise. I guess. Listen, let's save the talk for some other time. Where's Cai—um, Mr. Riordan?"

"The ambassador fled, pursued by one of the Hkh'Rkh."

Ambassador? Well, it would be interesting to learn about that later, too. "Was Caine hurt?"

"I do not think so. Major, could you leave some of your men here with us. And a radio?"

O'Garran laughed. "You want us to get some takeout food, as well? You're lucky we don't gut you here and now."

Darzhee Kut seemed confused. "But—are you not the security forces of whom Downing spoke?"

Downing? Security forces? Opal squatted down. "Darzhee Kut, I'm afraid I don't know what you're talking about."

His claws sagged, then came back up. "You have not heard. You are not part of the forces Richard Downing is sending."

"Sending for what?"

"To protect us from the insurgents and the Hkh'Rkh."

"What? Why protect you from your own allies?"

"Ah, again you do not know. We Arat Kur surrendered ten minutes ago. But the Hkh'Rkh did not. They are—they are in sun-time. All of them."

Opal stared at Darzhee Kut but did not see him, could only hear her thoughts moving like a flume pushing through the smoke and dim orange emergency lights. *Okay, gotta secure the HQ. Particularly since these are the senior staff. If they die, the situation could spin out of control. Well, further out of control. Besides, it's good to have a place to fall back on. But I've gotta find Caine. He's out there, unarmed, with a pack of mad-dog killer Sloths after him.*

"Okay, I'm leaving a dozen of my men with you. Wu, you and your detachment stay here: provide security. And if they need your radio, let them use it. Within reason."

Darzhee Kut bobbed. "I thank you, Major, but I must ask one more thing."

"What's that?"

"Do you have any medical supplies?"

"I'm not sure our supplies would be of any help to you."

"Actually, a few of your more common anesthetics are somewhat effective on our biochemistry as well."

"What do you need them for?"

"For administering to First Delegate of the Wholenest, Hu'urs Khraam."

"Is he badly injured?"

"He is dying."

Presidential Palace compound, Jakarta, Earth

Barr turned to say something to Rulaine when Caine heard the saw-toothed supersonic ripping noise again. Chunks of the work-shed's double-layered sheet metal were suddenly flying like buzzsaws around the interior. Several hit Barr, whose head bounced off the back wall, his falling torso sliced open from the left clavicle to the right floating rib. Daylight—suddenly present in the last two minutes—streamed in the holes like spotlights.

Caine looked up. "Jesus Christ."

Trevor rolled up to one knee and peered out one of the larger holes, his body behind an empty oil drum. "Damn coil gun. Wonder where they have it mounted?"

Caine started moving to better cover. "Might not be mounted. I've seen some Hkh'Rkh elites big enough to carry them dismounted as squad-support weapons."

Stosh's eyes widened but he said nothing.

Trevor crouched down again. "Pretty quiet."

Caine agreed, then silently amended, *Too quiet.*

A few rounds banged in from the front, followed by another spray of the bug-zapper rounds which ripped the door clean off its hinges. Then silence again.

Caine low-crawled to Barr's body, took the hotjuice canisters out of his gun, scavenged the ammo and other canisters off his web gear, started tossing them to the others, always glancing toward the shed's small rear window.

Trevor must have seen him looking that way. "What are you thinking?"

"That last volume of fire was pretty weak, compared to the stuff that got the last of the insurgents, and now, Barr. At first it sounded like they had two coils gun out there, but we only heard from one just now."

Trevor nodded. "They're flanking us, putting one of those damn bug zappers at our rear. Caine, you and I—we're going to cover the back entry of this little deathtrap." Trevor went prone, started low-crawling over long-unused rakes, hoes, and hoses. "If Tygg doesn't find us soon, this could get a lot worse before it gets better."

"Oh, I think you can count on that." Stosh smiled.

"Stop scaring the new guy," muttered Cruz.

"Don't worry about me." Caine wiped sweat, flicked a shower of it into the dust as he crawled behind Trevor. "I'm about as scared as I can get."

Stosh was remarkably cheery. "Guess we'll see about that."

Presidential Palace, Jakarta, Earth

"Major, my *real* GPS is working now." O'Garran frowned at the unit. "Although God knows how."

"Bet they seeded this part of low earth orbit with station-keeping geosync-emulators as soon as the Arat Kur lost orbital control," Opal speculated. "What's the good word, Miles? Do we have Riordan's telemetry, now?"

O'Garran nodded, poked his head out the rear floor door of the largely shattered HQ building, evidently blasted by the last of a long daisy chain of demo charges that had started out beyond the walls of the compound. He squinted across a broad tree-framed esplanade and pointed. "One hundred forty meters that way. My best-guess map puts him in that old garden shed you can just see over there."

Opal came erect out of her crouch. "That's where we just heard a shitstorm of fire."

"That's right, ma'am. And there's another problem on the way." He handed her his binoculars, pointed to the northeast. She looked.

At least a dozen Hkh'Rkh were flanking the tool shed the long way around, staying off the esplanade and behind a facing row of low buildings. One was carrying a ponderous coil gun eminently capable of cutting the shed into tin strips. *Shit.*

Before Opal was fully aware of it, she was giving orders. "Little Guy, set up squad two as the base of fire to cover our advance across the open ground toward the shed. Squad one is splitting into three fire teams: number one with me, number two with you, number three with the squad's senior remaining NCO. Running leapfrog advance. Propellant mixes at the hottest and grenades—"

"Major?"

"What?"

"That's what I want to ask you: what? As in, what the hell are you doing?"

"What does it look like I'm doing? I—we—are going to rescue Cain—Mr. Riordan."

"Major, all due respect—because I know you're bulletproof—but that's almost one hundred forty meters of open ground."

"Which we can cross before those Hkh'Rkh get that coil gun in position to hit the shed, if we move now."

"Seems like we could be sticking our necks way out on this one. We could take a lot of fire."

"Why? Have they seen us yet? Do you see any other forces?"

"Well—"

"Right. Me neither. The bad guys who are still hitting that shed are probably just a light pinning force with regular assault rifles, keeping our guys pinned down while those other Sloths bring up their one big piece of artillery to finish off the humans they've trapped."

O'Garran looked out at the esplanade, saw the Hkh'Rkh disappear behind the building that would screen them from being seen by the humans in the shed, but which would also screen the tunnel rats from being seen by them. "Seems right, but there's a lot we don't know."

"Little Guy, there's always a lot we don't know. That's where luck and boldness come in." Opal looked at the Chinese fire team behind her. They were alert, terribly afraid, even more terribly committed. "On me. Run when I run. Drop when I drop. Got it?"

One of them nodded. The other two looked at him.

O'Garran looked at the hedges and arbors framing both the north and south edges of the esplanade. "Ma'am, I just don't know about—"

Poor Little Guy. Such an old lady. She didn't hear the rest of O'Garran's tactical reservations. She was out the door and into the swirling dust, with one sharp phrase tossed over her shoulder:

"Cover me!"

Presidential Palace compound, Jakarta, Earth

Trevor had extraordinary eyes. "I've got movement, back by the Arat Kur HQ."

It took Caine a moment to see it. A small group, running directly toward them. Humans, from their size and their gait. Then they dropped, and a second group of four persons appeared running behind them, moving about twenty meters beyond the first group before dropping. Then a third was visible—

"Looks like reinforcements," commented Trevor, sounding like he was trying to control a surge of ecstasy and relief.

It did indeed look like reinforcements. And as the first group moved up and ran beyond the third, now no more than fifty meters away, it also looked like they were being led by a woman. A woman who looked remarkably like—

Caine stood: *shit.* "Opal!"

❖ ❖ ❖

Trevor's mind locked up. *Opal? Where? Ohmigod—* "Jesus, what the hell is *she* doing here—?" *Which is a bullshit question because you know the answer: she's here to save Caine's sorry ass.*

And she was coming across the open ground too fast, too directly, not sending scouts into the arbor she was paralleling. *Jesus Christ, Opal. Get down, get under some cover!*

Caine's shout matched his thoughts. "GET DOWN! COVER!"

❖ ❖ ❖

Opal heard a voice roaring at her from the shed. *That's Caine! But—*

He's calling for cover. He probably needs covering fire. Shit. They must be rushing him from the rear! We've gotta flank the shed, get around it to draw down on the bastards—

She didn't wait for the third team to advance past her. "Follow me!" she shouted, and rolled up into a sprint toward the concealment of the south arbor.

✧ ✧ ✧

Trevor saw Opal jump up to lead the first group in an off-sequence advance—and saw her go down just as quickly, suddenly obscured by a blood-red mist.

✧ ✧ ✧

Caine barely heard the thunder-splitting drill of the coil gun which the Hkh'Rkh had evidently positioned in the south arbor.

He thought as he moved. *Out the door, selector switch on the grenade tube to full automatic, pull the arming distance back to zero: contact detonation.*

The first step carried him out the doorway, with good momentum.

I'm out of time.

His second step became a forward roll. The supersonic crackle of more coil gun projectiles sped over and past him. He rolled to a stop, facing in the direction of the fire and, with a slight sideways jog of the gun, squeezed the trigger. The three grenades arced into the south arbor's clutter of bushes and trees with a rapid *foomfoomfoom.*

The three answering explosions were a bit more ragged. Some rounds hit a harder surface than others. But they erupted as a rough row of smoky orange flashes—one followed almost immediately by a short, loud sputter of similar blasts: secondary explosions. Someone's ammo had gone up. *That buys me one second, maybe two—*

Riordan yanked a smoke grenade off his web gear, nulled the fusing timer, heaved it a third of the distance to Opal. It was fuming and pluming as it left his hand. Then a quick roll to the left, and another grenade, thrown farther along that same trajectory—just as the splintering cracks of coil gun rounds started spatting overhead again.

❖   ❖   ❖

Trevor jumped up as the three tube-launched warheads went off, saw Caine heave a grenade. *Good: he's putting down a path of smoke to get to her.* "Stosh: get up here now!" *Gotta wait, watch*—Caine threw another smoke. Still no counterfire from the south arbor.

Keep waiting...

Just as Stosh came shoulder to shoulder with him, the coil gun resumed its shrill screaming. Trevor heard the crackling of the supersonic rounds, made his eyes follow the path of the sound his ears had detected, saw disturbance in the underbrush. Dumping his magazine at it, he yelled. "Suppression!"

❖   ❖   ❖

The volume of human fire erupting from the shed flowed into a high tide just as the skies broke again and the rain came down in sheets. Opal could sense, more than see, feet running past her, streaming up into the south arbor that had hidden the second squad of Hkh'Rkh and their coil gun.

And then a face was over hers, close, almost nose to nose. That nose was dripping rain onto her nose. It was a nose she knew as well—maybe better, now—than her own nose. She smiled. "Caine."

Then the firing, which had apparently moved around to the other side of the shed, ebbed, died away like a tired tide. *Good. It's going to be all right, just as soon as I get my breath back*—

Oh Christ, I'm such a liar. Even to myself.

❖   ❖   ❖

The smoke from the grenades swirled around them, the drifts struggling up against the battering rain. It washed the dirt off Caine; it washed the blood away from the two gaping holes in the front of Opal's right torso. It kept washing more blood away. He forced himself to smile, touch noses—she liked that—and lifted his head to call for help, hoping he'd discover a way to do so without alerting her to the severity of her wound.

Trevor came up, took one look, turned away, cupping his hand over the audio pickup on his headset, speaking urgently.

Looking down again, he saw she was smiling. "Caine," she said again, her eyes very bright, brighter than he had ever seen them, other than the time in the deputation module, right before her first interstellar shift, right before they first made love.

He held her hand. "We'll get you something for the pain." Caine held her hand more tightly. "And don't worry; you're going to be all right."

She tried to laugh through her tears, couldn't, gasped against the pain. "Not me—not me that I'm crying for."

"Then who—?"

She shook her head. "For the baby."

He hadn't heard her correctly. "For the what?"

"For our baby."

His eyes and nostrils suddenly ached and stung all at once, and his vision became as blurred, as if he were looking through a rain-drenched windshield. He wiped a hand across his eyes, leaned over to smile reassuringly.

But she was dead.

✣   ✣   ✣

Trevor looked at Opal, at Caine kneeling, back to him, the rain hammering his soaked shirt flat against him. And all he could think was: *you never deserved her.*

It was bullshit—pure, irrational bullshit—to think that, to feel that. But that was all he could think or feel.

"Trevor. Here, mate. Look who I found!" It was Tygg's voice, speaking to him from the end of some long tunnel.

Trevor turned, saw Tygg, whose ready smile seemed to shoot off his face sideways, as if slapped out of existence. "Trev, what is it? What's happ—?"

And then another face was in front of Tygg's. He thought he might be hallucinating, but then he saw that this face was just as rainsoaked, as tired, as his own. "Elena." He didn't think to say it, but he heard his voice make those sounds.

She looked at him, then over toward Caine and the body, and back to him. She closed her eyes, turned away.

"Sir"—it was Winfield, now—"we've got things under control. We—that is, Commander Ayala and your sister—linked up with Lieutenant Tygg in the first courtyard and got the drop on the Sloths that were working their way behind you. I think we've pretty much secured this part of the compound."

"Good."

Trevor felt Elena's hand rest gently on his shoulder. He wished he didn't need it, was glad she had placed it there, wished it was his father's.

Winfield didn't stop. "Rulaine went back with Cruz to reorganize the insurgents, assign some new leaders to replace the ones we lost. Where's Stosh?"

"Back in the shed."

"What's he doing?"

"Nothing. He's dead."

Chapter Fifty-Two

Darzhee Kut watched as the human called Wu rose, apparently receiving a call from his superiors. As soon as he had moved out of ready earshot, Hu'urs Khraam spoke weakly. "Darzhee Kut, come closer. I cannot see you."

"I am here, Hu'urs Khraam. Here is the claw of your rock-son."

"Would you had been. No matter. This day, you are. Is Urzueth Ragh there as well?"

"I am, Esteemed Hu'urs Khraam."

"Then bear witness to what I decree. Darzhee Kut, I name you Delegate Pro Tem, plenipotentiary in regard to our presence in this system. It is to be explicitly understood that this confers authority over the fleet as well, just as I possess. Urzueth Ragh, forgive me for not naming you to this responsibility, but at this hour, the song we need is that of a diplomat, not an administrator."

"I harmonize, Esteemed Hu'urs Khraam." Darzhee

743

thought that he had never seen Urzueth Ragh look so nervous, or relieved, in all the years he had known him.

"Darzhee Kut, it falls to you to perform the final task we must perform." The old Arat Kur was silent.

"Esteemed Hu'urs Khraam, I do not know the task to which you refer."

"Do you not? Darzhee, they—the humans—they must never learn what we know of them. They must never learn it of themselves. This is a mercy to both our races."

"But Hu'urs Khraam, when you surrendered our ships, surely you understood they could not help but learn. They would go through our computers, our records, and they would discover that—"

"And that is why you must give the order, the Final Directive, that will protect the secrets kept in the deep caves of the Homenest, Darzhee Kut. And you must remind your rock-siblings what the Wholenest needs of them in this dark hour."

"Hu'urs Khraam, I cannot do this."

"Darzhee Kut, you must. You *must*—and it is late. My father sings; I have not heard him for so long. I know the harmony. It is a minor—"

Hu'urs Khraam breathed in sharply. The breath escaped slowly, as it will from a corpse.

Darzhee Kut looked up at Urzueth Ragh. "He could not mean it, rock-sibling."

"Certainly he did, rock-sibling."

"But our promise to surrender to the humans, and all the lives of our own—"

"Rock-sibling, Darzhee Kut. They matter not. The fleet must be destroyed."

Presidential Palace compound, Jakarta, Earth

Caine looked up from Opal's bone-white face, turned to look for people he knew—for Trevor in particular—but he was surrounded by insurgents, some Australian commandoes, some very short Chinese soldiers. *So where is everyone I know? Are they all dead? Who are these people? How long have I been here, with her?*

He saw the garden shed, remembered it: maybe, with the rain coming down, Trevor and the others had gone back in there. Caine rose, remembered his weapon, reached down slowly, lifted its strap over his shoulder. He let his feet take him to the shed and through the doorway he had sprinted out of to try to save her life ten minutes or ten hours or ten days ago.

The only person he saw was Stosh. Dead Stosh, with his tongue protruding slightly from his faintly smiling lips and a hole where the base of his neck had been. There was no light except for the dark gray haze that came from skies heavy with clouds and smoke. Rain drummed on the tin roof and he went to look out the back door.

"Caine."

It was a strangely familiar voice. He turned, saw Elena sitting on a gardener's stool, behind one of the empty oil drums.

"Elena." She usually made him feel nervous, excited, perplexed—but now, he could not feel anything. Would have felt guilty, had he felt anything. "Elena," he said again.

She rose and approached him slowly, the way people do with stray animals that might either bolt or attack. When she got next to him, she squatted down.

For a long time they were silent, looking at the floor; then each other, then out the door. Out the door where Opal's body lay unseen, hidden from view by the doorframe. To Caine, it felt like that corpse was stretched across the packed dirt floor between him and Elena.

Whose knotted hands clenched as she exhaled forcefully. "Caine, I don't know what to do, what to say. I shouldn't *say* anything, not here, not now. But—"

Caine nodded. "But we might not be alive in five minutes." He looked up as a flight of missiles roared overhead, fell and blasted in the city south of them.

She closed her eyes, looked away, nodded. "Whatever we don't say now might never get said. And it's not just about us. If only one of us lives, gets back to Connor—"

Caine matched her nod, looked down at his bloodstained hands. There was no good place to start, so he began with the question that had puzzled him the most. "Why didn't you tell me earlier—on Mars, or at the Convocation—about us? About how we fell in love on the Moon?"

She kept looking past the torn doorway into the rain. It was a long time before she spoke. "How could I? By the time they woke you, brought you back after thirteen years and reintroduced you at Parthenon, you were already involved with—with Opal. And I didn't know how or if to approach you at all, because I had never been able to find out why you disappeared, what had really happened to you. So after Parthenon and Dad's death, I searched to see if there was any new information about where you'd been up until then. But I didn't want to push too hard, since it was pretty mysterious, the way you had just popped back into the world again. And the lack of information told me that my suspicion about why you disappeared fourteen years ago was correct. It wasn't because you had fled from me, from us. No. Something had happened to you. Something strange, dangerous."

"What do you mean?"

"Caine, you were a writer and analyst who had left a well-marked trail. Which came to a sudden and abrupt end the same day you didn't show up for dinner and the rest of our life together. By the time I recovered from that and started trying to find out more about you and what you were doing, I discovered that most of the data was no longer available. And what information still existed about you was suspiciously general. It was as if someone had conducted a thorough campaign to profoundly diminish any trace of you, but without erasing all record of your existence. Probably because complete erasure would have attracted attention all by itself.

"And who was I to attempt to learn about you from people you knew personally? I wasn't family, I had no rights. Our relationship was so sudden and so short that you had probably never mentioned me to anyone. And given who *I* was, I could hardly make those inquiries without attracting all the wrong kind of attention."

Caine agreed with a slow, shallow nod. "Because you figured that if someone had erased so much about me, they'd be watching for anyone who came looking for that lost data."

"Exactly. And what if one of those watchers learned that it was Nolan Corcoran's daughter who had come looking? If you were alive somewhere, that was the kind of connection which could have endangered not only my father, and me, and you, but Connor."

Connor. Caine closed his eyes. "Does Connor know?"

"That you're his father? No."

"What have you told him?"

"That I met a man who I loved, but couldn't remain with. I couldn't say more than that for the same reason I couldn't ask too many questions about your disappearance. It was too full of dangerous unknowns."

Caine put out his hand toward Elena. She took it slowly. "There are so many other things to say, to ask," he said hoarsely. "But today is..." His hand and his voice fell away as his eyes slipped back toward the front door, out toward the dying rain.

"I know," Elena said, "I know. But after today, we'll have time. All the time we need."

Presidential Palace, Jakarta, Earth

Darzhee Kut closed with Urzueth to keep his words down to a faint chittering. "We must not destroy the fleet. If we use the devices of the Final Directive— either the ones in our ships, or those in our bodies—it will trigger the very apocalypse they were meant to prevent."

"Darzhee Kut, granted that Hu'urs Khraam made you Delegate Pro Tem with his dying breath—but have you slipped into sun-time?"

"No. I see with well-shaded eyes, Urzueth Ragh. Think of what our Final Directive means. We are convinced that the humans must not be allowed to learn what we know of their past, their proclivities. They

must not discover that we broke the Twenty-first Accord
and invaded their homeworld not to correct a border
dispute, but to arrest their species' growth, to preempt
their ability to lay waste to our Homenest—again. If we
now use the Final Directive, the humans will be con-
fronted by a mystery. That we had obviously planned,
from the outset, to destroy even ourselves to deny them
any access to our technology, our culture, but most
especially, our history. It is wrong—terribly, perfectly
wrong—to believe that such an act of self-destruction
will bring greater safety to the Wholenest. Do you not
see the greater danger that will arise if we carry it out?"

Urzueth Ragh seemed ready to reject the line of
reasoning, then stopped. Darzhee Kut could feel him
thinking, expanding the game board of the scenario,
opening areas in which he had not yet thought to play.
Darzhee Kut felt and saw him make the fateful move
to full comprehension. "Ah. They will not rest until they
have solved the mystery. And so they will find out about
their past, anyway. Perhaps more surely."

"Precisely. Some of them, such as Riordan, have come
to know us and our behavior well enough to rightly
expect that we might, under the current circumstances,
peacefully and tractably surrender, and that we are not
intrinsically deceitful. But if we carry out the Final
Directive, they will have an act that sharply contradicts
both those expectations, and in which hundreds of them
will die along with us."

Urzueth hummed agreement. "Which will only
amplify the rage they feel over our sneak attack upon
their homeworld. They will think us a race of oath-
breakers and will thus feel justified in doing whatever
they will and can to our kind."

"All too likely. But worse, there will be the few, the thinking few, who will not react as the many, but will instead curl into their shells of reflection and wonder. Why did the Arat Kur do these things? Why did they attack us by surprise? Why were they willing to break the Twenty-first Accord and so attract the wrath of the Dornaani? How were they ready to destroy themselves in such complete unison when they were defeated? And why did they have suicide cysts where we could not readily find them?"

"That presumes they will know to look for the suicide cysts."

"But they are sure to do so, Urzueth. How could we effect such widespread self-destruction without them? And once they have discovered the cysts, they will have a mystery so profound that defies any reasonable explanation. The humans might hum to themselves that they can conceive of reasons for why we broke the Twenty-first Accord and attacked. They can even understand why *individuals* of our species might choose suicide over the possibility of abuse, even torture, on a lost battlefield. But premeditated, simultaneous, and universal self-destruction? And with no radios to coordinate it? And even among those of us for whom surrender will, in all probability, be safe?"

Urzueth Ragh buzzed slowly, meditatively. "They will see the preparation, and so discern that we had determined from the beginning that, if we were defeated, we needed to conceal something from them—even at the expense of all our lives and equipment."

Darzhee Kut bobbed. "Just so. They will eventually

debrief survivors here or elsewhere who could reveal what we must now keep hidden. For if the humans learn that we knew of them in prior millennia, when their birthright was to burrow the dark between the suns just as we did..."

"...then they will ask why their legacy did not stay among those stars." Urzueth clicked his mandibles. "Whereas if we do *not* employ the Final Directive, then they will have no reason to ask such questions."

Darzhee Kut harmonized. "If our actions fit what they expect, they will be without impetus to seek for the unexpected in us. Our resignation to surrender and negotiation will fulfill that expectation. Conversely, our self-destruction would be a goad to them, a deed that they will seek to understand, and in so doing, almost certainly learn the full truth of their past. Under the present circumstances, they could then easily become *more* dangerous than we imagined. They would see themselves as the one silently, secretly oppressed species among the stars, long kept from knowledge of themselves, and now invaded to preempt the resumption of their birthright. Like nestlings just discovering the idea of justice and having it violated, how will they act? What will they do to oath-breakers and skulkers such as us?"

Urzueth emitted a faint, ululating two-toned whistle in a minor key. "First Rock-Mother," he prayed/blasphemed. "We will have given rise to the very thing we strove to prevent."

Darzhee Kut harmonized and watched him closely.

Mobile Command Center "Trojan Ghost One," approaching Indonesia, Earth

"Mr. Downing, update from OPCOM."

Good. The more we know, the better we can negotiate. "Synopsis, please."

"Admiral Silverstein reports that the enemy flotilla which engaged Rescue Task Force One is dead in space. He has multiple nuke-pumped X-ray laser missiles targeted on every shift-capable hull and capital ship. He will soon be handing control over to Rear Admiral Vasarsky's Tango Echelon. He has also detached enough Gordon-class sloops to control the drones we now have covering the Arat Kurs' orbital flotilla. Initial boarding operations are underway in both areas of engagement. He hopes they will be concluded by the time Tango Echelon arrives."

"Then Silverstein is slingshotting out after Halifax?"

"Yes, sir, but he hardly needs to. Admiral Schubert's first report indicates that the Arat Kur belt fleet is almost one hundred percent incapacitated. The few hulls still capable of maneuver were overwhelmed by the first wave of drones and high-yield ordnance and were destroyed. However, it is unclear if Schubert's own boarding teams will be able to safely commandeer the remaining enemy hulls. Time to intercept is long enough that the Arat Kur might be able to regain control, necessitating their destruction."

Downing couldn't quite be comfortable with the report. Case Timber Pony and Case Leo Gap had worked *too* well, had been too seamless in their synergistic timing and effect. Innumerable contingency plans had been drawn up for dealing with high, partial, even low levels of success, but there had been no time to spend contemplating such a speedy and complete triumph. Something had to be amiss, about to go wrong…

"I also have reports via fiber-com in Jakarta that a mix of indigenous insurgents, infiltration teams, and tunnel rats have entered the presidential compound and provisionally secured the enemy headquarters."

Already? If anything, the successes threatened to get out of hand, were occurring too quickly. "Do we have reliable units inbound on their HQ?"

"Yes, sir. Pathfinder elements dedicated to that target are the Twenty-second SAS, B squadron, and A platoon of the Spetsnaz Sixteenth Brigade. Both are hitching rides with A company of Second Battalion, First Air Cav."

"Their ETA?"

"Ten minutes."

Downing looked down at his watch, did the math. That was too soon, now, given the change in plans these rapid successes necessitated. "Tell those units to orbit the compound and secure the surrounding airspace. They are to delay final approach and landing until we arrive to lead them in."

"Sir?"

"Relay those orders, Lieutenant. I don't want the arrival of possibly overeager elite troops to fuel the confidence—and vengeance—of resistance fighters. That could turn a nice, calm surrender into a slaughter. We will lead our elite formations in and set the tone as *diplomatic*, not military. Make sure they understand that. And tell the pilot we need to move up our ETA to Jakarta as much as possible."

"Yes, sir."

Alnduul swayed gently toward him as the high-speed command VTOL bucked with a sudden surge of acceleration. "Are you quite sure that this change is safe, Mr. Downing?"

"You mean the speed of our approach?"

Alnduul's outer lids nictated slowly. "I mean our direct entry into an unsecured combat zone."

Downing felt a brief spasm of contempt for the Dornaani Custodian, pushed it off with a shrug. "There is some risk involved. That is the nature of war, after all."

Downing felt as though the large, dark pupilless eyes were dissecting his words, his intents, his psyche. Then they blinked. "So it is. My apologies, Mr. Downing."

"Your apologies? For what? For asking about the degree of risk?"

"For forgetting what it feels like."

Downing felt his eyebrows rise. "It must be nice to live in a world where that's something you can forget."

"Nice? Perhaps. But worrisome, also."

"Worrisome?"

But Alnduul had turned to look out the small window to his right, the blue and white of sky and clouds a roiling concave moiré reflected upon his eyes. Downing waited, but the Dornaani did not speak again.

Presidential Palace, Jakarta, Earth

"Have you contacted our ships yet?"

"We have not, Darzhee Kut," answered the communications specialist.

Urzueth Ragh moved closer to him, hummed his query softly. "I do not understand. If you are determined to keep the fleet from destroying itself, why are you so eager to contact them with news of Hu'urs Khraam's death?"

"Because if they hear of our capitulation without also learning that the Final Directive is rescinded, the ship masters will presume it is in effect and scuttle their ships."

Urzueth's answering buzz was anxious. "It may occur anyhow, Darzhee Kut. If our rock-siblings are boarded before they can restore their systems, they are likely to destroy themselves, probably with humans aboard. And soon, down here, they will start finding some of our fully isolated troopers becoming sluggish, sick. And you know what they will find."

Darzhee Kut nodded. "Within forty-eight hours, all their potential prisoners will die of a noncontagious virus that first renders them unconscious and then kills them by producing fatal toxins out of body tissue."

"And because we have no way of reaching all of them, thousands will die within the same day or two. The humans will, as you say, realize that it is not a disease at all, but a suicide method. So let us reconsider. Why not be safe and destroy the ships, as well? If we cannot prevent the humans from discovering our planetside force's numerous suicides, then we might as well destroy the concrete answers the humans might find on our spacecraft."

Darzhee Kut snapped his claws. "No. If we can keep the planetside casualties to a minimum, we can explain that the troopers who killed themselves simply feared capture and torture. We must spend all our energies striving to contact our units. To that end, ask the humans to find Riordan and bring him back here."

"Why?"

"Because he will help us, and the humans still have radios. We can use those to contact our rock-siblings. If we can prevent even half of our units and ships from following the Final Directive, the suicides of the remainder may appear to be more an aberration than a plan."

Urzueth Ragh's antenna snapped erect as he spun away. "I shall inquire after Riordan with all speed."

"Delegate Kut." It was the first time anyone had ever addressed him with that honorific; it was thrilling and horrible at the same time.

"Yes, Communications Master T'yeen?"

"I have the ship *Greatvein.*"

"Who is on the channel? Fleetmaster R'sudkaat?"

"No, Delegate Kut. As you requested, Senior Sensor Master Tuxae Skhaas."

"Excellent. Tuxae Skhaas?"

"Yes, Speak—*Delegate* Kut."

"I must first sing a song of mourning. Hu'urs Khraam's voice no longer echoes in the rocknest."

There was a very long pause. "We are ill-fated to be alive to hear such notes, Delegate Kut." The sorrow in Tuxae's voice was deep and genuine.

"I have a very new song for your antennae alone, Tuxae Skhaas."

"I listen, ready to harmonize, Delegate Kut. But your radio has very limited range, and the path of our orbit will soon carry us beyond each other's reach."

"So I will be frank. We must not scuttle the fleet."

"We—have I heard you correctly, Delegate Kut?"

"You must unlearn the hymn we all sang together when we left Homenest. And you must teach this new atonality to all the other ships that you can reach: we must not follow the Final Directive."

Chapter Fifty-Three

"Trev?"

"Hmm?" Trevor Corcoran kept his eye on the scope of the Remington M167 he had retrieved from Gavin's body. *Almost eight minutes since I've seen a Sloth, but I'm in no rush. Six bagged and counting. And that last one—Stosh would have been proud of that shot: four hundred eighty meters if it was a centimeter. Single round, center of mass. The bastard went down like a poleaxed ox. Welcome to Earth, motherfucker.*

"Trevor." Tygg's voice was subtly more insistent.

"Yeah, what is it?"

"A report, Captain."

Yeah, that's right. I'm a captain now. Probably will keep my rank after this shindig. Glories and medals, too. O, be still my beating heart—

"Heart." "Heart" made him think of Opal, which made him stop thinking. When he opened his eyes, he found the view down the scope alien, strange, as if he had never seen it before. "Okay. Okay." He blinked,

757

felt like he was coming out of a general anesthetic. "What's the sitrep?"

Tygg, his sand-colored beret wet and rumpled close to his head, was at his left shoulder, his eyes steady, assessing. "Best if you come down to hear it, sir."

"Yeah, okay."

"And we can put Cruz on overwatch up here, give him the Remington. Don't you think?" Tygg's hand was already gently cupping the forestock of the long weapon. Trevor noticed that the Aussie's eyes never blinked.

Trevor nodded. "Yeah—I'm done." Tygg nodded, averted his eyes as if suddenly embarrassed. Trevor started down the narrow stairs that led from the small fieldhouse's observation cupola into its shattered atrium. Faces looked up at him, looked quickly away. His impulse was equally divided between a desire to hide his own face from them and to tell them to fuck off. Frozen into immobility between these two diametrically opposed urges, he managed to simply descend, silently, into their midst.

"Reports," he ordered.

Ayala started. "Outer perimeter secure. Our biggest problem is locals wanting to get in and trash this place. It's pretty ugly out there."

"What about the hunter-killer squads the Sloths sent out?"

"Scattered reports. Lots of them are still active, but running out of steam. A lot more have been wiped out. Some tried to lift their own vehicles to make a run for orbit or elsewhere. We really don't know. Our flyboys were too busy shooting them into small fluttering pieces."

Trevor nodded, turned to O'Garran. "Relief forces?"

"According to the latest fiber-com update, ETA is now six minutes."

"Vertipads?"

"Secured. Lieutenant Winfield and most of Commander Ayala's SEALs are working as cadre with ex-military insurgents to maintain a dedicated overwatch on the 'pads."

Trevor was preparing to move on to Rulaine for the internal security report, heard O'Garran clear his throat. "Something else, Sergeant?"

"Yes, sir. Although we're expecting the SAS and First Air Cav to be the first wave in, according to my latest intel update, their landing has been redesignated as the arrival of a 'high-security diplomatic mission,' not a part of the general assault."

"Who's leading this diplomatic mission?"

"I have no word on that, sir. But the Confederation clearance classification is listed as 01A1B."

Jesus. "Sergeant, you are to send all your remaining forces to the vertipads. I want them deployed as two concentric perimeters, placements and range at Lieutenant Winfield's discretion. And Sergeant O'Garran?"

"Sir?"

"You stay with us."

"Yes, sir."

"Bannor?"

Rulaine swept an arm out over the esplanade. "Interior is all quiet. No sniping incidents, not even any thermal signatures that aren't us or human workers. The undercover insurgents among the staff have made contact with us, confirm our suspicions that the only Hkh'Rkh left within these walls are the three we have captive and the dead."

"And the Arat Kur?"

"Most are holed up in their billets or are back near Lieutenant Wu in their headquarters."

"Any resistance from the others?"

"Not a peep. External reports tell the same story. The Arat Kur have ceased all offensive operations. Possibly due to illness."

Trevor swiveled back toward Rulaine. "Illness?"

"Yes sir. Scattered intel suggests that here, and at their other cantonments, an increasing number of Arat Kur are acting sluggish, distracted."

Caine's voice arose, was aimed into the rest of the crowd, not at Trevor. "Those of you with the infiltration teams or the fiber-com. Did you hear anything about plans to use a chemical weapon on the Arat Kur?"

"No, sir." Ayala shrugged. "Scuttlebutt is that no one ever got genetic samples of the Arat Kur."

Caine nodded. "Yeah, I believe it. All throughout the insurgency, the exos occasionally retreated, but they never left their dead behind for analysis. The one time I saw them retreat without all their bodies, they called in an air strike and burned the *kempang* down to bedrock."

"So the Roaches get sick. What of it?"

"Maybe nothing, Trevor—but if a whole lot of them are succumbing to some kind of disease or malaise right now, it might not be coincidence."

"Trev." It was Elena, her voice coming from behind, not much more than a whisper. "Caine is also the ambassador to the Arat Kur. If something's going on, he should be back in their headquarters, staying in touch with what's left of their leadership."

Trevor picked up his CoBro assault rifle. "Fine.

We'll escort you to Cockroach central. Tygg, Rulaine: on me."

Wholenest flagship *Greatvein*, Earth orbit

Tuxae kept his claws very still as R'sudkaat approached. "Yes, what is it now, Tuxae Hu'urs?"

"Esteemed Fleetmaster, I have a message from Darzhee Kut."

"A message to me? From him? Very well. What is it?"

"Delegate Kut sends his compliments and informs you that the Final Directive has been rescinded."

For a long moment, R'sudkaat did not move. Then he started forward, claws half raised. "Rescind the Final Directive? And since when is Kut titled Delegate?"

"Since Hu'urs Khraam sang his last note, some minutes ago."

R'sudkaat rocked back as though struck between the eyes, which roved in the direction of H'toor Qooiiz's empty couch, as if searching for some rock-sibling who would sing a different song than this, would negate and drown out the dirge that Tuxae sang. "This cannot be."

"So I thought also, but it is true. The ground staff has verified his death, as well as Hu'urs Khraam's conferral of the title Delegate Pro Tem upon Darzhee Kut."

R'sudkaat was very still. Then: "Preposterous. Hu'urs Khraam would never put the fleet under the direction of Kut. Magma and rotting meat: he is but an Ee'ar!"

Tuxae kept his antennae and claws very still and elected not to point out that he, too, was of the Ee'ar caste. "So he is. But now he is our Delegate in this place, as well. And he orders that we rescind the Final Directive."

R'sudkaat looked at Tuxae closely, who heard the sifting-sand sound of his commander's lenses compressing with the intensity of their focusing. "No," R'sudkaat hummed slowly. "No. I will not do so. Kut's order shows that he is not our Delegate, but rather that he is a tool of the humans."

"R'sudkaat, with respect, you must comply."

"I will not take orders from an upstart Ee'ar."

"I am afraid you must."

R'sudkaat raised a claw high, haughty. "You have slipped into sun-time, Tuxae Skhaas, if you think I will abandon our orders and our mission on the word of an Ee'ar. And now I must instruct you to relinquish your post. Until such time as a Nestmoot can be held to determine your complicity in this attempt to subvert the orders and due authority of this fleet, you are relieved of your duties."

"With respect, R'sudkaat, it is I who must now relieve you of your duties."

R'sudkaat's antenna wiggled, but there was no mirth in his voice. "Tuxae Skhaas, your audacity is singular. Comply or I will summon Enforcers."

"You need not. They are already here. Turn around."

R'sudkaat did so, discovered H'toor Qooiiz and six Enforcers standing two meters behind him. "Please come with us," H'toor Qooiiz asked softly.

Stunned, R'sudkaat scanned the bridge: expressionless eyes stared back at him. He turned quickly back toward Tuxae Skhaas. "Have you all gone mad? Have you forgotten the songs of our mothers and their great-grandmothers before them, back unto the rebirth of the Homenest? These are humans—*humans!* The great despoilers. If they take us captive, they will have access to our best technology, our drives, our weapons. We will be enabling them to cut another swath of terror through the stars. They will invade Homenest, take hostages, experiment upon us, torture us, make labor slaves out of the entirety of our race!"

"They are more likely to do so if, in destroying ourselves, we destroy their boarding teams as well. As might begin happening any moment. We have word that the ships of our counterattacking fleet are even now being commandeered by human troops."

"But—"

"With respect, Fleetmaster R'sudkaat, I cannot have this discussion at this time. We must try to send this instruction to Orbitmaster Edkor Taak's flagship. Please accompany the Enforcers. H'toor Qooiiz, please remain with me."

"Orders, Shipmaster Tuxae Skhaas?" H'toor Qooiiz's voice was a melody of liquid laughter.

"Given the approach of the humans, my first orders will probably be my last."

"Then they had best be good ones."

"Truly spoken. Can we reach the Orbitmaster's command ship with this radio?"

"We can try." H'toor Qooiiz's response was unconvincing, but after fifteen seconds of waiting, the channel crackled and cleared. Orbitmaster Edkor Taak responded personally. He was unsurprised by the news of Hu'urs Khraam's death, was startled by the naming of an Ee'ar to the position of Delegate, and fell into a long silence upon hearing that the Final Directive was rescinded. Then, in a slow voice, Orbitmaster Taak announced, "Before complying, I will speak to this Darzhee Kut myself."

"He is no longer in my radio range; perhaps he is in yours."

"We have no radios remaining other than this one, and we are too far from . . . planet . . . to exchange . . . or messages."

"Orbitmaster Taak, I believe we have little time to—"

H'toor Qooiiz clicked a negation, looked up at him. "He has passed out of the range of this radio."

Mobile Command Center "Trojan Ghost One," over southern Java, Earth

"Any word from RTF 1?"

"Boardings are underway, Mr. Downing. About forty percent of the opposing fleet's ships have been taken by Joint Spec Ops forces. No sign of resistance whatsoever, even though some of the Roach boats are starting to get their computers back online."

"Their belt fleet?"

"They were at longer range. Judging from Admiral Schubert's last report, he's anticipating first rendezvous in about two hours. And it's about thirty minutes before our ground-launched teams reach the ships in orbit around Earth."

"Are we anticipating any problem if either of those enemy formations get their systems running?"

"Not really, sir. We already have their hulls ringed with missiles and ordnance that caught up to them, retroboosted, and is now station-keeping with them in lethal proximity. If they so much as frown at us, they're ash. Nothing but good news for us, sir."

Downing looked over at Alnduul, who had not

spoken for ten minutes, whose head had inclined to stare down at the Jakartan metroplex that was rushing up at them. *There's always risk,* he had told the Dornaani. That was another way of saying that, in war, the news is never "all good." Downing stared at his watch for the third time in the past thirty seconds, wondered why he was so anxious, why he felt it to be so desperately necessary to link up with the Arat Kur leadership, why he couldn't think past the one thought that was pushing all others aside. *Land this thing, damn it; land it* now.

Presidential Palace, Jakarta, Earth

"Any word?" asked Darzhee Kut when he was sure no humans were close enough to hear.

"About the fleet or Riordan?"

"Either. Both."

"Nothing on the fleet," answered Urzueth Ragh. "None of our ships are in radio range any longer. The human Wu is unwilling to share much information, but I believe that Riordan was already on his way when I asked."

The first good news in an hour. But Urzueth did not seem encouraged. "What distresses you?"

"On this day, what does not? But just this moment, I was reflecting that even if your countermand of the Final Directive reaches our ships, their masters may not elect to follow the orders of an unknown Delegate."

Darzhee Kut bobbed once. "Yes, but at least they cannot scuttle their ships immediately. Not until they restore full computer control."

"Darzhee Kut, why do you place this importance upon their computers?"

"Because the instructed means of scuttling is to sabotage the antimatter or fusion containment fields."

Urzueth Ragh angled to look at him sideways. "Rock-sibling, Shipmasters have other means at their disposal."

Darzhee Kut felt his intestine twitch. "What do you mean?"

"Darzhee Kut, surely you have not forgotten that the humans are not the only ones who possess nuclear ordnance—"

Mobile Command Center "Trojan Ghost One," over southern Java, Earth

"Oh, Christ—Mr. Downing!"

The bump of the VTOL's hasty landing coincided with a panicked, almost electric pulse that jumped so hard through Downing that he felt pain at the rear of his skull. But there was relief, too. The bad news had finally arrived. "What is it, Lieutenant?"

"Sir—the Arat Kur are destroying their ships."

So. Not as harmless as they seemed. "How many?"

"I don't know, sir. It's going on right now—six, seven, eight."

"How?"

"Nukes, sir."

"And our boarding teams?"

The lieutenant turned very pale very quickly. "Our—?"

"Yes, Lieutenant. What about our boarding teams?"

Flagship USS *Lincoln*, Sierra Echelon, RTF 1, cislunar space

Ruth Altasso turned to Ira. Lateral lines, straight and stacked like the slats of a washboard, stretched across her forehead. "Admiral, Commander Dugan on tac comm one. Urgent."

Damned straight it's urgent. His teams are on those hulls. "Put him through. What's the count, Ruth?"

"Nine scuttled so far, sir. Dugan is online."

"*Lincoln* actual. Go."

"Admiral—"

"I know what's happening, Tom. Don't waste time with a sitrep."

"Okay." A long pause. When Tom Dugan spoke again, he sounded more like a green second looey than a seventeen-year veteran with the Teams. "Ira, what do I do?"

Good God, now SEALs are asking me what to do? "Secure the prisoners. Isolate them from all systems."

"Impossible, Admiral. On most hulls, I've only got two squads of boarders. That's twenty-two troops for hulls that are often more than two hundred thousand kiloliters in volume. And my men don't have intel on floor plans, standard complement, or command circuitry. My guys are working blind, and from what I can tell, they can't figure out how the Arat Kur are blowing their ships. I was in contact with Joe DeBolt when the smallish hull he took went up. His squads had corralled all the Roach bastards. Nobody threw a self-destruct switch or anything like that." Dugan stopped for a moment, then resumed. "Orders?"

Ira clenched his molars. *I know what you want me to say. And, God forgive me, you're right, because we just don't know how they're doing it. Hell, if they set this up as a worst-case contingency, they might not even need access to their ships' systems—*

Ira discovered that Altasso was looking at him. "Skipper, for all we know, the Arat Kur could have implanted themselves with remote triggers."

Ira closed his eyes. *Great God, does she read minds, too?*

"Sir." It was Dugan again, tense. "Orders?"

"Are your men still buttoned up?"

"All suits are still sealed, sir."

"Do they have control over internal systems? Such as bulkhead doors?"

"In most cases, yes sir."

Eyes still closed, Ira felt himself creating generations of hatred and mistrust as he allowed the next order to ride out of his mouth on the crest of one long sigh. "Remove the Arat Kur from their ships. Immediately."

Silence. "'Remove'? Sir, don't you mean—?"

"Commander, I know what I mean and what I said. Have your teams secure themselves to interior fixtures with lanyards. Then open the airlocks. Then open the bulkhead doors. All of them."

Presidential Palace, Jakarta, Earth

Darzhee Kut noticed the small human soldiers guarding the ruined headquarters crouch cautiously, then snap upward into a respectful, oddly erect and rigid stance. A superior approaching? Riordan, perhaps?

Larger humans with long, wicked-looking rifles swarmed through the door, followed by Trevor Corcoran.

Who had changed. Darzhee Kut had his claw half raised in greeting, but brought it down: he was suddenly fearful, more fearful than he had ever been around the Hkh'Rkh. He did not know humans well, but everything he had learned told him that there was death in Trevor Corcoran's eye. Not hatred, not outraged pride, not fury. Just cold, passionless, implacable death. Death for Darzhee Kut, for Arat Kur, for all exos—maybe for anyone. Darzhee shivered back into his carapace. That was Trevor Corcoran's face, but that was no longer Trevor Corcoran.

But arriving behind Corcoran was Riordan, his head turning, seeking, insistent, pushing past the human warriors into the room, over the body of the Hkh'Rkh that had guarded and then attacked him, still seeking—and stopped, staring in the direction opposite Darzhee Kut. His head and eyes were aimed straight at the silent, faintly fuming tank of Apt-Counsel-of-Lenses. Riordan's eager, ready expression bled away. For a moment—just a moment—Darzhee Kut thought his eyes were going to match Trevor's own.

"Caine Riordan!" As Riordan turned his head in the direction of Darzhee Kut's call, some measure of engagement came back to his eyes. "Caine Riordan, we need—"

"Radios. Yes, we've heard about the ships. And your soldiers, are they also—?"

"Yes. It is a perverse contingency plan discussed by some of our leaders," Darzhee Kut lied. "But I believe we can stop my forces from following them—many of them, at least. But I have no way to reach them. I need radios—"

But Caine was already turning away, shouting to the other humans—

❖   ❖   ❖

Caine faced Trevor. "Darzhee Kut is now in charge here and trying to ensure that the rest of Arat Kur surrender goes smoothly. He needs a long-range radio in order to communicate with his people, and tell them it's safe to cooperate with us." Caine saw Elena enter the room, felt a flash of misgiving at having her here, shouted over Darzhee Kut's continuing, and somewhat shrill, entreaties. "And we'll need to patch him through to his ships if he's going to stop them from being scuttled."

Trevor nodded to one of the SEALs with him, who promptly unshouldered a radio and moved toward Darzhee Kut. Darzhee Kut bobbed appreciatively, glanced up, but then the focus of his eyes seemed to go past Caine, as though he had seen something just behind—

Caine's back flared, felt like it was splitting, shattering, with flame gushing in and up along the fracture lines. He staggered forward, heard a soundless roaring in his ears, and then shouting all around him:

"JesusChristCaineShootthatmuthafuckingBelaythat-HelphimOhGodnoCaine."

Caine felt himself sway, caught his balance with a sidestep that half turned him. Apt-Counsel's tank was only two meters behind him, beaded with condensation, wisps of vapor wreathing it in white curlicues, a broad, smoking tube where one of the external manipulator arms had been mounted only a moment before. Caine reached behind, felt wet metal protruding from the right side of his back, felt his balance going again as people rushed in at him from every direction. He took another half step, confident he'd straighten up properly this time...

And found himself falling forward, turning, seeing a whirl of faces: Elena, Trevor, Darzhee Kut, Opal—*Opal? No, not here—and not now. Strange how slowly things move when you fall, when you can't help yourself, when you feel yourself slipping away into unmarked time once again.* Since this morning, he had been reunited with a lover and lost her, learned of the infant growing in her and lost it, rediscovered a lover he had forgotten and child he had never known and now was losing those, too. Because, unfortunately, at this cusp of victory, he had been killed.

As Caine fell forward—faces looming, hands rushing in—he smiled at the banality of his final thought: *Such a busy day.*

Off Lada Bay, Sunda Strait, Earth

The young ocean sunfish circled the fluttering object warily, vaguely recognizing in its downward progress the undulations of a jellyfish: preferred prey. But ultimately, the ocean sunfish flinched away, discerning that this was not a food source after all.

The tattered sleeve of Michael Schrage's uniform, made a colorful motley by service and unit patches, continued its slow-motion descent toward the sandy bottom where the mouth of Lada Bay kissed the Sunda Strait. It was the last piece of wreckage or debris from *Elektronische Kriegsgruppe Zwei* to come to rest. All the others had reached the bottom, and, like this, were too small to ever be of significance to historian-divers or curiosity seekers. None of the VTOLs' flight record-ers survived the catastrophic hits by Arat Kur orbital lasers; no member of the flight survived to tell their tale. The few cells that remained of Schrage's body carried no encoding that marked them as the remains of one of the thousands of humans who had, on that day, courted and were embraced by certain death in the performance of selfless acts against invaders. In Schrage's case, it had involved placing his ship over Dortmund's and Thandla's to give them the extra seconds they needed to ensure that the submarines could safely complete their decisive ascent. That this act was arguably the fulcrum upon which the balance of the battle had tipped made it no greater a sacrifice than the thousands of other sacrifices which had been offered up in the streets, airspaces, or waters around the island of Java.

As the tattered uniform sleeve neared the bottom, a sand shark, attracted by a faint scent of blood, snatched away a shred of skin which clung, scorched and fused, to the partial sleeve. Then, with a swirl of fabric, the sleeve met and flattened long and slow against the muddy sand. The shark swam testily off, disappointed at the meager pickings.

For no greater nourishment or savor resided in the unmissed flesh of unsung heroes.

COUNTERATTACK
Part Two

June 12–14, 2120

Part Two

Chapter Fifty-Four

Far Orbit, Sigma Draconis Two

Caine awakened into a gasp before he was aware of the pain, and that it was peaking: a searing stab that started a few inches under and behind his right floating rib and shot straight up to his scapula. As he exhaled the slowly diminishing pain out of his body, Caine felt a residual ache curl up—sullen and persistent—in the place the stabbing sensation was vacating.

Well, it wasn't like the Ktor nicked me with a pen knife. He remembered a doctor reading off a list of his injuries as he faded in and out of what seemed like postsurgical anesthesia: *"... deep dorsal penetration resulting in transfixing laceration of the latissimus dorsi, splintering fracture of T5, highly localized pulmonary laceration, and multiple lacerations of the liver. Extensive peripheral trauma is observed throughout the right thoracic..."*

He remembered losing focus then, sinking back into the black, and wondering: *Where is Elena? Where is everyone?*

He swam back up out of the lightless depths some time later and remembered hearing himself ask. *"How long?"*

Both the answering voice and the room's ambient sound were markedly different. *"You mean, before you're ambulatory?"*

"No. How long have I been unconscious?"

"Well, strictly speaking, you haven't been fully unconscious since—"

Suddenly, Elena was there in place of the doctor or orderly or whoever. She took his right hand in one of hers, laid the other smooth and firm along his cheek, as though she were poised to hold him harder, to keep him awake, in this world, with her.

"I'm sorry," he said.

"For what?"

"For worrying you. And for being such an easy target."

She smiled and cried without blinking or making a sound.

And was gone.

And now he was here, without her. Wherever here was. He vaguely remembered being strapped in for shift, a surgical nurse beside him, just in case the shock of transition made him flinch, reopened his wounds.

But that was all he remembered, other than occasionally awakening and trying to separate the conflicting feelings that seemed to clutch his heart, paralyze his tears, shackle his joy: mourning for Opal, longing for Elena, and recurrent guilt at the way the first emotion was so easily overridden by the second.

But as if avenging her rapid passing from his heart, he could feel Opal haunting everything he saw, every breath he drew. For all he knew, he might not be breathing at all had she not drawn the fire that would certainly have been unleashed against Caine, Trevor, and the others who had cowered in that shed in Jakarta.

There was a faint knock at the door. *Thank God. I don't care who it is, just . . .* "Come in!"

Downing entered.

Oh. Great. The Lying Bastard himself.

"Awake at last, I see. How are you feeling?"

"Well enough, I suppose." *And thanks for nearly getting me killed again. Asshole.*

Downing drew up a chair. "I'm glad to see you're alert and ready to move about."

Caine knew the tone. "Okay, how much have I missed?"

"So, you know you were in cold sleep, again?"

"It seemed a good guess. I just don't know how long."

Downing looked sheepish. "Caine, what's the last thing you remember?"

"Coming up out of the postsurgical anesthesia, I think. No, wait. I remember someone else, an orderly—" Downing was looking at the floor, a study in discomfort. Caine sighed, wanted to keep hating him but also knew that Richard had been following orders and doing his job. "Okay, how much time have I lost now?"

"Caine, I suspect the first thing you remember is the preoperative review at the time of your second surgery."

"*Second* surgery?"

"Yes. We did what we could right after you were hit in Indonesia, but we lost you on the table."

Caine thought he might vomit. "I was dead?"

"In another few minutes, they would have called the clock and pulled up the sheet. So we had to put you in a cryocell until we could get a different medical team to join us. They were far more advanced, and performed the second surgery."

"Stateside?"

"Er . . . no, spaceside."

"What?"

"Caine, do understand. Not only did we have to rendezvous with the second surgical team as swiftly as possible, but the entirety of the World Confederation Council insisted that you be sent with the invasion fleet to Sigma Draconis. Your unique relationships with so many of the—"

"Whoa, hold on. Sigma Draconis? Invasion fleet? Where the hell am I?"

Downing sighed. "You are in far orbit around the Arat Kur homeworld. We arrived a few days ago."

"And just where on the calendar are we?"

"It's June 12, 2120. You've been unconscious almost constantly for the last five months. The second surgical team did not reach us until late April. We were well underway to bring the war to the Arat Kurs' doorstep, and so they had to catch up. Your recovery was dicey and you were kept in postsurgical cryogenic reduction. Not full cryosleep, but the safest way to monitor an uncertain recovery."

Caine could hardly think through what felt like the hailstorm of mental blows he'd just received. "Then why—why the hell am I even here? Why didn't you leave me on Earth, with Elena, with Connor, with—?"

"I told you. The Consuls insisted you accompany us. Besides, you couldn't stay on Earth, Caine. The surgical team arranged to meet us on the way to

Sigma Draconis. And frankly, you'd still be in cryogenic reduction, recovering, if our mission here hadn't hit—well, a snag."

"So I guess I'm going to have a working recovery before I get to go back home."

"I'm afraid so, Caine. I've brought you this"—Downing held up a datastik—"to help you catch up on what's been going on over the last five months. Can I get you anything else?"

"No—yes! Is Elena here, too?"

"I'm sorry, Caine, but no. This fleet is only carrying essential personnel. Only you were deemed an indispensable asset, if our interactions with the Arat Kur became—problematic."

"Yeah, well, if I'm so indispensable, why couldn't the second surgical team have operated on me before we left Earth, rather than chasing us across umpteen light-years to—?"

But Downing was shaking his head. "No, Caine, you don't understand. The second surgical team was not on Earth. In fact, it would have taken them longer to get there than meet us on the way."

Caine felt something cold moving in the general area of his incision, told himself—somewhat desperately—that it was just his imagination. "The surgical team wasn't on Earth." He knew the answer to his next question before he asked it. "So it was the Dornaani?"

Downing nodded. "They sent a small diplomatic packet to join our fleet on the way to Sigma Draconis Two. It was also carrying their surgeons and equipment. To whom I am quite sure you owe your life."

Seems I owe lots of people my life: first Opal, now the Dornaani. Meaning I've got twice as many debts as I can reasonably repay. I've only got the one life, after all.

"Caine, are you all right? I know it's a beastly lot of shocks to absorb—"

"No, Richard. I'm okay. But it sounds like our situation with the Arat Kur isn't, so I'd better get reading, hadn't I?" Caine shook the datastik meaningfully.

Downing's answering smile was rueful. "I suppose so. But you don't need to get started straight away—"

"Yes. Yes, I'd better." Caine felt his patience slipping as picked up the bedside dataslate. "It will give me something to do other than think about a son I should be meeting, and the two women I should be visiting with flowers." *And whether or not I should keep hating your guts, duty and orders be damned.*

Downing cocked his head. "Bouquets for two women?"

"Yes, Richard." *Did he really not understand?* "One bouquet to bring to Elena's door, and another for Opal's grave."

Downing grew pale. Caine looked away as the computer brightened.

A moment later, he heard Downing close the door behind himself.

✧   ✧   ✧

The next morning, when Downing returned and knocked on the door—reluctantly, cautiously—Caine was already up and dressed, staring at the dataslate's screen. It looked as though he'd been reading from it most of the preceding night. "So, it seems we've been pretty busy getting some payback from the Arat Kur while I was napping."

"Yes, although I think what's distressed them most

is having us show up at their homeworld without a fraction of the warning they were expecting."

Caine nodded. "Speaking of their homeworld, I see from the battle reports that only two days ago, they were still fighting to retain control of their orbital space."

Downing nodded. "The Arat Kur defense drones kept our lads on their toes for quite a while."

"Any losses?"

"Some, but not heavy. Lord Halifax was a step ahead of our opponents all the way." Downing leaned back. "Which means they are now helpless at the bottom of their homeworld's gravity well. Which led everyone to expect that they'd finally be willing to discuss surrender terms. But instead they're not even returning our communiqués. That's why Visser and Sukhinin finally agreed to rouse you a week early. There are military pressures—strategic pressures—that make it essential we make some progress in regard to negotiations."

Caine nodded, turned away from his dataslate. "I think part of the problem with the negotiations is that there's a puzzle piece we're missing. And because of that missing piece, we're not fully understanding what we're seeing."

"To what are you referring, specifically?"

"I mean we've got too many unanswered questions about why the war-averse Arat Kur were so eager to fight us in the first place, and why it seems that the Ktor were laying the groundwork for this invasion of us long before we came to the Convocation."

Downing leaned back. "What's got you thinking about that?"

"Well, as soon as we realized that it was the Ktor who were almost certainly behind the Doomsday Rock, I started to wonder if they recruited the Arat Kur as their 'plan B' when it failed."

"Interesting notion. But why the Arat Kur, specifically?"

"Because I suspect the Ktor were quite aware of the Arat Kurs' prior knowledge—and fear—of our species as age-old destroyers."

Downing leaned forward. "Caine, do you really think there's anything to those folk myths of their lower castes?"

Caine glanced sideways at him. "The Arat Kur—Darzhee Kut, Hu'urs Khraam, others of the higher castes—made oblique references to what humanity had done, had been, before now. As if they were afraid of what we might do to them now because of something we'd done to them in the past."

"Maybe—or maybe you just misunderstood what was being said, or the translators garbled their intent."

"Perhaps. But how do you explain their suicide systems?"

Downing frowned. "Technical intelligence and prisoner interviews both agree that the suicide cysts of the Arat Kur *do* seem to be nonstandard equipment. But the Trojan bug wiped out any data that might have shed light on whether those suicide systems were part of a concerted plan or a harebrained option spearheaded by a cabal of superstitious and senile extremists, as the senior surviving Arat Kur claim."

"Of course they'd fabricate a story like that. They'd want to make their mass-*seppuku* look like an aberration, not their standard operating procedure."

"So you believe that they really did know about humanity long before?"

"Yes, particularly given some of the comments I overheard."

"It's an interesting theory, but it does have one rather large flaw, don't you think?"

"Which is?"

Downing couldn't help smiling. "Well, it's all predicated on the idea that the great 'destroyers' of their race came from Earth. But we weren't exactly flying about the cosmos, squashing mammalian beetles twenty thousand or even ten thousand years ago, were we? If I recall my history, I think the ancient Egyptians or Chinese were still striving mightily to perfect basic crop irrigation, rather than building interstellar invasion forces."

Caine didn't smile. "Remind me: how old are the human ruins I found on DeePeeThree?"

Downing stopped smiling. "Twenty thousand years. Give or take."

"No matter how much you give or take, they weren't made by, or for, any humans who called Earth 'home.' Couldn't be, for the historical reasons that you've provided. Yet there the ruins sit, created and extant in the same general epoch in which the cognoscenti of the Arat Kur insist that humans were destroying their civilization."

"And that's why the natives on DeePeeThree knew humans on sight," he said slowly.

"Hell, they were even able to point out the insignificant yellow speck that is our home star in their night sky." Caine carefully swung his feet down to the floor. "Look, life since the Parthenon Dialogs has been more like an opera than reality. In the course of a single year, we experience first contact, jockey for political equality with other races, are invaded, fight free, and now stand panting on the threshold of our future among the stars. But what we've overlooked is that no matter how much it may feel like it, this is *not* the beginning of the story. The story—whatever that is—began thousands of years ago. This only seems like the beginning to us because it is where we enter—or maybe reenter—the tale."

Downing felt his frown deepening. "Fair enough. So let's say some humans who did not live on Earth attacked the Arat Kur ten or twenty millennia ago. And so they have a sore spot for us. How does that change how we deal with them, here and now?"

"Firstly, we're dealing with a species which has conceived of us as 'the enemy' for longer than we've had writing. We're not a military opponent. We're their iconic bogey-men. That might complicate negotiations a bit.

"But secondly, the bigger multimillennia context should prompt us to ask this: what other ancient agendas, animosities, initiatives might be in play here? To us, it is all terrifyingly and wondrously new. But to the Dornaani, the Ktor, the Slaasriithi, and maybe the Arat Kur? And maybe even the natives of DeePeeThree? Richard, we have fallen into the common trap of seeing ourselves at the center of the universe: all that goes on around us somehow has us as its subject and *raison d'etre*. But in reality, all the events, all the plans, all the acts we interpret as intentionally malign—or benign—to us may, in fact, have almost nothing to do with our species. Or, in the case of the Arat Kur, have nothing to do with us as we are now."

Downing imagined Nolan's ghost grinning at him over Caine's shoulder. "What do you mean, 'as we are now'?"

"I mean, as Earth-born humans who, after five thousand years of relatively intact and complete history, are the brand-spanking-new entrants into the cosmos. But others in that cosmos might recollect some other batch of humans that was grabbed off Earth, bred for purposes both noble and nefarious. Some of whom may have been on Delta Pavonis Three, and some of whom may have done to the Arat Kur exactly what the Arat Kur say they did."

"And, of course, the Dornaani must know the whole story."

"Or a whole hell of a lot of it. And that could be crucial as we try to jump-start the negotiations with the Arat Kur. Because since Alnduul is here with us, that means there's someone in the room who *does* know the bigger story. From their own admission, the Dornaani have been Custodians for about seven thousand years, and it's a surety their histories stretch back well before then. That means that they must have a damn good idea of what was going on in this stellar cluster ten thousand years ago."

"Well, since we've got Alnduul on board, it will be easy enough to put questions to him."

"As if one ever gets straight answers out of the Dornaani. Which reminds me. When the Dornaani made their first contact with you, were they just as enigmatic as they've been since then?"

Downing scoffed. "It was blasted freakish. A message

coming out of nowhere, tight-beamed at an IRIS-DoD satellite."

"Richard, don't play coy with me. It had to have been a lot stranger than that, given the package they left waiting for you in deep space."

Oh damn. He's figured it out...

Caine nodded. "Because they had to smuggle you the device that you put into my arm on Mars, after those two Russians attempted to 'assassinate' me. Which was pure theater, all so you could get me into surgery and slip that Dornaani device into my arm. Tell me, was it Alnduul himself who came to our system, bearing strange gifts?"

Richard looked down. *No use concealing it now.* "No. I don't know if any of them even came within an AU of any of our planets. We simply received a signal directing us to deep space coordinates. We retrieved the device and a few instructions for its implantation and for subsequent communications with them. We learned what the implant did, and set up the eventual rendezvous for the delegation to be transported to the Convocation."

"And the device itself—implausibly perfect for your purposes, wasn't it? Almost like they knew what you needed to make Case Timber Pony work. A secret plan that they should have been completely unaware of."

So, you've wondered too? "It was as if we had ordered it from a catalog. Case Timber Pony would have been an uncertain—and damned messy—business without it."

"Yes, but Case Timber Pony was just one, penul- timate ploy in a long string of traps and tricks. If they knew how to provide what you needed for Case

Timber Pony, then they had to be aware of the other plans, as well."

Downing nodded. "They were. They never mentioned the different plans, but it was as if they had tapped into Nolan's strategic stream-of-consciousness. If it hadn't been for their implication that they knew what he had wanted, I would not have approved of the implantation or their other offers to help us protect ourselves in the event that the Convocation went as badly as it did. But try as I might, I've not been able to get Alnduul to tell me *how* they found out about—"

In answer to a soft knock on the door, Caine said. "Come in."

Ben Hwang entered, nodding at the two of them. "Good to see you awake, Caine. How are you feeling?"

"Just a little stiff, Ben. Thanks for asking. Draw up a chair?"

"Thank you, but no; I have to get back to the lab. Just wanted to see how you were doing and pass a report on to Mr. Downing. And ask him a question."

Richard nodded. "What's the question, Ben?"

Hwang scratched the back of his head. "Richard, is it true that we have some new visitors in-system?"

My, news travels fast. "Yes, Ben. A Slaasriithii ship showed up about two hours ago. The Dornaani seemed to be expecting it, and have vouched for its *bona fides*."

"Any guess why they decided to enter a war zone? I was under the impression that the Slaasriithii are pretty retiring. They were certainly the least communicative species at the Convocation."

Downing shrugged. "I was just as surprised at you, but the Dornaani speculate that with the hostilities winding down, they want to be on hand for whatever happens here, possibly initiate some kind of formal contact with us."

Hwang nodded. "Any chance we're going to get a look at one, arrange a meeting? It would be a good opportunity to get some samples of their—"

Downing smiled. "I'll let you know as soon as I learn anything relevant, Ben. Besides, I would think you have enough exobiology challenges on your hands already." Richard felt his smile slip. "About which, how's the reconstruction coming?"

Hwang avoided Downing's eyes. "Completed. We have reverse-engineered the original Arat Kur virus that they adopted for their suicide cysts."

"Well done. What was involved?"

"The tricky work was all up front. In order to understand the virus, we had to map the Arat Kur genetic structures. Like human smallpox, the virus mimics natural cells present in the Arat Kur body—the circulatory system, to be specific. The virus has almost exactly the same genetic template as normal Arat Kur cells, so the body's defenses don't recognize it as an intruder and the immune system's hunter-killer cells don't activate."

"How had the Arat Kur modified the original organism?"

"To make it useful as a suicide device, the Arat Kur simply turned off its ability to produce viable airborne infectants and slowed its reproductive process."

Downing's voice was very quiet. "And its broader weapons potential?"

Hwang studied the floor. "The original virus was one of the most contagious and lethal of all their plague bugs. As such, it was the first they sought to eliminate, which they accomplished almost a thousand years ago. Consequently, almost no modern Arat Kur have any immunities against it, and they have long since ceased retaining any extensive ready supplies of, or production facilities for, the vaccine they developed over eight hundred years ago."

Downing kept his voice level. "Total estimated effect on an infected population?"

"Ninety percent fatalities." Hwang rose, looking glum. "I'll have warhead-volume stocks of the Arat Kur virus within a day, maybe two." Hwang opened the door, nodded. Caine nodded back.

Richard spoke soon as the door had closed after Hwang. "Actually, while we're on the topic of the Arat Kur, I'm rather hoping you'll help us by trying to talk to one today."

"Darzhee Kut?"

Downing looked down. "The debriefing team feels that it has run out of options. Permissible options, that is."

Caine was on his feet quickly. "Why? Won't he talk to anyone else?"

"Not productively. And I think it's important you try to communicate with him before the debriefing team convinces Visser or Sukhinin to allow them to use—well, impermissible options."

Caine left the room in a rush.

Chapter Fifty-Five

Far Orbit, Sigma Draconis Two

Darzhee Kut heard the cycles of sound in his head repeat, welcomed the familiar cadences and tones, told himself he was glad there was nothing to distract his attention from the mostly random waves of submusic that washed over and through his mind.

A strange thumping rang against the room's hatch. At first, Darzhee Kut thought the ship might be in distress, that the sound was the precursor to disabling or destruction. But no: it was just a modest, steady thumping.

And then he realized that it must be a person, requesting entrance, "knocking" on the door. Darzhee Kut roused out of his trancelike stare into the room's far corner. For many days, he had not heard a knock on a door. When his questioners entered, they gave no warning. They determined when he slept, when he ate, when he was allowed to speak, when not. They arrived at different times, in different numbers, with different questions. And they never, ever, addressed him by name or title, although they often left one of their number behind. He was rarely allowed to be alone. Whether that was out of consideration for his species' monophobia or to prevent him from doing harm to himself was unclear.

But a knock on the door. One would not knock unless one was intrinsically conferring the right of choice to the person on the other side of the door, whether to admit the visitor or not. And that meant it was not improbable that, at last, he was being visited by—

He chittered a permission to enter. Caine Riordan appeared through the opening hatch. "Darzhee Kut," the human said. It sounded more like a question than a greeting.

"Caine Riordan."

"I am glad to see that you are well."

"What you see is that I am alive. 'Well' is a more relative term."

Riordan came closer. "Did they—the debriefing team—mistreat you in any way. *Any* way?"

"No," Darzhee had to admit, "they did not. But I had hoped I might be able to tell you so earlier."

Riordan looked away. "I was not able to come before now. My injuries were—severe."

Darzhee felt his eye-lenses constrict in concern. "But you are well now, Caine Riordan?"

The human smiled. "As you observed, 'well' is a relative term. I am recovering."

"I am glad to hear it. I would be interested to hear of other things, as well. Specifically, there are questions I have pondered these long months, for which I have been unable to deduce answers."

"Questions such as . . . ?"

"Such as how, only a few weeks after the Convocation, Earth already had a complex sequence of deceptions ready for us, and how it was already prepared to wage war?"

The human leaned his back—carefully—against the wall. "I can't share all the details with you, but for quite some time, influential persons had realized that it was very likely that we would encounter exosapients and that we might quickly find ourselves at war with them. So, starting about five years ago, serious war preparation began, mostly under the cover of other activities. Antimatter production was increased to ensure extensive operating surpluses. There was a major influx of discretionary funds funneled surreptitiously into the construction of new classes of capital ships, stockpiles of nuke-pumped X-ray laser drones, a new generation of control sloops, defense ships cored out of asteroids, massive cislunar drone inventories, expansion of commando units with zero-gee training, cutting-edge vertibirds and interceptors. It was necessary to establish many of these industries outside our home system. In particular, we developed a great deal of dirtside and spaceside industry in Delta Pavonis, using the system-wide quarantine that was in place from 2118 onward as an intelligence blackout curtain behind which we could conceal these activities."

"I suppose that would explain why the Ktoran's human collaborators were largely unaware of these activities. You are to be congratulated on your talent for deception. We were too often taken in by your ruses and decoys. But the loss of your fleet near Jupiter: there were no decoys there."

Riordan nodded. "There couldn't be. We knew you'd

have ample time to conduct post-action forensics once you were in our home system, so there, everything had to be authentic. So we accepted those losses in advance, and figured that the fight-to-the-finish you got at Jupiter would further convince you that our desperation was absolute. And if you picked up any survivors of those craft, that was exactly what they believed."

Darzhee Kut bobbed, but there was one thing that still mystified him—had mystified all of his rock-siblings. "These notes ring true and obvious, now that we see how they were sounded, and why. But I am still perplexed: how did your relief fleet know to come to Earth when it did, and how did it arrive so quickly? I remember that you had one shift-carrier—the *Tankyū-sha Maru*— accelerating to preshift velocities when we arrived in the system. But it only shifted out less than an hour before your whole fleet shifted in to counterattack us in cislunar space. How is that possible? Our intelligence on your shift capabilities is not in error. It takes at least thirty-two days for you to build up sufficient kinetic energy to initiate your shift. How did your counterattacking fleet do it in mere minutes?"

The human smiled. "It didn't have to build up the kinetic energy. The fleet was already traveling at preshift velocity."

Darzhee Kut saw the answer—so simple, so elegant— with great suddenness. It was as though he had been deaf, but now regained his hearing from this clap of revelatory thunder. "Roof rock. Now I see it. Your ships were all preaccelerated. They were merely awaiting the word to return to your home system."

"Just so. We used the same strategy to cut other key communication intervals down to minutes or hours.

For instance, when you arrived in Barnard's Star, you may remember detecting a shift-vessel almost fully preaccelerated, in the far outer system?"

"Yes, of course. The *Prometheus*, I believe."

"Correct. And when it shifted, it went straight to Ross 154."

"Which we sent part of our fleet to interdict."

"As we would have, in your place. But that's why there was already *another* preaccelerated shift carrier waiting in Ross 154."

"And the ship from Ross 154?"

"It hopped to the system we designate as Lalande 21185, which is where we had stashed all the ships and crews you thought you destroyed at Barnard's Star. That unit—Relief Task Force One—immediately began to load all ordnance and units, and secure for pre-shift acceleration. That was on November 26. They attained preshift velocity on New Year's Day, and then they waited."

Darzhee Kut bobbed. "They waited for the *Tankyū-sha Maru*, the shift-carrier that jumped out from your home system on the day of their attack. Which must have had a time-based estimate of where your fleet was in Lalande 21185. And so it was able to deliver the message swiftly."

"Correct. And when Relief Task Force One arrived near Earth, that started the clock ticking for all the surprises we sprung on you on Java."

Darzhee Kut considered. "Even without the Dornaani device in your arm, you might have won."

Caine shrugged again. "Possibly. But it would have been a much, much costlier battle."

"True. Caine Riordan, I must ask. How many of

my rock-siblings in space had their songs stilled by the Final—by their own claws?"

The human seemed to study him closely. "Less than a dozen of your major ships refrained from destroying themselves after the surrender."

"Which your people no doubt saw as treachery, as a ploy to lure your boarding teams to their deaths."

"Yes, it seemed that way."

"Did they not understand that it was not our intent to destroy your people? That, because your computer virus paralyzed our ships, we had no way to scuttle them until *after* your soldiers had commandeered them?"

"Some knowledgeable—and calm—people concede that your actions may not have been intended to harm us. But even they do not understand why all the Arat Kur would be so determined to kill themselves."

"But you do."

"I might."

"You must! You heard our discussions in the headquarters, the careless talk. You know that we remember your race, and what it did, even if your own people do not."

"Darzhee Kut, in the epoch during which you claim your race was destroyed, the people of Earth had not yet even learned to navigate the oceans of our planet."

"Then it may not have been humans from Earth, but descendants of populations taken from there in earlier times. But what does it matter which star the ravagers of my planet were born beneath? Their blood is your blood."

"How can you be so sure?"

"How can I not? I have seen the pictures painted

in the deepest refuge-caves. There is no mistaking the shape of your species depicted as our destroyers, more than fifteen thousand of your years ago." He stilled his claws. "And now you are back among the stars. But enough of the past. What has happened since you defeated the forces we brought to your home system?"

"The smaller fleet you sent to Ross 154 destroyed our military facilities there, and then withdrew after deploying a Hkh'Rkh shift-carrier for raiding down the Big Green Main. Meanwhile, the Slaasriithi stepped up pressure along your common border, putting you on the defensive."

Darzhee Kut couldn't decide whether he should be amused or annoyed at the human's claims. "And how would you know all this? You speak of places more than a dozen shifts distant from your homeworld."

The human stared. "The Custodians have been most helpful with intelligence."

Darzhee Kut felt a small, coiling worm-twist in his abdomen. "The Custodians are to remain neutral."

"Unless the Twenty-first Accord is violated. Which you did. And the Dornaani are too busy to correct all the recent abuses to the Accords on their own."

"So you have been deputized by the Custodians?"

"That isn't possible, since we were never confirmed as members of the Accord."

The abdominal squirm doubled. "Then you are operating without constraint?"

"We are, but that would ultimately be your doing, wouldn't it? We tried—very hard—to convince you that we should be made members of the Accord. You refused."

Darzhee Kut let his limbs slump. "When the truth

is sung clearly, there are no counterpoints with which it may be confounded. It is as you say: we are the architects of our own problems."

"I am glad you see it that way, Darzhee Kut. And I am hoping that you can convince your leaders to see the current situation similarly."

"Why? Are we to journeying to meet representatives of the Homenest? And you wish my assistance?"

"That is correct."

"I am flattered, but, in truth, you do not need me. The Homenest's leaders have adequate translation devices and they will listen to your words."

"They have not done so thus far."

Darzhee Kut felt the wormlike sensation move up higher, into his second stomach. "You speak as though you are already in contact with them."

"We are."

The worm twitched its tail as he asked the next, inevitable question, suddenly dreading the answer, on the verge of vertigo, the universe suddenly adrift and unsteady. "Where are we?"

"We are in a far orbit about your homeworld."

Darzhee Kut rose slowly from his comfortable crouch. "That cannot be. By counting meals and sleep cycles, I estimate it has been ninety-five days since we departed your home system."

"That's an excellent estimate, Darzhee Kut. This is the ninety-third day."

"Then it is impossible for you to have reached Homenest, or what you call Sigma Draconis Two. Even for us, with our greater shift range and shorter preacceleration times, it would take much longer to make such a journey. And for your ships, the fastest way to reach us still required nine shifts. The better part of a year."

"You know the star charts, and their strategic implications, perfectly, Darzhee Kut. But that is not the course we took to get to Sigma Draconis Two."

Darzhee found that the six claws holding him up were tense, quivering. "It is the only one you can take, the only one possible for your technology."

"For our technology, yes. For Dornaani technology, no."

Darzhee Kut felt the cold floor come up under him, slap his belly-plate. "They modified your engines."

"No, just the Wasserman field-effect generator. And they could only do it to certain of our shift-carriers—the Commonwealth, Federation, and Union designs were advanced enough to make use of the greater control and precision of the Dornaani guidance, containment, and navigation systems."

Darzhee Kut saw the room again, as if it was reappearing from out of a fog. "So, you made deep-space shifts."

"Correct. From Earth we shifted to a deep space site with two carriers—one from TOCIO, one a commandeered CoDevCo ship—carrying nothing but fuel. They served as tankers for the rest of our fleet, which shifted on to V1581 Cygni2."

"Which is only eight light-years from Homenest."

"Eight point two five, to be exact."

Rotting flesh and plague, it is true. Humans are hovering over Homenest. The ravagers had returned, after having repulsed an invasion of their homeworld. Darzhee Kut felt lower digestive juices rise through the valves that led into his first stomach, clamped them

down. "How many ships?" It came out sounding like
a pebble-choked gargle.

Riordan shrugged. "Five shift carriers—two Commonwealth, two Federation, one Union—fitted to
capacity with capital ships, ordnance, transatmospheric
attack craft, commandos. And we used two of your
shift-carriers, as well."

Darzhee Kut felt his eyelenses grind against each
other until they were a quivering, locked collection
of plates. The world was an amber blur. "Two of *our*
shift carriers?"

"Yes, one of which was your orbital flotilla's command ship. We loaded it with a mix of our warcraft
and yours."

"But surely none of my rock-siblings would help
you by—"

"No. The Dornaani provided us with control interfaces. We are running the craft ourselves."

Darzhee Kut half-turned toward the wall again.
Zkhee'ah Drur the Elder had once observed that
while one is yet alive to complain of misfortune, the
greatest of all misfortunes has not yet occurred. But
this turn of affairs seemed very close to disproving
that ancient axiom. "I take it that using our ships has
made the invasion of our systems much easier."

"Yes, although there wasn't much of a fight in V1581
Cygni2. Only minor defense elements were present,
no shift ships. But lots of useful intelligence. Then we
shifted here. That was a sharper fight."

"I'm surprised you won."

"Well, since your leaders didn't think we could
hop straight into their laps, they kept most of your
defense fleet at AC+54 1646-56. That's the system

that controls the route you, and they, presumed we would have to take."

"That is only one shift away from Homenest, for our ships."

"Precisely. That's why we had to hit you hard and fast here in your home system. We didn't want anyone shifting out and calling for help. So we used the ships we captured from you as lures."

"Lures?"

Riordan nodded. "We made it seem like they were still your ships, returning from Earth. Your ships and command personnel took the bait. All but delivered themselves to us on a silver platter."

"The story you tell is not possible. You would not have been believed, for you did not have our passwords."

Caine Riordan looked away. "Actually, we did."

Darzhee Kut rose on his front claws. "They were not stored in our computers, and those of my rock-siblings who had been entrusted with the knowing of them would never have surrendered them willingly to you."

"They didn't surrender them—willingly."

Darzhee Kut's antenna yanked into his carapace reflexively. *Sun-timing, blood-drenched savages.* "Your race is unchanged."

Riordan nodded. "That may be true. But this time, it was my race's homeworld that was threatened, invaded, fought over. Between the resentment over that, and a widespread feeling that the Arat Kur deserve whatever happens to them, there have been several acts—crimes—against your rock-siblings which are terribly wrong."

"And will those who performed these actions pay for them?"

"Maybe. Or they might get medals. It is too early to say. At any rate, once we engaged your home defense fleet, the battle lasted about four hours."

"That's all?"

"That's all. We had all your codes and passwords. Also, from your intact ships, we got a pretty complete picture of how you train your personnel, how you fight wars, how you try to trick adversaries, what you fear and how you try to minimize your weaknesses. Accordingly, our fleet was carrying a quadruple load of extremely heavy ordnance, particularly tactical nuclear missiles and nuke-pumped X-ray laser drones. Altogether, it made for a fairly short battle. Which was good, given how close your other fleet is."

"And that is why you need me to talk to my leaders. Because despite your victory, you have limited time."

"Exactly. If we assume that you, too, keep preaccelerated ships as waiting couriers, then news of the attack here could have arrived at AC+54 1646-56 two days ago. Now, best guess and captured intelligence both project that there will be a minimum two-week delay between the time your other fleet gets the message and their earliest arrival here. Which means capitulation must be secured before then."

Darzhee Kut stared at the human. "And why do you think I will help you to enslave my people? And probably destroy them?"

Riordan rose, came closer, sat within reach of his claws. "Darzhee Kut, I am trying to keep your people from *being* destroyed. That's why I need your help."

"Your tunes are discordant. If my people refuse to capitulate, it is because they are gambling—rightly— that you humans will not want to land and fight in our subterranean home. And it would take a long time—too long—to bomb us into submission, living as we do miles beneath the surface. Besides, I doubt the Dornaani will allow that."

"Darzhee Kut, everything you say is true, but you must convince your leaders to surrender."

Darzhee Kut remained silent, hoped the human had learned that this was a polite rejection of his exhortation.

Riordan hung his head a moment, and then looked up. His eyes seemed oddly lusterless. "Very well. You'll need to see this." He produced a palmtop, pushed a button on its screen.

Which winked awake, showing four humans holding down a limp Arat Kur, a fifth squirting a mist into its alimentary openings and eyes. It did not seem particularly painful, but the Arat Kur flinched away.

The scene changed, and a timecode at the bottom indicated that just under three hours had elapsed. The Arat Kur was now moving listlessly, unsteadily, ultimately staggering to a halt against a wall.

The next scene was arresting. The Arat Kur was writhing in the far corner, chittering in a puddle of its own filth. Its shell was peeling, its eye covers seemed dry and unable to close, and the soft tissue around its mouth had become a faint, crusty mauve.

Oh First Mother of us all, no—!

The last scene confirmed Darzhee Kut's fear. The Arat Kur—now barely recognizable as such—spasmed, shuddered so hard that one of his back-plates sprang free, exposing his endodermis to air, fluid spraying. He shrilled, antennae jerking in and out of their sleeves asynchronously. Then a blast of circulatory and digestive fluids erupted from both his mouth and his alimentary endpoint and he was still. The image froze. According to the timecode on the bottom, eight hours and thirteen minutes had elapsed since he had been exposed to the mist.

By all Mothers— He looked directly into Riordan's eyes. "No. You would not do this."

"I would not do any of this. But my people would."

Judging from the disease-ravaged Arat Kur corpse frozen on the palmtop's screen, evidently they would. "You recreated the plague."

"Yes. Using cyst samples, we reverse-engineered it to its original state. Here's how I believe the military will deliver it: our fleet would take up station-keeping for sustained bombardment of your homeworld. Ultimately, we will overwhelm your defensive systems. Fairly easy, now that we understand their particular vulnerabilities.

"In the midst of this barrage, we will seed in some plague rockets with penetrator warheads. Most will explode and deliver the pathogen via aerosol dispersion upon attaining subterranean chambers. Follow-up missiles will probably burrow right in behind them, carrying a payload of microbots which, once released, will carry packets of the disease at least fifty kilometers from the impact site and start disseminating it based on sensor contacts with primary vectors for infection: water supplies, foodstuffs, breeding crèches."

Breeding crèches: Darzhee Kut's second stomach partially refluxed into his primary stomach. He looked at the disease-ravaged corpse frozen like death itself on the palmtop's screen. "And was it necessary to use innocents as test subjects?"

The human shrugged. "I wonder if the word 'innocent' applies to anyone involved in this war. However, the three prisoners who were subjected to the test were among those who had capitulated on false pretenses, in order to ambush and kill our boarding teams when we overwhelmed your forces at V1581 Cygni2. At any rate, beyond the question of innocence, a live test was deemed necessary by our generals."

"And you agree with them?"

Caine looked away. "I've stopped agreeing with any of this—what my people do, and what your people do—a long time ago. However, there is a certain grim logic behind their decision."

"Which was to make sure that it worked in a 'field trial'?"

Caine nodded. "And there was concern that if your leaders did not receive irrefutable evidence of the disease and its course—precisely how it works, right down to the smallest details of the changes in Arat Kur biochemistry—then they might question whether we had really reengineered it. They could have conjectured that we were bluffing: that we found the cysts, realized what they implied genetically, but were unable to actually produce the pathogen."

Darzhee Kut's claws sagged. The human was probably right. "But with precise clinical observations of the stages of the disease, a genetic map of the virus in all its various stages, and this—demonstration—of its weaponization, then they would know that you had created the organism and observed it through a full course of its life cycle in a host."

"Yes."

"As you say, I revile the decision, but I fear that

your generals may have been right in their apprehension: just as they were ruthless enough to develop and test the virus, the leaders of the Wholenest might well have been willing to gamble the billions of Arat Kur on the homeworld by 'calling your bluff,' as you say. And they will discover that you shall do to us what we, in your system, repeatedly refused to do to you—despite the incessant urging of the Hkh'Rkh."

"A just remonstration. But here's a just question for you to consider in return. If your leaders regained an advantage, would they not return to Earth and now do exactly what the Hkh'Rkh urged them to do?"

"Yes, probably—but Caine Riordan, you must know that I would never agree to such an atrocity."

"Unfortunately, you do not speak for the Wholenest, any more than I speak for the World Confederation. We must guess what those above us will do, based on the events and fears which have now accumulated. And I know this. If your fleet returns before you surrender control of your defenses and communities to us, then it is we who might well be destroyed. We cannot expect to gain the upper hand against your race a second time. So our victory must be won now, or become a disastrous defeat, ending in the reinvasion of Earth."

Riordan leaned forward urgently. "Even the most moderate of my people are willing to take any steps necessary to ensure that you do not invade us again. Most will simply accept your surrender and sufficient concessions. But some—and their voices are growing louder and more convincing with every passing hour—counsel that there is only one way to be sure." The human looked meaningfully at the image on the screen of his palmtop.

The dirt-cursed Hur *and their caste-stubbornness! Do they really think that the humans would hover over Homenest with no better weapon than a bluff?* "After what happened to the fleet they sent to invade Earth, the Wholenest leaders still will not listen?"

Riordan shook his head. "They refuse to believe our story of what transpired on Earth. Their answer to the first communiqué—the only response we have ever received from them—was that it was 'impossible' that we had repulsed your invasion, and therefore, they suspected that our arrival in your home system was part of an elaborate ruse to get them to surrender when they did not actually need to. They told us they would not respond again unless it were to speak to Hu'urs Khraam."

"I am not he."

"No, but you are the one he designated Delegate Pro Tem at the minute of his death. You are senior among the Arat Kur who have survived; who but you may speak?"

"My caste is insufficient. I am but an Ee'ar. They will not listen to me. It was why the Shipmasters did not listen to me when I rescinded the—when I called for them to desist scuttling their vessels. It will be no different here."

"You cannot know that if you do not try."

"I am weary of trying and failing. But I will try... try..." Darzhee Kut felt his claws, and then his legs, begin to grow numb. It was the onset of fugue-torpor, induced by the emotional shock of what he had seen, had heard. How to explain that to a human? "Depression and mental shock" explained the sensation, but wholly missed the physical inescapability of the phenomenon, once its onset had commenced. "But later. I . . . am weary. For now. Find someone else. To speak to the leaders. Of the. Wholenest."

He turned to the wall, and allowed the cycles of sound to build within his inner ears, taking comfort and refuge in the waves of smoothly repetitive tones he heard/felt/tasted there—since he was now capable of little else.

Through those sine-waves of solace, he thought he heard Caine Riordan speak again. "Darzhee Kut, if you do not speak, your planet—your race—may die. Please, consider again: speak to your world, to your people."

Darzhee Kut tried to listen more closely to Caine, but fell into the rhythm of the soothing cycles, wandered lost among the rolling peaks and valleys of the gentle tones manufactured by self-created changes in the air pressure between his own multiple ear-drums.

Chapter Fifty-Six

Far Orbit, Sigma Draconis Two

The guard saluted as Caine left the room, then smartly resecured the hatch with the crisp, focused motions of a rating who was being observed during inspection. *How the hell do they even know I held a rank?* Caine returned the salute, turned the corner to return to his room—and came face to face with Alnduul.

"It is pleasant meeting you here, Caine Riordan."

"It pleases me to see you also, Alnduul. What brings you to the secure section of the ship?"

"You do, Caine Riordan. It is where I was told I would find you."

Ah. "Will you walk with me as I return to my quarters?"

"I would be glad to walk with you, Caine Riordan, but I bring news that Confederation Consuls Sukhinin and Visser wish to meet with you in the forward conference suite. I hoped we might walk there together."

And work a little of that subtle Dornaani discursive magic as we go, eh? "Let us walk, then."

As they walked, Caine waited, counting off the seconds. Had he been asked to guess, he would have predicted a prefatory fifteen-second silence.

Just as Caine mentally ticked off "seventeen," Alnduul asked, "The Arat Kur persist in their refusal to return your communiqués?"

"So I am told."

"And Delegate Kut cannot intercede?"

"He does not believe he can. And he seems to have become physically indisposed. I witnessed something similar when he was isolated prior to our rescue at Barnard's Star. But this time, there was no apparent causal trauma."

"I see. And you? Are you quite well?"

"Er...yes." Caine wished Alnduul had asked one of his maddeningly oblique questions, instead. This jarringly sudden—and apparently dispassionate—shift to personal pleasantries made Riordan wonder if Dornaani calm also concealed an almost sociopathic detachment. *You tried talking to the Arat Kur? No progress? Ho hum, I suppose their species has to die, then. Such a pity.* But Caine simply added, "I'm okay."

Alnduul nodded. "Clearly, the hepatic regrowth agents are proving efficacious. This is gratifying to me."

"Well, that's nothing compared to how gratified my people must be that you decided to come to Earth after all."

"I regret having to deny my intent to travel to Earth after the Convocation, but Mr. Downing asserted that possible leaks in your intelligence structure made it imperative that my visit remain a secret. Had the Arat Kur learned of our presence, they might have become far more cautious. Consequently, the outcome of the conflict might have been far less decisive."

"You must have brought a fair amount of equipment with you as well."

"We did, but why do you so conjecture?"

"Well, it stands to reason, given how you were able to accede to our request to give our ships the ability to counterattack the Arat Kur. I imagine that it requires a number of fairly bulky subsystems to modify our carriers for shifts to and from deep space."

Alnduul's eyelids nictated once. "Apologies, but I must correct your surmise, Caine Riordan. It was not your leaders who asked for the deep space shift modifications. We Custodians offered this assistance. Indeed, it was one of the primary reasons I was sent to your world."

"So you didn't come in the role of a diplomat, but as a techno-military adviser."

"Let us say my mission was multifaceted."

"With an emphasis on ensuring that we could adequately defend ourselves."

"In truth, I was not overly concerned about the success of your defensive efforts. After considerable study, we were confident that, once the device in your arm came within a few meters of a suitable computer, the Arat Kur defeat was certain."

"So what was your primary mission?"

Alnduul waved lazily about him. "To see to your arrival here. Dornaan wished to be certain of swift success against the Ktor, and this necessitated that we keep our strength massed near our borders with them. The Slaasriithi are not particularly experienced or adept at military endeavors, so it fell to us to provide Earth with the means of sending her most advanced shift-carriers on a strategic counteroffensive into Arat Kur space."

"And here we are."

"It is as you say. And our plans have largely unfolded as we envisioned. Your attack has caught the Arat Kur off-guard and they have lost the military initiative. I feel confident that they will never regain it and that you will use this moment to cripple their ability to make war for several decades to come. And it is a near-certainty that, upon learning of the capitulation of the Arat Kur homeworld, the Ktor will propose a truce and the process of rapprochement will begin."

"Well, let's hope the Arat Kur will surrender." Riordan watched Alnduul's face for any sign of a matching concern, any hint of alarm that the subtle charnel smell of genocide was seeping into the void left by the Arat Kur's diplomatic silence.

But Alnduul merely responded, "Let us so hope. But regardless, your mastery of the situation is clear and the outcome is certain. And most gratifying."

"Gratifying in what way?"

"Is it not obvious? Your foes thought to defeat you with surprise attacks and trickery, but found themselves overmatched by your own cunning use of the same tactics. You have indeed proven the wisdom of your race's the axiom that, sometimes, one must fight fire with fire."

Caine started. "You used that same phrase, right after Convocation, when you tried to warn me that war might be coming. And Nolan Corcoran used it just after Parthenon." He turned to watch Alnduul's features. "I've always wondered: did you use that phrase because Nolan had used it in conversation with me, several times before?"

"We Custodians are privy to many conversations between humans. It is difficult to keep track of all of them."

Caine stopped walking. "Alnduul, don't play games with me. I've tolerated your many oblique intimations and fortune-cookie axioms, but this time—this one time—I want a straight answer. You knew Nolan said that to me right before he died, didn't you?"

Alnduul's eyelids nictated once, slowly. "I—*we*—did."

Caine spoke through the shiver that had spread cold fingers across his back. "We were alone when Nolan said it. No one else heard."

"Yet we know."

"But how—?"

Alnduul's hand came up. "I answered your question. It was insightful and has revealed much to you. It suggests much more. But I will not answer questions pertaining to our methods."

But suddenly, Caine was sure. "It was Nolan's implant, wasn't it?"

Alnduul's lids fluttered.

"That organism in his chest wasn't just to help his heart, was it? It gave you a means of exerting subtle control over him, possibly through timely alterations of body chemistry—"

Alnduul's lamprey mouth straightened into a ghastly rictus. "We would not do what you imply."

"No? Isn't that just the kind of long-term strategy you'd use to control the Hkh'Rkh, maybe even the Arat Kur?"

"Nolan Corcoran was a balanced being and a visionary

among your kind. We control only those organisms which we deem, after long observation and innumerable confirmations, to be irremediable destabilizers of their own and others' environments."

"Yet you Dornaani manage to get humans to add all sorts of implants to each other, don't you?"

"Our perspective on these—interventions—is that we provide assistance when it is essential, and only to ameliorate crises that would not have occurred had it not been for our own failings as Custodians. Nolan Corcoran should never have had to intercept what you call the Doomsday Rock. Your planet should never have been left defenseless after Convocation. We attempted to compensate for these failures using the smallest, least obtrusive, methods at our disposal."

"So you say. And I still don't understand how the hell you pulled off getting that organism into Nolan years before you even contacted us."

Their walk had finally brought them into the busy corridors of the command disk at the bow of the shift-carrier. "There is much you do not understand about us yet, Caine Riordan. It is probable that this will ever be the case. We prefer it that way."

"In other words, you prefer that we humans remain easier to control. Excuse my bluntness. Allow me to rephrase: Our ignorance of your methods makes us easier to 'guide in positive directions.'"

"Yes, although that is not the reason for remaining reticent in regards to our methods."

"Then what *is* the reason?"

Alnduul looked squarely at Caine, who believed he had started to understand enough of the facial expressions of the Dornaani to read this one. A mighty attempt to repress impatient paternalism. "Caine Riordan, you have learned you have a thirteen-year-old son, have you not?"

"I have."

"And, assuming he has been trained in its use and safety, would you trust him with that sidearm?" The Dornaani's eye's flicked down at the Unitech ten-millimeter that had been issued to Caine as a mandatory part of his daily dress.

"Well—if there was sufficient reason, yes."

"Let us say you had been fortunate enough to know your son as a two-year-old, a 'toddler,' in your vernacular. Would you have trusted him with your sidearm at that time?"

"I would have to be insane to do such a thing."

"As we would have to be insane to entrust humans with all our methods, our secrets, and our technologies. Of course, restricting access to objects does not reduce the curiosity of the two-year-old, nor their eagerness to handle objects that they associate with those older then they—even if told that the objects would be lethal to them."

Caine didn't want to smile, but found he couldn't keep the corners of his mouth from rising slightly. "So, you're telling me not to get too big for my diapers."

Alnduul's nose and mouth puckered together in puzzlement, then unfurled into an amused twist. "Beings that can laugh at themselves, particularly their own foibles, stand the greatest chance of attaining wisdom." He stopped at the door to the conference suite. "Enter first. I will join you shortly." His mouth still twisted, Alnduul spread his arms very slowly, but angled them toward the human, thereby converting the generic Dornaani farewell gesture into a very personal one. "Enlightenment unto you, Caine Riordan."

Caine spread his arms in return. "And unto you, Alnduul."

Whose lids nictated once before he turned and moved away with the strange grace of a flat- (and slightly web-) footed ballet dancer. Caine watched the strange silhouette recede for a moment before turning to enter the conference suite.

The dominant feature of the room—the vast arc of the gallery viewport—was mostly filled with the black of space. The stars were faint against the contrasting brightness of Sigma Draconis, which was mirrored in the polished teak conference table and bathed the chrome fittings in rusty gold. In the lower left quadrant of the near-panoramic viewport was a small but bright gibbous ball: the second planet, Homenest. A few particularly bright stars seemed to be in motion around it, all tracking in roughly the same direction: various other ships of the fleet, tucked extremely close to each other, most at intervals of less than a thousand kilometers. The vastness of the room was not only magnified by this window unto infinity, but by the small number of occupants, which left it an empty, echoing cavern.

Caine started toward the two figures situated on a small platform overlooking the observation gallery which followed along the lower edger of the viewport. "Hello," he called toward them, "I came as soon as I heard you needed me."

The biggest silhouette turned, revealed its face: Sukhinin. The shorter one beside him did so as well: Visser. And down in the gallery, revealed in the gap between them—

Caine stopped in midstep. "What the hell is *that* doing here?"

"Caine—now, be calm. We had to—"

The faint wisps of vapor tendrilling off the side of the Ktoran environmental unit looked serpentine, viperous. "I don't care what you had to do. Get that thing out of here." Two Marine guards—one Canadian, one US—were also down on the gallery level, standing slightly behind the Ktor. Its treads and outsize water-tank made it too large to fit on the platform upon which the two Consuls stood.

"Mr. Riordan," Visser's syllables were Berliner-precise and clipped, "my sincere apologies. We had hoped to get word to you that Ambassador Apt-Counsel-of-Lenses was going to be joining us."

Caine did not want to move closer—which was why he forced himself to advance down to the droplet-beaded environmental tank. "Apt-Counsel is not an ambassador; he is an assassin. Although for all we know, in his culture, those might be the same profession."

The translator rendered Apt-Counsel's voice as a soothing baritone. "With respect, Mr. Riordan, I seem to recall learning that you were involved in combat yourself that day. Even though you were an ambassador."

"Yes, I was involved in combat—after my Hkh'Rkh 'guards' tried to filet me and I had to flee the command center. What was *your* excuse?"

"From what I heard of your conversation with Darzhee Kut, you were attempting to secure further capitulations and seizures of Arat Kur shift-hulls. The more of those which fell into human hands, the greater the peril to our allies and ultimately ourselves. I acted to disrupt, and hopefully defeat, that process."

"So you took on a combat role without being forced into it or physically provoked or endangered."

"At that one instant, yes."

"Sorry, Apt-Counsel. Diplomatic immunity and status is like virginity: once you give it up, you can't get it back."

Sukhinin had flushed a very dark shade of red. "*Da*, Caine. This is how it has ever been, as it should ever be. But . . ."

"But you've made an exception this time, haven't you?"

Visser straightened her five foot, five inches to ramrod attention. "The World Confederation's Council did not wish to, but ultimately, we had no choice. Ambassador Apt-Counsel-of-Lenses is the only representative of his species anywhere near Earth—"

—so far as you know or he admits—

"—and his diplomatic credentials were among the dozen or so presented to us at Convocation as possible future liaisons. He is authorized to speak for his people, and may thus be instrumental in ending this war, particularly if he can help persuade the Arat Kur that they must concede. We had no choice but to reextend his diplomatic privileges. He has given his word that he will not abuse them again."

So now he's promised he'll behave. I feel safer already. Aloud: "So, now he's going to help us?"

"I will do what I can to bring an end to these hostilities," Apt-Counsel supplied.

"Oh, good—because I was afraid you might be here to stab us in the back. Just a figure of speech, you understand."

Caine had the impression that Visser was going to stamp her foot. "Mr. Riordan, please!"

"It is quite all right, Consul Visser. I can hardly expect Mr. Riordan to feel otherwise. Although, for my part, Mr. Riordan, I am glad to see that you are on your feet and almost recovered."

"Why? Looking to get in a little more target practice with your trick arm?"

"Mr. Riordan, you may find it improbable, but, since my side lost, I am glad that you survived my attack. I am sorry to have made it at all."

"Sure. None of us likes failure."

"No, Mr. Riordan. That is not my reason. I accept that in war there must be loss of life and, often, duplicity. But that makes it no less regrettable. In your case, had you been killed in Jakarta, it would have made no difference to the current outcome. And so, your death would have been pointless. I am glad, therefore, in retrospect, that you survived."

"How very rational of you, Apt-Counsel."

"Despite your clearly sarcastic intent, I thank you."

Always the unflappable smooth talker, aren't you, Apt-Counsel? If I remember my Bible stories a-right, some other indefatigable plotter of humanity's downfall evinced that very same attribute, along with being the Prince of Lies. Caine turned to Sukhinin. "So, has Apt-Counsel managed to thaw the current state of affairs with the Arat Kur?"

The Russian, his hair streaked with far more white and gray than when Caine had last seen him, shook his head; his jowls waggled to emphasize the negative. "No, nothing yet. He has tried to contact the leadership of the Wholenest. They will not respond."

"Not even to ask for proof of his identity?"

"No response whatsoever."

"That is hardly surprising, Mr. Riordan," explained Apt-Counsel. "Since the Arat Kur have not seen Ktorans any more than your race has, you yourselves could manufacture a device such as my suit to dupe them. And how would they know the difference until it was too late? The Arat Kur seem to be quite suspicious of such attempts at deception."

Caine kept his focus on Sukhinin. "And that's it? No other insights from our esteemed and trustworthy Ktoran ambassador?"

"Nothing, except he too agrees that the situation is hopeless."

"He *what*?"

Apt-Counsel rolled about a foot closer to the platform. Caine watched for the angle of the manipulator arm, saw that it had not been replaced. And saw that the other arm was missing as well: a prudent precaution. "We Ktor have dealt with the Arat Kur far longer than you have. We know their speciate tendencies and characteristics. They do not act or decide rashly, but once they have, they are slow to change."

Sukhinin's eyes narrowed slightly. "Caine, you know how this standoff must end. Even if we wished to do otherwise—and I do not intend to leave this system until the Arat Kur are no longer a threat—we are under orders from the Confederation Council. The final contingency, which was approved unanimously, is quite clear."

"Wholesale murder of an entire species."

Visser closed her eyes. "Mr. Riordan, none of us like this alternative, but we have already exceeded the maximum time allowed for negotiation and capitulation. We must act in accordance with our orders. And as

Apt-Counsel has pointed out, we may have less time than our analysts originally conjectured."

"Oh? How so?"

Apt-Counsel's voice was smooth and unperturbed. "Your command staff's assessment on the disposition of the Arat Kur fleet in AC+54 1646-56 presumed that it would either be completely preaccelerated, or completely in defensive station-keeping. We have observed that Arat Kur defense postures are not always so uniform. For instance, the majority of their fleet might remain in a ready posture, but a small number of hulls might be preaccelerated, to function either individually as couriers, or collectively as a small strike squadron."

"And do we think that a small strike squadron could destroy us so easily?" Caine looked from Visser to Sukhinin.

The Russian frowned and shrugged. "Who can say? And what if the Arat Kur have not used all their drones here? What if some are still hidden, such as we had on Luna?"

"But I thought that the number of drones we destroyed here met, and even slightly exceeded, the numbers we expected to find, based on captured Arat Kur force-deployment rosters."

"*Da*, that is true. But what if their line commanders were not provided with full accountings of the reserve forces? If that is the case, a small strike squadron could arrive, activate a second wave of hidden defense drones, and damage us so badly that we cannot finish our job here."

Caine nodded, but thought, *Something's not right here. Apt-Counsel has got Visser and Sukhinin panicked. Me too, almost. And that means we're probably not thinking clearly.* He turned to the Ktor. "I find this all a bit strange, Mr. Ambassador."

"Admittedly, it would be unusual for the Arat Kur to have a strike force preaccelerated—"

"That's not what I mean, Apt-Counsel. I mean, aren't you supposed to be the Arat Kurs' ally?"

There was a long silence. "Yes."

"Then I'm a little puzzled. I understand why you are trying to help us contact the Wholenest leadership, but I don't see how sharing your knowledge of Arat Kur military protocols is consistent with your role as their 'ally.'"

"My earlier misdeeds made it incumbent upon me to make an extraordinary show of good faith. Strategically significant revelations were the only way I could readily earn your trust. Also, by presenting all the dangerous and uncertain military variables, it underscored the volatility of the situation. That, in turn, would logically make both parties see the urgency of reaching a peaceful settlement as quickly as possible. Unfortunately, I did not foresee that I would be ignored or rebuffed by the Arat Kur leadership."

Every explanation seems plausible, but still—

The door opened. Ben Hwang entered, Darzhee Kut after him. Alnduul brought up the rear. Sukhinin, seeing Darzhee Kut, straightened, suddenly a redoubtable general of the Motherland. Caine could almost see the absent uniform and the litter of medals jostling for position on the left side of his chest. "Dr. Hwang, Ambassador Alnduul, at best, you failed to request permission to enter. At worst, you have brought a sworn enemy into a highly classified briefing and discussion."

Darzhee Kut's claws scissored and waved fitfully, far more animated than they had seemed to Caine only half an hour earlier. It was as if the Arat Kur had awakened out of a haze or a drugged state, just as he had when he recovered from his extended isolation on board the auxiliary command module. "Please. Do not dismiss me. I wish to talk to the Elders of the Wholenest."

Sukhinin shook his head. "Talk is over. Now we finish what you started."

"But I have rested enough and emerged from fugue. I am able to speak once again. I cannot be sure Homenest will listen to me, but I must try."

Before anyone else could respond, Apt-Counsel spoke. "Delegate Kut, it pains me to observe that the only thing which has changed between now and the weeks prior is that Mr. Riordan has visited you. And from that visit, you may have inferred or learned what the humans can now do to your planet, and how close they are to carrying it out."

"What if that is true? Is that not a reasonable motivation to speak?"

"It is also a reasonable motivation to advise your leaders to do what they have not tried yet: to engage the humans in negotiations for the purpose of stalling long enough for a strike force to arrive."

Yeah, Apt-Counsel, but if you're his ally, then why aren't you helping him achieve that deception? Is this another attempt to prove your good faith by helping us—or are you jumping ship, maybe with an eye to eventually courting us as allies, the way you did at the Convocation?

Caine instinctively flinched away from that explanation. If anything, it was too simple, too obvious. But

Apt-Counsel's "observations" had galvanized human anxiety, had focused their attention upon the horrible necessity of ending the war with an act of genocide.

So, behind the first smokescreen of fear, Apt-Counsel might be indirectly trying to once again curry favor with humanity. But that, too, was too easy to foresee. So what was Apt-Counsel trying to achieve, behind both smokescreens, that would benefit the Ktor?

Darzhee Kut was rotating to face Caine, claws raised in appeal. "Riordan, please. I must speak to the Elders."

I've got to intervene, but I've got to make sure that I'm not stepping into a trap. With the Ktor, there was always the unseen dagger, the half-lie that wasn't clear enough to call attention to itself when first uttered. Such as Apt-Counsel's earlier claim that he only back-shot Caine to prevent the humans from capturing the Arat Kur ships. In retrospect, that was rubbish: when the Ktor had attacked, the radio was already being made available to Darzhee Kut. So eliminating Caine was no longer a military objective when the Ktor attempted it.

Caine's thoughts snagged on another troubling detail. *Apt-Counsel's attack also removed me before I could intercede in regard to their ground force suicides. So, another way to look at his actions would be this: after the Arat Kur ships were already lost, he was still willing to kill me to make sure that even the planetside Arat Kur died. But why?*

One tentative answer offered itself. *The Arat Kur suicides and ship scuttlings do have one thing in common. They ensured that human and Arat Kur would share an intense mutual hatred, that they would no longer wish to communicate their thoughts or intents to each other except through weapons of mass destruction.*

A reasonable hypothesis, insofar as it explained why Apt-Counsel attacked Caine five months ago. But it did *not* explain why he would help humans now. Indeed, if the Ktor objective was to keep enmity absolute and war perpetual between the two races, Apt-Counsel was defeating his own purpose. If the Arat Kur were exterminated, there would be no further interspeciate conflict to exploit.

It doesn't add up. I'm missing something. And Caine felt that as each sliver of a second slipped past, the undeterred momentum was building toward atrocity. *I've got to do, to say, something, if only to buy some time.* He turned toward Sukhinin, unsure what he was going to say, but sure that he had to intervene before—

Ben Hwang's voice was quiet, just above a whisper, in his left ear. "Caine, do you have a moment?"

Damn. "Not really, Ben. What's it about?"

"The Ktor."

"Oh?" *"Know thy enemy"—so always take the time to learn about them. Even now. No, particularly now.* "Sure."

Ben gestured toward the reading lounge with a bend of his head, moved in that direction. Caine followed, making an apologetic gesture toward Sukhinin.

Hwang turned to face him as soon as they were in the small lounge. "I'm sorry I didn't have this sooner. With the push to reverse-engineer and then manufacture the Arat Kur virus—"

"I know. Not much time for the other projects you

had going. But we don't have much time now, either. What do you have on the Ktor, Ben?"

"More mysteries, I'm afraid. I've had our three top xenophysiologists and macromolecular chemists working on simulations and biochemical models which would show how the exhausts from the Ktor environmental unit could be produced as the waste products, the 'exhalations,' of an ultra-cold-temperature organism."

"And they're still stumped."

"Worse than that. They've concluded that, according to the laws of biological heat and energy exchange as we understand them, these gases simply do not fit with any foreseeable model of life based on methane, ammonia, or hydrogen fluorine. And so far as we know, those are the only three low-temperature compounds which are flexible and volatile enough to serve as the building blocks of a subzero, non-carbon-based biochemistry."

"So what does that mean?"

"It means that either my team is not up to the task, or that these gases aren't what the Ktor 'exhale.' And we know for sure they can't be the gases they actually 'inhale.'"

"How?"

"Because that gas mix can't do the job of transmitting the necessary reactants to a cold-climate organism. The per molecule potential energy of cold weather gases is a great deal lower than those which are predominant in higher temperature regimes. So, according to our models, low-temperature creatures would logically need a very reactant-rich atmosphere, comparatively speaking. Unfortunately, the mix coming out of those oversized hot-water heaters couldn't sustain a mouse-sized organism."

Caine nodded, thought. "How confident are you of the team's abilities?"

"Two were Nobel nominees. The third is a laureate."

"I see. So, if we assume that your tragically under-skilled team isn't at fault, then all your findings add up to—what?"

"The first mystery."

"There's another?"

"Yes." Hwang's tone became a little more formal, a little more measured. "We have noted some oddities in Ktoran artifacture."

"Their artifacture? Where did you find any of their artifacture lying around?"

"It was not lying around. It was embedded in your back."

Of course. The manipulator arm would be a piece of invaluable forensic data. "Go on. What's the mystery?"

"Its manner of production. We have subjected all of its components—the metal, plastic, and carbon-composite fittings—to extensive analysis. Everything from gross physical measurement to subatomic scans."

"And?"

"And the lab studies return normative results on the probable fabrication processes involved in its construction. It's just lightweight steel, with all the expected amounts of carbon, trace elements, surface annealing and ion-bonding. And atomic analysis shows that the polymers in the plastics are not synthetics. They were clearly derived from natural petroleum products. In other words, fossil fuel deposits."

Caine frowned. "Wait a minute. If the Ktor come from a world where the life-forms are not carbon-based, then how the hell is it possible for them to have access to fossilized hydrocarbons?"

"That's just the problem. It shouldn't be possible, not unless the Ktor decided to go to our kind of environment to mine the components used in the creation of this object. And furthermore, they must have also decided to manufacture the arm there, too."

"What leads you to that conclusion?"

"Because given the building blocks of life in a cold-climate biochemistry, and the indigenous atmosphere, ores, and temperatures which they imply, we should be observing different trace elements. We should also be detecting telltale signs of the different kinds of manufacturing processes which would be developed by, and used in, environments where the mean temperature is someplace south of minus-eighty Celsius. And to reemphasize your point, there shouldn't be *any* fossil fuel deposits on their planets, at least not the carbon-based variety that are used to make plastics."

"Well, as you said, Ben, they might have simply gone to a world like ours to harvest those resources."

"Yes, but why *would* they? In order to travel to other worlds, the Ktor had to leave their own first. That makes it a certainty that, long before being able to mine *other* worlds, they had to evolve the equivalent of plastics using their own methods and resources. Meaning, by the time they had access to fossil fuels, they would no longer need them."

Caine nodded. "And we would certainly expect to see some use of their own plastic equivalents in their artifacts."

Hwang shrugged. "It's what one would expect. But almost every piece of their machinery scans—and looks—like something we ourselves would have manufactured."

"Like something we ourselves—?" And Caine felt his mind stop, spin, access a piece of data that he knew was significant even before he could reason out why. He found himself seeing the wisps of vapor curling away from Apt-Counsel's life-support unit, found himself hearing his words again: *"Since the Arat Kur have not seen Ktorans any more than your race has, you yourselves could manufacture a device such as my suit to dupe them."*

Caine stood up slowly. "Of course. Jesus Christ, of course."

Hwang rose. "What—?"

Caine did not hear the rest; he was already through the doorway, heading straight for Apt-Counsel, but not seeing him. Instead he could almost see pieces of the puzzle in the air before him, coming together, revealing probable answers.

Sukhinin saw Caine approach, smiled, raised a hand. "*Gospodin* Riordan, we were—"

Caine didn't even look at him, but came to within a meter of Apt-Counsel before stopping. "Ambassador Apt-Counsel, you have been kind enough to share your insights regarding Arat Kur military procedure and mindset. I wonder if you would be kind enough to indulge one more request for your counsel. At this point, what would you recommend we do?"

The treads on the Ktoran life-support unit reversed briefly, as though a reflex to back up had been overridden at the last second. "As a general principle, I would recommend that you adopt a policy of patience and lenience toward the Arat Kur. But I must concede that, logically, I don't see how you can extend any more patience and lenience than you already have."

"Ambassador Apt-Counsel, if I didn't know better, I'd say it sounds like you're agreeing that we should exterminate the Arat Kur. As their ally, I'd expect to you to arguing steadfastly against such an outcome."

"I did so as long as I had arguments that might reasonably stay your hands. I have consistently pleaded for clemency and patience, but with each passing day, your control over the Arat Kur grows increasingly uncertain and they remain obdurate and uncommunicative. Your leaders believe their antipathy to be unremitting and thus conclude that the Wholenest would launch a genocidal reprisal against you, if given the chance. I would suggest alternate perspectives if logic revealed any. But it does not."

"So you assert that humanity would be the target of a genocidal reprisal if we were to spare the Arat Kur?"

"It is a common-sense projection. You have reproduced the virus which can decimate their race. You also possess examples of their technology and will soon have reverse-engineered those systems with the greatest strategic significance, achieving near or full military parity with them. This means that if they are to strike back, they must do so soon, and with great finality: enough to cripple your civilization to the point of being unable to return to their Homenest."

Caine nodded slowly. "And then there's the unspoken variable, the one which no one told us about before all this started: the Arat Kur fear of humans in particular."

Apt-Counsel's translator made a sound that mimicked a sigh—poorly. "Sadly, this is true. And since the Accord forbids member-races from revealing information pertaining to any race other than itself, only the Arat Kur could reveal that they identify homo sapiens as the destroyer race of their prehistory."

"A belief which made them extremely dependable allies, didn't it?" Caine asked. "They were already committed to the outcome you desired: cripple Earth. And their misguided motive for doing so—preventing the return of the human destroyers—meant that no cost was too great, no subterfuge too base, no act too extreme. You were able to recruit a race of fanatics."

Sukhinin's frown had nearly pulled his eyebrows beneath his brow line. "Are you saying the Ktor put the war in motion with the final objective of exterminating us?"

"Maybe not extermination. But bashing us back a few centuries? Sure. It was only logical that they'd try again."

Visser snapped, "What was their first attempt, then?"

"Their first attempt was the Doomsday Rock, Ms. Visser. You've read the classified reports. Now ask *him* about it."

Visser looked at Apt-Counsel, whose empty arm servos whirred faintly, like an amputee trying to shrug with a missing shoulder. "I am not disposed to discuss such wild accusations."

Visser edged forward, not breathing. "Do you deny it?"

"I am not disposed to discuss it."

Sukhinin was transitioning from pink to red. "*Shto?* I have seen the briefings and Downing's recent speculations, but—is this possible?"

Caine rubbed his chin. "That would be a good question to ask Nolan, or Arvid Tarasenko. They both had years to think about the implications of discovering that an alien mass driver had been used to push the Doomsday Rock at us. Oh, but wait. They're both dead—and both within forty-eight hours of us announcing the existence of possibly hostile exosapients at the Parthenon Dialogs. Strange coincidence, that."

Sukhinin shrugged. "Yet, autopsies showed that both men did die of natural causes, Caine."

"That's not quite accurate. The autopsies were not definitive. They simply discovered nothing that our medicine recognizes as foul play. So 'natural causes' was the default finding, particularly after investigations into their deaths found no evidence pointing to the typical rogue's gallery of terrestrial actors: rival states, megacorporations, terrorists." He looked pointedly at Apt-Counsel. "But in the last few weeks, I've started wondering if we were looking too close to home, all along."

"And how is it that we could have had a hand in these events?" the Ktor asked.

"I'll get to that in a moment, Ambassador Apt-Counsel. But first I want to understand why it's equally acceptable to your plans to have the Arat Kur eliminated instead of us."

Darzhee Kut's claws clacked in sharp surprise. "What are you saying, Caine Riordan?"

"Well, look at where we're all standing and how we got here, Darzhee Kut. First, you invade our world, and the Ktor are your advisors behind the scenes. But when your campaign goes to hell in a handbasket, who are the Ktor helping now? And they're not merely helping us, Darzhee Kut. In the past thirty minutes, Ambassador Apt-Counsel has been justifying, exonerating, even indirectly encouraging us to unleash a plague that could wipe out your whole race. Now why would he do that—unless this was always a part of his plan?"

Apt-Counsel sounded amused. "First I am attempting to exterminate humanity, Mr. Riordan. Now I am attempting to exterminate the Arat Kur. Please make up your mind."

"Oh, there's no contradiction there, Ambassador Apt-Counsel, because, as I said, I think either outcome would suit Ktor's long-term strategy."

Visser shook her head once. "Where is the sense in that, Mr. Riordan?"

"Admittedly, the sense is hard to see—unless you step back from the trees of current events to survey the larger forest of what lies ahead. Which provides the perspective from which we can ask this question: What if the Ktor are not so much worried by humanity, or the Arat Kur, but by a synergy of the two?"

Ben Hwang nodded immediately. "Yes. The Hkh'Rkh were not good allies for the Arat Kur. We would have been a much better fit. Humanity is not as rash as the Hkh'Rkh, yet is almost as militarily experienced, and we advance—in terms of exploration, settlement, technological development—much faster than either race."

"Then what would we offer to such an alliance?" Darzhee Kut sounded more worried than shocked.

"Stability, efficiency, level-headed analysis, high rates of production," replied Caine. "Darzhee Kut, I know it is hard to think of your dreaded destroyer race as your allies, but I suspect that this was part of what the Ktor wished to prevent. Because if our two species ever became unified against their objectives, we would have been a formidable obstacle. But the full extermination of one race by the other—or the cycle of vengeance that would be spawned by a failed attempt—would ensure that such an alliance could never be forged."

Darzhee Kut's claws made a surprised castanet sound. "You said this was only part of what the Ktor wished to prevent by prompting you to destroy my race. What is the other part?"

Caine looked at Apt-Counsel's silent environmental tank, then at Alnduul. "They wanted to ensure our estrangement from the Dornaani." He saw Alnduul's mouth coil about its own center. *He's* smiling? *Of course. He knew all along.*

Sukhinin leaned his rather furry fists forward to meet their shadowmates on the reflective table-top. "Caine, explain how this could happen. It was the *Dornaani* who made it possible for us to be here above the Arat Kur homeworld. And did so their own free will."

"Yes, but that doesn't mean they have sanctioned genocide."

Visser looked—somewhat anxiously—at Alnduul. "Perhaps not, but we have not concealed our plans and contingencies from the Custodians. They have known from the start what we were prepared to do."

"Yes," agreed Caine, "but if they had intervened, then would they learn as much about us, get as accurate a measure of who we humans are, right now? Our actions—our *independent* actions—are what define us. So, if we decide, on the advice of the Ktor, to initiate genocide, what will the Dornaani have learned?"

Darzhee Kut's translated voice was a murmur. "That you are indeed the great destroyers we feared."

"Precisely. And that is exactly what the Ktor want, because if they can't eliminate us, then they want to ensure that the Dornaani will decide that we cannot be trusted."

"And what would that achieve?"

"We would become pariahs, Vassily, like the Ktor. And so, to whom else would we be able to turn?"

"You mean—as *allies*?"

"That's exactly what I mean, Ms. Visser. Think it through. We exterminate the Arat Kur. We become the great savages of this region of space. Our bid for Accord membership is rejected. The Ktor sympathize, probably extending similar condolences to the Hkh'Rkh, who violated the Twenty-first accord by violating a homeworld—"

"And so they build an alliance of outcasts which can undo the Accord." Vassily was nodding, looking at the Ktor's tank as if it held a mixture of piranha and sewage.

Visser's nostrils had flared and stayed that way. "In that scenario, it would not even require warfare to undo the Accord. With only the Slaasriithi remaining as members, the Accord would become a travesty. It would lack both material power and political legitimacy." She turned to Apt-Counsel. "Ambassador, were these your plans?"

"Consul Visser, surely you cannot expect me to either confirm or deny. Either response would provide you with information, whether negative or positive, about my race's long-term diplomatic strategies."

Visser looked as if she were about to spit at the

misting tank. "I will take that to be an affirmative, Ambassador—despite your evasive sophistries. It will be made widely known among our highest command staff that all your counsel is to be reevaluated, in light of your apparent duplicity and hostility—which compassed even the possible extermination of the human race."

Apt-Counsel's voice sounded thoroughly unruffled. "You must do as you see fit, Consul Visser. But I assure you of this. Had there been any risk of genocide against your planet, Ktor would have interceded. Aggressively. We would have considered an act of genocide against you to be tantamount to an act of genocide against us."

Sukhinin looked as though he was struggling with a sudden up-rush of bile. "With all due respect, Ambassador Apt-Counsel, you cannot expect us to believe you are so charitably concerned with the survival of our species when you also tried to destroy it with a space rock."

Caine nodded slowly. "Yes, Vassily. Actually, we can believe him on this one point—although charity would have nothing to do with his desire for our survival. If the Arat Kur, or anyone else, had brought a true campaign of genocide to our homeworld, it *would* be the equivalent of bringing that invasion to the Ktor homeworld." Caine smiled, kept a wary eye on Apt-Counsel. "In fact, it wouldn't have merely been the *equivalent* of depopulating the Ktor homeworld. It would have been *exactly* that. Because to depopulate Earth *is* to depopulate the Ktor homeworld."

Sukhinin frowned. "I do not understand."

The Ktor almost sounded amused. "When did you know?"

"I was pretty sure when I came back from talking to Dr. Hwang."

Visser's voice was sharp. "Gentlemen. What are you talking about?"

"I'll show you," said Caine. "Crack open his environment tank."

"*What?!*"

Caine turned to the American Marine. "Corporal, I carry the rank of Commander, am declaring this a combat situation, and am issuing you a direct order. Crack open the Ktor's environment tank."

Apt-Counsel's tone was languid. "There is no need for violence. I will happily comply."

Chapter Fifty-Seven

Far Orbit, Sigma Draconis Two

The tank came apart so easily, it was difficult to believe it had ever been an apparently seamless container. After a brief burst of air escaping, Apt-Counsel emerged like a decathlete on the half-shell, stepping free of a sensor-laden body suit, a face piece that might have been a sophisticated VR vision unit falling aside as he did so. Naked, tall, trim, almost perversely well-defined, he stood at their center, evidently unperturbed by having both his human body and identity so completely exposed. His voice reinforced the impression. "It is so constraining in there, particularly these last few months. Presuming I was under constant observation, I was not able to leave the tank. Although this is an unfortunate turn of events, it is pleasing to be done with this charade and to anticipate the prospect of real food. I wonder—do you have olives?"

Visser and Sukhinin seemed unable to speak; the Marines had their hands on their weapons; Darzhee Kut had backed up until the rear of his shell rested

lightly against Alnduul's legs. Caine did not take his
eyes off the Ktor but smoothly unholstered his weapon,
snapped the safety off, and centered the red dot of
the aimpoint laser two centimeters above the navel.
"Dr. Hwang."

"Yes?"

"Please go at once to the CIC. Inform Admiral
Silverstein that we have a situation in the conference
suite requiring the utmost discretion and the immediate
presence of armed personnel with the highest levels
of clearance. Also tell him that it is our collective
opinion that under no circumstances whatsoever are
any biological weapons to be launched at the Arat
Kur Homenest, at least not until all the parties here
present have been fully and satisfactorily debriefed.
Please also convey a description of the Ktoran ambassador's true form and that it is the shared opinion of
the persons in this room that he is not to be trusted
in any matter, to any degree. And lastly, if any firearms are discharged in this room, it is to be sealed
and flooded with suppressive gas. Does anyone wish
to amend or alter my message?"

Silence, then Hwang said, "Caine, in the time it
takes for me to run to the CIC—"

"Ben, I think it best that we don't put that kind of
message on the intercom. We want to keep this as low
profile as possible. All the way under the scuttlebutt
radar, if we can. Please go with all speed."

Caine steadied the gun with his left hand as the
door opened and closed.

The Ktor smiled. "You didn't request olives."

"All in good time, Ambassador Apt-Counsel."

"Let us dispense with assumed names as well as

appearances. I am Tlerek Sirn of the House Sheth-kador."

"I can't say that I'm pleased to meet you. How-ever, this makes it pretty clear how you were able to influence events on Earth long before the war, before Convocation, even before Parthenon. And not only can you walk among us, you had access to Earth as well, legitimated by the Accord."

Sukhinin looked at Caine with wide eyes. "*Shto?*"

"Read the fine print of the delegation's report, Vassily, and look at the text of the Eighteenth Accord. The current Custodians, the Dornaani, were unable to cover all their duties alone, so they were allowed to tap one additional race for assistance in monitor-ing and policing new and uncontacted races. That was the perfect cover for their Ktor 'helpers' to put ships in our system, to infiltrate agents, to start the Doomsday Rock in our direction—all with complete plausible deniability."

"Do you still deny this?" Visser asked the Ktor, her voice tightly controlled.

Shethkador raised his right hand in the classic palms-up sign of uncertainty, his middle finger's oddly long, tapering fingernail raised like a dagger toward the ceiling. "Did I *ever* deny it? I seem to recall indicating that I was not disposed to discuss it."

Caine nodded. "Very well, Ambassador Shethkador, we'll leave that discussion for another time. But unless you want us to discuss your speciate origins openly with the entirety of the Arat Kur—or perhaps, the whole Accord—you will now send your *genuine* identity codes to the Homenest leadership."

Sukhinin started, then nodded. "Of course. This

zjulik gave them a false confirmation code when he 'attempted to contact' them."

Shethkador stared out at the stars, at Homenest. "I suppose there is little reason to refuse you this accommodation."

Caine smiled. "And every reason to comply, if you want us to keep your speciate identity a secret."

Shethkador looked away. "Keeping our identity is of no consequence to us."

"Lie. If it wasn't important, you wouldn't cooperate in *any* way."

"You are quite wrong. We stand to lose nothing by having others know our identity."

"Nice bluff—but I was born on the planet that invented poker. You want that secret kept because what the Arat Kur claim is true: humans *are* the killer species they fear, the ones in their legends. But it was you—the Ktor—who were still traveling between the stars, who were slaughtering other races before we were even wondering about how to build pyramids. And if the Arat Kur were to learn that, I wonder how they might start rethinking their positive opinion of you, and their negative opinion of us."

Shethkador turned and smiled—and Caine noticed that there were flecks of blood or red mixed into his eyes' light amber irises. "You have admirable skills, Mr. Riordan, but remember to be measured in your requests. It is useful, but not essential, that our speciate identity remains undisclosed. If you make the price of your silence too high, you will receive no concessions at all."

Caine smiled back, wanting to squeeze the trigger. "So it was you—the Ktor—who almost obliterated Homenest."

"It would seem that way."

"And the locals on DeePeeThree? Them too?"

Shethkador's smile broadened. He shrugged. "Who can say?"

Caine pursued. "Don't be coy. There are no other alternatives."

"No? There's always the possibility of yet another group of humans. If two, why not three? Or five?"

Caine shook his head. "Because if you believed that, you wouldn't suggest it. You give away no useful information. You'd only bring up the possibility of other human enclaves if you thought it would sow uncertainty and confusion into our planning."

Shethkador smiled back. "Impressive. One point for you."

"More than one."

Shethkador's eyebrows elevated slightly. "Oh? How so?"

"By just now admitting that there are only *two* groups of humanity, you've told me something else. That you have fairly intact records of the actual history of our species, of how it was that we were in the stars twenty millennia ago, who brought us there, and what we were doing, and why. Otherwise you wouldn't be so sure that there *weren't* other groups."

Shethkador's eyebrows lowered. "And therefore, you have deduced a third and final piece of information."

Caine studied Shethkador's utterly expressionless features and then nodded. "That you're not going to share the smallest bit of that history with us."

Shethkador smiled again. "Such a clever low-breed. It would be interesting to examine your DNA."

Caine tried to suppress—but couldn't—the shudder

that rippled from the center of his spine out in all directions.

Visser had stepped forward and aggressively planted herself in front of Shethkador. "You will do more than contact the Arat Kur homeworld; you will agree to cease and desist from any interference in our affairs. Which is to say, you will now observe the Accords to which you have pledged yourself."

Shethkador looked down at her; his smile became a mirthless laugh. "As if any of the races do observe the Accords—with the possible exception of the rather inane Slaasriithi. Although I suspect that even they may bend the rules from time to time. Perhaps by providing a few key pieces of data on other races?" His smile broadened; his eyes narrowed into hers.

Christ. He knows that the Slaasriithi passed us intelligence on the location of the Arat Kur homeworld.

Visser blinked. "I would not know anything about that."

"Of course not." He nodded, smiled wider still, looked away. "At any rate, I will make no agreement which limits Ktoran freedom of action. And I think you must ask yourself if exposing our identity is truly in your best interests. Have you considered the cost to yourselves? You may see yourselves as different from us, but your history—your very recent history—argues differently." Seeing Visser's lowering brow, he shrugged and provided examples. "The active and then passive extermination of the indigenous peoples of three continents; your biosphere held hostage to absolute thermonuclear destruction as a pawn in the game of empires; the death camps of countless regimes while you were in the first flower of your glorious atomic and information ages; and, less than a century ago, your benign toleration of what you called the 'megadeath.' What horror have you not perpetrated against yourselves in the recent past? By extension, what horror will you not perpetrate against others, particularly other species whose ways, appearances, biologies are so different and daunting to such rude minds and sensibilities as yours? Will revealing our speciate identity make heroes of you, or to borrow your metaphor, will revealing us tar you with the same brush?"

Shethkador seemed ready to yawn, but continued. "Besides, if you elect to tell other races that we are, in fact, human, we will deny it. And unless you make me a testamentary zoo-specimen—which would bring about a war you could not win—you will have no evidence to support your claim.

"But this is all moot. Your genes are ours, and so are your deeds. You cling to the differences in our behaviors. But other species will not note these distinctions. They will be subtleties that your exosapient allies will silently brush aside in view of the greater truth. That the most bloody deeds of your recent past resonate with our own. In short, they will see that—first, last, and foremost—you are us."

Caine shook his head. "They will also see that the Dornaani allowed events to unfold this way so that we would be the ones to spare, even save, another race—and so redeem ourselves. And eventually, when the inevitable day of revelation comes—when all masks are dropped or stripped away—we humans of Earth will be remembered and seen for what we can be at our best, not at our worst."

Shethkador waved a hand at Caine's retort. "Oh, that

may occur too, I imagine. But do not forget that the Dornaani also used you in the prosecution of this war because they understand us as a species. Human social evolution is unique in that our race has achieved the maximum, even optimum, balance of violent aggression and social cohesion. Again, consider your recent past. What other race could teeter so long, and yet not topple over, the brink of nuclear self-extermination? And all in the name of ideals, which were simply the facades behind which you hid your national prejudices, racial fears, and innate savagery. They are the blinds behind which you hid your appetite for the horrors you had made and amidst which you lived. Who else could have been shrewd enough, versatile enough, resilient enough—and brutal enough—to stalemate us in this war? It is not chance that you were the ones to foil our plans. You have a saying that eludes me now, about how you extinguish wild-fires, that you ... er—"

"Fight fire with fire." Caine finished for him, his stomach growing smaller, harder.

"Just so. You were the Dornaani application of that principle: using humans to fight humans."

It could not be mere chance that Alnduul had invoked this same axiom—that of fighting fire with fire—back at Convocation and again less than half an hour ago. He had foreseen this coming from Shethkador, had subtly primed Caine for the revelations of this moment. *Suggesting that full control, and full understanding, of this war and our place within it has never been wholly ours, not even when we thought we were taking the initiative.*

Perhaps Shethkador had seen some trace of surprise or discomfiture in Caine's face: his voice was suddenly less histrionically jocular and detached, almost became earnest. "Accept what the Dornaani have accepted about us. We, as a species, are not instruments of enduring peace. We are engines of perpetual war. And together, we would be unstoppable."

"And apart?"

The Ktor smiled. "You have an expression: 'war to the knife.' Only one of us may prevail." Shethkador stared straight at Caine for a long moment, then around at the rest of the group's glittering, somber eyes, and finally—with a smile and a shrug—looked out toward the stars.

Caine nodded to himself. *And so that is our future: the fire that fights fire. And that fight will become Earth's redemptive trial by fire. The struggle that will simultaneously expiate humanity's past deeds and prove our future promise.*

That macroscopic glimpse of humanity's futur-escape goaded Caine to reexamine and reconceive the "serendipitous" events that had helped humanity prevail in the war. Had the first, fortuitous meeting between himself and Darzhee Kut truly been a matter of chance? Had the Hkh'Rkh disdain and, ultimately, disregard for the Arat Kur been hormone-enhanced? Had similar hormonal tinkering amplified the humano-phobia of the leading Arat Kur castes into a fatally dismissive blind-spot? Were any of these occurrences *truly* serendipitous—or merely instances of Dornaani manipulation?

Caine pulled pack from the steep slope unveiled by that thought. *If you start thinking that way, soon you'll see Dornaani covert control in every event, every random factor of human existence. But how do*

*I—how does anyone—distinguish between the two?
How do we go about sorting out the actual Dornaani
intents and intrusions from the noise, the illimitable
static, of routine human affairs? I guess Downing's
IRIS is still going to have plenty of work to do.*

Sukhinin—during the two silent seconds that had
compassed Caine's thoughts—approached Tlerek Shethkador. He drew himself up straight, shoulders back,
head high. "We would die before allying with you."

The Ktor smiled, did not look away from the stars.
"Your words may well be prophetic, Consul Sukhinin."

Caine adjusted his grip on the handgun. "So tell
me. If we're so promising as allies, then why not try
to recruit us from the start, openly, instead of trying
to blast us back into the bronze age with an asteroid?"

That brought Shethkador's head around. "Because we
did not approve of the outcome of the events of the
Twentieth Century. Two prominent forms of autocracy
were routed. The impotent rot of pluralism and equality
had almost completely perverted the natural order, of
survival of the fittest. You were intent on protecting
and preserving the weak, both nations and individuals,
all in some fawning worship of these inane concepts
you've derived from your laughable mystery cults."

"What 'inane concepts' are you referring to?"

"Empathy. Justice. Compassion. Each one is a means
of decaying the essential truth of strength and power."

"So, was Nietzsche one of you?"

"No, but we hoped his wisdom would become predominant. Alas, it did not. Not in the last century,
nor this one. So, seeing how quickly you were moving
toward the stars, we deemed that you would be an
impediment, rather than an adornment, to our plans."

"So you decided to kill ninety-five percent of our population."

"Our estimates were only eighty percent. But no matter. The cattle had grown soft and the herd needed culling. You would have recovered in two or three centuries. We made sure that the asteroid we directed toward Home was large enough to significantly damage but not destroy you. The resulting waves and geological perturbations would have wiped out the epicenter of the linked viruses you called 'humanism' and 'paidiea.'"

Darzhee Kut's claws clacked. "Paideia?"

"The virtue of civic duty and sacrifice, usually associated with Pericles' funeral oration in the Peloponnesian War." Caine looked at Sukhinin. "Pretty much spoken in the shadow of the Parthenon."

Sukhinin nodded. "*Da*, and it was why Nolan chose that location for the meeting. To remind us all how much of that work is still left undone."

Caine nodded. "And in order to do that work, we have to be in the Accord. And if the Accord is to endure, the price we have to pay right now is silence. We let the charade continue. We act as though the Ktor are not human."

"So we lie?"

"No, Vassily. We follow the implied spirit of the Accord. It is not our business to reveal information about any race other than our own. But it's also the smartest thing we can do, in this instance."

The door opened. Hwang and a dozen security personnel entered, Bannor Rulaine at their head. "Is this the—gentleman—we are to escort to special quarters?"

Caine nodded. "That's him. And good riddance."

"A strange farewell," observed Shethkador. He smiled

as the two shortest commandoes—Miles O'Garran and Peter Wu—pulled a restraint jumper up around his ankles. "This would be a better parting platitude: 'until we meet again.'"

"I hope not."

"I predict otherwise." With the Ktor's arms wrapped tight against his body, the security detachment frogwalked him out of the room. Caine did not lower his sidearm until the door had closed behind the detail.

Even Alnduul seemed to relax slightly, then turned to the humans in the room. "There is one more item of importance. The final name by which the Accord is to address your polity. World Confederation was only a tentative term, was it not?"

Visser nodded. "That is correct, Alnduul. Since we were summoned to the Convocation, though, there has been much talk of settling upon a more species-specific, a more inclusive, term: Human Confederation."

Alnduul's lids nictated slowly. "I would suggest you consider a different term."

Sukhinin stared at the Dornaani. "Now you will tell us what to call ourselves?"

"I merely offer a prudent suggestion. Consider, you are planning to call yourself the Human Confederation. Yet, what is the Ktor, but another human?"

Sukhinin shrugged. "So perhaps we are simply more precise. 'The Earth Confederation,' maybe?"

Caine thought. "What about the Terran Confederation?"

Vassily looked over, perplexed. "Terran? From the Latin? Why this?"

It was Visser who answered. "Caine is right. Latin is not any nation's language anymore, so any name derived from it is less likely to arouse cultural jealousies."

Hwang nodded. "It is also wise not to use a name too closely associated with any one world. If we include 'Earth' in the title, we are emphasizing one planet above the others. What about the Moon, Mars, DeePeeThree, Zeta Tucanae? If we choose a title that fails to implicitly include all our worlds, I think you may be only one generation away from rebel groups chanting 'no Confederation without representation.'"

Visser nodded. "I agree. But your point brings another issue to mind. We cannot know how our government will evolve, or if all of our peoples and polities will have equal, or any, representation within the blocs that comprise our state. Even now, some nations and groups choose not to. Can we truly claim ourselves to be a 'confederation,' then?"

"What would you suggest?"

Visser reflected upon Sukhinin's question for a moment. "I think the closest English term is 'consolidated.' It would mean that we are all together—all one political entity—but it does not attempt to define or imply any universal set of political relationships: merely solidarity."

"I agree," Sukhinin said softly. "But if we make no statement of political accountability and equality, then what makes us different from a mob? 'Terran Consolidation' could be a fine title for the empire of a ruthless dictator, no?"

Caine felt something rise up from values learned at his family's kitchen table, something which would have made his history-professor father proud. "Republic. We call it a republic."

Visser frowned. "Not all states will like this."

"With respect, that's too damned bad. A republic is representative pluralism, yes? So is the bloc structure, even if all the constituent states are not, themselves, republics. But one of the implicitly understood principles of a republic is that its social contract is the supreme authority, and may be fashioned and evolved only by representatives of the people. It puts the rule of law above both the vagaries of the *vox populi* and the dicta of would-be tyrants. And isn't that what we want? Isn't that what Nolan was urging, on his last day? To take a stand—at least this *one*—to use a global government not merely as a mechanism for enhanced security, but as an instrument for social good?"

Sukhinin was smiling for the first time in the past hour. He put a hand—Caine had to actively dispel the hackneyed association with a bearish Russian "paw"—on his shoulder. "Nolan could not have said it better. He would be happy today, to have heard you say this." Sukhinin squeezed his shoulder and his eyes grew shiny. "Nolan was right about you. Every bit. If there is a heaven—and, *bozhemoi*, I hope there is—he is surely smiling down on you right now."

Caine gave a brief, and he hoped humble, nod, but thought, *That assumes that Nolan is wearing wings above us, rather than in chains below. Just how many good-intentioned lies can you tell before even those prosocial prevarications earn you a one-way ticket to a personal, or mythological, hell? Probably equal to the number of angels that can dance on the head of a pin....*

"So we will recommend our polity to the Accord to be named the Consolidated Terran Republic?" As the first word of the title began rolling off Visser's tongue, it sounded tentative. It had been graven in stone by the time the last syllable emerged.

Caine looked at the persons in the room, committed their locations and facial expressions to memory. *I will be able to say—and record—that this was the first time our collective name for ourselves was uttered. That this was the founding moment and vision that would become our touchstone and hope throughout the long trial by fire that now stands before us. And in so recording it, pen a rebuttal to the stylish cynicisms of the modern age: that not all declarations are banal; not all acts are futile; not all beliefs are pointless—and that I have lived the truth of that in this past minute.*

And in the time it had taken to reflect upon the significance of the moment, the moment was past. That was, after all, the nature of moments. *By the time we can reflect on events, they are behind us. The present is like a vertical line in geometry, with the past stretching limitlessly to the left, and the future immeasurably to the right. But existing upon the line of the present means we are eternally perched upon a single point, an imaginary unit of measure that has no width. Just the way a "historical" moment is so narrow a sliver of time that it appears and disappears in the same instant. It has no epic dimensions and so casts no epic shadow at the moment it passes us. Only when it becomes a momentous object of the past—or future—does it acquire shape, mass, opacity.*

Visser approached Darzhee Kut. "Delegate Kut, might I invite you to accompany us to the captain's ready room? It would be the most appropriate place for us to begin our attempts to recontact your government."

Darzhee Kut chittered out a string of affirmatives, turned just before he, Visser, Sukhinin, and Hwang exited. "I will look forward to our next meeting, Caine Riordan."

"As will I, Darzhee Kut."

As the door closed, Alnduul moved in the opposite direction, toward the observation gallery and the star-littered expanse before them. Caine asked his back. "How much did you know?"

"Of what would occur?"

"That, and the identity of the Ktor."

"Their stratagems and the flow of events we foresaw. Their identity was uncertain at best. We foresaw that the Ktor would attempt to destroy the Accord unless they could secure your cooperation. With you as a satrapy, the Accord could have been a legitimating structure for their ambitions. However, when you would not ally with them, they hoped you would either prove weak enough to be conquered, or savage enough to undertake atrocities that would make you pariahs. Like them. You have done neither, and they are not revealed. For the Ktor, the outcome is a stalemate."

"So nothing has really changed."

"Sometimes, when your adversary is trying to precipitate dramatic change, stability is the best victory. Besides, their stalemate is your gain. Your decision to desist from attacking the Arat Kur Homenest shall garner the humans of Earth the high opinion of the Dornaani and, I suspect, the Slaasriithi. Although provoked and holding apocalypse in your hand, you refused to unleash it. You are a promising species, after all. But history shows that you can also be mercurial at times, and wayward when it comes to following any single course for very long. Perhaps, this time, you will contemplate other species whose natural inclination is to quietly flourish in times of peace, rather than spectacularly soar in times of crisis. We shall see."

"Well, you must have suspected, or at least hoped, we'd be capable of restraining ourselves," observed Caine. "Otherwise, you wouldn't have invested so much effort and faith in Nolan. You watched him, helped his heart resist the damage he had received. Which means you knew how he received the damage. Which means you knew about the Doomsday Rock. Which means you knew the Ktor were behind it. Which means you knew the Ktor had a particular interest in and fear of Earth. Which means the identity of the Ktor really wasn't so uncertain, that they were likely to be huma—"

"Be still, Caine Riordan." Alnduul looked about furtively and in that second, appeared to be anything but a super-being. "The moment of revelations about the Ktor is past. Leave it so, and learn not to speak of it. One is never so alone as one thinks. And, yes, we knew of the damage to Nolan's heart, and what had caused it. And so we surmised what he must have seen, to become so fixed and certain in his purpose to lead your people to the stars. But those of us Custodians who had further suspicions had no proof—and still have none we can share—as to the intents and actual identity of the Ktor."

Caine gaped. "But today, just minutes ago, you saw—"

Alnduul's eyes closed. "Understand, Caine Riordan, amongst my people, particularly amongst my elders,

I am considered what you would call a hothead: impetuous, prone to unwarranted conclusions, willing to act as much upon instinct as evidence. What was revealed here today cannot even become official information within the ranks of the Custodians, let alone the Dornaani Collective."

"But—why not?"

"Because this knowledge, and indeed, the entire outcome of your war, is the fruit of a much-poisoned tree. Consider the procedural violations we committed in handling this conflict. We did not announce ourselves to the Arat Kur as soon as we landed upon your world. We provided your people—long before the war commenced—with the device in your arm, foreseeing this probable course of events. We enabled you to carry out a sneak counterattack upon the Arat Kur by using deep-space shifts. And we were willing to stand aside—or so it seemed—as you hovered above the Arat Kur Homenest, with the fate of their entire race in your hand." Alnduul closed his eyes wearily. "At best, what was revealed here today about the Ktor will be whispered in the ears of those few volunteers who are willing to be more 'proactive' in their Custodianship. But it cannot be entered into the records, nor openly acknowledged."

Caine felt nauseated. "Meaning that the Ktor are right in one regard. The Accord is founded, and runs, on lies."

Alnduul closed his eyes. "If that is true, then you may say the same of being a parent. It is founded on the telling of lies."

Again the paternalistic wisdom crap. "That's just not—"

"Attend, Caine Riordan. Think of yourself as having an infant child—"

"I wish I could." A vision of dying, pregnant Opal flitted through his mind, scissored at his heart.

Alnduul seemed to shrink inside himself. "Apologies. Profound apologies. Let me rephrase. Think of small children you have seen about you in Indonesia, and elsewhere. Children who are scared, are hungry, possibly even mortally wounded. And they ask their parent: 'Progenitor, will I be safe? Will I be fed? Will I live?' And the parent, knowing the truth to be in the negative—what do they say?"

Caine looked down. "They lie."

"Just so. And they must. It is a kindness to the child, no less so than a palm placed upon a fevered brow, or lips upon a face streaked with tears. And so, Caine Riordan, do not answer now, but think upon this. Is no lie a justified means to a good end? Is existence so black and white as that? It would be comforting and simple if such were the case—but is it?"

Alnduul stepped back and his mouth puckered slightly: a melancholy smile? "Enlightenment unto you."

Caine lifted his arms in response. "And unto you, Alnduul. I hope we shall meet again."

Alnduul, who had started to turn after the farewell, half turned back toward him: "We shall. Indeed, we must."

Chapter Fifty-Eight

Far Orbit, Sigma Draconis Two

Caine looked from Sukhinin to Downing as they rose. "Are you at least going to monitor the meeting?"

Downing shook his head. "The Slaasriithi specifically asked that their first contact with us be unrecorded."

"And that it be with you alone," Sukhinin said through his playfully malicious smile.

Caine found he was impatient for them to leave. *It's harder to act like I'm not nervous than it is being alone.* He made sure his answering smile was lopsided, his tone ironic. "Yeah, that's me: Speaker to Exos."

Sukhinin picked up his briefing materials. "Better you than me, *cheloveck*." There was a very slight tremor under their feet. Half out of the room, the Russian cast one eye back at the light over the airlock. The red light flickered, became yellow. "Well, they have arrived. Good luck. Don't get eaten by aliens."

"Hah, hah, Vassily. Go away."

"I hear and obey, *Gospodin* Riordan." A cough of laughter and he was gone.

Downing sounded more serious and more sympathetic. "Their representative should just about be ready. They breathe an almost identical mix of gases, so neither of you will need suits. When they signal that their representative has debarked and they have undocked from this module, our shuttle will leave as well. You've removed your transponder anklet?"

"And my collarcom. I don't like that requirement, Richard. Did they give any explanation?"

"As to why there are to be no transmissions of any kind while the two of you are out here? No, but they were firmly, if gently, insistent."

"Firmly but gently insistent." That's a pretty good descriptor for every one of our few, brief exchanges with the Slaasriithi.

Downing continued. "I suspect they just want to create an environment that is—for their species, at least—optimally private, even intimate."

"Yes. Like two scorpions in one high-tech bottle."

"Nonsense. They are simply very careful. They have suggested some general discussion before direct contact. The idea is that you acclimatize to their discourse first, then to them. Or so goes the theory." Downing looked up sharply, beyond Caine's shoulder.

Caine turned. The green light over the airlock had come on.

Downing straightened up. "Your show, now." He smiled, put out a hand. "Try not to muck it up."

Before he could rethink the reaction—before he could recall Downing's lies, manipulation, withheld secrets—Caine had offered his own hand in response to the unpremeditated amity that he felt in Richard's gesture.

Downing's smile widened, then seemed to falter, along with his eyes. He turned quickly, exited with a backward wave as the hatchway into the Commonwealth—or would it now be Terran?—corvette sealed with a shrill hiss. A moment later, Caine felt a slight shudder in the module, as though something were pressing down on the roof of the room: the counterspin boosters. The fractional centrifugal forces that had provided a faint pseudo-gravity diminished, were gone.

All alone in a can in space, weightless and adrift. But no, not quite alone. Caine looked at the iris valve at the other end of the chamber. No reason to be apprehensive. So far, the Slaasriithi were the most honest—if reclusive and enigmatic—allies that Earth had. It was beyond thinking that there should be any danger from them, particularly here. Their recently arrived ship was enveloped by the entirety of the human fleet, and fully exposed to the scrutiny of Alnduul and the Custodians. And yet—

"You are present, the-Riordan-called-Caine?"

Caine rose—and felt quite stupid. He was still alone, so for whom was he standing?

"I am."

"And you are alone?"

"As you requested. May I ask to whom I am speaking?"

"My full name is cumbersome for your tongue and quite long. Perhaps you would consent to call me Yiithrii'ah'aash."

I will if I can. "I am pleased to meet you, Yiithrii'ah'aash." Caine had the sensation of his tongue being poised to stumble over the downhill slalom of syllables, was surprised to get to the end of the word without major disaster. "While I doubt I could pronounce it just yet, I would be happy to learn your full name and what it means."

"This is most gracious and we appreciate it. However, we would defer this to some other time, if this is acceptable."

I had good enough manners to try; he has good enough manners to let me off the hook. We're off to a good start. "Of course, Yiithrii'ah'aash. I would appreciate knowing your title, however."

"It translates quite imperfectly into your language, the-Riordan-called-Caine, and it is not so much a title as a denotation of present function. One term for it would be 'facilitator'; another might be 'liaison-symbiote.' I do not know your language well enough to determine which more accurately reflects my role in this meeting."

"You seem to know our language quite well—" And then Caine realized that the voice was not a machine equivalent. "Yiithrii'ah'aash, you are speaking to me without the benefit of a Dornaani translator?"

"This is correct."

"How did you—?"

"The-Riordan-called-Caine, we, too, are a species renowned for our curiosity, so it is with regret that I must decline to answer your questions. I am under fairly restrictive time constraints. Suffice it to say that it was my honor to be selected to become fully familiar with the speciate self-reference materials that you presented at the Convocation."

Good grief, that would mean—"You became familiar with *all* those materials?"

"This is so."

"That was a great deal of work, Yiithrii'ah'aash."

"It was a great honor and illumination. We Slaasriithi regret to have given you such limited information in return, and it is for this reason—among others—that this meeting was deemed advisable as soon as it was practicable."

"I'm sorry. I do not understand."

"My apologies. I will elucidate. It was our desire to communicate directly with you at the Convocation. However, in the months preceding that gathering, envoys from the Arat Kur arrived at one of the contact points along our shared border, urgently requesting dialog with our representatives. Their intent, plainly put, was that we should help them deny human admission to the Accord."

Son of a—"But how could they do so without revealing details of our race, without violating the privacy stipulations of the Accord?"

"Your bafflement reprises our own. However, in telling us about humanity, the Arat Kur demonstrated that they had a far greater awareness of the ancient history and inhabitants of this region of space than we did. Based on their reaction to your candidacy for membership in the Accord, humanity seemed to be the epicenter of their species' fears. When we refused to commit to an *a priori* rejection of your candidacy, we discovered that their fears of you quickly became fears of us."

"Because you had indirectly supported us?"

"That, too, but subsequent information prompted us to reconsider the possible causes of the Arat Kur's diminished congeniality."

The end of the sentence dangled like a baited hook. "And what new causes came to light, Yiithrii'ah'aash?"

"There are several, but most share a common root. It is conjectured that, in some time past, your race and mine were, if not allied, then at least affined."

Caine smiled at the archaic usage.

Yiithrii'ah'aash's voice skimmed and glided in an oddly liquid fashion over the English phonemes and idioms. "As Convocation approached, we projected that any ready exchanges between us, or strong support for your candidacy, could make the Arat Kur—intemperate."

Caine understood. "Because if they interpreted your friendship toward us as a prelude to alliance, they'd preemptively move to a war footing, escalating what might have been a salvageable situation."

"Yes, this was our thinking. We regret and apologize for its profound flaws."

"You couldn't have known that they had already prepared themselves for war," Caine pointed out.

"Embarrassingly, we did not even consider it a possibility. It was too uncharacteristically precipitous and aggressive for their species."

"Convocation was beyond anyone's power to salvage," Caine said with a shrug. "However, I have since learned that your ships were commerce-raiding all along the Arat Kur border during the war, keeping more than a third of the Wholenest's military assets tied up in fear of a large-scale incursion."

"That is so."

"Well, that was an immense help, and my leaders wish to express their immense appreciation for it. With this war behind us, we can initiate the kinds of cultural exchange I'm sure both our peoples would welcome."

"This is a most interesting proposition, and one which we must discuss at some later date. However, our time now grows short. Perhaps it would be wise for us to conclude this dialog with a brief meeting."

Or maybe not. I've faced enough anxieties, real and imagined, for one year, thank you. But Caine said, "Yes. I would like that."

The green light above the airlock's iris valve flashed three times and went out. The portal opened with a breathy squeal and Caine stepped forward, glad for the speed with which this was happening, that his mind had less than one second to spin within the maelstrom of primal fears that he had come to associate with first contacts. *What will they look like? What will they smell like? Will I lose my composure, run gibbering into a corner because what I have seen is something that humans should never have seen, should never have encountered? Will I unwittingly insult them? Will I fail my race by seeming stupid, inept, rude, too aggressive, too passive, too silent, too loquacious? In short, how can you control the encounter and win the day, when the rules of the game change every time you play it?*

However, Caine stopped in mid-stride—because there had been no way to be ready for what he saw. Because he did feel like running into a corner, gibbering, the universe tilting and making less sense with every passing second.

Yiithrii'ah'aash glide-walked through the doorway with precisely the same rolling gait as the natives Caine had met on Delta Pavonis Three. The familiar smallish and tightly furred head of that species—shaped more like a brazil nut than an almond—rode smoothly atop

the equally familiar and improbably long ostrich neck.
The body was closely furred and wasp-waisted. The
long gibbon's-arms swung easily alongside the oddly
flanged hips and dog-jointed legs. Prehensile finger-
tentacles extended in some form of greeting and the
knee-length bifurcated tail was shorter than those
Caine had seen on Delta Pavonis Three. However, a
few purposeful coiling and flexing motions indicated
that it was still a functional appendage.

The Slaasriithi was not a Slaasriithi. It was a Pavonian.
Or Pavonians were Slaasriithi. Caine wished he could
close his eyes until the pointless debate in his head
subsided. Whoever, or whatever they were, they were
the same species. He opened his eyes—*damn, I guess
I did close them*—and discovered that Yiithrii'ah'aash
was holding something out to him. Caine, reached out
to receive it. A small, recently harvested branch with
small green leaves. It was subtly fragrant, familiar—

*It's an olive branch. Where did they get this? And
is this a sign of peace? Or*—and Caine could not tell
whether his next insight was profound or paranoid—*are
you telling me you know many of our secrets, including my code name? Are you telling me you know the
tale of how, when Odysseus finally came home to his
own family and his own life, he returned to a bedroom
which was built around an olive tree: a sign of life, hope,
fruitfulness, closure?* Caine couldn't decide whether,
in receiving this branch, he was being encouraged to
see himself as coming full circle, his wanderings and
wonderings at an end, or whether he was being pitched
headlong into another odyssey of mysteries and risks. He
looked from the leaves back to Yiithrii'ah'aash, and was
surprised to find three irregularly shaped eyes staring

at him from either slanted facet of the edge-on, furry brazil-nut that was his head.

Caine swallowed. "I know you. I mean, we—your people and I. We have met before." *How erudite.*

"Ah, you refer to your experiences on Delta Pavonis Three."

Okay, so I guess everyone knows about that *"secret," now.* "Er—yes."

Yiithrii'ah'aash's tendril-fingers spread straight and flat to either side. The gesture of negation was so clear that Caine almost expected him to shake his head as well. "That was not us."

Caine simply stared at the contrary evidence before his eyes.

Yiithrii'ah'aash's tendrils unfolded into a slow-motion writhe of baby snakes. "Allow me to clarify. As Neanderthal is to you, what you met on Delta Pavonis Three is to us. We cherish it and call it ours, but it is not *us.*"

"But it communicated with me, and knew about—things." *Such as, which star we come from.*

"Be at ease. Understanding will come when you visit us."

"When I what?"

Yiithrii'ah'aash looked at him. Caine felt the small hairs on his spine stand in response to the eerie familiarity of the purring sound that Yiithrii'ah'aash made deep in his chest. "Was I not clear? I said that you shall understand all when you visit us. For you shall visit us, the-Riordan-called-Caine. And soon. Very soon."

"Is that an invitation, a request, or a prophecy?"

Yiithrii'ah'aash just stared.

And purred more loudly.

Epilogue

The voice of Vruthvur, Senior Coordinator of the Custodians, burbled through the humid, comforting darkness of the ship's most private Communitarium. "Alnduul, members of this council have expressed some concern in regard to your management of the assistance we provided the humans in the recent war. More than one observer feels that your success owes as much to luck as it does to logic and methodical planning."

Alnduul settled deeper into his couch. "I must remind you of the rules of contact and engagement imposed upon us Custodians at the start of this operation. Until the war commenced, we were prohibited from making direct contact with anyone but Downing, once Corcoran's decease was confirmed. This severely limited our ability to influence or even be aware of, human strategic decisions."

"Do you feel we should have made more open contact, exerted more direct control?"

"These two variables are quite different. More open contact? Yes—but with the Earth Confederation as a whole. Conversely, exertion of more direct control was not a practicable option and, if detected, would have played into the Ktor hands."

Vruthvur's voice remained patient, serene. "Why so?"

"Because if the humans had learned that we were manipulating their governments from within, they would have rejected us as allies. Sooner or later, they would have aligned themselves with the Ktor. Moreover, I am of the opinion that more direct control would have hindered rather than helped the humans' prosecution of the war. Long before hostilities commenced, Corcoran's strategy of losing the first battles in order to later be in a position to win the war was well underway."

The Coordinator's voice was slow. "I do not understand what you mean by this phrase, nor how Corcoran's strategy impacted our planning."

"Venerable Vruthvur, as you may recall, Nolan Corcoran came to our attention during incident 2083B—the 'impending asteroid collision' crisis that the humans refer to as the Doomsday Rock."

"I do recall this."

"Then you may also recall that, by the time he had come to our attention, and we were able to situate proximal surveillance and security assets, that he had already begun to set plans in motion for humanity's accelerated move toward the stars."

"My recollection is unimpaired, Alnduul. What do you adduce based on this preamble?"

"We presume to guide events, Vruthvur. But Corcoran moved too decisively, and was too strong a mind, for that customary approach to be practicable. He crafted a set of subtle, interlocking plans without any input—active or passive, direct or indirect—from us. And it is well that we were too late to succumb to the temptation of attempting such influence. It would have ruined his extraordinarily bold and insightful plans."

"So you imply that Corcoran—and through him, the humans—were truly in charge of the situation?"

"I do not imply this. I state it unequivocally."

A new voice intruded: Menrelm, whose pointed inquiries often produced more irritation than enlightenment. "How can this be? The humans had not yet even attained interstellar capability at that point."

"True, but after the asteroid crisis, some of their leaders now had evidence of its attainability, because they had discovered the impending collision had been engineered by interstellar intruders. Corcoran's consequent strategic deductions were not merely inspired, but proleptic. He reasoned that if Earth had already been the target of an attack, it would be again. He further reasoned that once a proper First Contact occurred, a second attack on Earth would follow soon after, since a new target is best attacked when it is small, weak, or disoriented. He further conjectured—correctly—that Earth, having been watched, would face opponents who would not merely have technological advantages. They would also enjoy advance intelligence on humankind, its capabilities, forces, deployments."

"He could hardly conclude otherwise," Menrelm commented, "given what he found on the asteroid."

"Precisely. Consequently, it was central to Corcoran's strategic planning to presume defeat as an inevitable outcome of the initial engagements, and so he orchestrated a strategy to fit that inevitability."

"You are saying he wanted Earth's forces to be defeated?"

"No. He simply started from the reasonable presumption that they inevitably *would* be defeated. His strategy was based on that presumption."

"In what way?" Vruthvur's tone suggested both surprise and interest.

"To apparently lose the initial engagements, giving the enemy the victories that were the reasonable, expected outcomes. However, he crafted a cunning set of deceptions, so that, even while these victories took place and opened a path to the human homeworld—a situation so dire and desperate that his enemies could hardly suspect it as a ploy—he had conserved the majority of Earth's best forces, which, upon a signal, returned to catch the invaders embroiled in the difficult task of occupying and controlling the humans' home system. It was a bold stratagem."

"It could have led to disaster, had any of its elements failed significantly."

"I believe he knew this, Menrelm. I believe he also was absolutely convinced—and correctly so—that any attempt at standard meeting engagements between Earth's fleets and those of a more advanced enemy would be no less disastrous. The humans would have spent their best equipment, personnel, and most of their reserves without profit. Consequently, Corcoran was not reckless or overconfident. He chose an unconventional and risky plan that *might* work, over a conventional campaign that was *certain* to fail."

"And you felt it wise for us to follow his lead?" asked Menrelm, with the faintest hint of incredulity.

"I felt it was unavoidable. He had already secured

a web of influence and alliance that used international rivalry as the impetus to expand more rapidly into space and attain interstellar capability, as well as to fuel the modest arms race that produced over ninety-five percent of the space defense assets that Earth has now. Our external influence, at its best and most direct, could not have achieved one-tenth of what Corcoran's own initiatives accomplished, all of which were informed by his 'lose the first battles' strategy. If we were going to follow Corcoran's lead—and we had little choice, unless we wished to fight Earth's battles for it—then we were also committed to following his plan. It was too intricate and nuanced to survive any attempts at modification."

"Even once he died?"

"Particularly then. With Corcoran gone, the plan was moving forward under its own inertia, with occasional assistance from Downing. To redirect their efforts at that point would have required direct and very obvious intrusion by us."

"Well," asserted Vruthvur, "it is fortuitous that Corcoran's plan survived him. And now that this war is behind us, we must call a new Convocation as swiftly as practicable."

"Why?" asked Alnduul.

"Firstly, to censure the Arat Kur and the Ktor. Secondly to issue a stern warning to the Hkh'Rkh that without properly altered behavior, they may have permanently forfeited the offer of membership they received. And lastly, we must induct the humans into the Accord as quickly as possible. Only once they have been offered and have accepted membership can we extend full protection and, also, control their tendencies to—"

"My apologies for interrupting, learned Vruthvur, but I think you may project in error if you presume that the humans will be as swift or grateful in their acceptance of an offer of membership now as they were at the first Convocation."

The Communitarium was still for a moment. "Explicate and illuminate, Alnduul," Vruthvur invited.

"Again, with apologies, I must remind this group of its decision to reject the human request for direct protection after the collapse of the Convocation. And you may remember why I counseled that we grant their request: because if they felt abandoned, and that they could not depend on us, they would not be so cooperative later on."

"Then it must be emphasized that we *did* save them."

"Did we? Our participation turned a hard and uncertain fight into a devastating rout of their invaders."

Menrelm sounded overtly impatient. "For which they should be grateful."

"Yes, and they are. But their gratitude is conditional and limited, now—just as our willingness to help was conditional and limited."

"And this portends what, Alnduul?"

"None may speak the future with certainty, Coordinator Vruthvur, but I speculate that, in the wake of this war, and living with the terror of their own possible extinction hanging unrelieved over their heads for several months, they will not now trust us as the guarantors of their safety."

"Do you fear they will return here later, to exterminate the Arat Kur?"

"No. That would not be their way. The human psyche and their political ethos could have excused or at least rationalized an act of infuriated, unthinking xenocide by a fleet at great remove from its violated homeworld, uncertain of its security, and with time running out. But to return and conduct xenocide in cold blood, having to fight every step of the way? This they will not do, for matters both ethical and practical."

"Then what are your misgivings, Alnduul?"

"I do not fear that they will preemptively attack others, but rather, will aggressively strengthen themselves. And they are in an extraordinary position to achieve this. They now have access to the most advanced Arat Kur technology. The humans will speedily copy and improve it, far faster than the Arat Kur, whose cultural predisposition is to slow, steady expansion and change."

"This means that, at least in military applications, they will soon rival the Slaasriithi as well."

"So I fear, Vruthvur. And there is more. The humans will realize, if they do not already, that it may be in their interest *not* to be members of the Accord, just yet."

"What?" Menrelm almost exclaimed, "You speak as if they are deranged beings."

"Not deranged: primal. And when we left them to fend for themselves against two foes, one of which was their technological superior, we caused a full reversion to primal reflex and thought. They will see this moment as a singular opportunity and will seize the freedom of action that is their right until their membership process is completed."

"And what can they do that we cannot stop?"

"There is nothing that we *cannot* stop, Menrelm, but there is much that I suspect we *would not* stop, as a matter of choice."

"Such as?" Vruthvur mused.

"Such as this: what if the humans were to expand beyond their pathways of allowed expansion? Not invading any other race's systems, just expanding farther into the unclaimed and unreserved extents. What would you do?"

"I would tell them they must desist and return."

"And if they politely pointed out that, while they prize their friendship with the Dornaani and are grateful to the Custodians, they are not yet members of the Accord, and therefore are not subject to its strictures? Then what would you do? Fire upon their ships? Inter their settlers?"

Menrelm's mouth became straight and brittle. "You are right. We would do nothing."

"And they know this already. They can read the political spoor left by this war clearly enough: the Arat Kur are now cowed and powerless. The Hkh'Rkh are safely trapped in a small cluster of systems by the limitations of their shift range. The Slaasriithi are passive and would be unwilling to even join our remonstrations. And we Dornaani? The humans have already begun to discern that we must rely upon them as the only energetic allies with whom we may counteract the machinations of the Ktor. We cannot afford to take aggressive or harsh actions against Earth, both because we have no legal right, and because it is contrary to our interests both as Dornaani and as the Custodians of the Accord."

Vruthvur spoke softly. "They will run riot in the near systems. They will rush outward, to consume as many unclaimed systems as they can before we can call the next Convocation and put the matter of their membership to a final vote."

Alnduul inclined his head. "This they will do. This we caused when we refused to provide protection for them after having been the ones to bring them to their first, and disastrous, Convocation. We erred, and we did not compensate them for being the victims of our error."

"There was wisdom in our actions, though," Menrelm insisted doggedly.

Alnduul's mouth twisted slightly. "The humans also have wisdom, which we might have heeded when we hastily chose to leave them to their own devices. They have a saying: 'err in haste, repent at leisure.'" Alnduul's mouth straightened again. "I suspect we shall now spend several long years repenting our hasty action, standing by as the humans take advantage of this moment."

"Is there nothing we can do, then?" asked Vruthvur.

Alnduul shrugged. "We can watch. And, maybe, learn." He stood and raised his arms. "Enlightenment unto you."

Dramatis Personae

R. J. Astor-Smath: Vice President of CoDevCo and senior overseer of Indonesian operations

Alfredo Ayala: SEAL Lieutenant Commander

Matthew Barr: ex-Secret Service agent

Chris Berman: SEAL Commander

Matilda Brahen: Ensign, USSF

The "Captain": Unnamed clone produced by Optigene Corp., subsidiary of CoDevCo

Elena Corcoran: anthropologist and IRIS operative

Nolan Corcoran: deceased Admiral, creator of IRIS and mastermind of Earth's defense

Trevor Corcoran: SEAL captain and IRIS operative

Carlos Cruz: SEAL rating

Djoko: CoDevCo security guard

Richard Downing: head of IRIS

Etienne Gaspard: European Union Consul

John Garvin: SAAS private, sniper

Hadi: Indonesian resistance fighter

Lord Thomas Halifax: Admiral, Commonwealth Joint Command, RTF 1

Benjamin Hwang: Nobel-prize winning Chinese-Canadian exobiologist

Bill "Jonesy" Jones: Admiral, USN

Heather Kirkwood: reporter

Moerdani: KOPASSUS captain, Indonesian Army

Miles "Little Guy" O'Garran: SEAL noncom

Ong Wei: captain of bulk container ship, and operative of the Taiwanese National Security Bureau

Opal Patrone: Army major and IRIS operative

Martina Perduro: Admiral, USSF

Cesar Pinero: captain of freighter *Maldive Reckoner*

Gray Rinehart: IRIS coordinator and Richard Downing's XO

Caine Riordan: IRIS operative, commander (USSF), and liaison to exosapients

Christopher "Tygg" Robin: SAAS captain

President-for-Life Ruap: President of Indonesia

Bannor Rulaine: Special Forces captain

Edward Schubert: Admiral, EUSF

Ira Silverstein: Admiral, USSF

Eimi Singh: corporate liaison for CoDevCo

Duncan Solsohn: CIA analyst

Vassily Sukhinin: Russlavic Federation Consul

Teguh: Indonesian resistance fighter

Sanjay Thandla: world-renowned computer expert

Mary Sue Tigner: captain and CO, SSBN *Ohio*, USN

Ulrike Visser: European Union Consul

Lemuel Wasserman: world-renowned physicist

Jacob "Jake" Winfield: SEAL lieutenant

Stanislaus "Stosh" Witkowski: SEAL chief petty officer

The Exosapients

Alnduul: Dornaani, Senior Mentor of the Custodians

Apt-Counsel-of-Lenses / Tlerek Sirn Shethkador: Ktoran ambassador/infiltrator

Darzhee Kut: Arat Kur of Ee'ar caste, Speaker to Nestless (exosapient liaison)

Graagkhruud, First Fist: Hkh'Rkh, field marshall

H'toor Qooiiz: Arat Kur, communications expert aboard flagship *Greatvein*

Hu'urs Khraam: Arat Kur, First Delegate

N'Erkversh, First Voice: Hkh'Rkh, overlord of the First Family

R'sudkaat: Arat Kur, Fleetmaster aboard flagship *Greatvein*

Tuxae Skhaas: Arat Kur, sensor operator and assistant shipmaster aboard flagship *Greatvein*

Urzueth Ragh: Arat Kur, Senior Administrator

Vrryngraar: Hkh'Rkh, great troop leader

Yaargraukh: Hkh'Rkh, Advocate (ambassador)

The following is an excerpt from:

RAISING CAINE

VOLUME THREE OF
THE TALES OF THE
TERRAN REPUBLIC

CHARLES E. GANNON

Available from Baen Books
October 2015
trade paperback

Chapter One

Far orbit; Sigma Draconis Two

Weightless, Caine Riordan escorted the Slaasri-ithi ambassador to the exit of the free-floating habitation module in which they had met. Nearing the docking hatch, the slender exo-sapient raised one gibbonlike arm to steady its zero-gee drift and raised the other to lift a tendril-fingered hand in farewell.

Caine returned the wave as the ambassador disappeared into its diplomatic shuttle and wondered, *Will I ever get used to being the point man during first contacts?* It didn't seem likely, not when every new species presented him, and humanity, with yet another disorient-ing surprise. In the case of the Slaasriithi, the surprise had been in their appearance. But not because they were ghastly—they weren't—but rather, because they were unnervingly familiar. Tightly furred, wasp-waisted, and with a roughly tetrahedral head perched atop an abbreviated ostrich neck, the Slaasriithi were identical to the primitive beings Caine had met on Delta Pavonis Three two years ago. But Ambassador Yiithrii'ah'aash had denied kinship between his race and that one—sort of. Leading Riordan to conclude that there was only one constant when conducting a first contact: each day ended with more questions and mysteries than it had begun.

As the hatch whispered closed, a muffled thump drew Caine's attention to the opposite end of the module: his own retrieval shuttle had completed its hard dock. A voice emerged from the speaker: "Sorry about the bump, Commander Riordan." The voice was mature, matter-of-fact: not one of the young, nervous pilots that predominated here in the recently pacified Sigma Draconis system. The Arat Kur locals, driven all the way back from their invasion of Earth, had put up a stiff fight before conceding. In consequence, there were now slightly fewer young pilots in the fleet, and those who remained were no longer quite so brash as they had been when they arrived. In short, they had grown up.

But this shuttle-jockey sounded like he had grown up quite some time ago. He expanded upon his brief apology: "Guess I'm getting a bit rusty."

"Hardly felt the bump," Caine lied politely. "Can I get out of this tin can, now?"

"No, sorry, sir. Another half hour and the xenomicrobiologists will be done with the quarantine protocol."

"I'm not 'sir.' Just 'Caine.'"

"Uh . . . not to seem contentious, sir, but it says right here on my orders that you are a full Commander, USSF."

"Really? I wasn't when I left the shift-carrier this morning." *Although, for all I know, Downing has put me back on the active duty roster. Again.*

"Well, sir, I wouldn't know anything about that. All I know is what I read in my orders."

"Fair enough. They keep changing my status back and forth so fast, I'm not sure of my title from day to day." *Or whether I'm a soldier, an intelligence operative, an envoy to exosapients, or just a civilian again.* "What about you? Navy?" Caine was slowly drifting back down toward the deck: the pilot of the retrieval craft had imparted a slow rotation to the module. As Caine's toes made contact, the whole world seemed to be sliding subtly, but perpetually, sideways: the Coriolis effect from the spin.

The shuttle-jockey corrected him. "No, sir. I'm not Navy. Commonwealth Survey and Settlement Office."

"You have a name?"

"Karam Tsaami."

Caine, in the course of his travels, met a lot of people whose names were unusual cultural mash-ups, even for this day and age. Still, this was one of the more peculiar combinations. "So you're, uh, Finno-Turkish?"

"By way of Toronto, yes." Tsaami's tone was distinctly wry. "And unless I'm mistaken, sir, you're the guy who reported first contact with the natives on Delta Pavonis Three at the Parthenon Dialogs two years ago."

Yes, the same natives who paradoxically, even impossibly, are dead-ringers for the Slaasriithi I just met with. "That was supposed to remain a closed-room debrief."

"Yeah, well, the story even reached me where I was ferrying, er, special payloads around the Delta Pavonis system."

"Special payloads?" Although officially civilians, a lot of SSO jockeys ferried covert operators around the colonies beyond Alpha Centauri. "You said you were stationed at Delta Pavonis?"

"Yup. That's been my home, on and off, for the past three years."

Three years? The pilot's voice suddenly

seemed familiar. "Hey, aren't you the guy who flew me out to the illegal CoDevCo facility on DeePeeThree?"

Karam Tsaami sounded pleased. "Yep. That was me. Been a long road since—Hold up. I've got incoming commo, highest priority." The five second pause seemed like ten minutes. "Commander, we're going dark. Admiral Lord Halifax just called the fleet to battle stations. An Arat-Kur shift cruiser just popped in-system. ETA fifty-five minutes."

"And we're going to hide?"

"Commander, given our size, our best chance in a shooting war would be to become invisible. But since we can't do that, we're going to become a motionless and inconsequential speck on a scanner filled with weapons-hot bogeys. So yes, we're going dark. Right now."

The speaker's glowing green indicator winked off. Then the module's lights did the same, leaving Riordan alone in the gently rolling darkness.

Except that, squinting, Caine now noticed a small red light, blinking alongside the hatch through which the Slaasriithi ambassador had exited. Riordan pushed off the floor, drifted to the hatchway: nothing but the aft airlock beyond it. So did the light indicate a pressure leak? A compromised seal?

No, he realized, leaning closer, *that's the activation light for an external commo jack.* So was someone actually outside the module, trying to reach him?

Caine punched the manual activation stud. "Hello?"

"Commander Riordan, is that you?"

"Yes. Who's this?"

"Bannor Rulaine, sir."

It made no sense that Bannor, a friend from the war, was floating just outside the airlock. To the best of Caine's knowledge, the ex-Green Beret should still have been babysitting an enemy agent back on the flagship, a liquimix battle rifle aimed at the Ktor bastard's midriff. "Bannor, what the hell are you doing out there?"

"Well, sir, I'm doing what our boss Mr. Downing told me to do: watch over you. I'm not alone: Miles O'Garran is here, too."

Little Guy, as well? Well, Downing certainly pulled the A-team off the benches for this overwatch mission. "So why the heck are you on the *outside* of the module?"

"We're here to make sure you had some unseen back-up. Just in case something went sideways."

"Which, thanks to the Arat Kur, has now occurred. You got the alert?"

"Loud and clear. And unexpected. I thought we'd accounted for all the Roaches' ships."

Caine suppressed a sigh. *That's because you're a few steps further down the clearance food chain. Just because we secured the Arat Kurs' home system doesn't mean we're out of the woods.* "Well, your overwatch job ended when the Slaasriithi left, so, get in out of the cosmic rays."

"Thanks, sir, but even cracking the outer hatch is contrary to the current black-out protocols. Opening the airlock to free space would produce a thermal differential that could show up on enemy sensors. Besides, our mission isn't over until Mr. Downing says it is. Oh, and Sergeant O'Garran just reminded me that this is a rare opportunity for us to work on our tans."

Yeah, tans which can be measured in double-digit REM per hour—the kind of tan which causes you to lose hair, and maybe a few years, if it goes on too long.

The green light flashed on the comm panel behind Riordan. "Hold on, Bannor: message coming in."

Karam Tsaami's voice was tense. "Commander, some big shot named Richard Downing wants to put you in the loop. The big loop. As in, patched through directly to Admiral Silverstein's combat information center."

"And when does this happen?"

"Dunno, sir. I'm just standing by like you are."

Riordan heard the weary tone of a long-term professional—a long-term *government* professional. Who had been his aerial chauffeur on Delta Pavonis Three two years ago. An extraordinary coincidence. *Or probably not*, Caine realized with a smile. "So, Karam, nice to have you ferrying me around during yet another first contact. Pretty small universe, wouldn't you say?"

"What? You don't like me?"

"Oh, I like you just fine, Karam. It's implausible coincidences that I'm not so fond of."

"Yeah, okay. I was your taxi driver to the CoDevCo compound on DeePeeThree because I had the right clearances. But now—well, things are different. When it comes to you, that is."

Huh? "Different how?"

"Caine, er, Commander, it's like I was implying earlier: you don't seem to realize how many people know your name, now. More to the point, you have no idea how many people are probably following your movements. Of course, being at the center of events during the invasion of Earth didn't help matters, if you were trying to stay off the radar."

"Not like I wanted that attention."

"Didn't say you did. You don't seem the type. But even before the fires had burnt out in Jakarta, a bunch of intel types were inviting lots of your prior official contacts to come have a nice quiet chat in a nice secluded place for a nice long time."

"Did they suspect some of you as moles?"

"Maybe, but mostly they were looking for folks with clearance who'd already had direct contact with you. They picked me to be one of the ship jockeys who could also watch your back. But you pretty much fell off the grid after Jakarta."

Did I ever. "That's because I didn't walk away at the end of the Battle of Jakarta. I rode out here to Sigma Draconis in an intensive-care cold cell."

"Ah. Sorry. I didn't know that you—wait: message coming through."

Tsaami was back on within the minute. "Okay, I'm jumping off the line. Mr. Downing is going to come on in a few moments with brief instructions. He's bouncing this one commo through my lascom and then cutting me out of the loop."

"Good talking to you, Karam."

"Yeah, likewise. We'll have to get a beer someday when you aren't on everyone's watch list."

The circuit switched channels with a pop. Downing's voice—crisp, urgent, and decidedly Oxbridge—crackled out of the speaker: "Caine, if you are reading this, you are to reply with a zero point two second coded lascom pulse with wavelength variation protocol Hotel X-Ray Seven."

Riordan did so, and then, after his pulse's variation fingerprint had cleared the security firewall, asked, "Richard, what the hell is going on? Why would only one Arat Kur ship shift into—?"

"No time now, Caine. You'll be receiving live-feed from my pick-up here in the intel situation room. Once you are in that loop, just listen. Do not send. It is unlikely that tight-beam emissions would register on enemy sensors, but we don't want to take a chance. In the meantime, stand by for emergency extraction by us, by the Slaasriithi, or to hear that we are relinquishing command authority over your team—Tsaami, Rulaine, O'Garran— directly to you."

Riordan increased the volume for Bannor's benefit. "So I'm waiting to learn whether or not the shit that's hitting the fan now will bury half the fleet. Or more."

Downing only replied: "Stay alert."

The circuit closed and then reopened,

unleashing a loud babble of orders, reports, and counterorders: the sounds of Admiral Ira Silverstein's CIC at red alert and weapons free.

Bannor commented through the external comm circuit: "They sound pretty panicked."

Riordan listened more carefully. "They're scrambling every drone and Hunter-class control sloop they've got on ready status. Problem is, this Arat Kur ship shifted in so close that they don't have the time to push out a full protective hemisphere around our shift-carriers. Whatever happens is going to be close, dirty, and very destructive."

"Makes me glad the Arat Kur only brought one ship."

Caine grunted agreement and listened to the staccato sitreps and flight ops chatter crackling out of the speaker behind him. He recognized Admiral Silverstein's voice laying down a barrage of orders: "I want those Boulton-class cruisers out in front and on our flanks. And Commo, you tell the shift-carrier captains that if I *don't* see them red-line their thrusters and un-ass this area of operations, I will personally come to each of their bridges when this is over and bust them down to ensigns. Nothing is more important than our shift hulls. *Nothing*. Signal Halifax on *Trafalgar* that we are now at eighty percent of maximum power output and stand ready to discharge spinal weapons and point defense fire lasers simultaneously."

"Sir," cried another familiar voice—it was communications officer Lieutenant Brill, if Caine remembered correctly—"I've got incoming signals from the enemy ship. Well, maybe it's *not* an enemy ship."

"Brill, give me clear data or I'll find someone who can."

"Sir, I think— Listen."

Yet another voice, this one unfamiliar, became prominent. "—ld your fire. I say again: hold your fire. This is prize-ship *Doppelganger*, transmitting on all frequencies, all codes: please respond. Repeat, hold your—"

"Damn it!" Silverstein shouted. "Captain Kagawa, this is Admiral Silverstein. You nearly had us soiling our duty suits over here. We were seconds away from frying that Arat Kur hull you've commandeered. Why the hell didn't you follow protocol and communicate immediately?"

Kagawa sounded harried. "Two problems, Admiral. The first was that the Arat Kur left us some viral surprises in the communications software."

"Damn it, I thought we'd purged all that crap."

"From the coding and management systems, yes, sir. But not from the physical interfaces.

The Roaches must have triggered this sleeper virus to activate when the shift drive was engaged without a passkey code. From the moment we came out of shift, we couldn't get the radios or lascoms to realign or transmit."

"Then why the hell didn't you stand off and pulse your power plants to send a Morse code mayday in the clear?"

"Well, sir, that's the second problem."

"More software issues?"

"No, sir. A diplomatic issue."

"A diplomatic issue?" Silverstein repeated.

"Yes, sir. Our ranking passenger—and he officially ranks me, once we entered this system—ordered that we maintain our approach even as we tried to regain control of our communications."

"What? Why? Damn it, who is this ass, anyway?"

"It is I," said another familiar voice, "Ambassador Etienne Gaspard, charged to lead the negotiations with the Arat Kur Wholenest. And now, apparently, I have been promoted to 'ass.' I am unfamiliar with the duties and prerogatives of that new rank, Admiral, but it shall figure prominently in my report of this event. Of that I assure you."

"What the hell is going on?" Bannor asked, evidently having heard the furor but not the specific words. "Are we being hit by the Arat Kur?"

"No," Riordan answered, "worse."

"Worse? What could be worse?"

"We're being hit by diplomats. Stand by to come in out of the sun, guys."

—end excerpt—

from *Raising Caine*
available in trade paperback,
October 2015, from Baen Books

BAEN BOOKS by
CHARLES E. GANNON

The Tales of the Terran Republic
Fire with Fire
Trial by Fire
Raising Caine (forthcoming)

The Starfire Series
(with Steve White)
Extremis

The Ring of Fire Series
(with Eric Flint)
1635: Papal Stakes
1636: Commander Cantrell in the West Indies

**To purchase these and all Baen Book titles in
e-book format, please go to www.baen.com.**